The Spellbinding Episodes of Phoebe and Her Unicorn

Complete Your Phoebe and Her Unicorn Collection

Phoebe and Her Unicorn
Dana Simpson

Unicorn on a Roll
Another Phoebe and Her Unicorn Adventure
Dana Simpson

Unicorn Crossing
Another Phoebe and Her Unicorn Adventure
Dana Simpson

Phoebe and Her Unicorn in The Magic Storm
Dana Simpson

Unicorn of Many Hats
Another Phoebe and Her Unicorn Adventure
Dana Simpson

Phoebe and Her Unicorn in Unicorn Theater
Dana Simpson

Unicorn Bowling
Another Phoebe and Her Unicorn Adventure
Dana Simpson

The Unicorn Whisperer
Another Phoebe and Her Unicorn Adventure
Dana Simpson

Camping with Unicorns
Another Phoebe and Her Unicorn Adventure
Dana Simpson

Virtual Unicorn Experience
Another Phoebe and Her Unicorn Adventure
Dana Simpson

Unicorn Famous
Another Phoebe and Her Unicorn Adventure
Dana Simpson

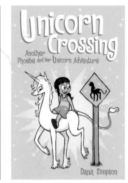

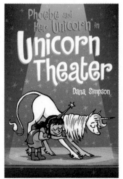

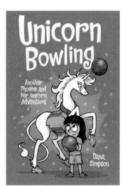

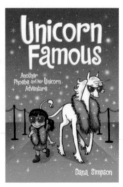

The Spellbinding Episodes of Phoebe and Her Unicorn

Dana Simpson

Featuring comics from *Unicorn vs. Goblins*
and *Razzle Dazzle Unicorn*

Andrews McMeel
PUBLISHING®

Unicorn vs. Goblins

Another Phoebe and Her Unicorn Adventure

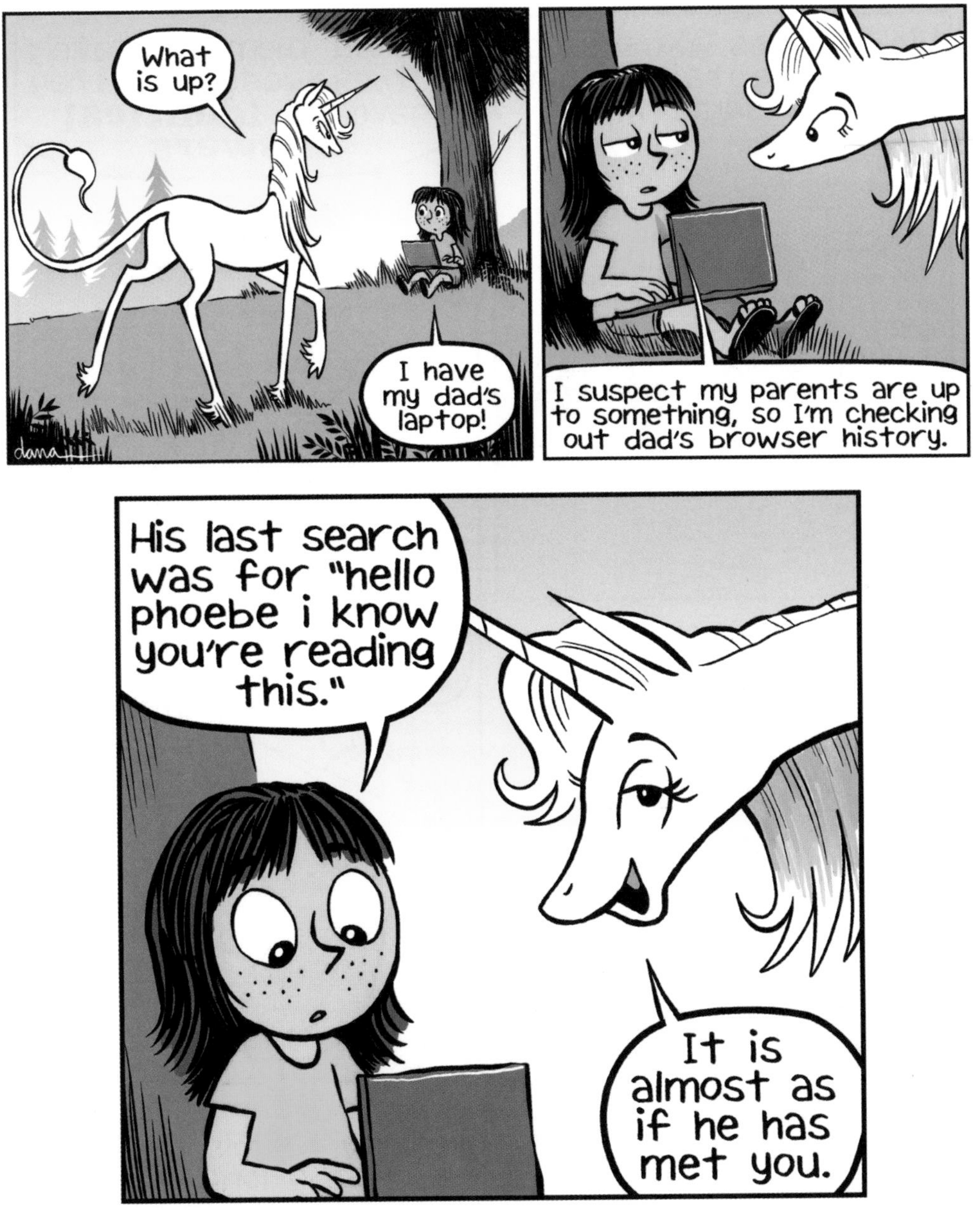
What is up?
I have my dad's laptop!
I suspect my parents are up to something, so I'm checking out dad's browser history.
His last search was for "hello phoebe i know you're reading this."
It is almost as if he has met you.
dana

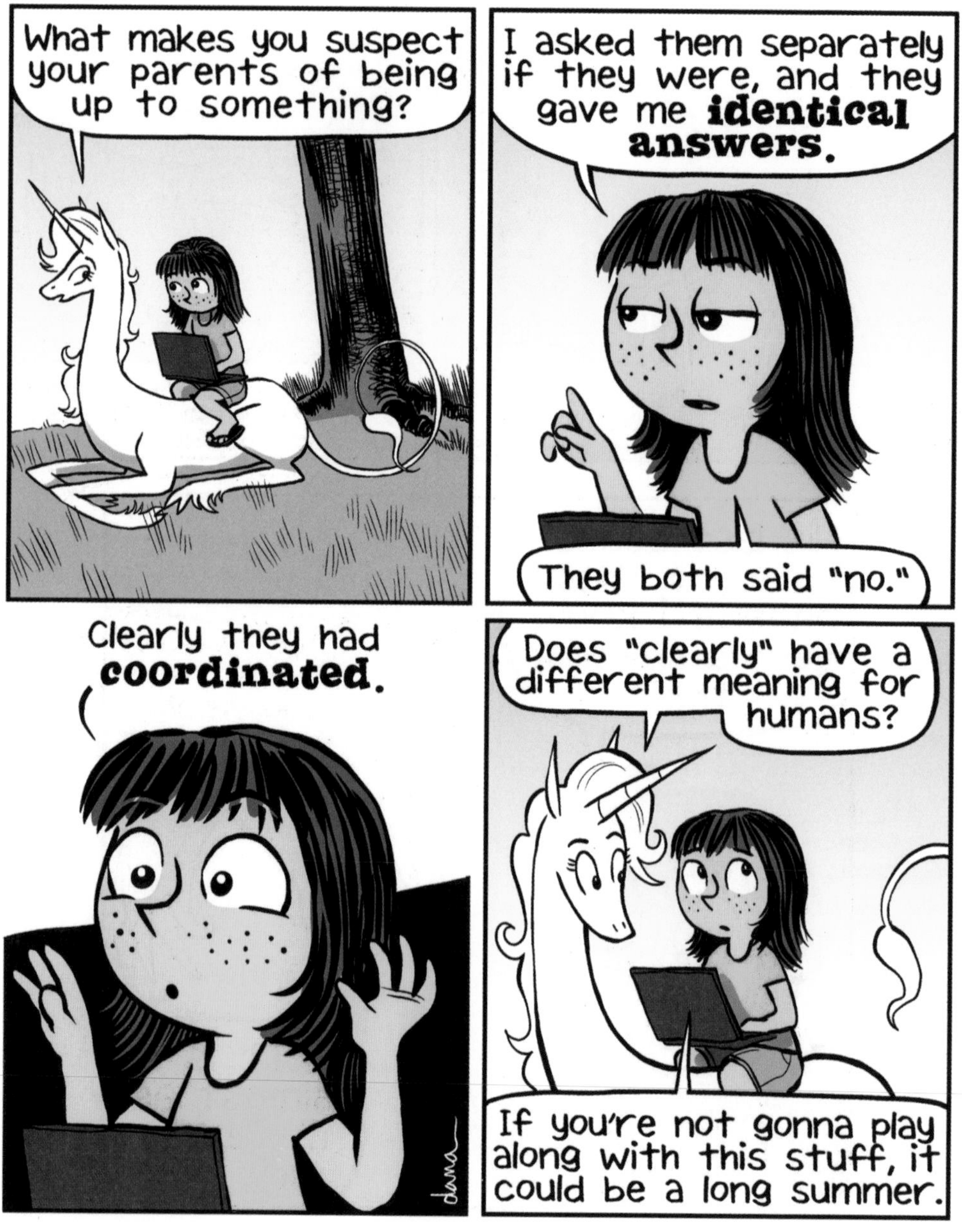
What makes you suspect your parents of being up to something?
I asked them separately if they were, and they gave me **identical answers**.
They both said "no."
Clearly they had **coordinated**.
Does "clearly" have a different meaning for humans?
If you're not gonna play along with this stuff, it could be a long summer.
dana

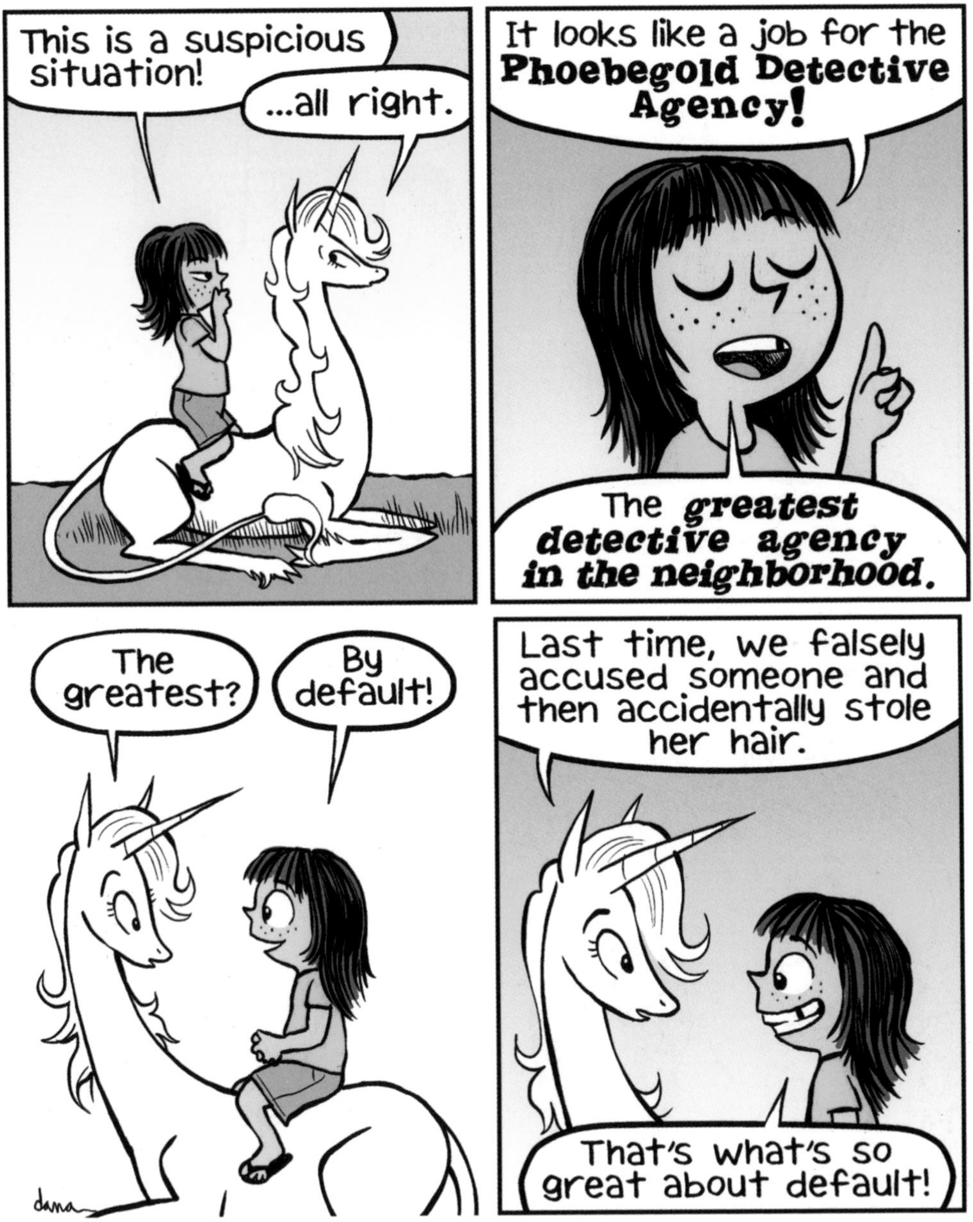
This is a suspicious situation!
...all right.
It looks like a job for the **Phoebegold Detective Agency!**
The ***greatest detective agency in the neighborhood.***
The greatest?
By default!
Last time, we falsely accused someone and then accidentally stole her hair.
That's what's so great about default!
dana

I shall cast a spell to amplify their conversation!

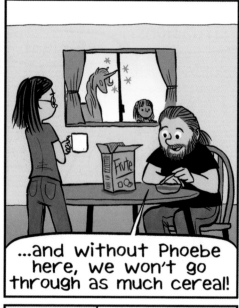

...and without Phoebe here, we won't go through as much cereal!

It can mean only one thing!

What?

Your parents mean to send you into exile for excessive cereal consumption!

Then we should start playing "law firm" instead of "detective agency."

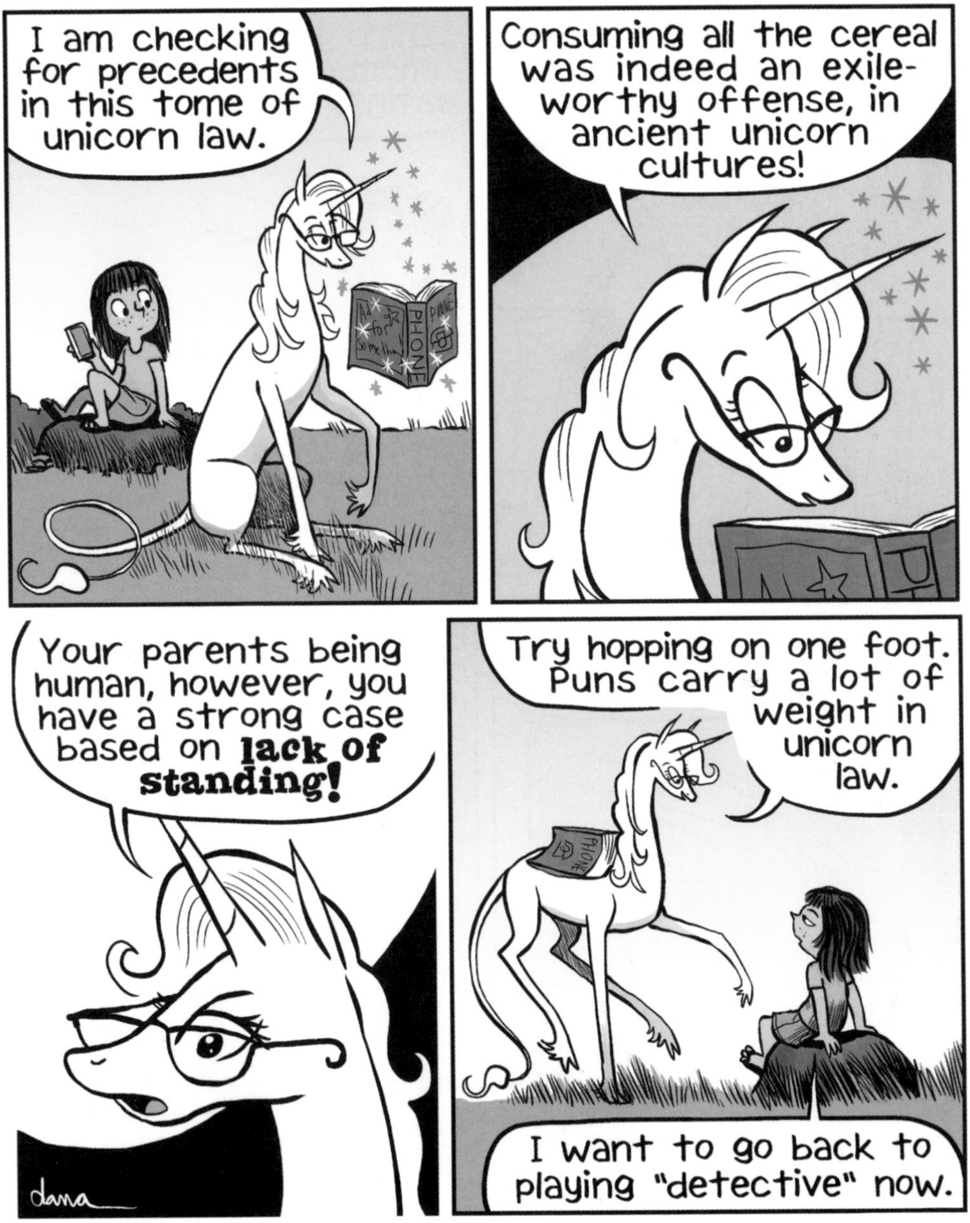
I am checking for precedents in this tome of unicorn law.
PHONE
Consuming all the cereal was indeed an exile-worthy offense, in ancient unicorn cultures!
Your parents being human, however, you have a strong case based on **lack of standing!**
dana
Try hopping on one foot. Puns carry a lot of weight in unicorn law.
PHONE
I want to go back to playing "detective" now.

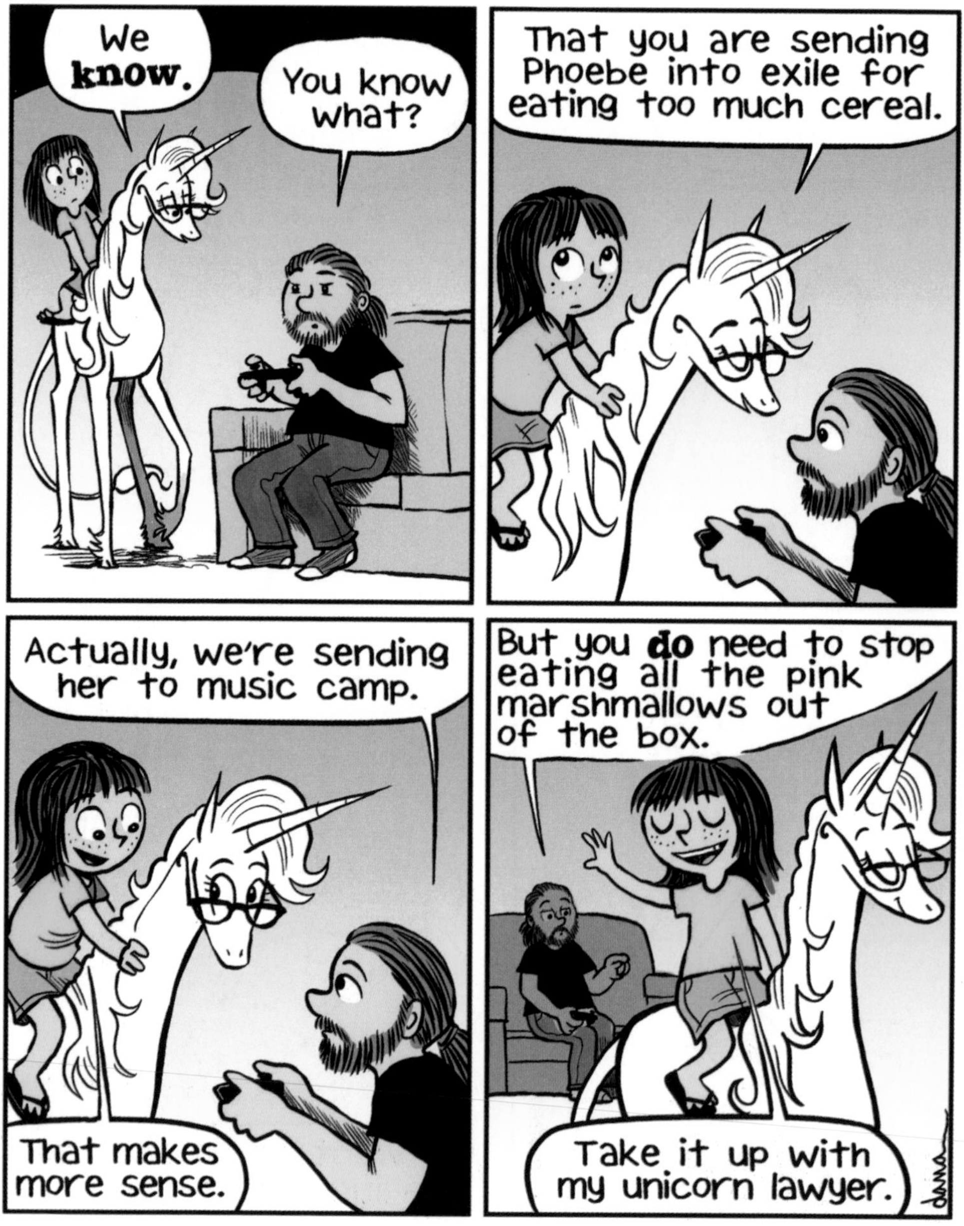
We **know.**
You know what?
That you are sending Phoebe into exile for eating too much cereal.
Actually, we're sending her to music camp.
That makes more sense.
But you **do** need to stop eating all the pink marshmallows out of the box.
Take it up with my unicorn lawyer.
dana

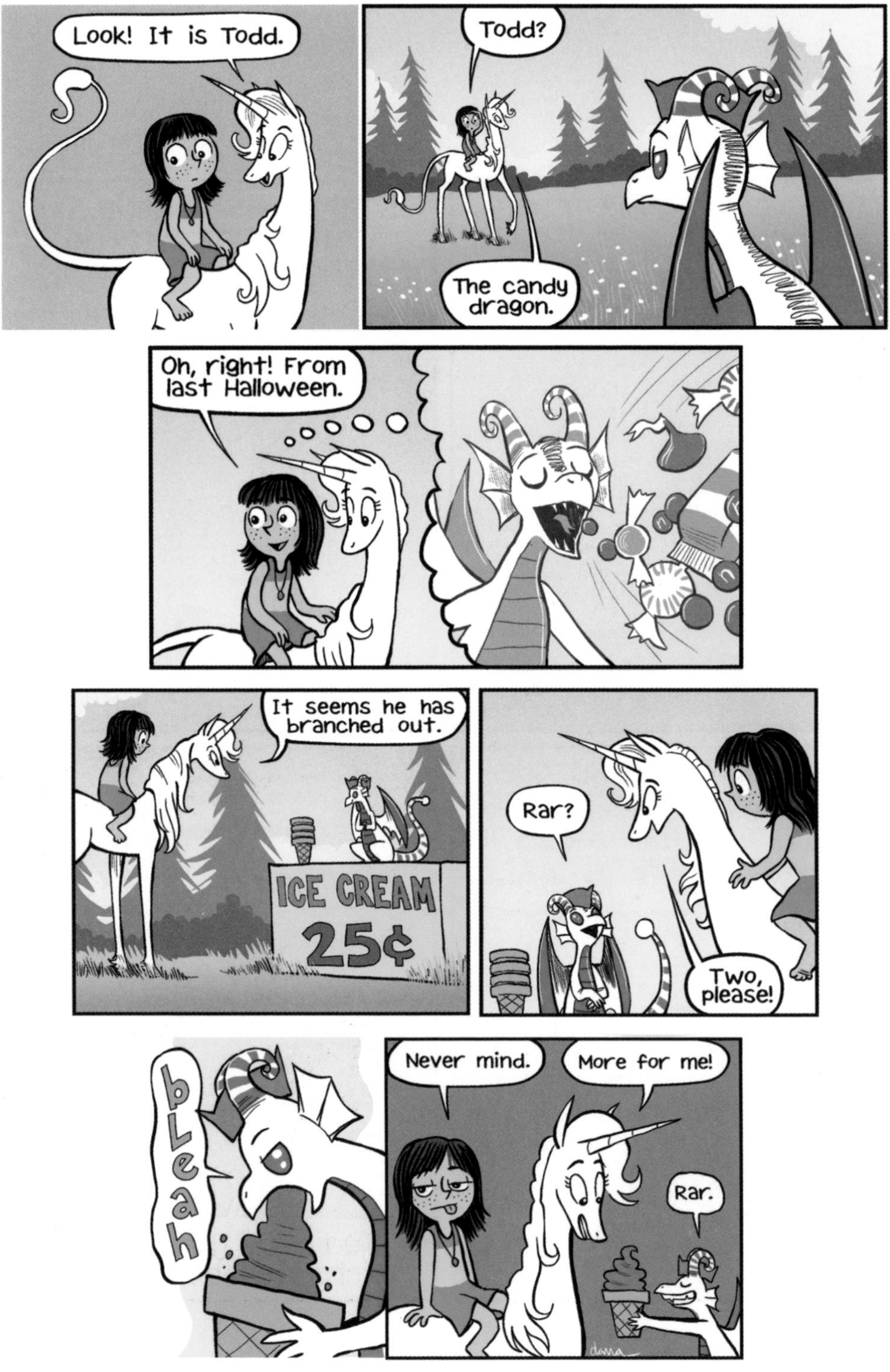
Look! It is Todd.
Todd?
The candy dragon.
Oh, right! From last Halloween.
It seems he has branched out.
ICE CREAM
25¢
Rar?
Two, please!
bleah
Never mind.
More for me!
Rar.

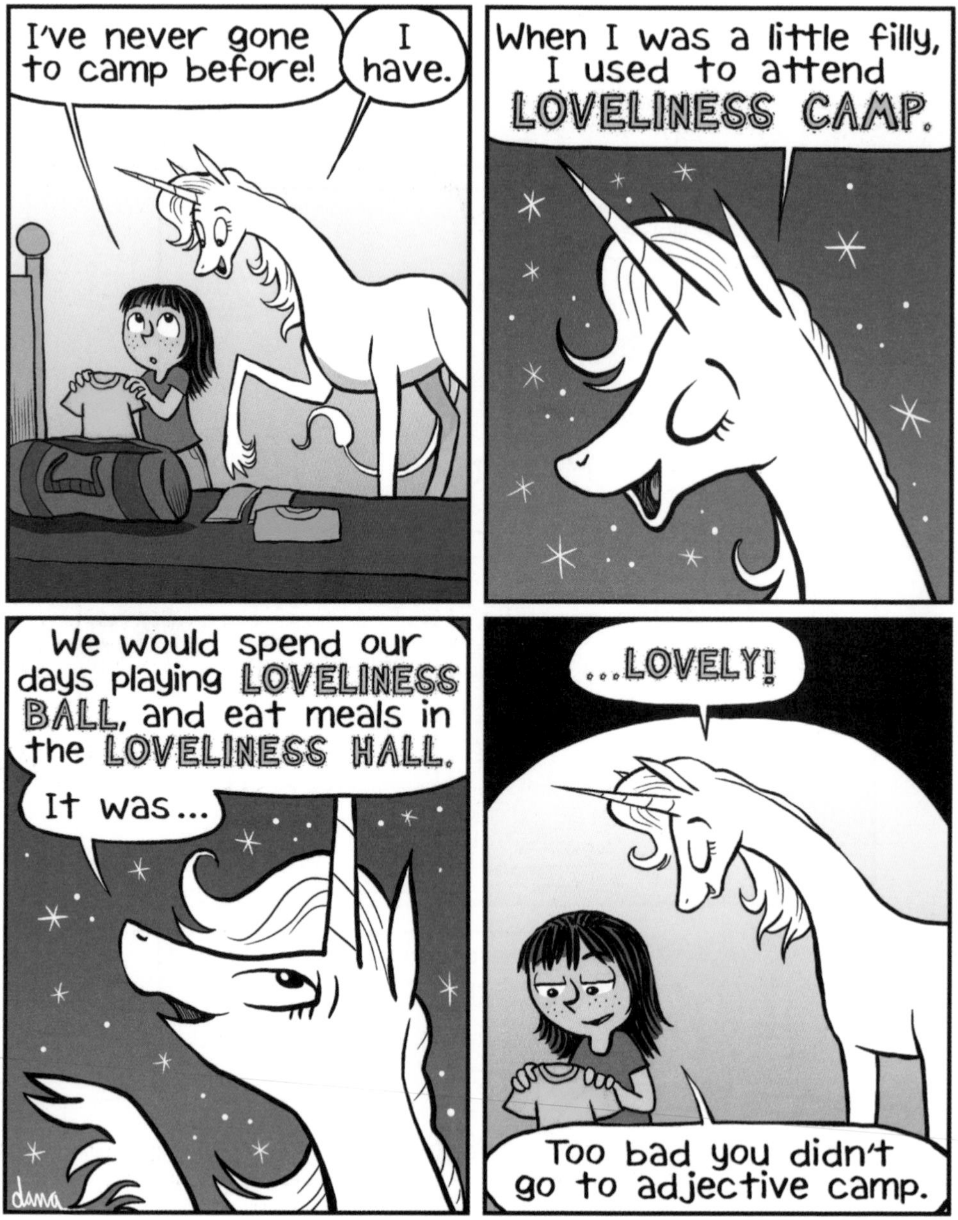

I've never gone to camp before!
I have.
When I was a little filly, I used to attend LOVELINESS CAMP.
We would spend our days playing LOVELINESS BALL, and eat meals in the LOVELINESS HALL.
It was...
...LOVELY!
Too bad you didn't go to adjective camp.
dana

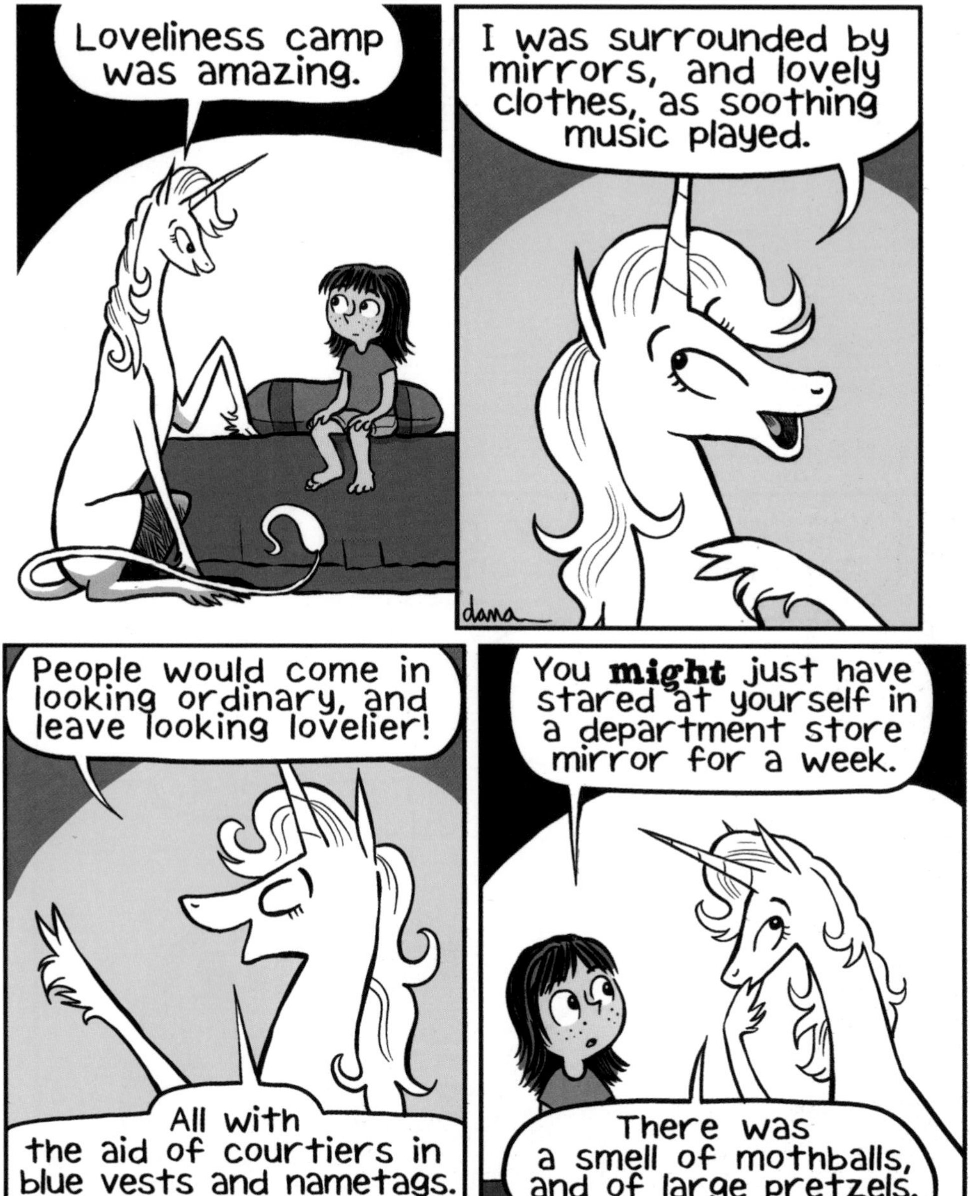
Loveliness camp was amazing.
I was surrounded by mirrors, and lovely clothes, as soothing music played.
dana
People would come in looking ordinary, and leave looking lovelier!
All with the aid of courtiers in blue vests and nametags.
You **might** just have stared at yourself in a department store mirror for a week.
There was a smell of mothballs, and of large pretzels.

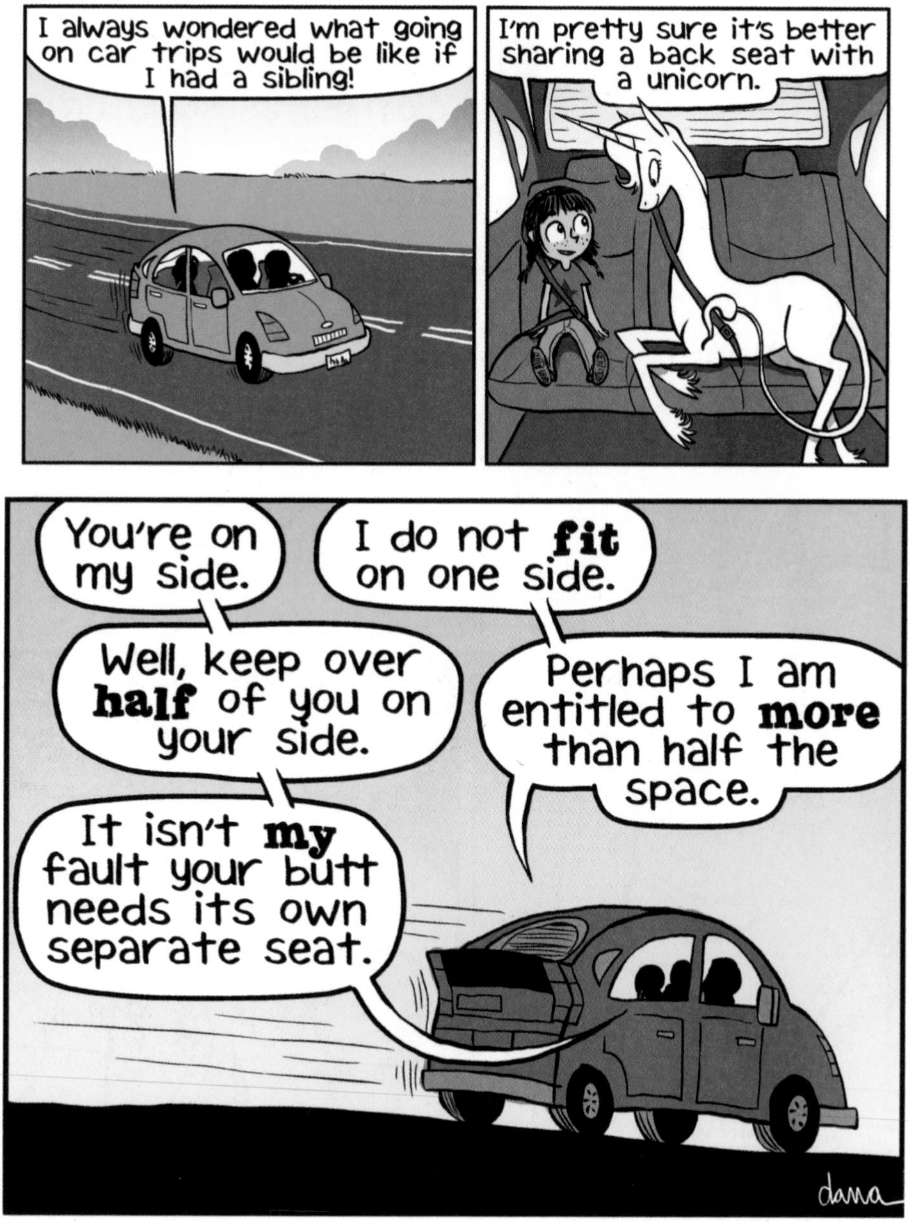
I always wondered what going on car trips would be like if I had a sibling!
I'm pretty sure it's better sharing a back seat with a unicorn.
You're on my side.
I do not **fit** on one side.
Well, keep over **half** of you on your side.
Perhaps I am entitled to **more** than half the space.
It isn't **my** fault your butt needs its own separate seat.
dana

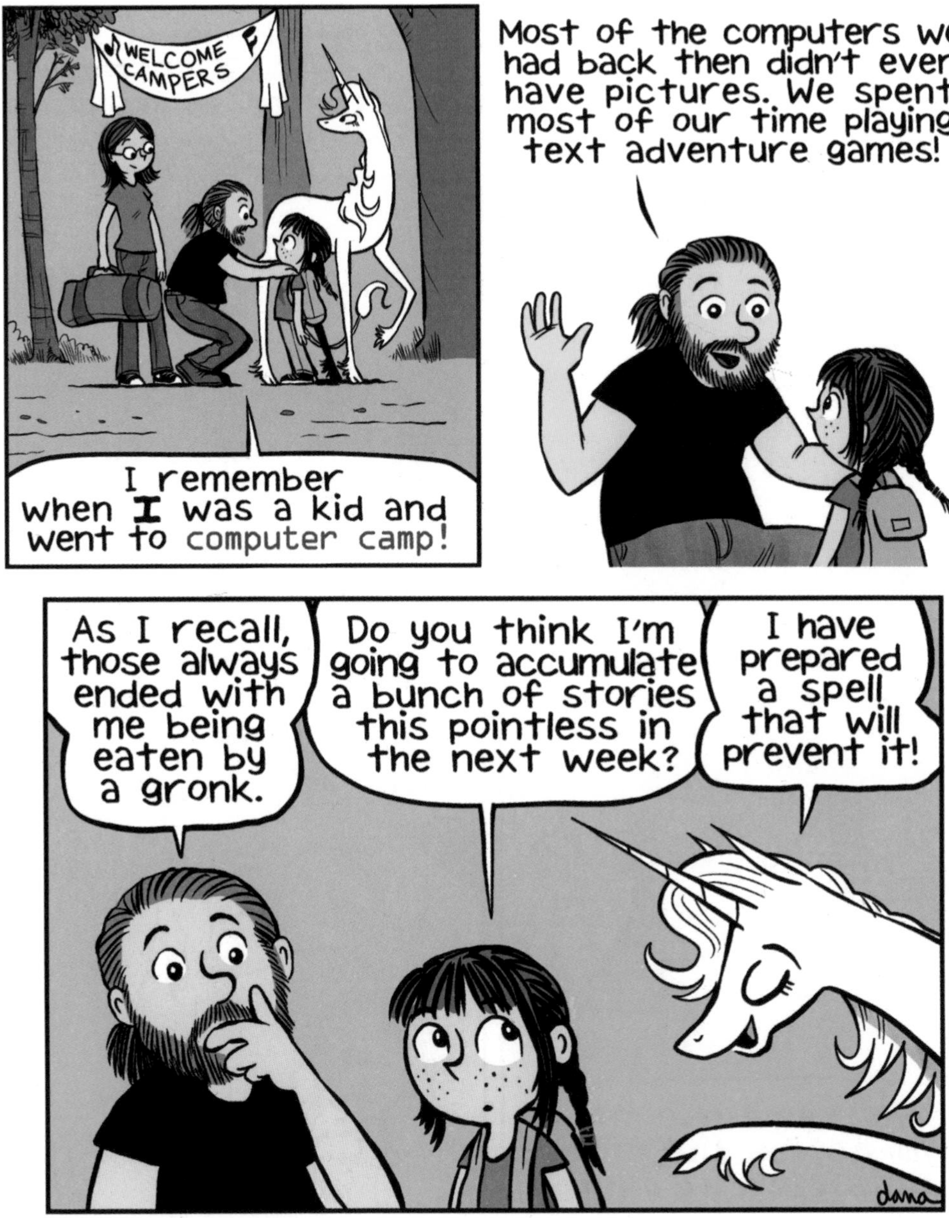
WELCOME CAMPERS
I remember when I was a kid and went to computer camp!
Most of the computers we had back then didn't even have pictures. We spent most of our time playing text adventure games!
As I recall, those always ended with me being eaten by a gronk.
Do you think I'm going to accumulate a bunch of stories this pointless in the next week?
I have prepared a spell that will prevent it!
dana

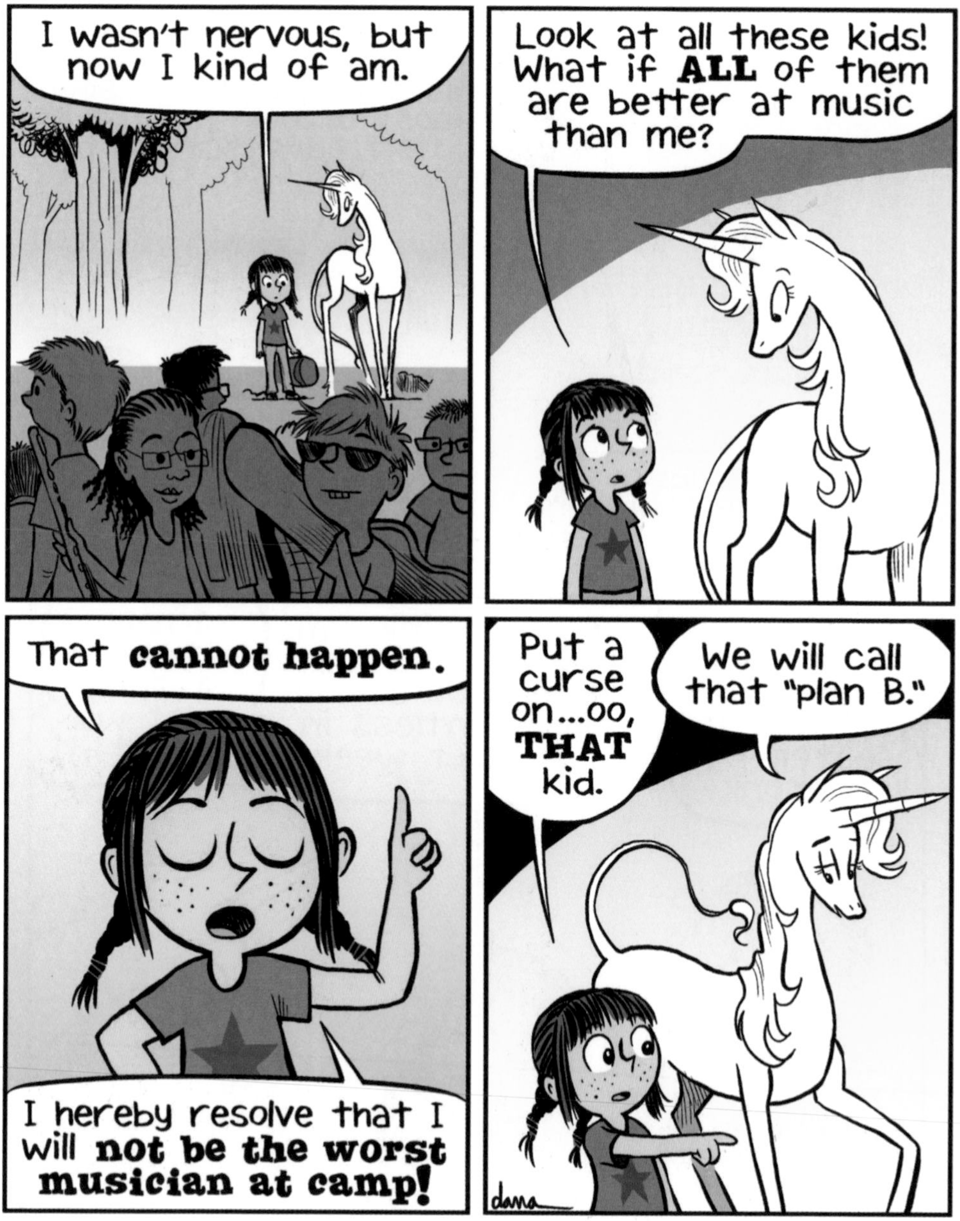
I wasn't nervous, but now I kind of am.
Look at all these kids! What if **ALL** of them are better at music than me?
That **cannot happen.**
I hereby resolve that I will **not be the worst musician at camp!**
Put a curse on...oo, **THAT** kid.
We will call that "plan B."
dana

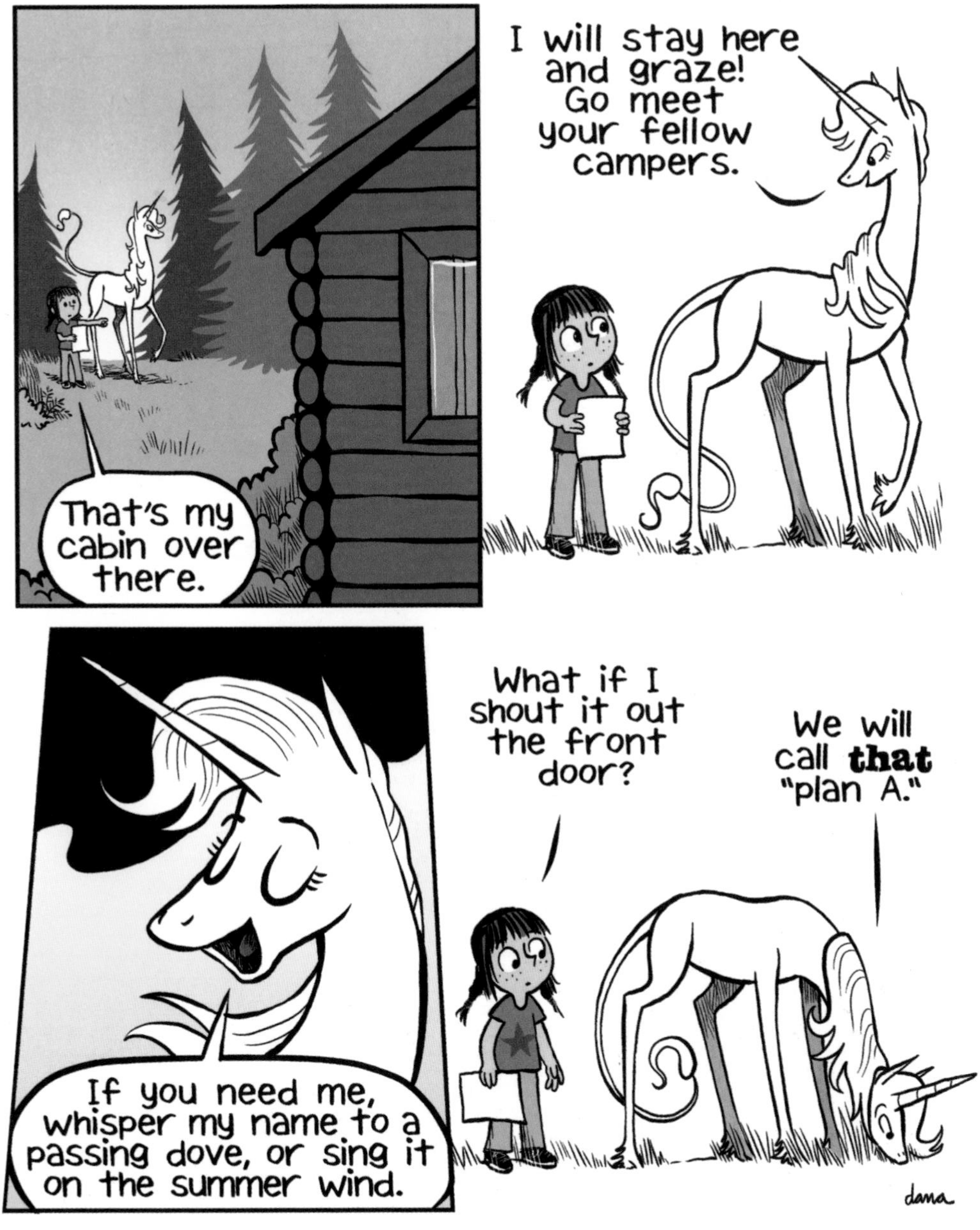
That's my cabin over there.
I will stay here and graze! Go meet your fellow campers.
If you need me, whisper my name to a passing dove, or sing it on the summer wind.
What if I shout it out the front door?
We will call **that** "plan A."
dana

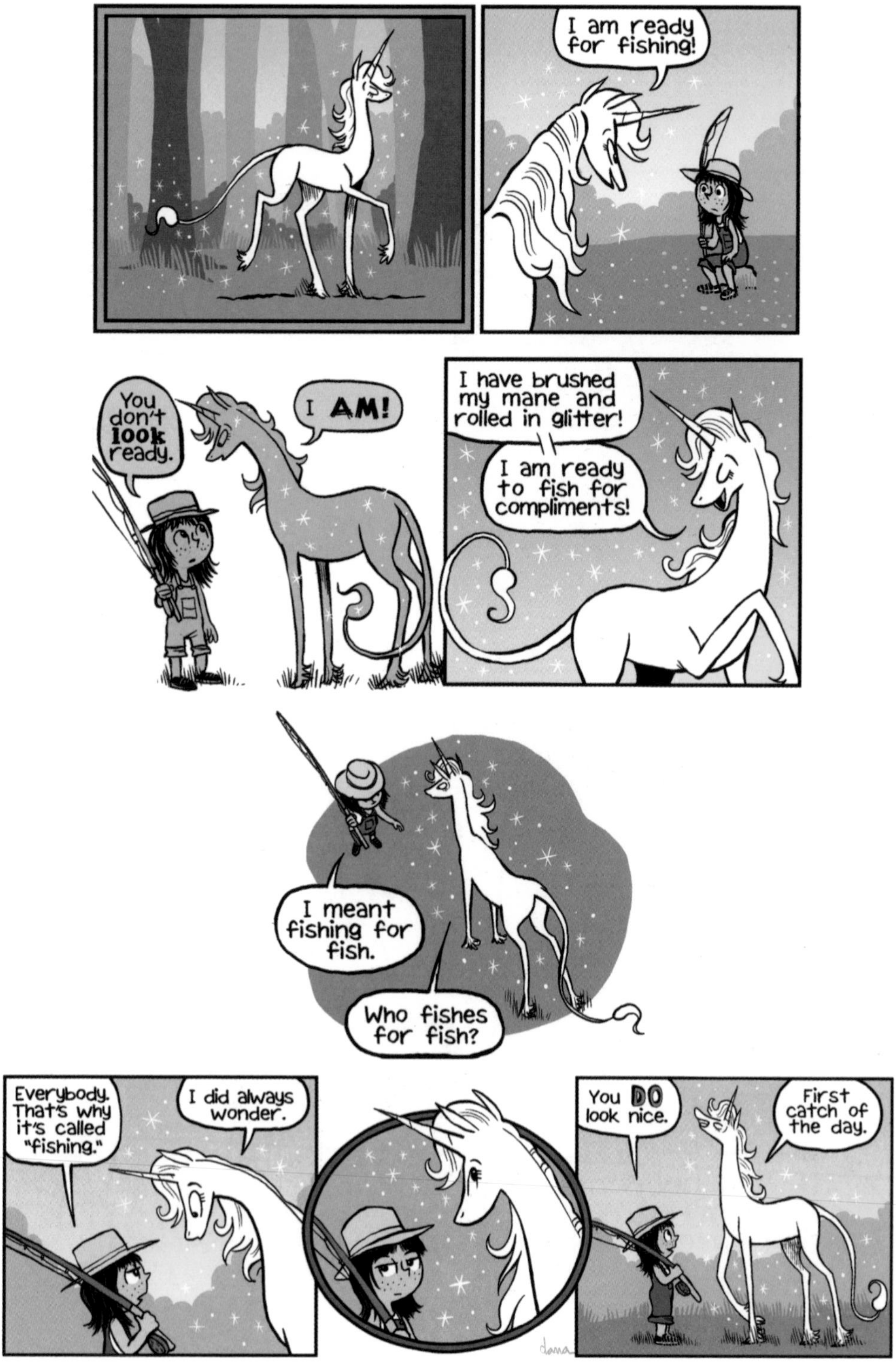
I am ready for fishing!
You don't look ready.
I AM!
I have brushed my mane and rolled in glitter!
I am ready to fish for compliments!
I meant fishing for fish.
Who fishes for fish?
Everybody. That's why it's called "fishing."
I did always wonder.
You DO look nice.
First catch of the day.

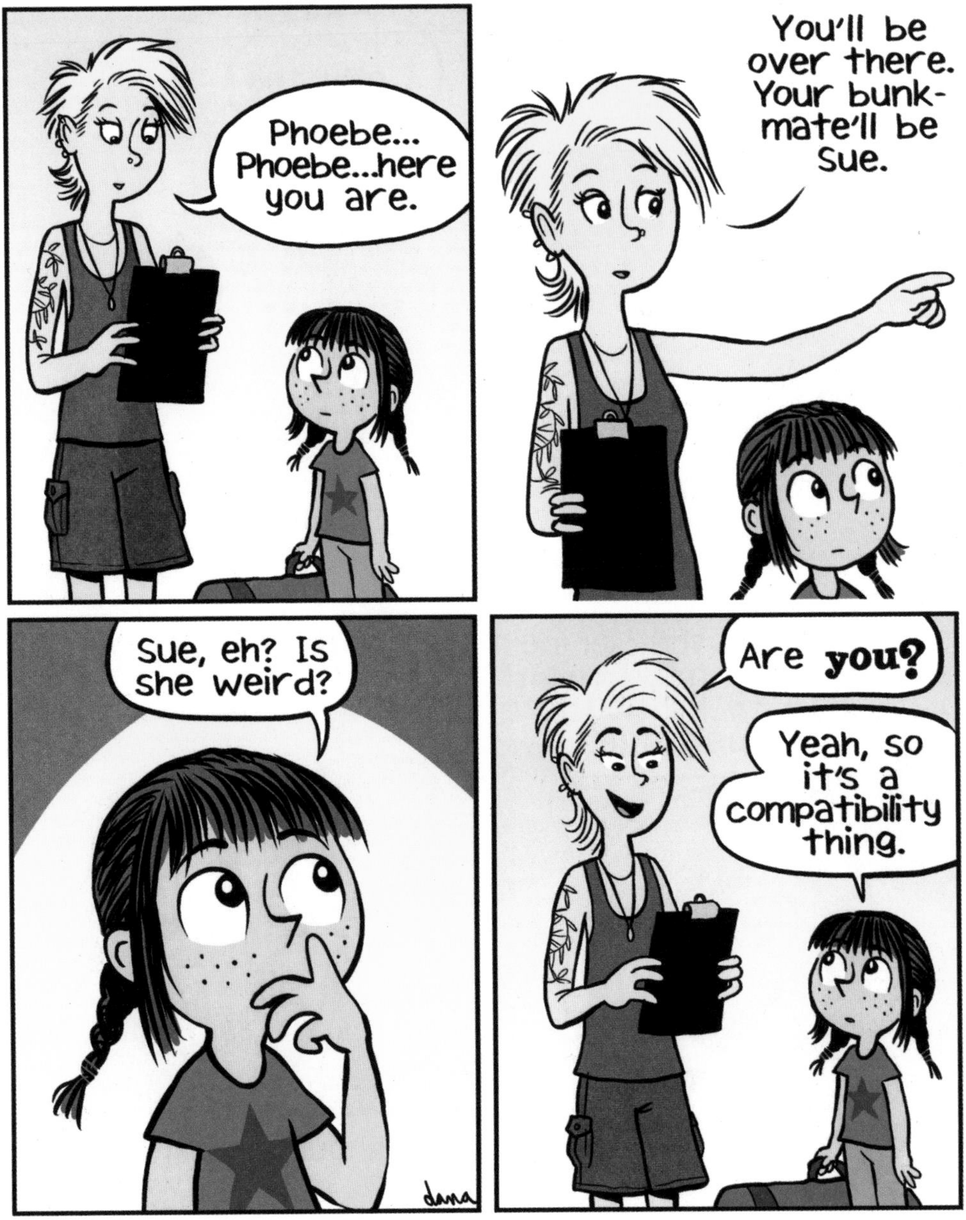
Phoebe... Phoebe...here you are.
You'll be over there. Your bunk-mate'll be Sue.
Sue, eh? Is she weird?
Are **you?**
Yeah, so it's a compatibility thing.
dana

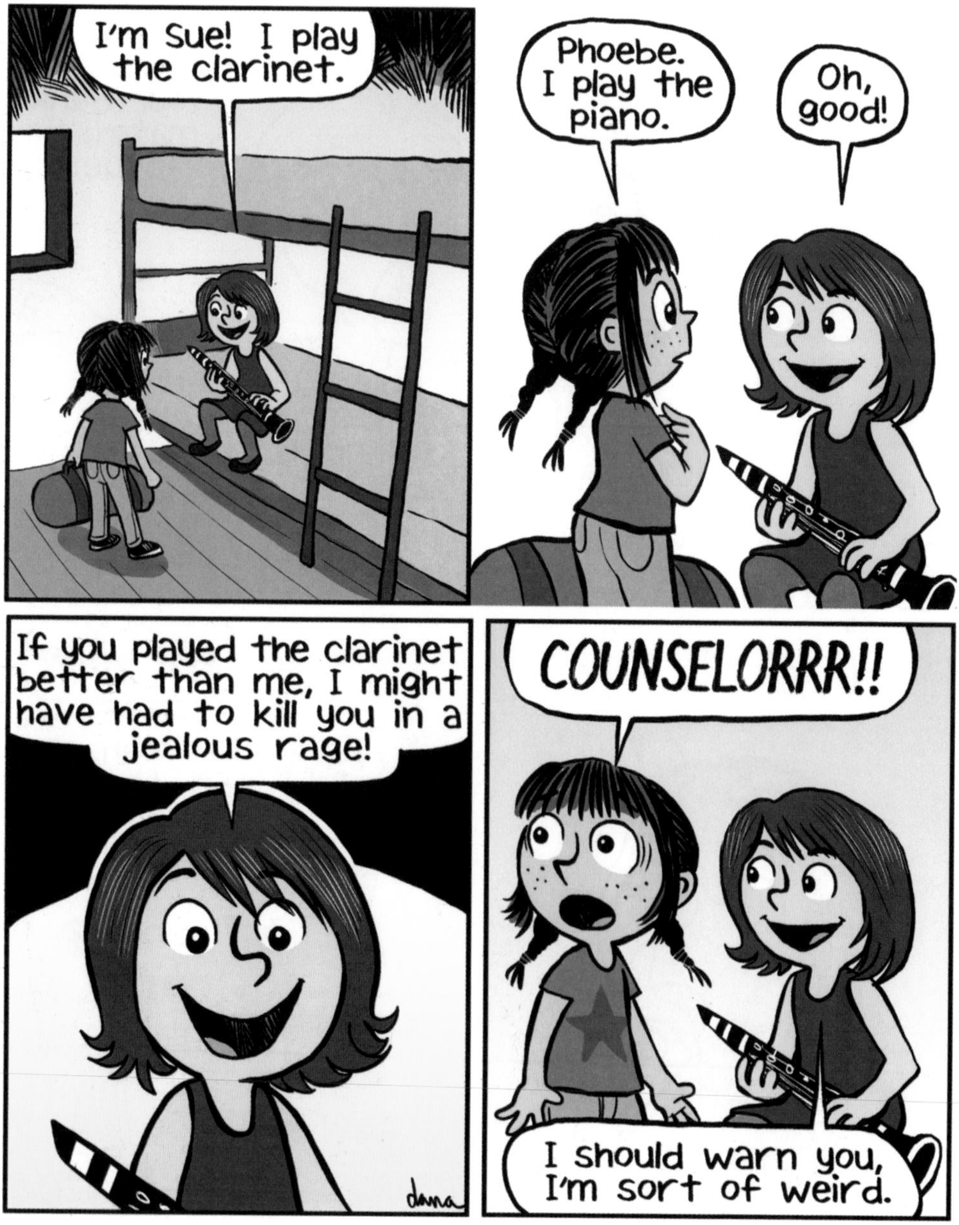
I'm Sue! I play the clarinet.
Phoebe. I play the piano.
Oh, good!
If you played the clarinet better than me, I might have had to kill you in a jealous rage!
COUNSELORRRR!!
I should warn you, I'm sort of weird.
dana

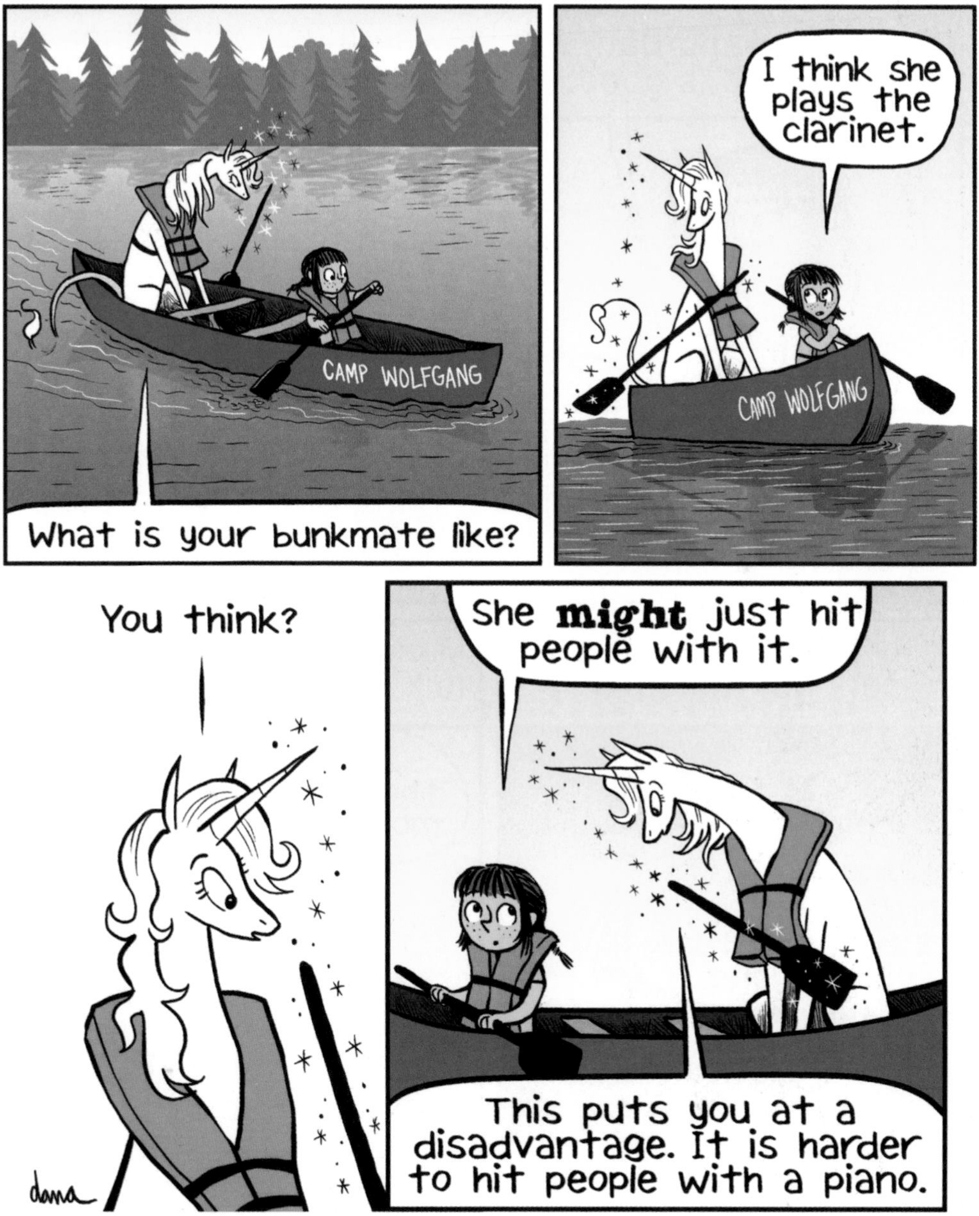
What is your bunkmate like?
CAMP WOLFGANG
I think she plays the clarinet.
CAMP WOLFGANG
You think?
She **might** just hit people with it.
This puts you at a disadvantage. It is harder to hit people with a piano.
dana

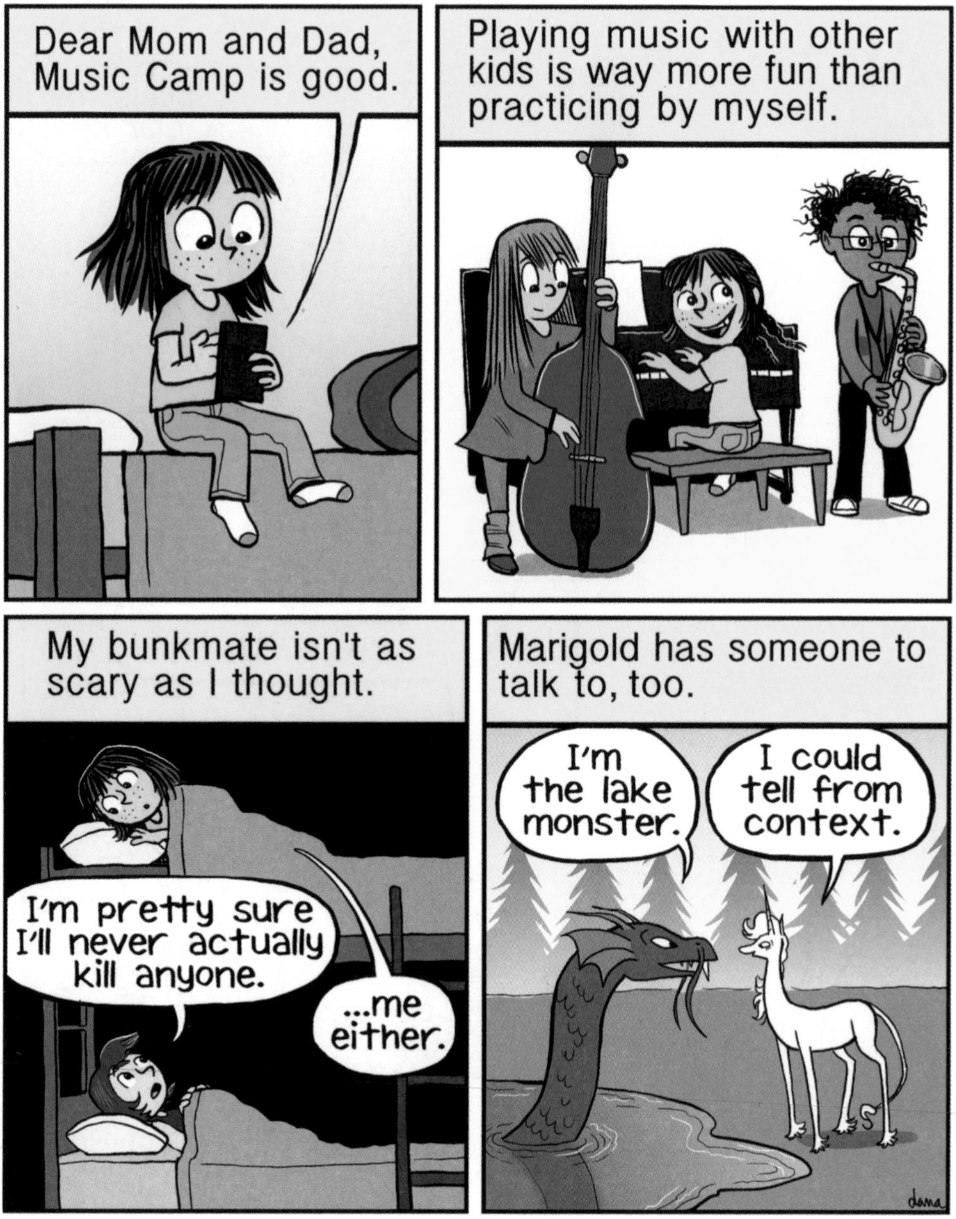
Dear Mom and Dad,
Music Camp is good.
Playing music with other kids is way more fun than practicing by myself.
My bunkmate isn't as scary as I thought.
I'm pretty sure I'll never actually kill anyone.
...me either.
Marigold has someone to talk to, too.
I'm the lake monster.
I could tell from context.
dana

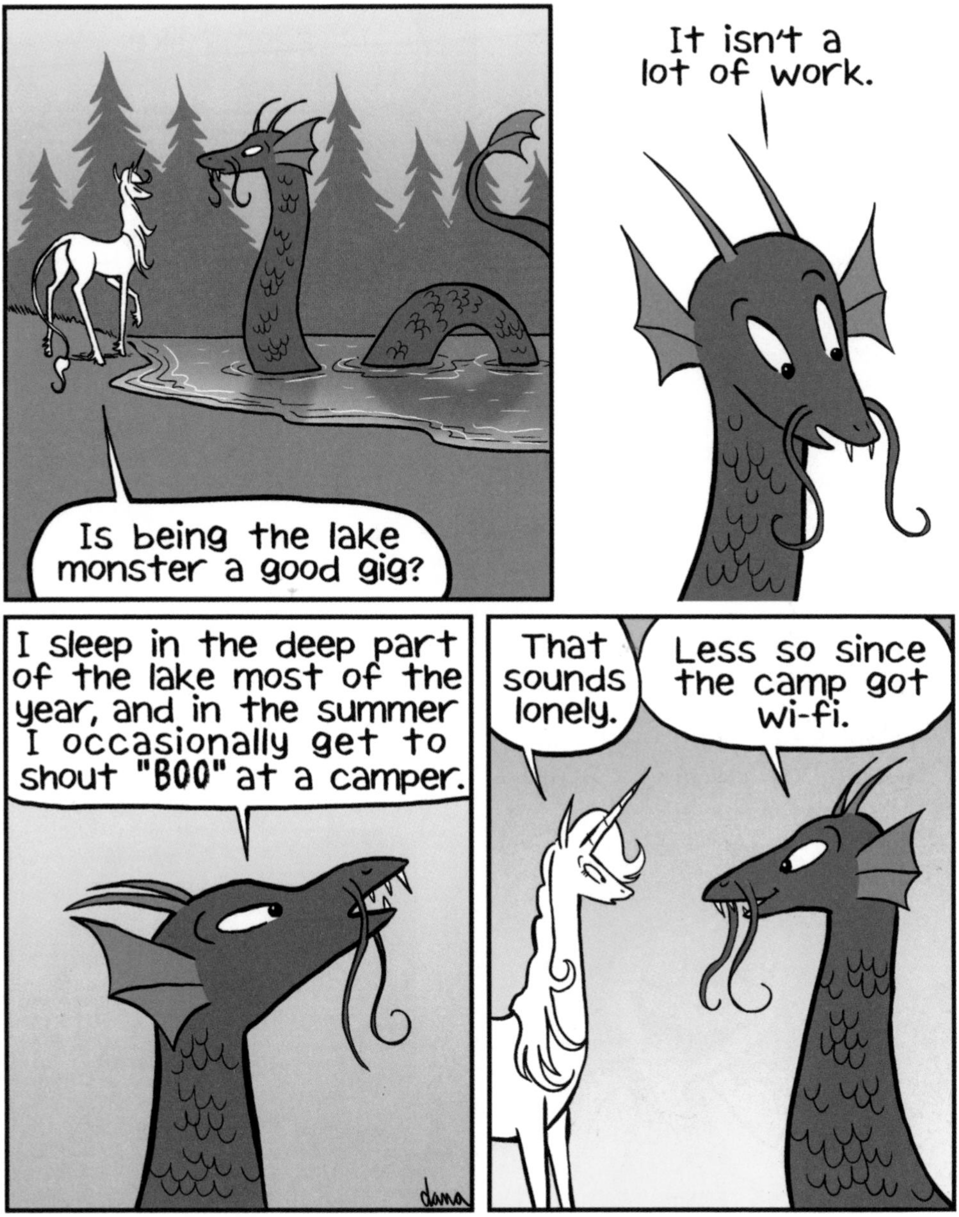
Is being the lake monster a good gig?
It isn't a lot of work.
I sleep in the deep part of the lake most of the year, and in the summer I occasionally get to shout "BOO" at a camper.
dana
That sounds lonely.
Less so since the camp got wi-fi.

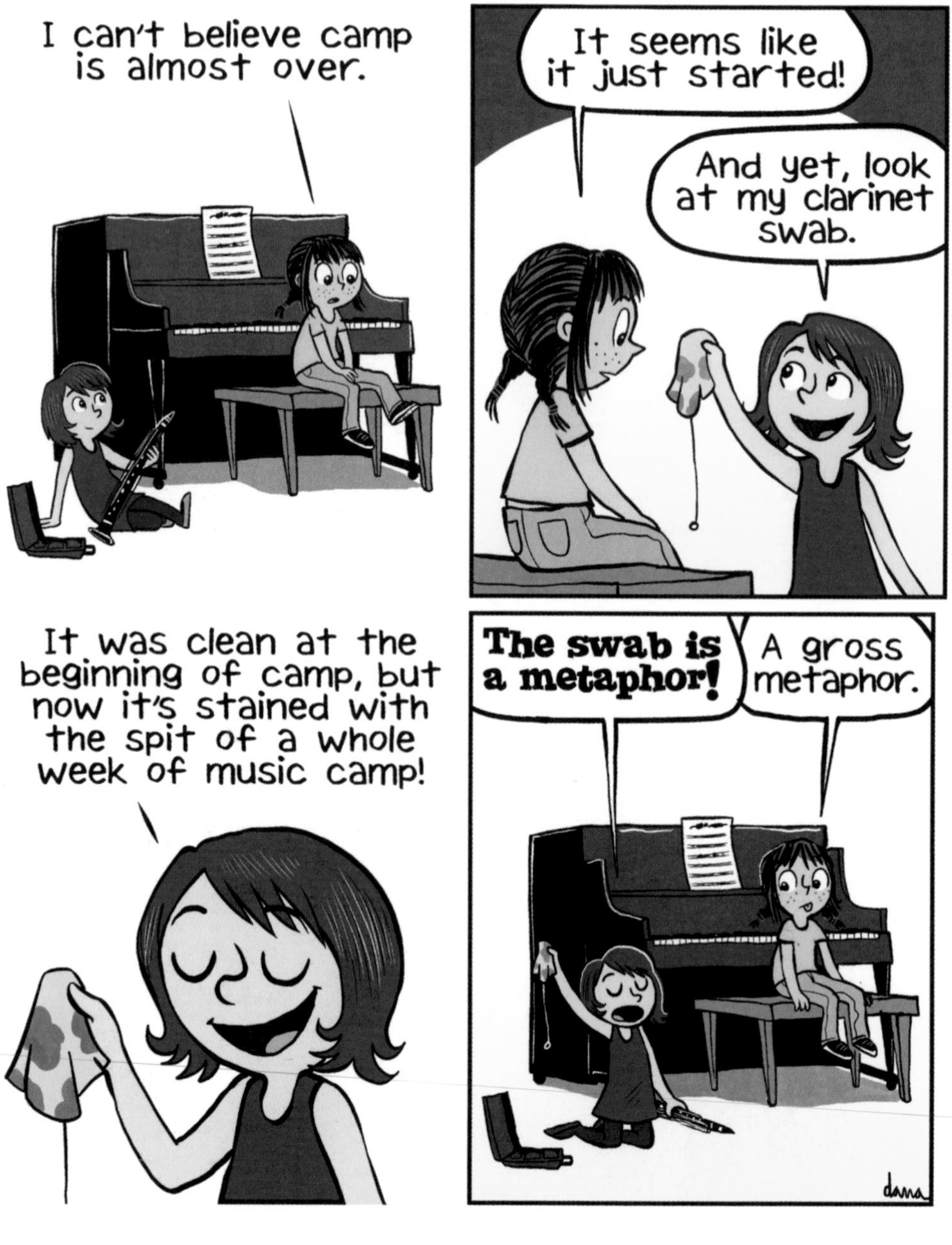
I can't believe camp is almost over.
It seems like it just started!
And yet, look at my clarinet swab.
It was clean at the beginning of camp, but now it's stained with the spit of a whole week of music camp!
The swab is a metaphor!
A gross metaphor.
dana

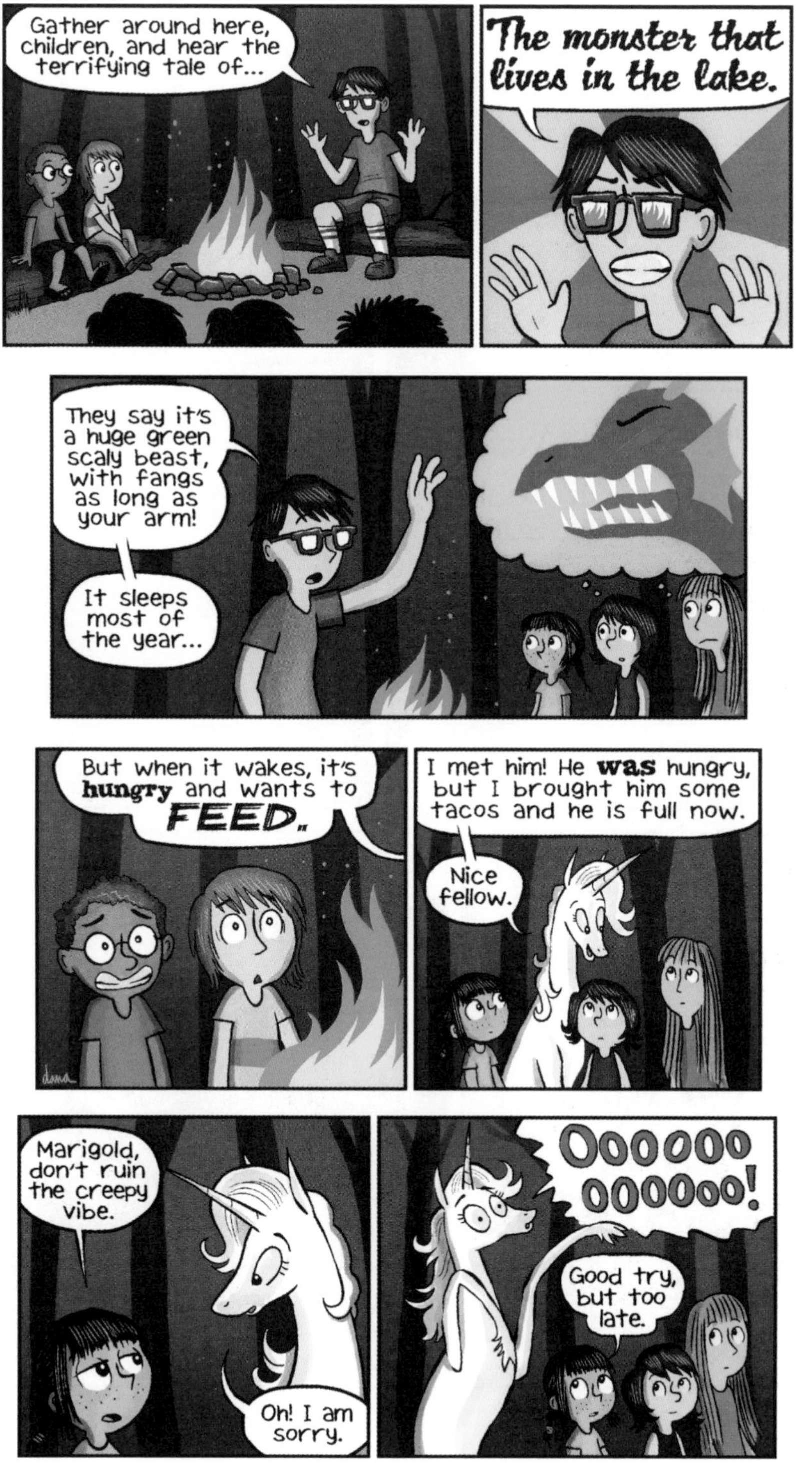
Gather around here, children, and hear the terrifying tale of...
The monster that lives in the lake.
They say it's a huge green scaly beast, with fangs as long as your arm!
It sleeps most of the year...
But when it wakes, it's hungry and wants to FEED.
I met him! He was hungry, but I brought him some tacos and he is full now.
Nice fellow.
Marigold, don't ruin the creepy vibe.
Oh! I am sorry.
OOOOOO OOOOOO!
Good try, but too late.

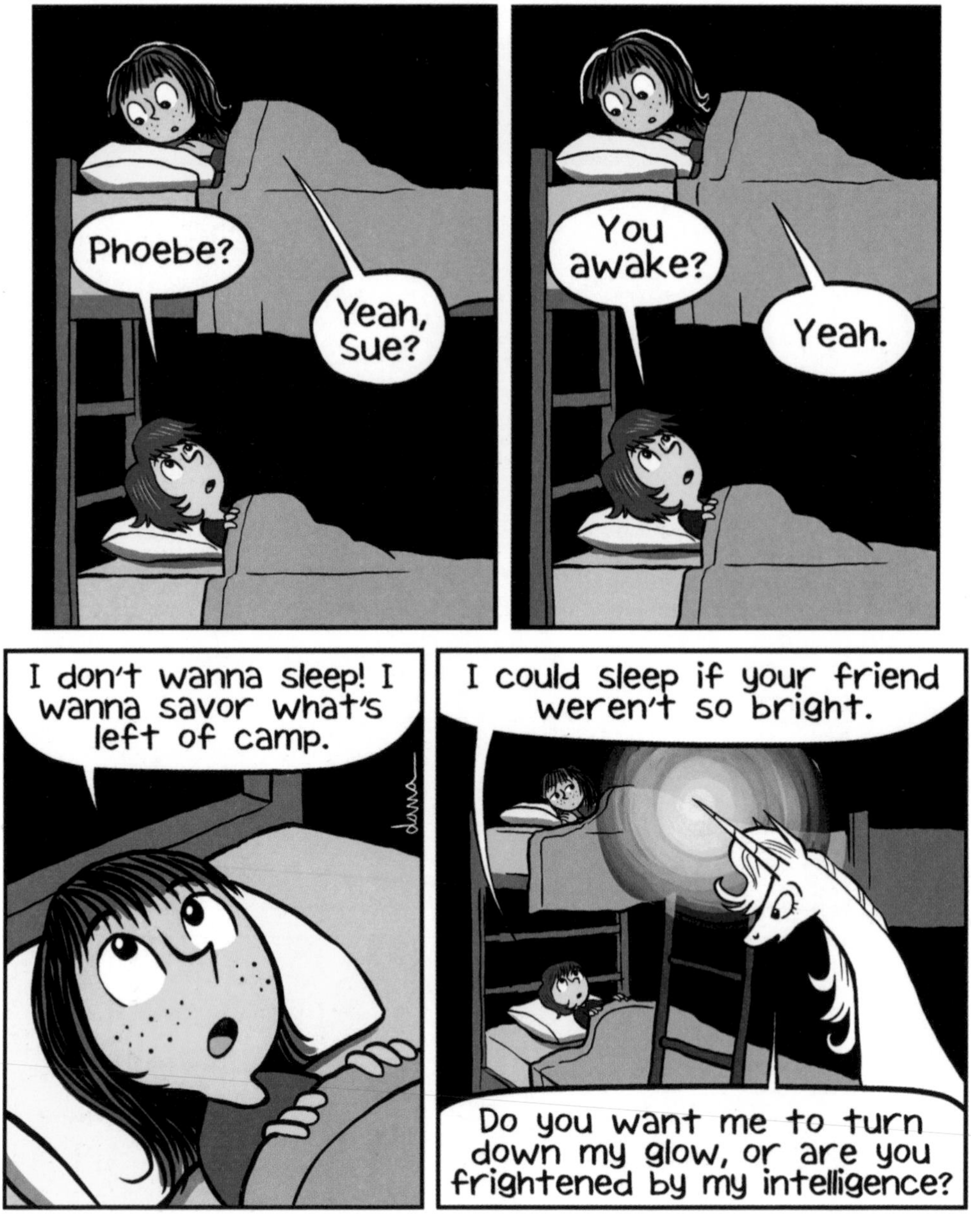
Phoebe?
Yeah, Sue?
You awake?
Yeah.
I don't wanna sleep! I wanna savor what's left of camp.
I could sleep if your friend weren't so bright.
Do you want me to turn down my glow, or are you frightened by my intelligence?

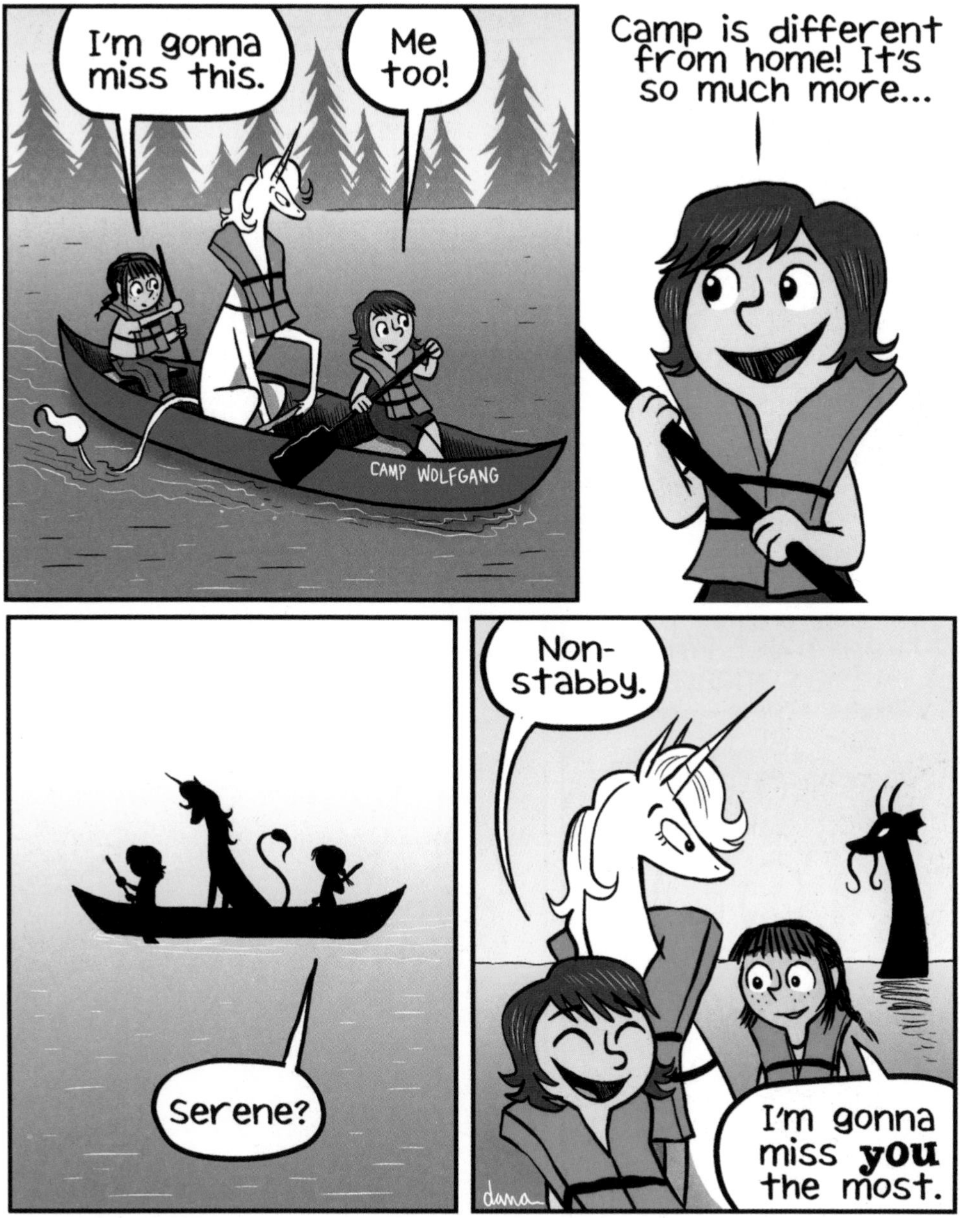
I'm gonna miss this.
Me too!
CAMP WOLFGANG
Camp is different from home! It's so much more...
Serene?
Non-stabby.
I'm gonna miss **you** the most.
dana

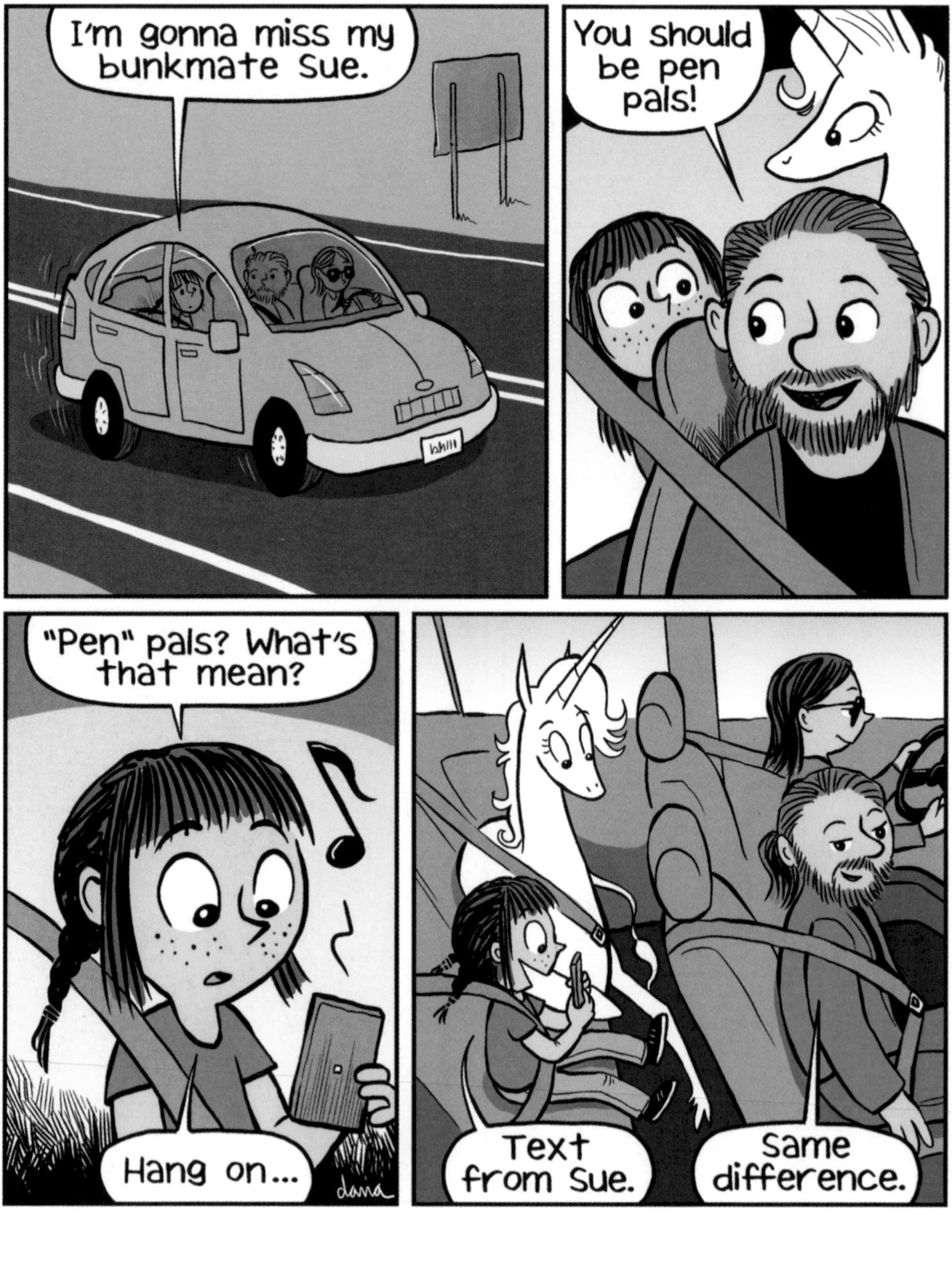
I'm gonna miss my bunkmate Sue.
You should be pen pals!
"Pen" pals? What's that mean?
Hang on...
dana
Text from Sue.
Same difference.

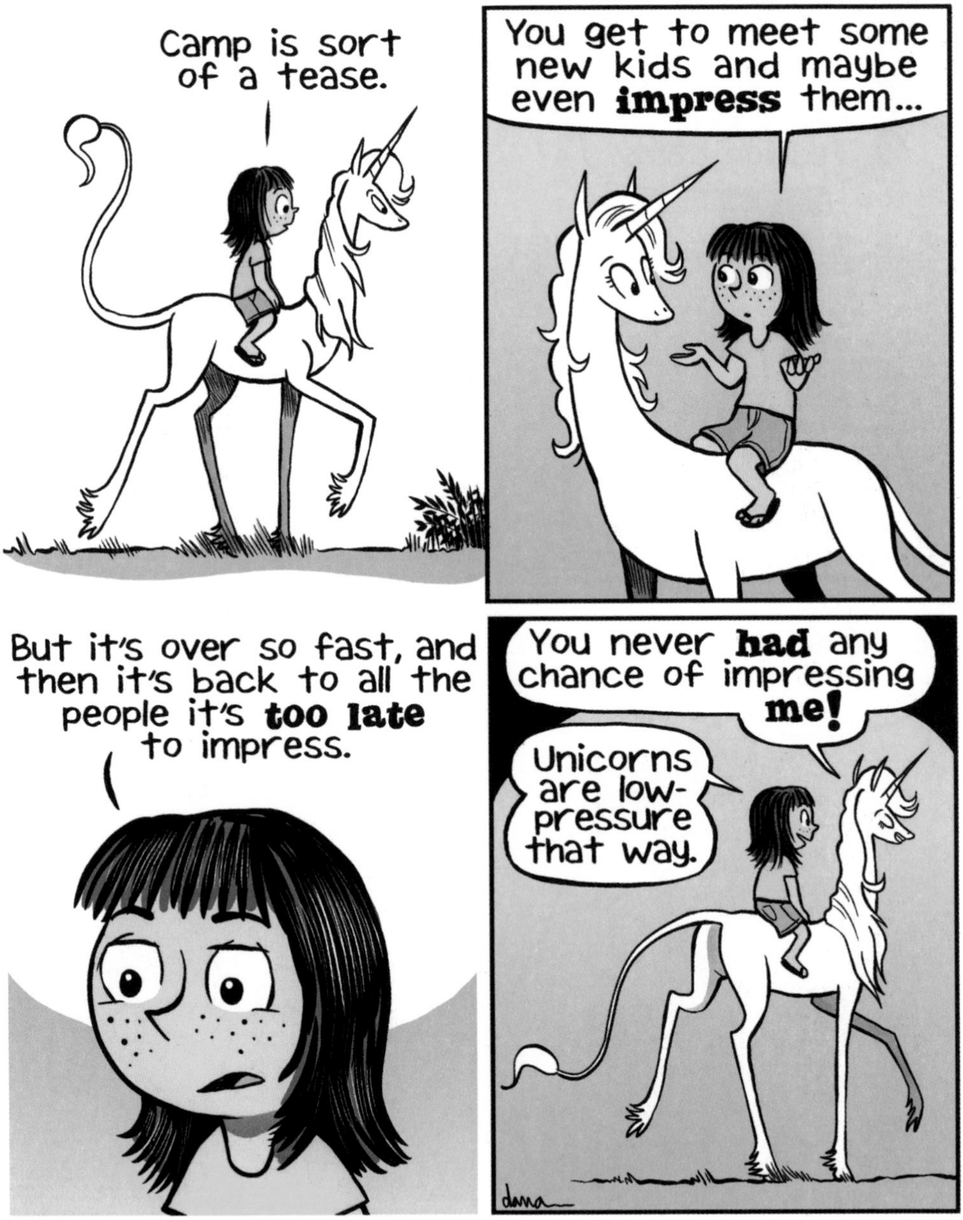
Camp is sort of a tease.
You get to meet some new kids and maybe even **impress** them...
But it's over so fast, and then it's back to all the people it's **too late** to impress.
You never **had** any chance of impressing **me!**
Unicorns are low-pressure that way.

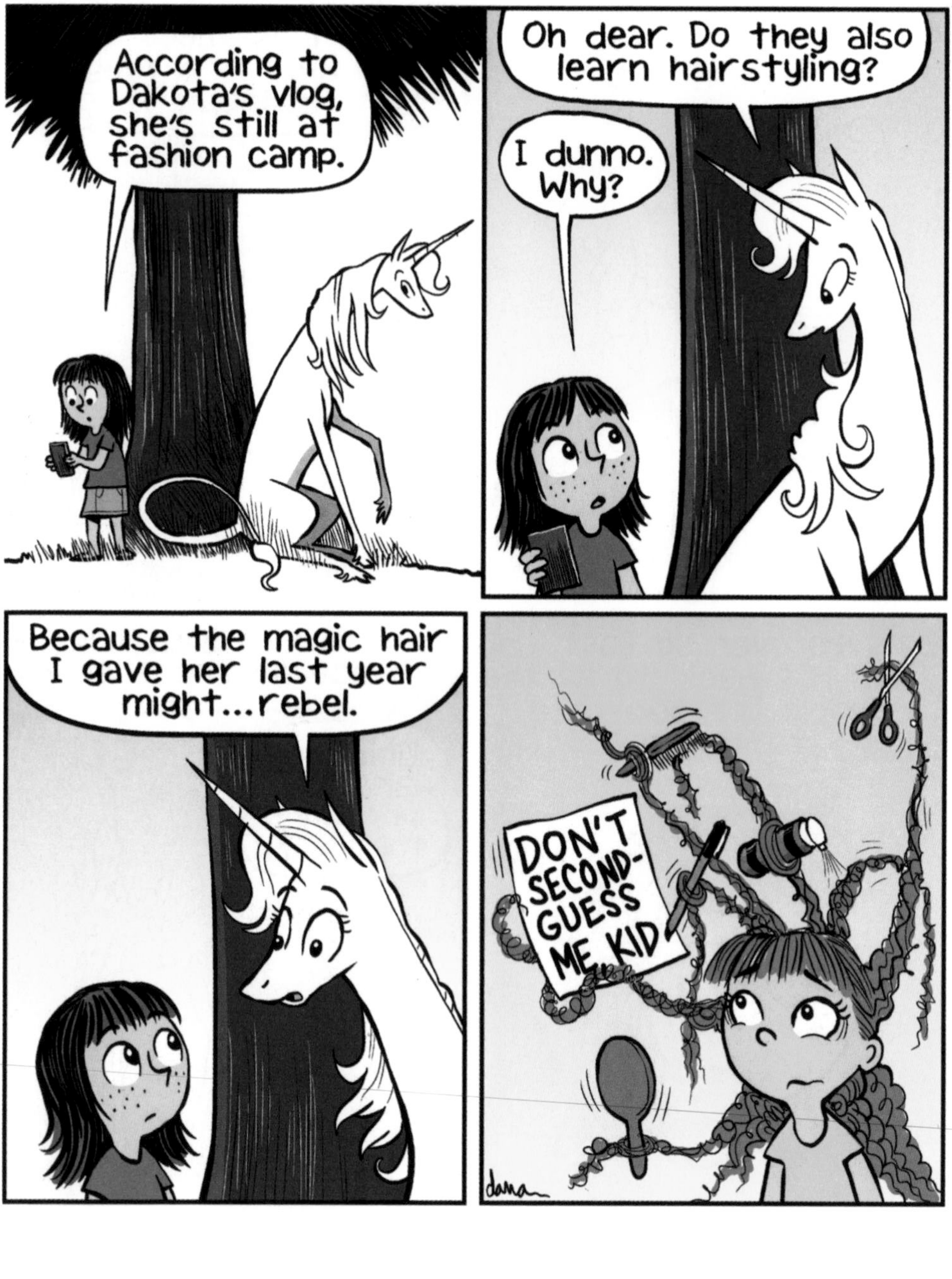
According to Dakota's vlog, she's still at fashion camp.
Oh dear. Do they also learn hairstyling?
I dunno. Why?
Because the magic hair I gave her last year might...rebel.
DON'T SECOND-GUESS ME, KID
dana

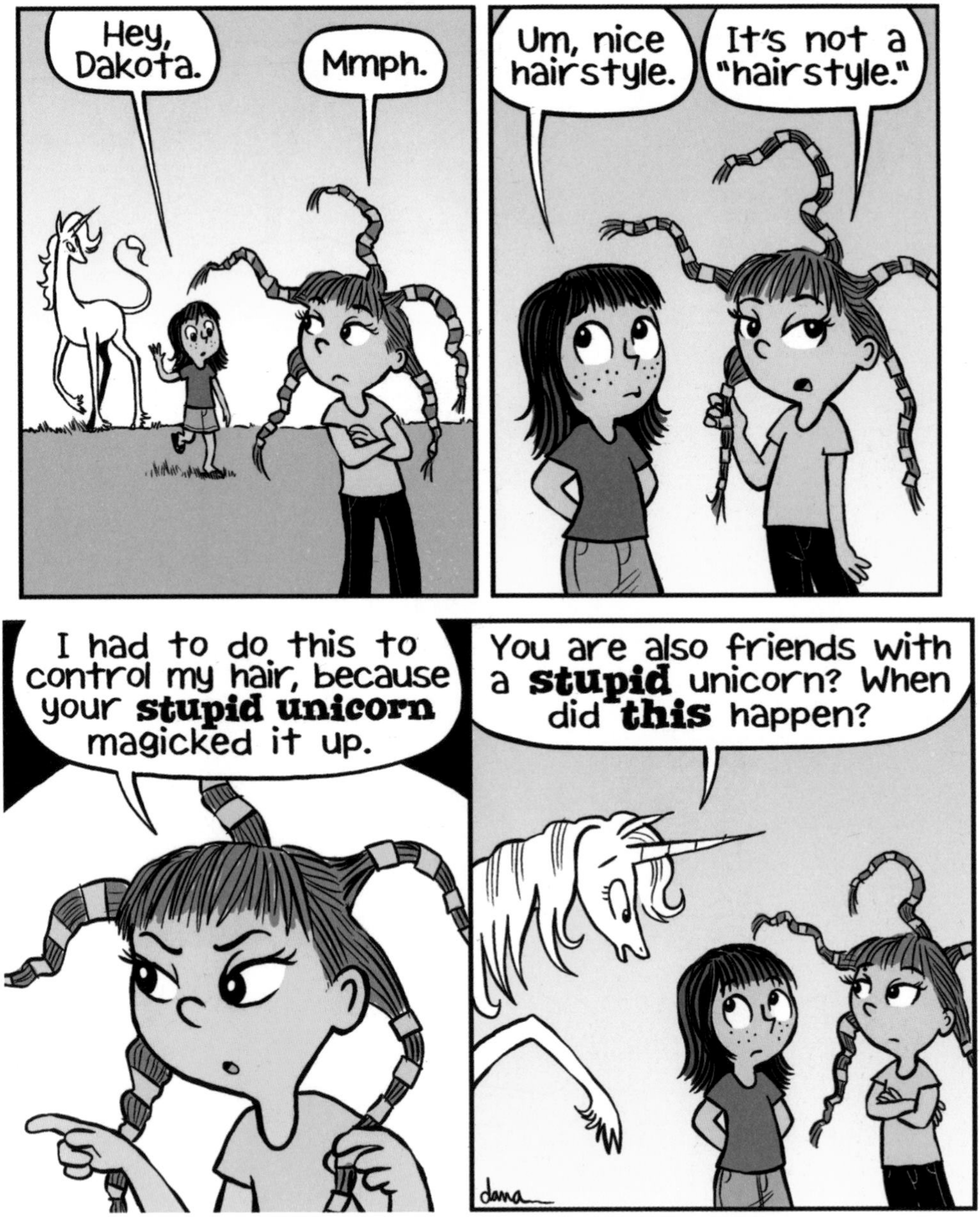
Hey, Dakota.
Mmph.
Um, nice hairstyle.
It's not a "hairstyle."
I had to do this to control my hair, because your **stupid unicorn** magicked it up.
You are also friends with a **stupid** unicorn? When did **this** happen?
dana

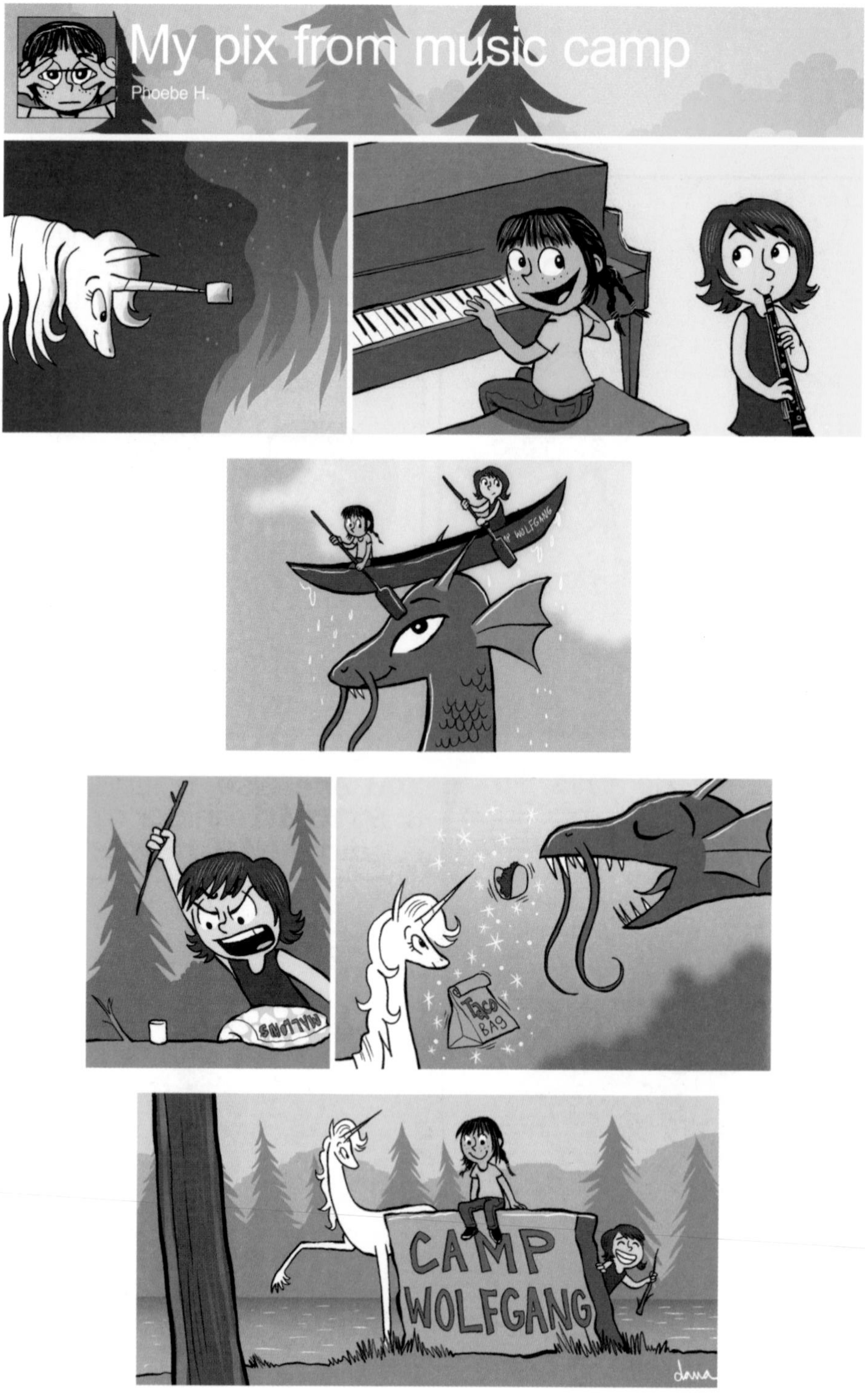
My pix from music camp
Phoebe H.
TACO BAG
CAMP WOLFGANG
dana

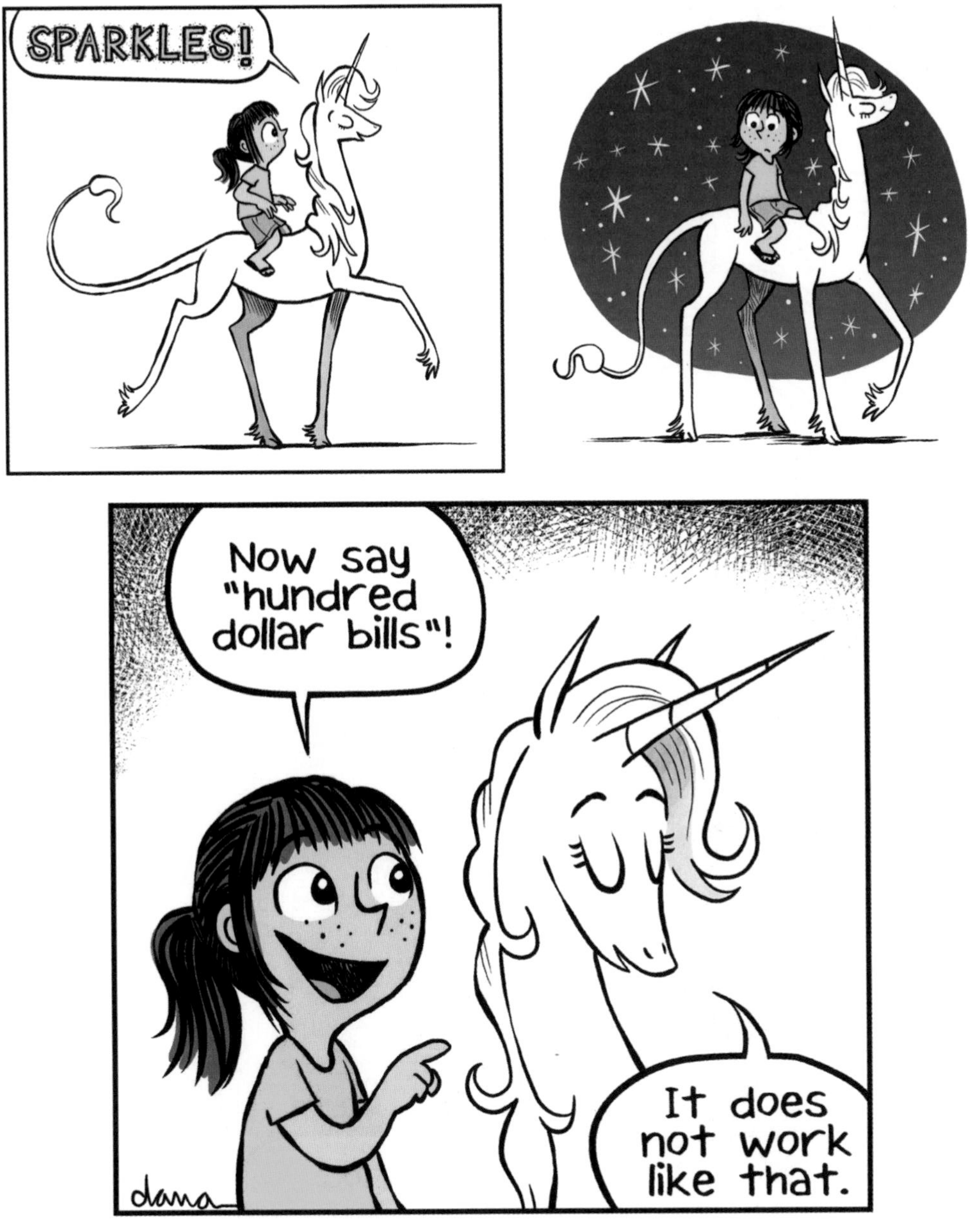
SPARKLES!
Now say "hundred dollar bills"!
It does not work like that.
dana

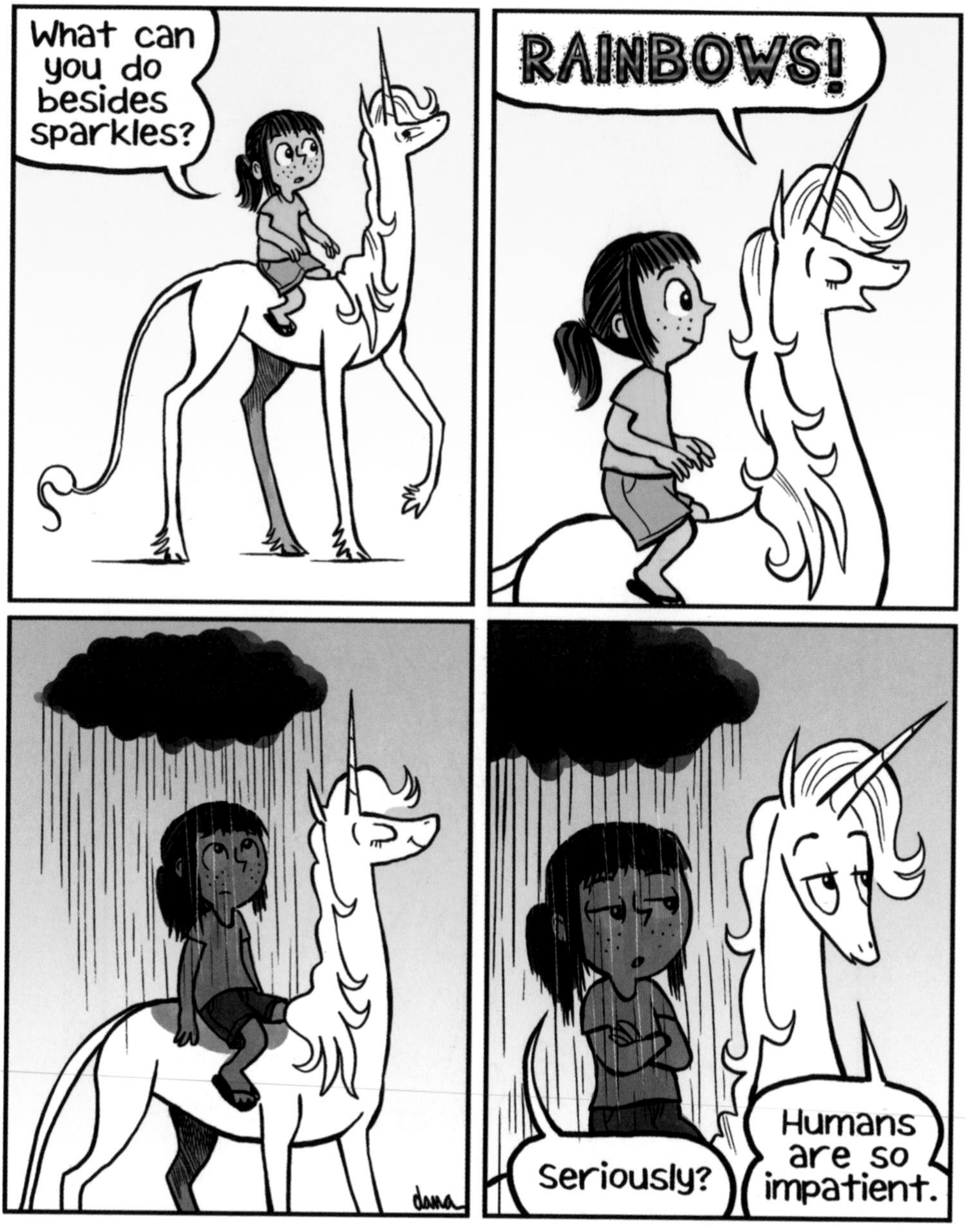
What can you do besides sparkles?
RAINBOWS!
Seriously?
Humans are so impatient.
dana

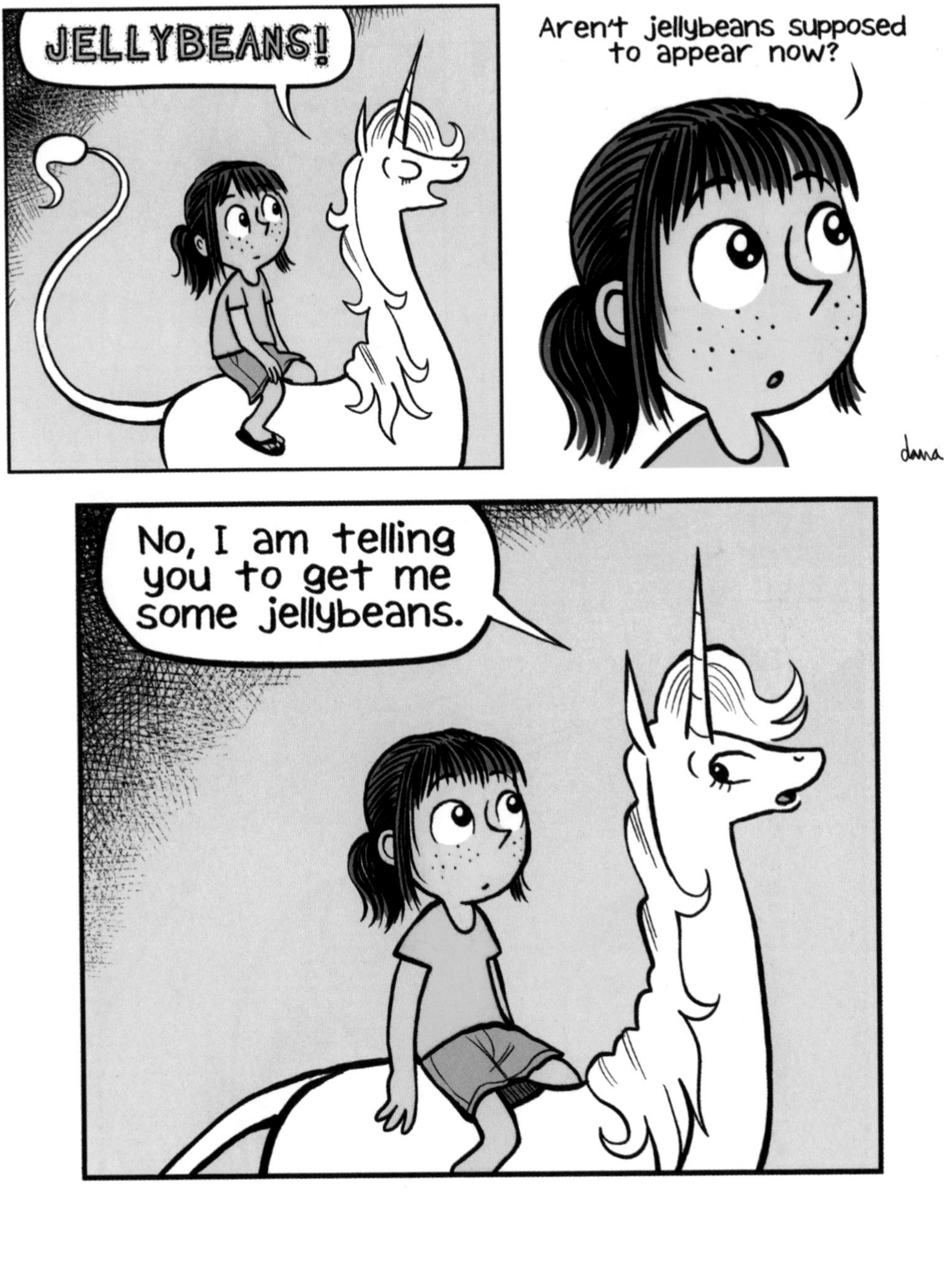
JELLYBEANS!
Aren't jellybeans supposed to appear now?
dana
No, I am telling you to get me some jellybeans.

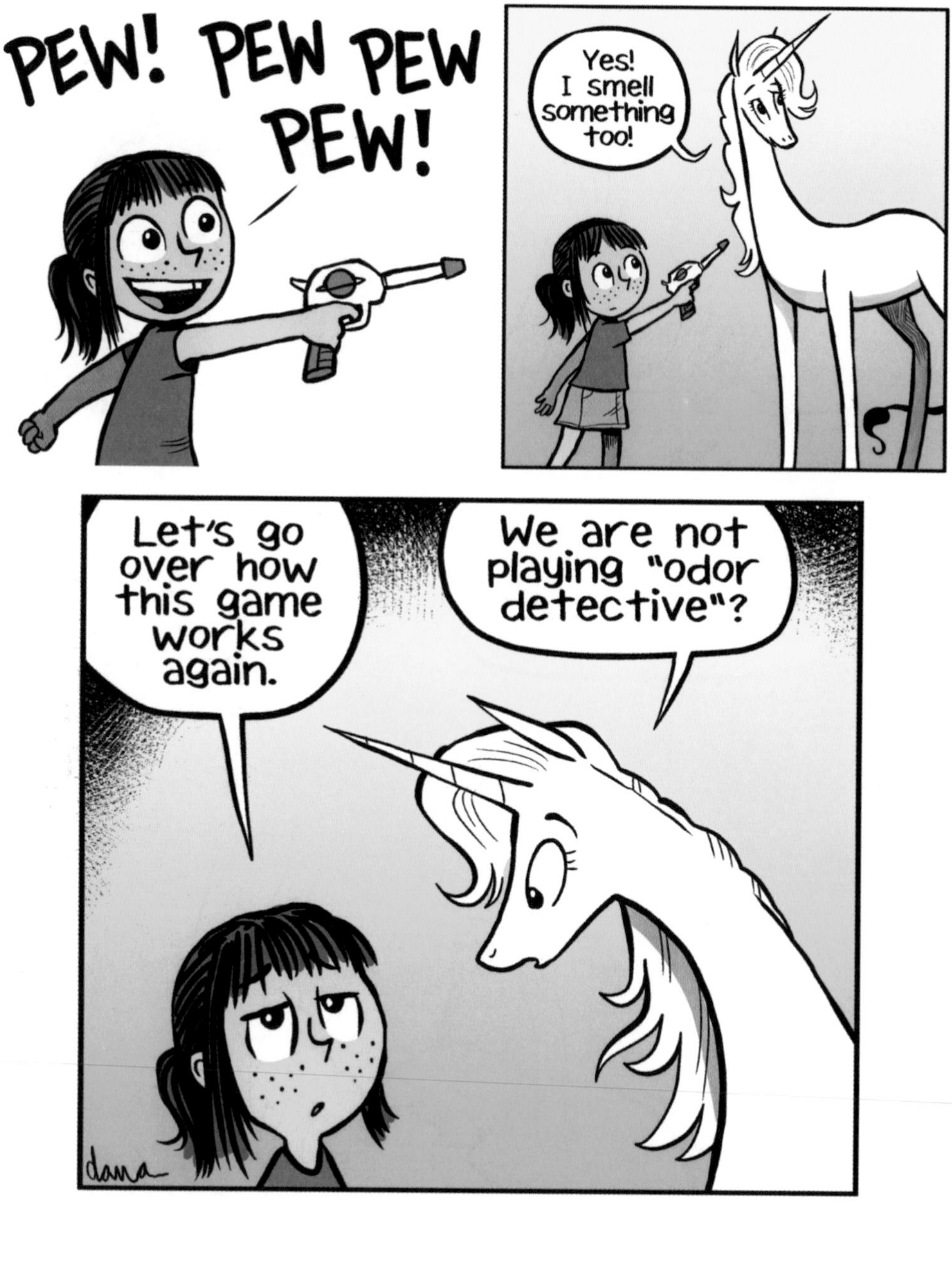
PEW! PEW PEW PEW!
Yes! I smell something too!
Let's go over how this game works again.
We are not playing "odor detective"?
dana

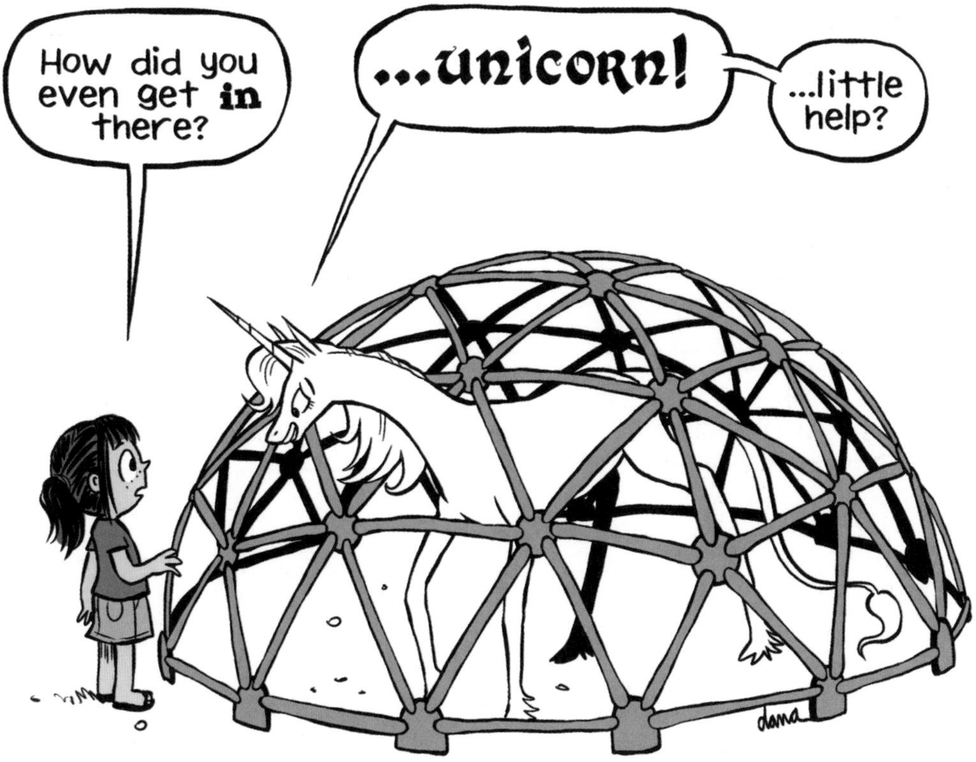
How did you even get **in** there?
...UNICORN!
...little help?
dana

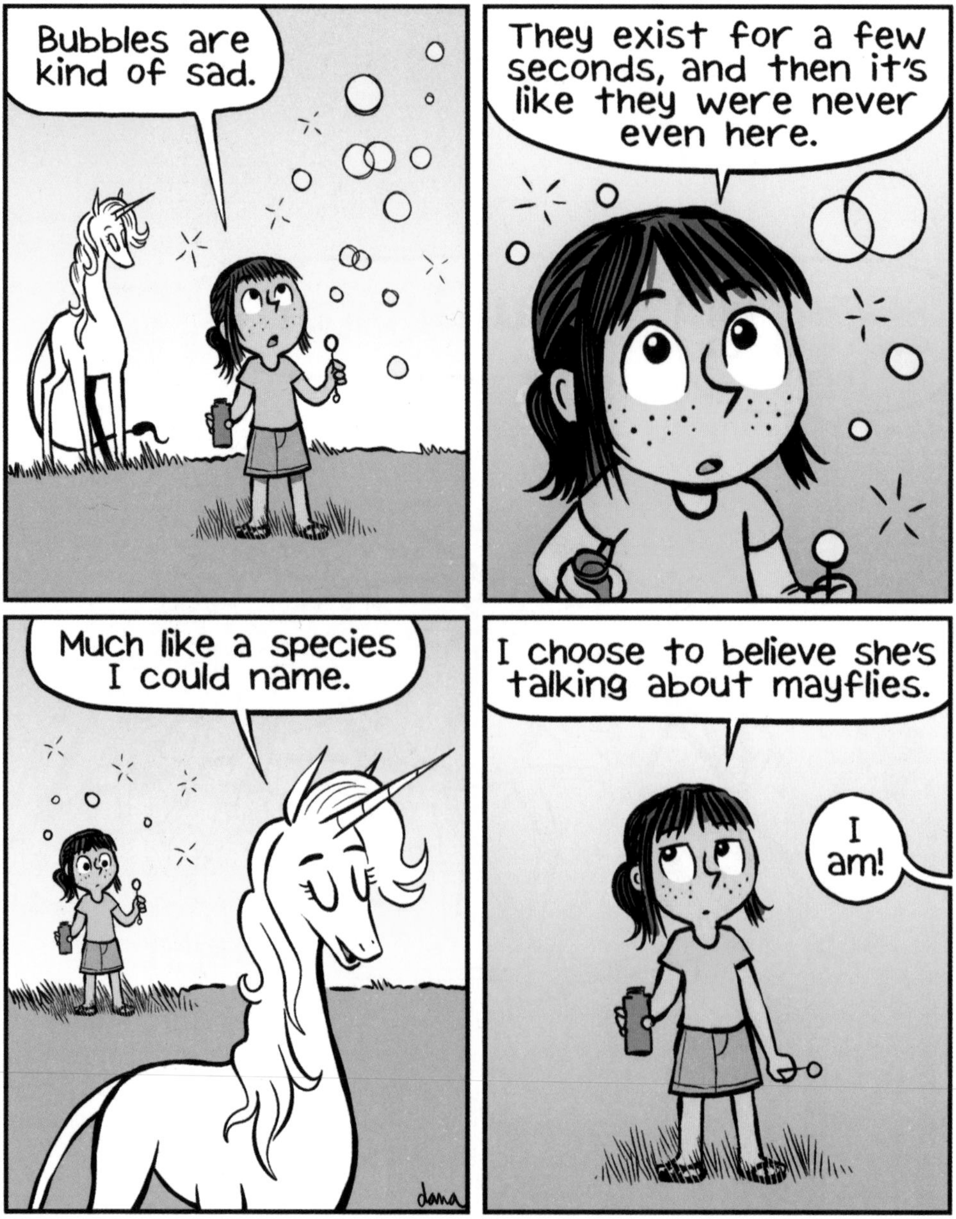
Bubbles are kind of sad.
They exist for a few seconds, and then it's like they were never even here.
Much like a species I could name.
I choose to believe she's talking about mayflies.
I am!
dana

I'd never even seen a firefly until last year when we were on vacation.
Little dancing lights. I begged my parents to move someplace that had them.
But here, there is a **UNICORN.**
Finding that out did change the equation.

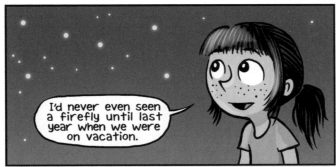

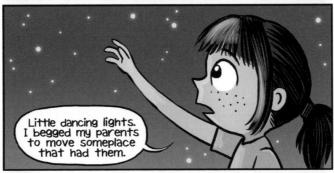

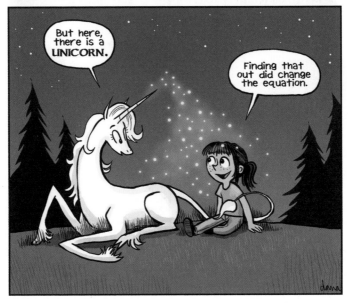

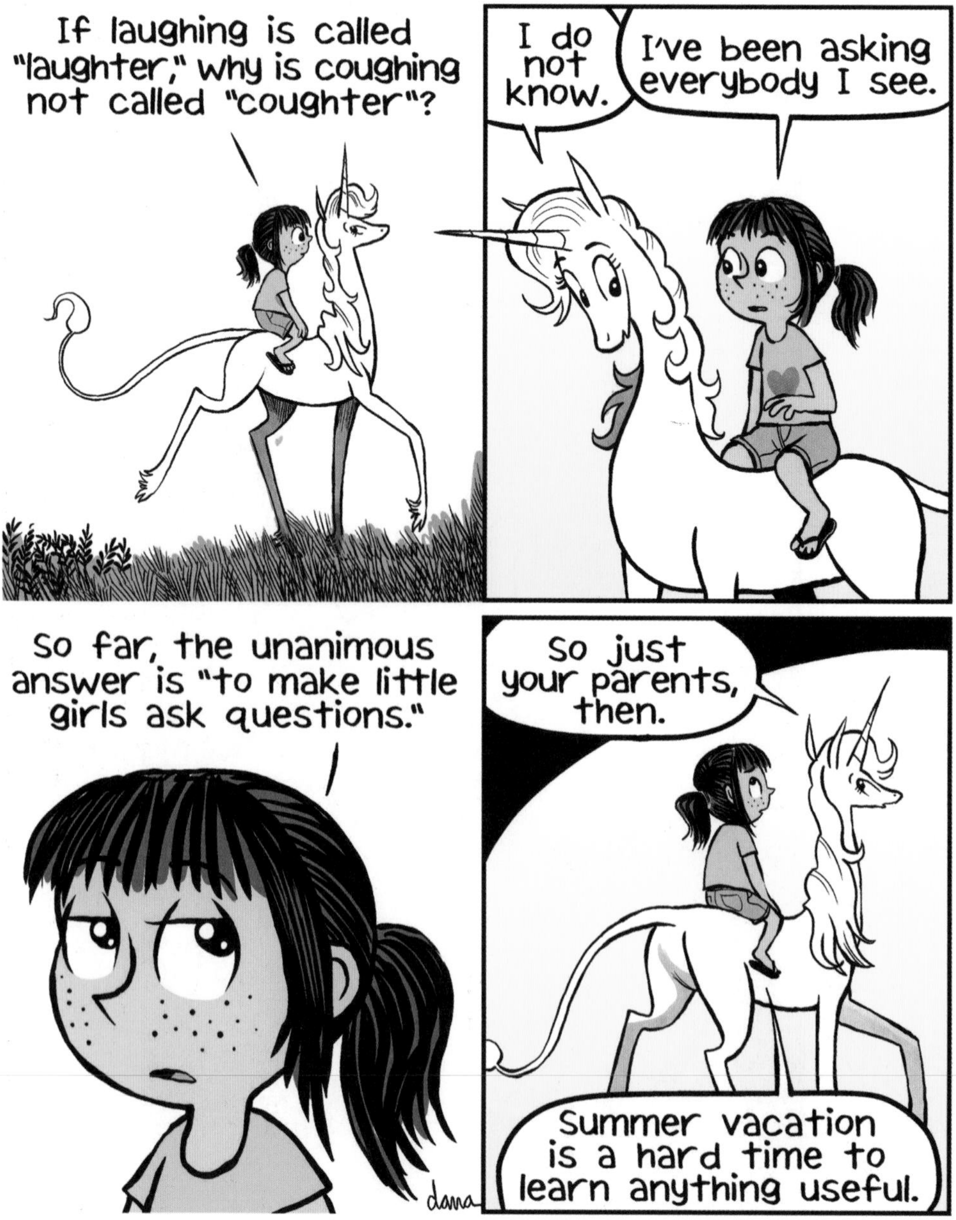
If laughing is called "laughter," why is coughing not called "coughter"?
I do not know.
I've been asking everybody I see.
So far, the unanimous answer is "to make little girls ask questions."
So just your parents, then.
Summer vacation is a hard time to learn anything useful.
dana

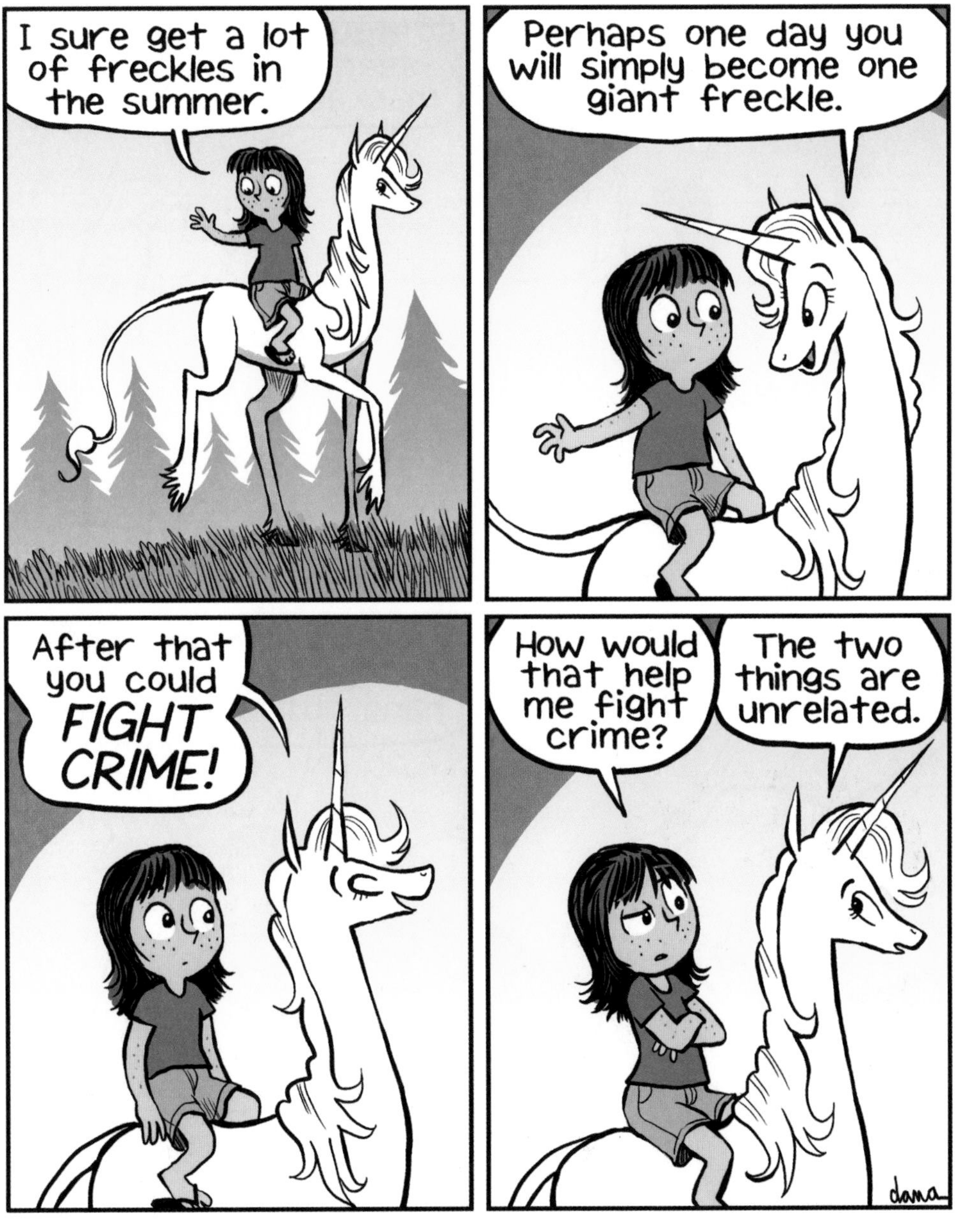
I sure get a lot of freckles in the summer.
Perhaps one day you will simply become one giant freckle.
After that you could FIGHT CRIME!
How would that help me fight crime?
The two things are unrelated.
dana

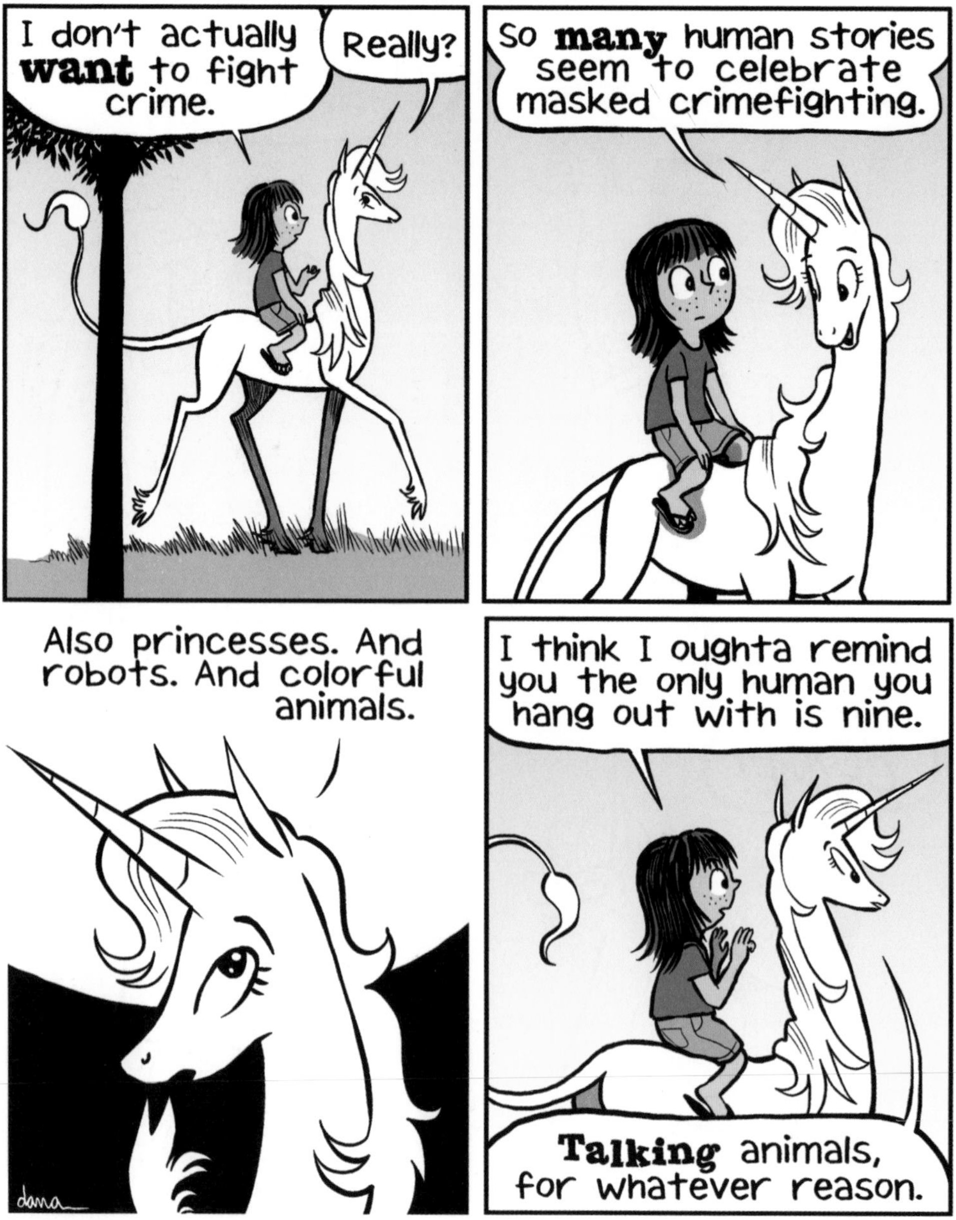
I don't actually **want** to fight crime.
Really?
So **many** human stories seem to celebrate masked crimefighting.
Also princesses. And robots. And colorful animals.
I think I oughta remind you the only human you hang out with is nine.
Talking animals, for whatever reason.
dana

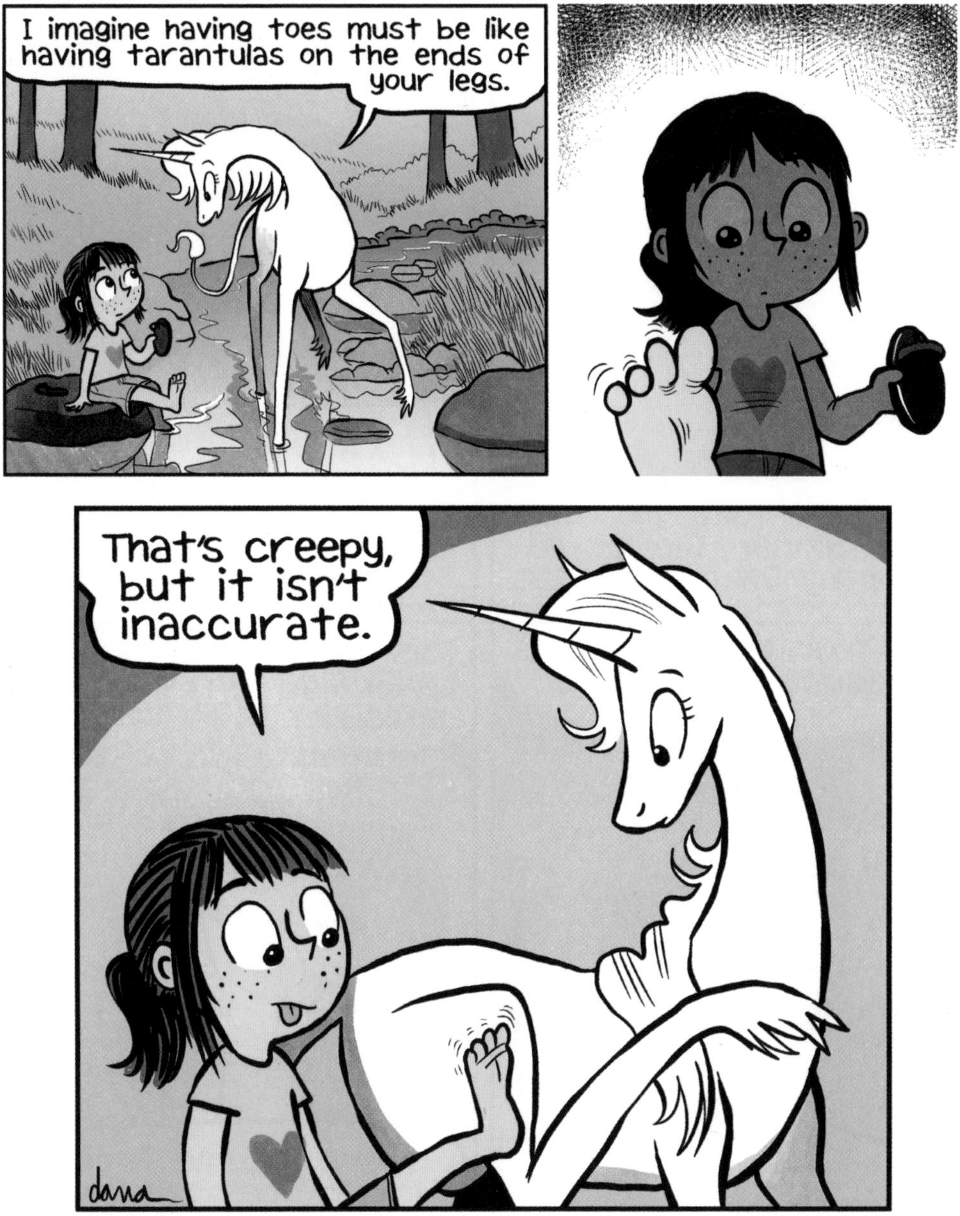
I imagine having toes must be like having tarantulas on the ends of your legs.
That's creepy, but it isn't inaccurate.
dana

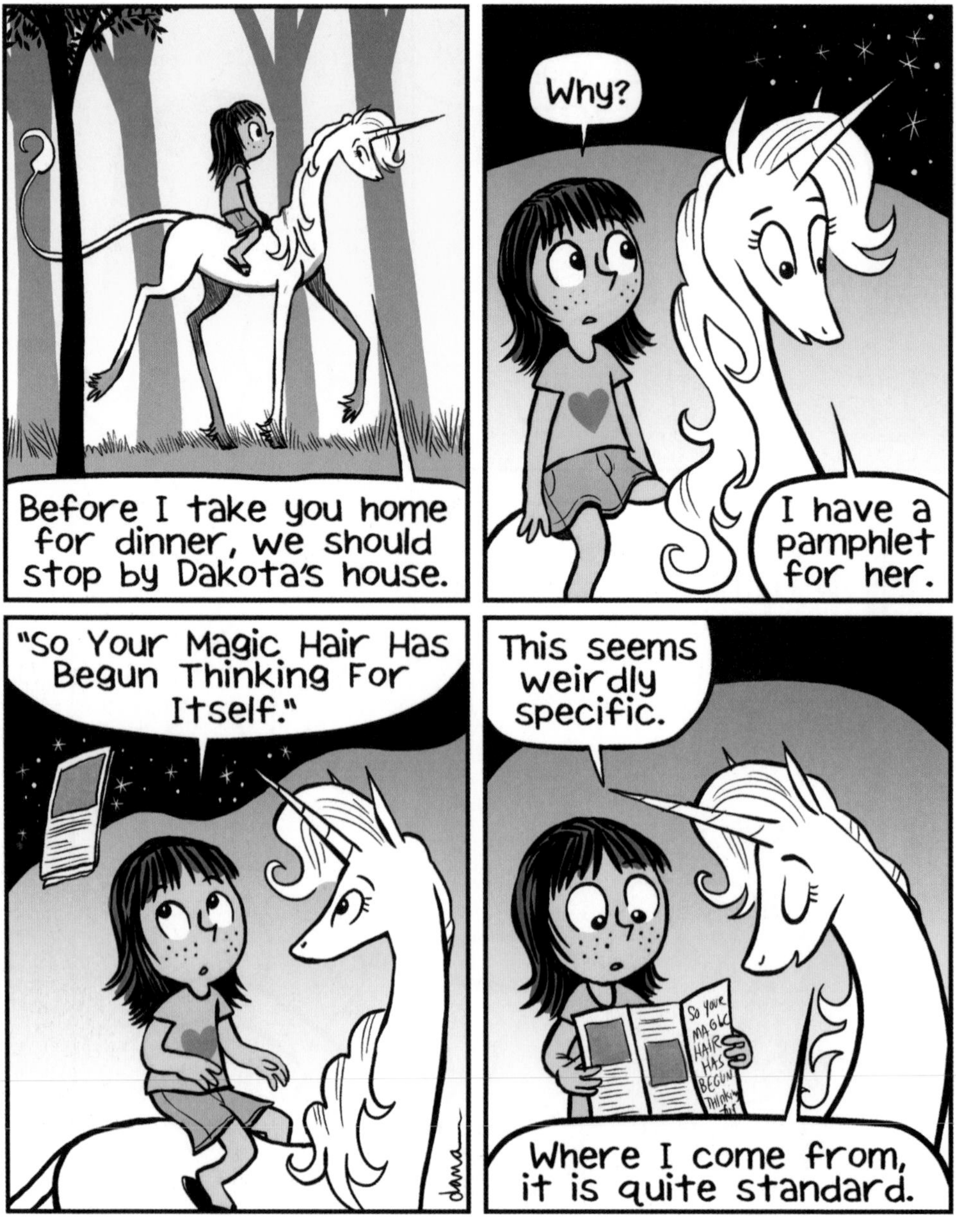
Before I take you home for dinner, we should stop by Dakota's house.
Why?
I have a pamphlet for her.
"So Your Magic Hair Has Begun Thinking For Itself."
This seems weirdly specific.
Where I come from, it is quite standard.

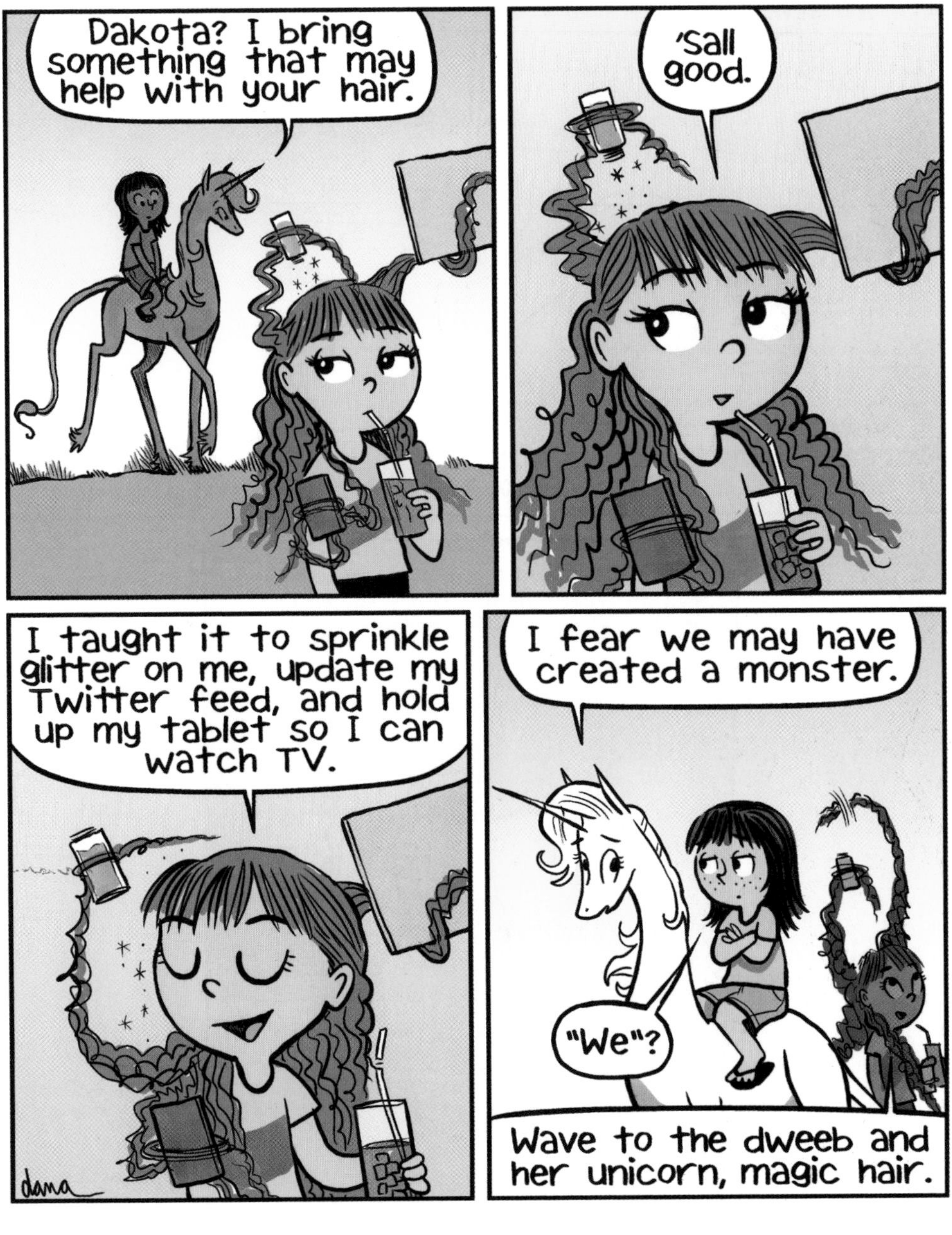
Dakota? I bring something that may help with your hair.
'Sall good.
I taught it to sprinkle glitter on me, update my Twitter feed, and hold up my tablet so I can watch TV.
dana
I fear we may have created a monster.
"We"?
Wave to the dweeb and her unicorn, magic hair.

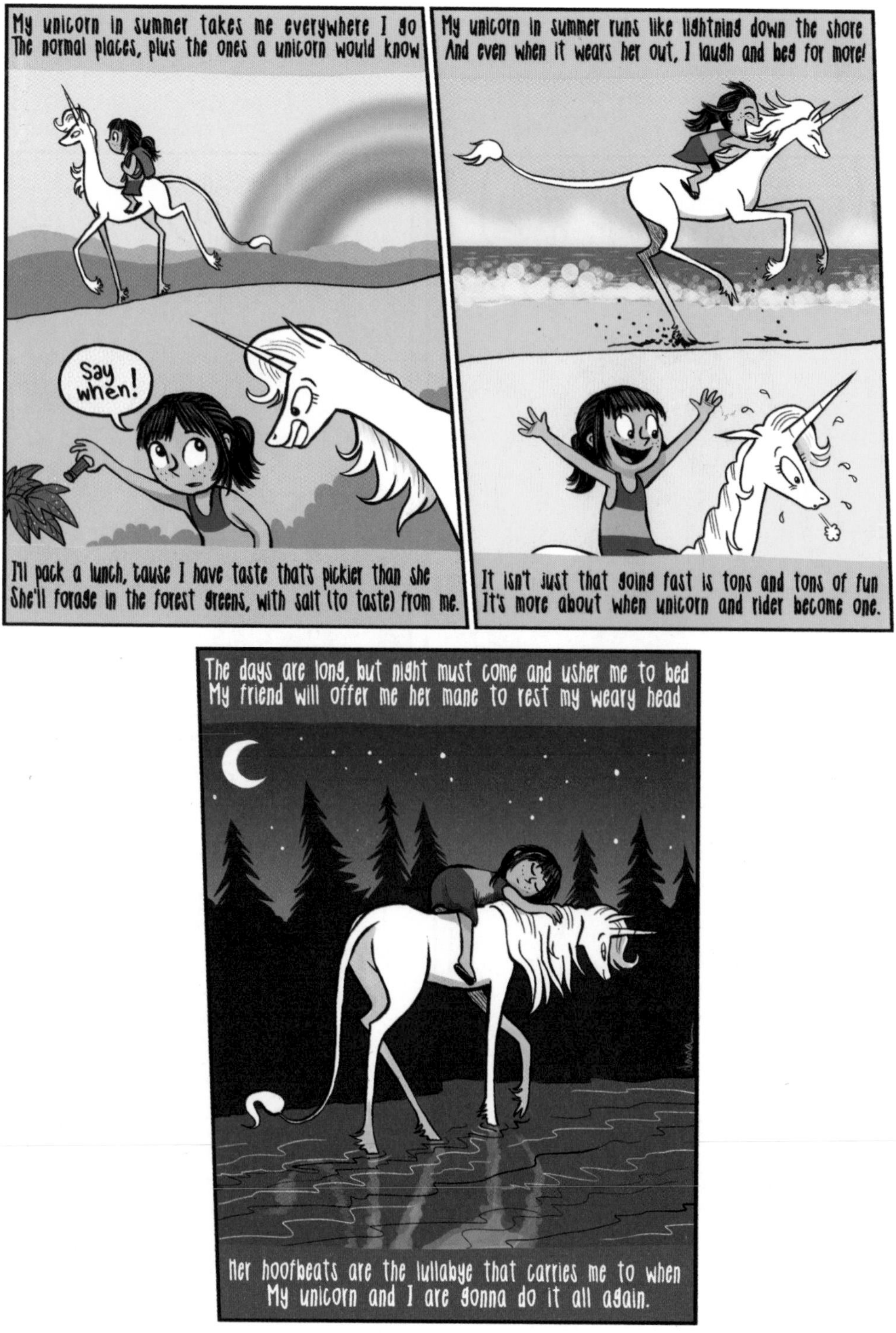
My unicorn in summer takes me everywhere I go
The normal places, plus the ones a unicorn would know
My unicorn in summer runs like lightning down the shore
And even when it wears her out, I laugh and beg for more!
Say when!
I'll pack a lunch, cause I have taste that's pickier than she
She'll forage in the forest greens, with salt (to taste) from me.
It isn't just that going fast is tons and tons of fun
It's more about when unicorn and rider become one.
The days are long, but night must come and usher me to bed
My friend will offer me her mane to rest my weary head
Her hoofbeats are the lullabye that carries me to when
My unicorn and I are gonna do it all again.

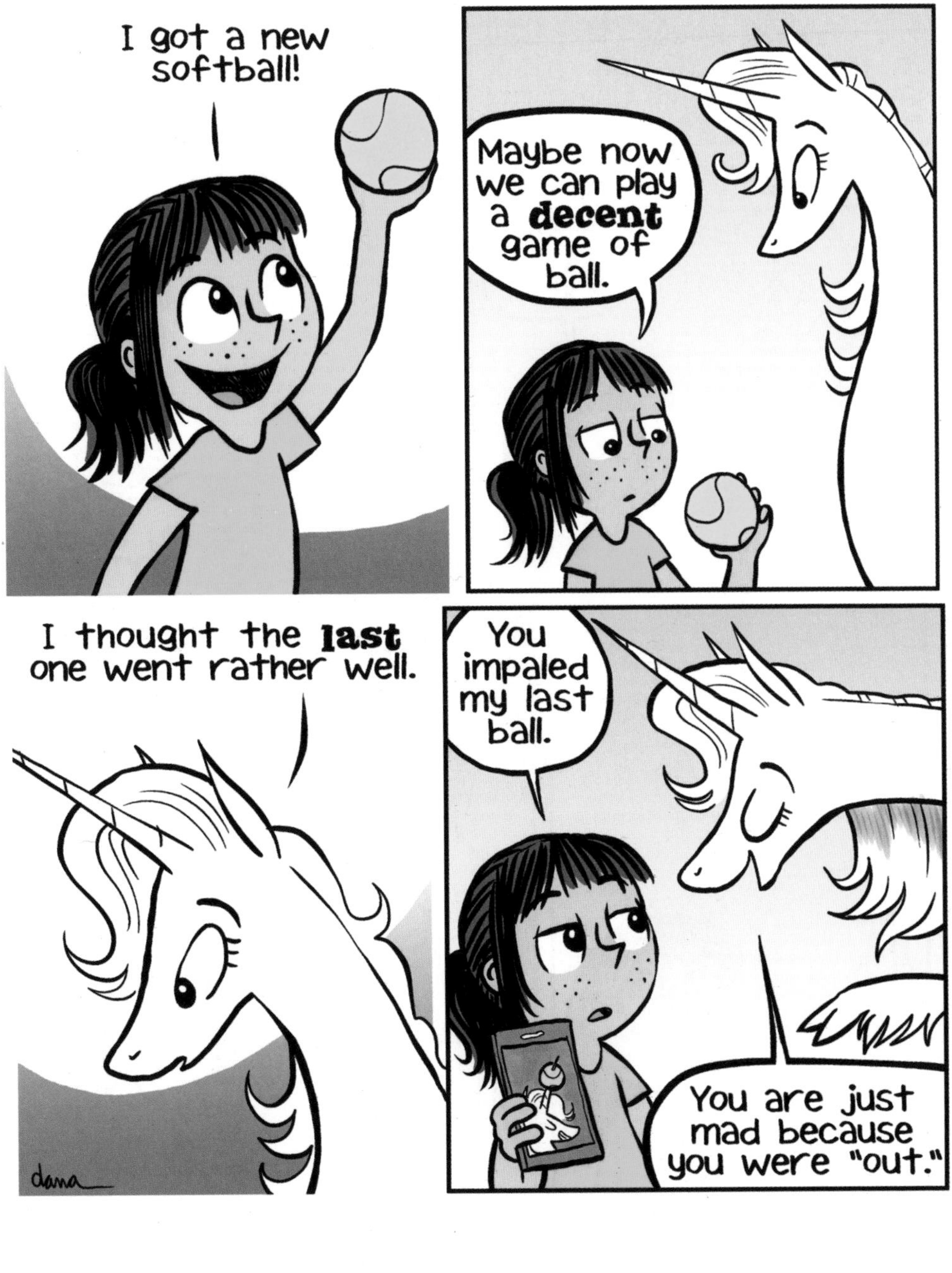
I got a new softball!
Maybe now we can play a **decent** game of ball.
I thought the **last** one went rather well.
You impaled my last ball.
You are just mad because you were "out."
dana

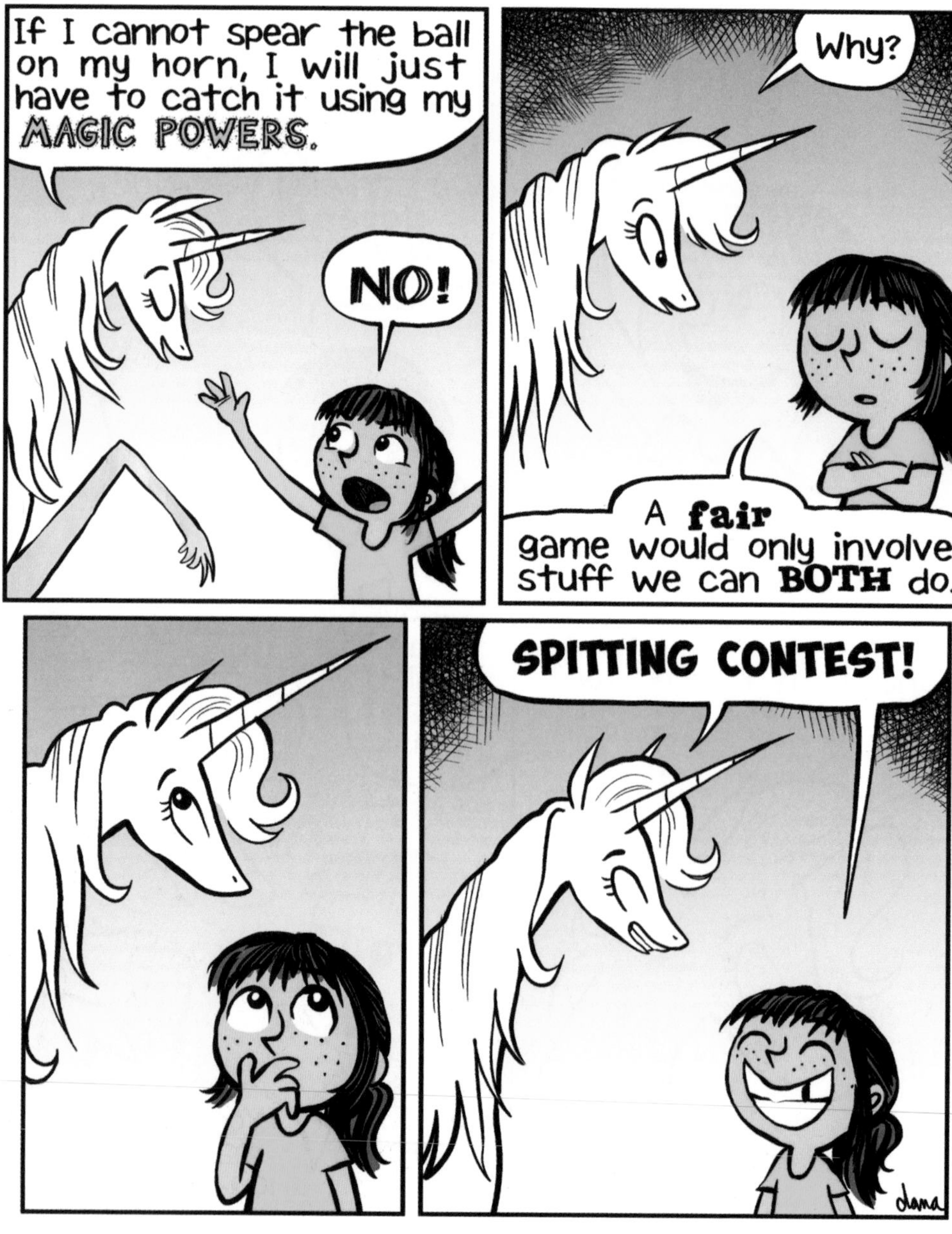

If I cannot spear the ball on my horn, I will just have to catch it using my MAGIC POWERS.
NO!
Why?
A **fair** game would only involve stuff we can **BOTH** do.
SPITTING CONTEST!
dana

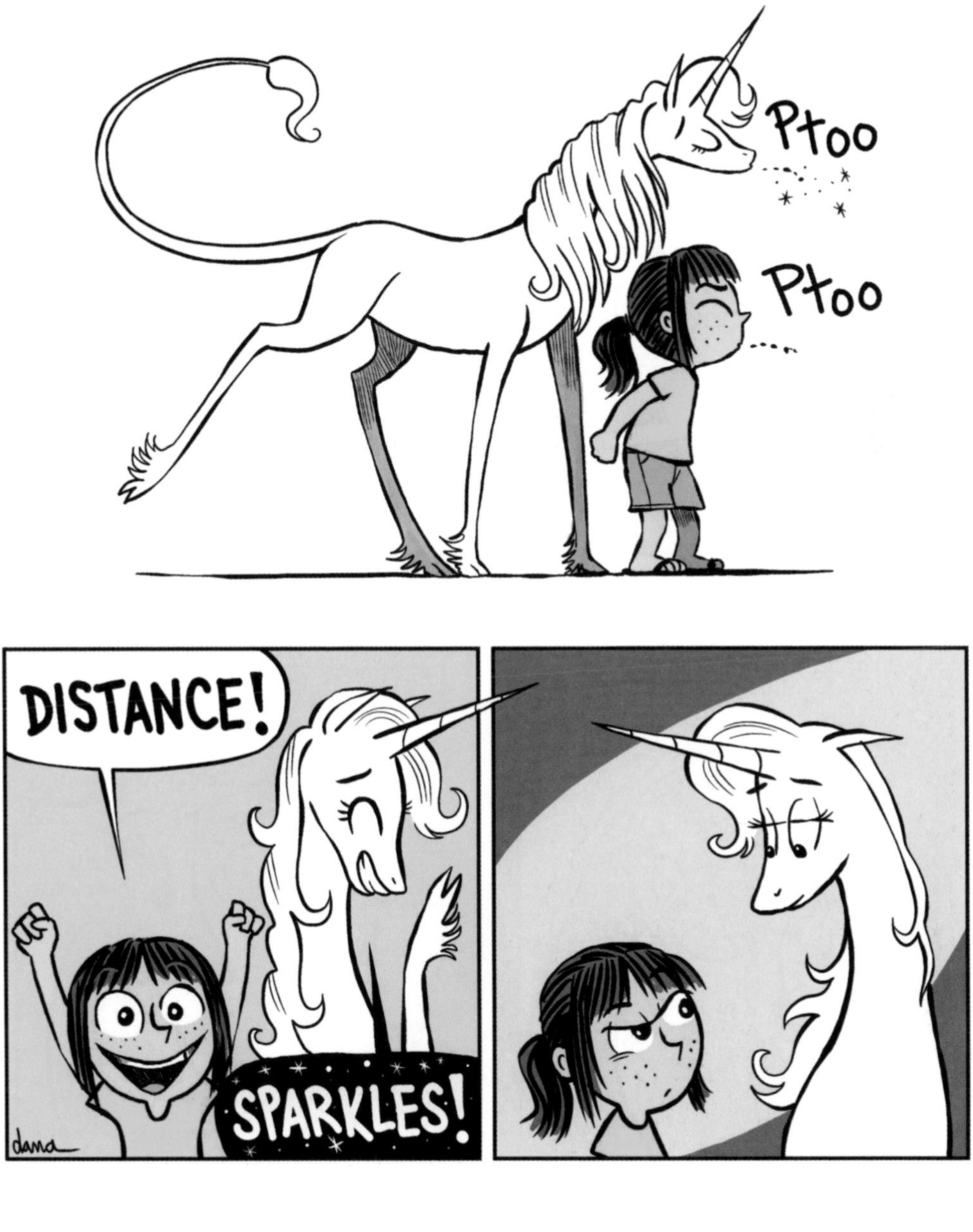
Ptoo
Ptoo
DISTANCE!
SPARKLES!
dana

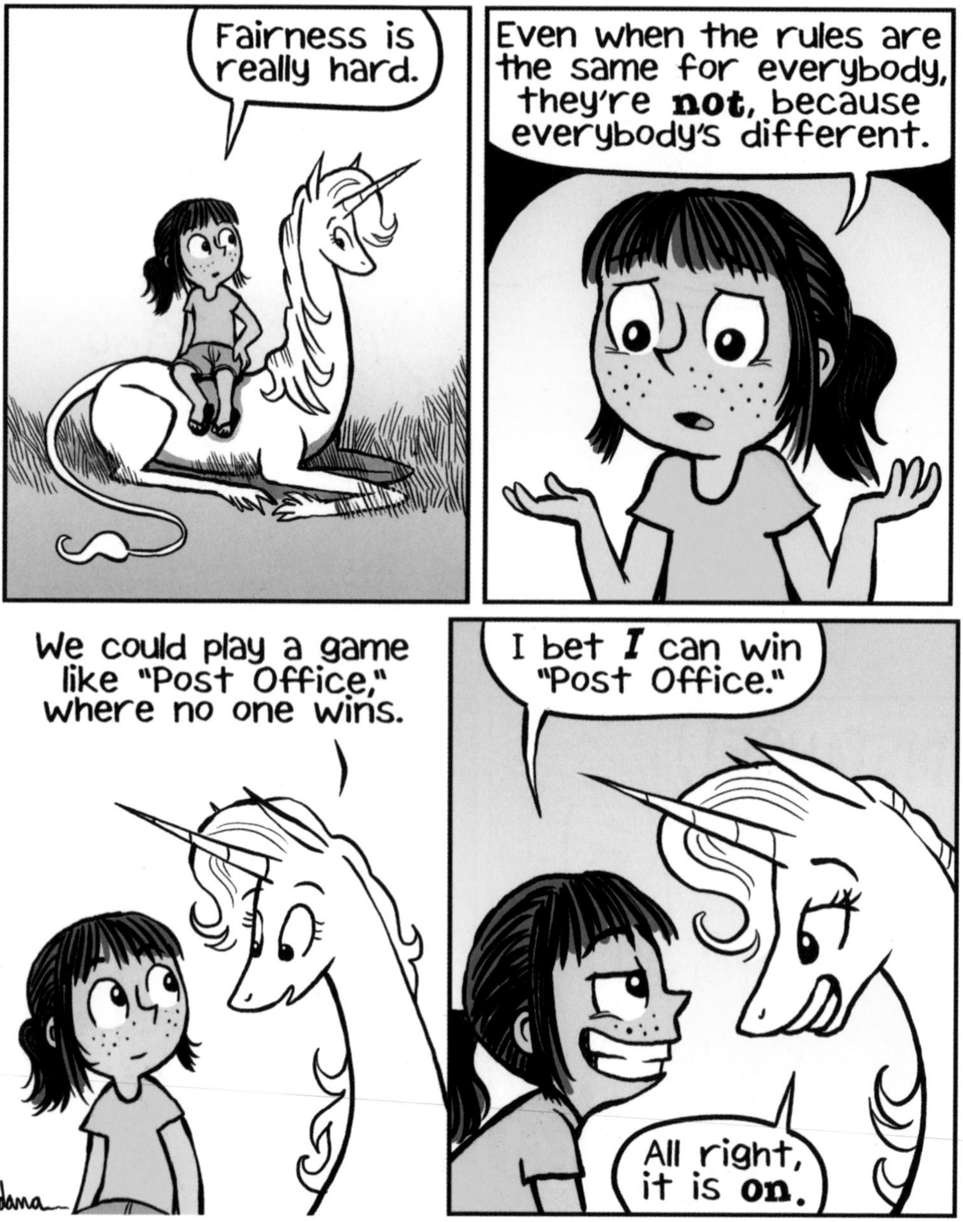
Fairness is really hard.
Even when the rules are the same for everybody, they're **not**, because everybody's different.
We could play a game like "Post Office," where no one wins.
I bet ***I*** can win "Post Office."
All right, it is **on**.
dana

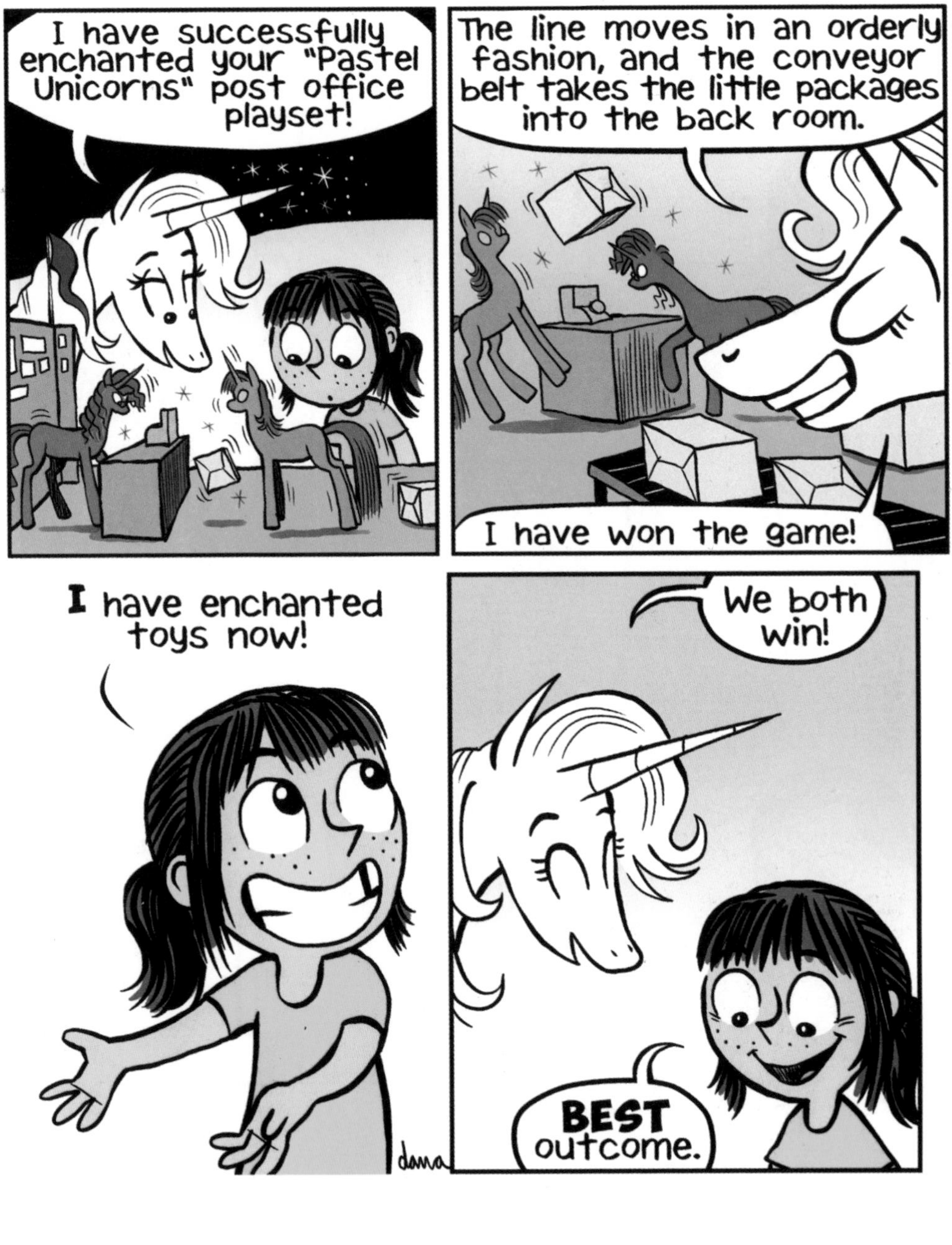
I have successfully enchanted your "Pastel Unicorns" post office playset!
The line moves in an orderly fashion, and the conveyor belt takes the little packages into the back room.
I have won the game!
I have enchanted toys now!
We both win!
BEST outcome.
dana

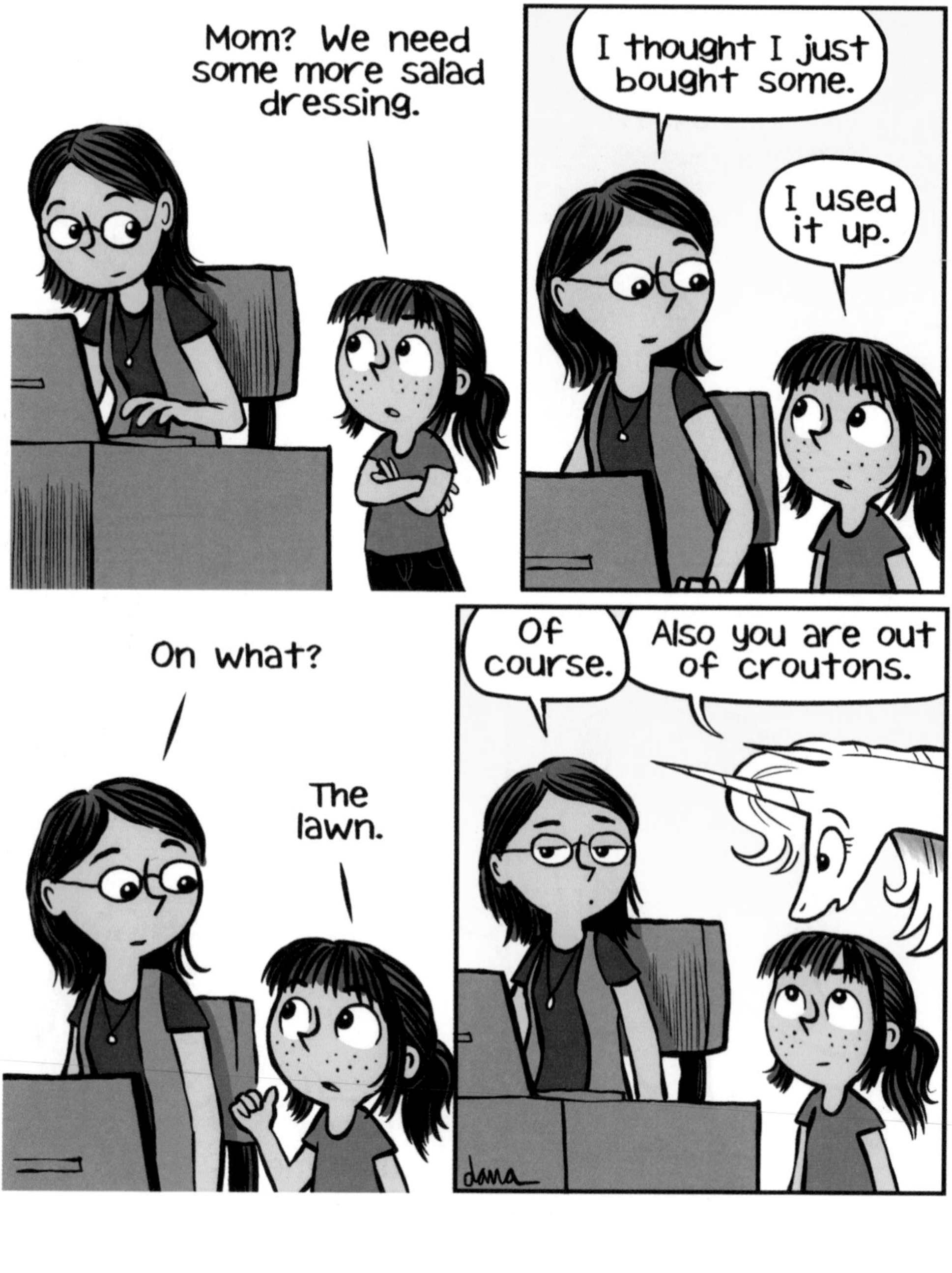
Mom? We need some more salad dressing.
I thought I just bought some.
I used it up.
On what?
The lawn.
Of course.
Also you are out of croutons.
dana

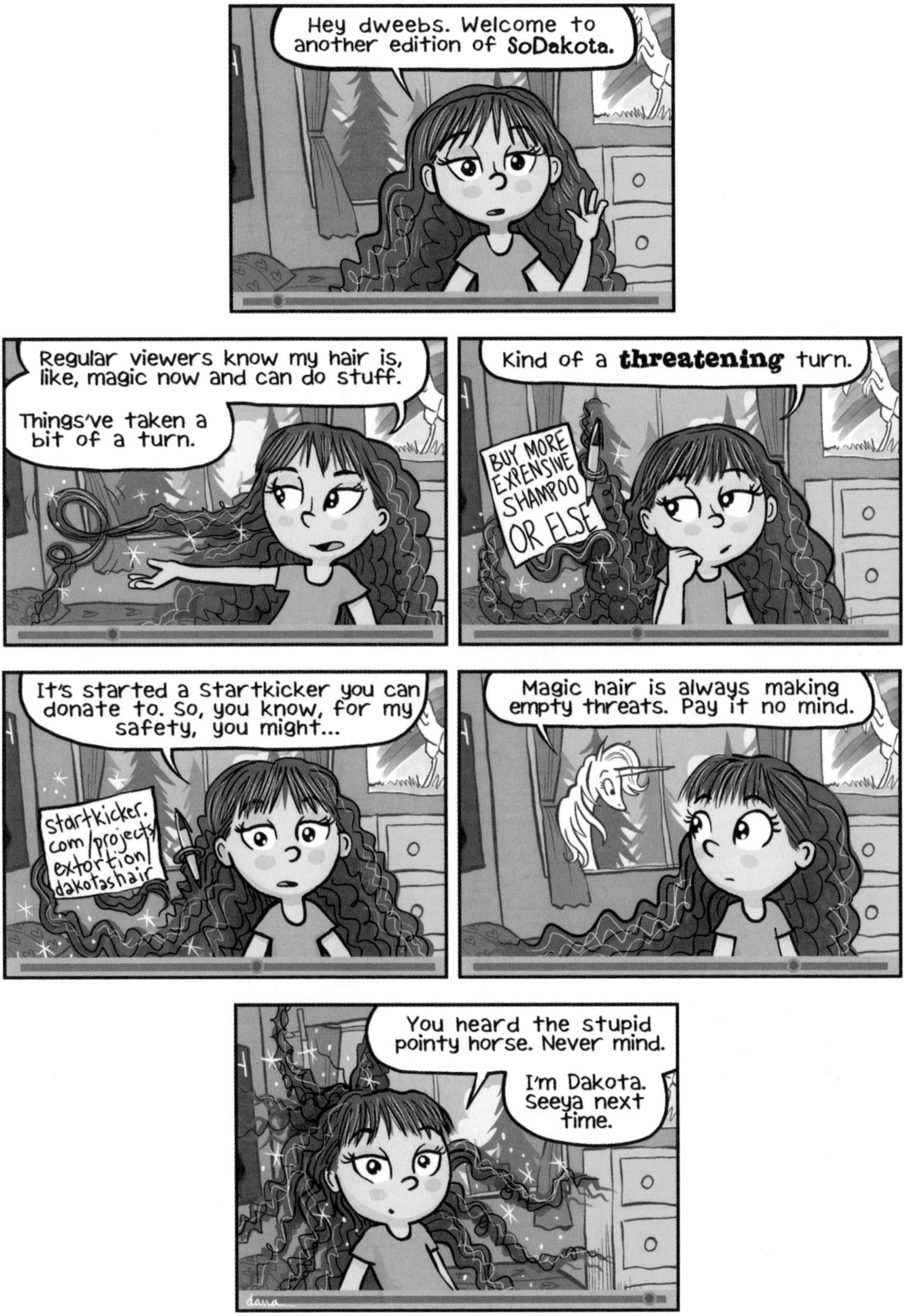
Hey dweebs. Welcome to another edition of SoDakota.
Regular viewers know my hair is, like, magic now and can do stuff.
Things've taken a bit of a turn.
Kind of a threatening turn.
BUY MORE EXPENSIVE SHAMPOO OR ELSE
It's started a Startkicker you can donate to. So, you know, for my safety, you might...
startkicker.com/projects/extortion/dakotashair
Magic hair is always making empty threats. Pay it no mind.
You heard the stupid pointy horse. Never mind.
I'm Dakota. Seeya next time.
dana

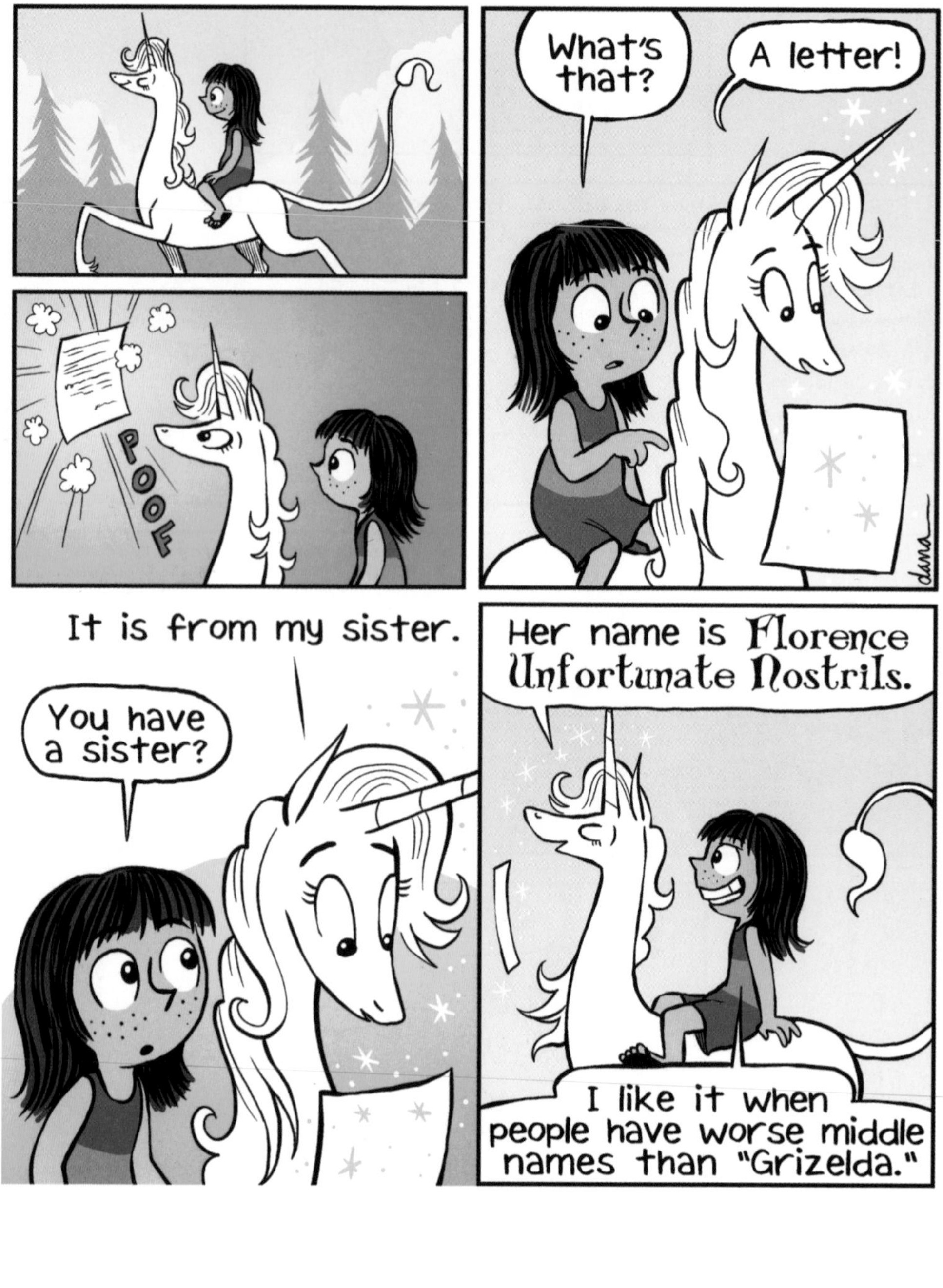

What's that?
A letter!
POOF
It is from my sister.
You have a sister?
Her name is Florence Unfortunate Nostrils.
I like it when people have worse middle names than "Grizelda."

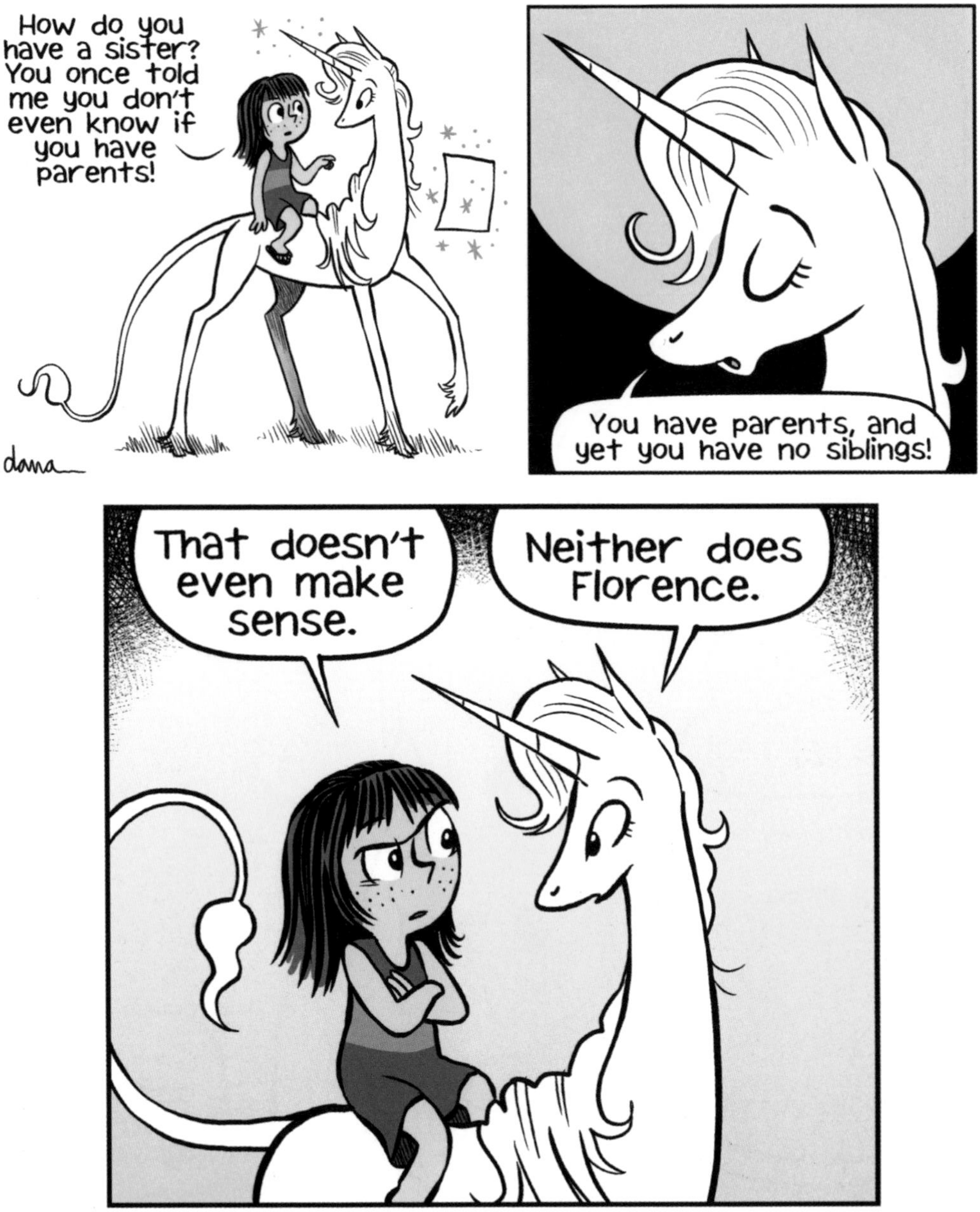
How do you have a sister? You once told me you don't even know if you have parents!
You have parents, and yet you have no siblings!
That doesn't even make sense.
Neither does Florence.
dana

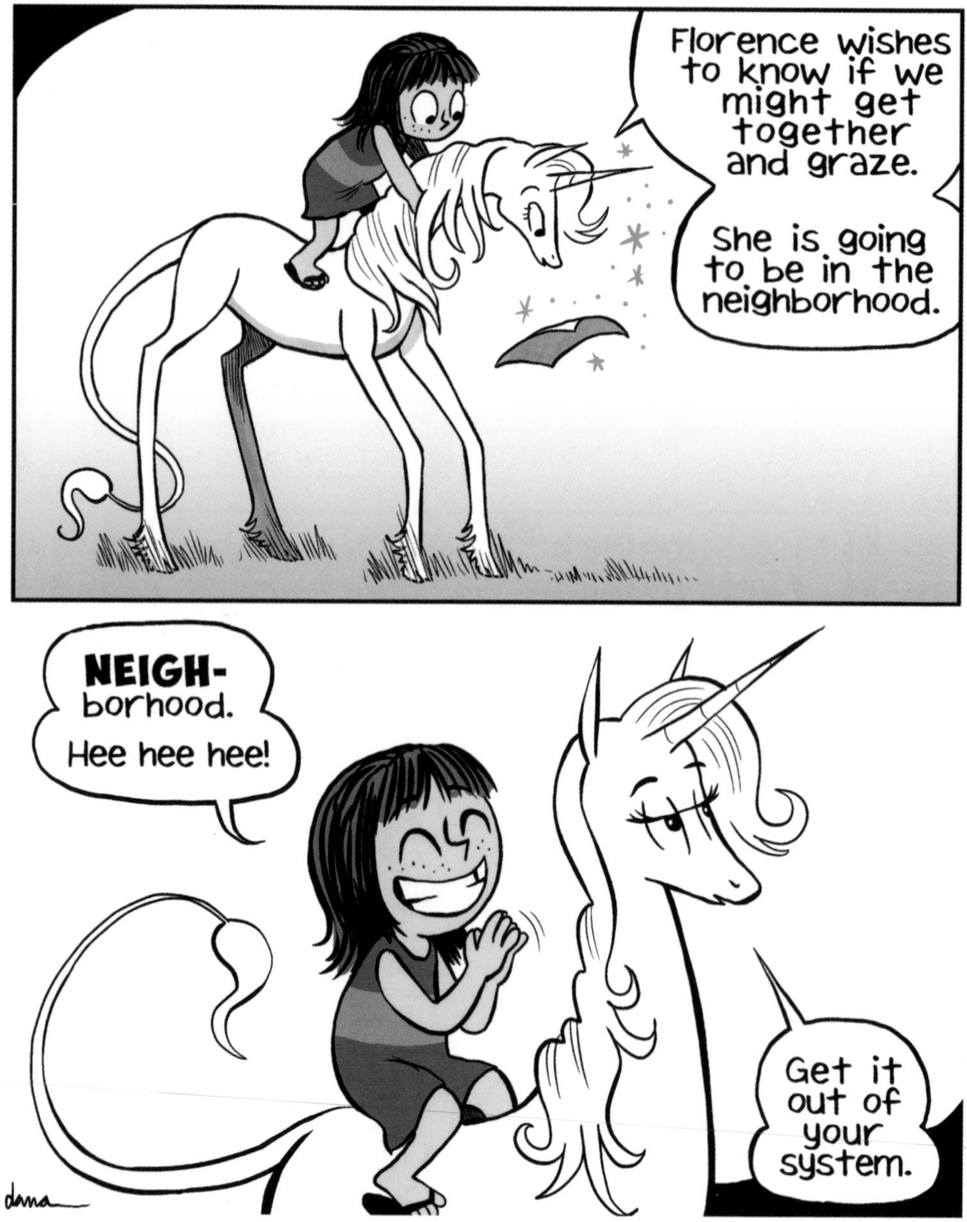
Florence wishes to know if we might get together and graze.
She is going to be in the neighborhood.
NEIGH-borhood. Hee hee hee!
Get it out of your system.
dana

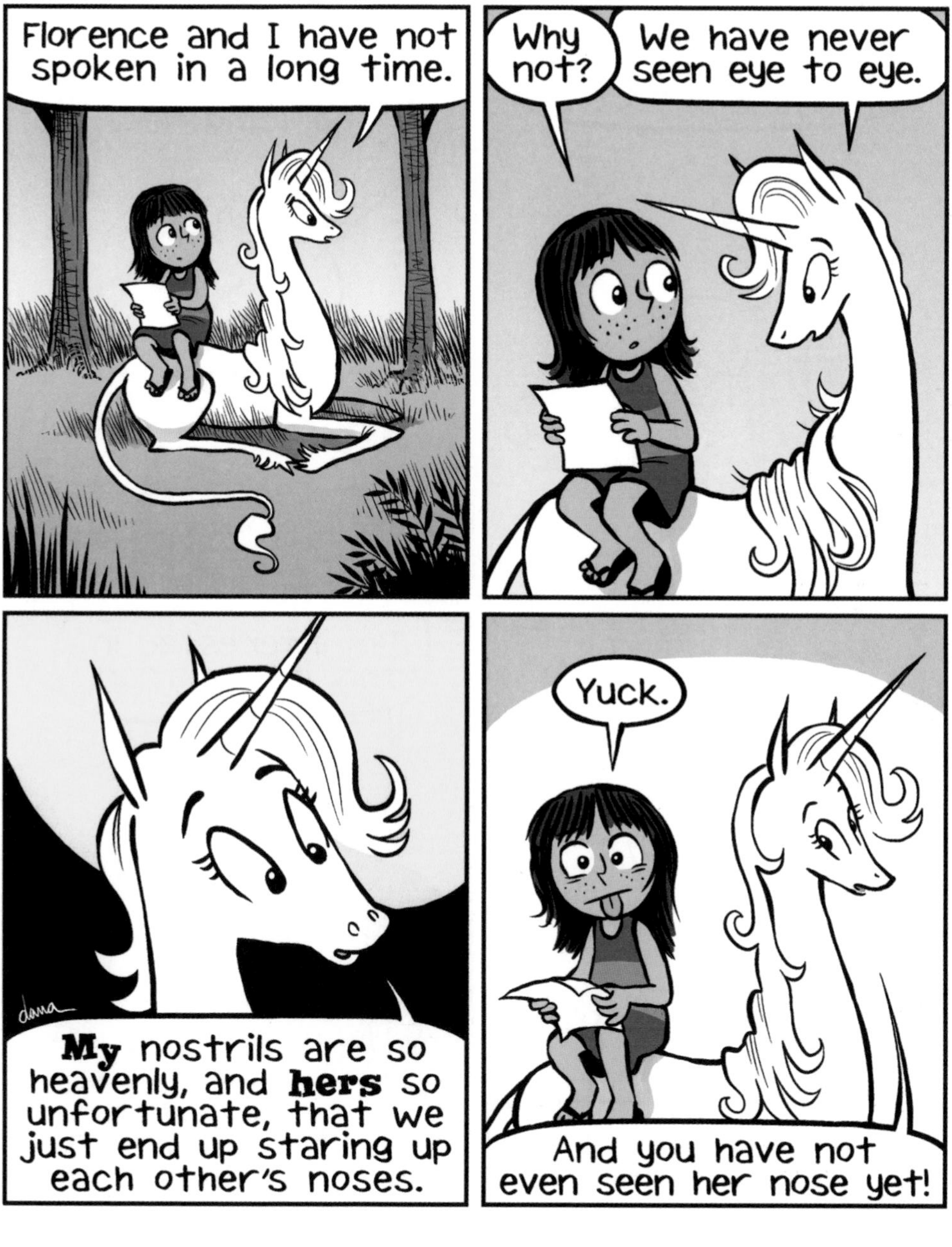
Florence and I have not spoken in a long time.
Why not?
We have never seen eye to eye.
dana
My nostrils are so heavenly, and **hers** so unfortunate, that we just end up staring up each other's noses.
Yuck.
And you have not even seen her nose yet!

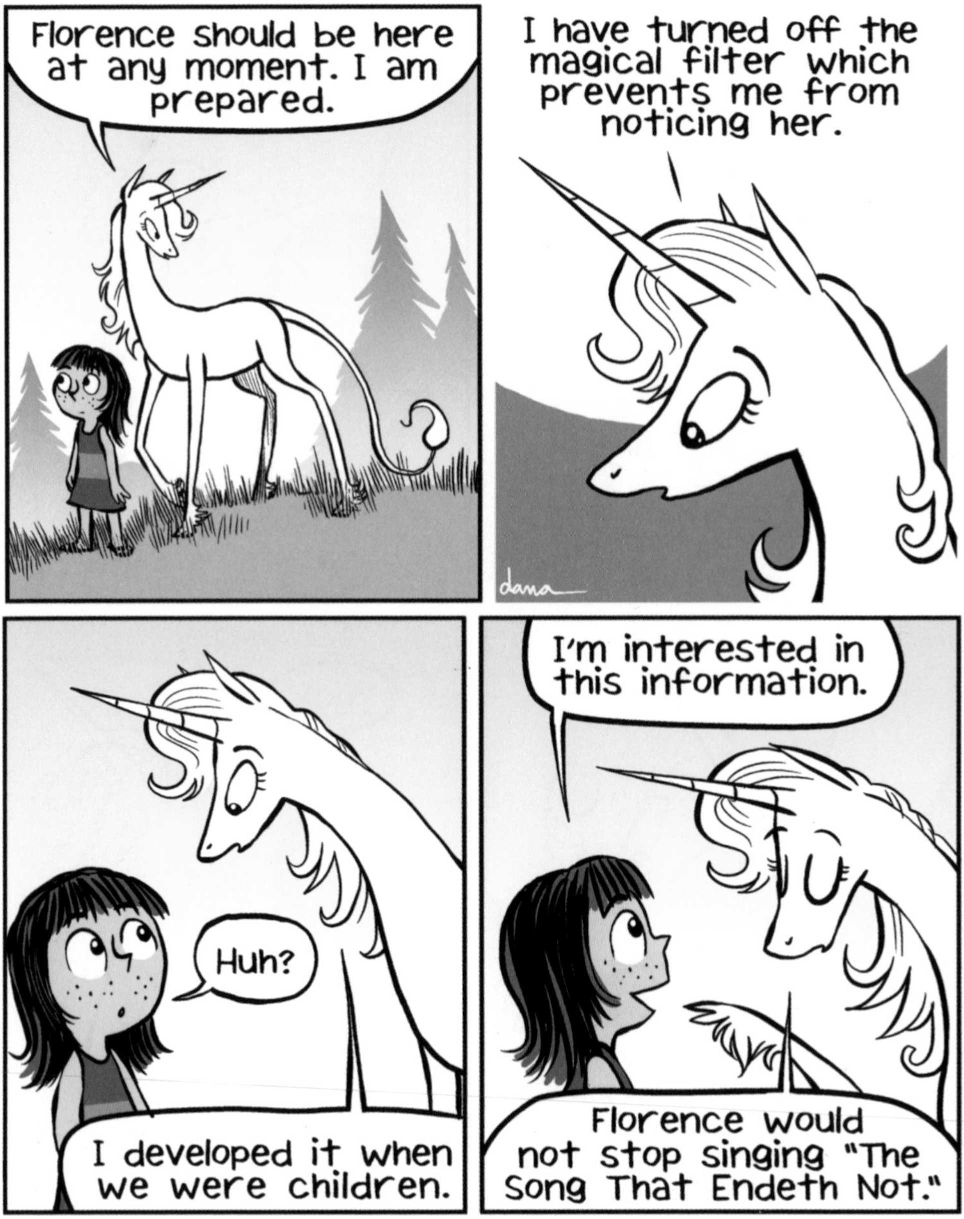
Florence should be here at any moment. I am prepared.
I have turned off the magical filter which prevents me from noticing her.
dana
Huh?
I developed it when we were children.
I'm interested in this information.
Florence would not stop singing "The Song That Endeth Not."

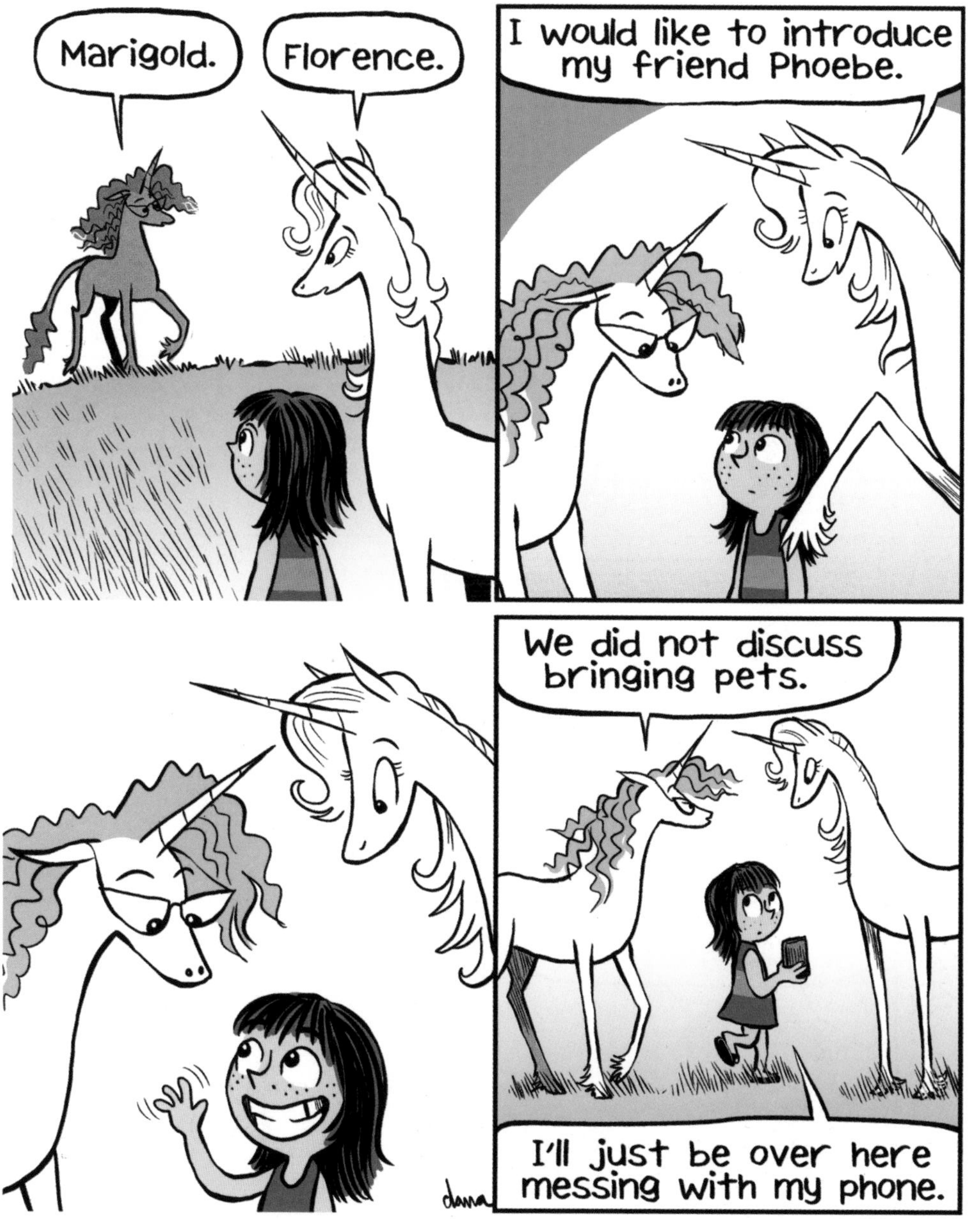
Marigold.
Florence.
I would like to introduce my friend Phoebe.
We did not discuss bringing pets.
I'll just be over here messing with my phone.
dana

They're making a "Pastel Unicorns" movie!

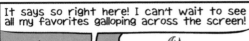

It says so right here! I can't wait to see all my favorites galloping across the screen!

It says the movie "contains no galloping."

Two minutes in, the unicorns become human, and enroll in Popular High School.

The title is "Pastel Unicorns: Skinny Pretty Non-Unicorns."

But...to play **that**, I'd need to get mom and dad to buy me an entirely **NEW** set of...

Adults are just messing with me, aren't they?

So are unicorns! It is just subtler.

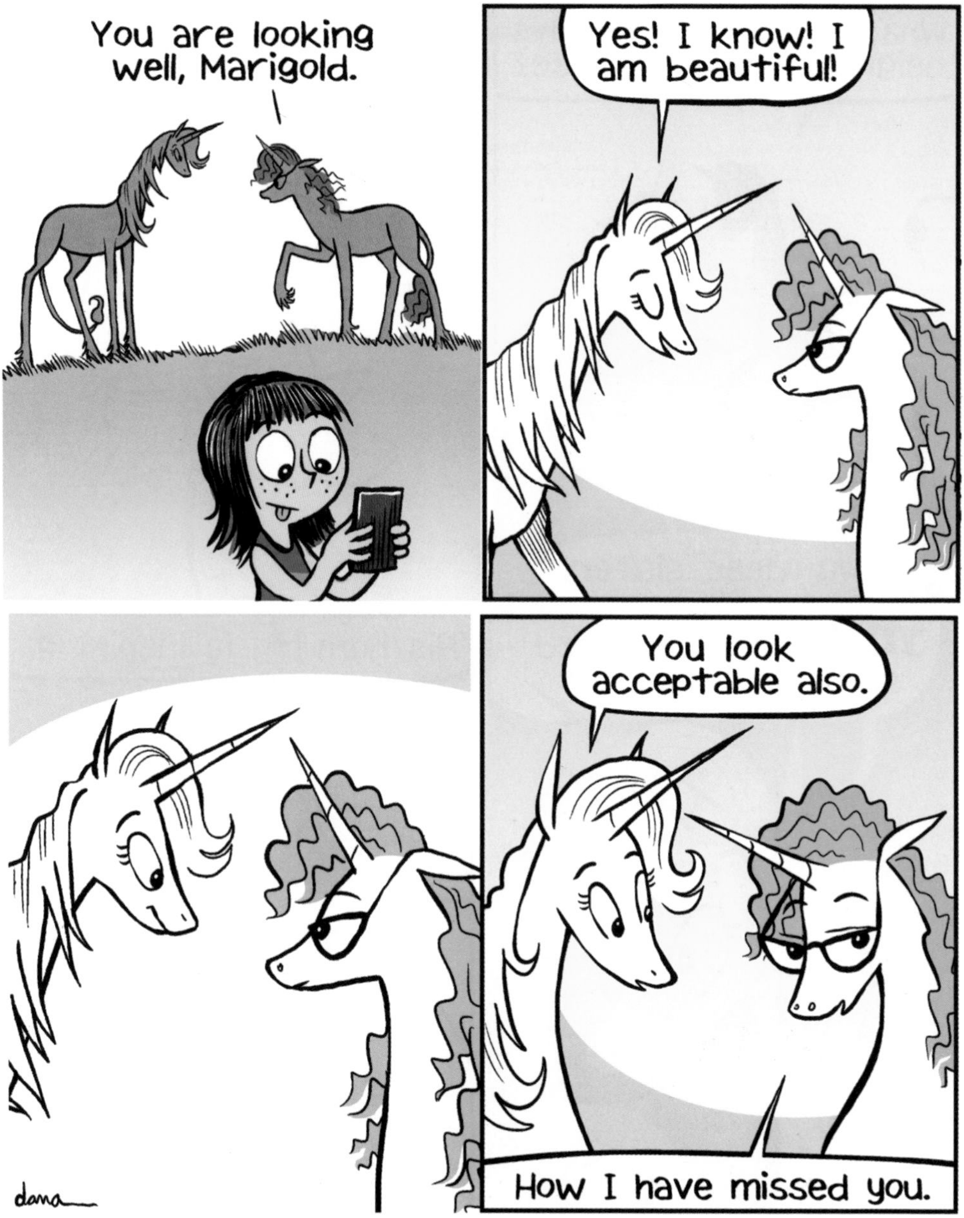
You are looking well, Marigold.
Yes! I know! I am beautiful!
You look acceptable also.
How I have missed you.
dana

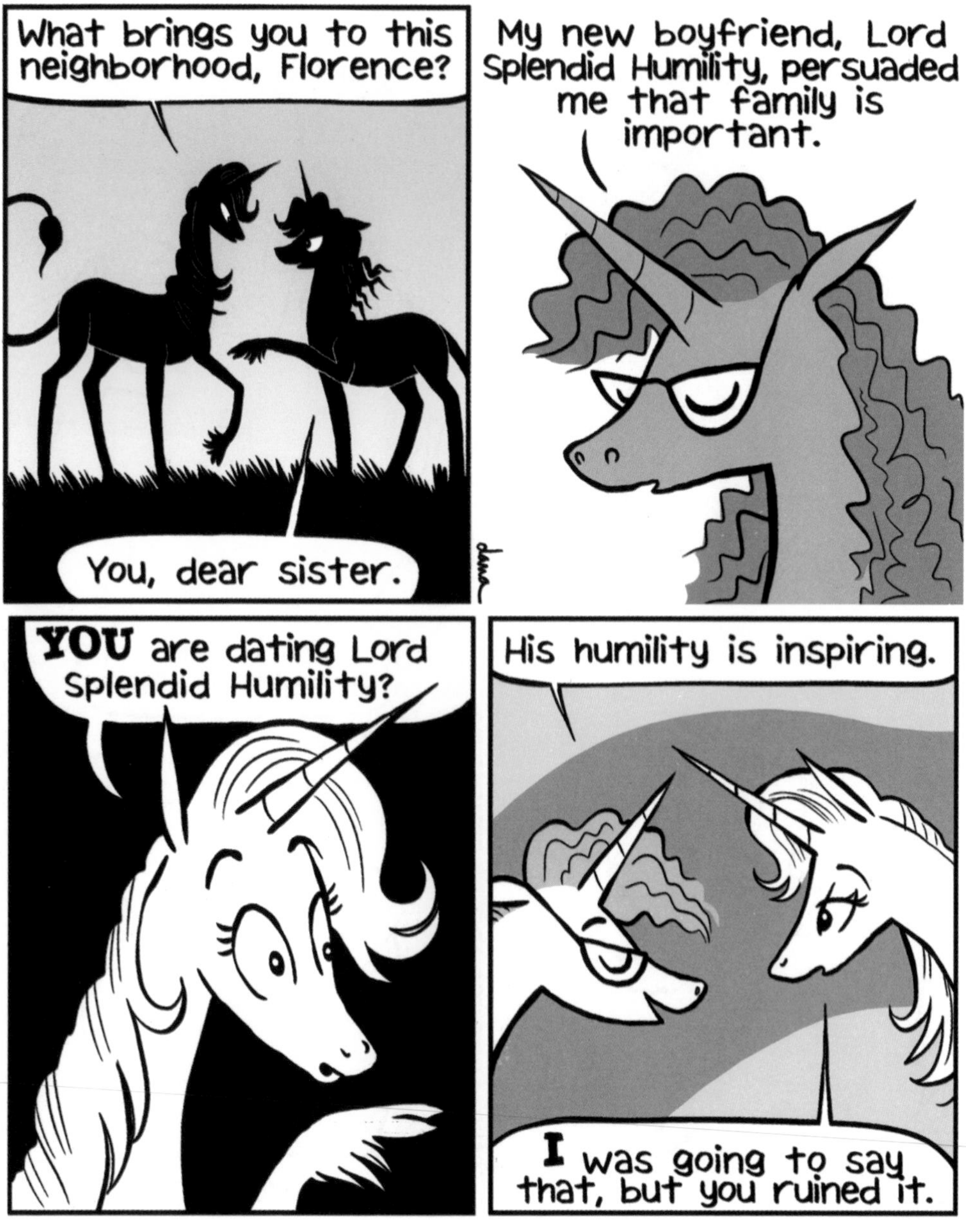
What brings you to this neighborhood, Florence?
You, dear sister.
My new boyfriend, Lord Splendid Humility, persuaded me that family is important.
YOU are dating Lord Splendid Humility?
His humility is inspiring.
I was going to say that, but you ruined it.

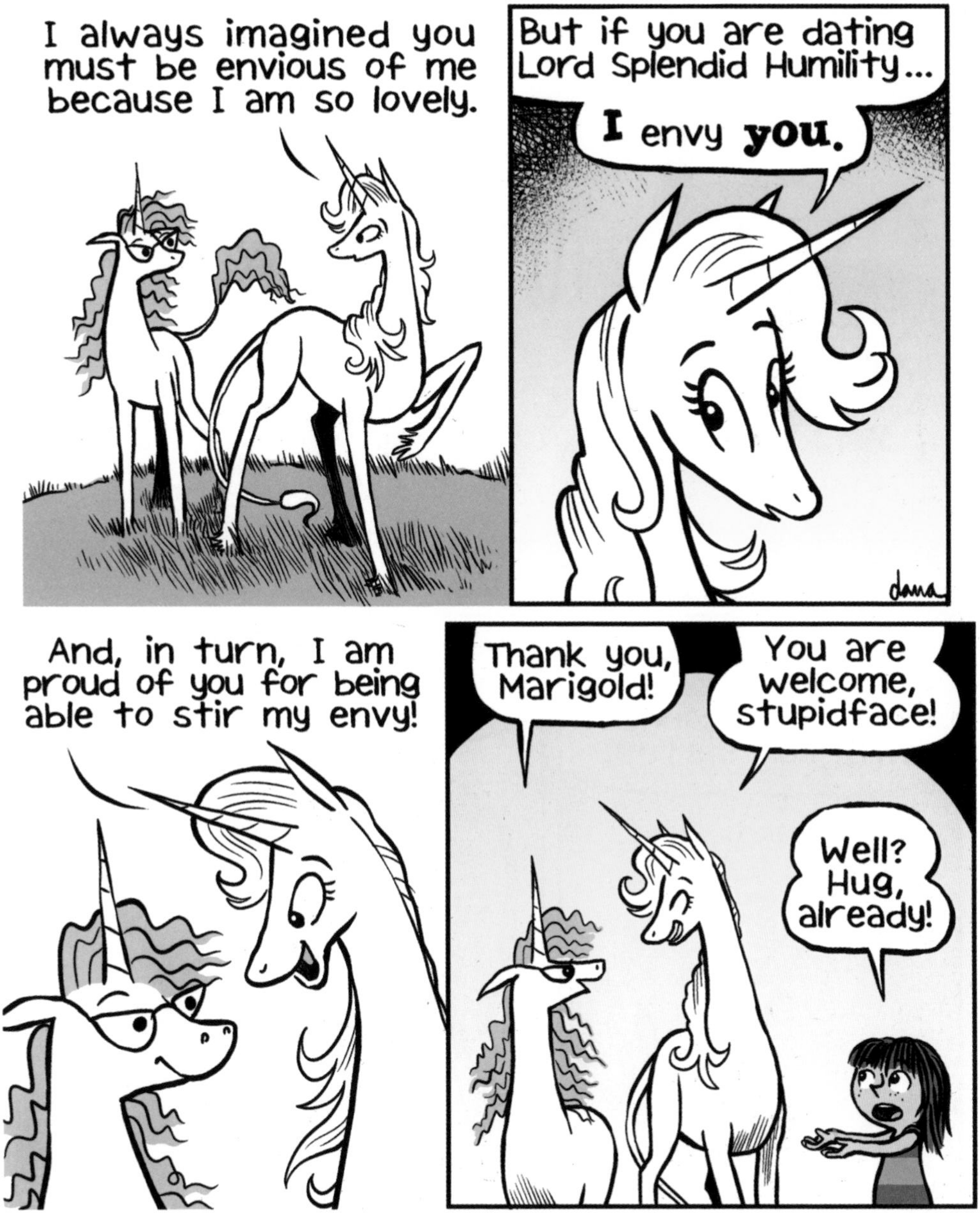
I always imagined you must be envious of me because I am so lovely.
But if you are dating Lord Splendid Humility...
I envy **you**.
dana
And, in turn, I am proud of you for being able to stir my envy!
Thank you, Marigold!
You are welcome, stupidface!
Well? Hug, already!

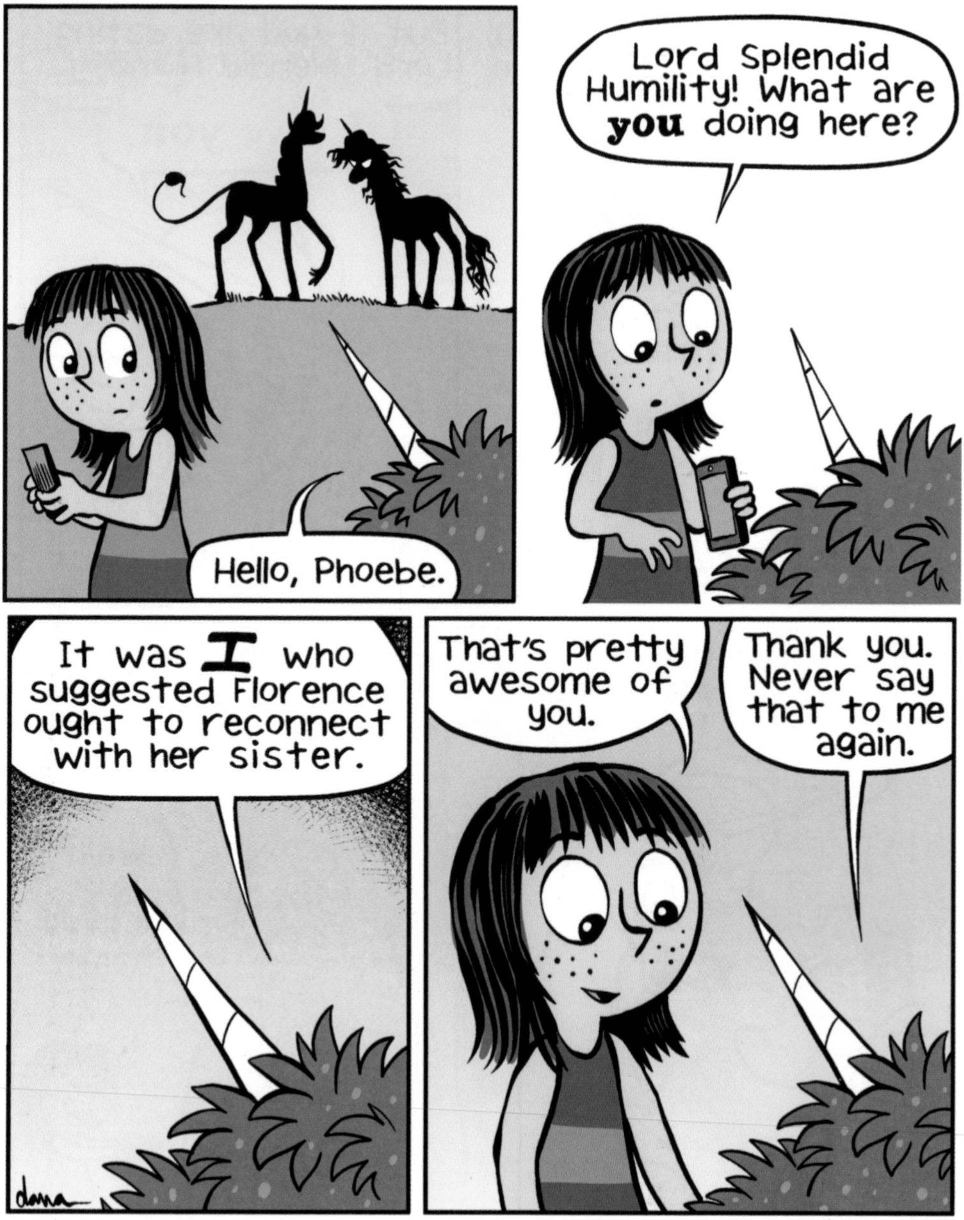
Hello, Phoebe.
Lord Splendid Humility! What are **you** doing here?
It was I who suggested Florence ought to reconnect with her sister.
That's pretty awesome of you.
Thank you. Never say that to me again.
dana

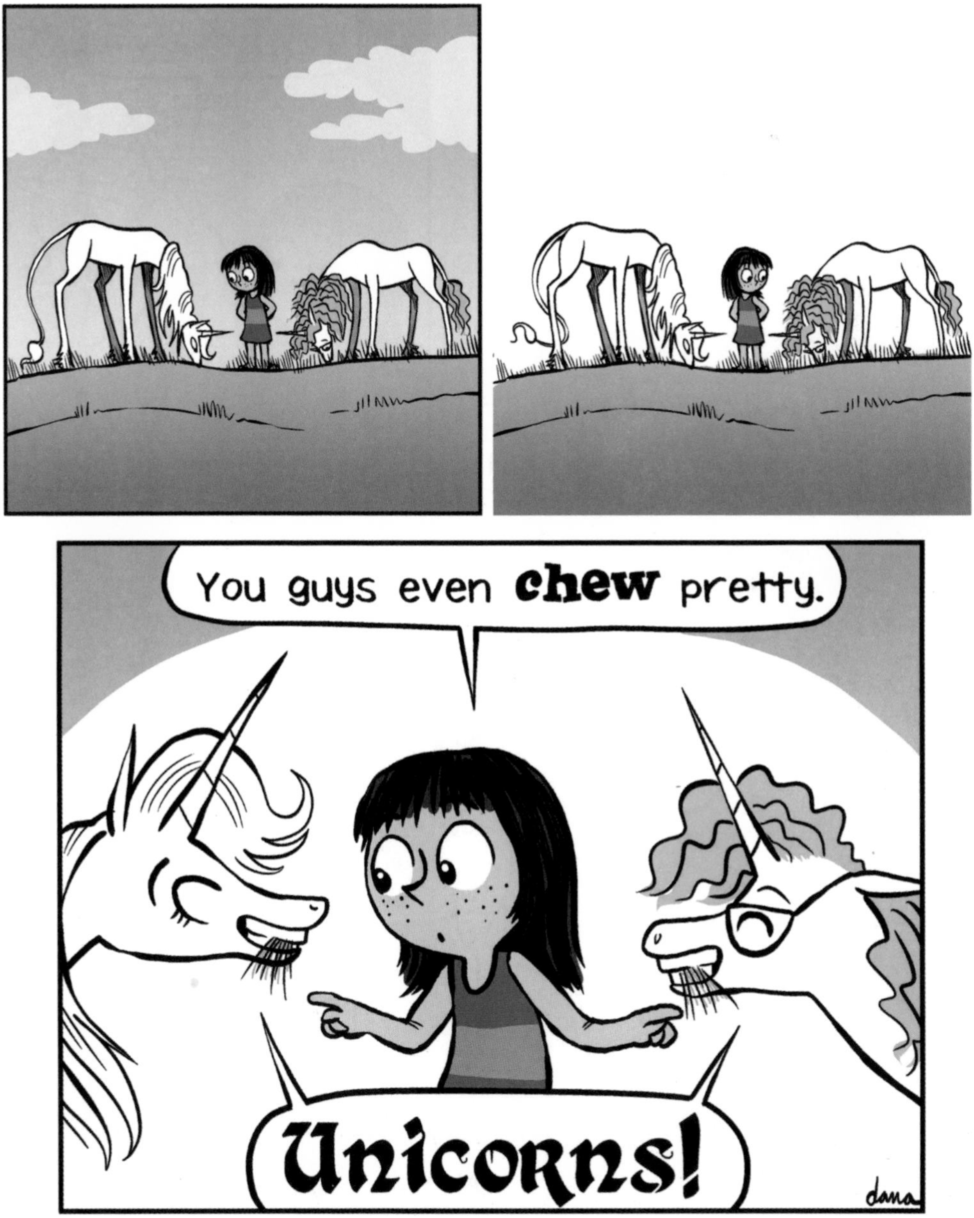
You guys even **chew** pretty.
Unicorns!
dana

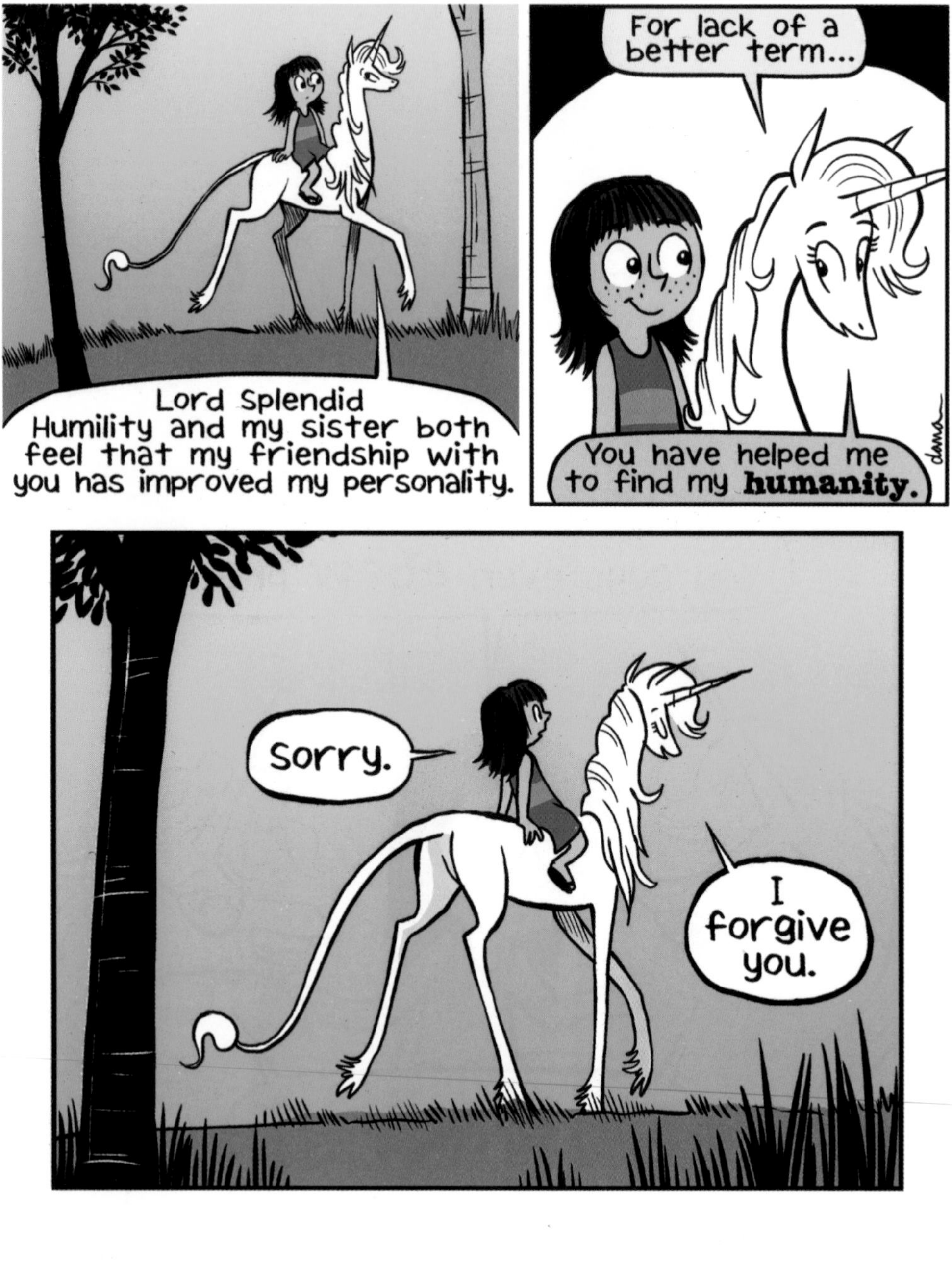
Lord Splendid
Humility and my sister both feel that my friendship with you has improved my personality.
For lack of a better term...
You have helped me to find my **humanity.**
Sorry.
I forgive you.

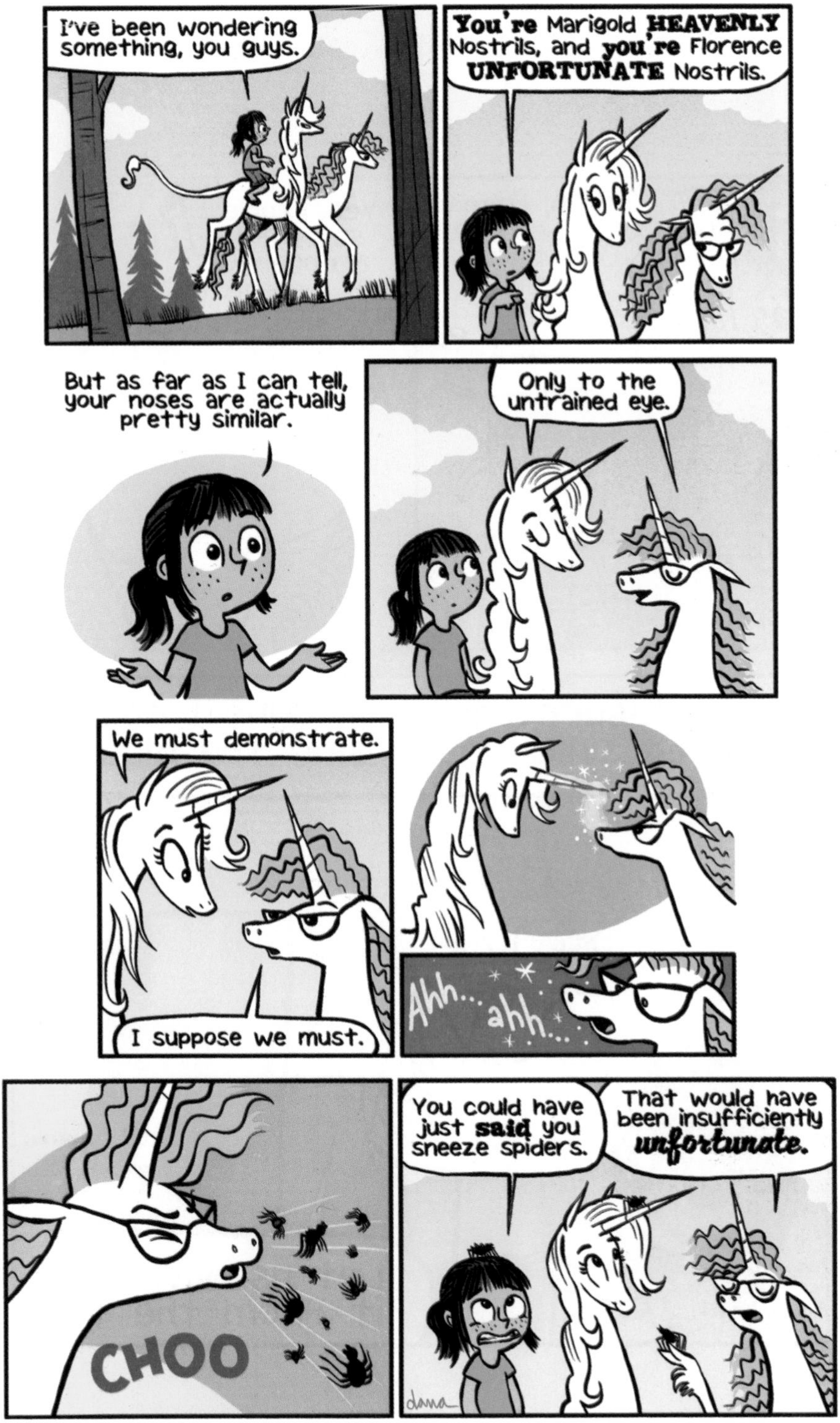
I've been wondering something, you guys.
You're Marigold HEAVENLY Nostrils, and you're Florence UNFORTUNATE Nostrils.
But as far as I can tell, your noses are actually pretty similar.
Only to the untrained eye.
We must demonstrate.
I suppose we must.
Ahh... ahh...
CHOO
You could have just said you sneeze spiders.
That would have been insufficiently unfortunate.
dana

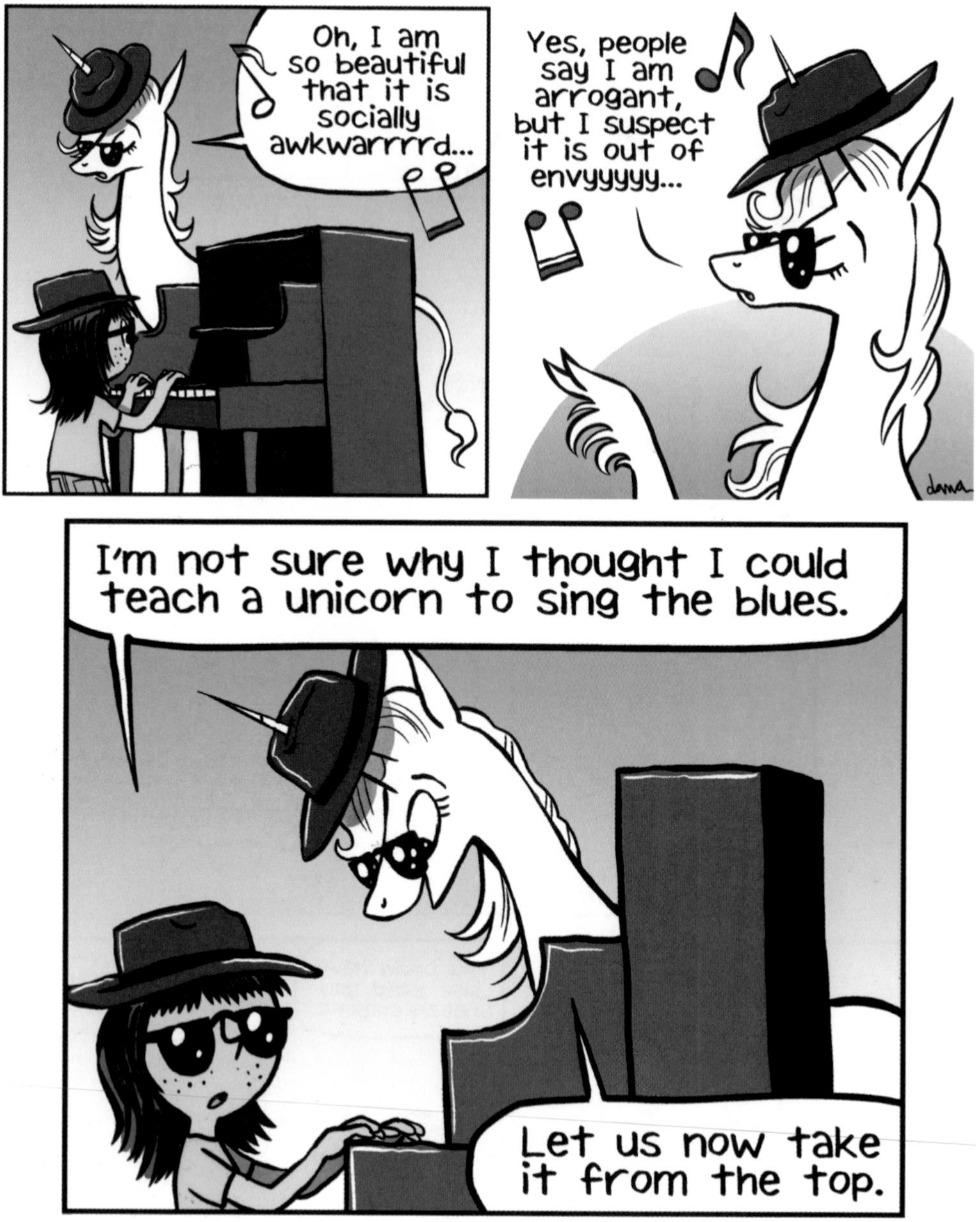
Oh, I am so beautiful that it is socially awkwarrrrd...
Yes, people say I am arrogant, but I suspect it is out of envyyyyy...
dana
I'm not sure why I thought I could teach a unicorn to sing the blues.
Let us now take it from the top.

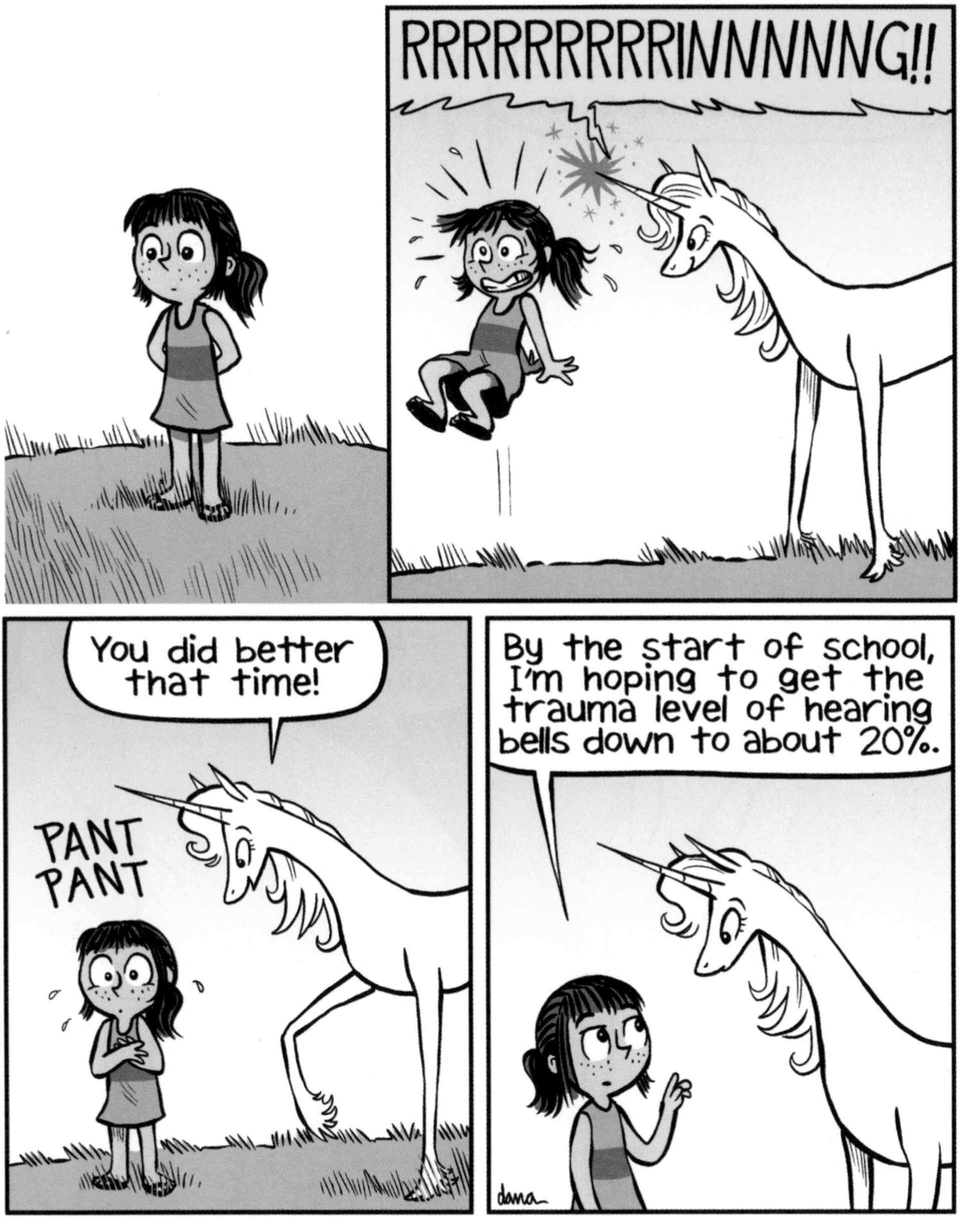
RRRRRRRRRINNNNNG!!
You did better that time!
PANT PANT
By the start of school, I'm hoping to get the trauma level of hearing bells down to about 20%.
dana

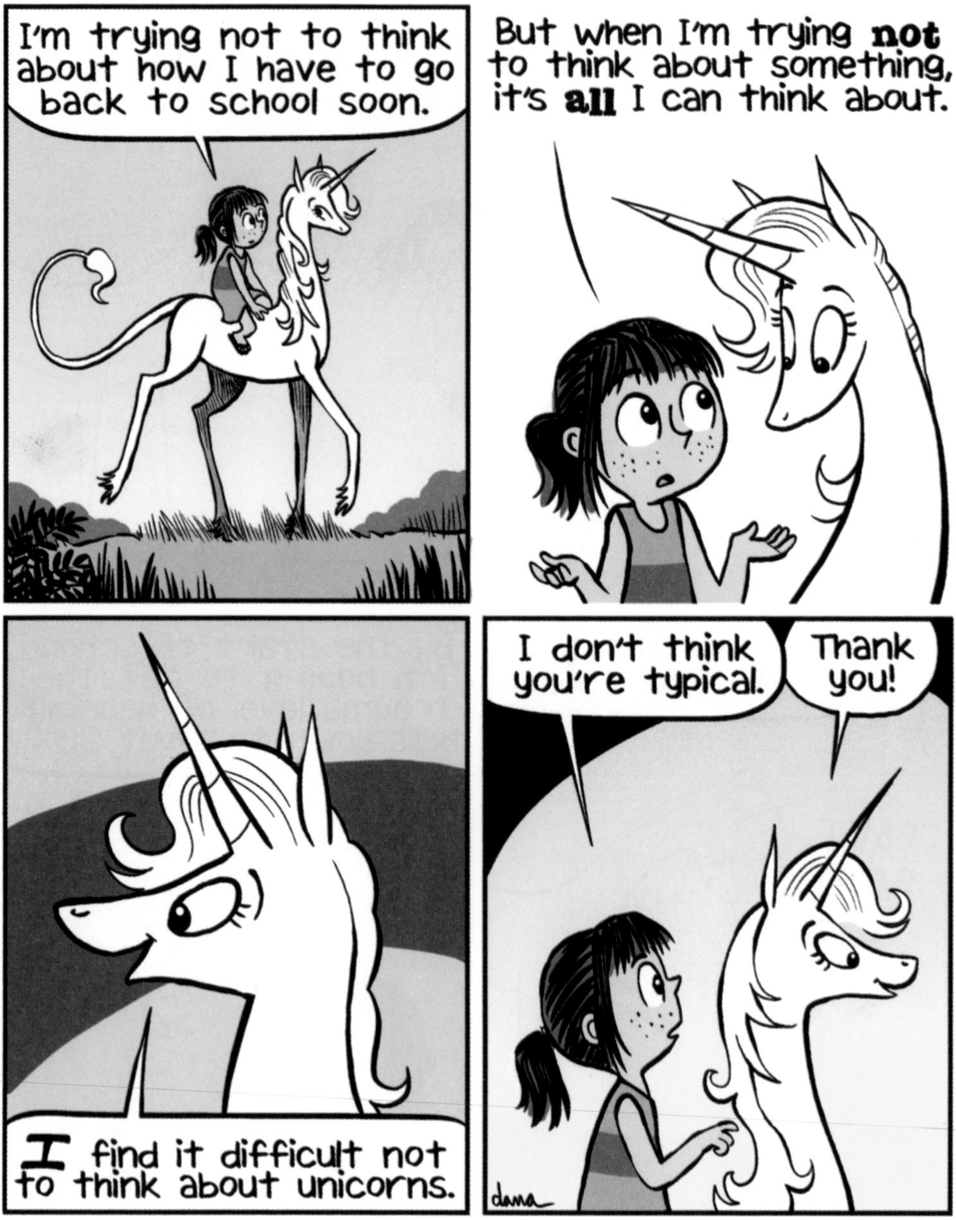
I'm trying not to think about how I have to go back to school soon.
But when I'm trying **not** to think about something, it's **all** I can think about.
I find it difficult not to think about unicorns.
I don't think you're typical.
Thank you!
dana

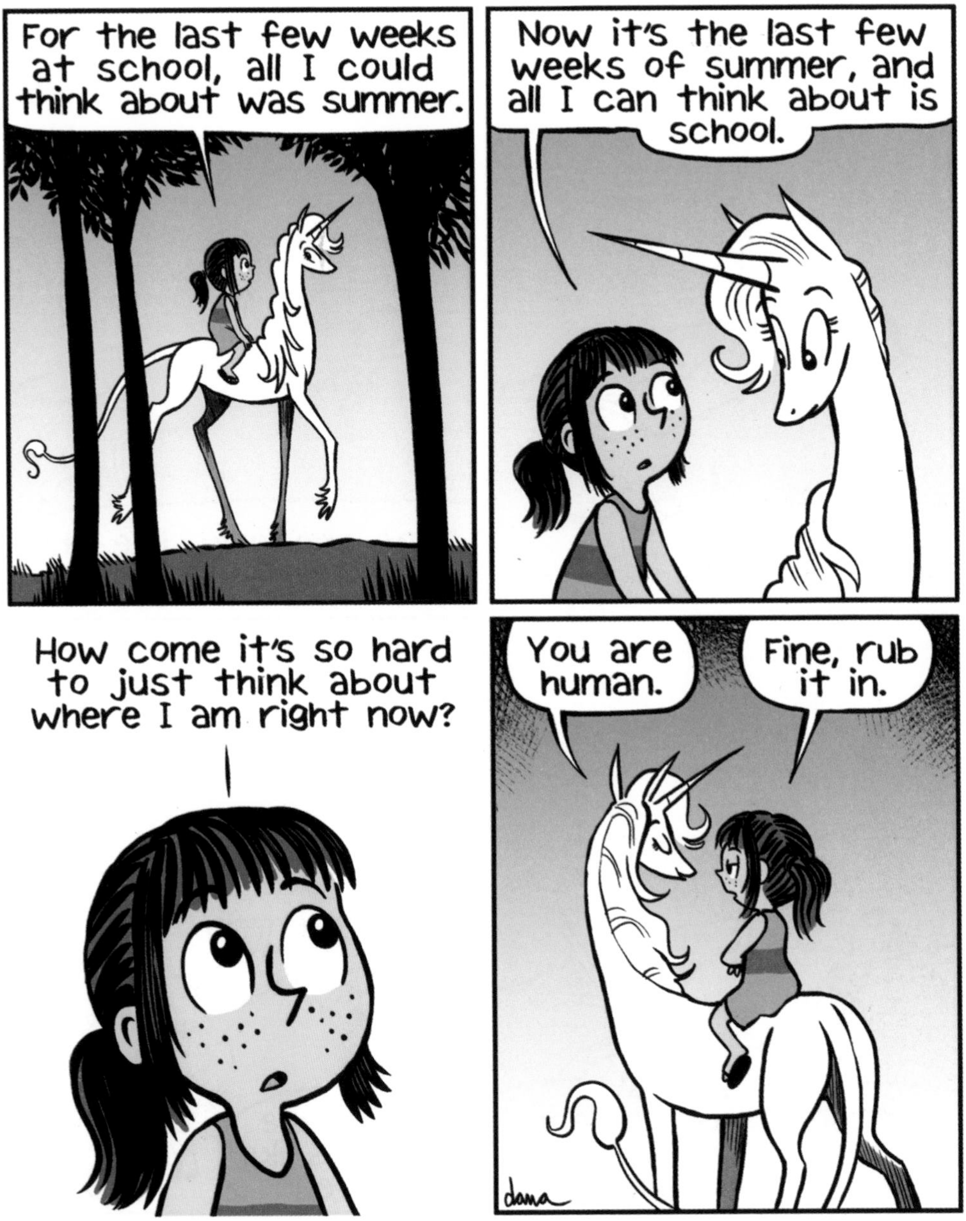
For the last few weeks at school, all I could think about was summer.
Now it's the last few weeks of summer, and all I can think about is school.
How come it's so hard to just think about where I am right now?
You are human.
Fine, rub it in.
dana

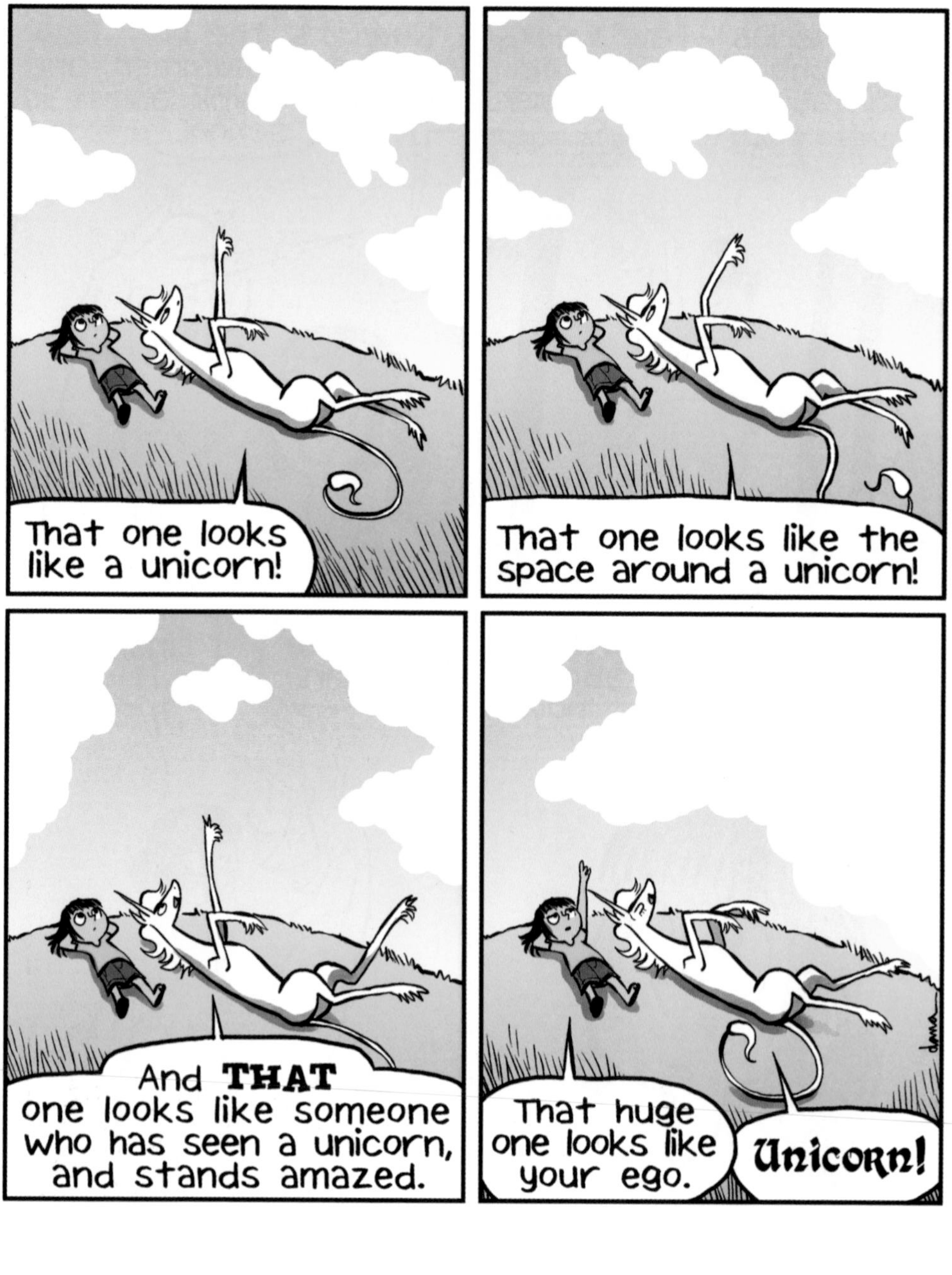
That one looks like a unicorn!
That one looks like the space around a unicorn!
And THAT one looks like someone who has seen a unicorn, and stands amazed.
That huge one looks like your ego.
Unicorn!

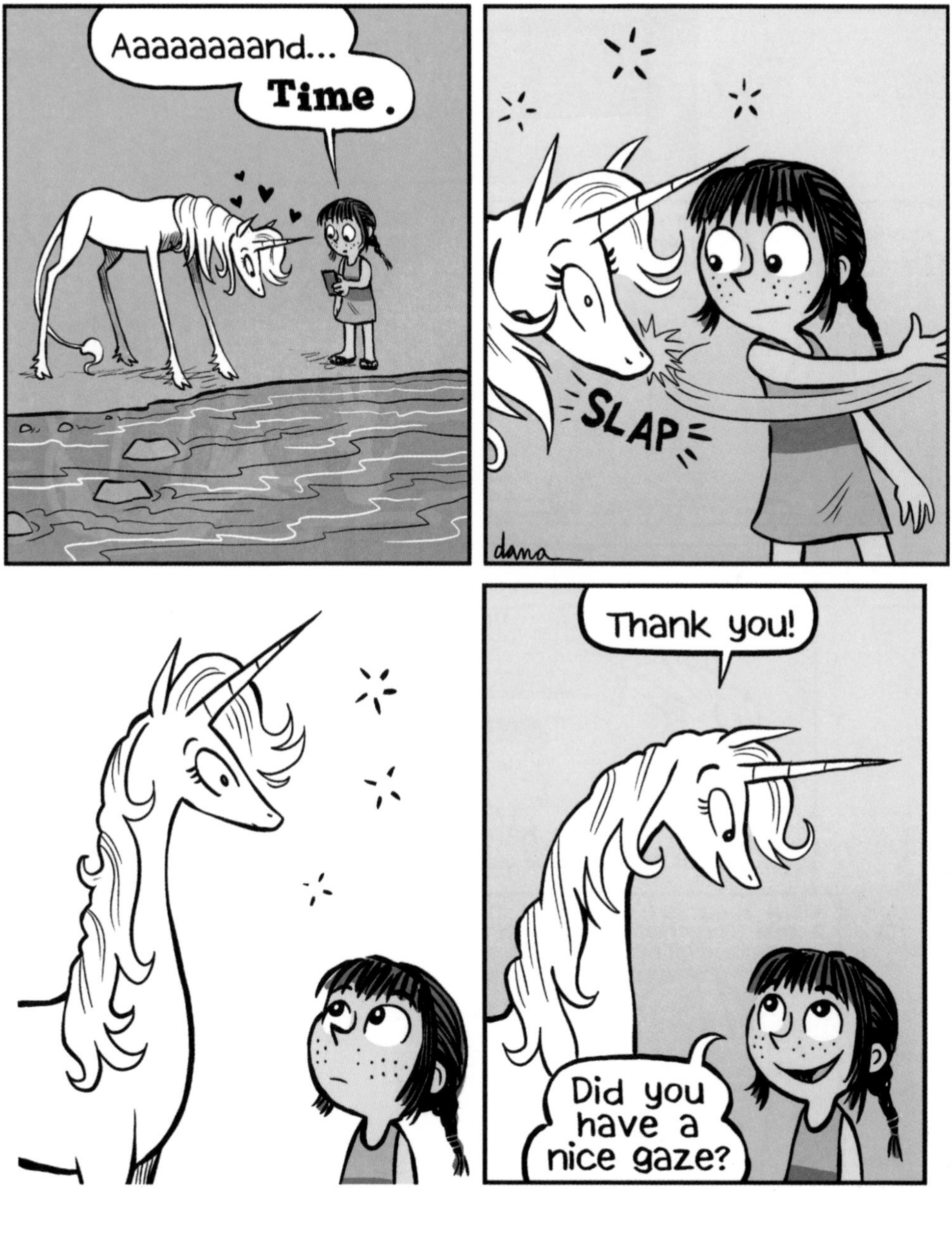
Aaaaaaaand...
Time.
SLAP
dana
Thank you!
Did you have a nice gaze?

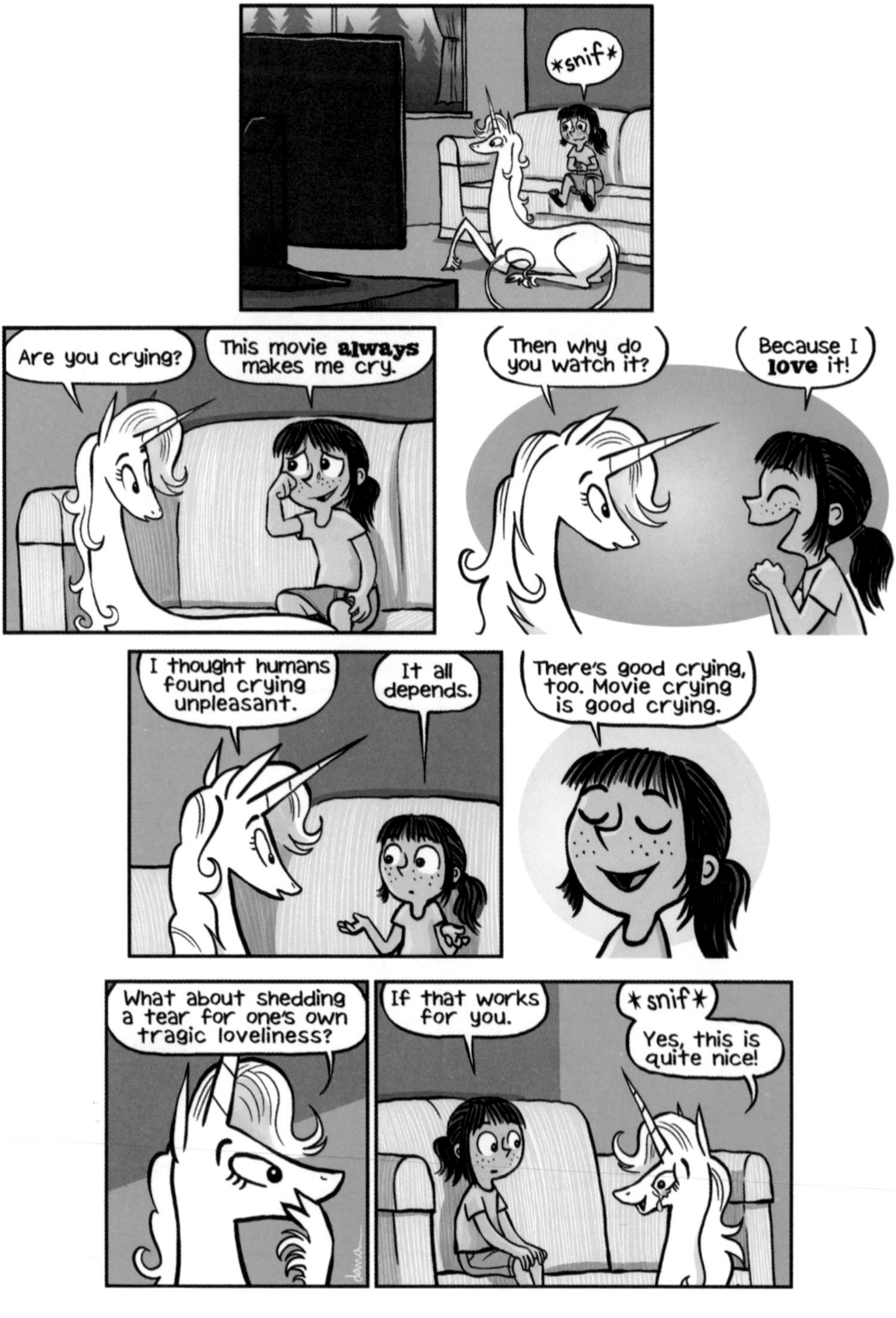
snif
Are you crying?
This movie **always** makes me cry.
Then why do you watch it?
Because I **love** it!
I thought humans found crying unpleasant.
It all depends.
There's good crying, too. Movie crying is good crying.
What about shedding a tear for one's own tragic loveliness?
If that works for you.
snif
Yes, this is quite nice!
dana

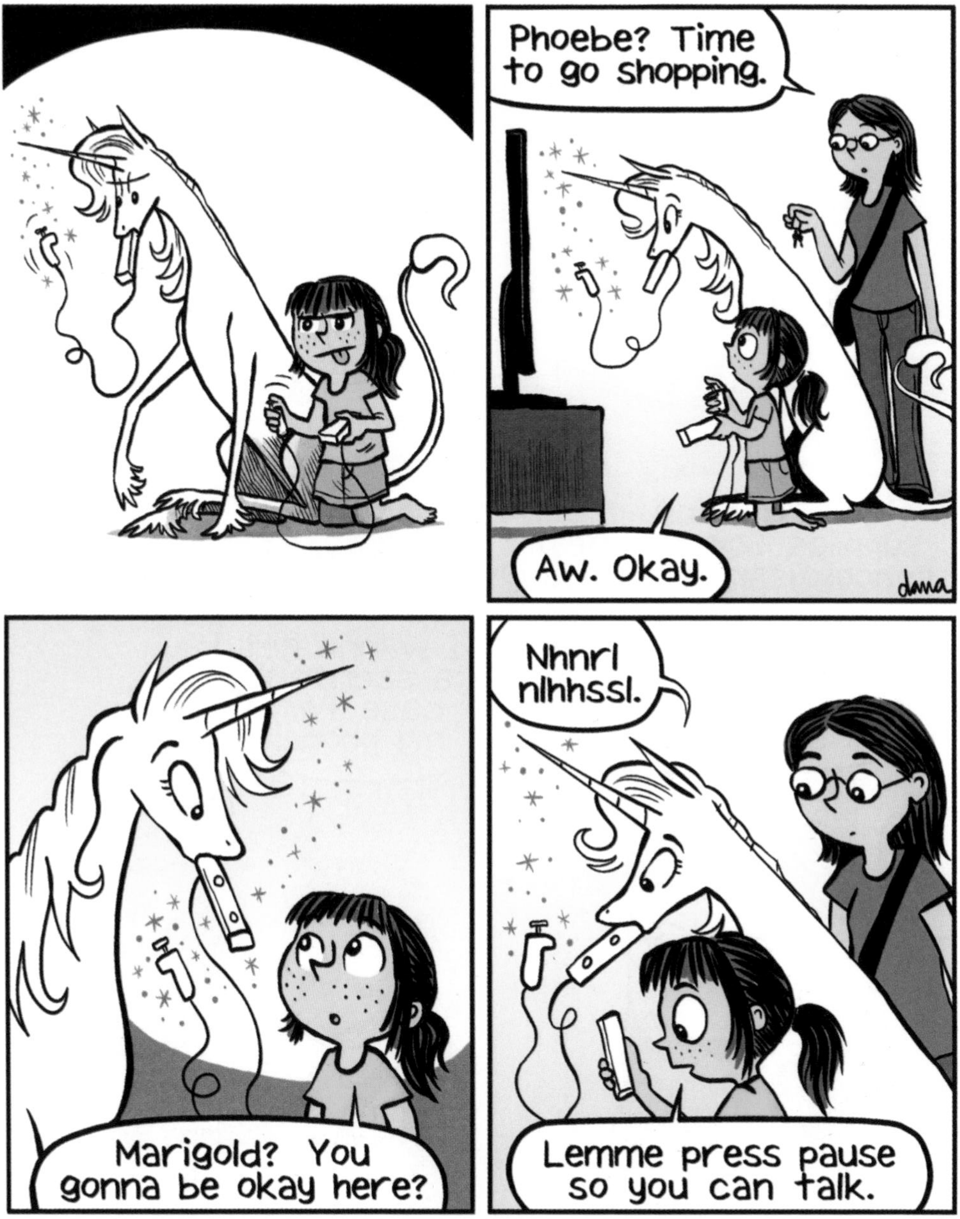
Phoebe? Time to go shopping.
Aw. Okay.
dana
Marigold? You gonna be okay here?
Nhnrl nlhhssl.
Lemme press pause so you can talk.

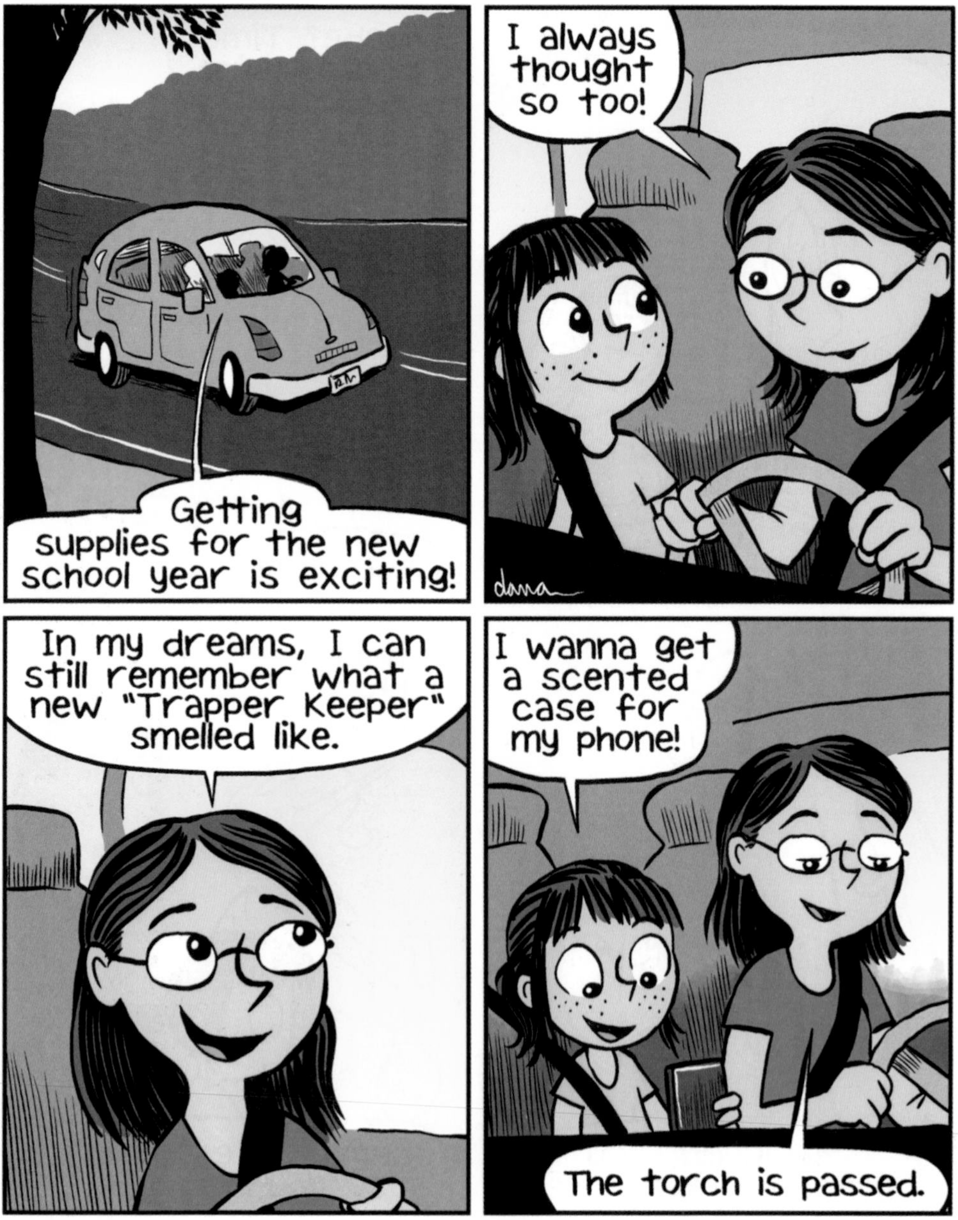
Getting supplies for the new school year is exciting!
I always thought so too!
dana
In my dreams, I can still remember what a new "Trapper Keeper" smelled like.
I wanna get a scented case for my phone!
The torch is passed.

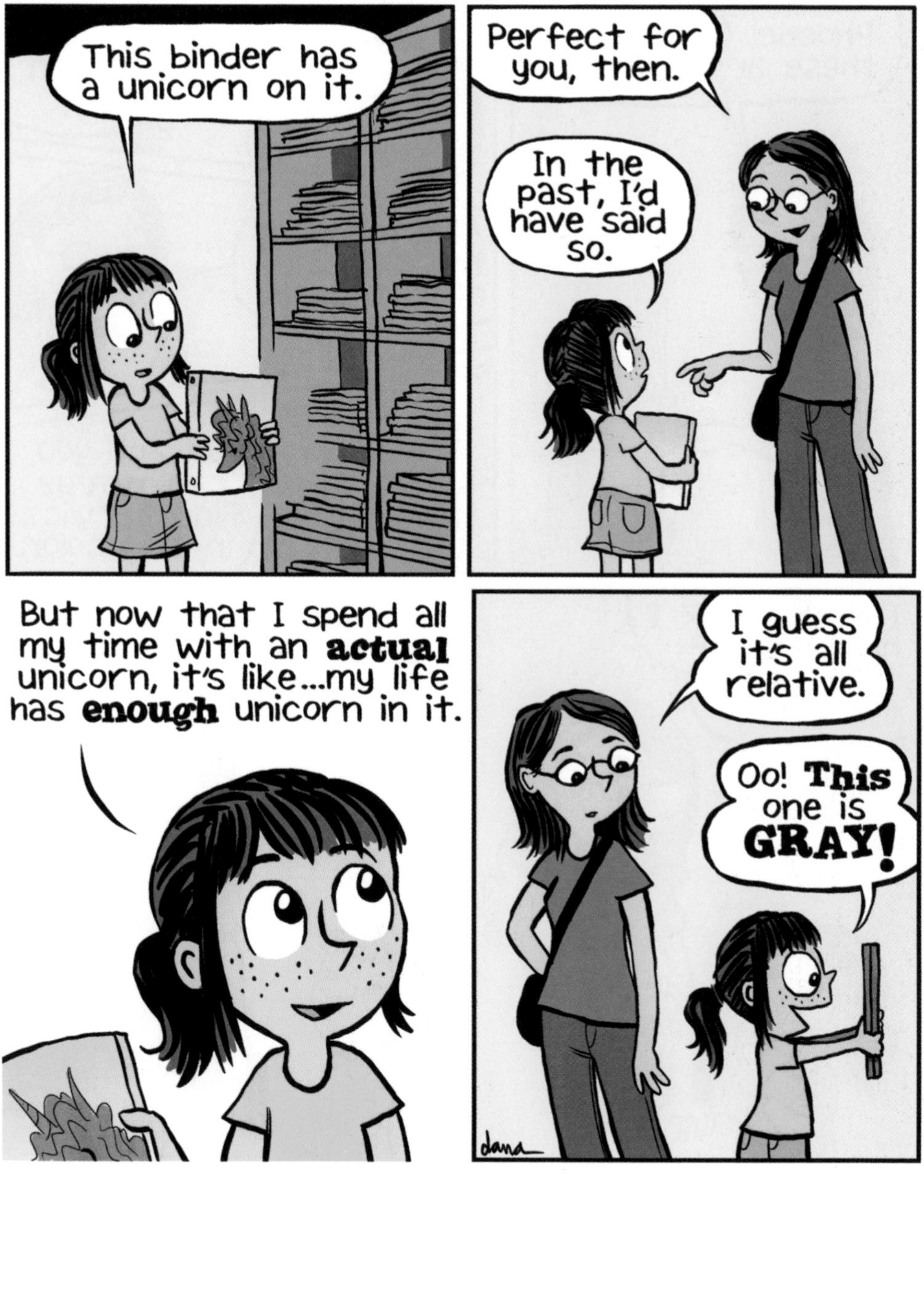
This binder has a unicorn on it.
Perfect for you, then.
In the past, I'd have said so.
But now that I spend all my time with an **actual** unicorn, it's like...my life has **enough** unicorn in it.
I guess it's all relative.
Oo! **This** one is **GRAY!**
dana

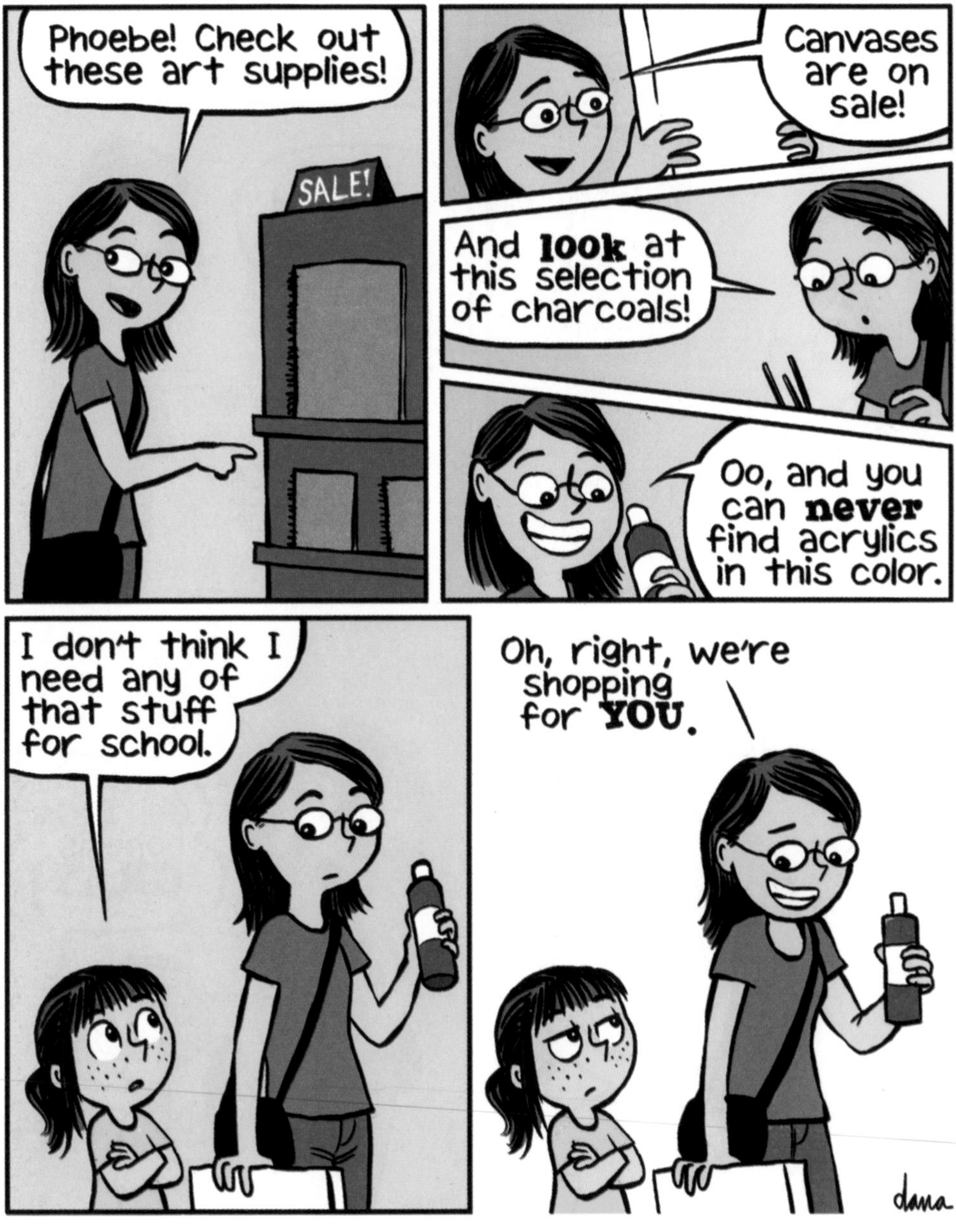
Phoebe! Check out these art supplies!
SALE!
Canvases are on sale!
And **look** at this selection of charcoals!
Oo, and you can **never** find acrylics in this color.
I don't think I need any of that stuff for school.
Oh, right, we're shopping for **YOU**.
dana

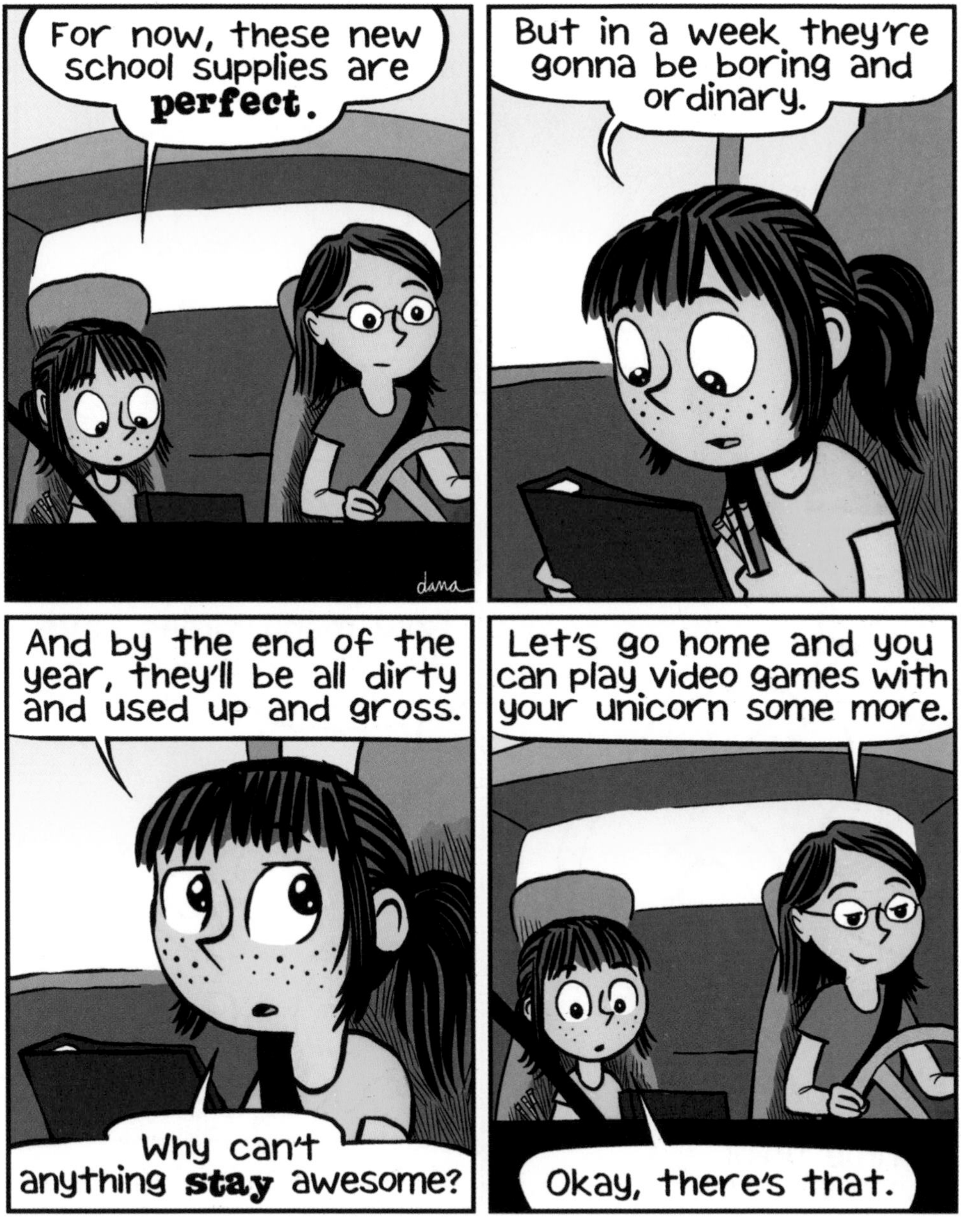
For now, these new school supplies are **perfect**.
But in a week they're gonna be boring and ordinary.
And by the end of the year, they'll be all dirty and used up and gross.
Why can't anything **stay** awesome?
Let's go home and you can play video games with your unicorn some more.
Okay, there's that.
dana

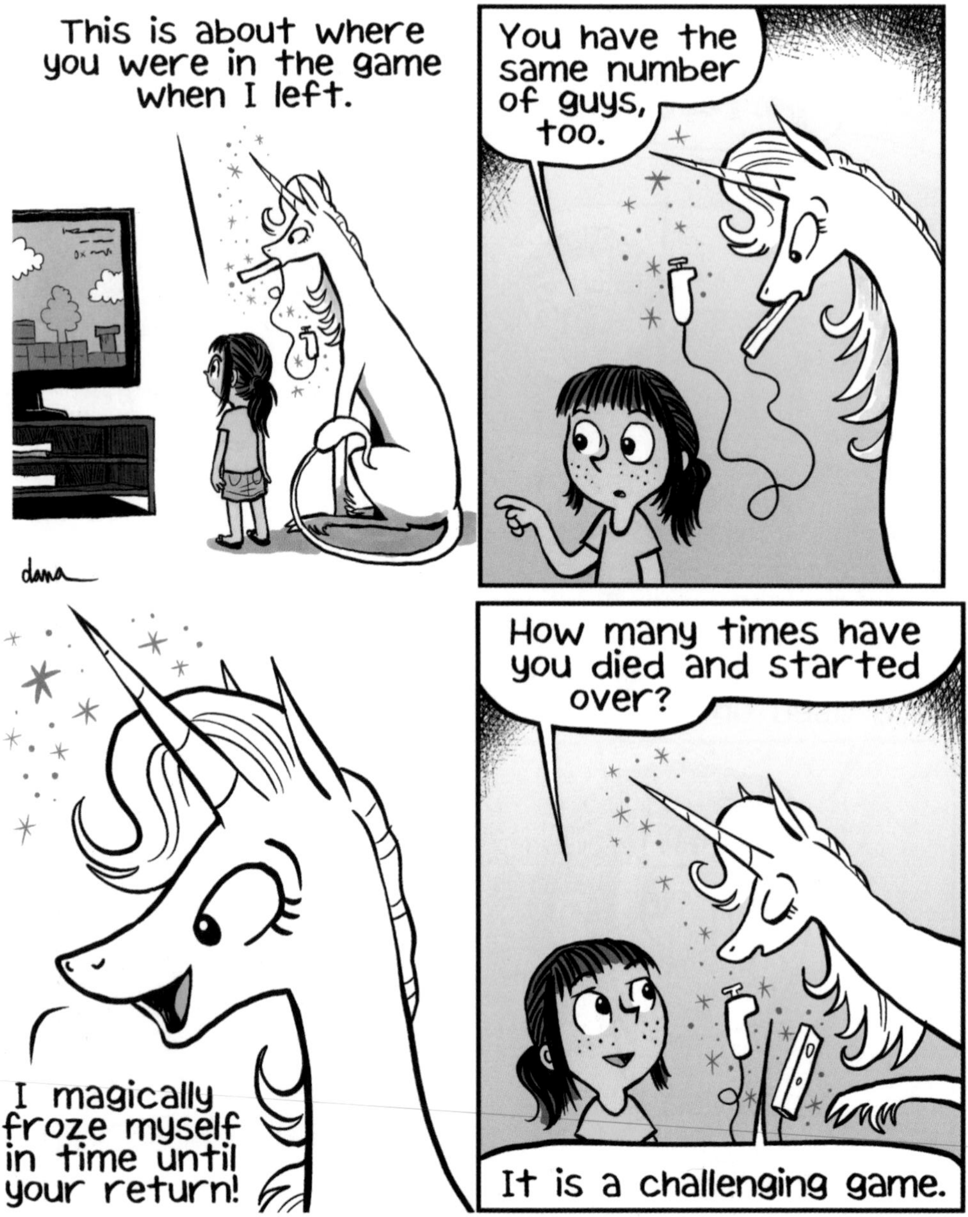
This is about where you were in the game when I left.
dana
You have the same number of guys, too.
I magically froze myself in time until your return!
How many times have you died and started over?
It is a challenging game.

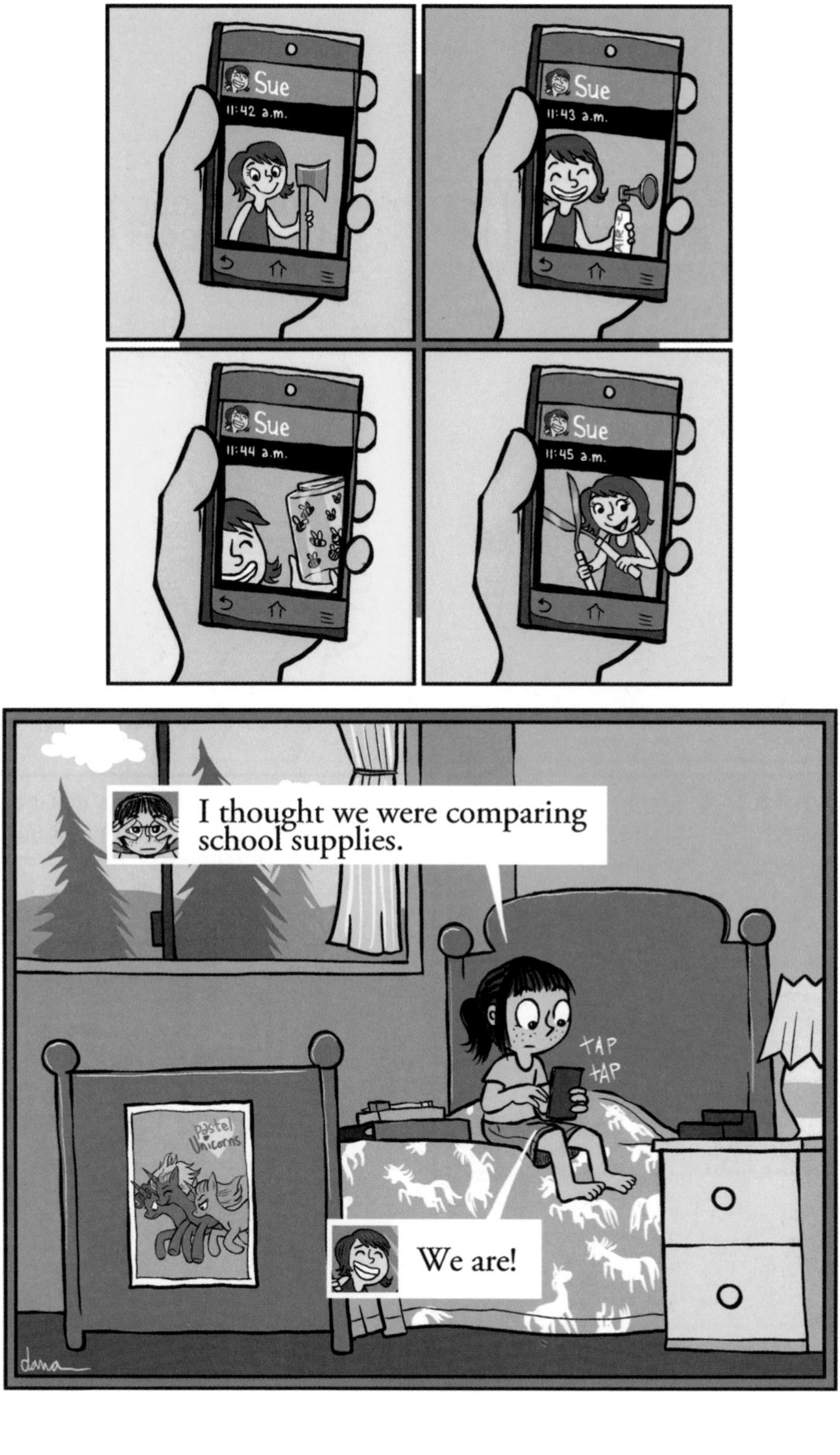
Sue
11:42 a.m.
Sue
11:43 a.m.
Sue
11:44 a.m.
Sue
11:45 a.m.
I thought we were comparing school supplies.
TAP TAP
Pastel Unicorns
We are!

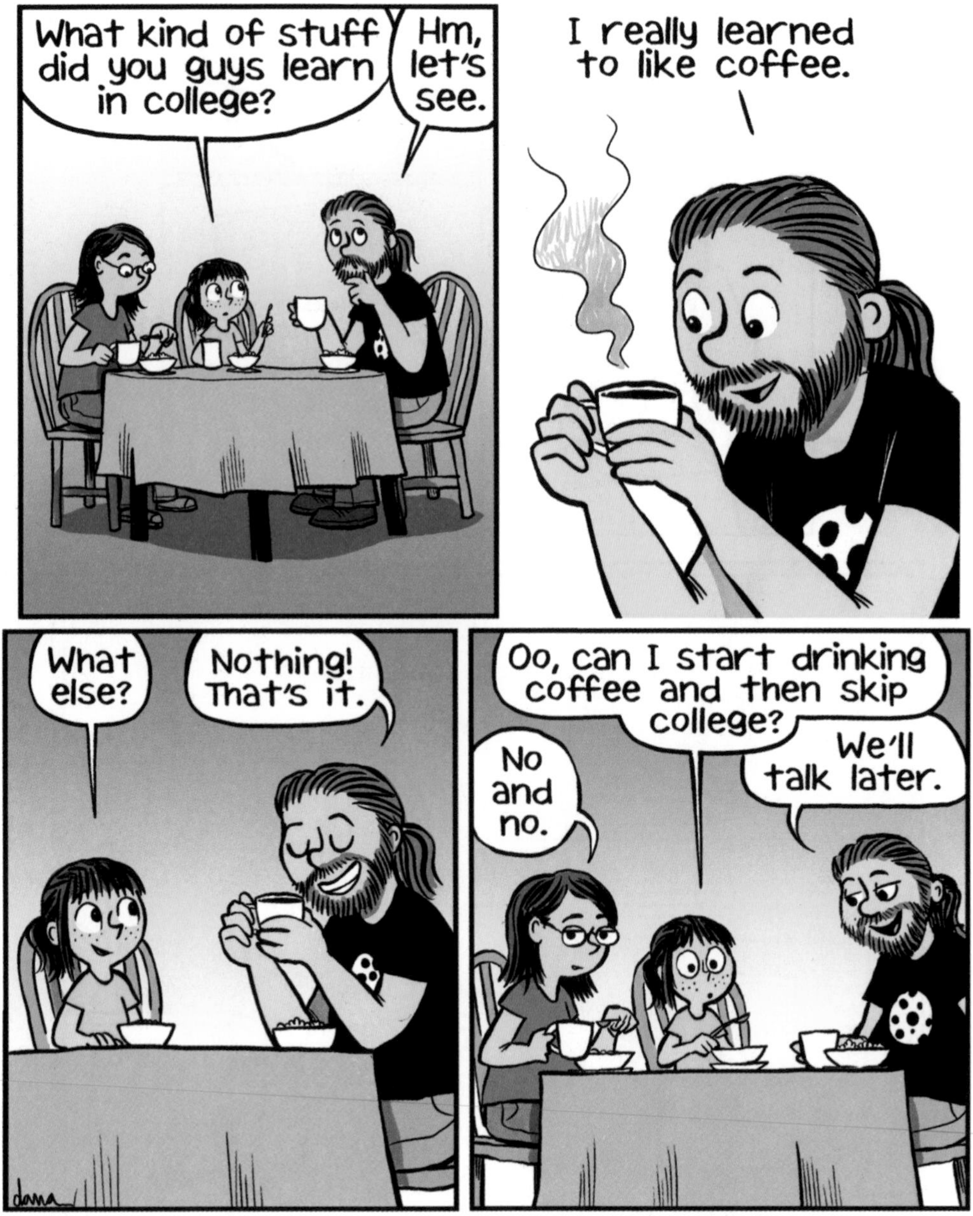
What kind of stuff did you guys learn in college?
Hm, let's see.
I really learned to like coffee.
What else?
Nothing! That's it.
dana
Oo, can I start drinking coffee and then skip college?
No and no.
We'll talk later.

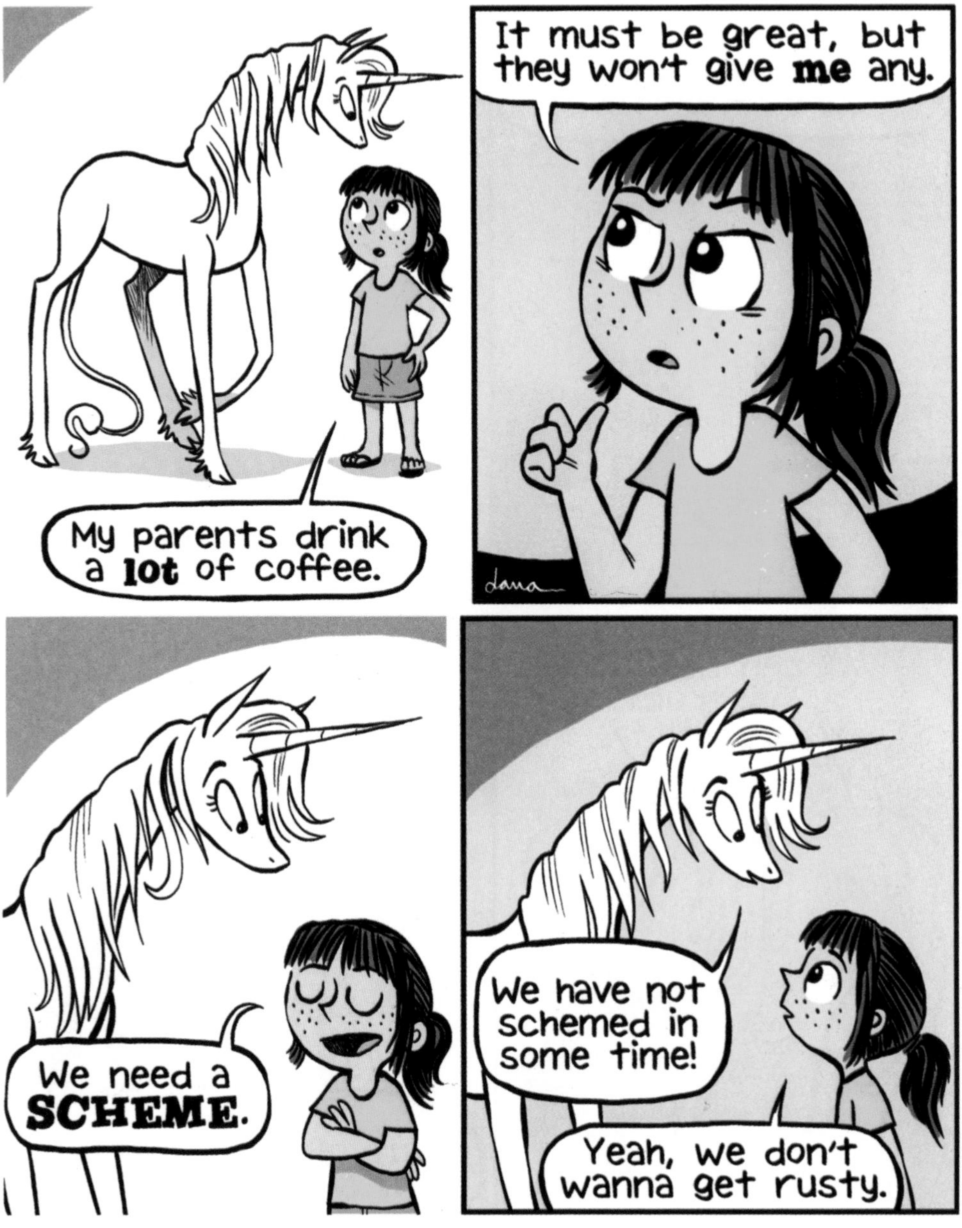
My parents drink a **lot** of coffee.
It must be great, but they won't give **me** any.
We need a **SCHEME**.
We have not schemed in some time!
Yeah, we don't wanna get rusty.

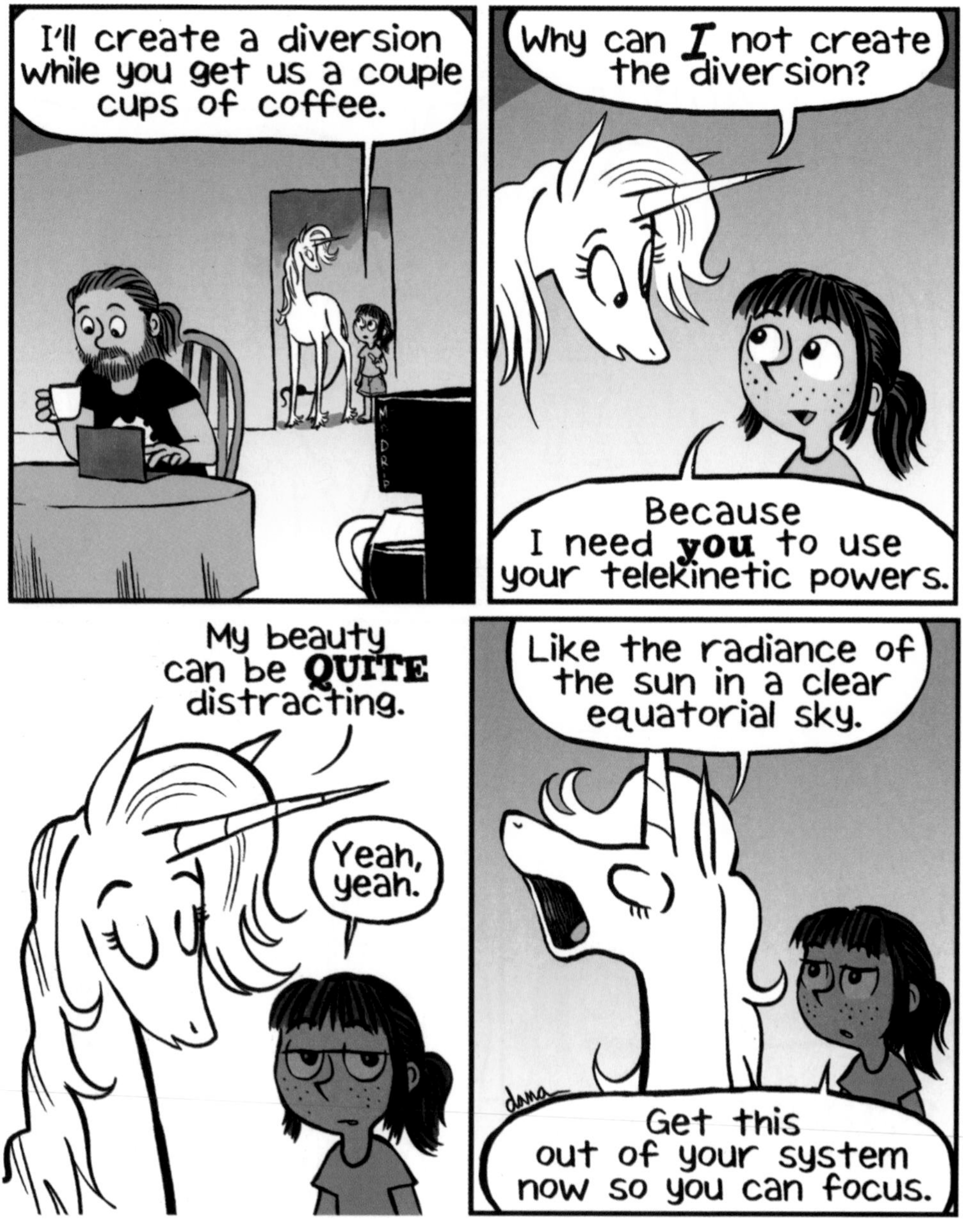
I'll create a diversion while you get us a couple cups of coffee.
Mr. DRIP
Why can I not create the diversion?
Because I need you to use your telekinetic powers.
My beauty can be QUITE distracting.
Yeah, yeah.
Like the radiance of the sun in a clear equatorial sky.
dana
Get this out of your system now so you can focus.

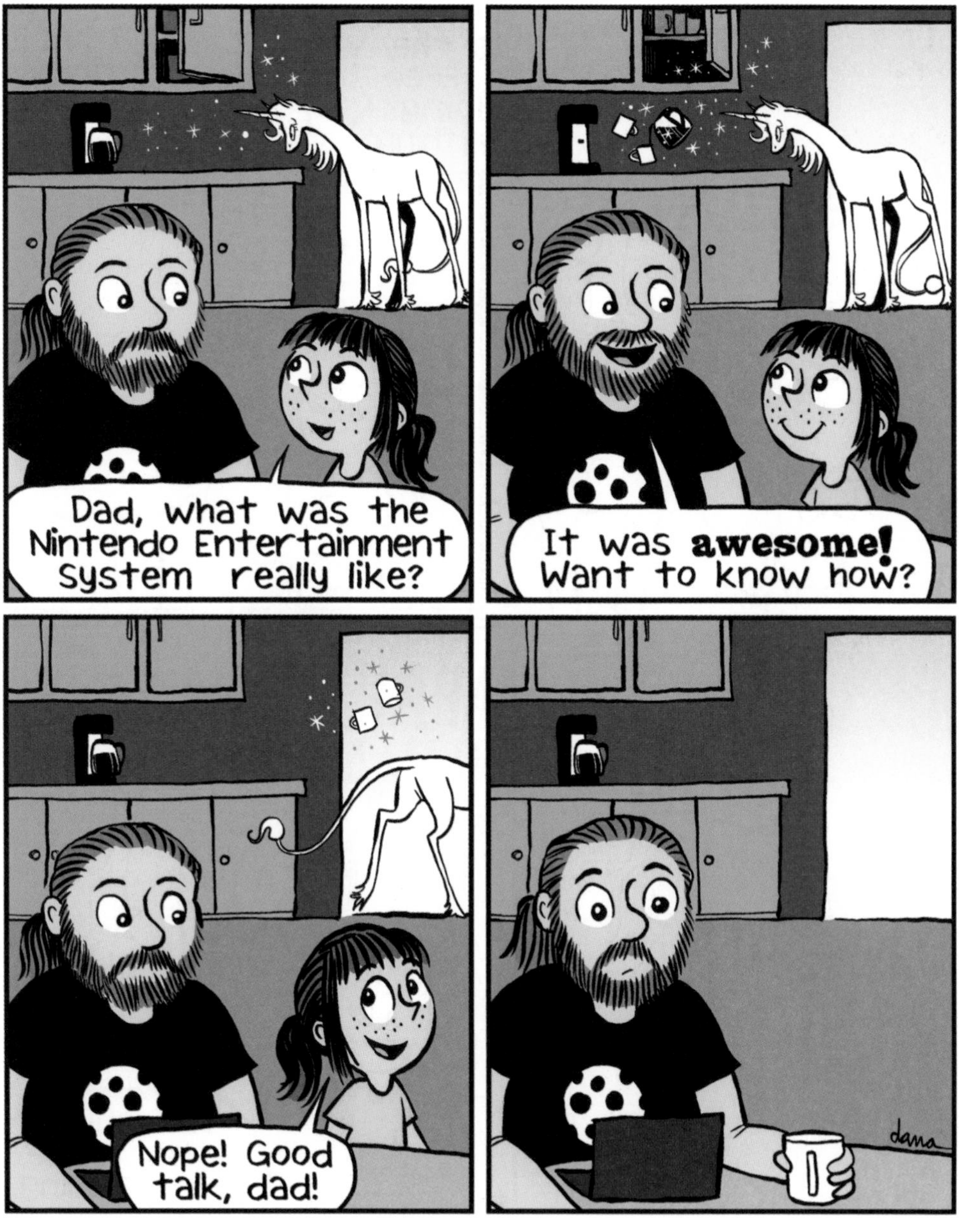
Dad, what was the Nintendo Entertainment System really like?
It was **awesome!** Want to know how?
Nope! Good talk, dad!
dana

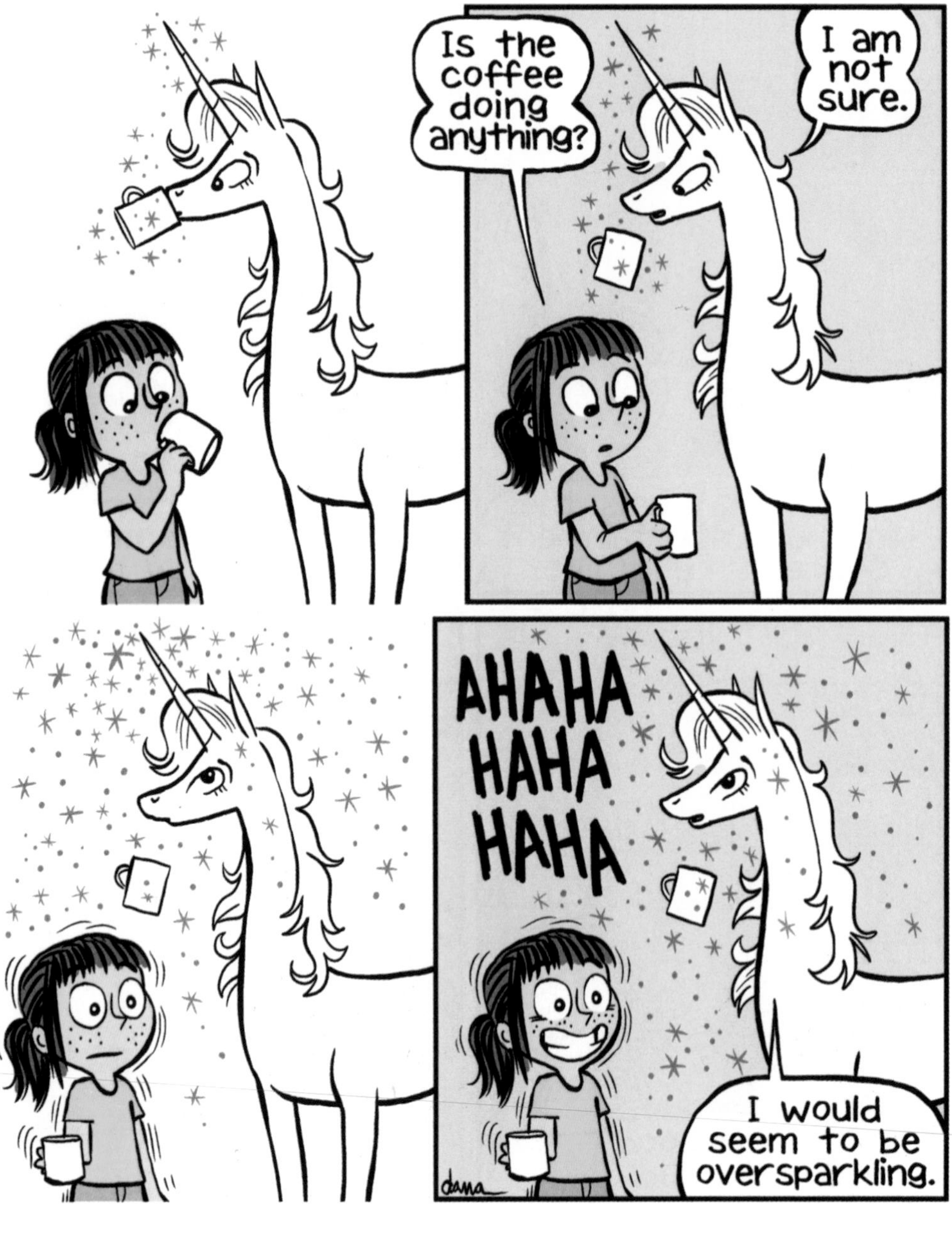
Is the coffee doing anything?
I am not sure.
AHAHA HAHA HAHA
I would seem to be oversparkling.
dana

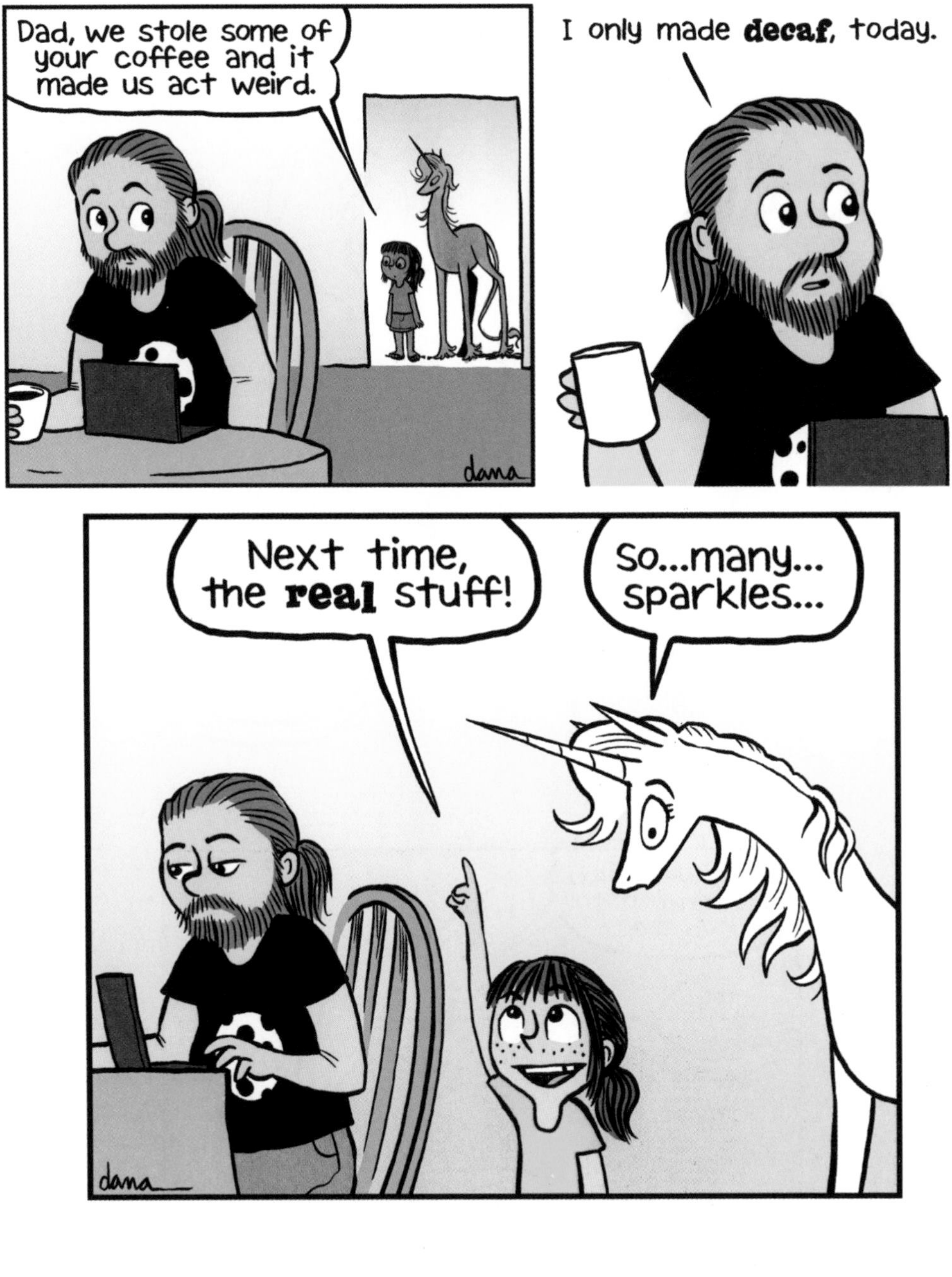
Dad, we stole some of your coffee and it made us act weird.
dana
I only made **decaf**, today.
Next time, the **real** stuff!
So...many... sparkles...
dana

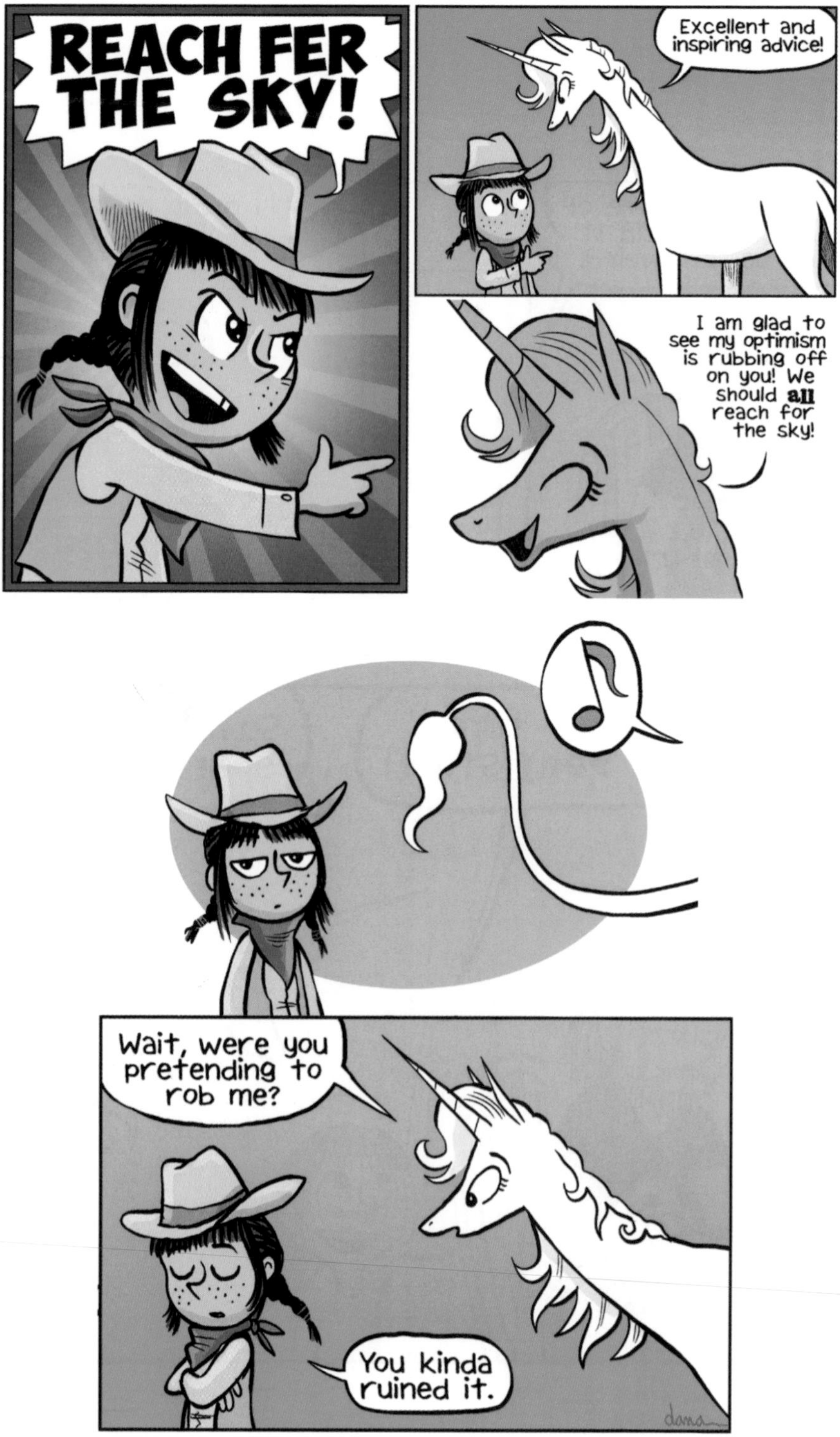
REACH FER THE SKY!
Excellent and inspiring advice!
I am glad to see my optimism is rubbing off on you! We should **all** reach for the sky!
Wait, were you pretending to rob me?
You kinda ruined it.
dana

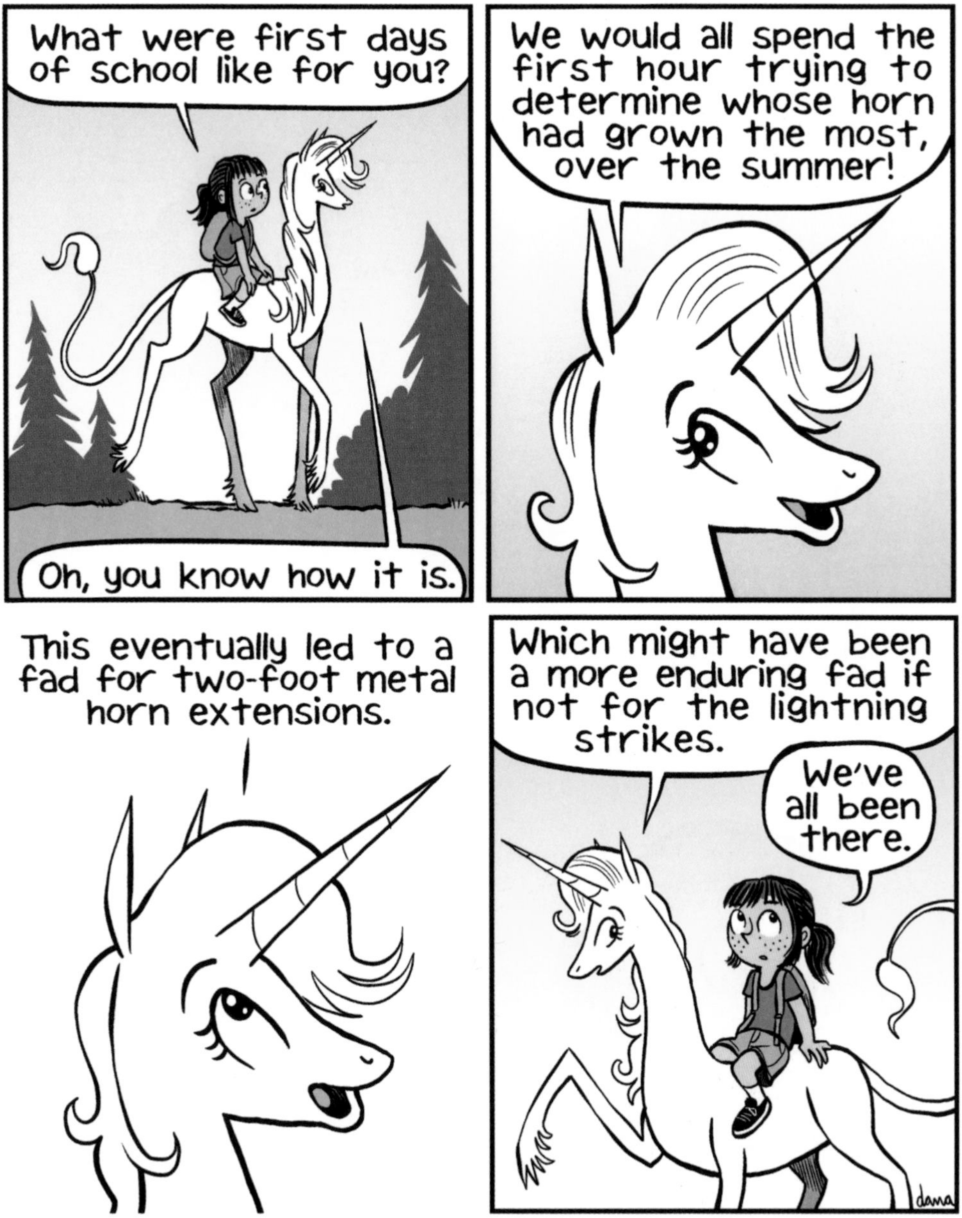
What were first days of school like for you?
Oh, you know how it is.
We would all spend the first hour trying to determine whose horn had grown the most, over the summer!
This eventually led to a fad for two-foot metal horn extensions.
Which might have been a more enduring fad if not for the lightning strikes.
We've all been there.
dana

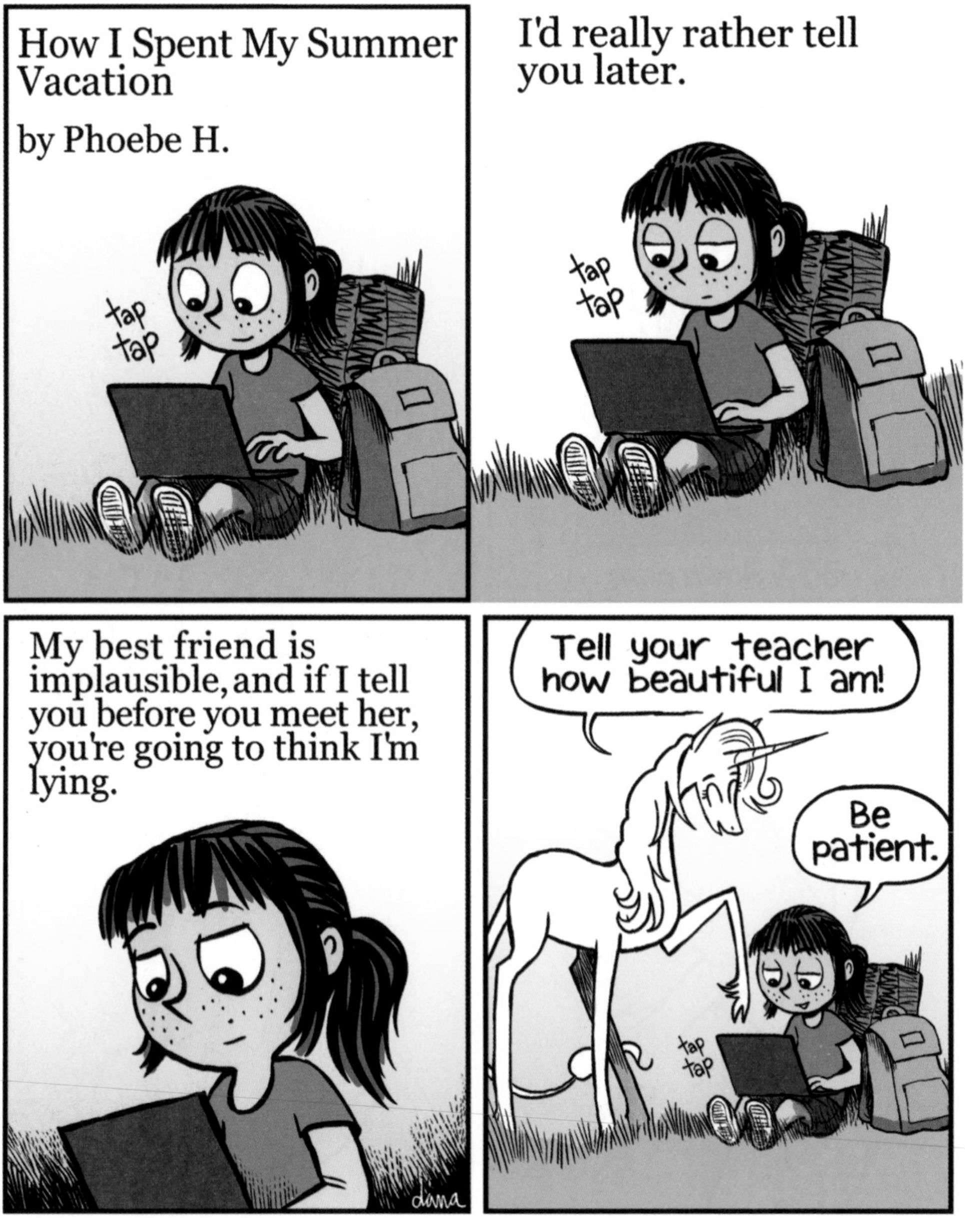

How I Spent My Summer Vacation
by Phoebe H.
tap tap
I'd really rather tell you later.
tap tap
My best friend is implausible, and if I tell you before you meet her, you're going to think I'm lying.
Tell your teacher how beautiful I am!
Be patient.
tap tap

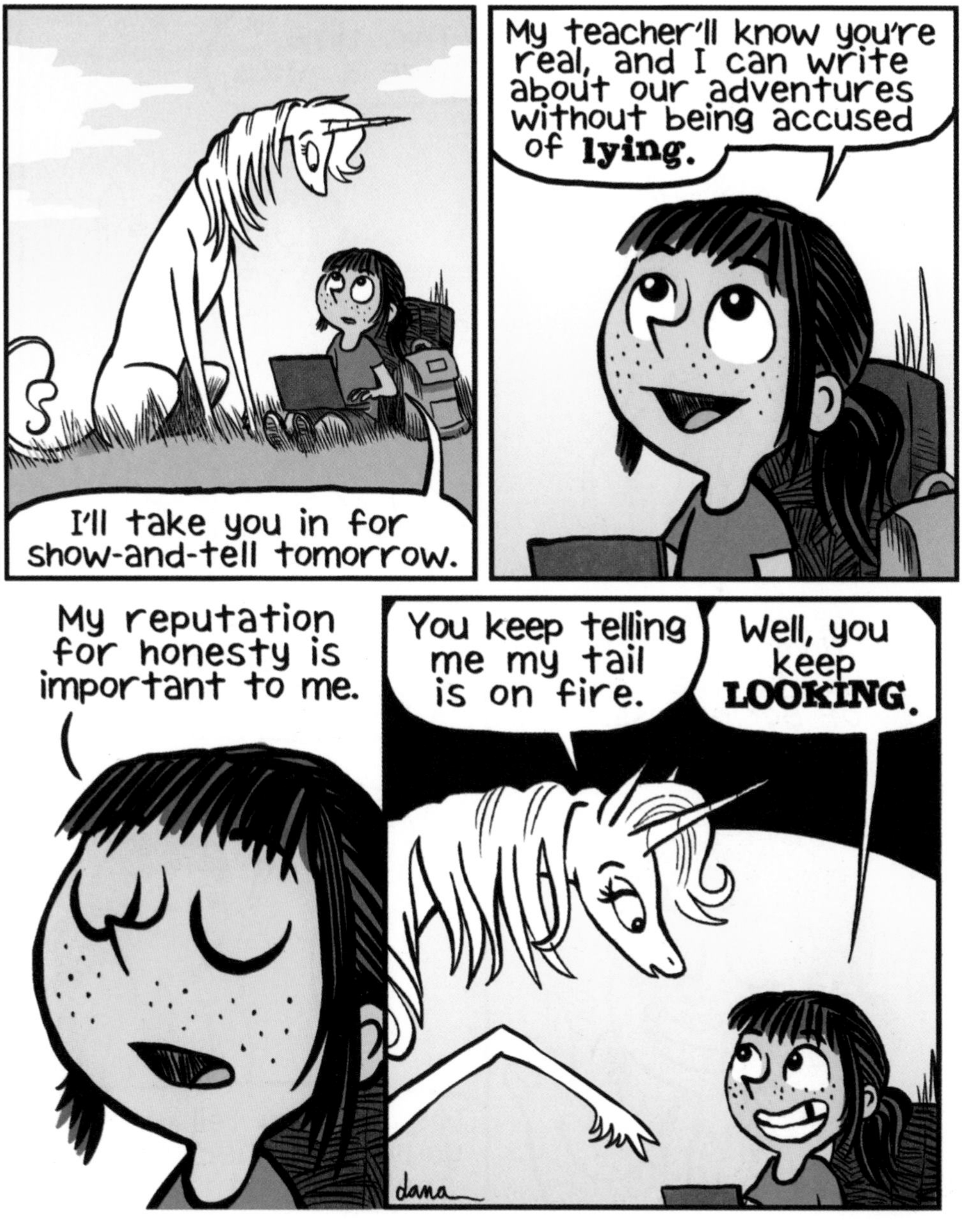
I'll take you in for show-and-tell tomorrow.
My teacher'll know you're real, and I can write about our adventures without being accused of **lying.**
My reputation for honesty is important to me.
You keep telling me my tail is on fire.
Well, you keep **LOOKING**.
dana

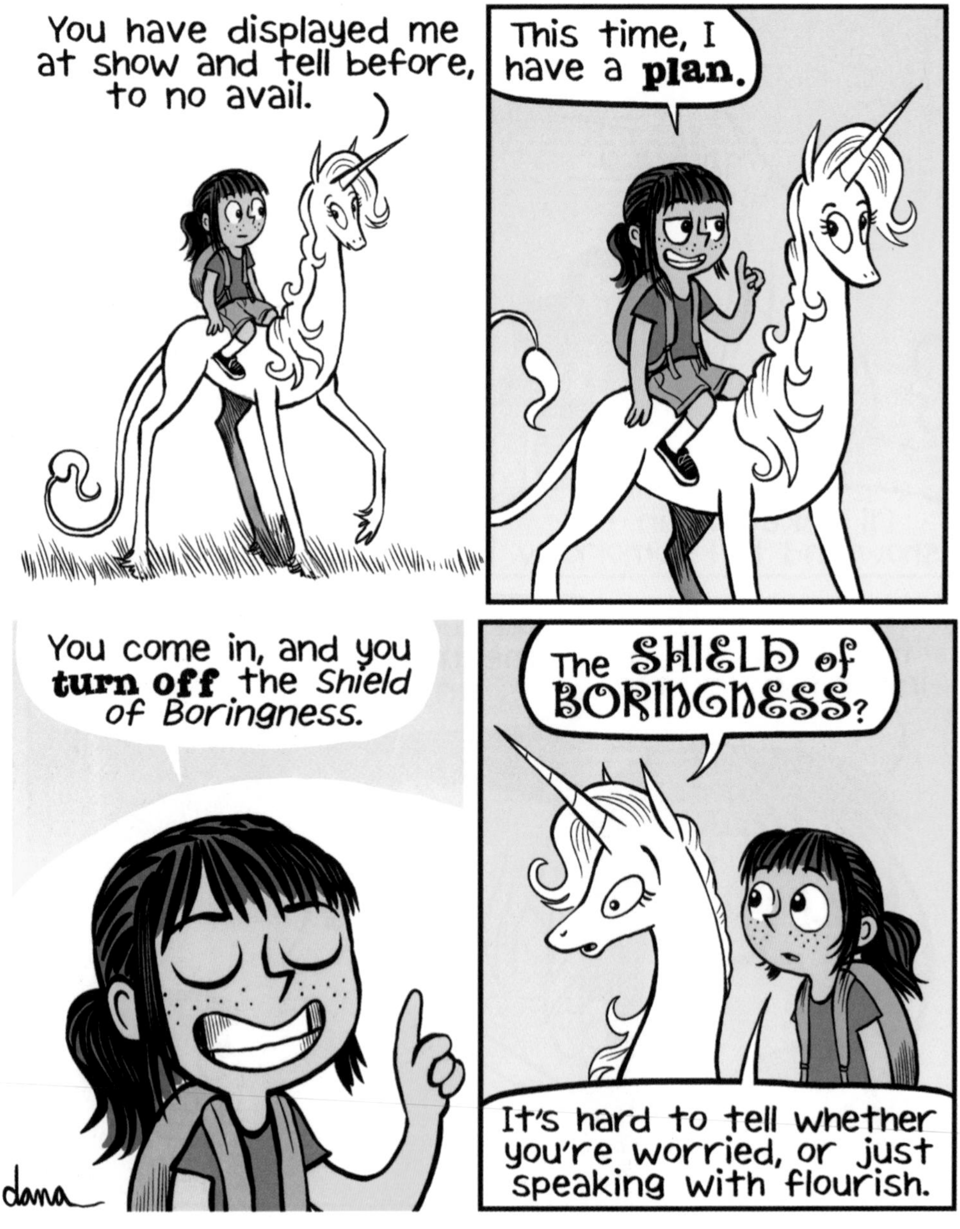
You have displayed me at show and tell before, to no avail.
This time, I have a **plan.**
You come in, and you **turn off** the *Shield of Boringness.*
The SHIELD of BORINGNESS?
It's hard to tell whether you're worried, or just speaking with flourish.
dana

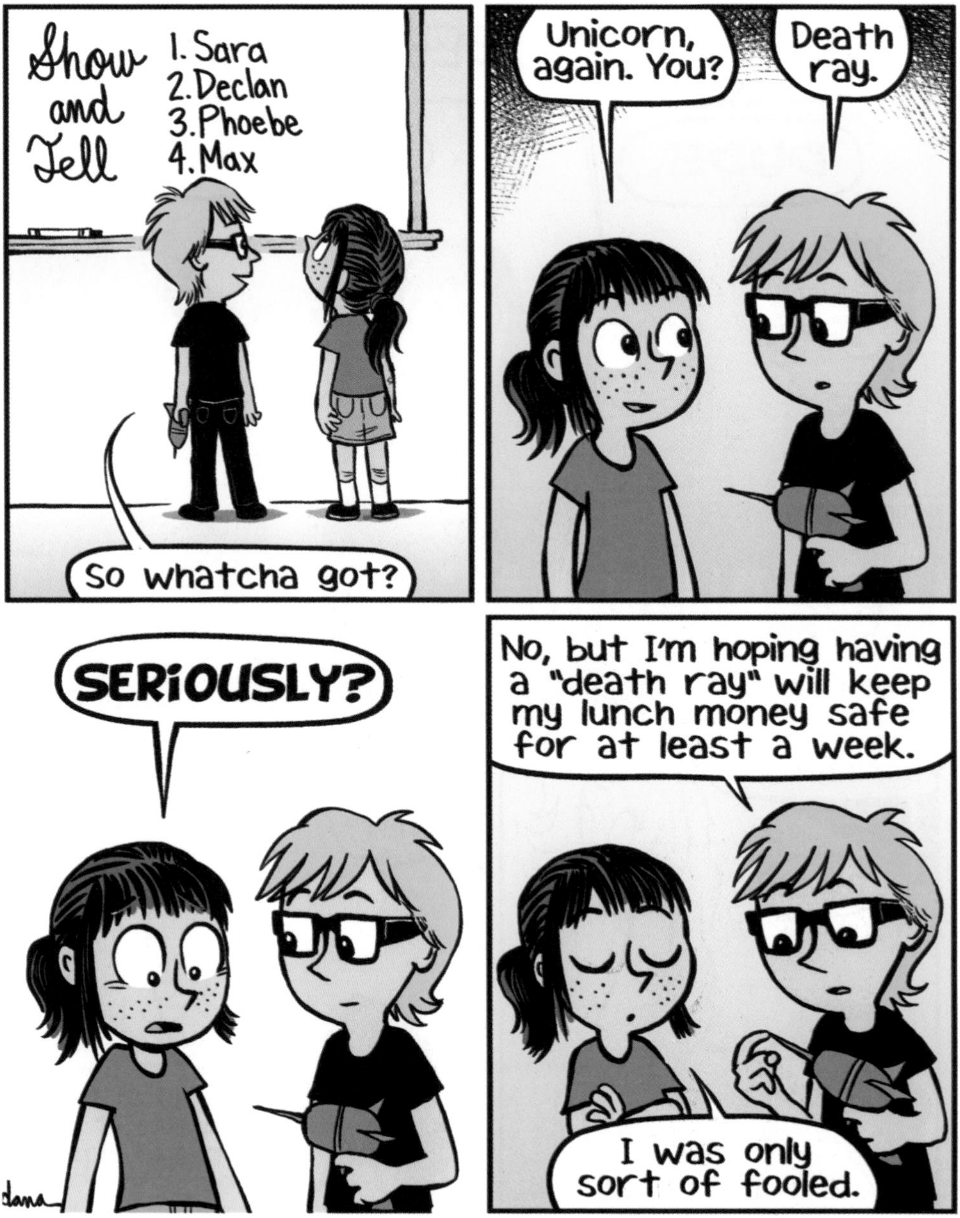
Show and Tell
1. Sara
2. Declan
3. Phoebe
4. Max
So whatcha got?
Unicorn, again. You?
Death ray.
SERiOUSLY?
No, but I'm hoping having a "death ray" will keep my lunch money safe for at least a week.
I was only sort of fooled.
dana

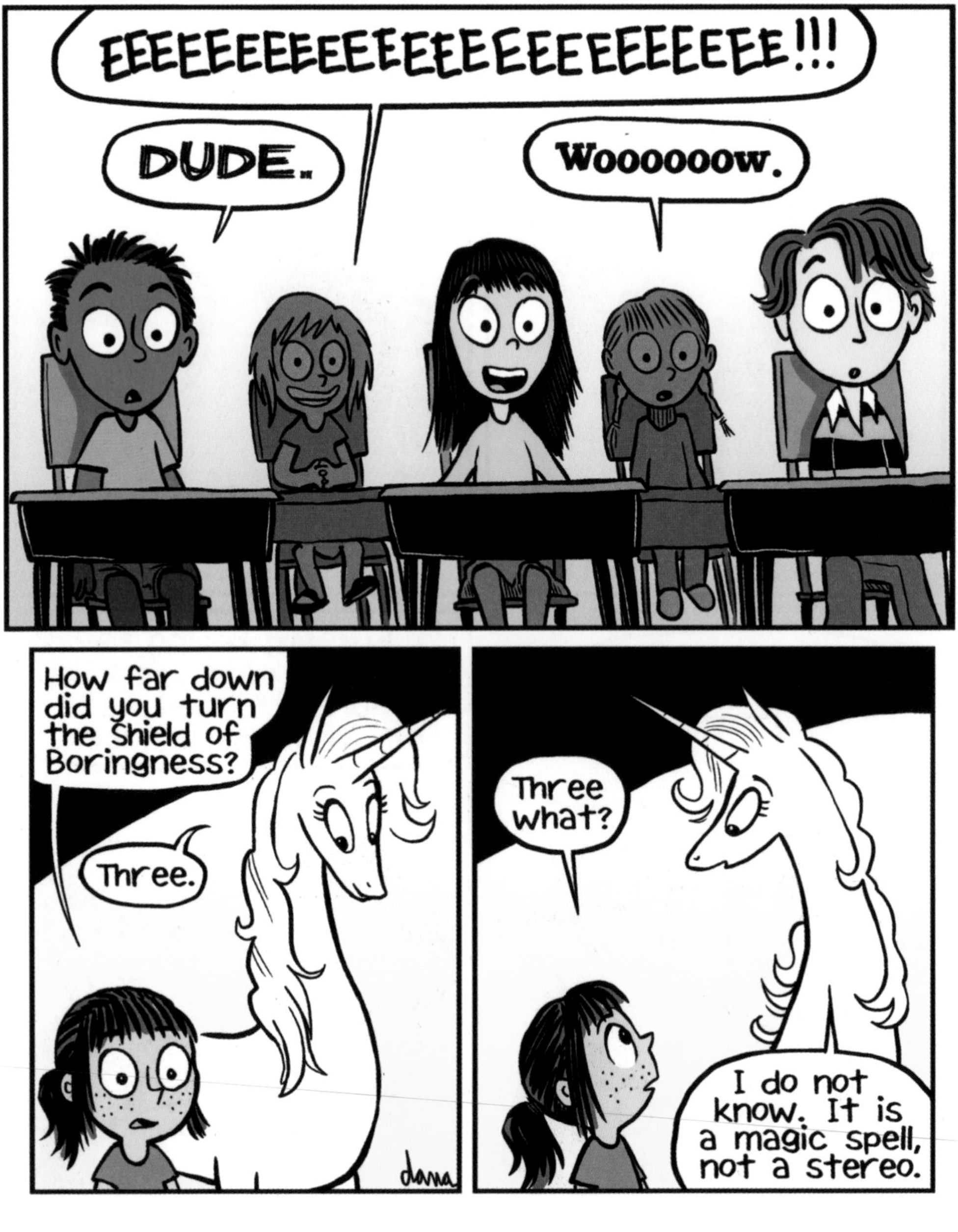
EEEEEEEEEEEEEEEEEEEEEEEE!!!
DUDE.
Woooooow.
How far down did you turn the Shield of Boringness?
Three.
Three what?
I do not know. It is a magic spell, not a stereo.

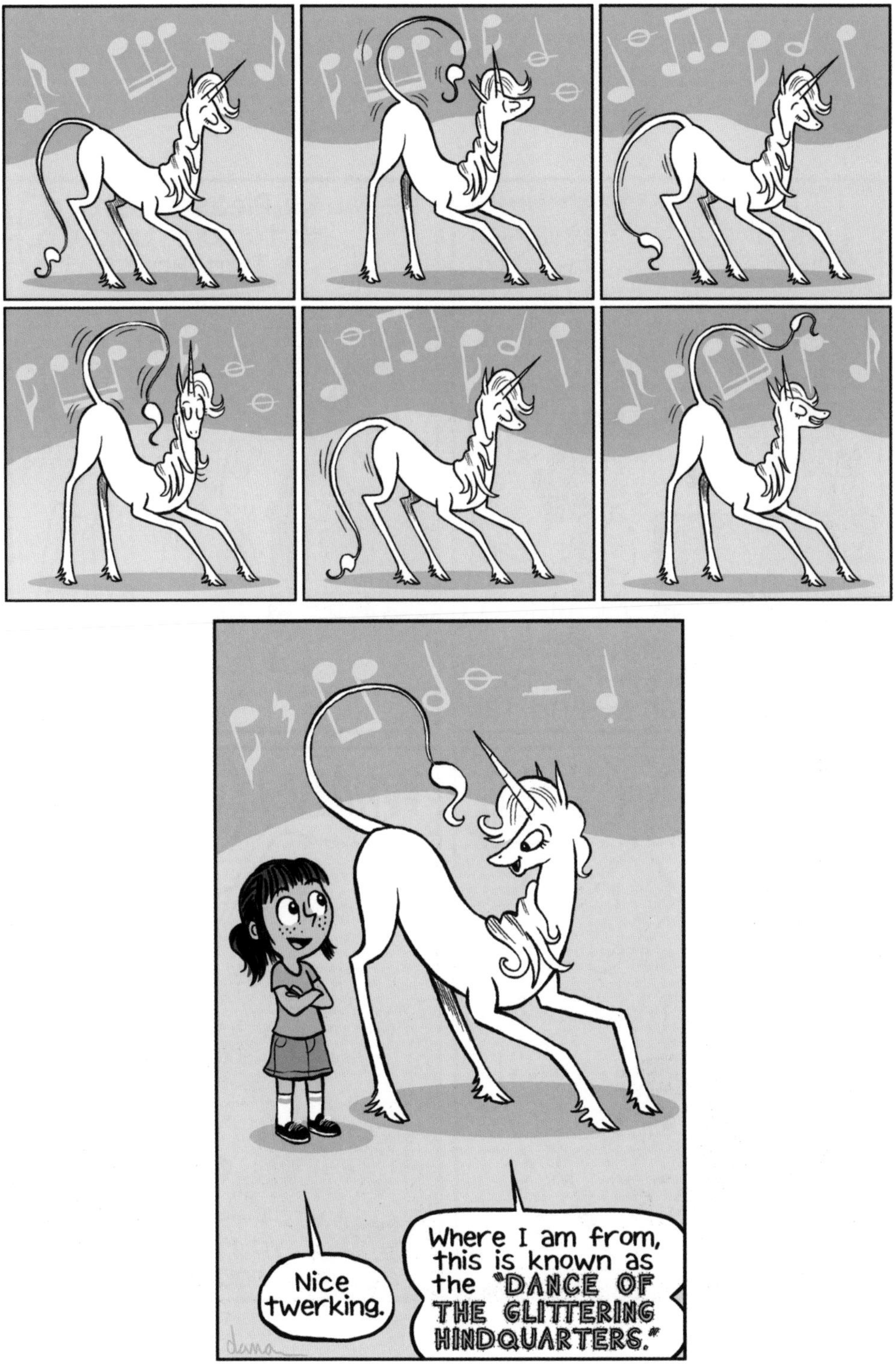

Nice twerking.
Where I am from, this is known as the "DANCE OF THE GLITTERING HINDQUARTERS."

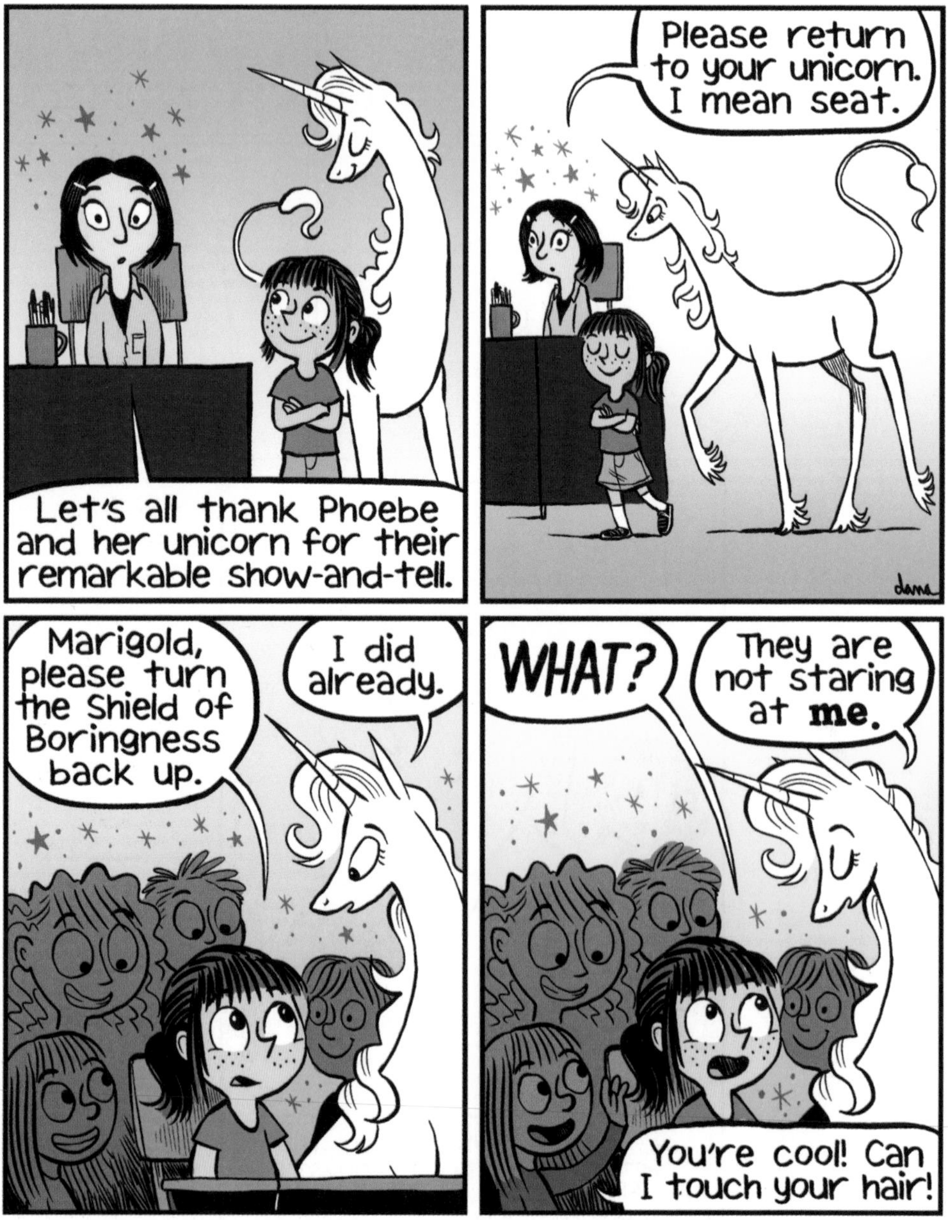
Let's all thank Phoebe and her unicorn for their remarkable show-and-tell.
Please return to your unicorn. I mean seat.
Marigold, please turn the Shield of Boringness back up.
I did already.
WHAT?
They are not staring at **me**.
You're cool! Can I touch your hair!

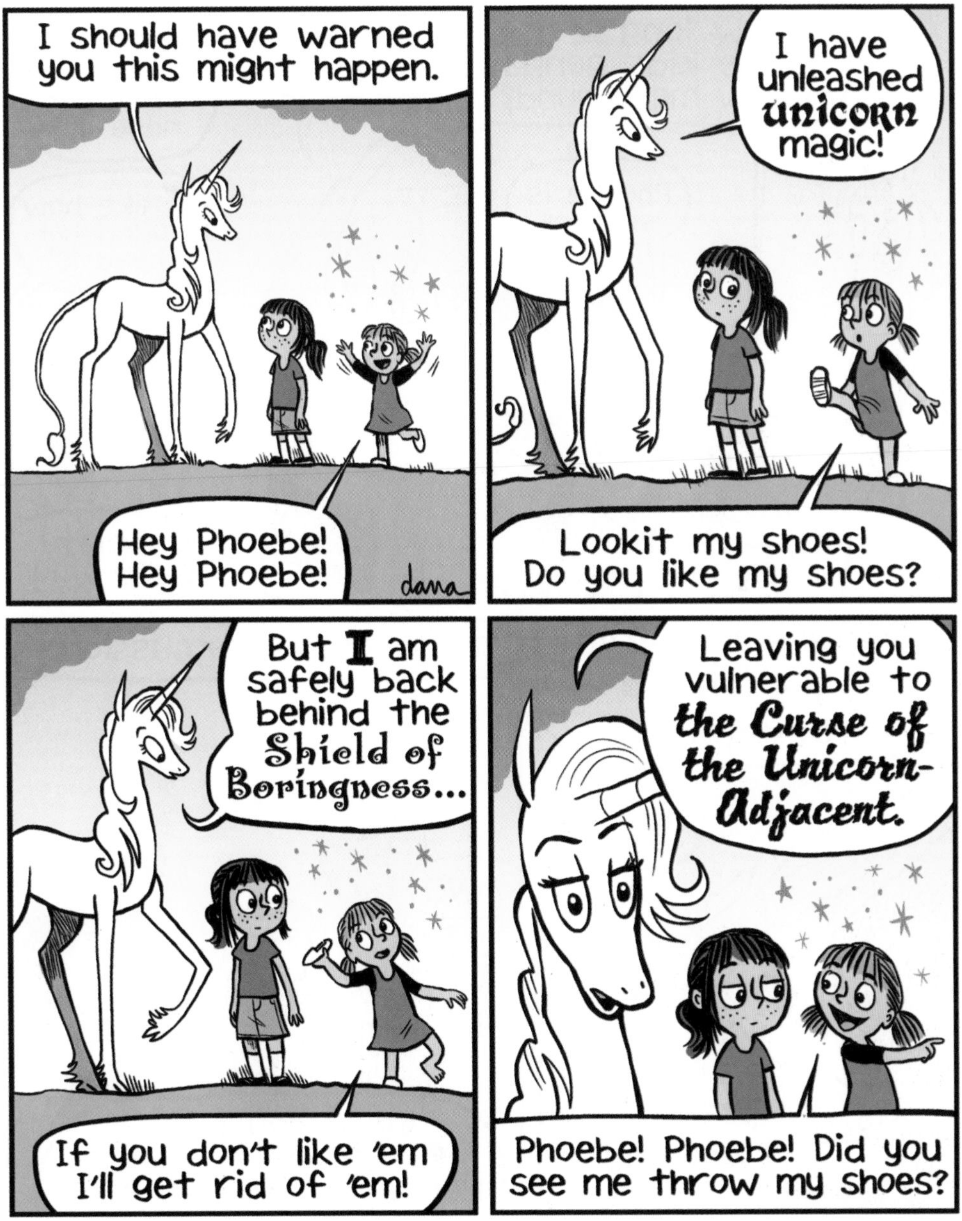
I should have warned you this might happen.
Hey Phoebe! Hey Phoebe!
dana
I have unleashed unicorn magic!
Lookit my shoes! Do you like my shoes?
But I am safely back behind the Shield of Boringness...
If you don't like 'em I'll get rid of 'em!
Leaving you vulnerable to the Curse of the Unicorn-Adjacent.
Phoebe! Phoebe! Did you see me throw my shoes?

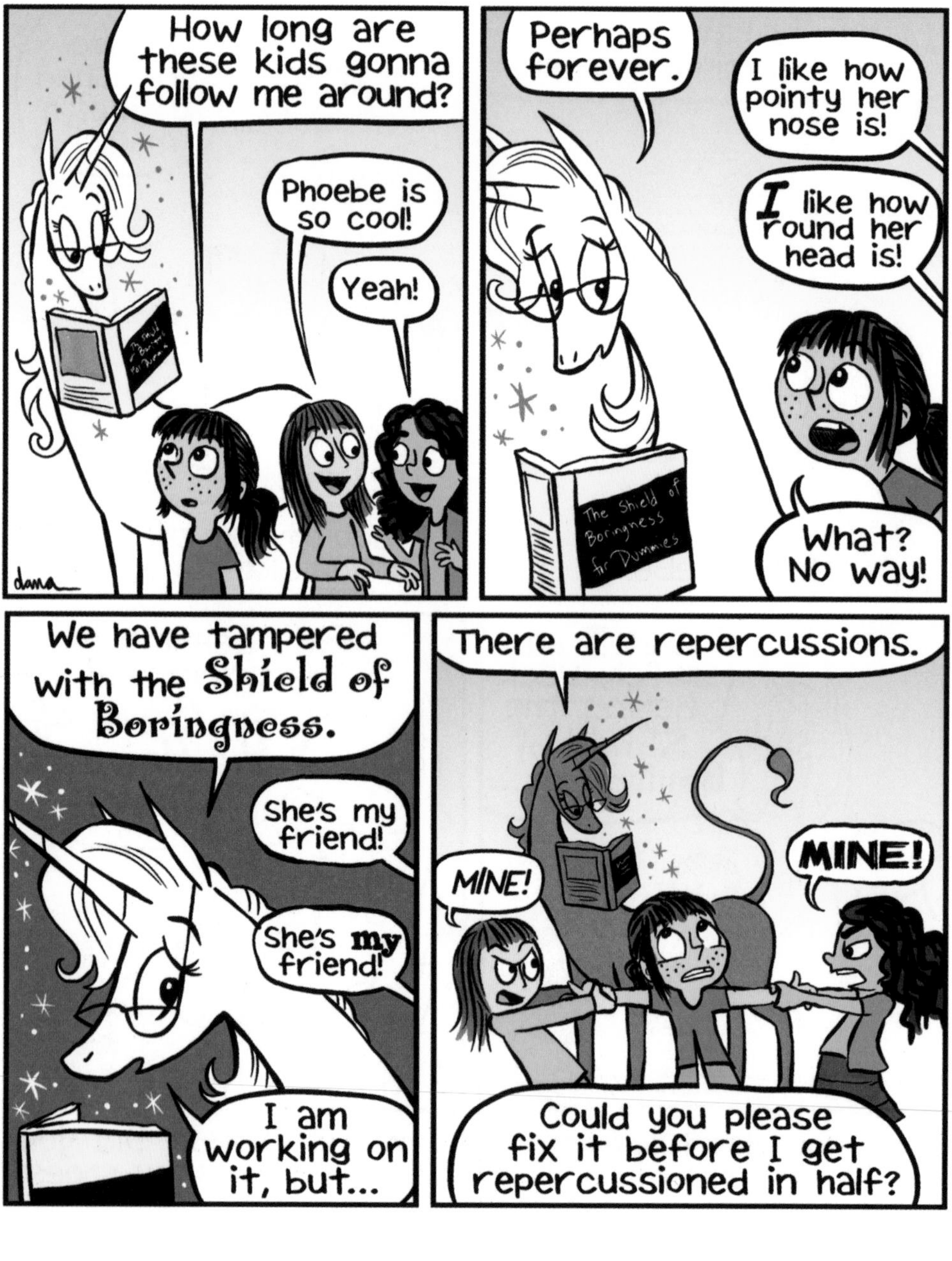

How long are these kids gonna follow me around?
Phoebe is so cool!
Yeah!
dana
Perhaps forever.
I like how pointy her nose is!
I like how round her head is!
The Shield of Boringness for Dummies
What? No way!
We have tampered with the Shield of Boringness.
She's my friend!
She's my friend!
I am working on it, but...
There are repercussions.
MINE!
MINE!
Could you please fix it before I get repercussioned in half?

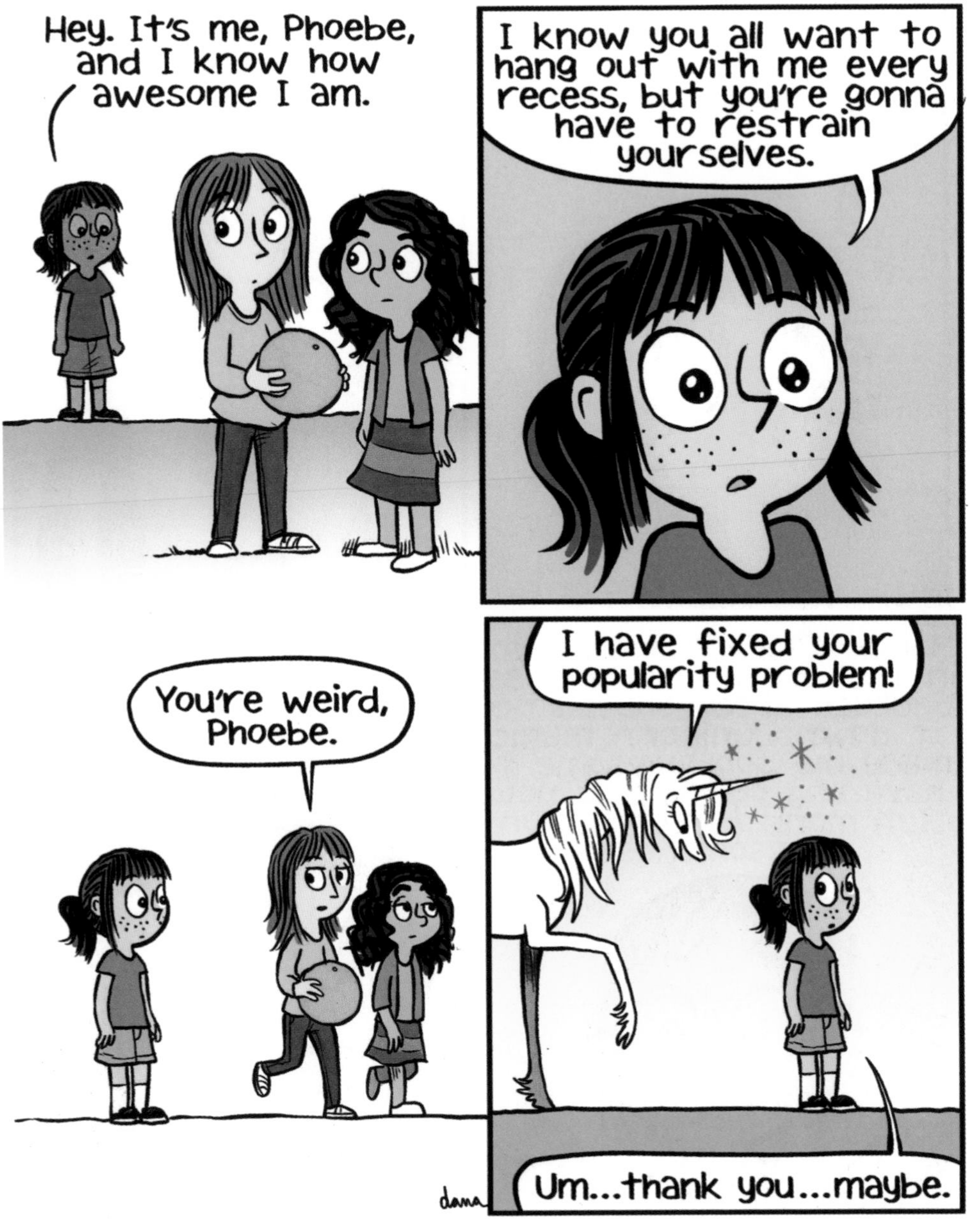
Hey. It's me, Phoebe, and I know how awesome I am.
I know you all want to hang out with me every recess, but you're gonna have to restrain yourselves.
You're weird, Phoebe.
I have fixed your popularity problem!
Um...thank you...maybe.
dana

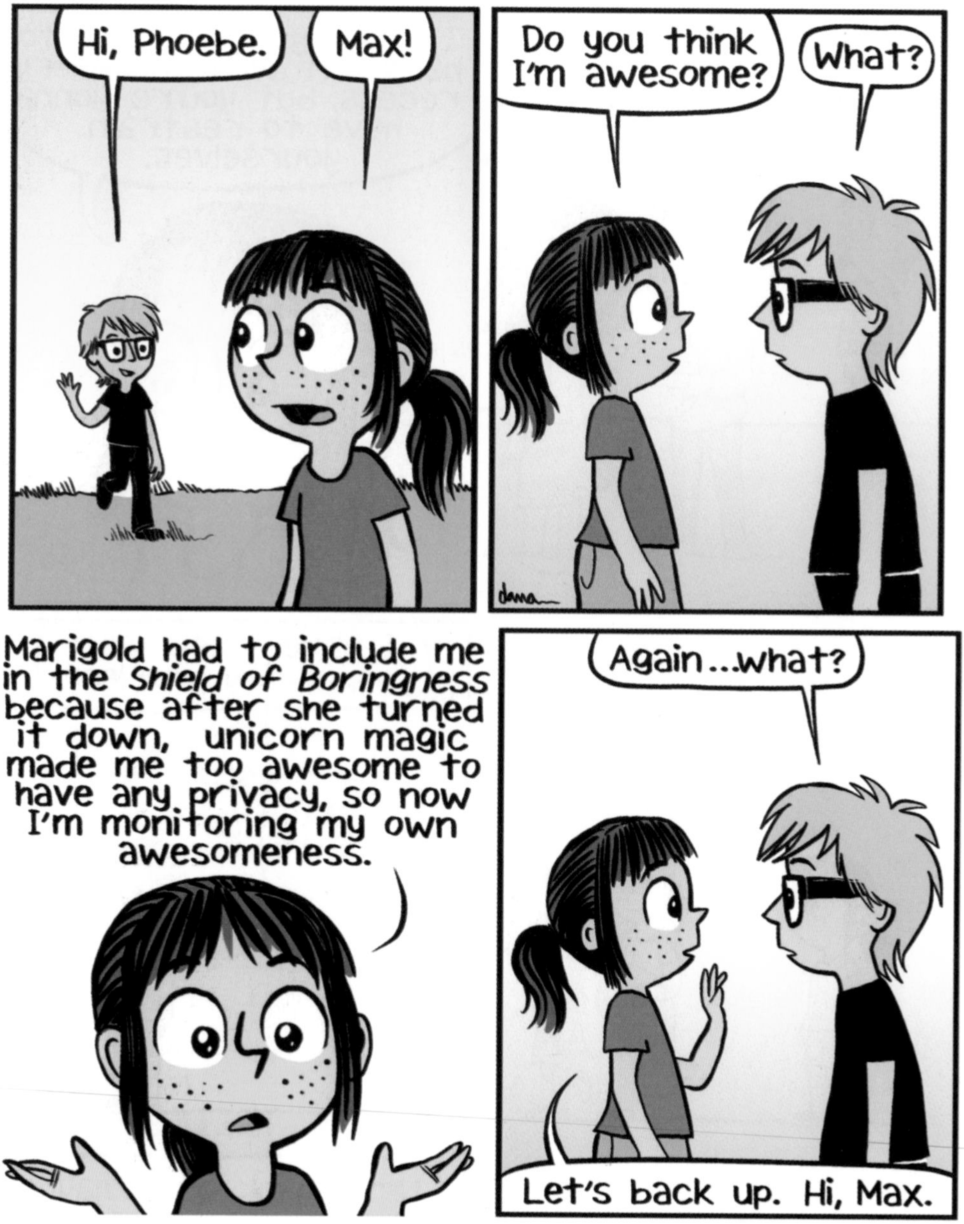
Hi, Phoebe.
Max!
Do you think I'm awesome?
What?
Marigold had to include me in the *Shield of Boringness* because after she turned it down, unicorn magic made me too awesome to have any privacy, so now I'm monitoring my own awesomeness.
Again...what?
Let's back up. Hi, Max.

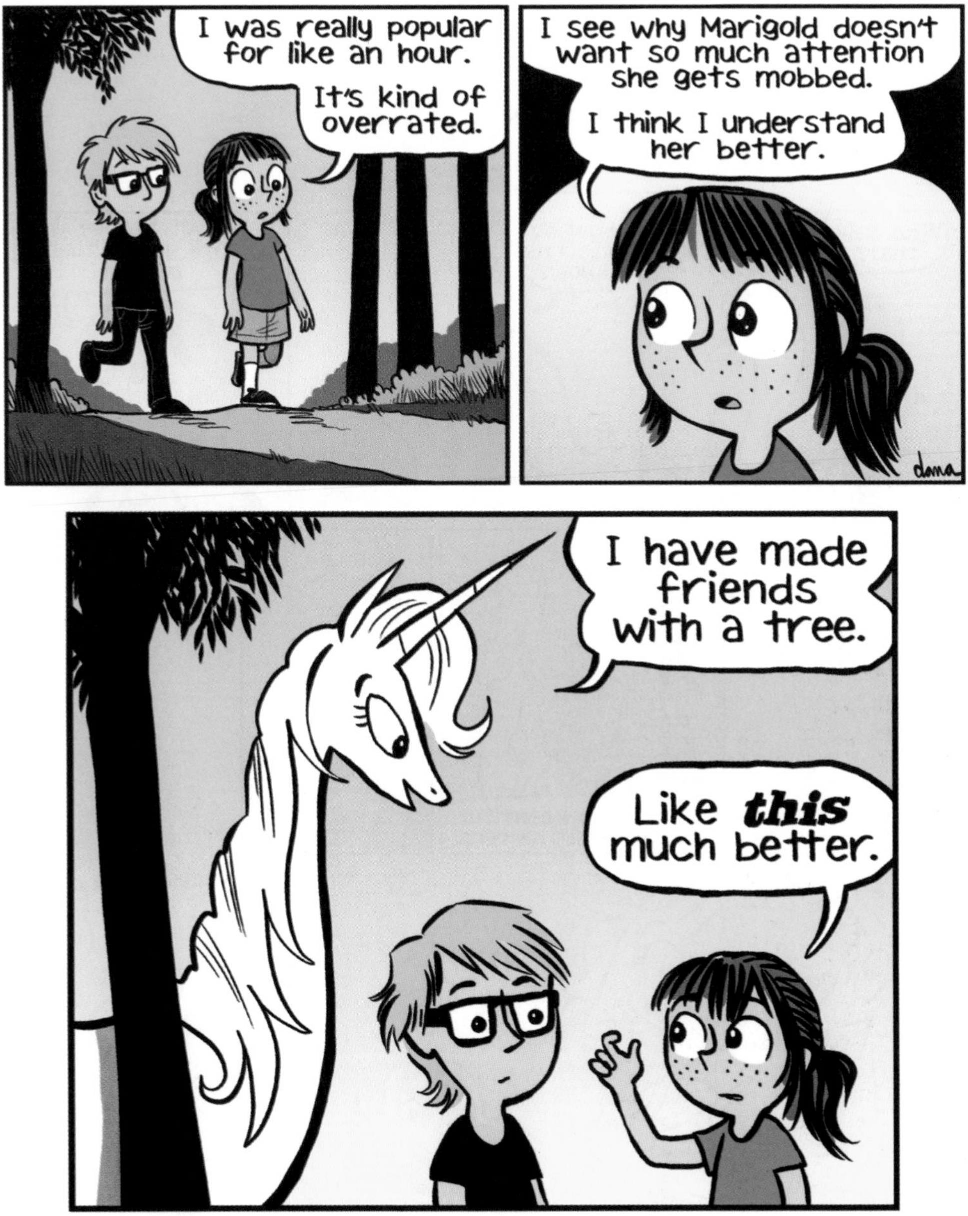

I was really popular for like an hour.
It's kind of overrated.
I see why Marigold doesn't want so much attention she gets mobbed.
I think I understand her better.
dana
I have made friends with a tree.
Like ***this*** much better.

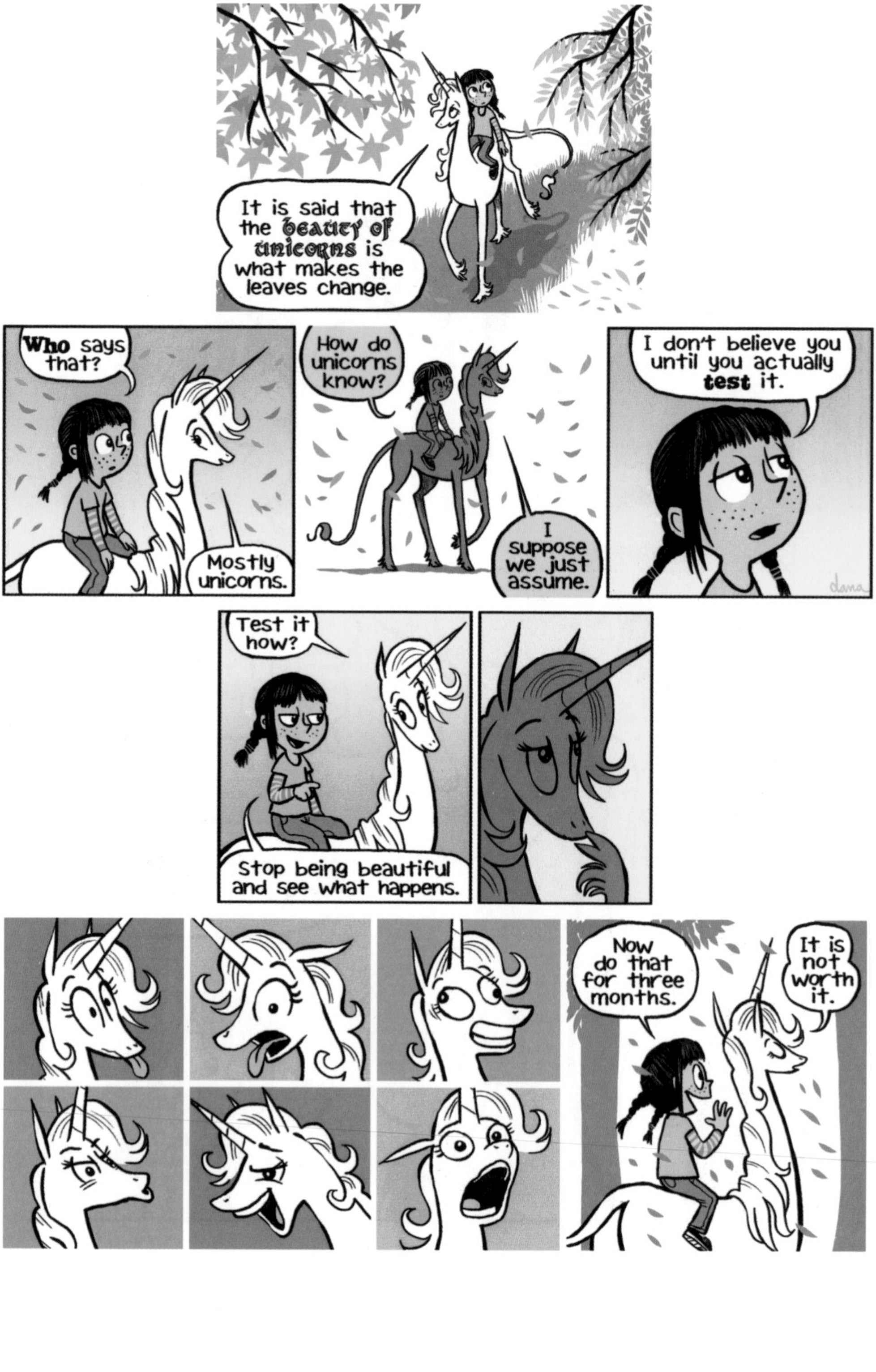

It is said that the beauty of unicorns is what makes the leaves change.
Who says that?
Mostly unicorns.
How do unicorns know?
I suppose we just assume.
I don't believe you until you actually test it.
Test it how?
Stop being beautiful and see what happens.
Now do that for three months.
It is not worth it.

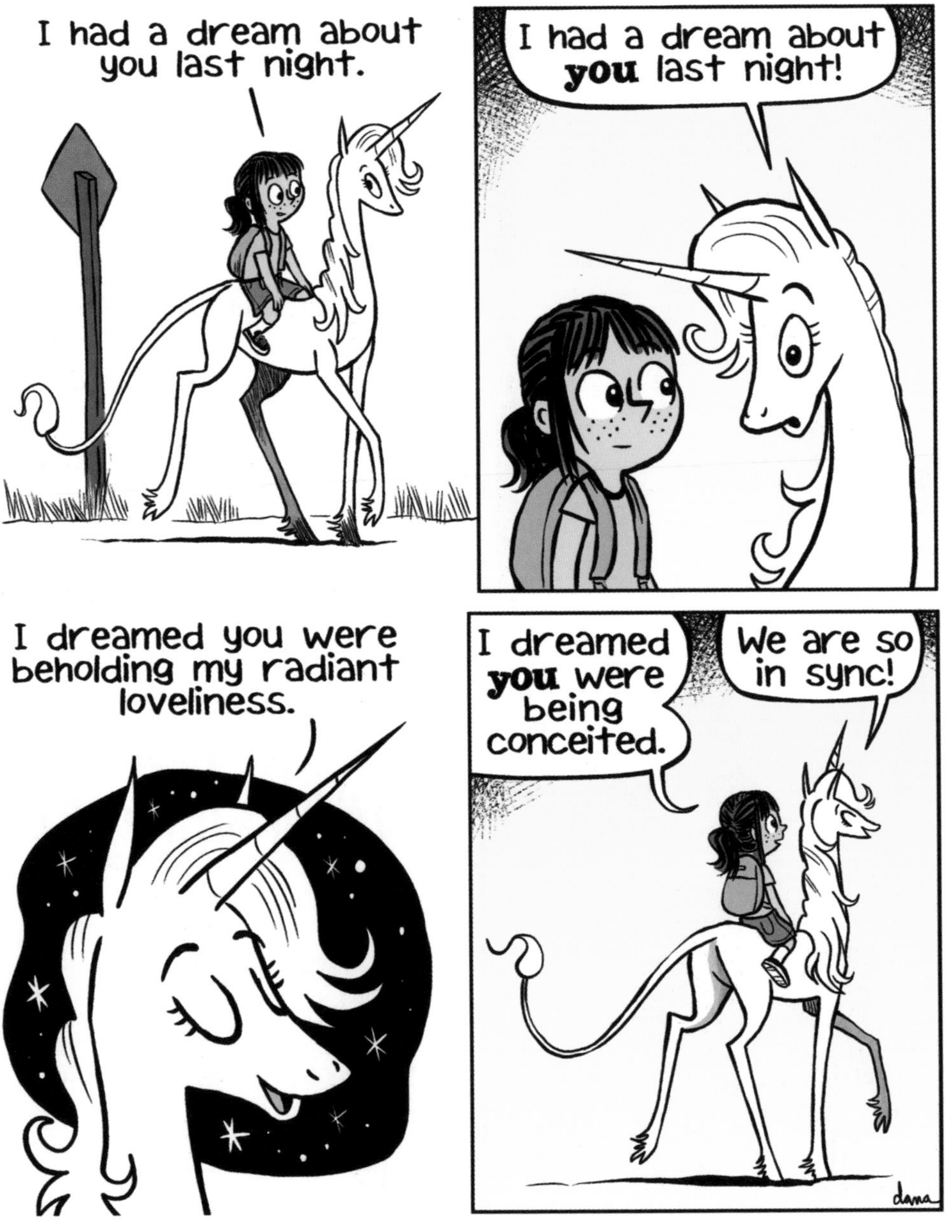
I had a dream about you last night.
I had a dream about **you** last night!
I dreamed you were beholding my radiant loveliness.
I dreamed **you** were being conceited.
We are so in sync!
dana

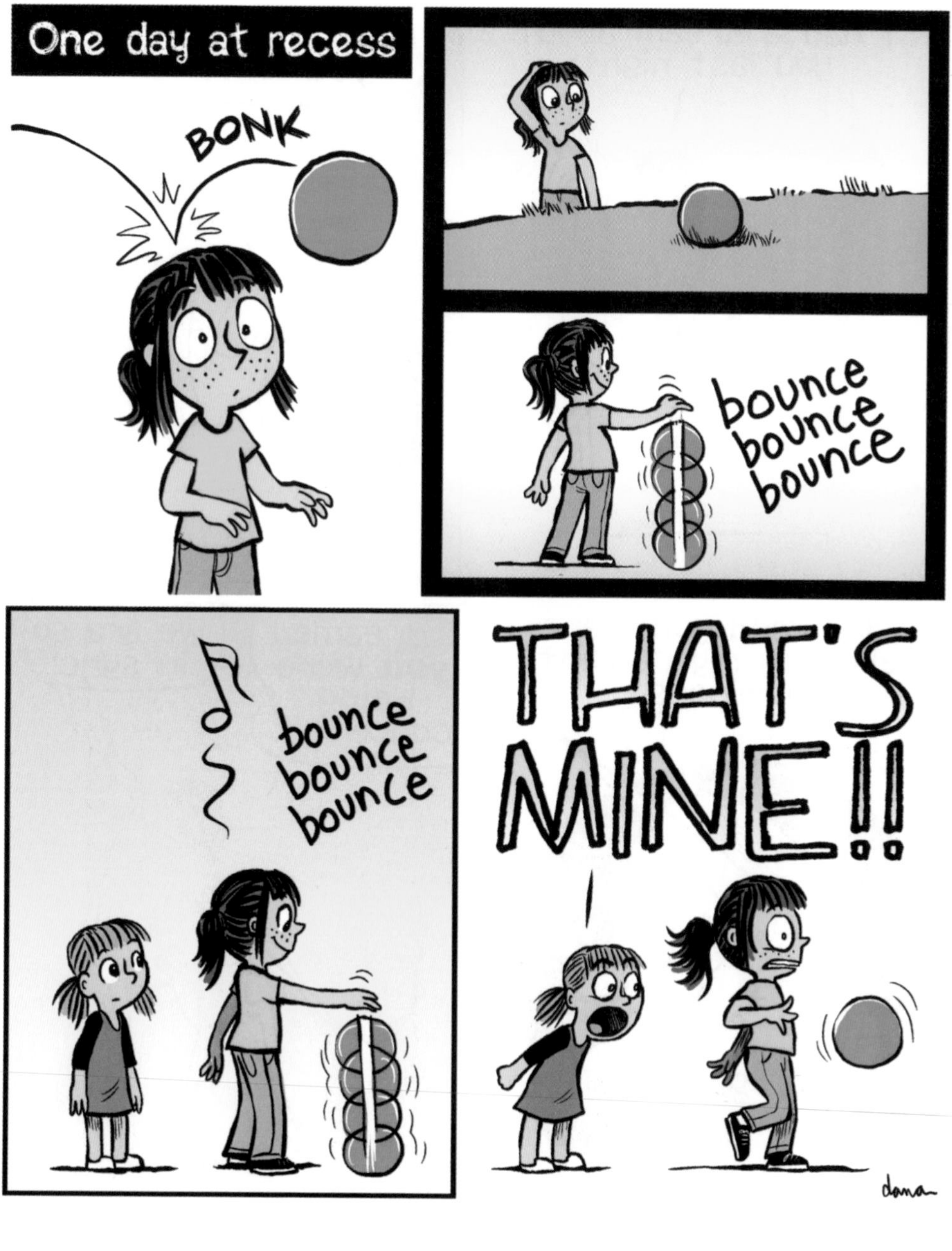
One day at recess
BONK
bounce
bounce
bounce
bounce
bounce
bounce
THAT'S MINE!!
dana

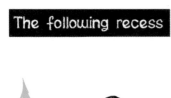
The following recess

YOU TOOK MY BALL AGAIN!!

If this is deliberate, it's verging on entrapment.

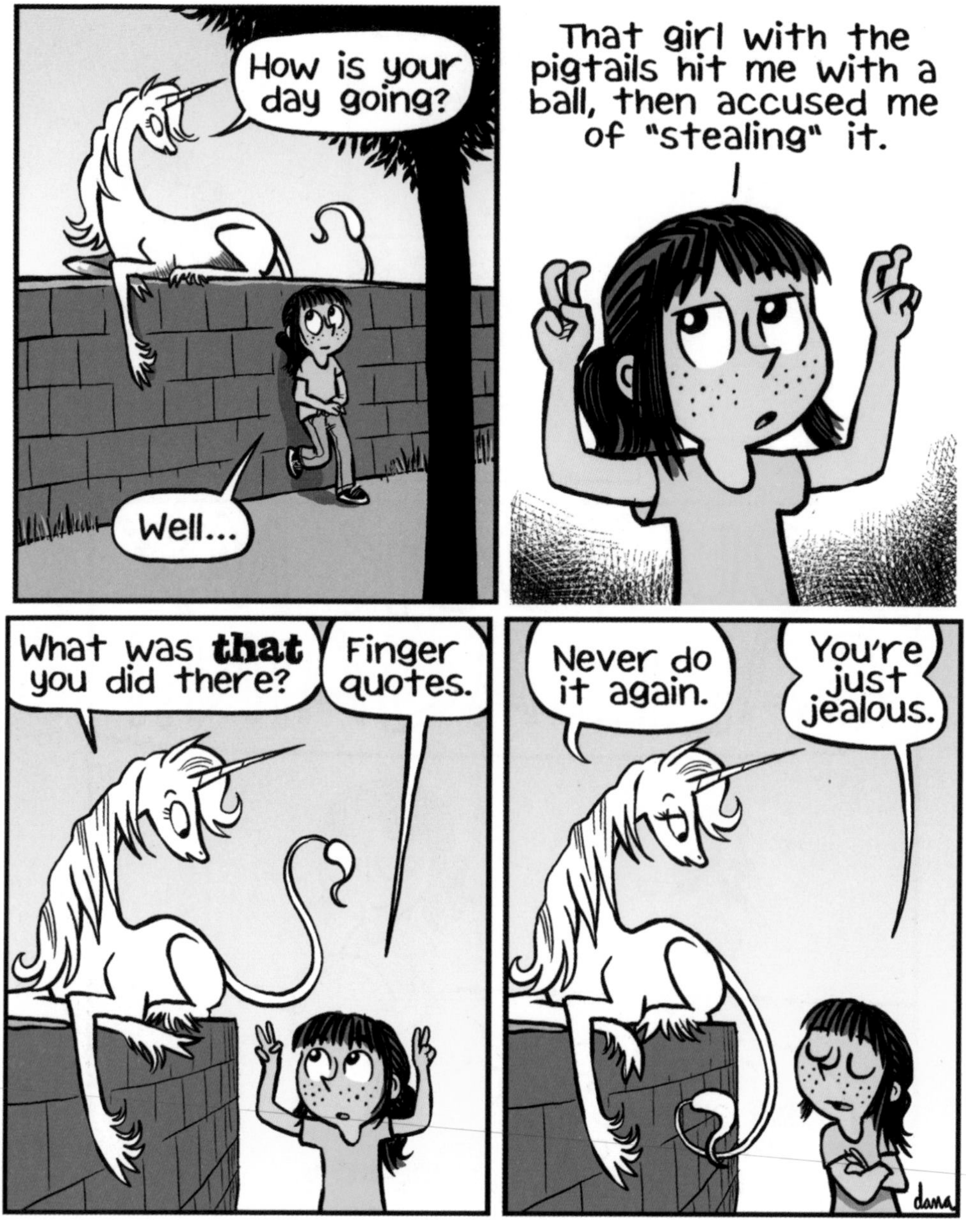
How is your day going?
Well...
That girl with the pigtails hit me with a ball, then accused me of "stealing" it.
What was **that** you did there?
Finger quotes.
Never do it again.
You're just jealous.
dana

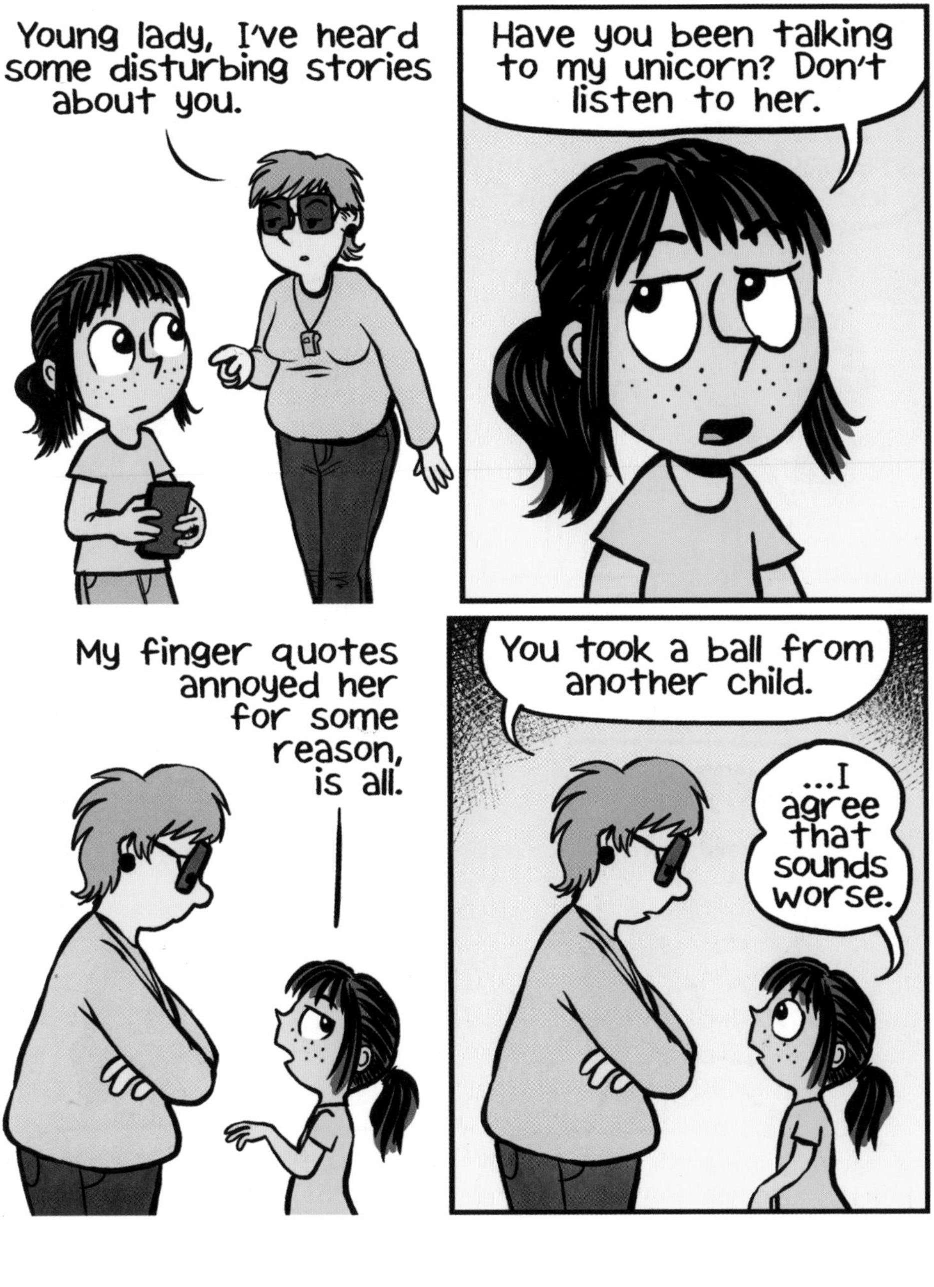
Young lady, I've heard some disturbing stories about you.
Have you been talking to my unicorn? Don't listen to her.
My finger quotes annoyed her for some reason, is all.
You took a ball from another child.
...I agree that sounds worse.

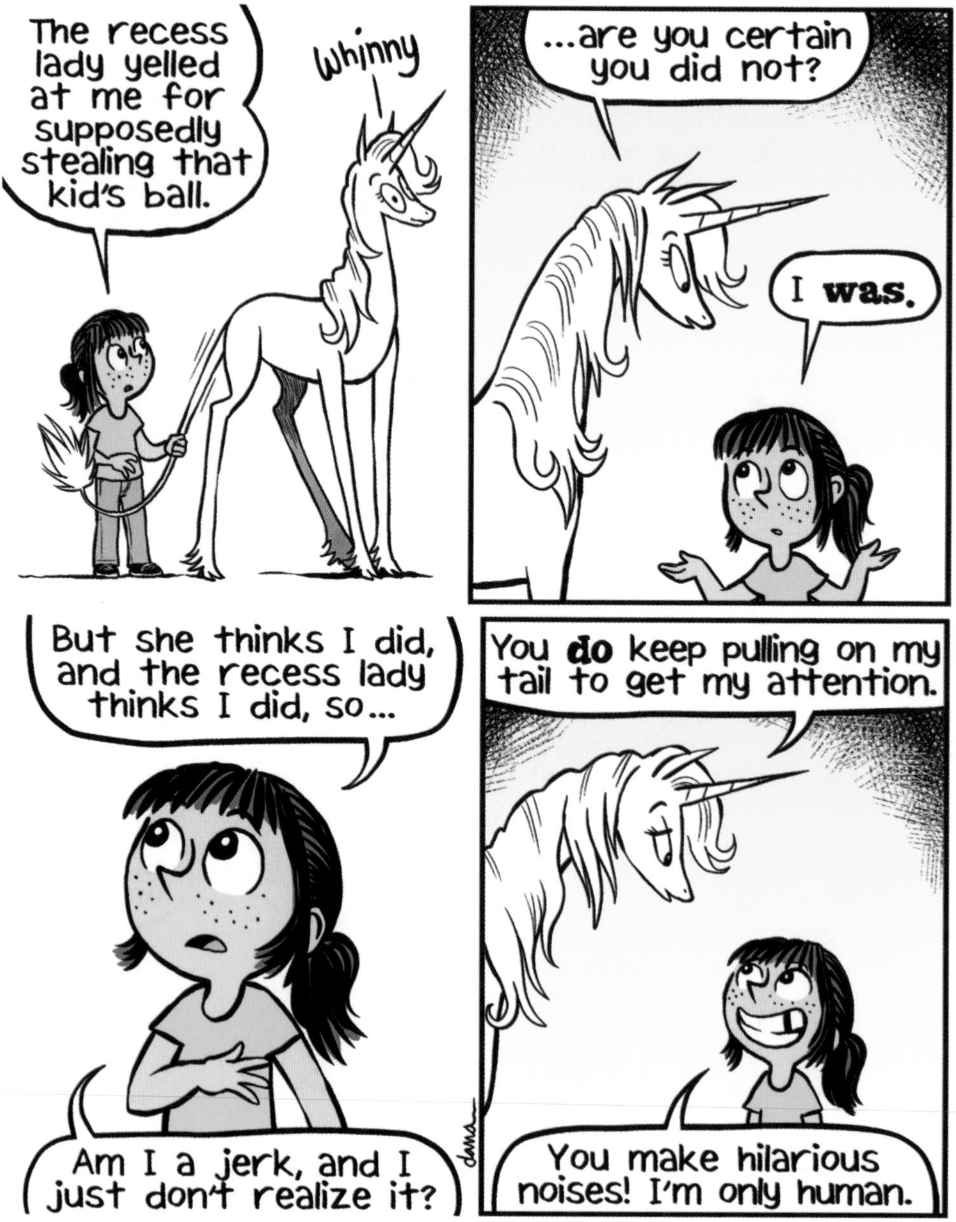
The recess lady yelled at me for supposedly stealing that kid's ball.
Whinny
...are you certain you did not?
I was.
But she thinks I did, and the recess lady thinks I did, so...
Am I a jerk, and I just don't realize it?
You do keep pulling on my tail to get my attention.
You make hilarious noises! I'm only human.
dana

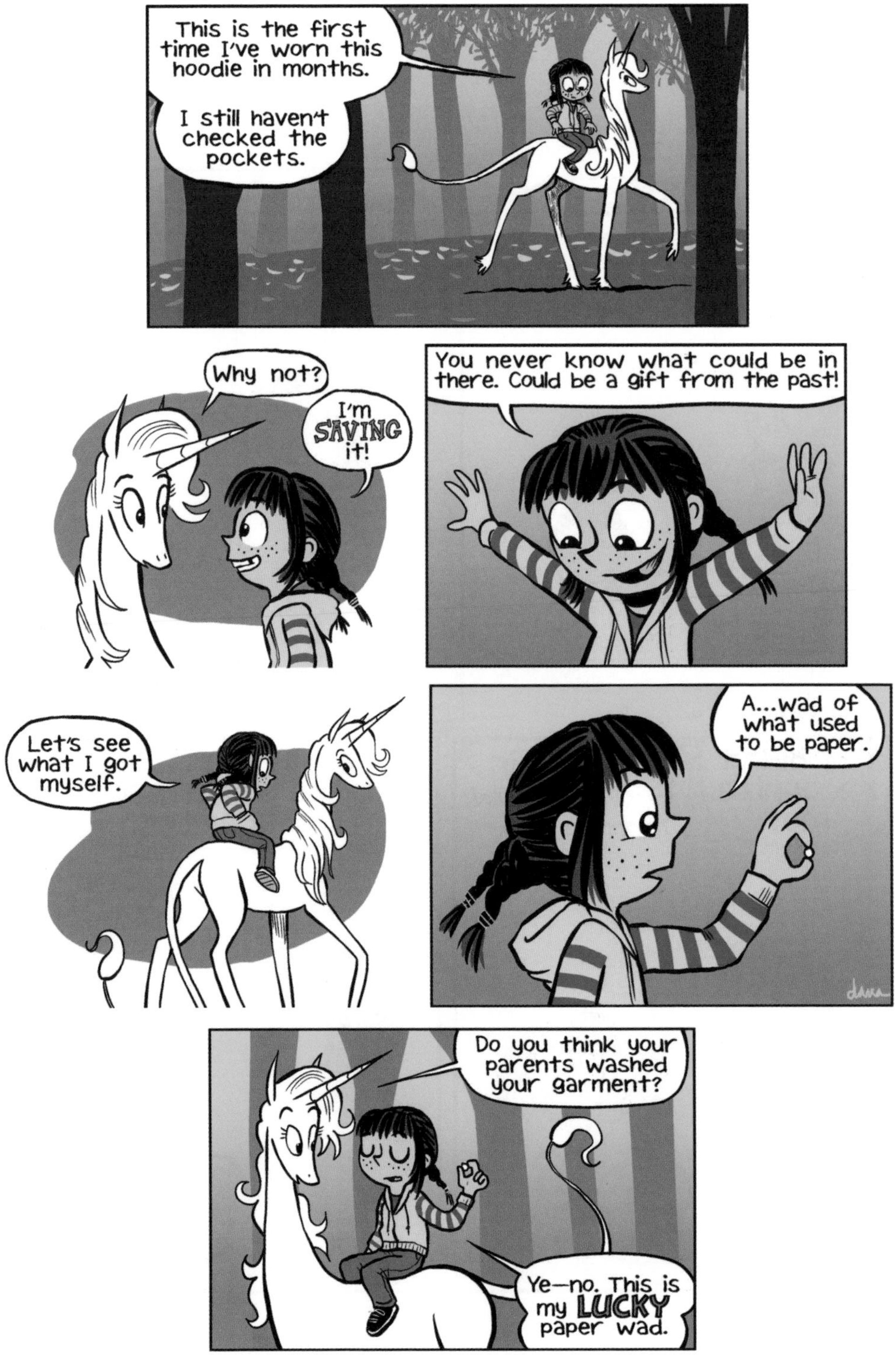
This is the first time I've worn this hoodie in months.
I still haven't checked the pockets.
Why not?
I'm SAVING it!
You never know what could be in there. Could be a gift from the past!
Let's see what I got myself.
A...wad of what used to be paper.
Do you think your parents washed your garment?
Ye—no. This is my LUCKY paper wad.

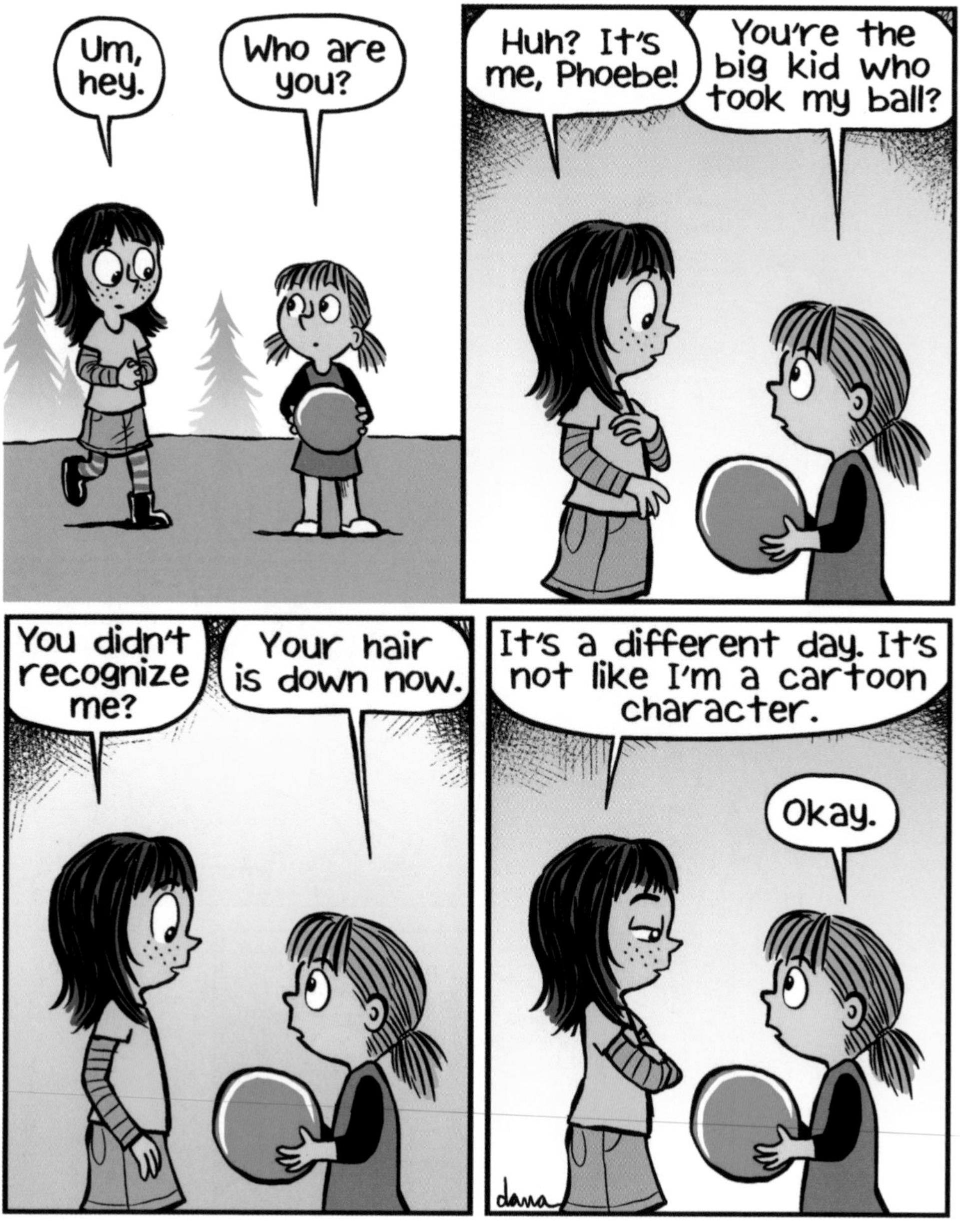
Um, hey.
Who are you?
Huh? It's me, Phoebe!
You're the big kid who took my ball?
You didn't recognize me?
Your hair is down now.
It's a different day. It's not like I'm a cartoon character.
Okay.
dana

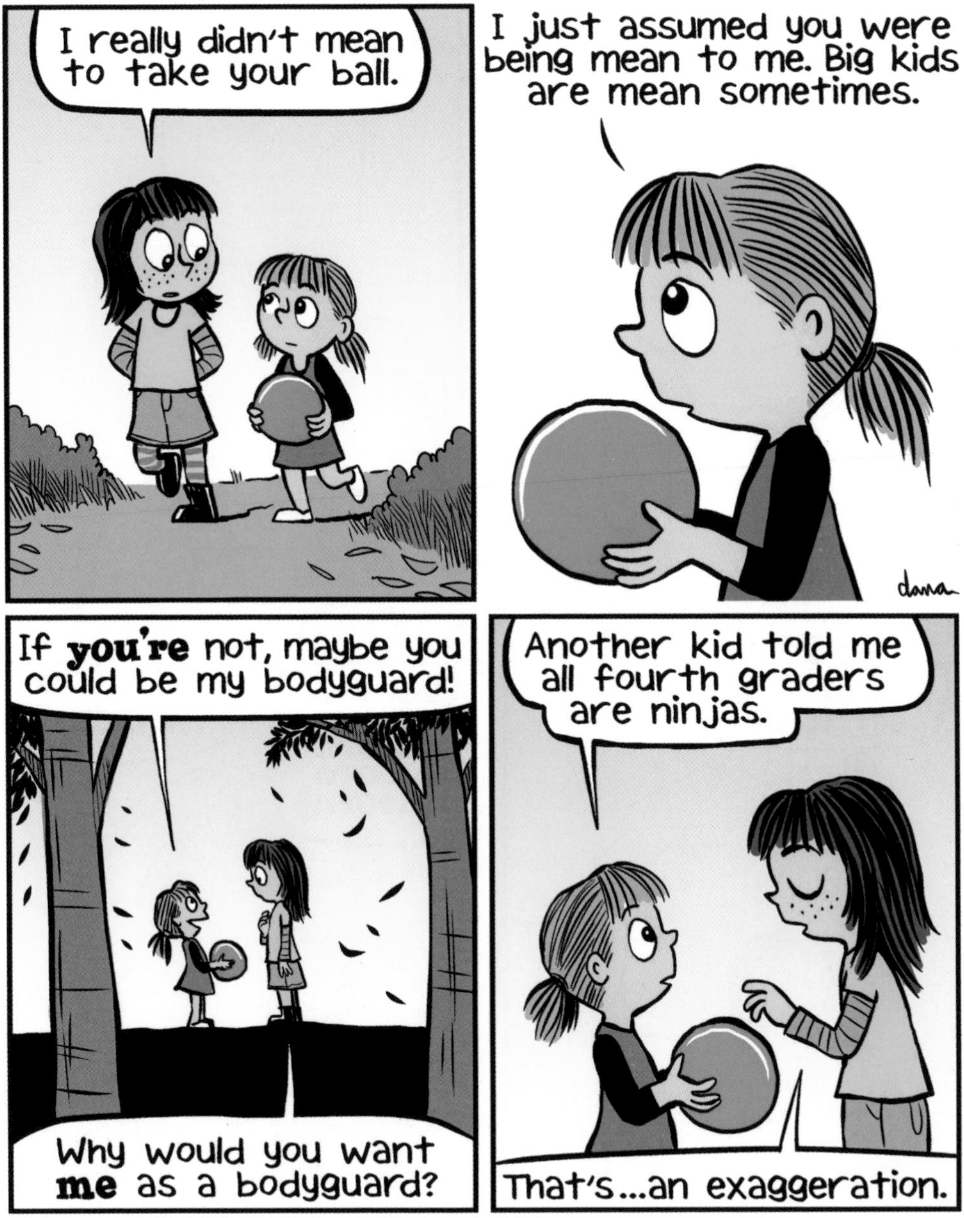
I really didn't mean to take your ball.
I just assumed you were being mean to me. Big kids are mean sometimes.
dana
If **you're** not, maybe you could be my bodyguard!
Why would you want **me** as a bodyguard?
Another kid told me all fourth graders are ninjas.
That's...an exaggeration.

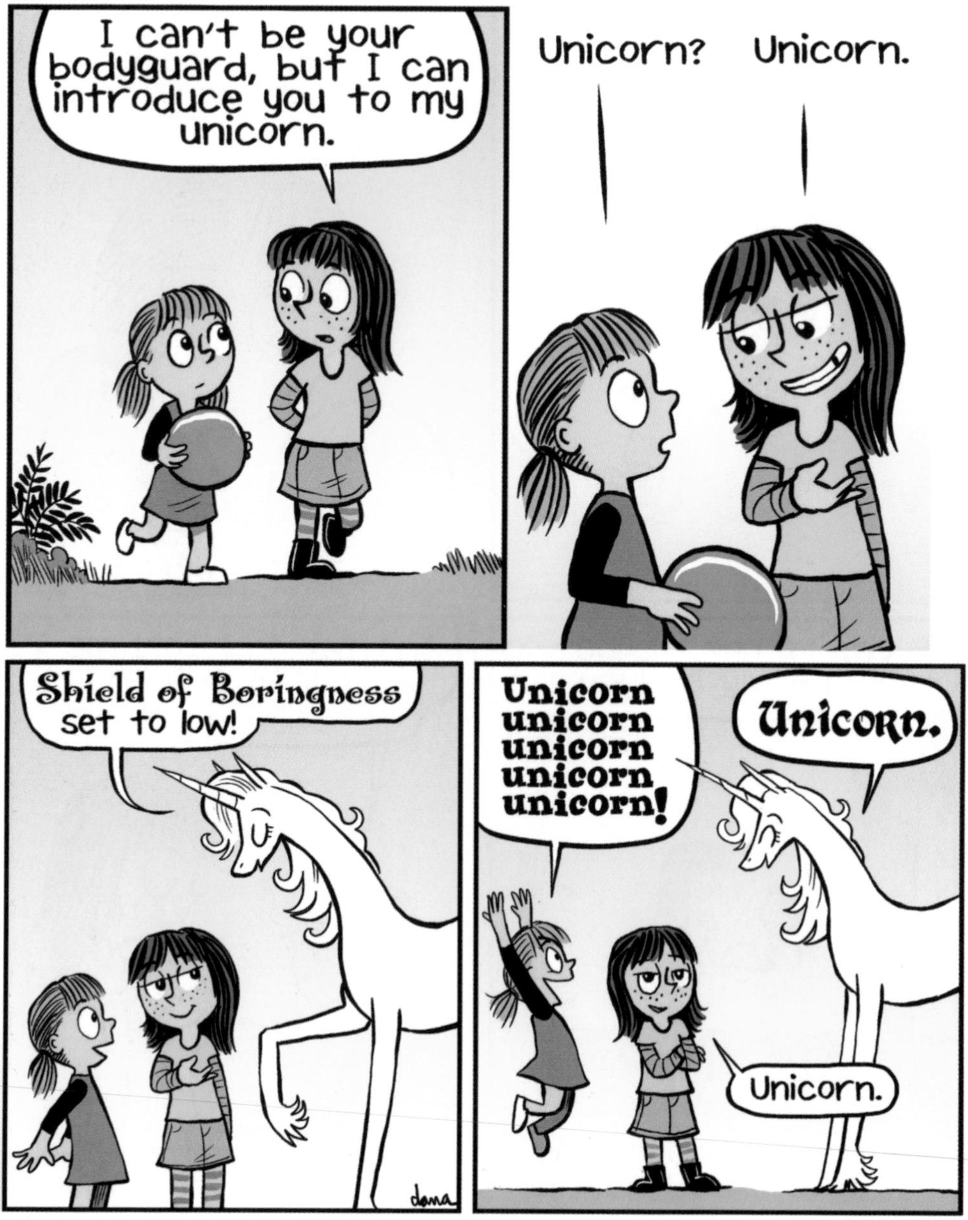
I can't be your bodyguard, but I can introduce you to my unicorn.
Unicorn?
Unicorn.
Shield of Boringness set to low!
Unicorn unicorn unicorn unicorn unicorn!
Unicorn.
Unicorn.
dana

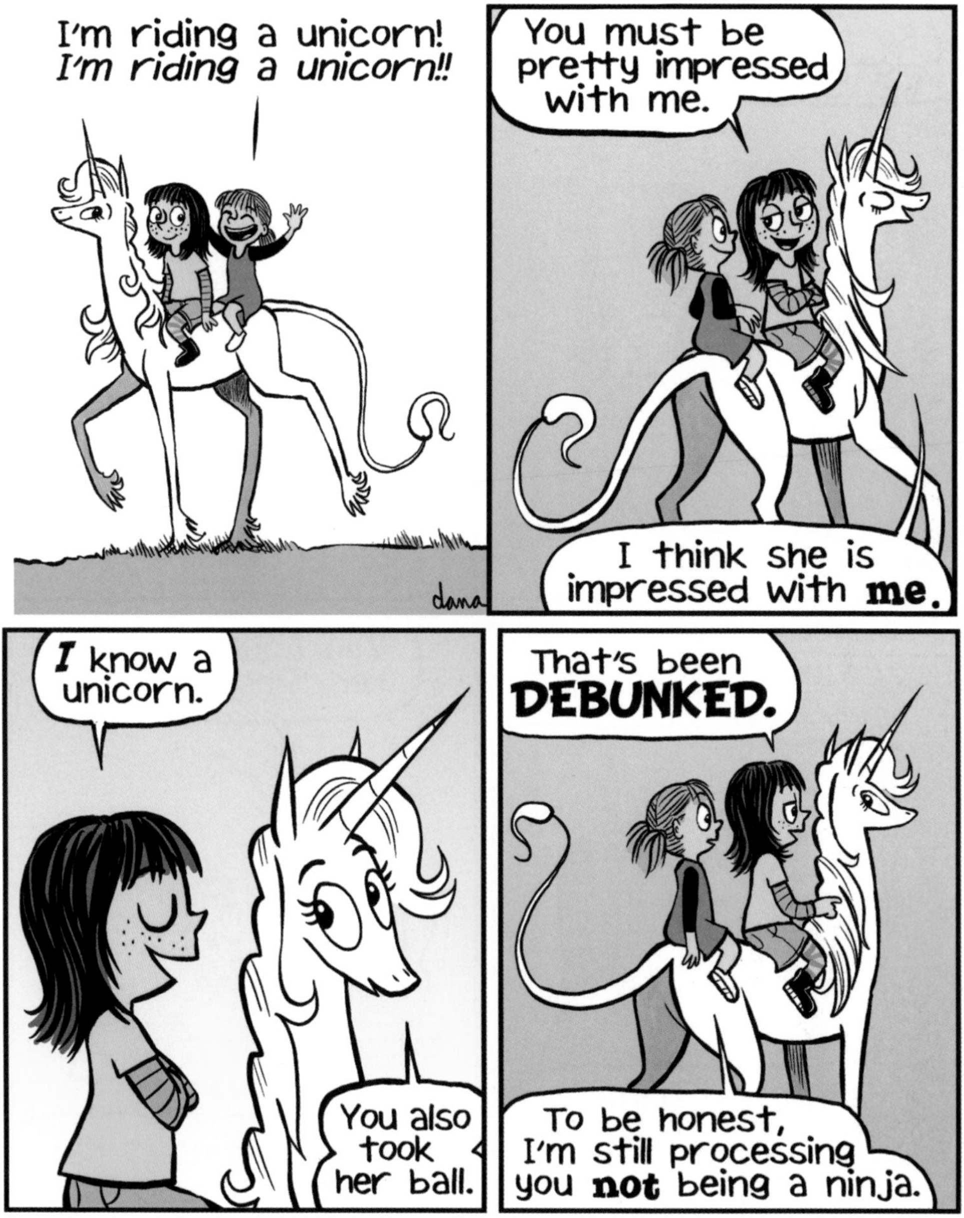
I'm riding a unicorn!
I'm riding a unicorn!!
dana
You must be pretty impressed with me.
I think she is impressed with **me**.
I know a unicorn.
You also took her ball.
That's been **DEBUNKED.**
To be honest, I'm still processing you **not** being a ninja.

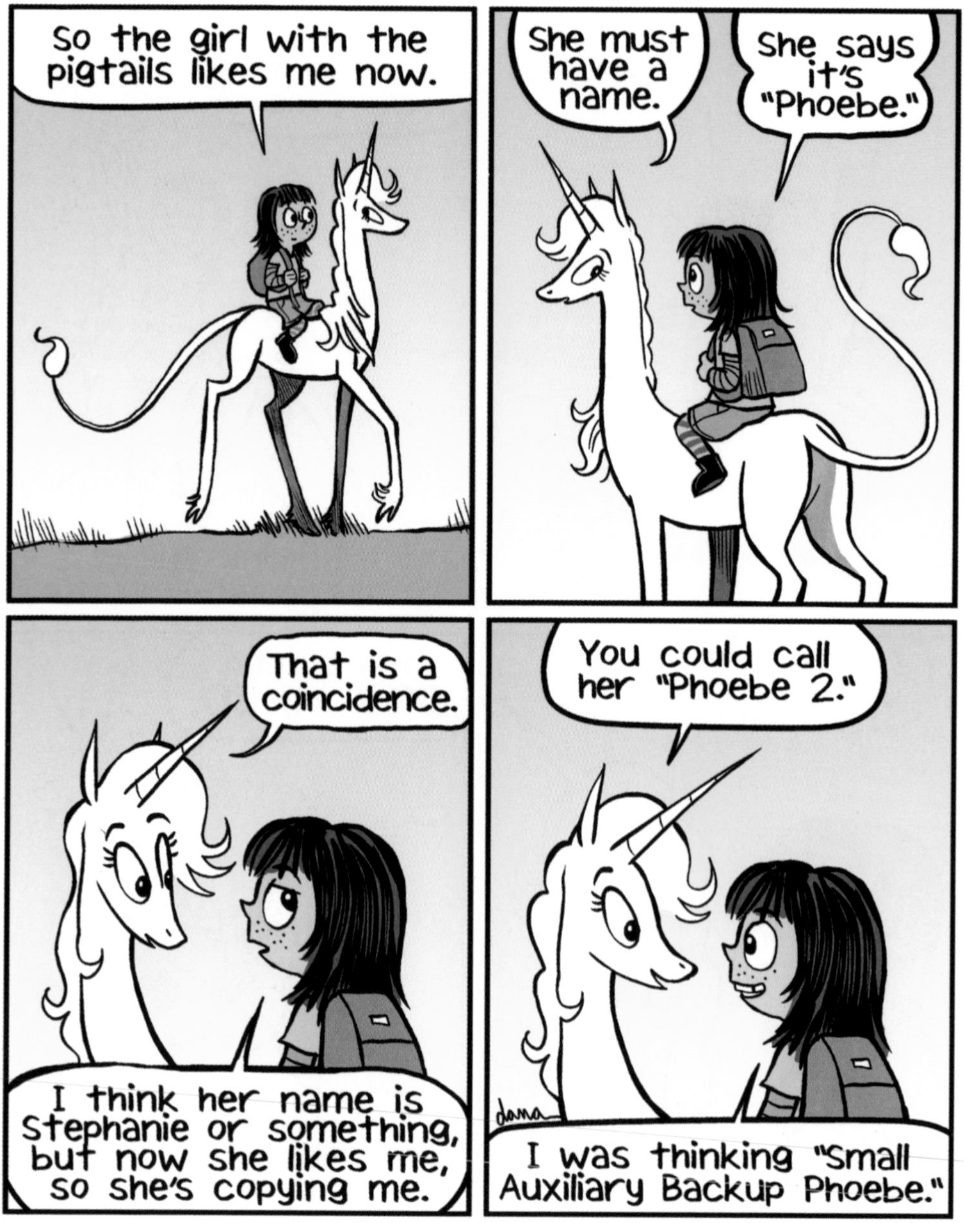

So the girl with the pigtails likes me now.
She must have a name.
She says it's "Phoebe."
That is a coincidence.
I think her name is Stephanie or something, but now she likes me, so she's copying me.
You could call her "Phoebe 2."
I was thinking "Small Auxiliary Backup Phoebe."
dana

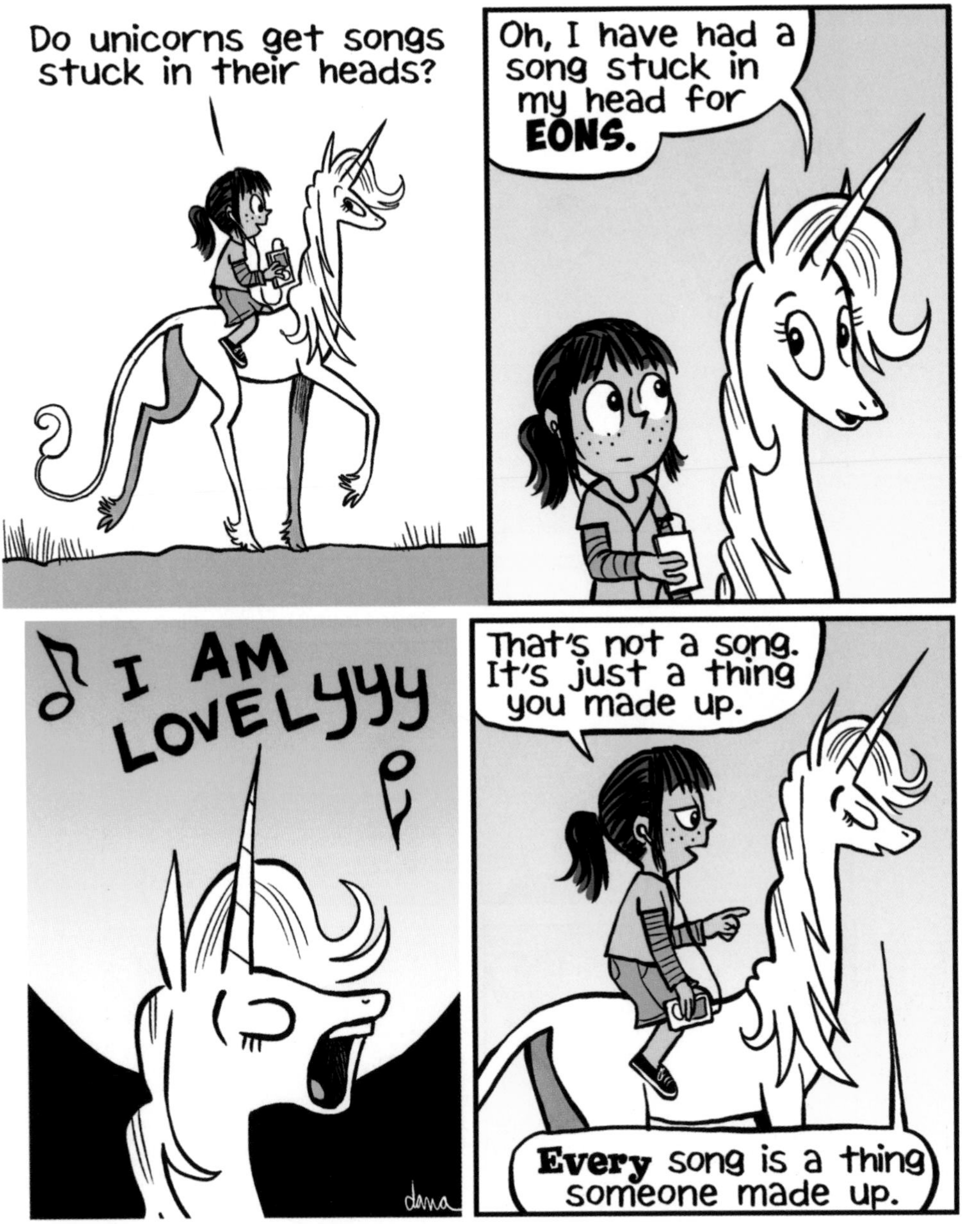
Do unicorns get songs stuck in their heads?
Oh, I have had a song stuck in my head for **EONS.**
I AM LOVELYYY
That's not a song. It's just a thing you made up.
Every song is a thing someone made up.
dana

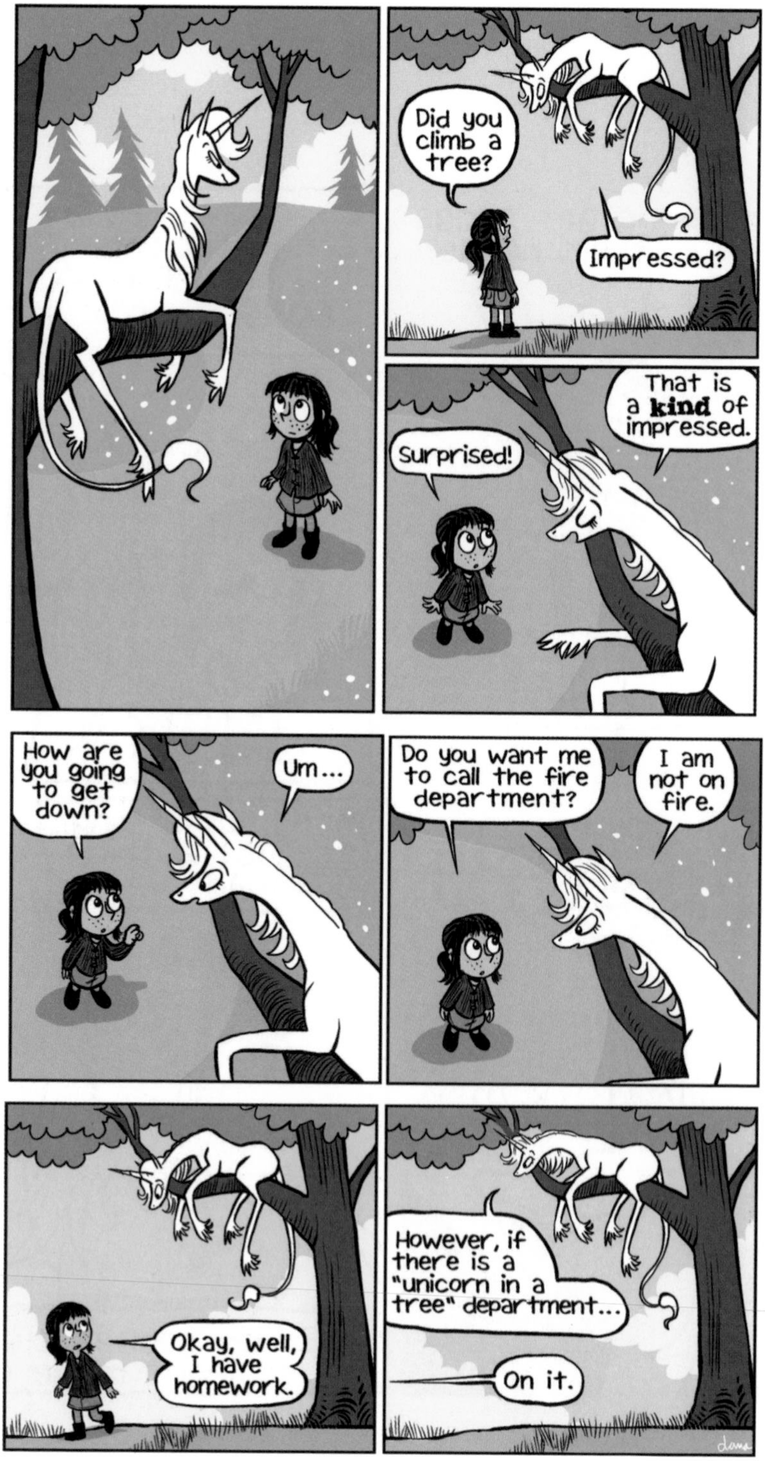

Did you climb a tree?
Impressed?
Surprised!
That is a **kind** of impressed.
How are you going to get down?
Um...
Do you want me to call the fire department?
I am not on fire.
Okay, well, I have homework.
However, if there is a "unicorn in a tree" department...
On it.

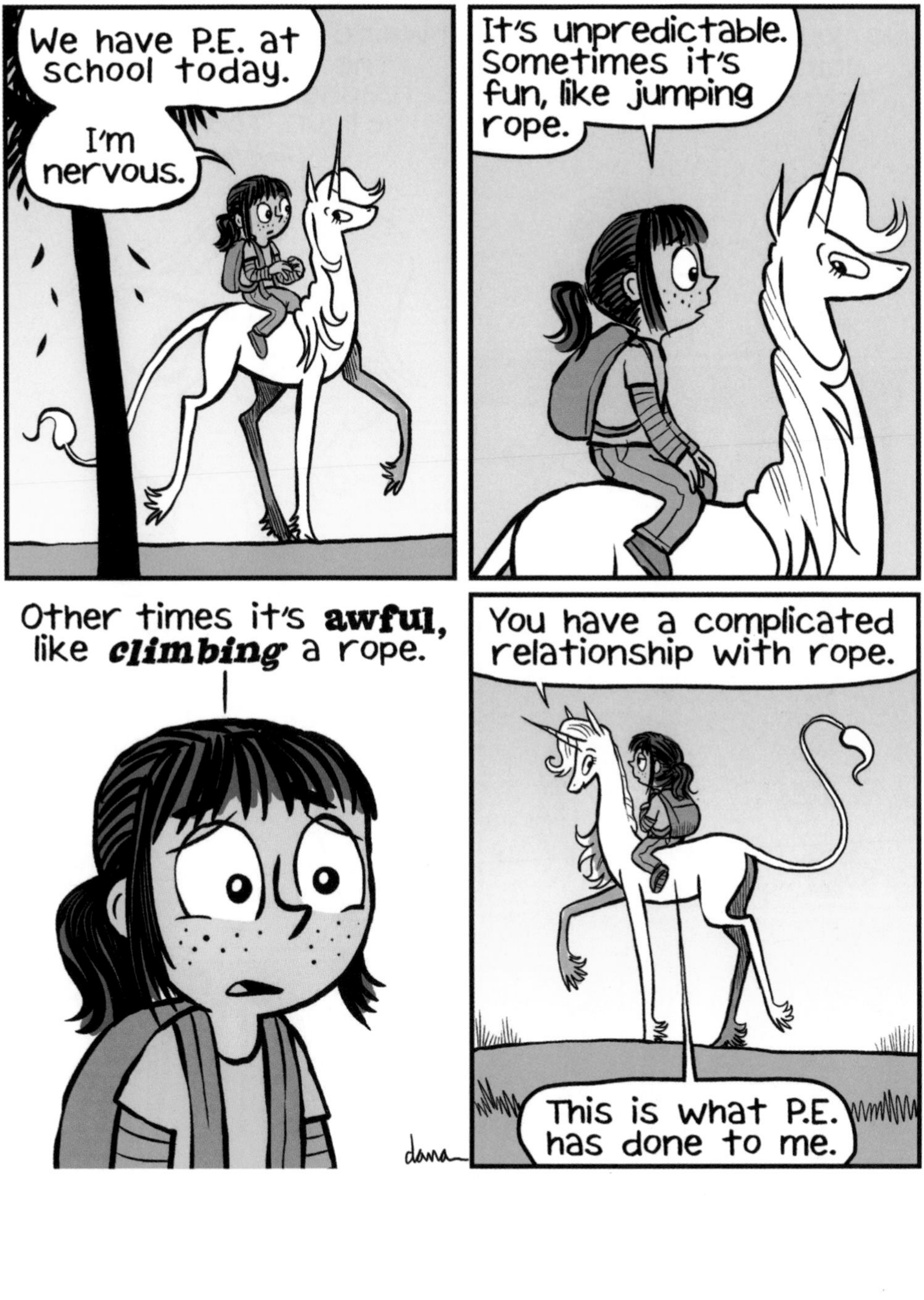
We have P.E. at school today.
I'm nervous.
It's unpredictable. Sometimes it's fun, like jumping rope.
Other times it's **awful**, like ***climbing*** a rope.
You have a complicated relationship with rope.
This is what P.E. has done to me.
dana

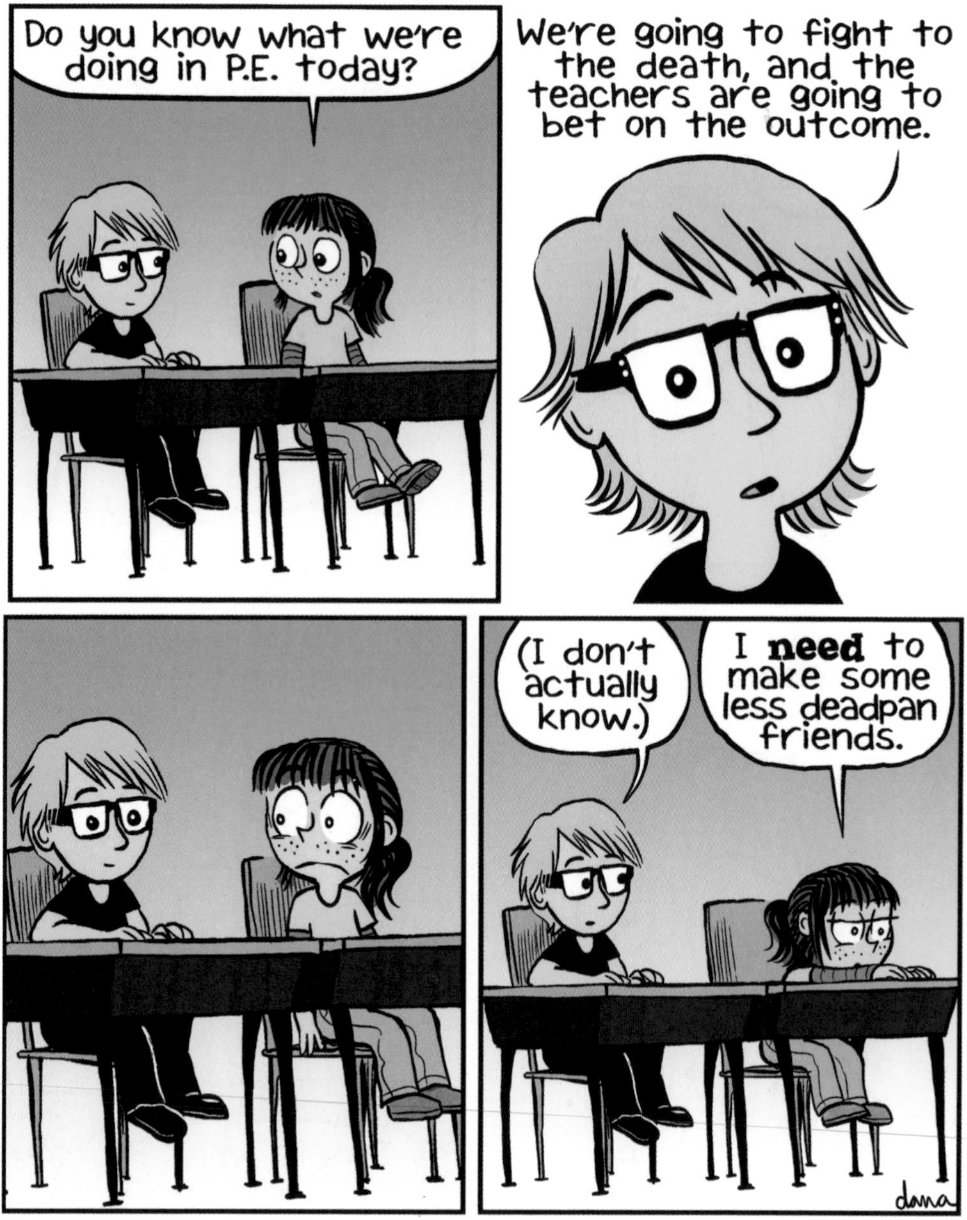
Do you know what we're doing in P.E. today?
We're going to fight to the death, and the teachers are going to bet on the outcome.
(I don't actually know.)
I **need** to make some less deadpan friends.
dana

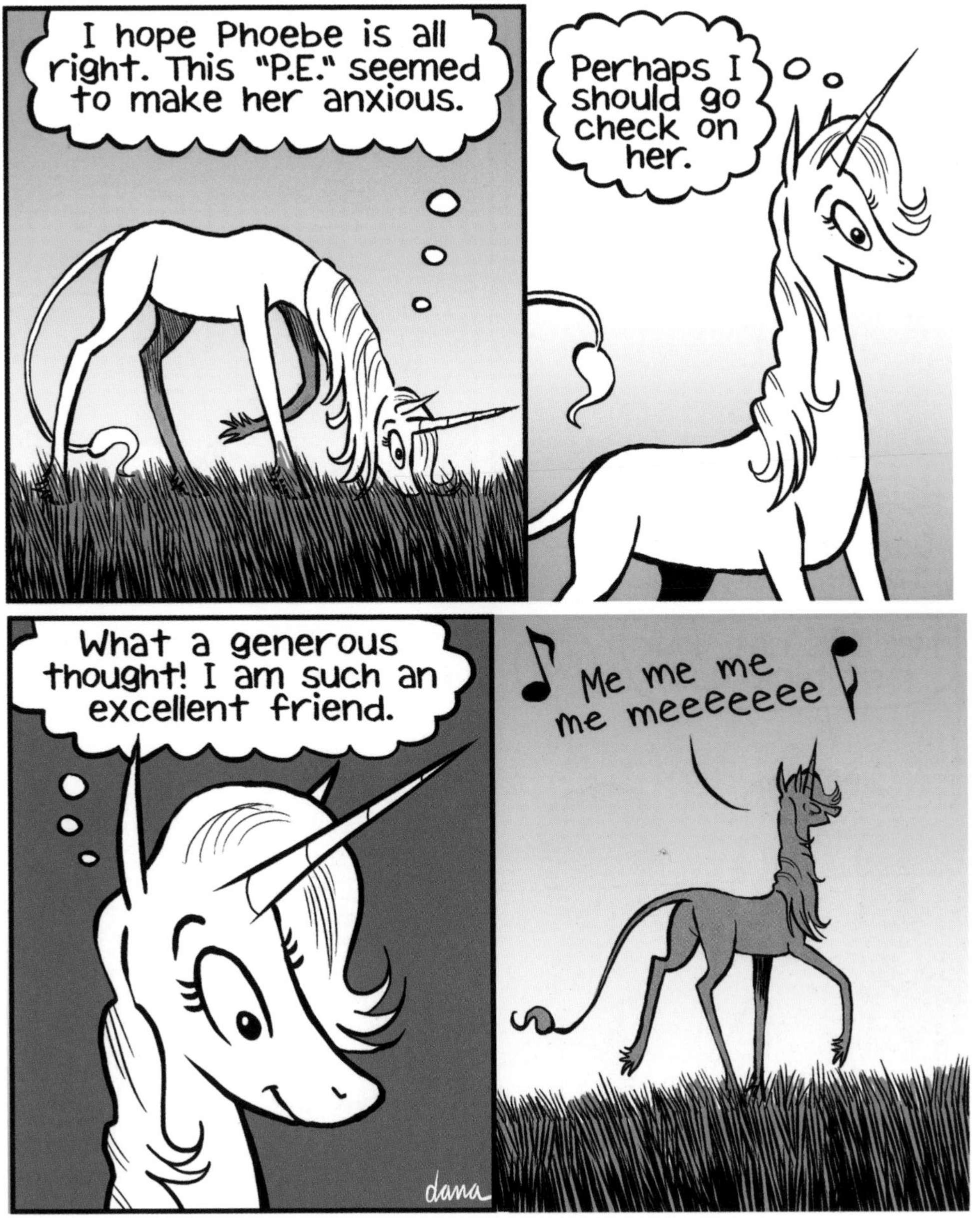
I hope Phoebe is all right. This "P.E." seemed to make her anxious.
Perhaps I should go check on her.
What a generous thought! I am such an excellent friend.
Me me me me meeeeeee
dana

I pick... Declan!

Dodgeball. It had to be dodgeball.

Getting hit with a ball hurts...and I always get picked last...and—

I pick Phoebe!

Me? It's not your last pick yet!

So?

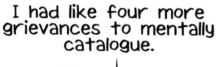

I had like four more grievances to mentally catalogue.

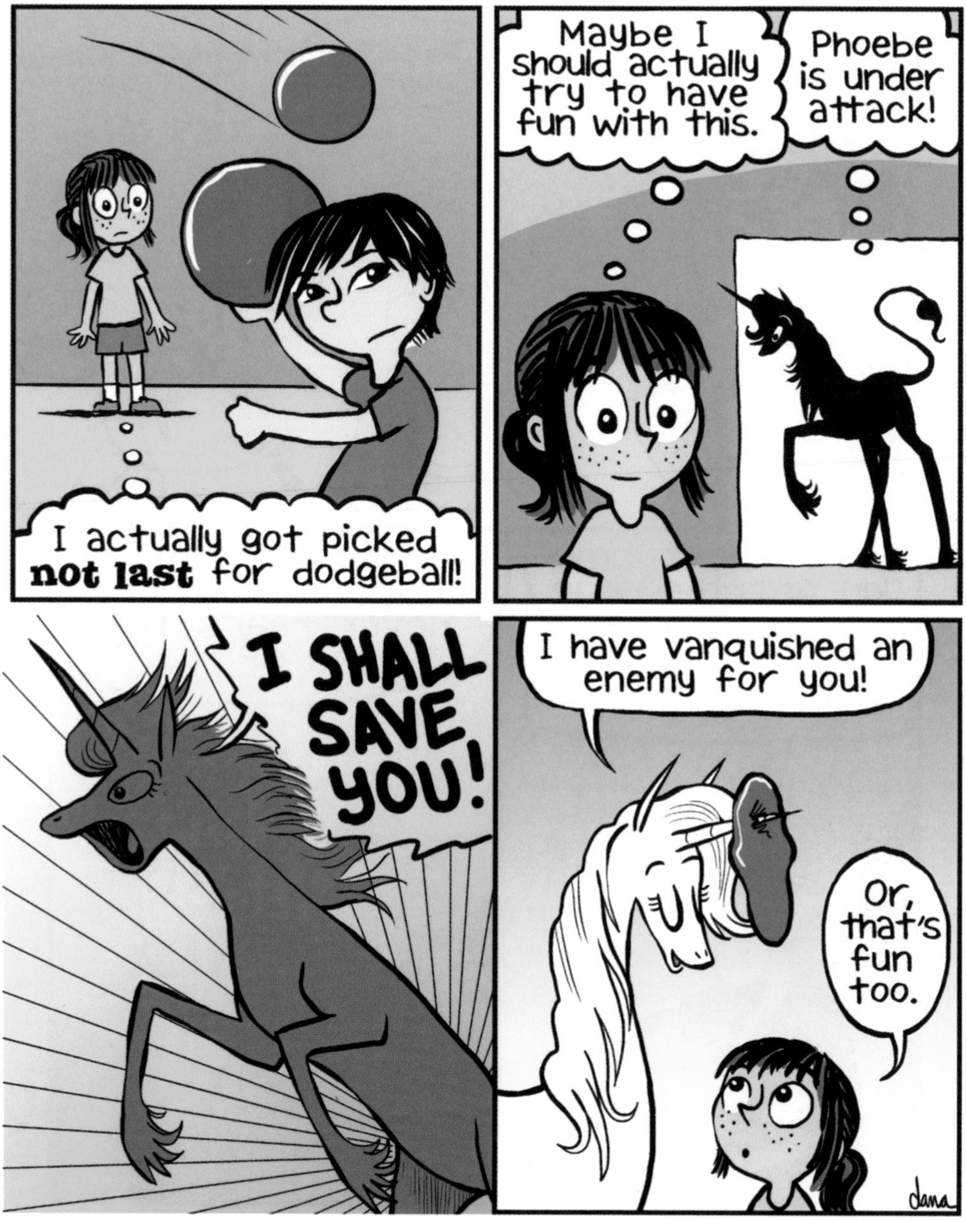
I actually got picked **not last** for dodgeball!
Maybe I should actually try to have fun with this.
Phoebe is under attack!
I SHALL SAVE YOU!
I have vanquished an enemy for you!
Or, that's fun too.
dana

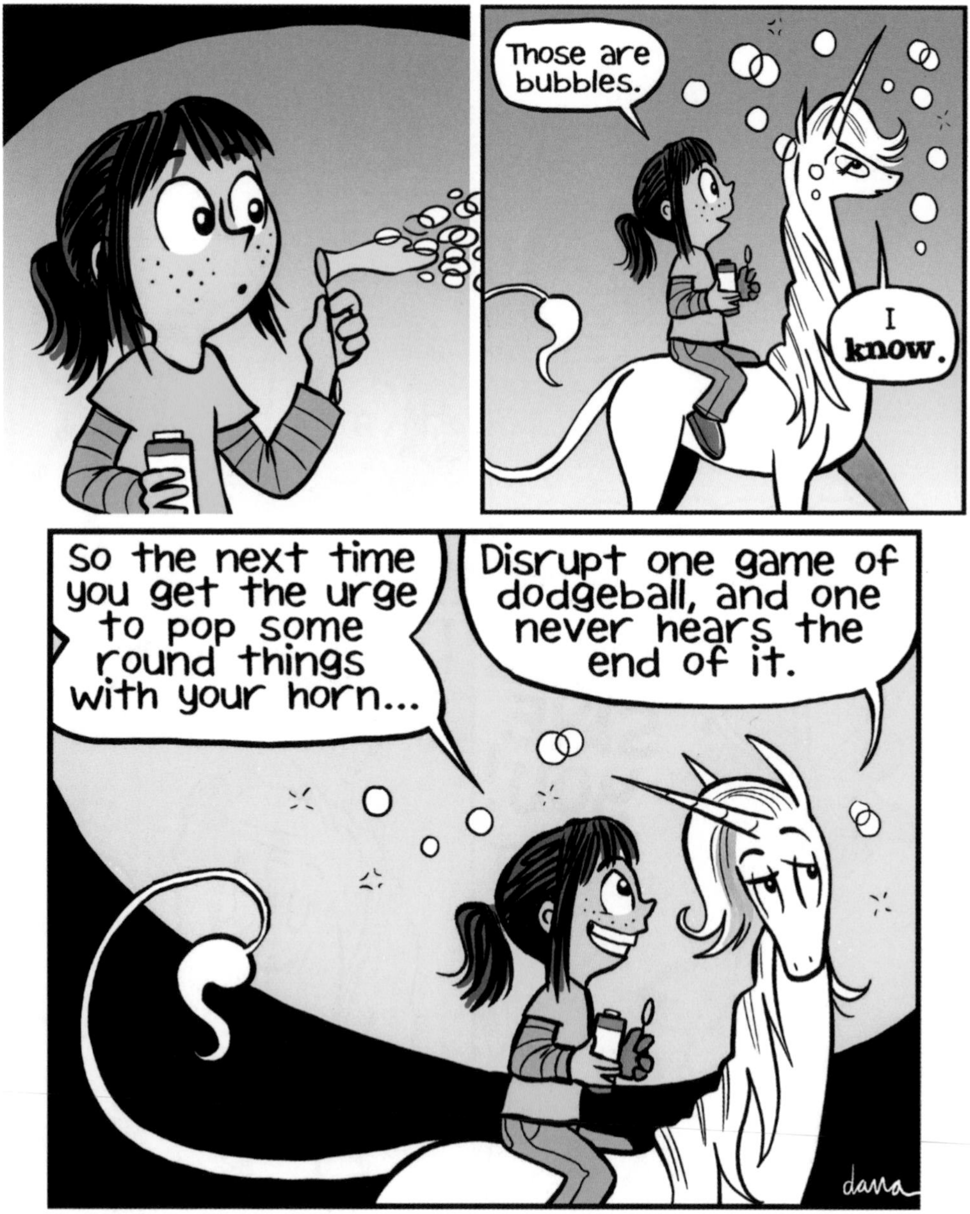
Those are bubbles.
I know.
So the next time you get the urge to pop some round things with your horn...
Disrupt one game of dodgeball, and one never hears the end of it.
dana

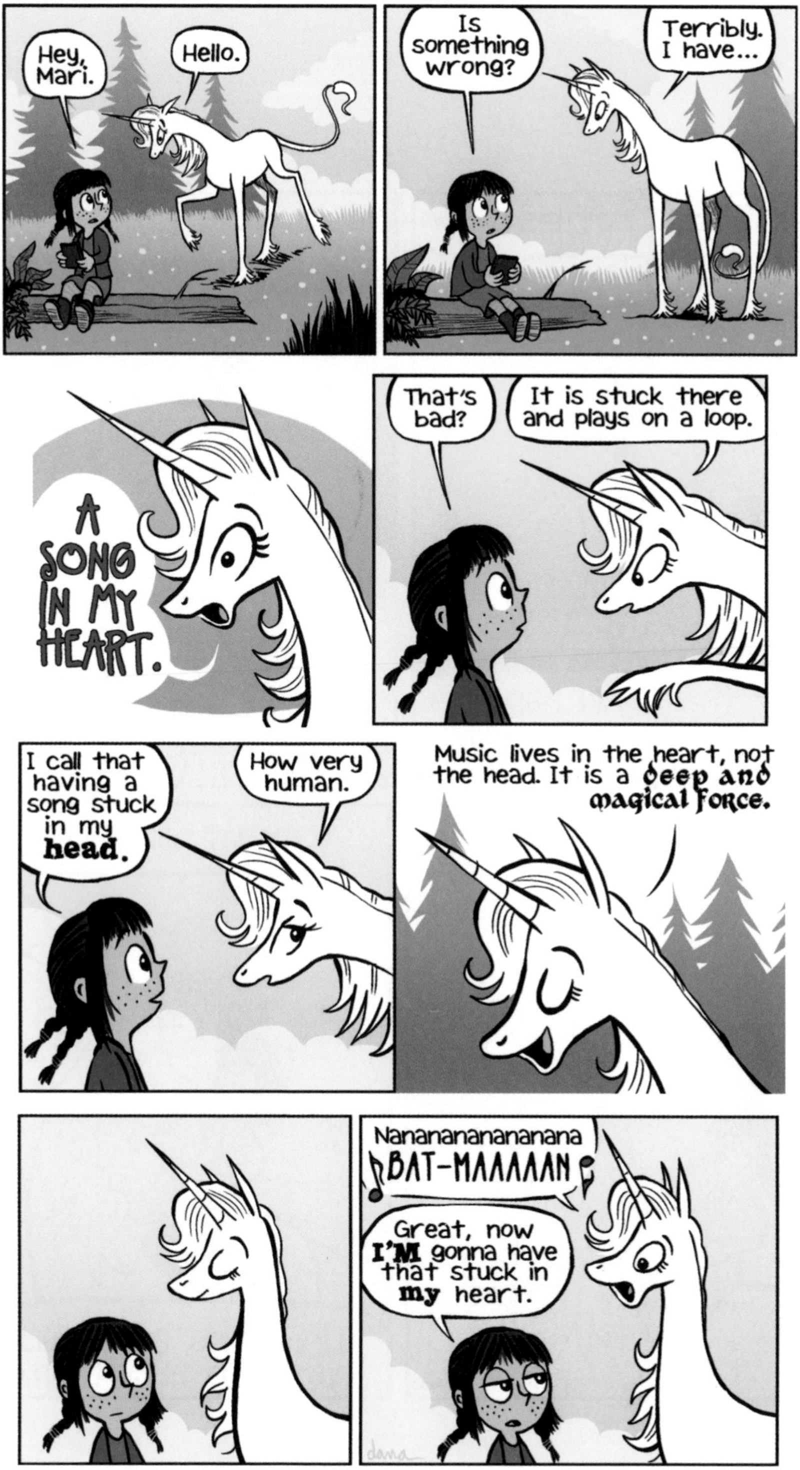
Hey, Mari.
Hello.
Is something wrong?
Terribly. I have...
A SONG IN MY HEART.
That's bad?
It is stuck there and plays on a loop.
I call that having a song stuck in my **head**.
How very human.
Music lives in the heart, not the head. It is a deep and magical force.
Nanananananananana BAT-MAAAAAN
Great, now **I'M** gonna have that stuck in **my** heart.
dana

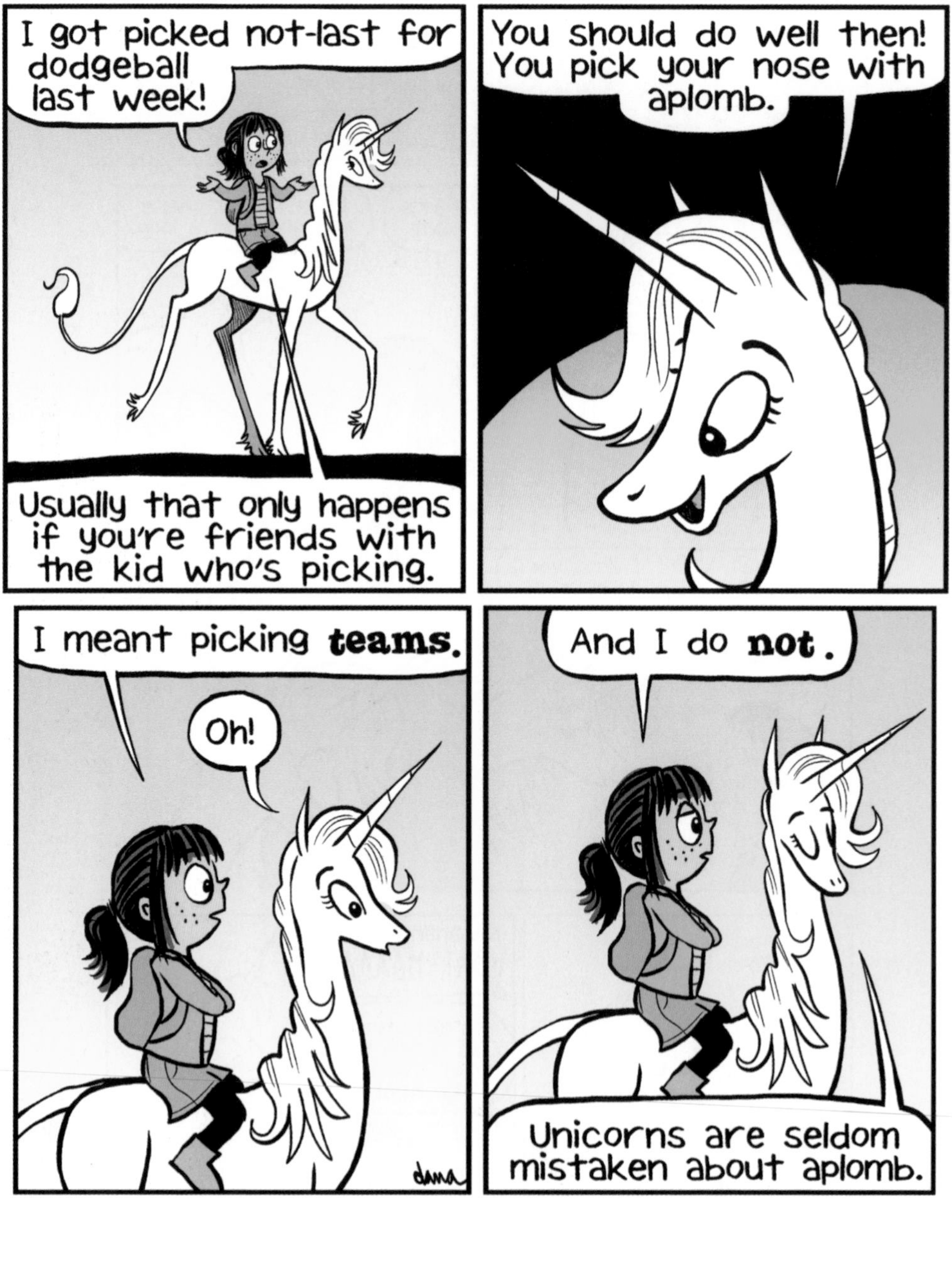
I got picked not-last for dodgeball last week!
Usually that only happens if you're friends with the kid who's picking.
You should do well then! You pick your nose with aplomb.
I meant picking **teams**.
Oh!
And I do **not**.
Unicorns are seldom mistaken about aplomb.
dana

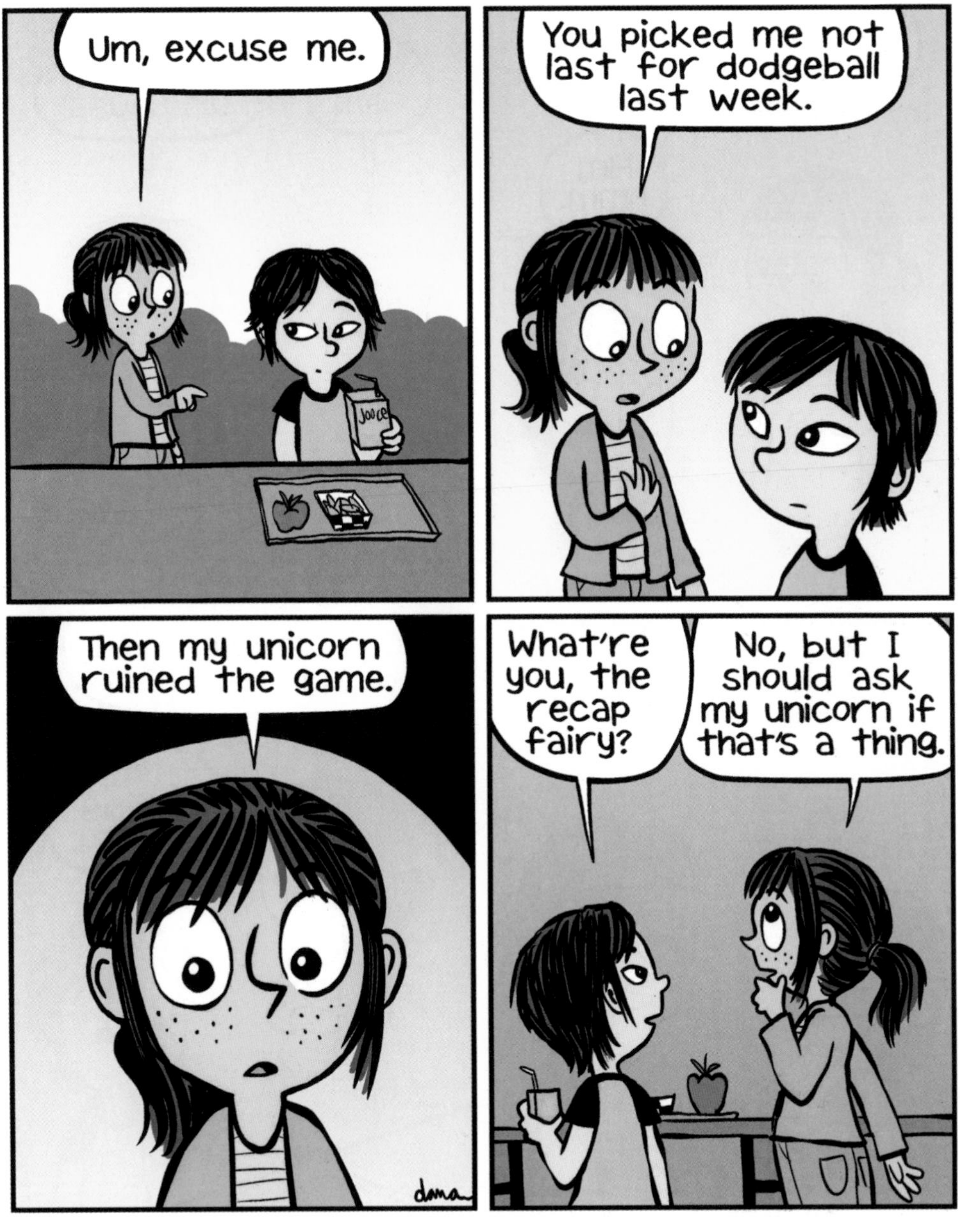
Um, excuse me.
You picked me not last for dodgeball last week.
Then my unicorn ruined the game.
What're you, the recap fairy?
No, but I should ask my unicorn if that's a thing.

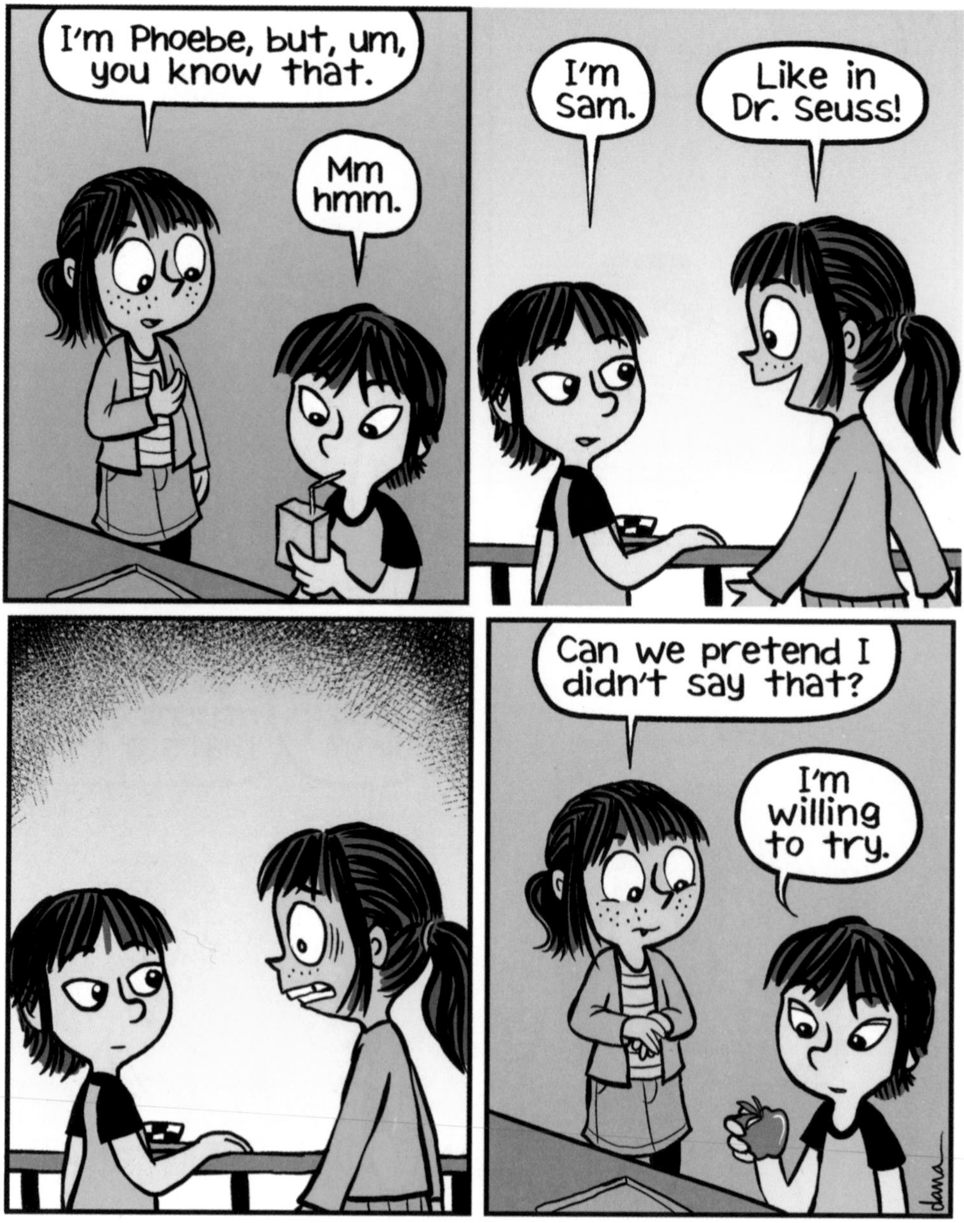
I'm Phoebe, but, um, you know that.
Mm hmm.
I'm Sam.
Like in Dr. Seuss!
Can we pretend I didn't say that?
I'm willing to try.
dana

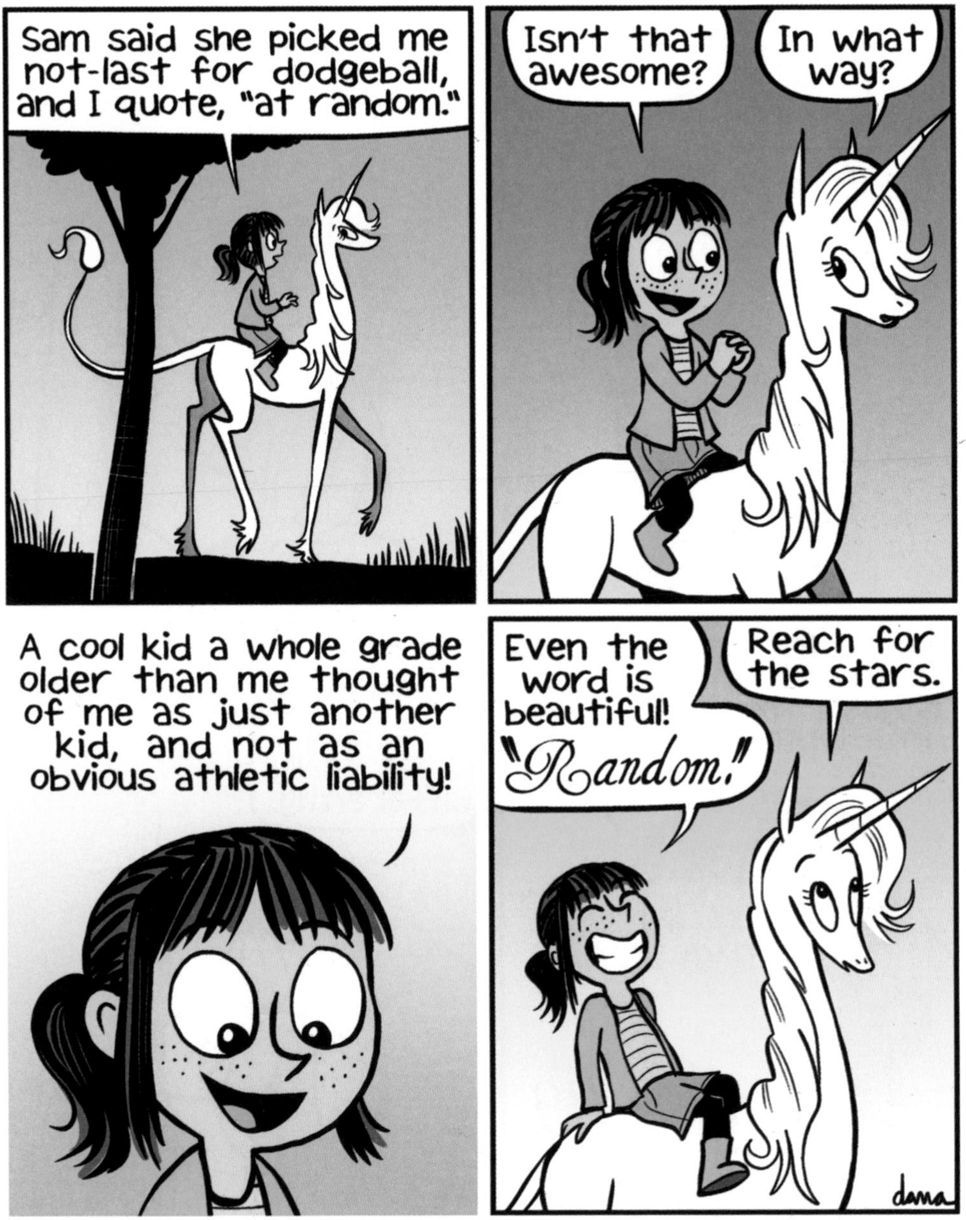
Sam said she picked me not-last for dodgeball, and I quote, "at random."
Isn't that awesome?
In what way?
A cool kid a whole grade older than me thought of me as just another kid, and not as an obvious athletic liability!
Even the word is beautiful! "Random."
Reach for the stars.
dana

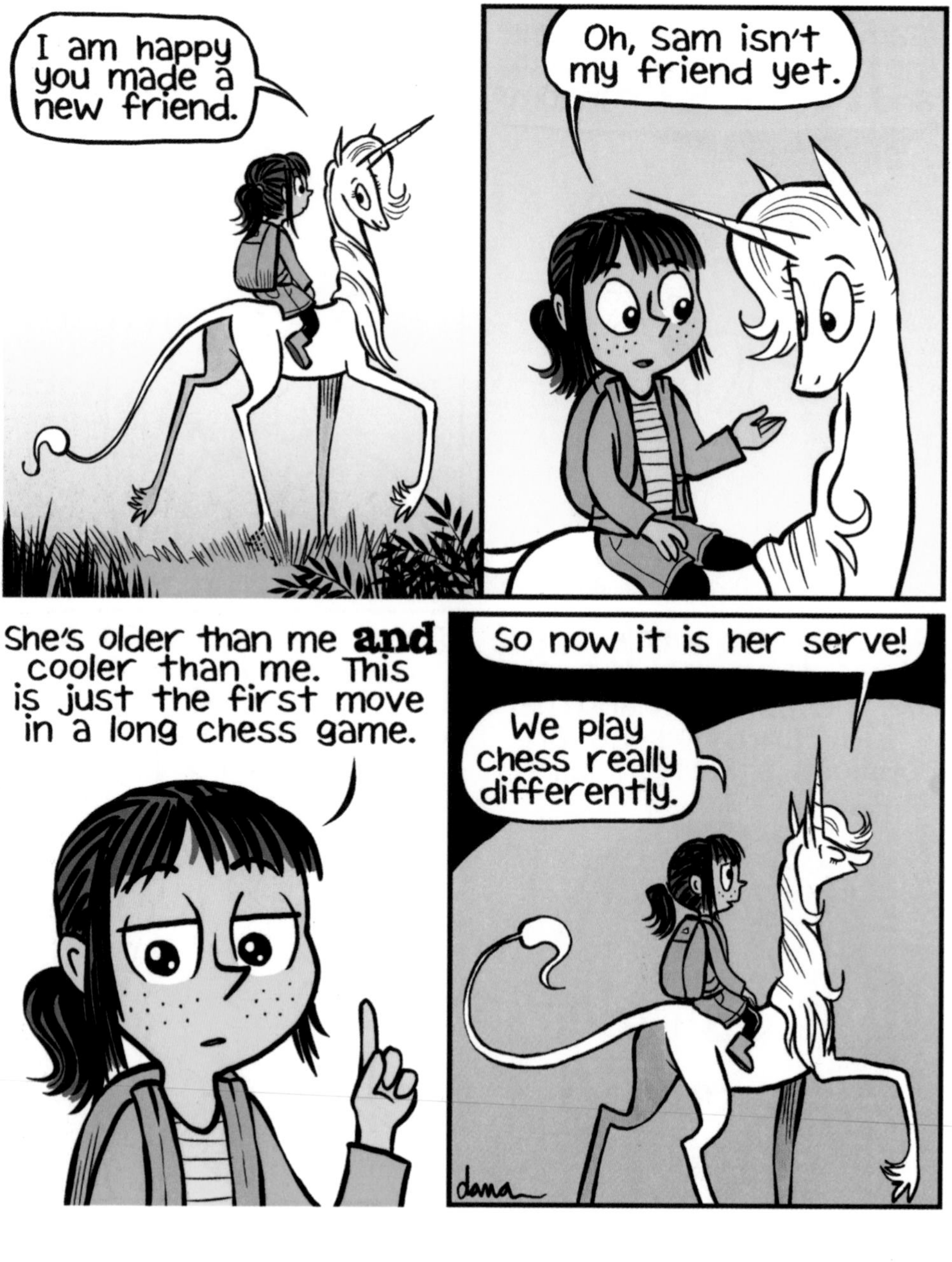
I am happy you made a new friend.
Oh, Sam isn't my friend yet.
She's older than me and cooler than me. This is just the first move in a long chess game.
So now it is her serve!
We play chess really differently.
dana

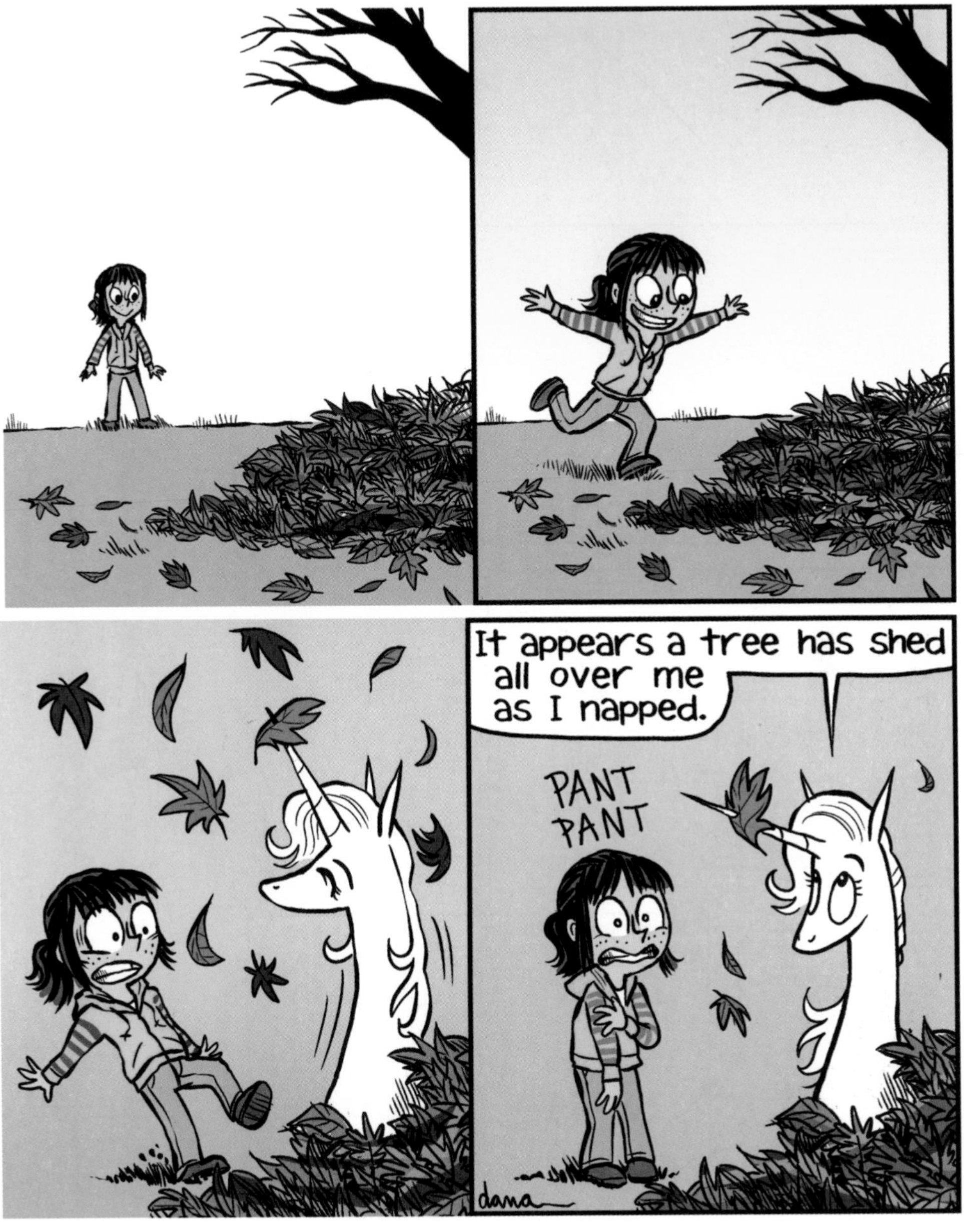
It appears a tree has shed all over me as I napped.
PANT PANT
dana

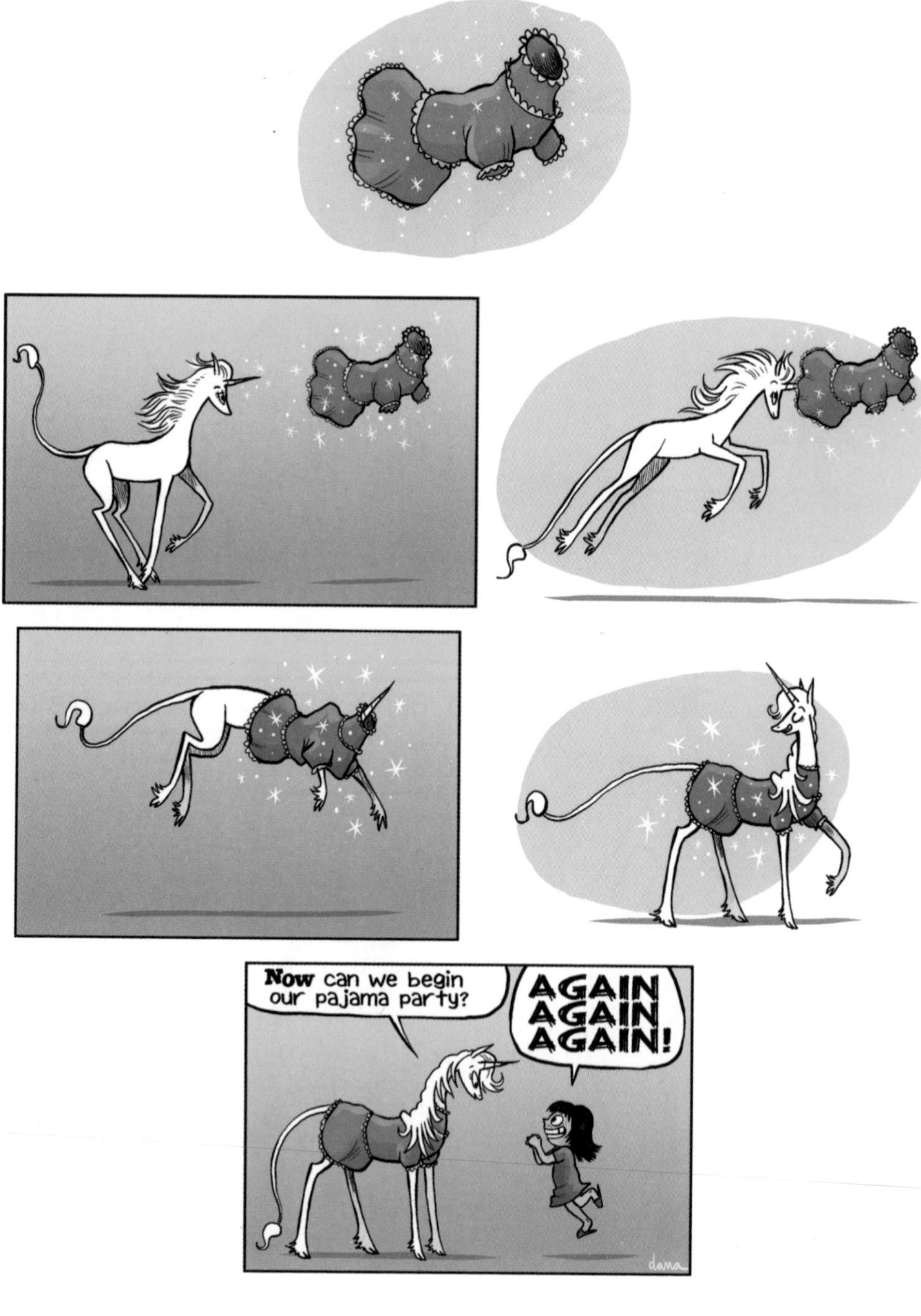
Now can we begin our pajama party?
AGAIN AGAIN AGAIN!
dana

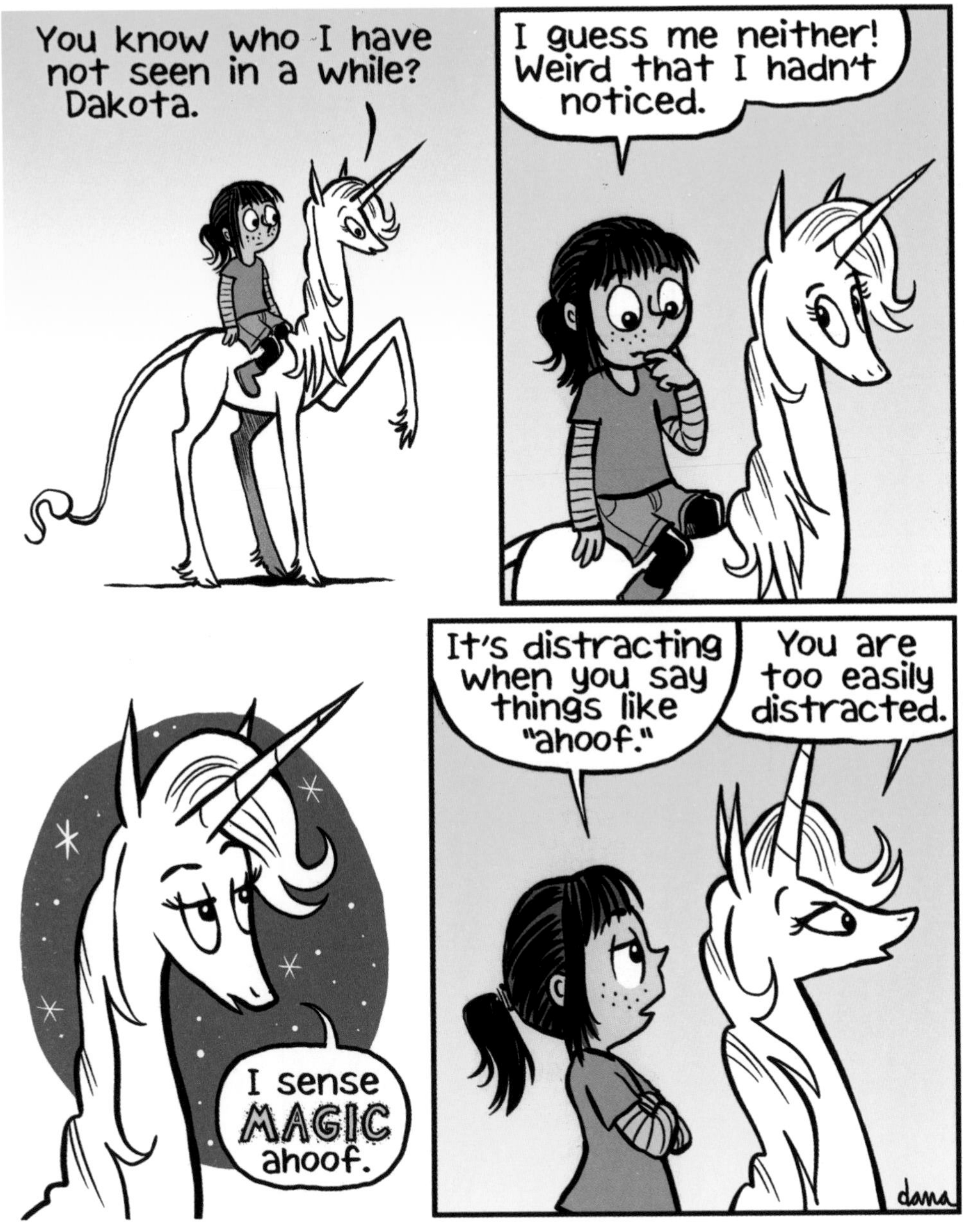
You know who I have not seen in a while? Dakota.
I guess me neither! Weird that I hadn't noticed.
I sense MAGIC ahoof.
It's distracting when you say things like "ahoof."
You are too easily distracted.
dana

I will check the area for enchantments.
beep beep
beep beep
I wanna go "beep beep" too!
That is sort of **my** thing.
dana

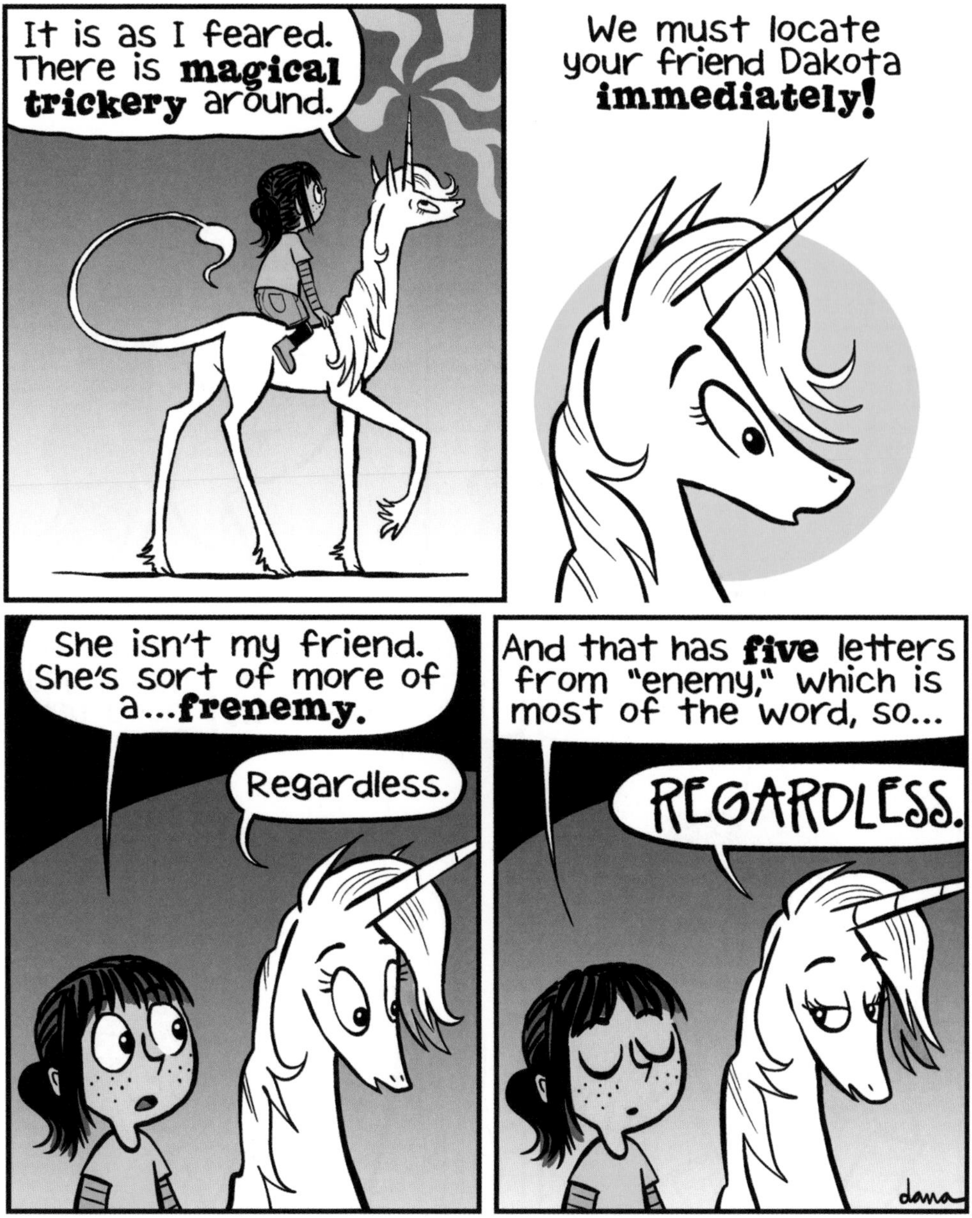
It is as I feared. There is magical trickery around.
We must locate your friend Dakota immediately!
She isn't my friend. She's sort of more of a...frenemy.
Regardless.
And that has five letters from "enemy," which is most of the word, so...
REGARDLESS.
dana

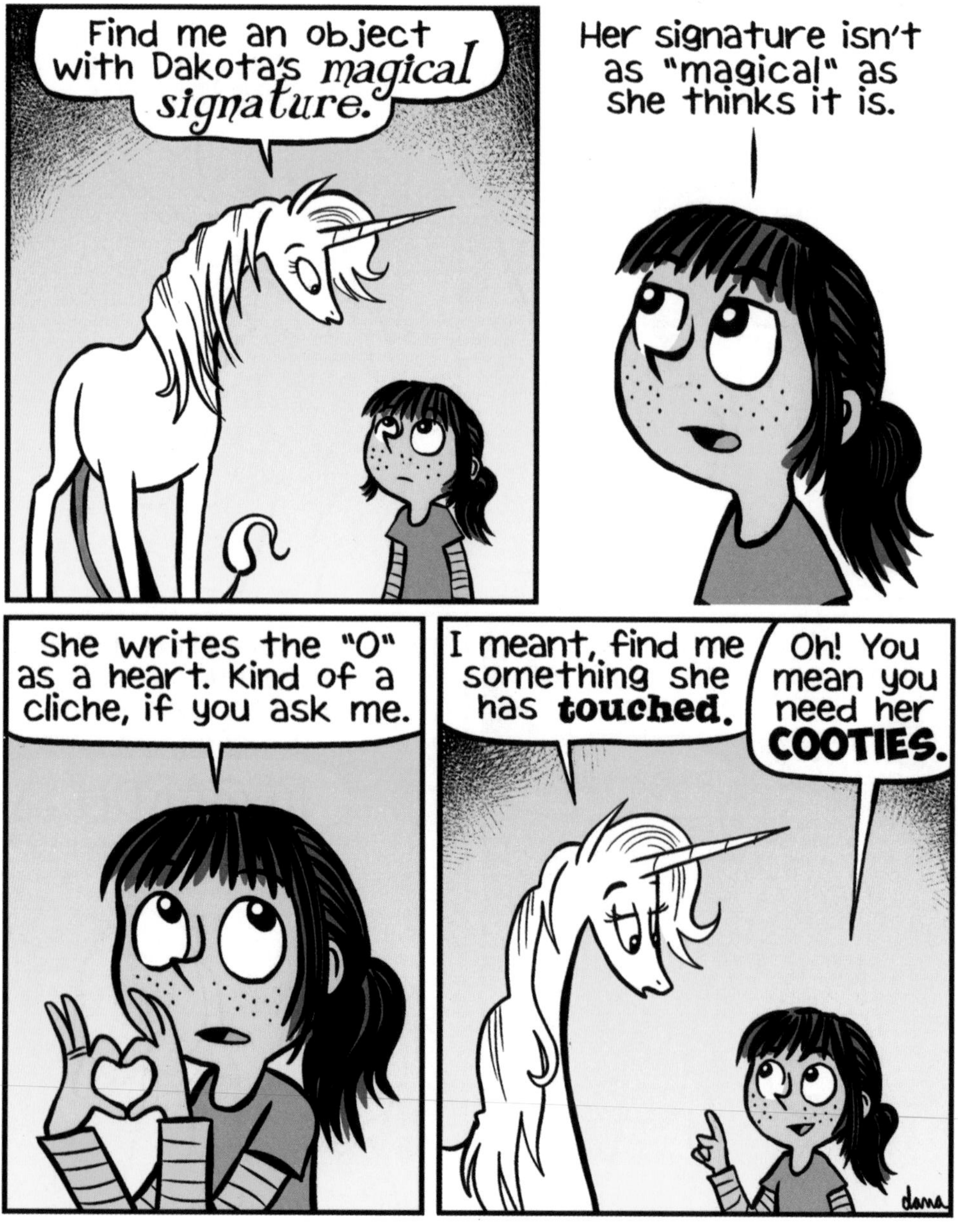
Find me an object with Dakota's *magical signature.*
Her signature isn't as "magical" as she thinks it is.
She writes the "O" as a heart. Kind of a cliche, if you ask me.
I meant, find me something she has **touched.**
Oh! You mean you need her **COOTIES.**
dana

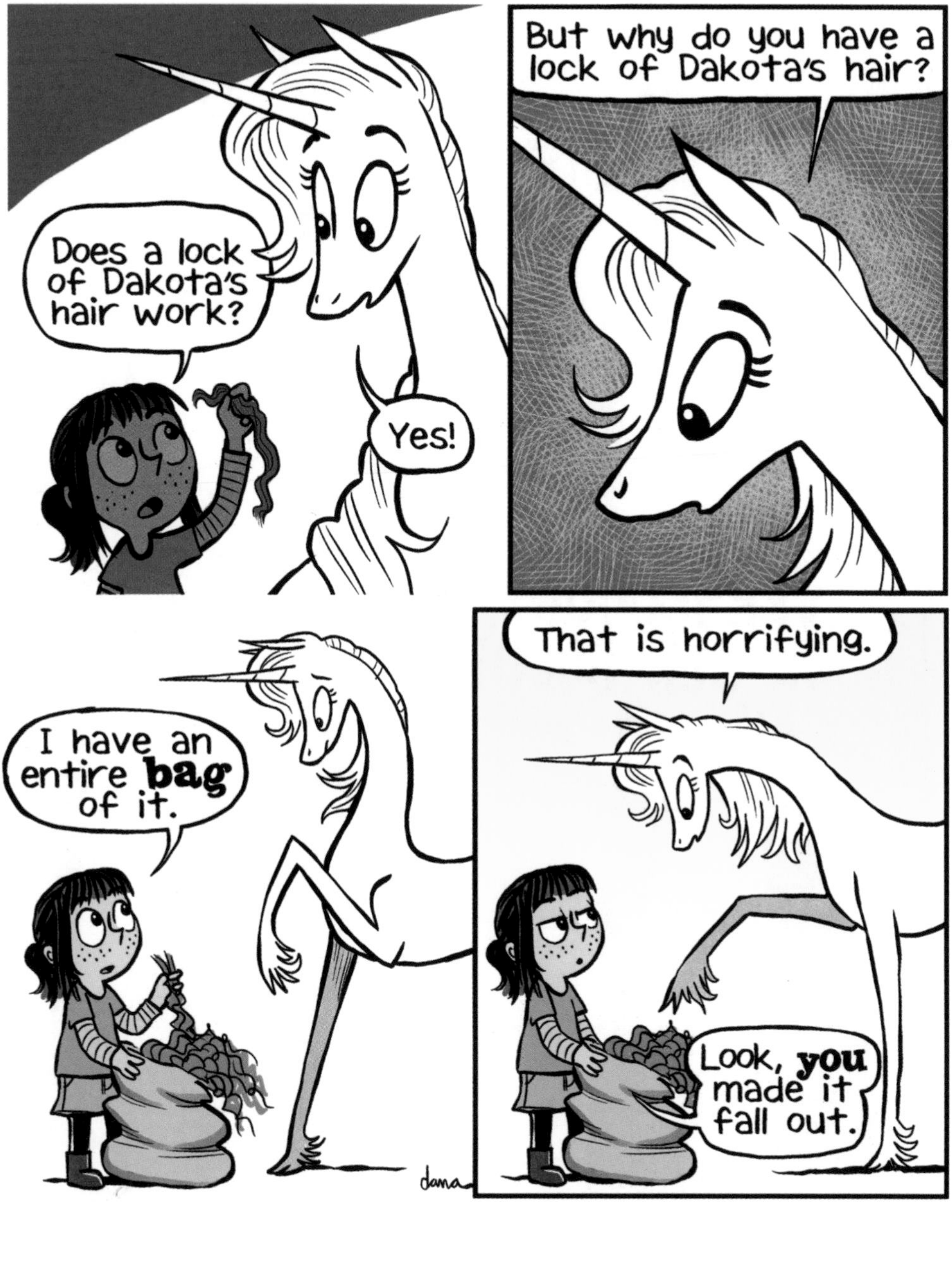
Does a lock of Dakota's hair work?
Yes!
But why do you have a lock of Dakota's hair?
I have an entire **bag** of it.
That is horrifying.
Look, **you** made it fall out.
dana

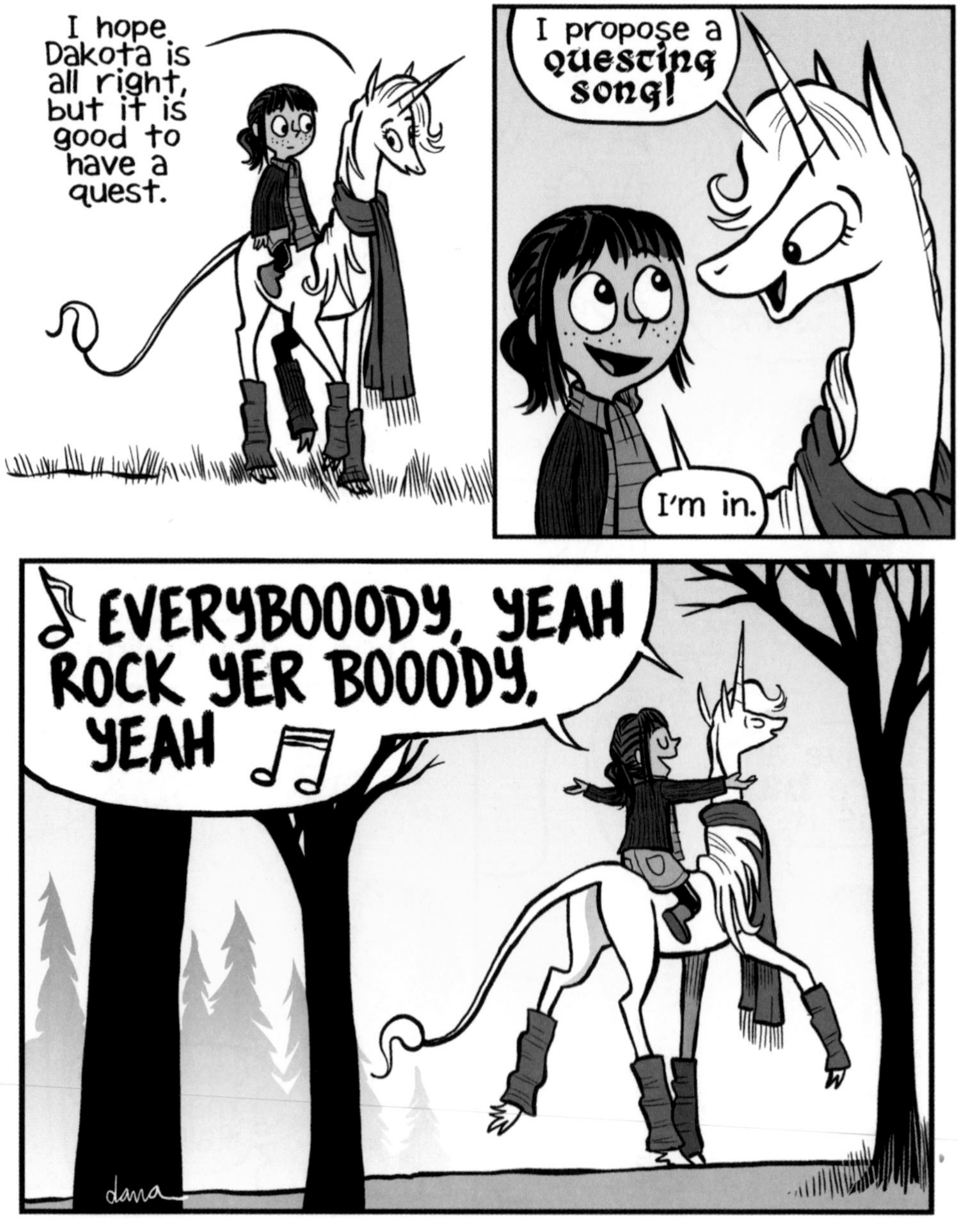
I hope Dakota is all right, but it is good to have a quest.
I propose a questing song!
I'm in.
EVERYBOOODY, YEAH ROCK YER BOOODY, YEAH
dana

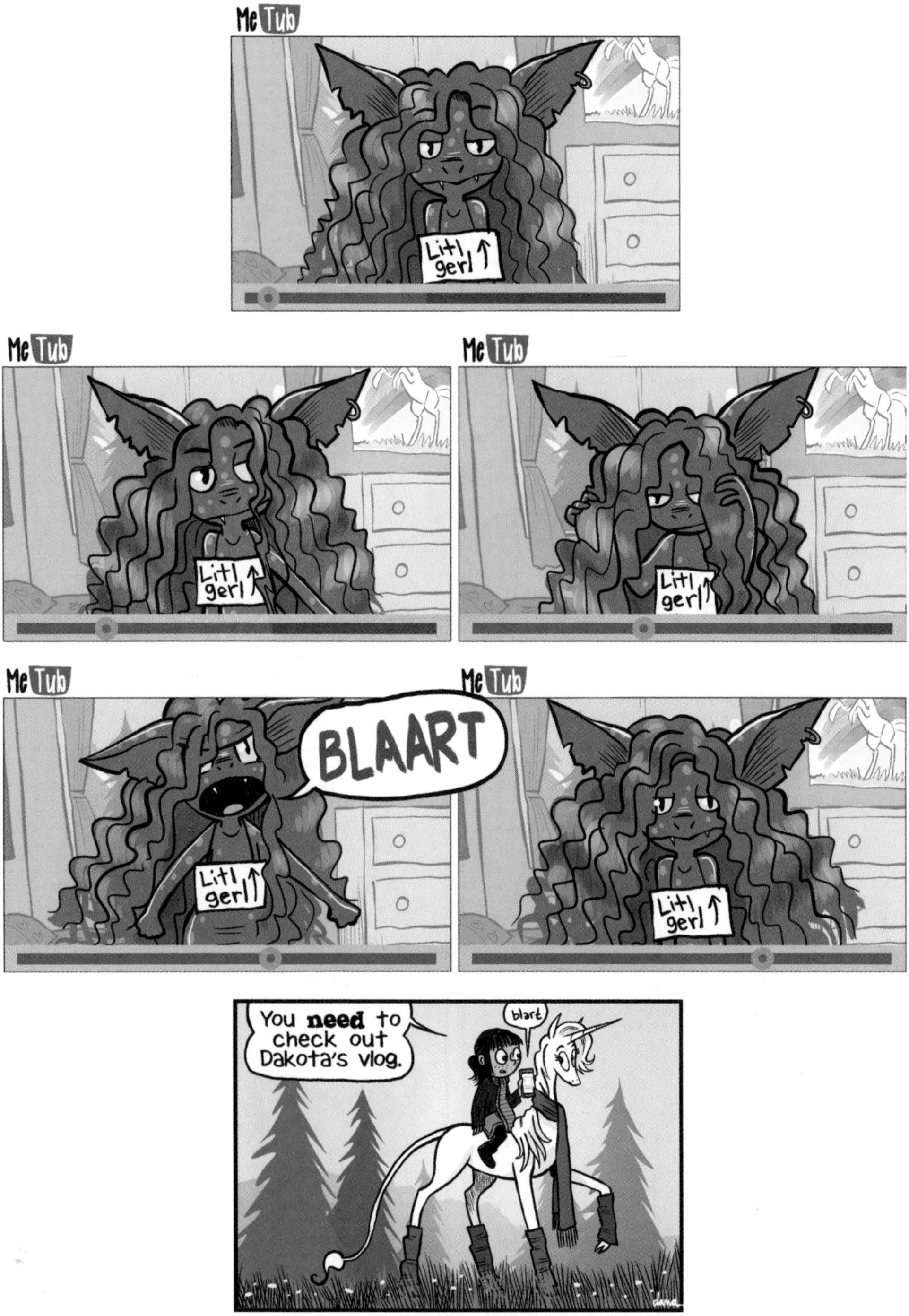
MeTub
Litl gerl ↑
MeTub
Litl gerl ↑
MeTub
Litl gerl ↑
MeTub
BLAART
Litl gerl ↑
MeTub
Litl gerl ↑
You **need** to check out Dakota's vlog.
blart

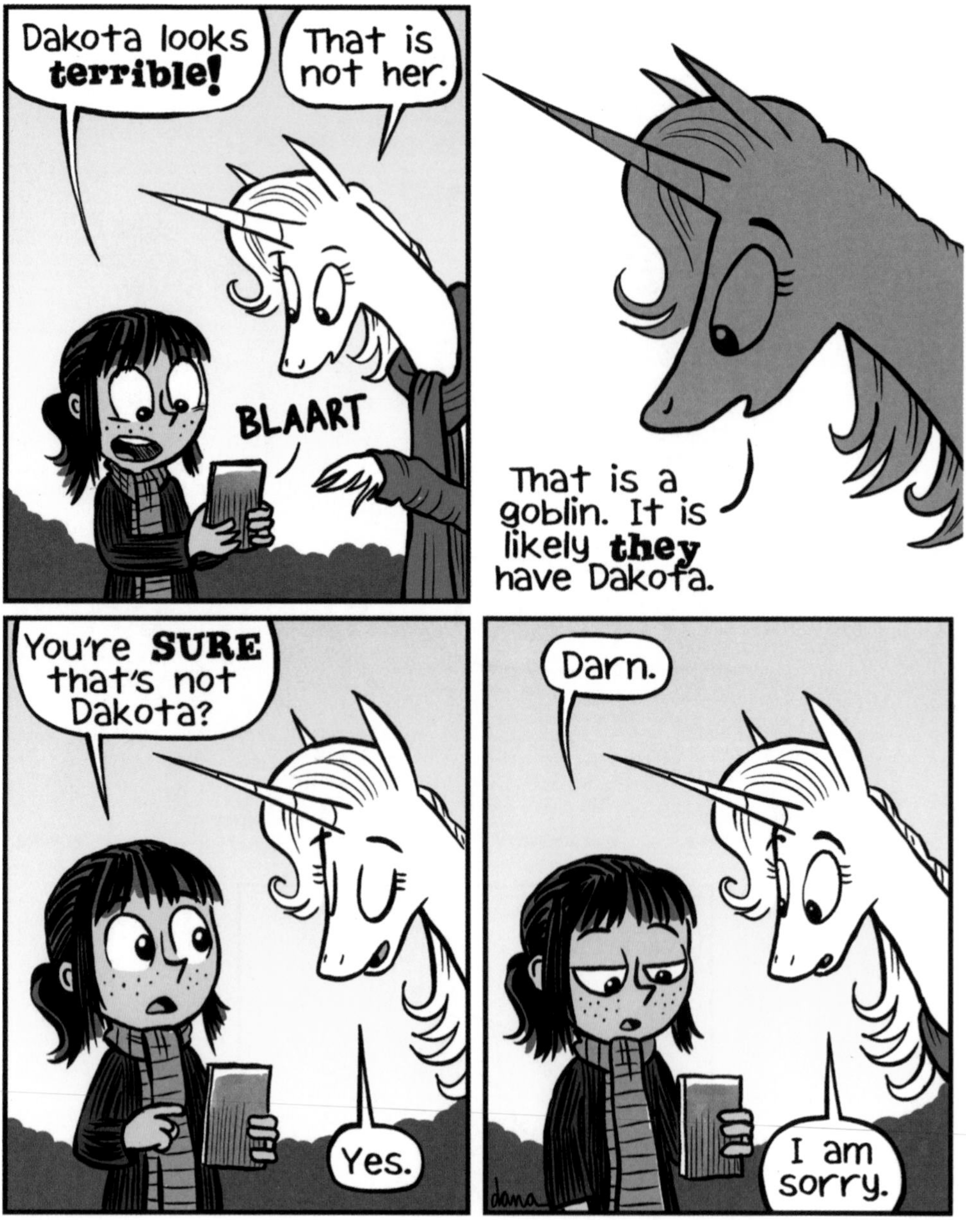
Dakota looks **terrible!**
That is not her.
BLAART
That is a goblin. It is likely **they** have Dakota.
You're **SURE** that's not Dakota?
Yes.
Darn.
I am sorry.
dana

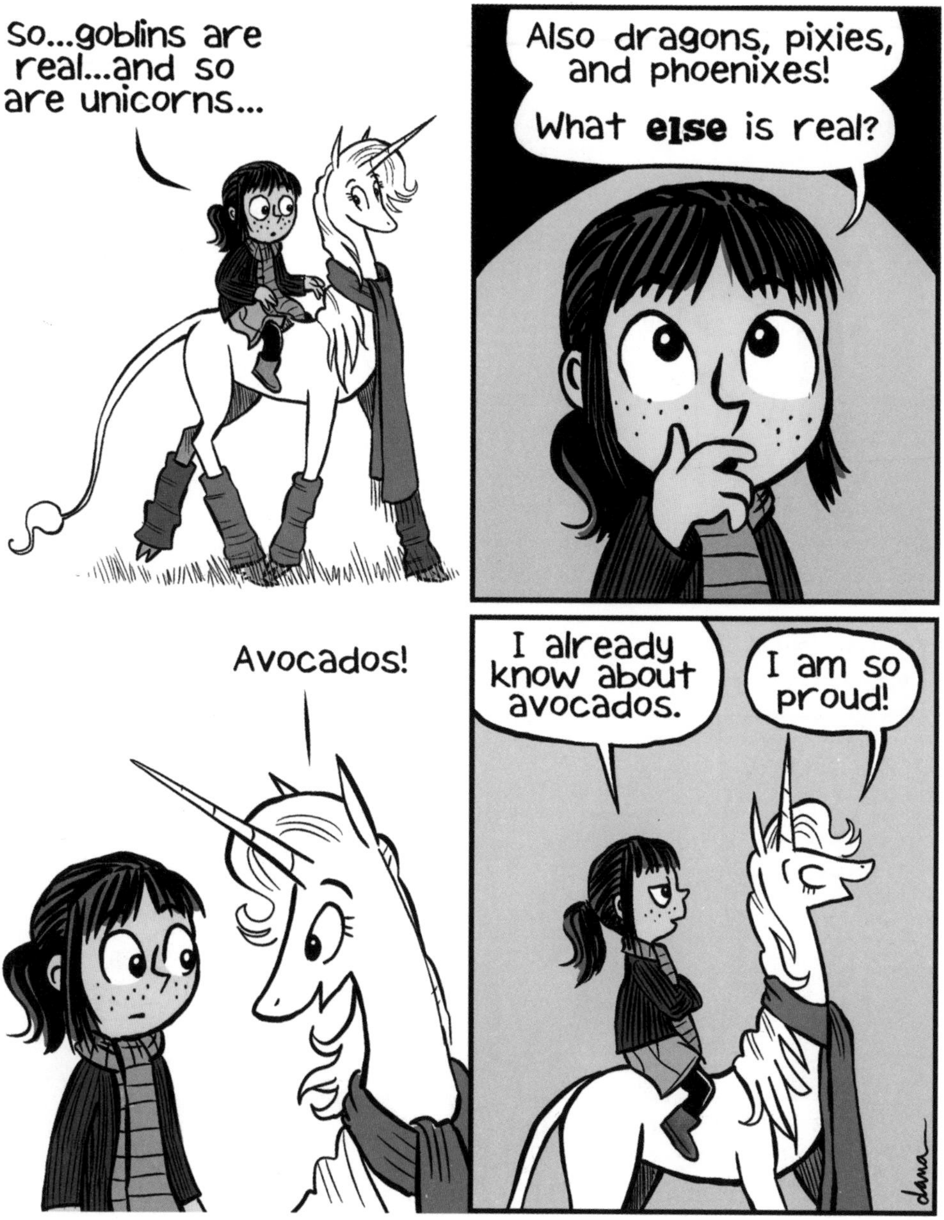
So...goblins are real...and so are unicorns...
Also dragons, pixies, and phoenixes!
What **else** is real?
Avocados!
I already know about avocados.
I am so proud!
dana

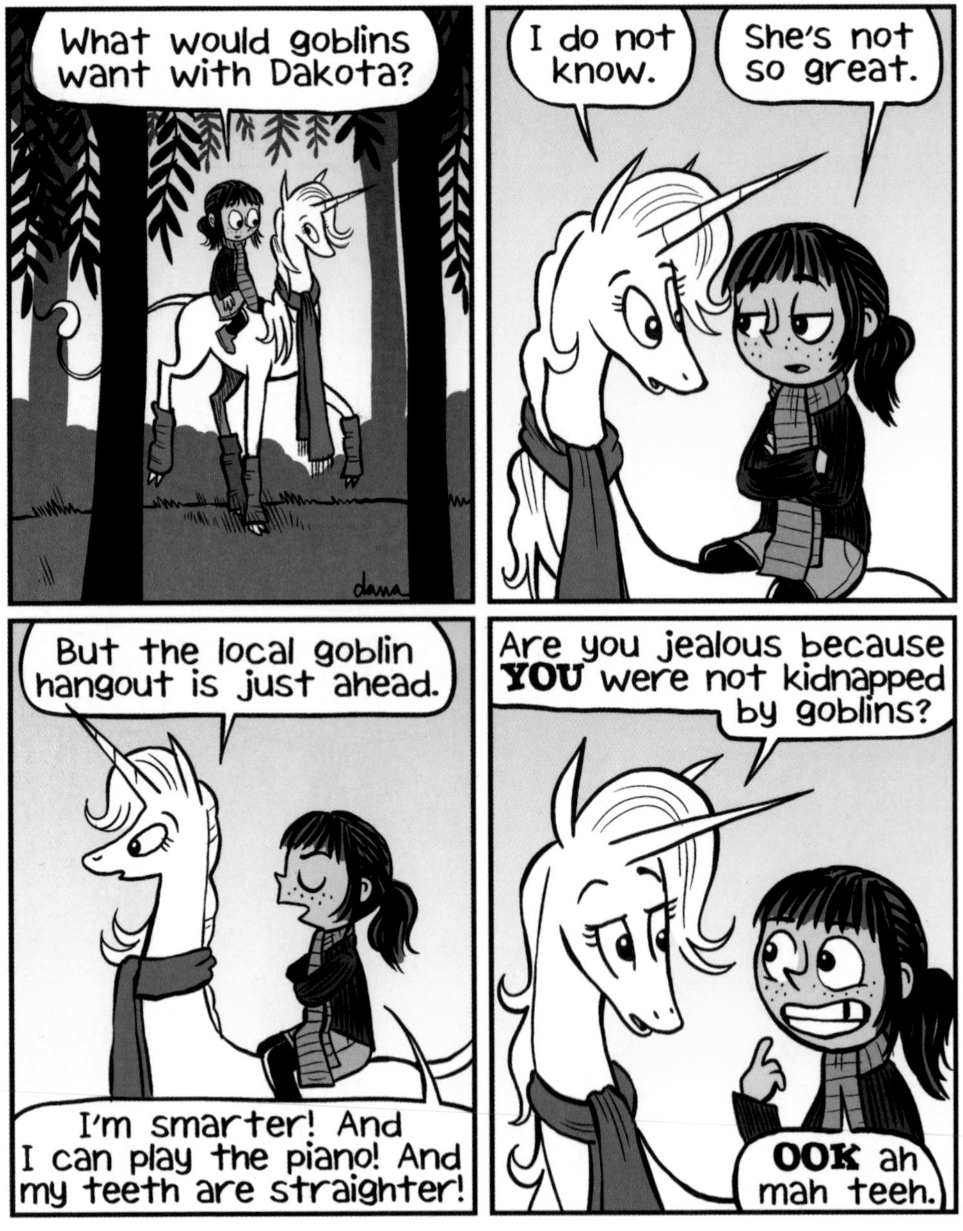

What would goblins want with Dakota?
dana
I do not know.
She's not so great.
But the local goblin hangout is just ahead.
I'm smarter! And I can play the piano! And my teeth are straighter!
Are you jealous because **YOU** were not kidnapped by goblins?
OOK ah mah teeh.

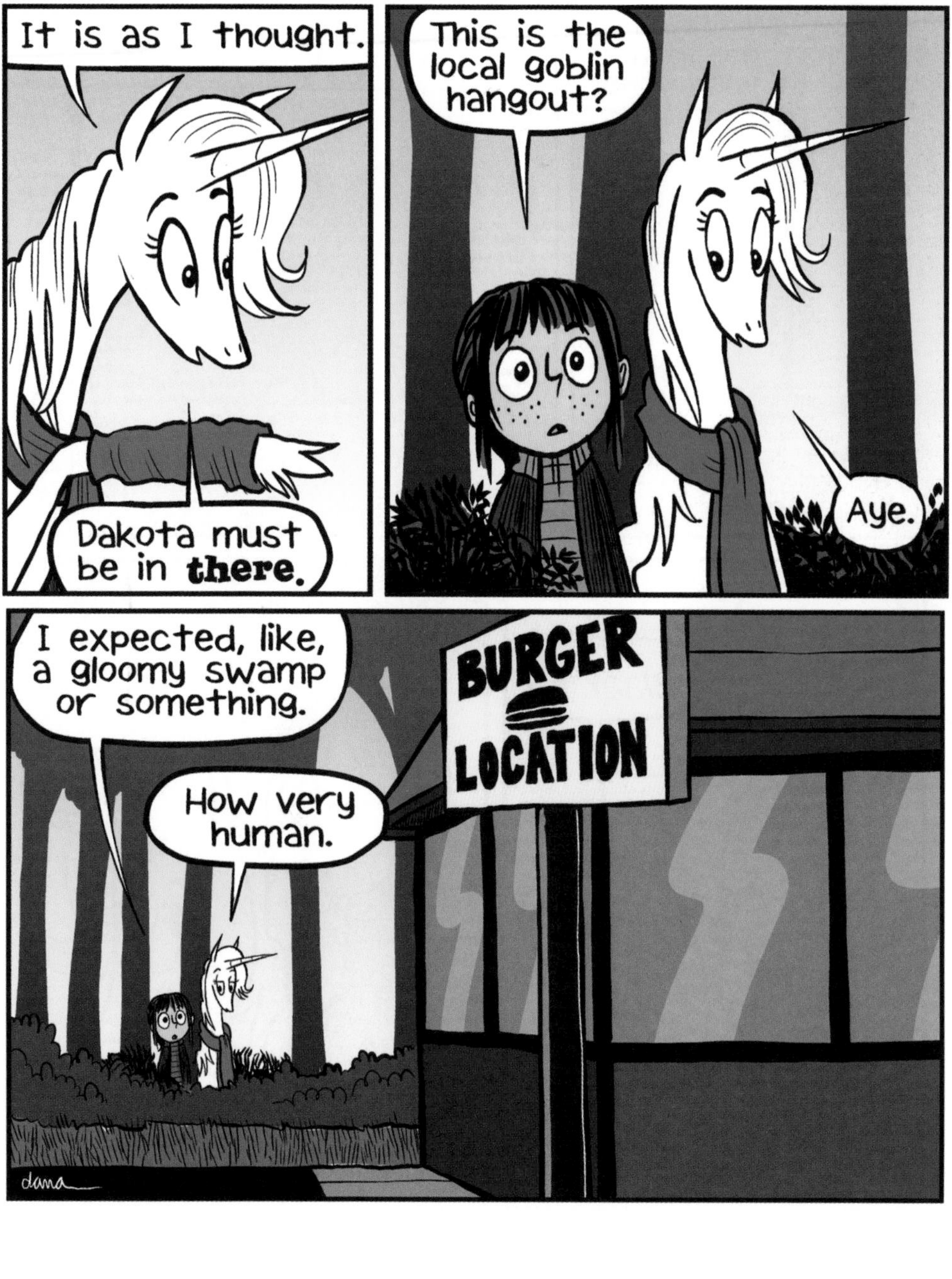
It is as I thought.
Dakota must be in **there**.
This is the local goblin hangout?
Aye.
I expected, like, a gloomy swamp or something.
How very human.
BURGER LOCATION
dana

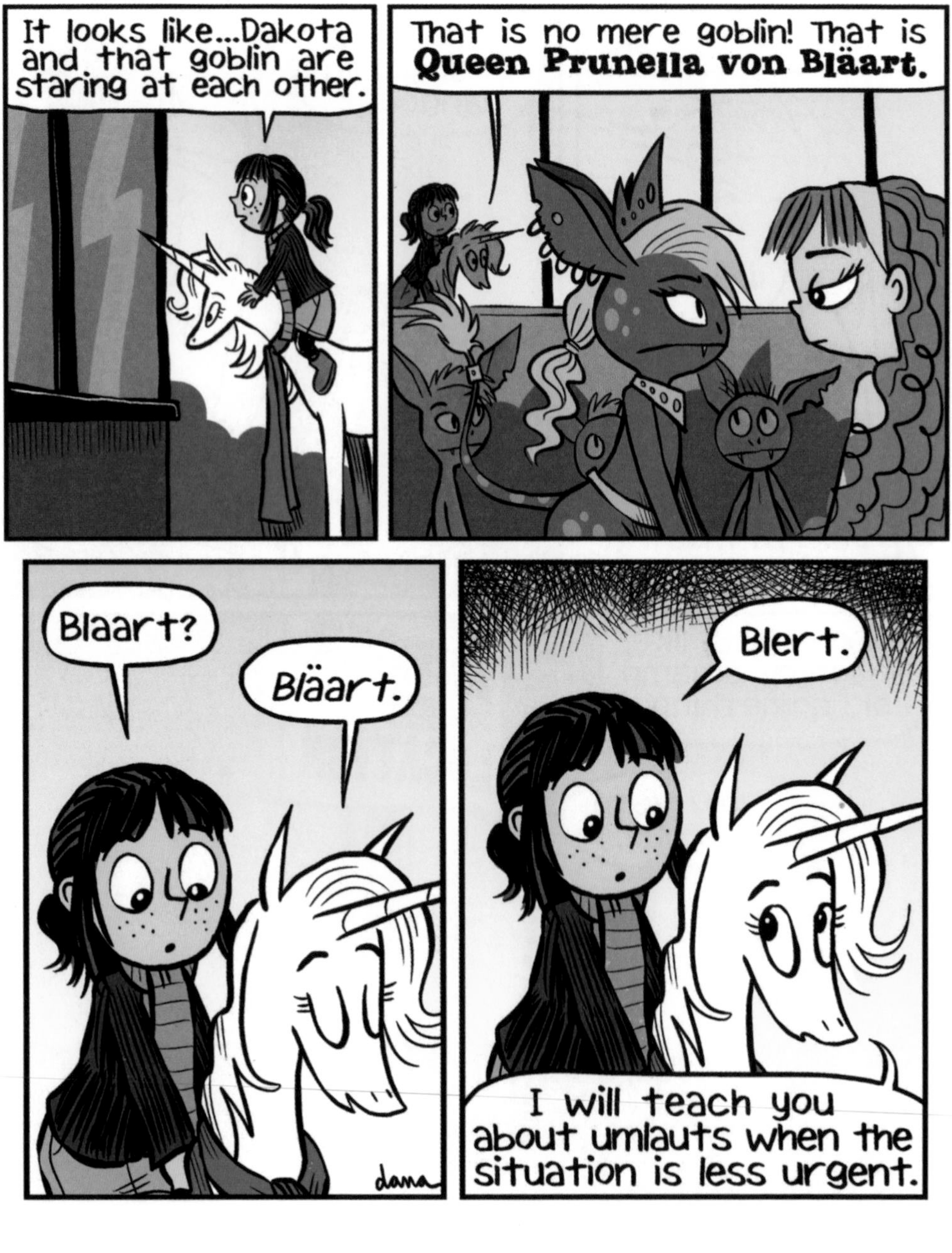

It looks like...Dakota and that goblin are staring at each other.
That is no mere goblin! That is **Queen Prunella von Bläart.**
Blaart?
Bläart.
dana
Blert.
I will teach you about umlauts when the situation is less urgent.

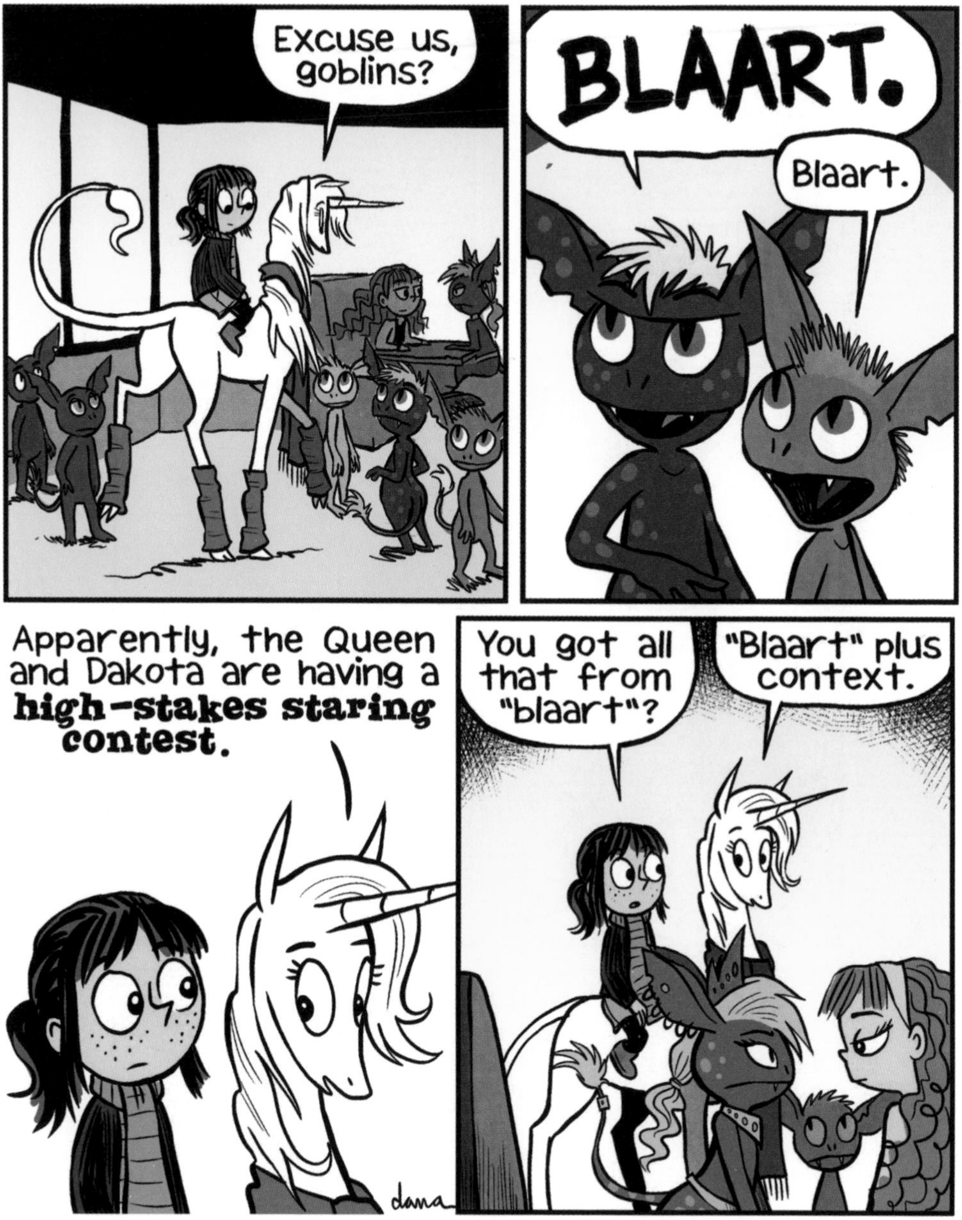
Excuse us, goblins?
BLAART.
Blaart.
Apparently, the Queen and Dakota are having a **high-stakes staring contest**.
You got all that from "blaart"?
"Blaart" plus context.
dana

A DAY IN THE LIFE OF A GOBLIN POSING AS A KID

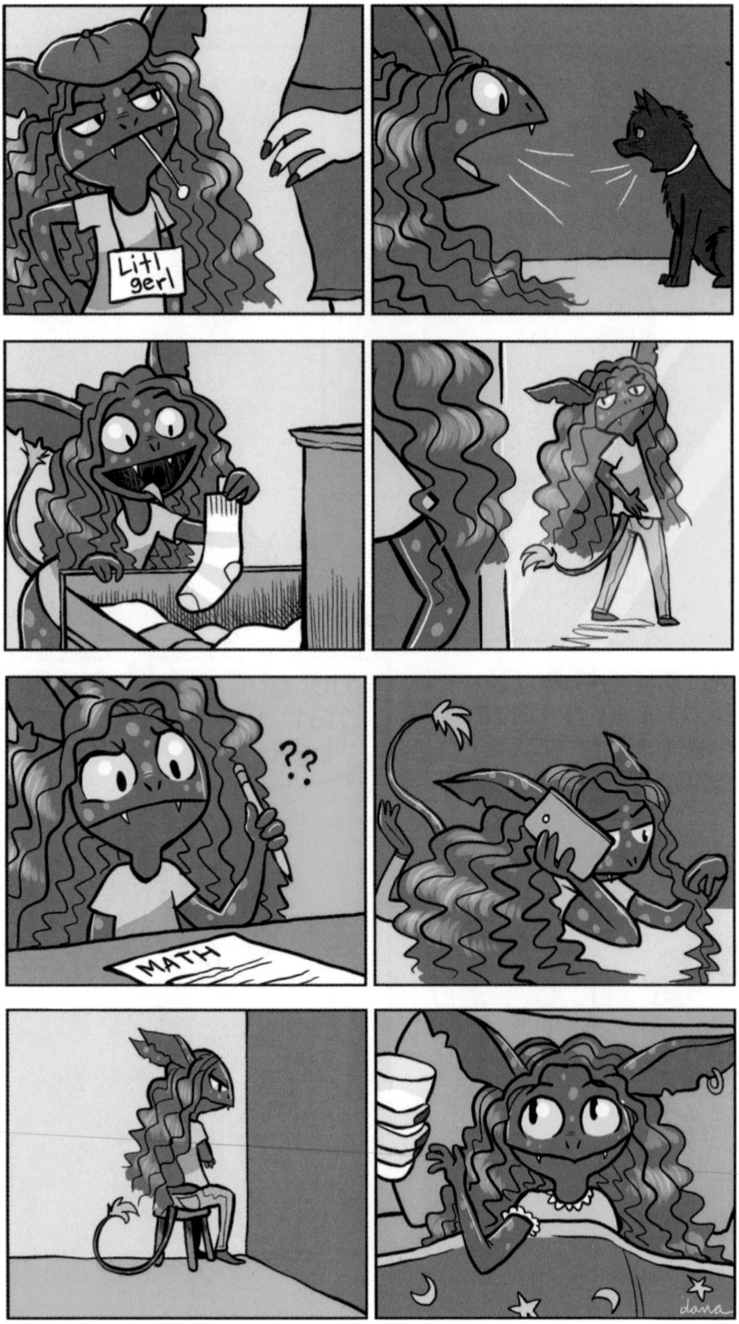

Litl gerl
??
MATH
dana

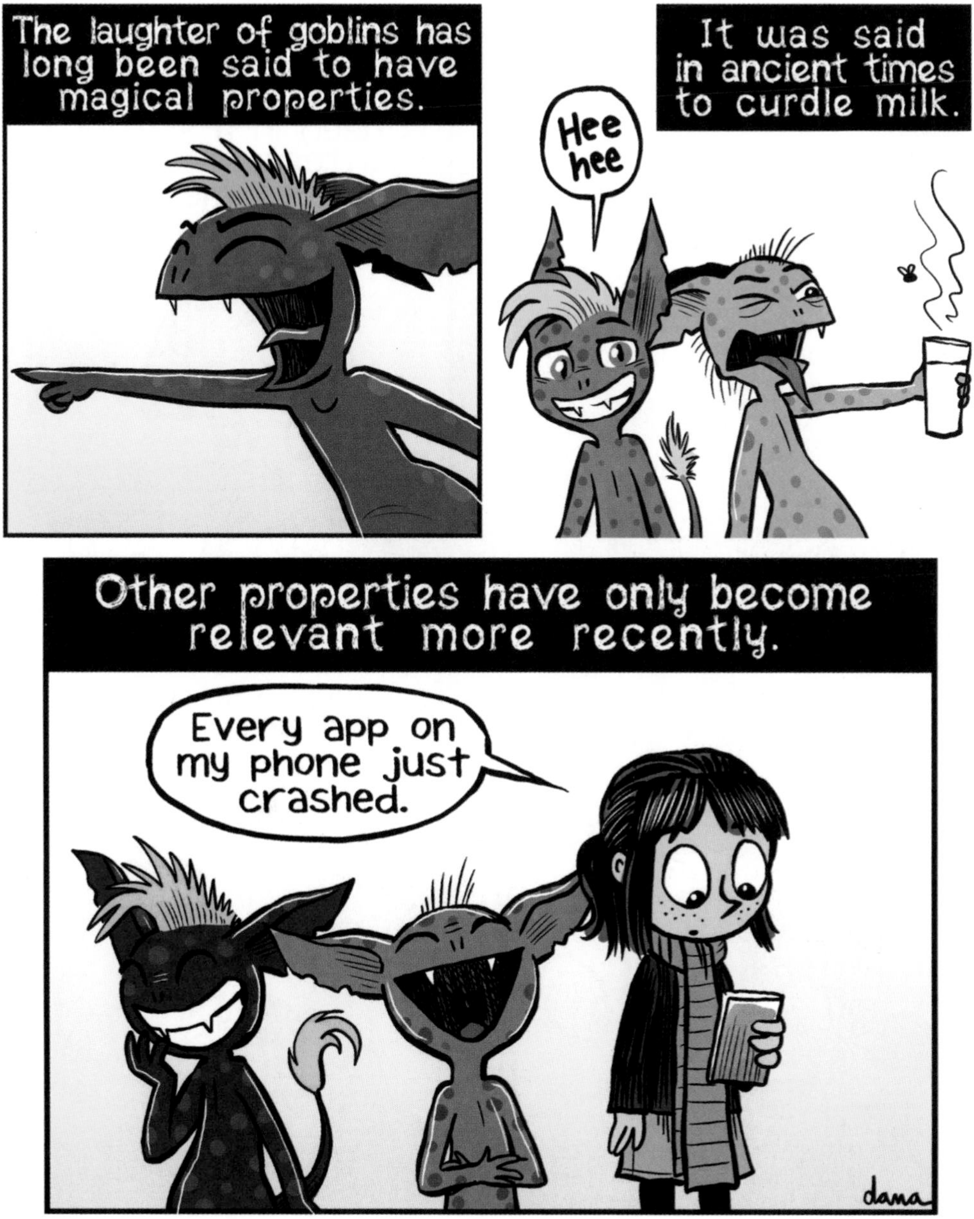
The laughter of goblins has long been said to have magical properties.
It was said in ancient times to curdle milk.
Hee hee
Other properties have only become relevant more recently.
Every app on my phone just crashed.
dana

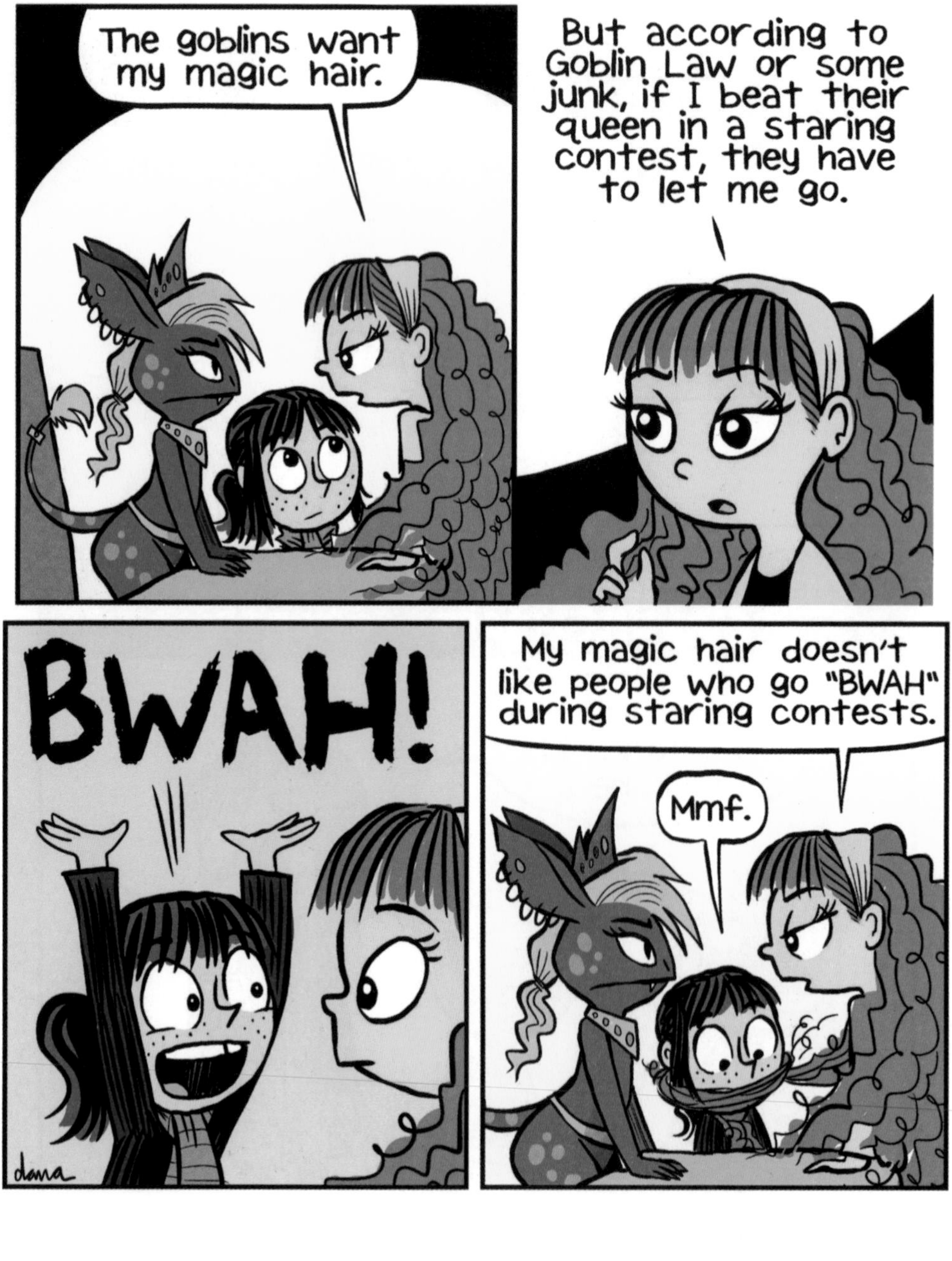
The goblins want my magic hair.
But according to Goblin Law or some junk, if I beat their queen in a staring contest, they have to let me go.
BWAH!
dana
My magic hair doesn't like people who go "BWAH" during staring contests.
Mmf.

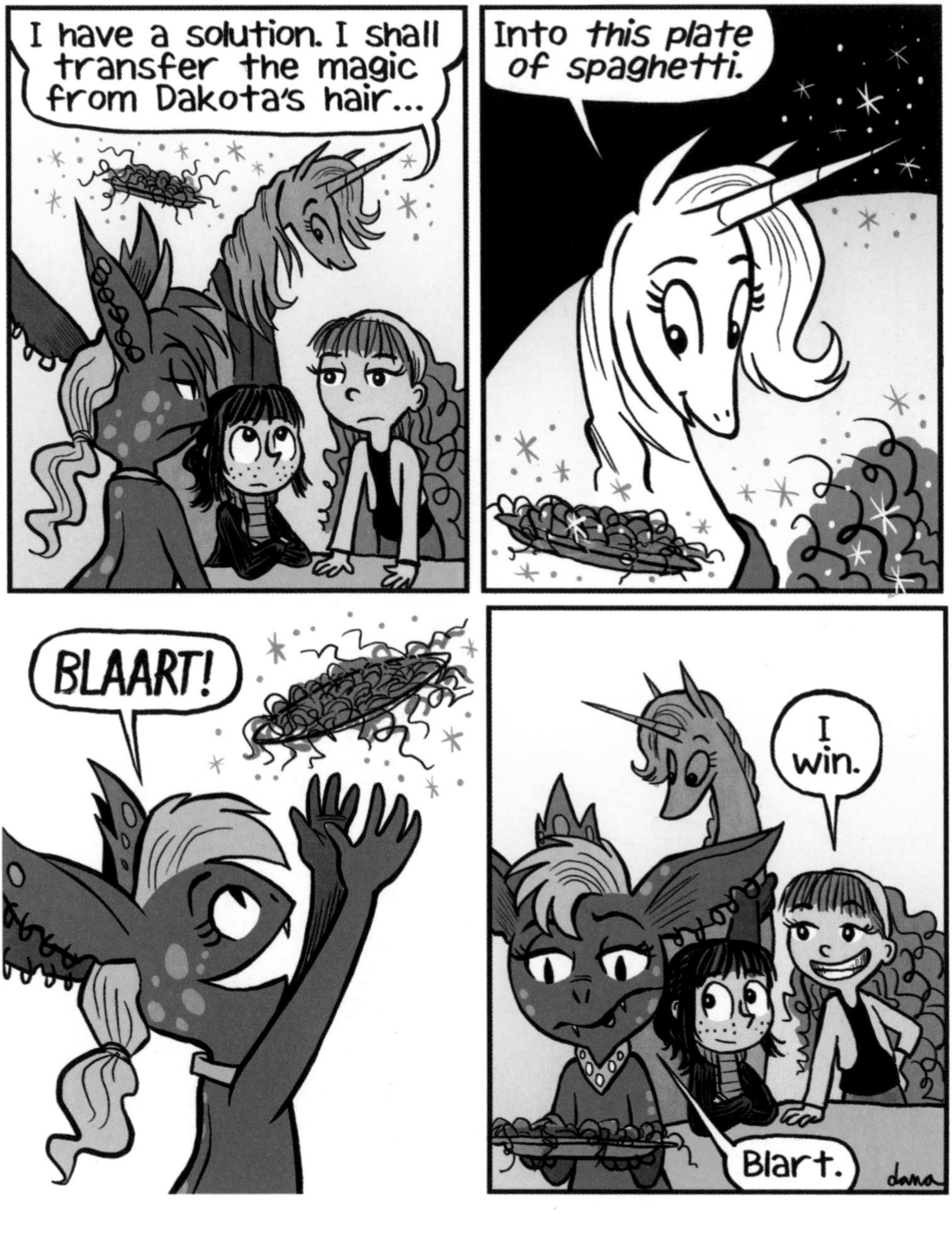

I have a solution. I shall transfer the magic from Dakota's hair...
Into *this* plate of spaghetti.
BLAART!
I win.
Blart.
dana

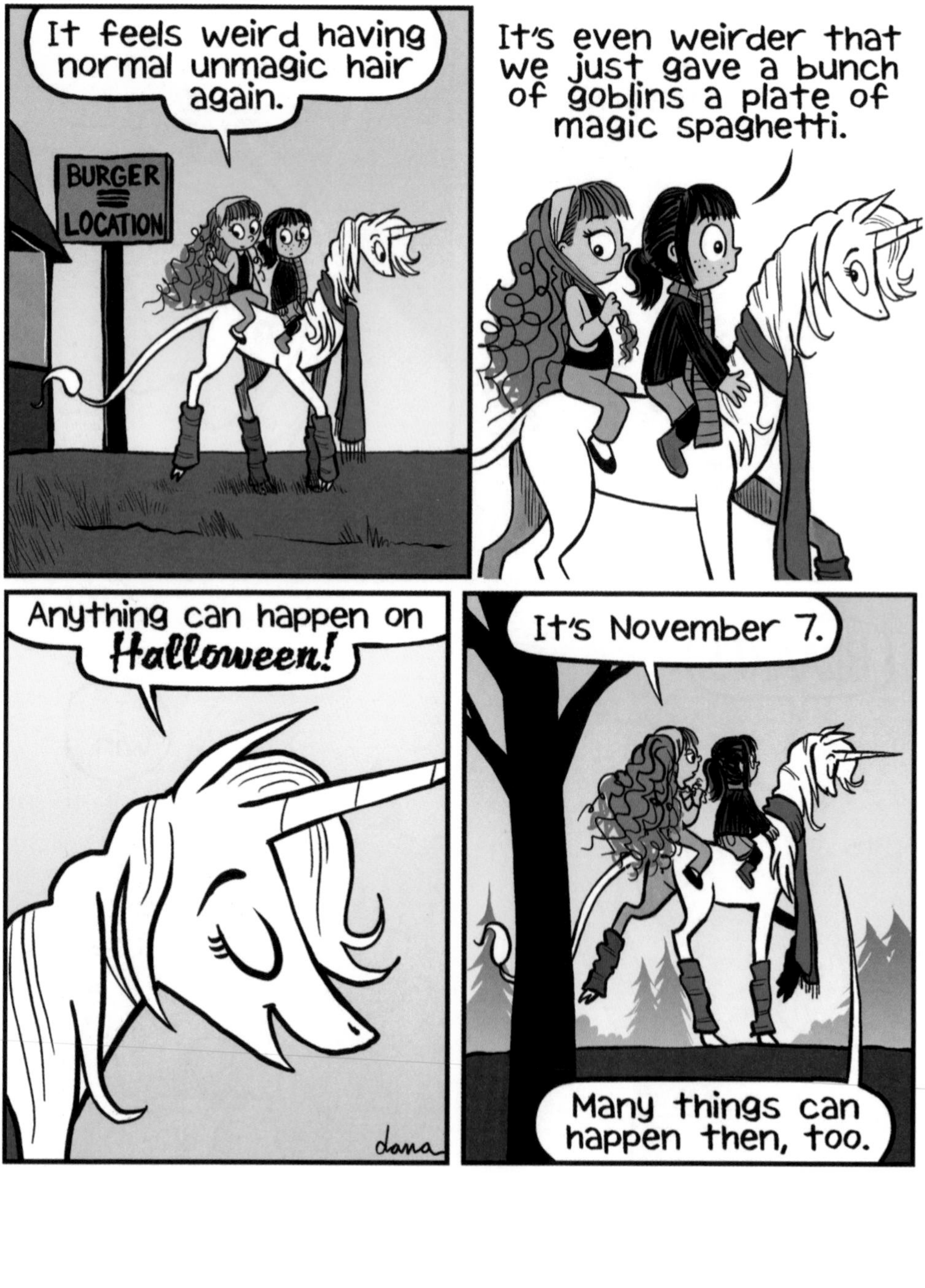
It feels weird having normal unmagic hair again.
BURGER LOCATION
It's even weirder that we just gave a bunch of goblins a plate of magic spaghetti.
Anything can happen on Halloween!
It's November 7.
Many things can happen then, too.
dana

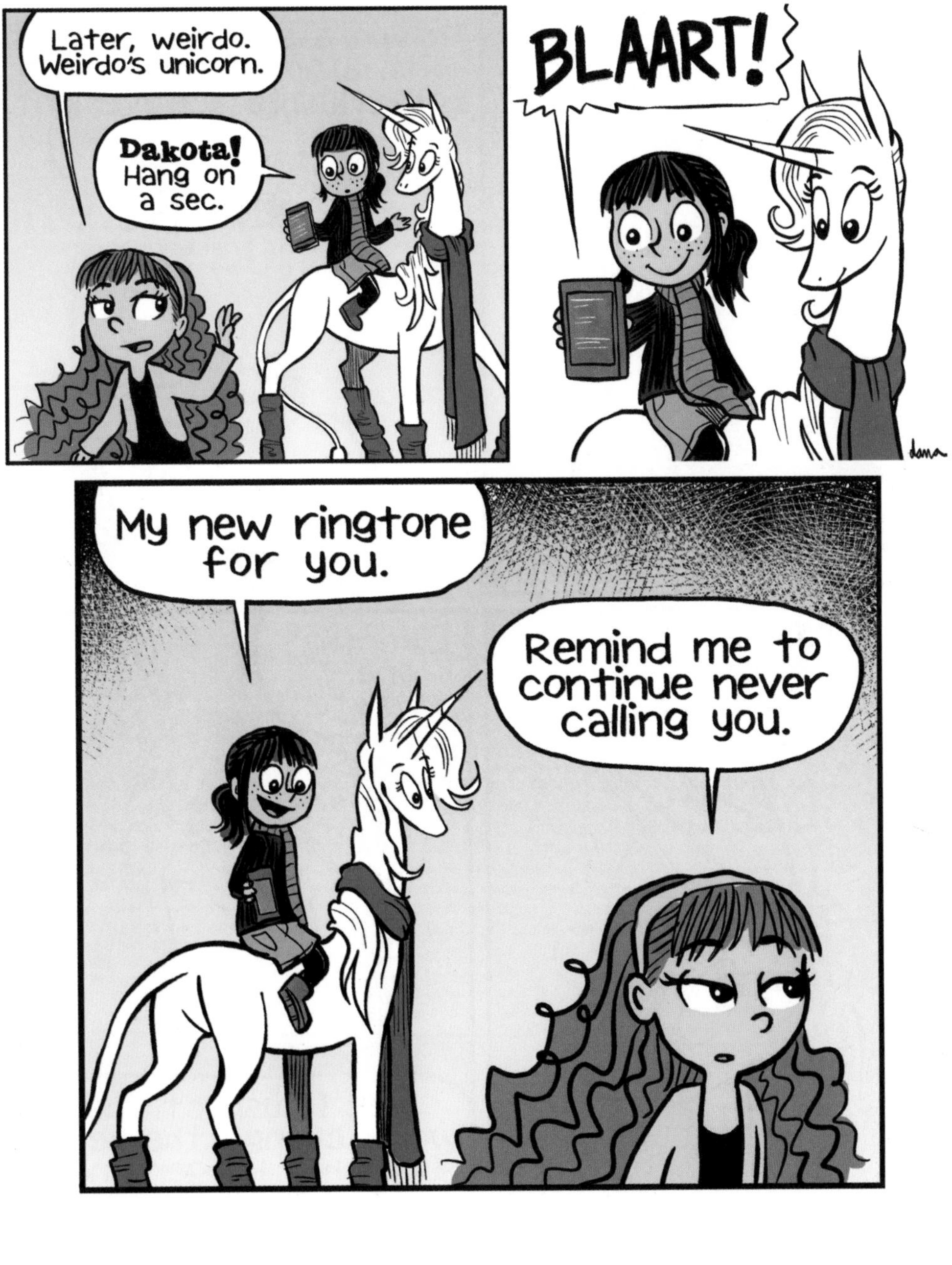
Later, weirdo.
Weirdo's unicorn.
Dakota! Hang on a sec.
BLAART!
dana
My new ringtone for you.
Remind me to continue never calling you.

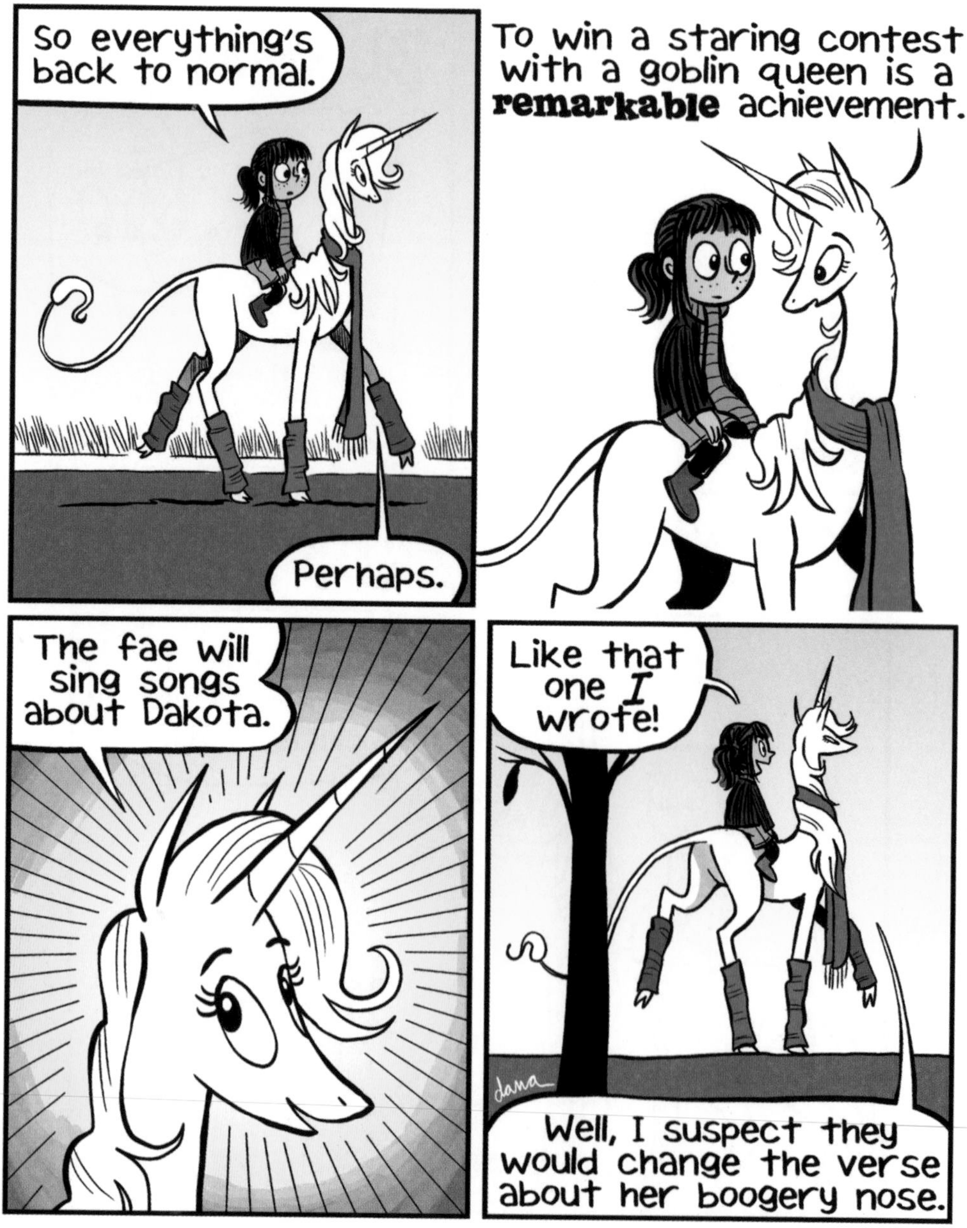
So everything's back to normal.
Perhaps.
To win a staring contest with a goblin queen is a **remarkable** achievement.
The fae will sing songs about Dakota.
Like that one *I* wrote!
Well, I suspect they would change the verse about her boogery nose.
dana

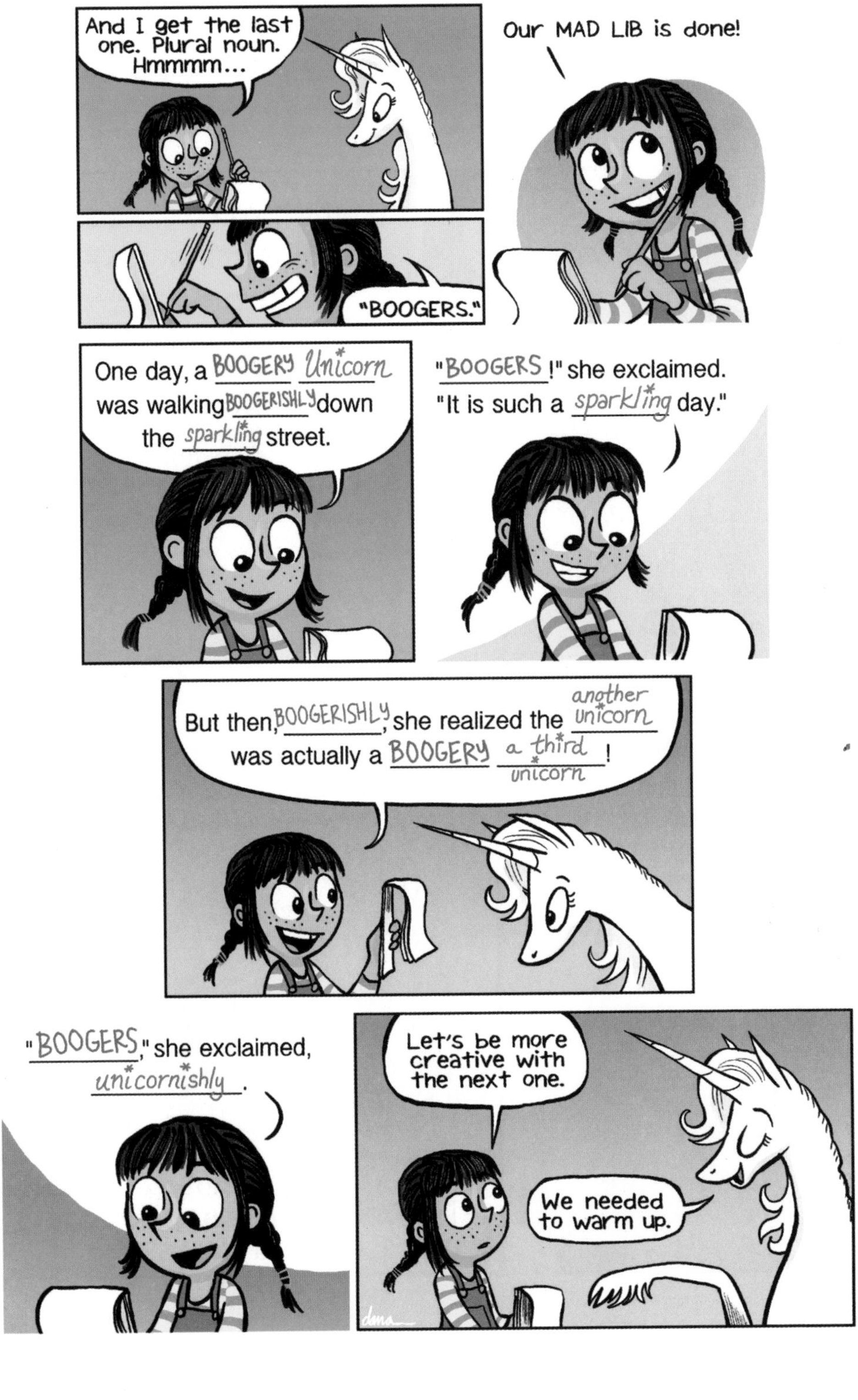
And I get the last one. Plural noun. Hmmmm...
"BOOGERS."
Our MAD LIB is done!
One day, a BOOGERY Unicorn was walking BOOGERISHLY down the sparkling street.
"BOOGERS!" she exclaimed. "It is such a sparkling day."
But then, BOOGERISHLY, she realized the another unicorn was actually a BOOGERY a third unicorn!
"BOOGERS," she exclaimed, unicornishly.
Let's be more creative with the next one.
We needed to warm up.

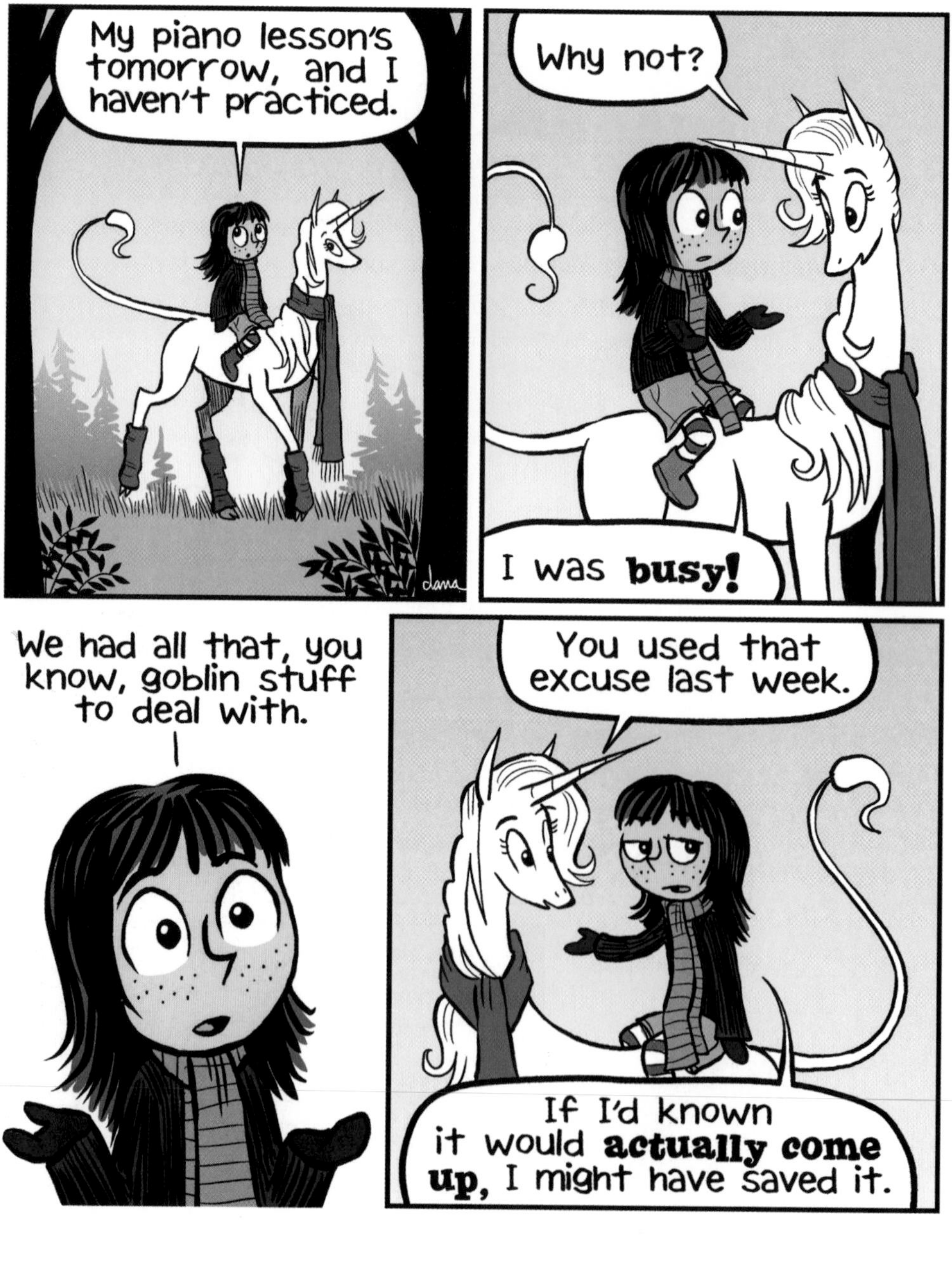
My piano lesson's tomorrow, and I haven't practiced.
Why not?
I was **busy!**
We had all that, you know, goblin stuff to deal with.
You used that excuse last week.
If I'd known it would **actually come up**, I might have saved it.

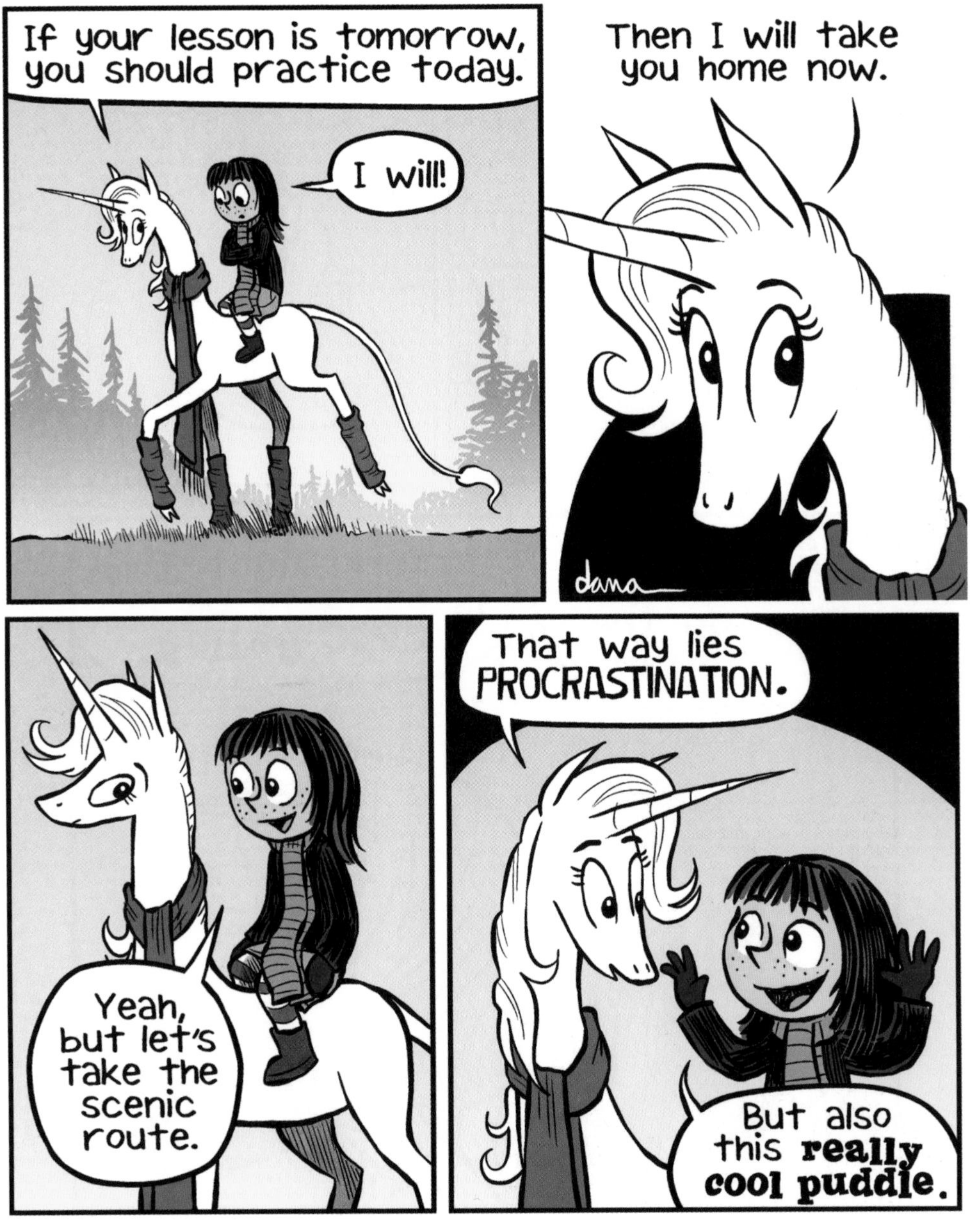
If your lesson is tomorrow, you should practice today.
I will!
Then I will take you home now.
dana
Yeah, but let's take the scenic route.
That way lies PROCRASTINATION.
But also this **really cool puddle**.

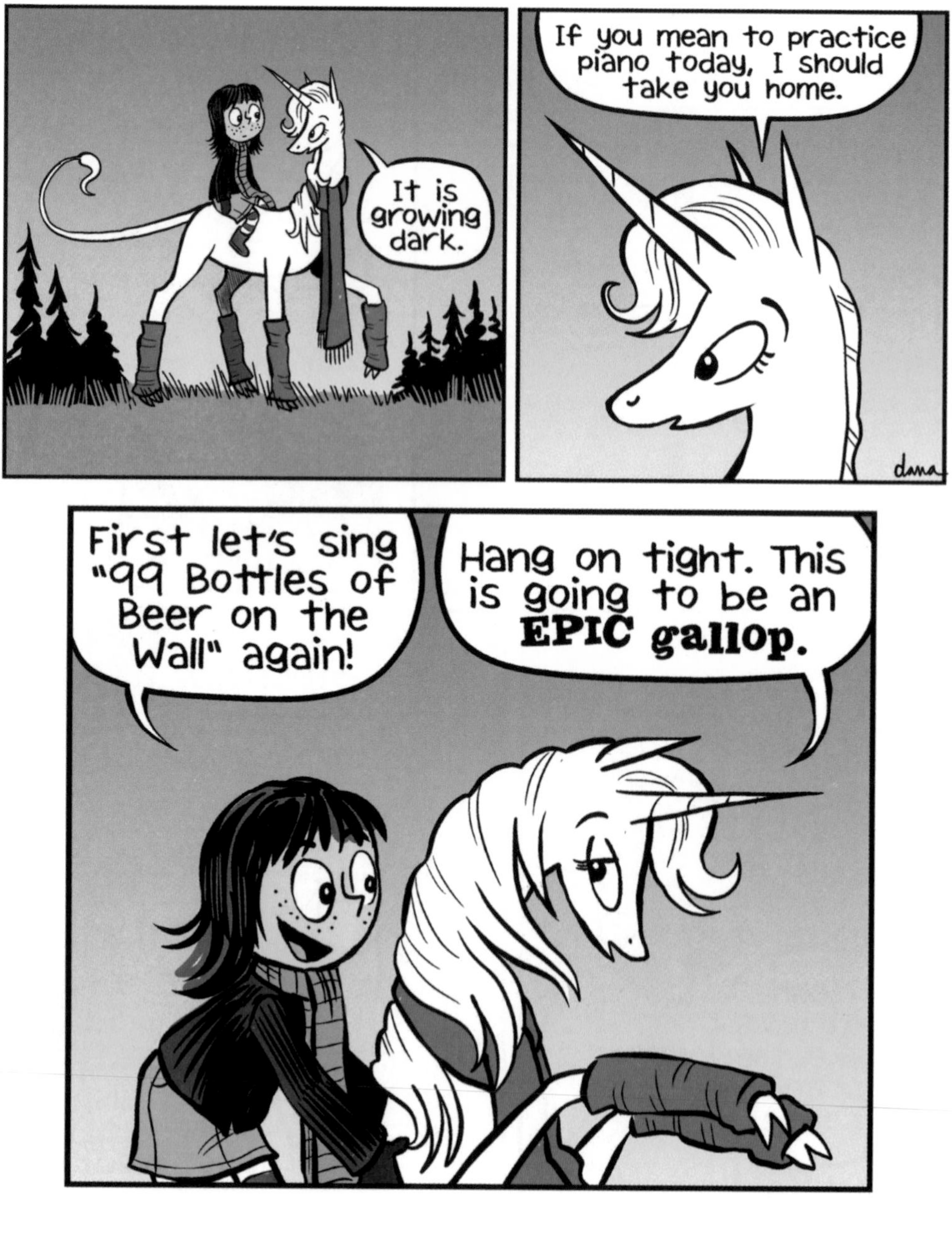
It is growing dark.
If you mean to practice piano today, I should take you home.
dana
First let's sing "99 Bottles of Beer on the Wall" again!
Hang on tight. This is going to be an **EPIC gallop.**

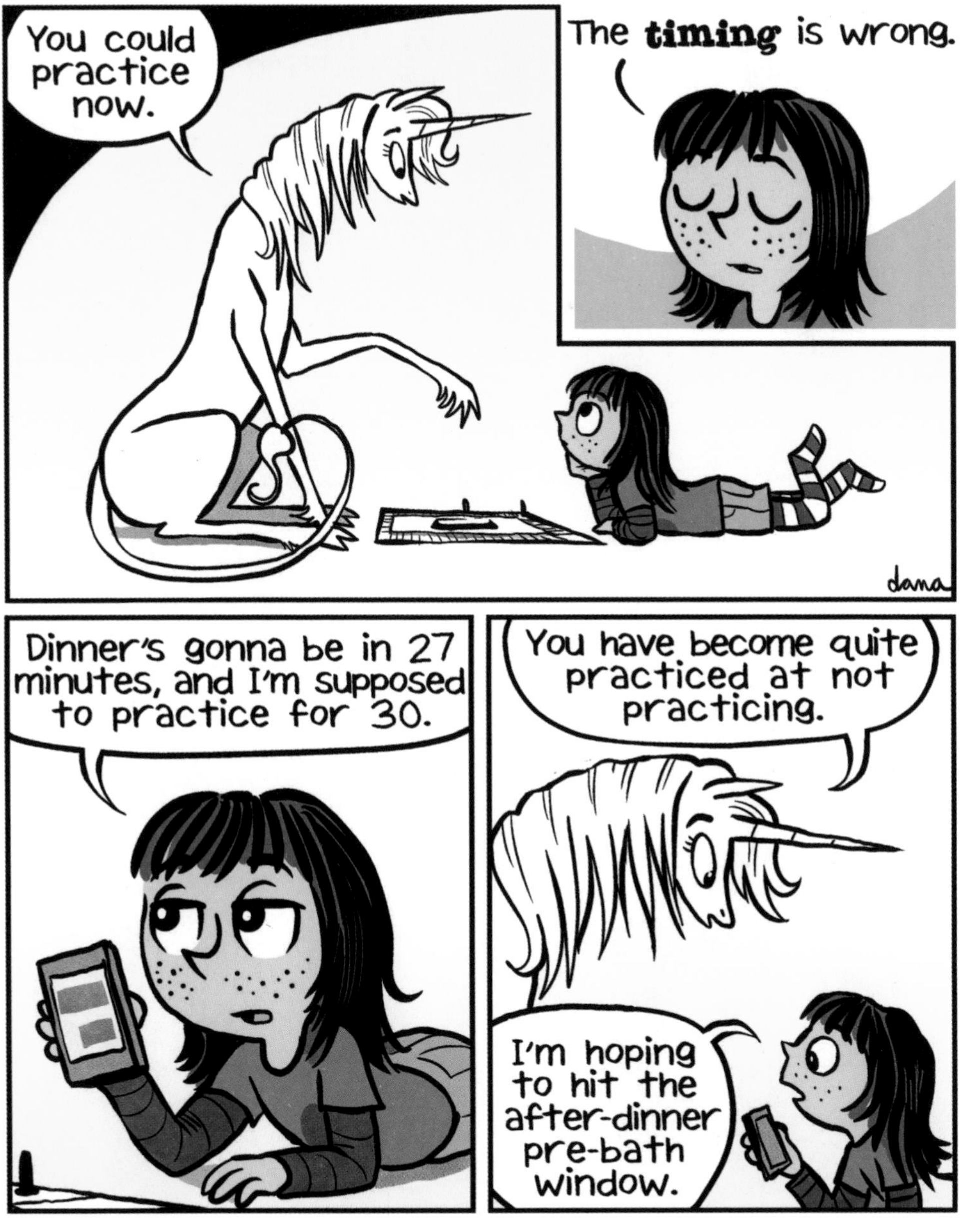
You could practice now.
The **timing** is wrong.
dana
Dinner's gonna be in 27 minutes, and I'm supposed to practice for 30.
You have become quite practiced at not practicing.
I'm hoping to hit the after-dinner pre-bath window.

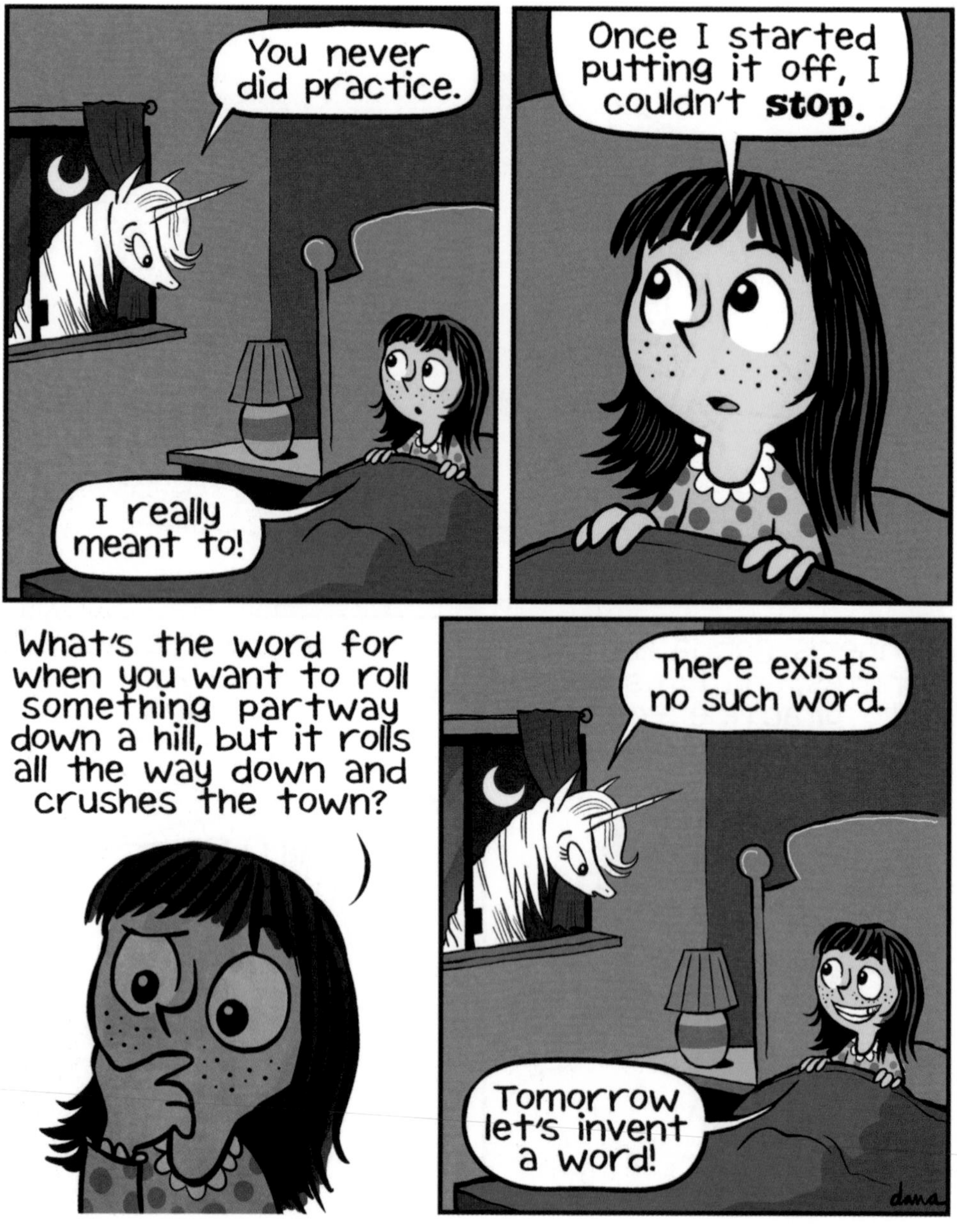
You never did practice.
I really meant to!
Once I started putting it off, I couldn't **stop.**
What's the word for when you want to roll something partway down a hill, but it rolls all the way down and crushes the town?
There exists no such word.
Tomorrow let's invent a word!
dana

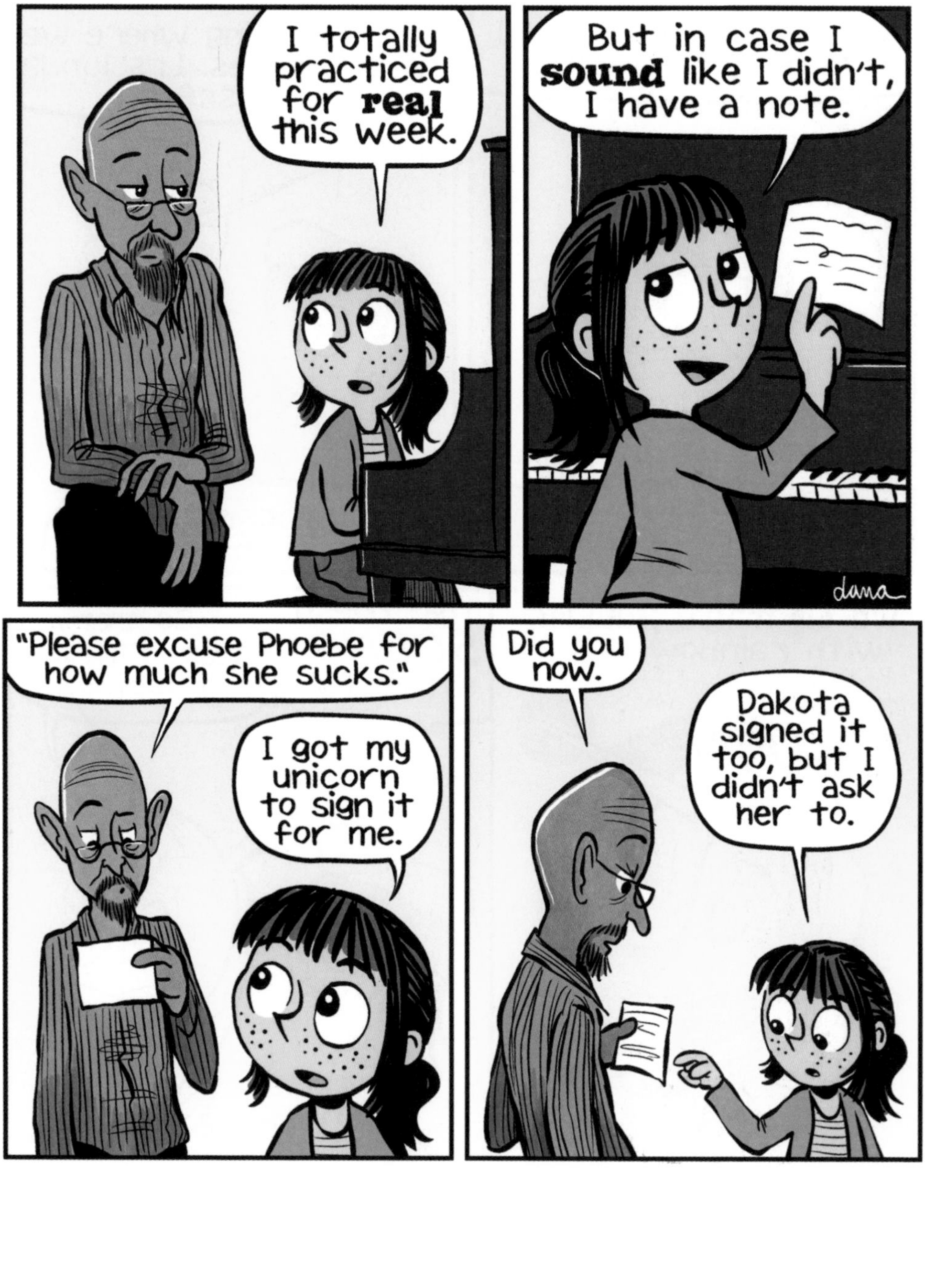
I totally practiced for **real** this week.
But in case I **sound** like I didn't, I have a note.
dana
"Please excuse Phoebe for how much she sucks."
I got my unicorn to sign it for me.
Did you now.
Dakota signed it too, but I didn't ask her to.

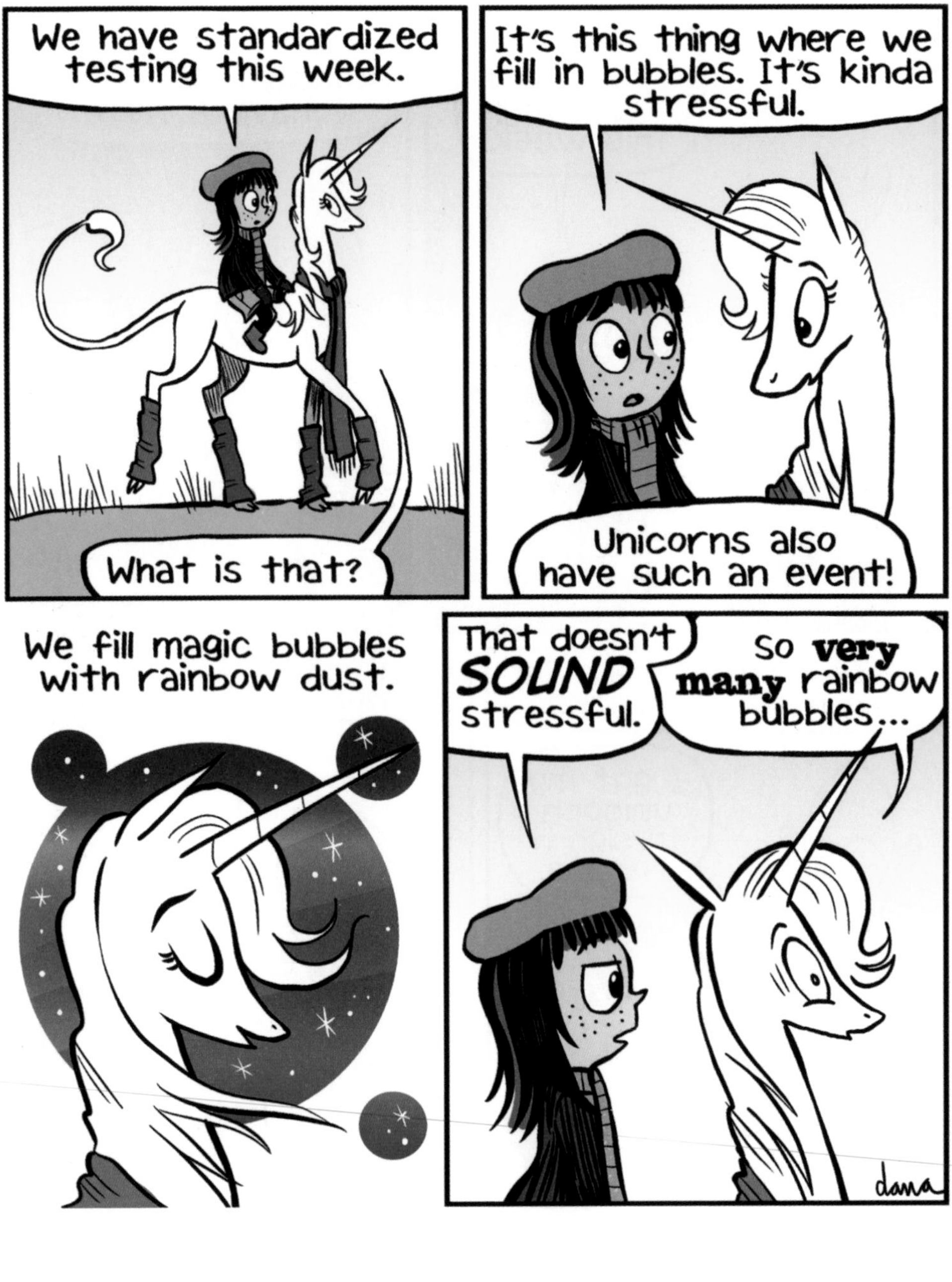
We have standardized testing this week.
What is that?
It's this thing where we fill in bubbles. It's kinda stressful.
Unicorns also have such an event!
We fill magic bubbles with rainbow dust.
That doesn't SOUND stressful.
So very many rainbow bubbles...
dana

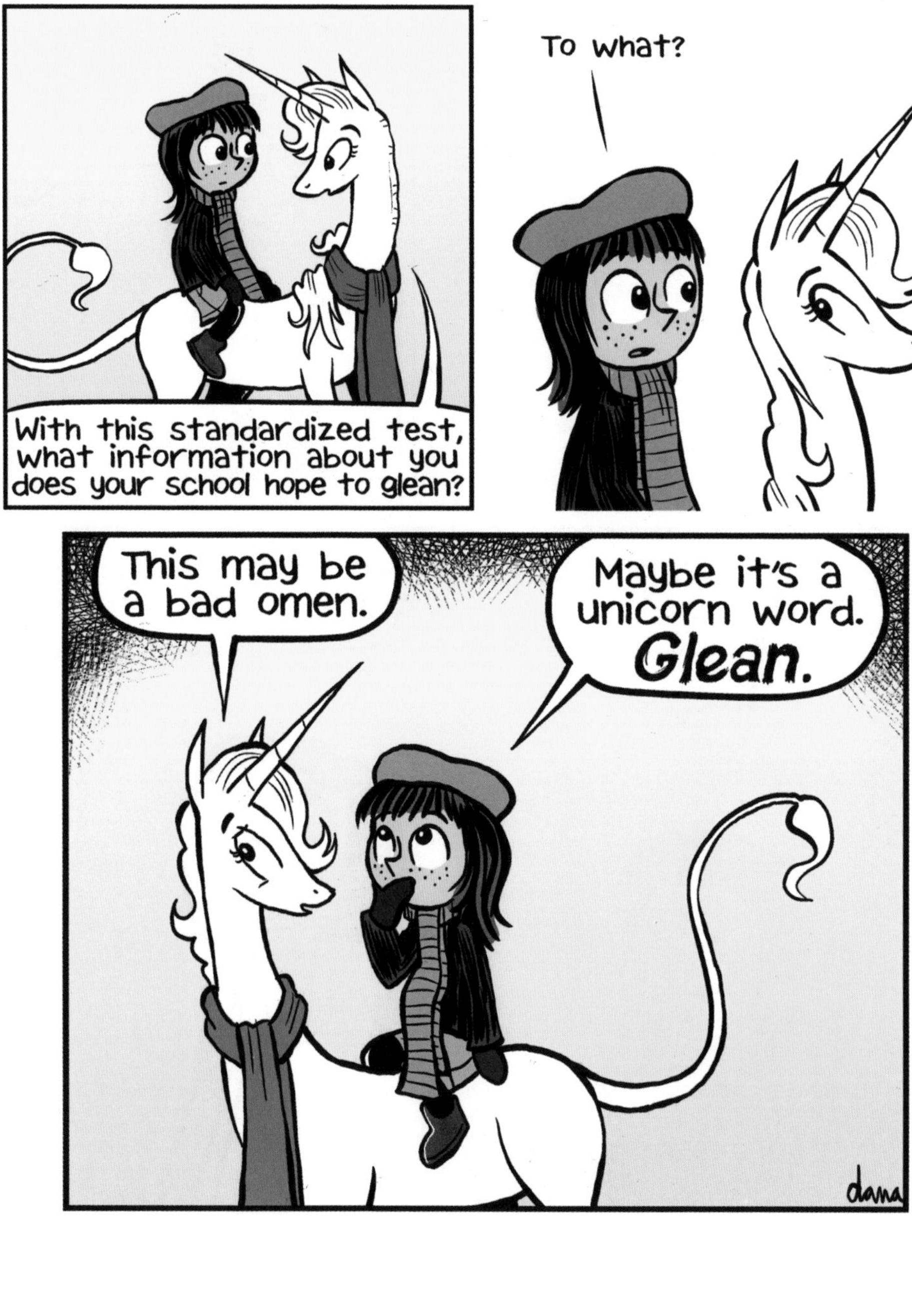
With this standardized test, what information about you does your school hope to glean?
To what?
This may be a bad omen.
Maybe it's a unicorn word. Glean.
dana

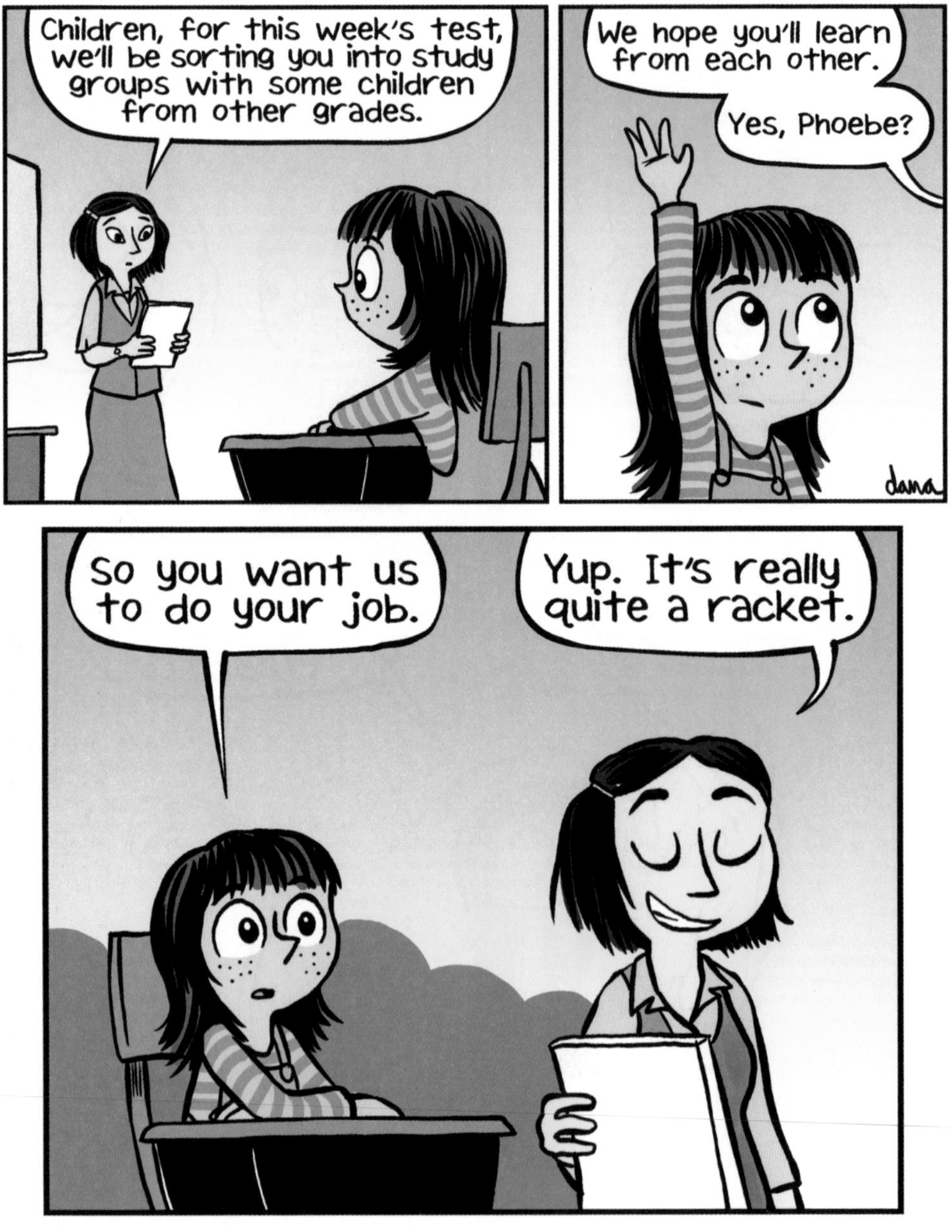
Children, for this week's test, we'll be sorting you into study groups with some children from other grades.
We hope you'll learn from each other.
Yes, Phoebe?
dana
So you want us to do your job.
Yup. It's really quite a racket.

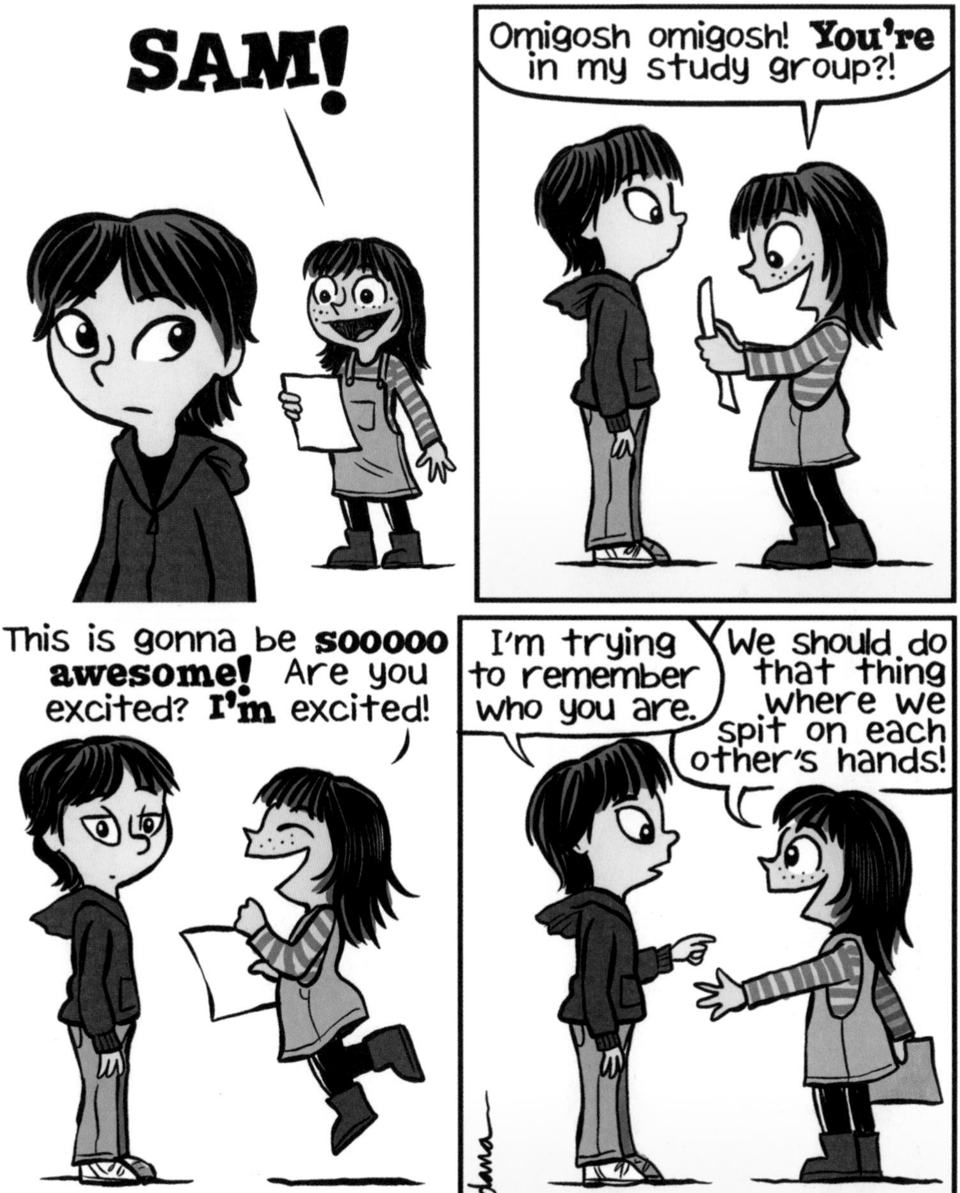
SAM!
Omigosh omigosh! You're in my study group?!
This is gonna be sooooo awesome! Are you excited? I'm excited!
I'm trying to remember who you are.
We should do that thing where we spit on each other's hands!
dana

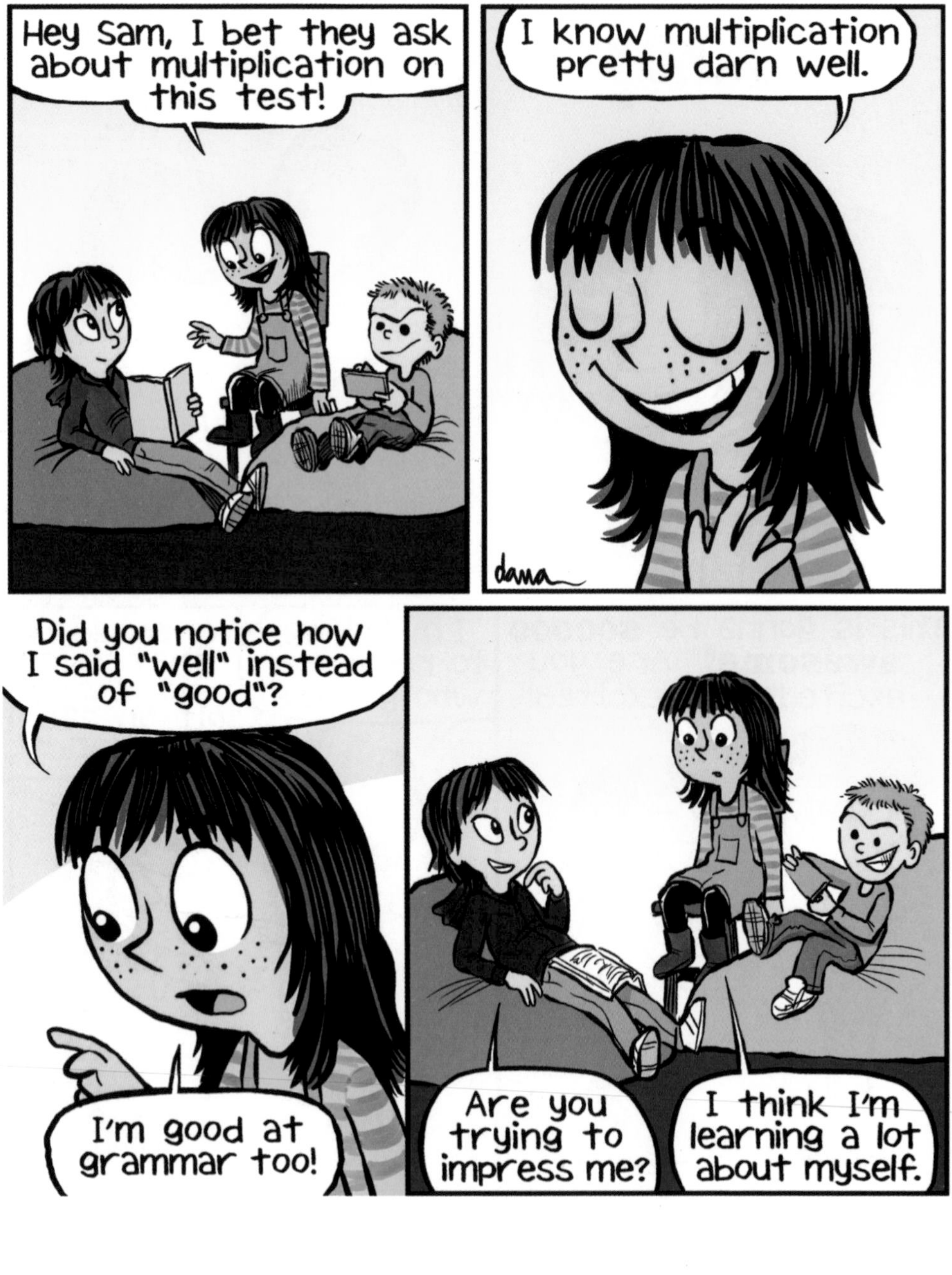
Hey Sam, I bet they ask about multiplication on this test!
I know multiplication pretty darn well.
dana
Did you notice how I said "well" instead of "good"?
I'm good at grammar too!
Are you trying to impress me?
I think I'm learning a lot about myself.

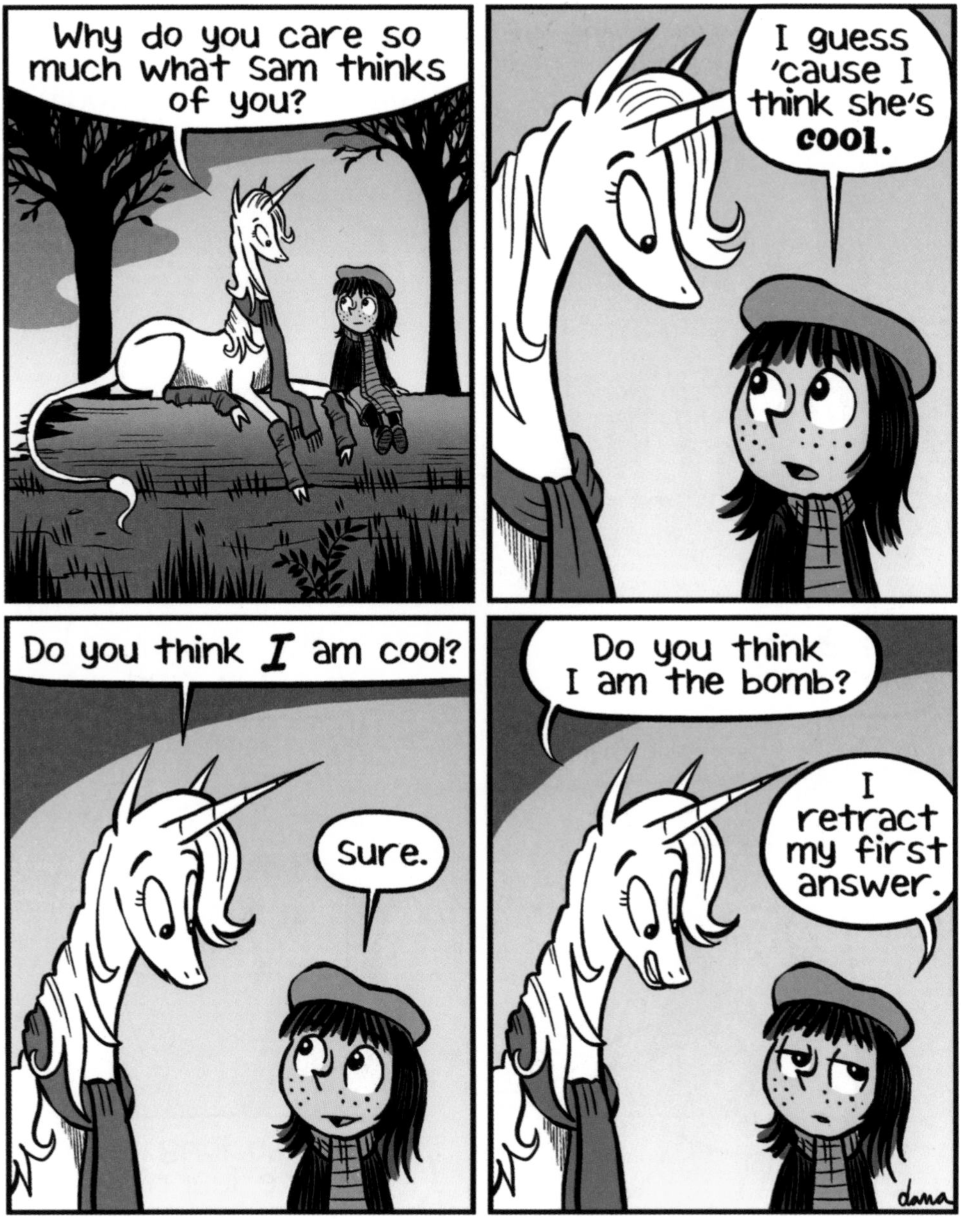
Why do you care so much what Sam thinks of you?
I guess 'cause I think she's **cool.**
Do you think *I* am cool?
Sure.
Do you think I am the bomb?
I retract my first answer.
dana

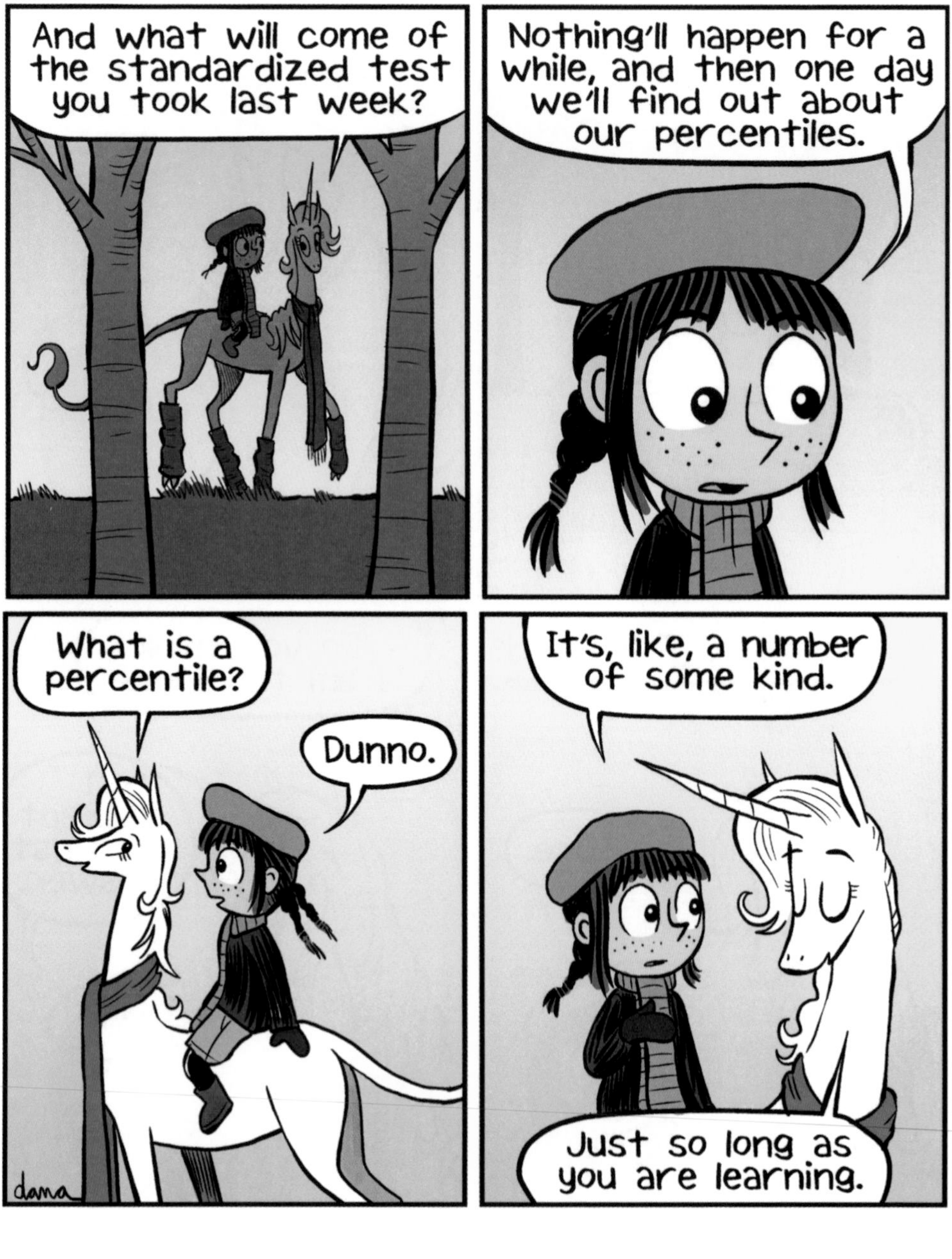
And what will come of the standardized test you took last week?
Nothing'll happen for a while, and then one day we'll find out about our percentiles.
What is a percentile?
Dunno.
It's, like, a number of some kind.
Just so long as you are learning.
dana

Let's Draw Some Supporting Characters

There are more characters than just Phoebe and Marigold! Here's a look at how I draw some of them.

Dakota and Max

Like Phoebe's, Dakota's head is based on a circle.

Max's is more of an oval.

Headband

Round little nose

Three eyelash lines... also, her eyes are seldom open all the way

Hair is mostly curly lines

Eyes are dots in his glasses

Wedge nose

Max's glasses have changed since the previous book! (He got new ones)

Both of them are a little taller and skinnier than Phoebe.

Hand on hip— she's always kind of striking a pose

Dakota's body is also based on circles

Max's body is based on an oval, like his head

Seldom looks up from his phone!

Always wears black

Todd the Candy-Breathing Dragon

No pupils

Curly horns

Pointy beak face →

Head and body based on circles (they're SO useful)

Dragon wings are a "hard" shape—I recommend practice

Todd is very small— here's Phoebe's hand for reference

His tail (and horns) are striped like a candy cane

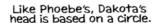

Florence Unfortunate Nostrils

Florence looks a lot like her sister Marigold Heavenly Nostrils in some ways, but there are also some big differences.

Her mane (and some of her tail) are wavy lines

Her glasses hook behind her ears

Always spiders, with Florence

Her nose is less pointy than Marigold's, and her nostrils are bigger

Florence is shorter than her sister, and the difference is mostly legs

Goblins

Your typical goblin

mohawk

Goblin heads are possibly the roundest

ragged-edged ears

slit pupils, like a cat

nostrils, but no real nose

fangs

their bodies are sort of pear-shaped, which is really two different-sized circles

Short, kind of bent legs

Queen Prunella Von Bläart

floppy hair

she has a unique eye shape, (but they all have big mouths)

The queen gets to have ornamentation

Goblins come in different heights, shapes, spot patterns...they probably vary as much as humans.

Questing Mix

Marigold might be able to survive on grass when she and Phoebe go on their quest to save Dakota from the goblins, but Phoebe will need something to snack on, and you will too! This special trail mix is easy to take along or to share with friends.

INGREDIENTS:

½ cup peanuts or other nuts

½ cup mini pretzels or 1-inch pieces small pretzels

½ cup semisweet chocolate chips

½ cup dried cranberries or cherries

¼ cup Goldfish crackers

¼ cup raisins

¼ cup sunflower seeds

INSTRUCTIONS:

In a large bowl, combine all the ingredients and toss to mix well.

The trail mix will keep in an airtight container at room temperature for at least 2 weeks.

Makes about 8 servings, about 3 cups.

Alice and the Unicorn

Not surprisingly, the unicorn makes an appearance in the works of Lewis Carroll, creator of the most delightful whimsy of the Victorian age. In *Through the Looking Glass and What Alice Found There*, Alice encounters a unicorn in a passage that captures the essential paradox of the legendary beast:

> ". . . He was going on, when his eye happened to fall upon Alice: he turned round instantly, and stood for some time looking at her with an air of the deepest disgust.
>
> 'What—is—this?' he said at last.
>
> 'This is a child!' Haigha replied eagerly . . . 'We only found it today. It's as large as life, and twice as natural!'
>
> 'I always thought they were fabulous monsters!' said the Unicorn. 'Is it alive?"
>
> 'It can talk,' said Haigha solemnly.
>
> The Unicorn looked dreamily to Alice, and said, 'Talk, child.'
>
> Alice could not help her lips curling into a smile as she began: 'Do you know, I always thought Unicorns were fabulous monsters, too? I never saw one alive before!'
>
> 'Well, now we *have* seen each other,' said the Unicorn, 'if you'll believe in me, I'll believe in you. Is that a bargain?'"

Razzle Dazzle Unicorn

Another Phoebe and Her Unicorn Adventure

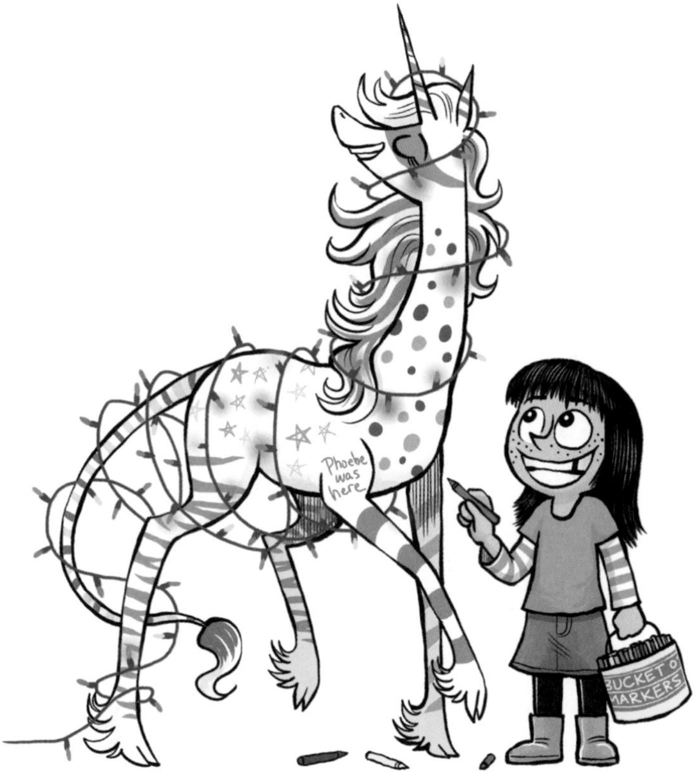
Phoebe was here
BUCKET O' MARKERS

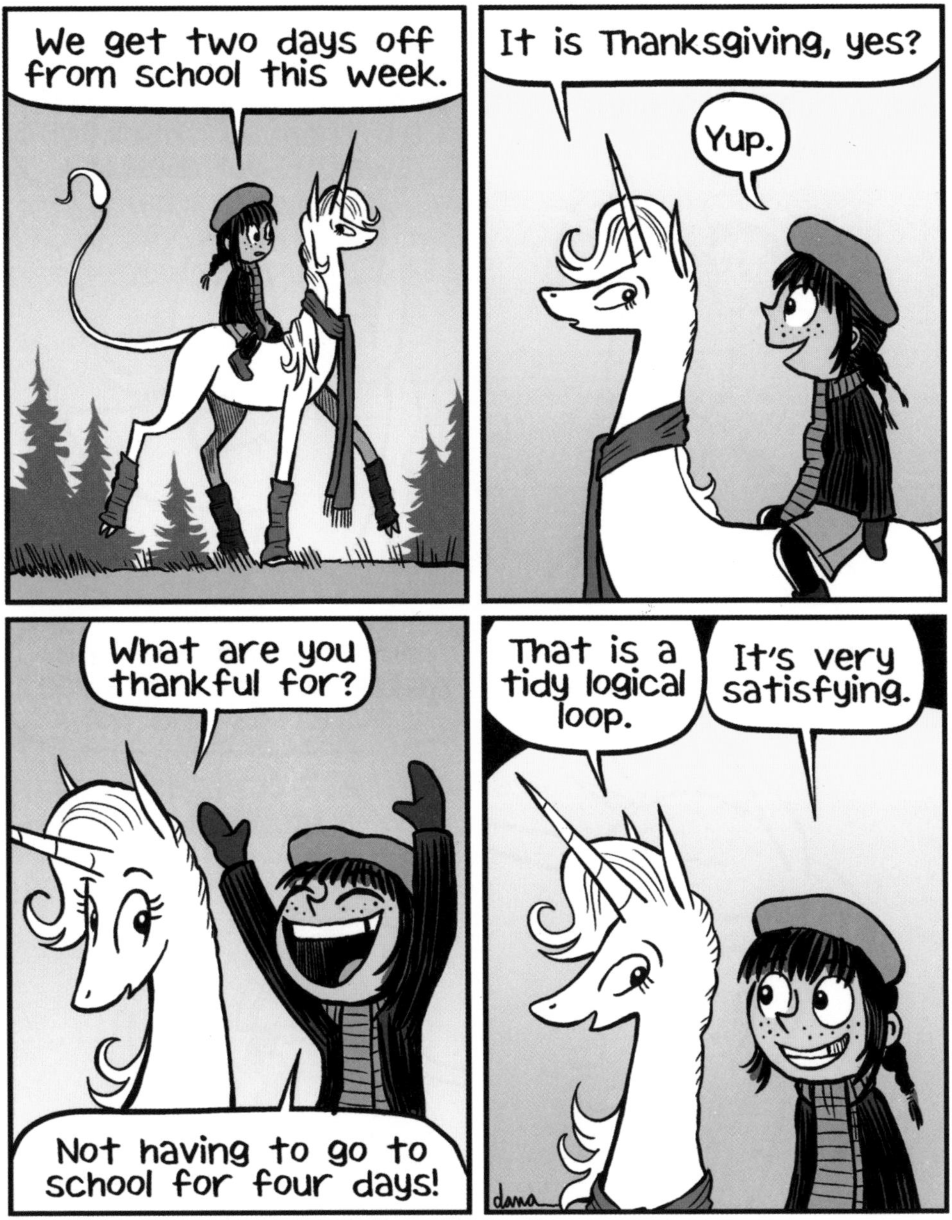
We get two days off from school this week.
It is Thanksgiving, yes?
Yup.
What are you thankful for?
Not having to go to school for four days!
That is a tidy logical loop.
It's very satisfying.
dana

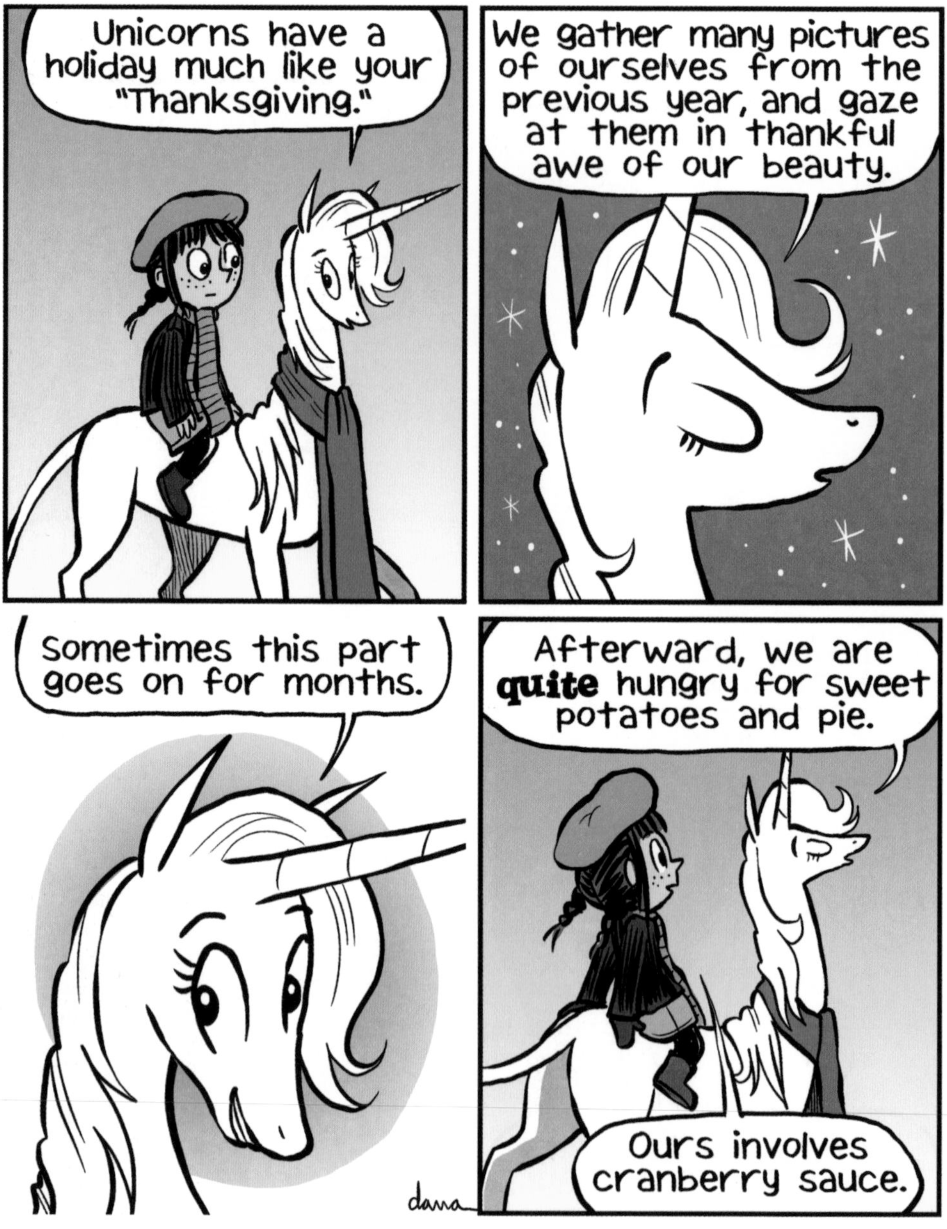
Unicorns have a holiday much like your "Thanksgiving."
We gather many pictures of ourselves from the previous year, and gaze at them in thankful awe of our beauty.
Sometimes this part goes on for months.
Afterward, we are **quite** hungry for sweet potatoes and pie.
Ours involves cranberry sauce.
dana

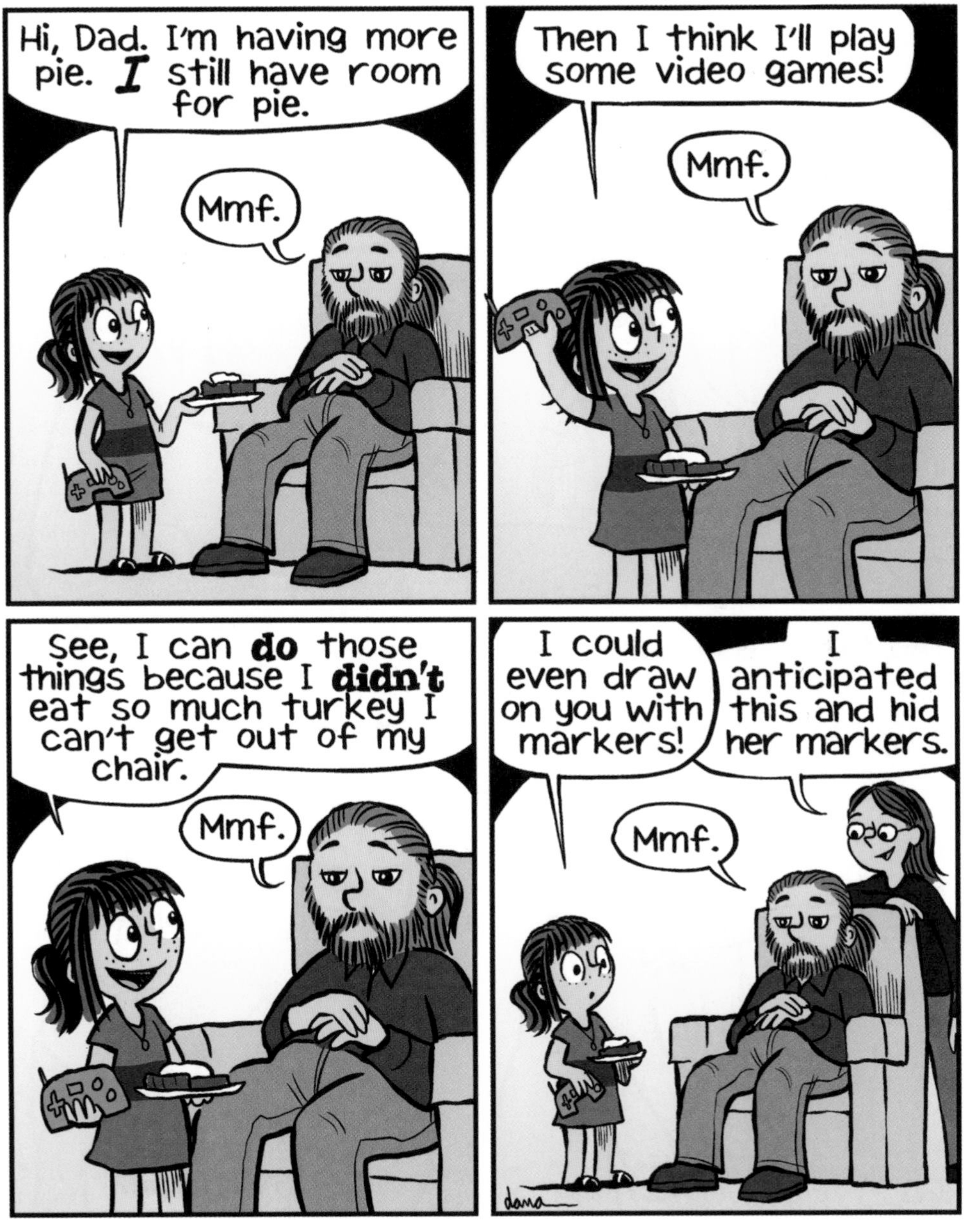
Hi, Dad. I'm having more pie. I still have room for pie.
Mmf.
Then I think I'll play some video games!
Mmf.
See, I can do those things because I didn't eat so much turkey I can't get out of my chair.
Mmf.
I could even draw on you with markers!
I anticipated this and hid her markers.
Mmf.
dana

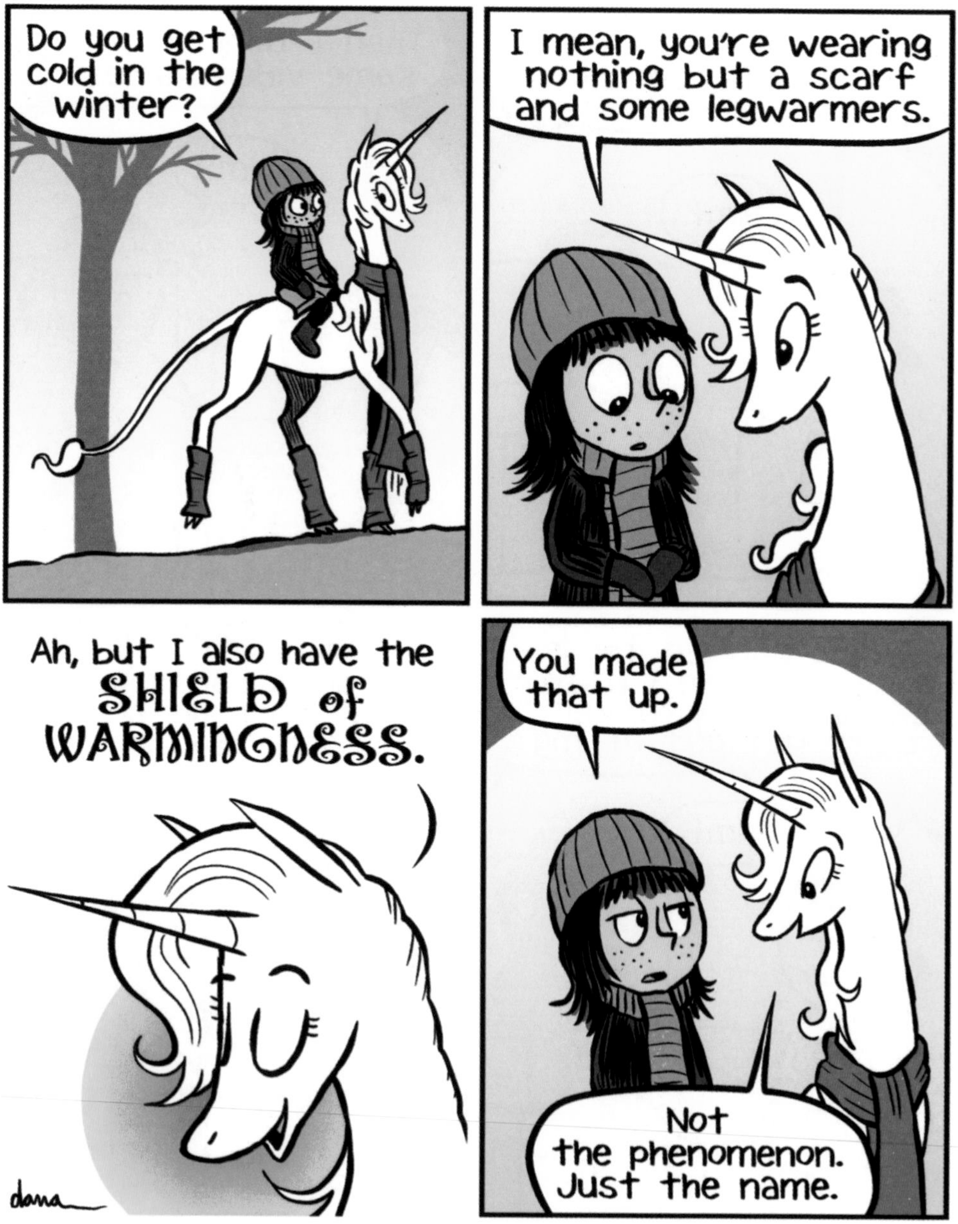
Do you get cold in the winter?
I mean, you're wearing nothing but a scarf and some legwarmers.
Ah, but I also have the SHIELD of WARMINGNESS.
You made that up.
Not the phenomenon. Just the name.
dana

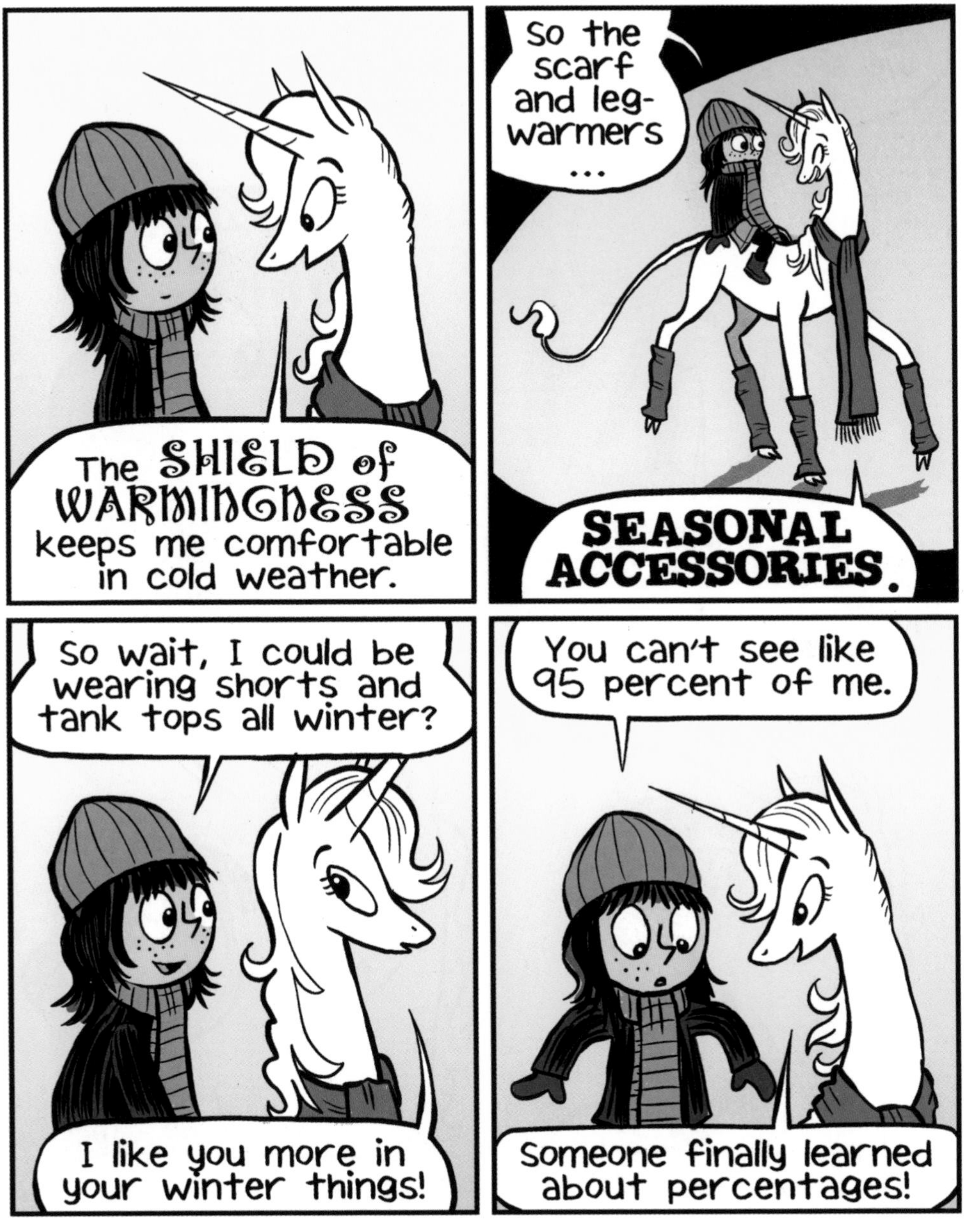
The SHIELD of WARMINGNESS keeps me comfortable in cold weather.
So the scarf and leg-warmers ...
SEASONAL ACCESSORIES.
So wait, I could be wearing shorts and tank tops all winter?
I like you more in your winter things!
You can't see like 95 percent of me.
Someone finally learned about percentages!

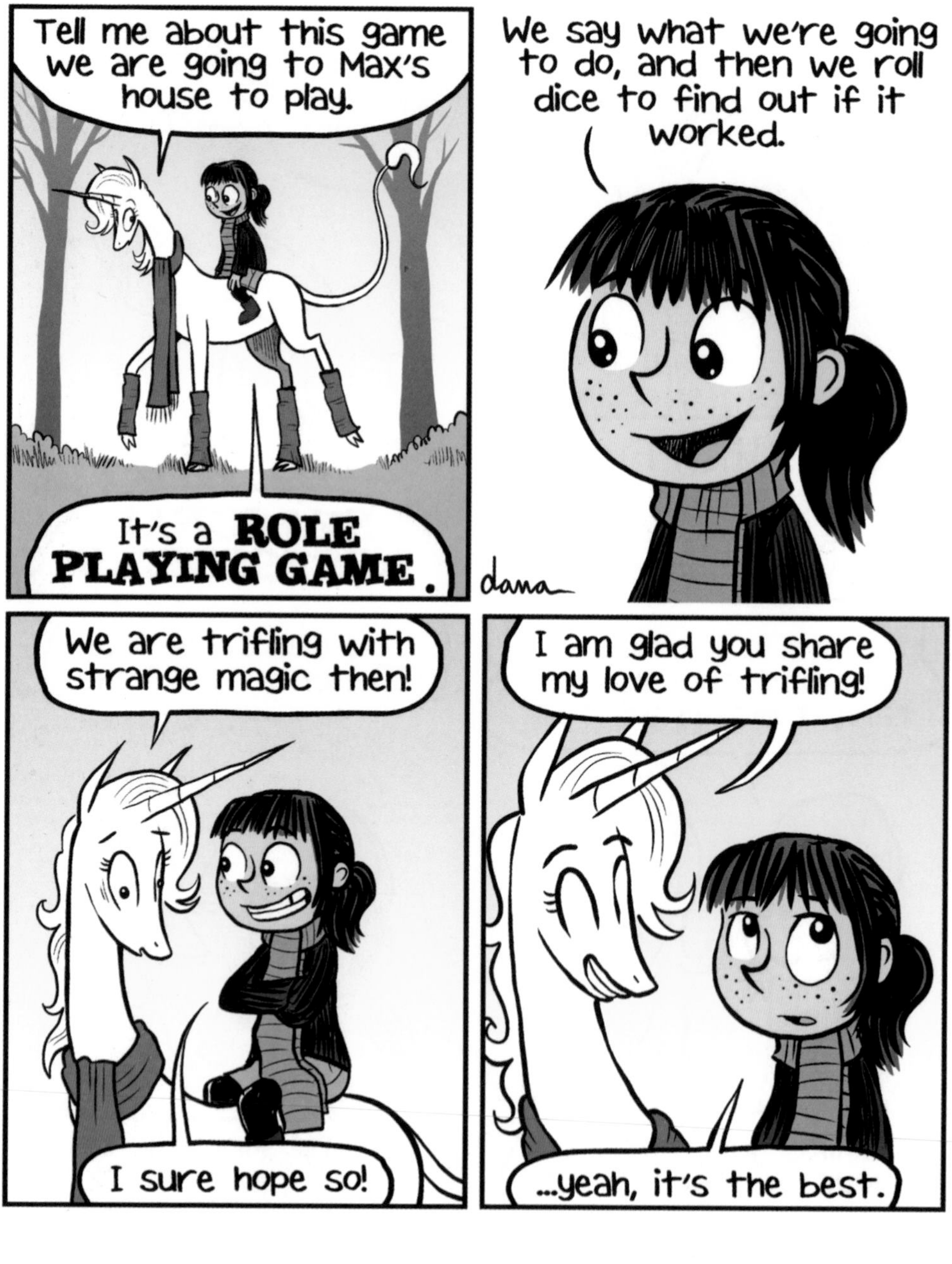
Tell me about this game we are going to Max's house to play.
It's a **ROLE PLAYING GAME**.
We say what we're going to do, and then we roll dice to find out if it worked.
dana
We are trifling with strange magic then!
I sure hope so!
I am glad you share my love of trifling!
...yeah, it's the best.

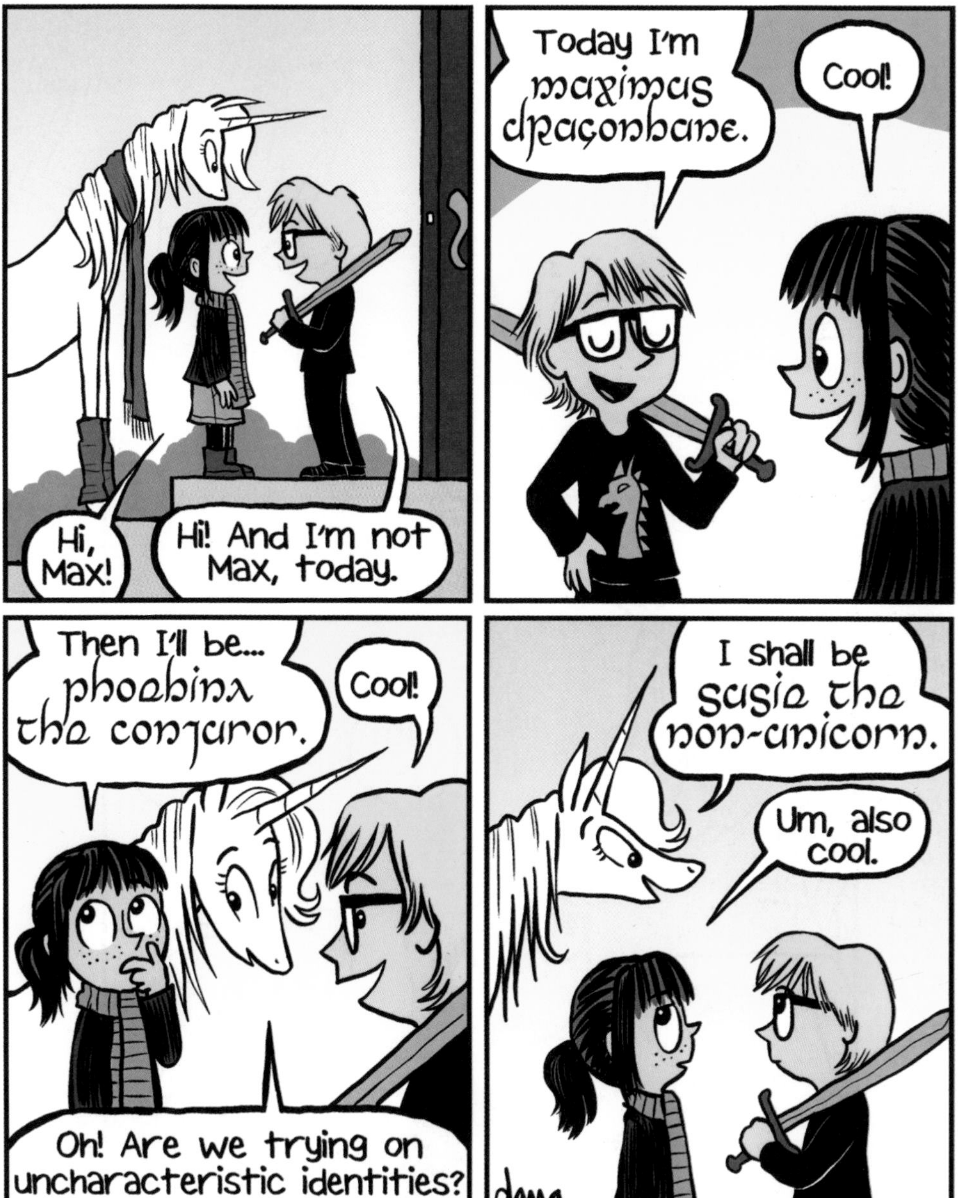
Hi, Max!
Hi! And I'm not Max, today.
Today I'm maximus dragonbane.
Cool!
Then I'll be... phoebina the conjuror.
Cool!
Oh! Are we trying on uncharacteristic identities?
I shall be susie the non-unicorn.
Um, also cool.
dana

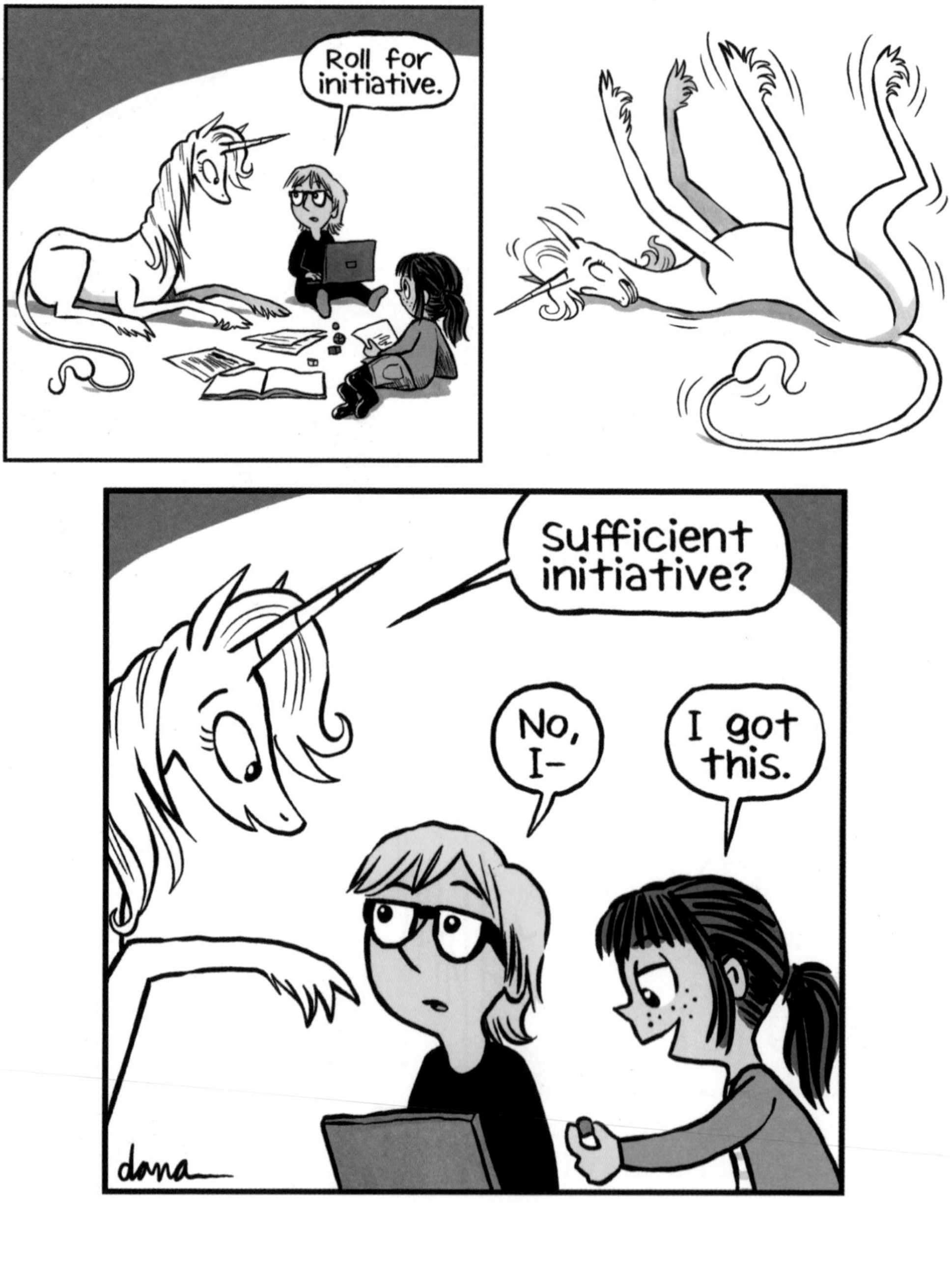
Roll for initiative.
Sufficient initiative?
No, I-
I got this.
dana

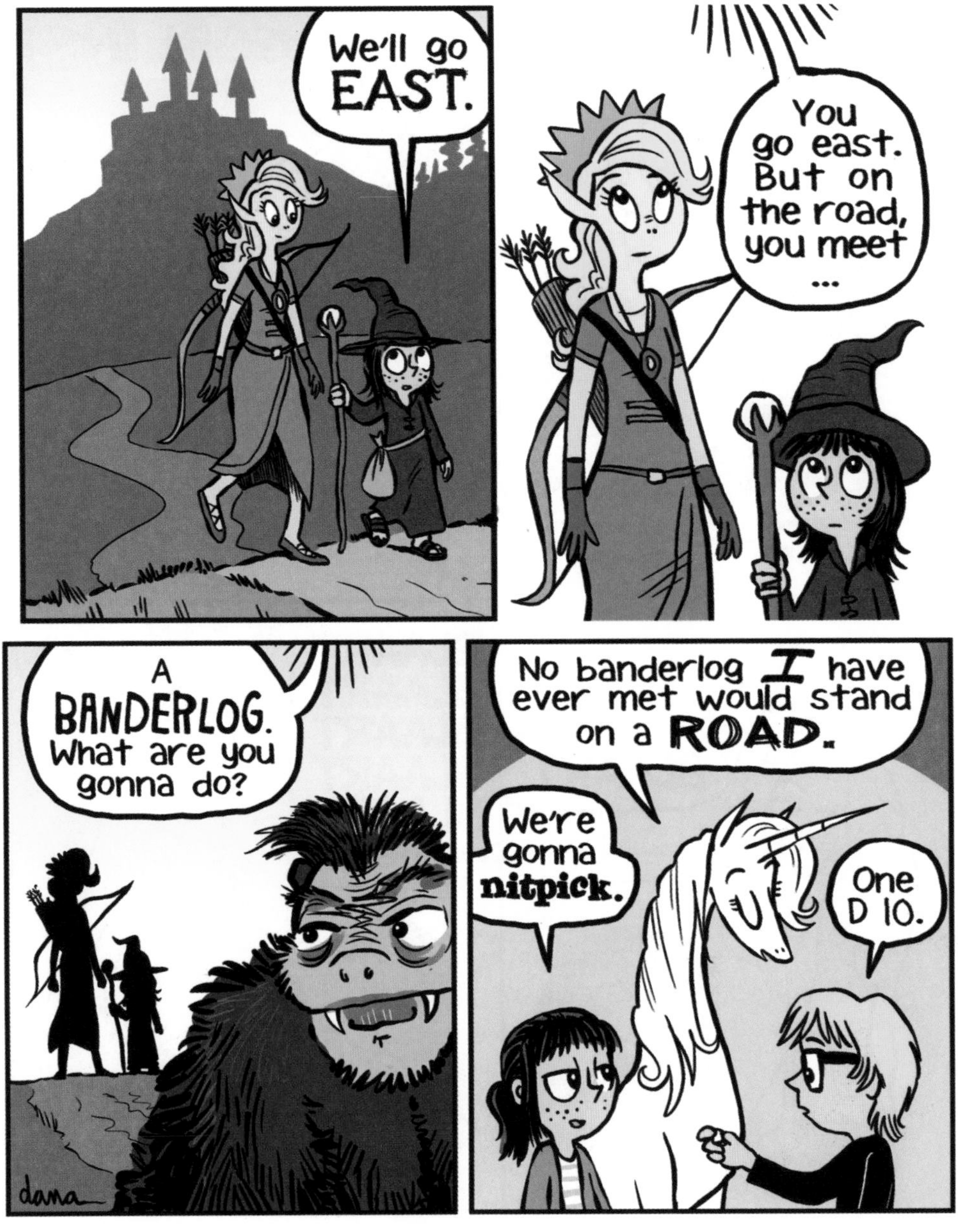
We'll go EAST.
You go east. But on the road, you meet ...
A BANDERLOG. What are you gonna do?
dana
No banderlog I have ever met would stand on a ROAD.
We're gonna nitpick.
One D 10.

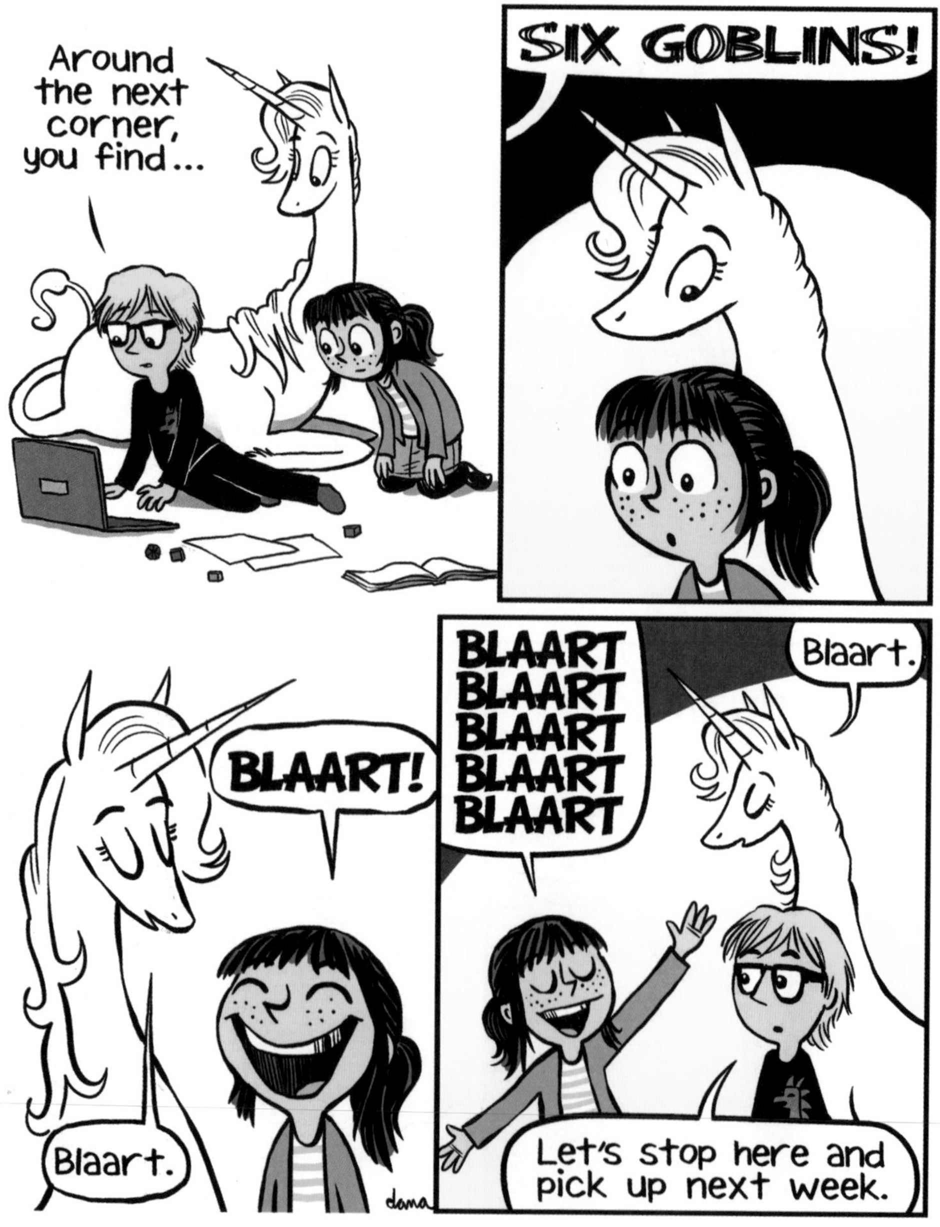
Around the next corner, you find...
SIX GOBLINS!
BLAART!
Blaart.
BLAART BLAART BLAART BLAART BLAART
Blaart.
Let's stop here and pick up next week.
dana

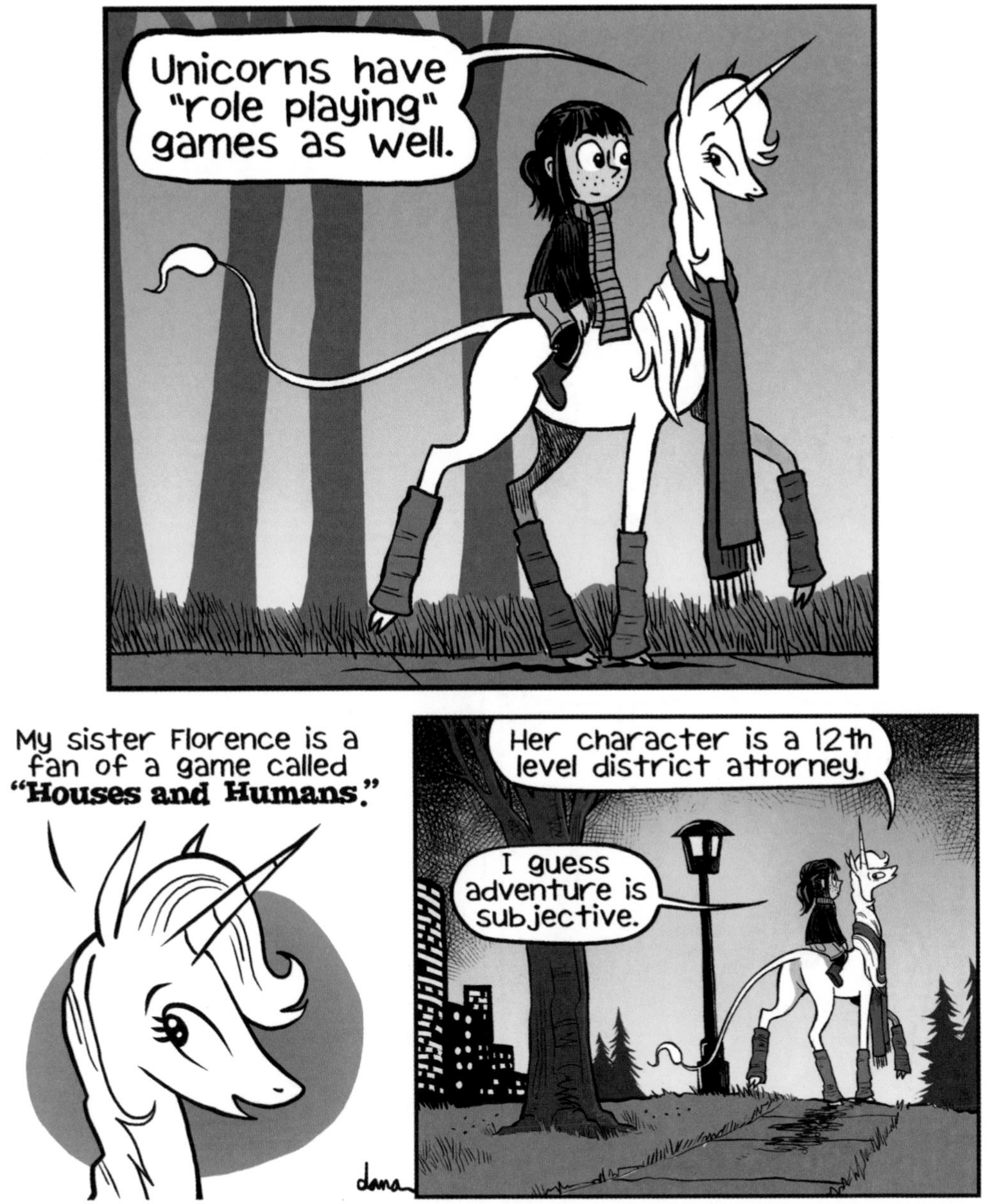
Unicorns have "role playing" games as well.
My sister Florence is a fan of a game called "Houses and Humans."
Her character is a 12th level district attorney.
I guess adventure is subjective.
dana

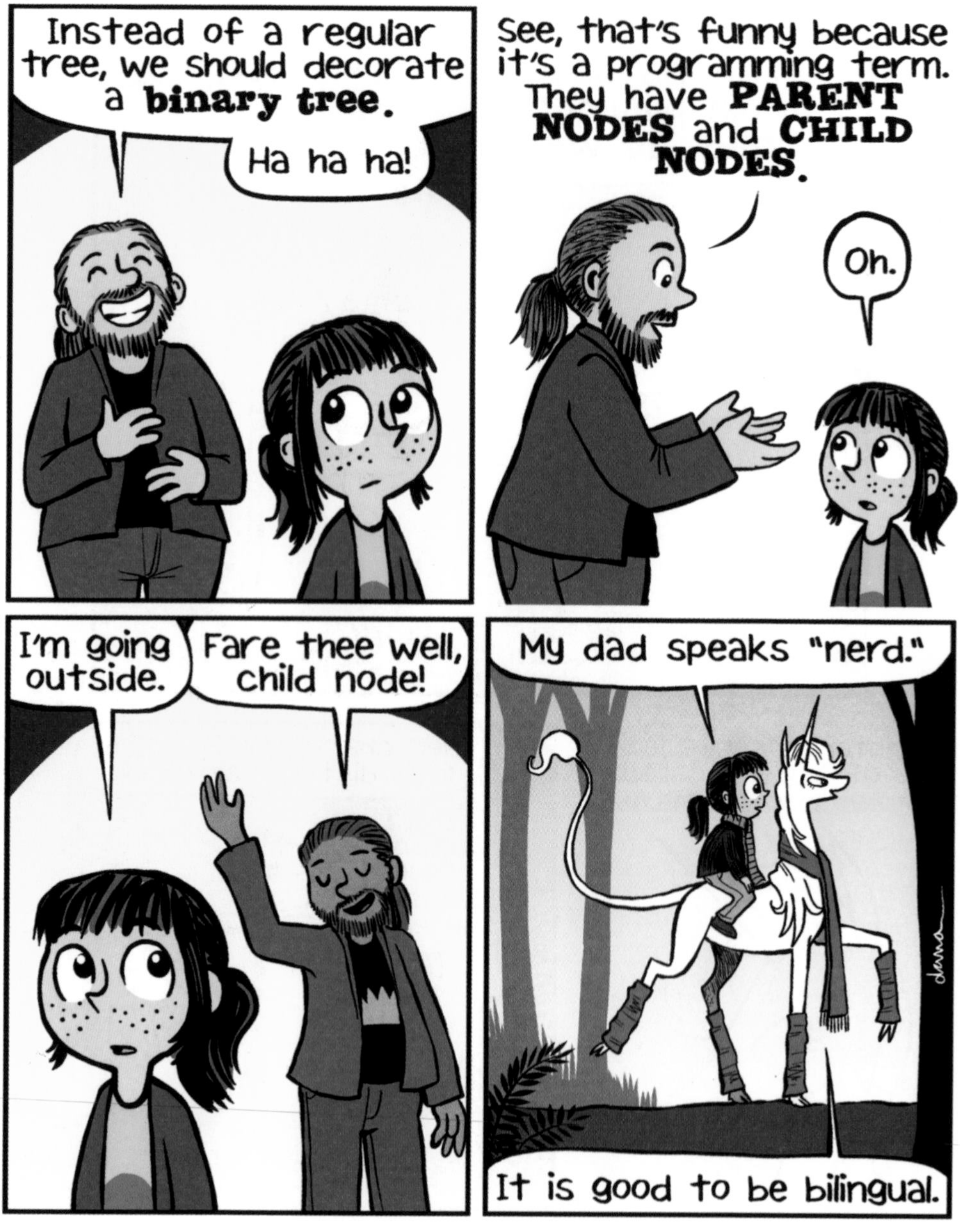
Instead of a regular tree, we should decorate a **binary tree**.
Ha ha ha!
See, that's funny because it's a programming term. They have **PARENT NODES** and **CHILD NODES**.
Oh.
I'm going outside.
Fare thee well, child node!
My dad speaks "nerd."
It is good to be bilingual.

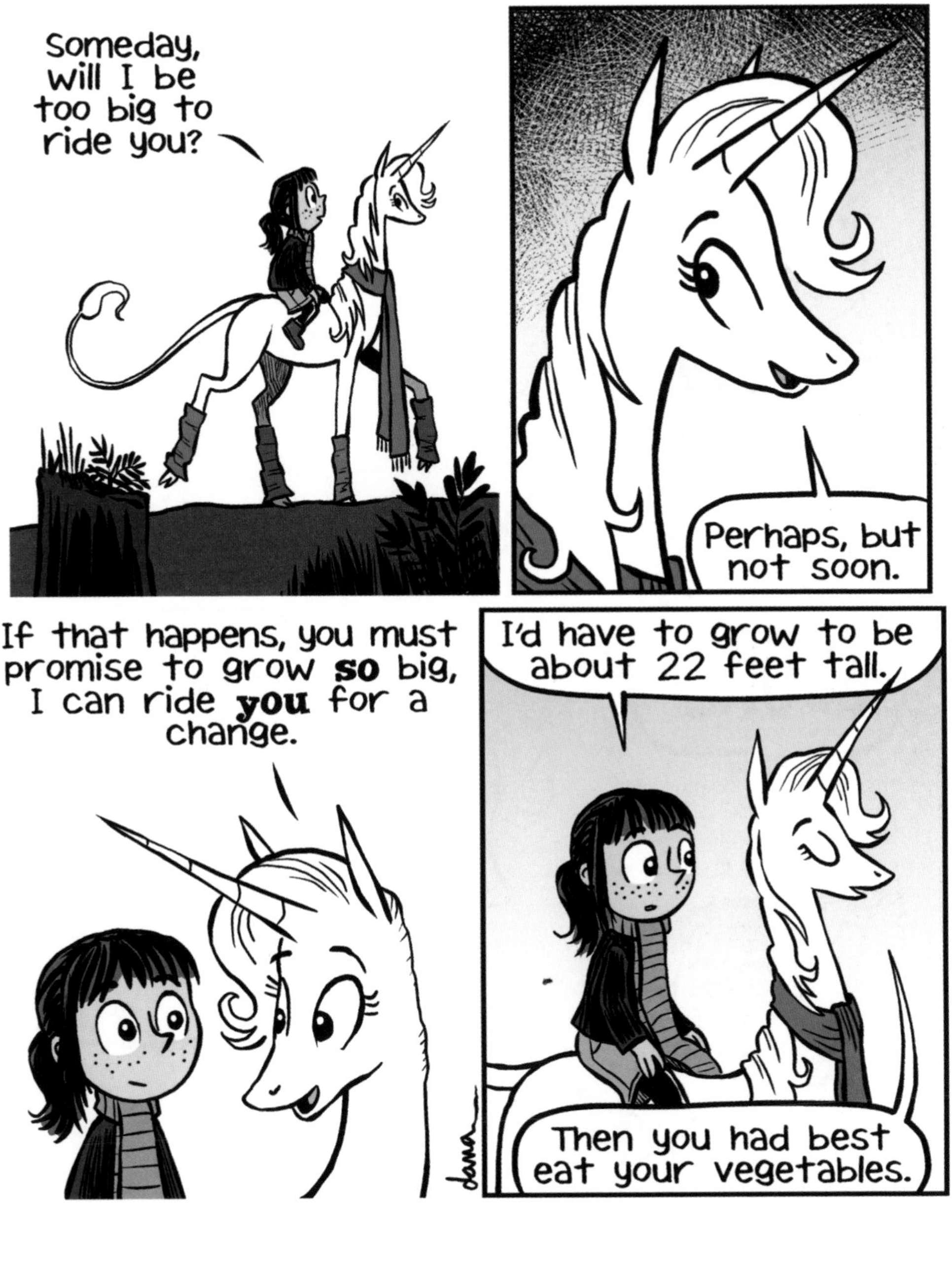
Someday, will I be too big to ride you?
Perhaps, but not soon.
If that happens, you must promise to grow **so** big, I can ride **you** for a change.
I'd have to grow to be about 22 feet tall.
Then you had best eat your vegetables.
dana

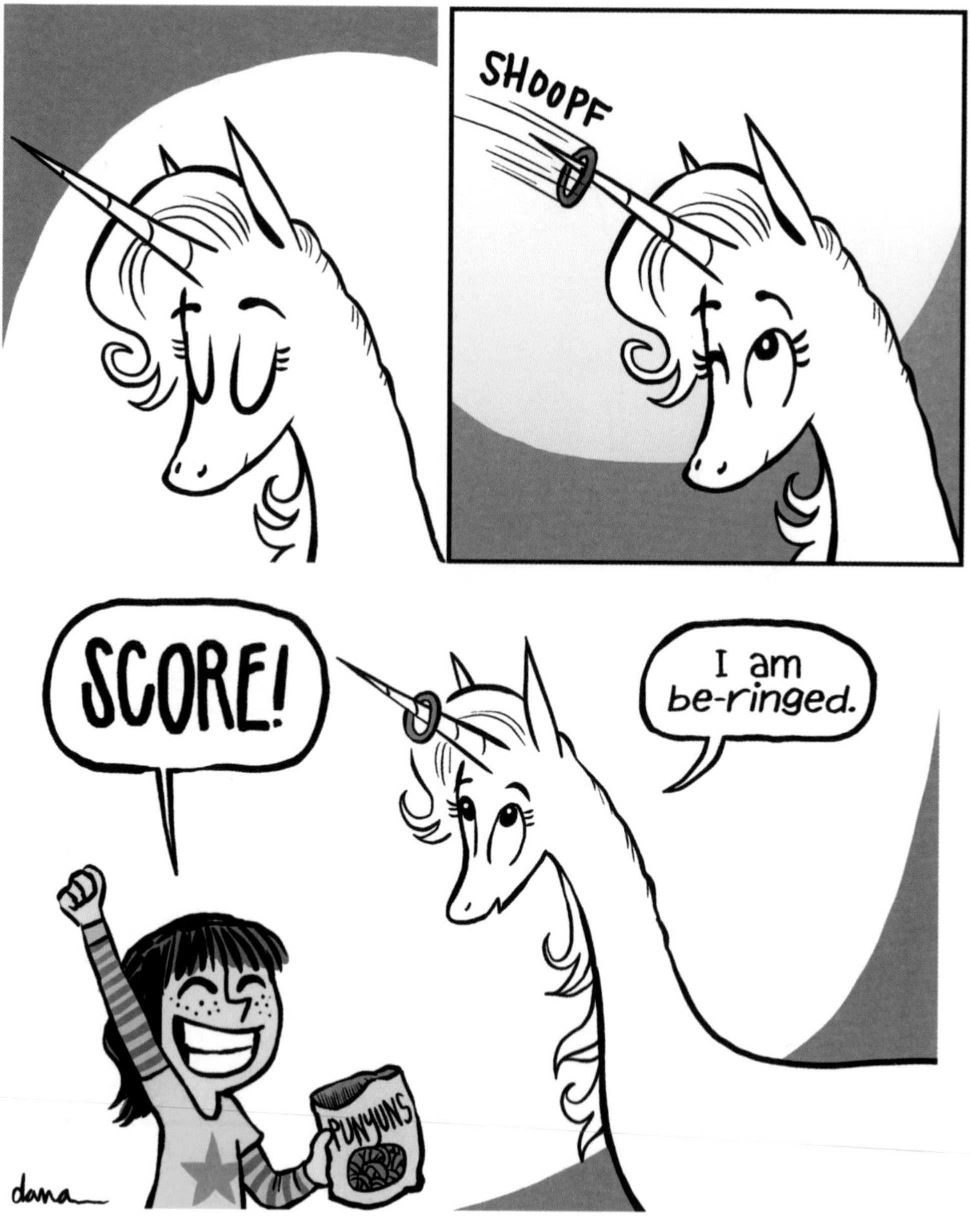
SHOOPF
SCORE!
I am be-ringed.
PUNYUNS
dana

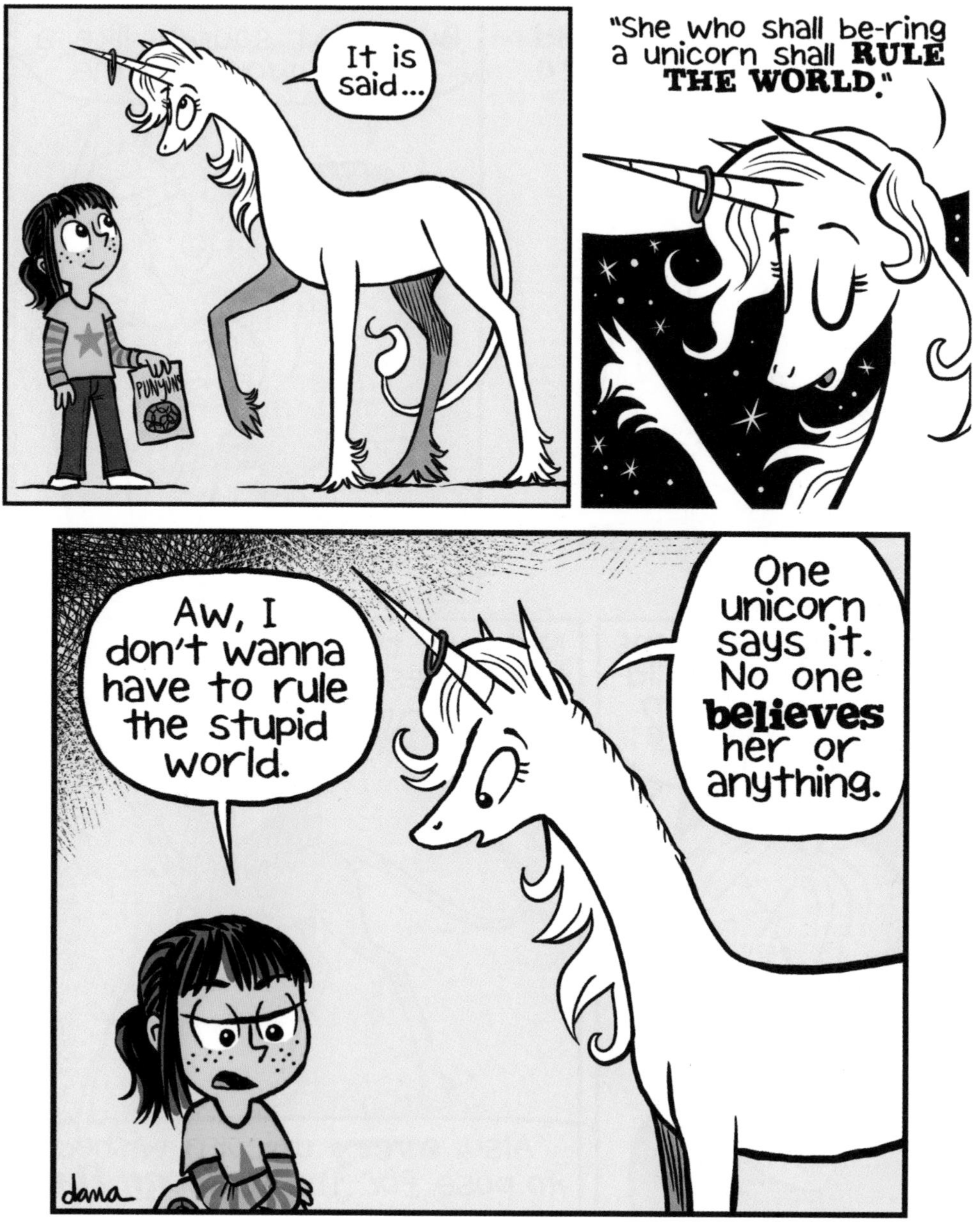
It is said...
"She who shall be-ring a unicorn shall **RULE THE WORLD.**"
Aw, I don't wanna have to rule the stupid world.
One unicorn says it. No one **believes** her or anything.
dana

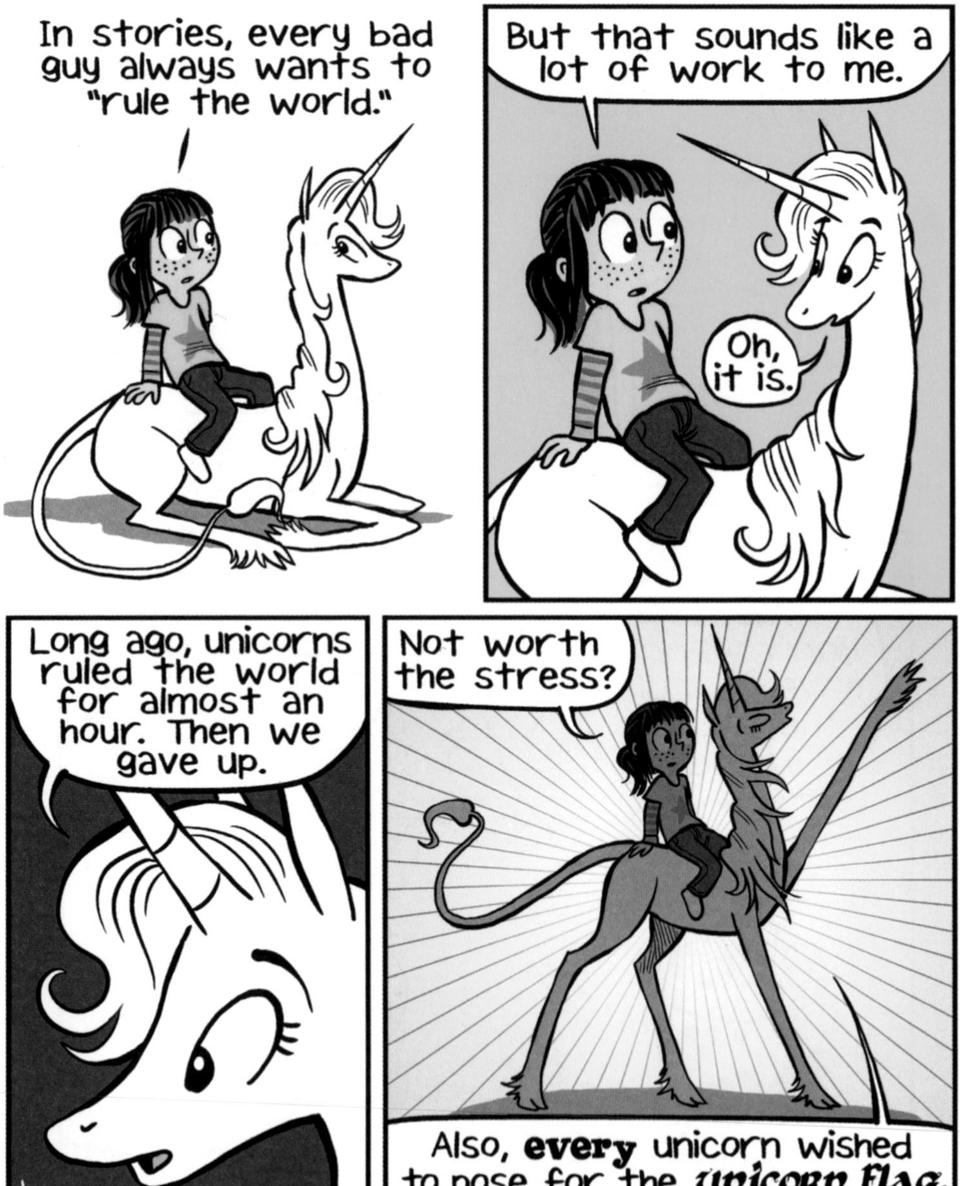
In stories, every bad guy always wants to "rule the world."
But that sounds like a lot of work to me.
Oh, it is.
Long ago, unicorns ruled the world for almost an hour. Then we gave up.
dana
Not worth the stress?
Also, **every** unicorn wished to pose for the *unicorn flag.*

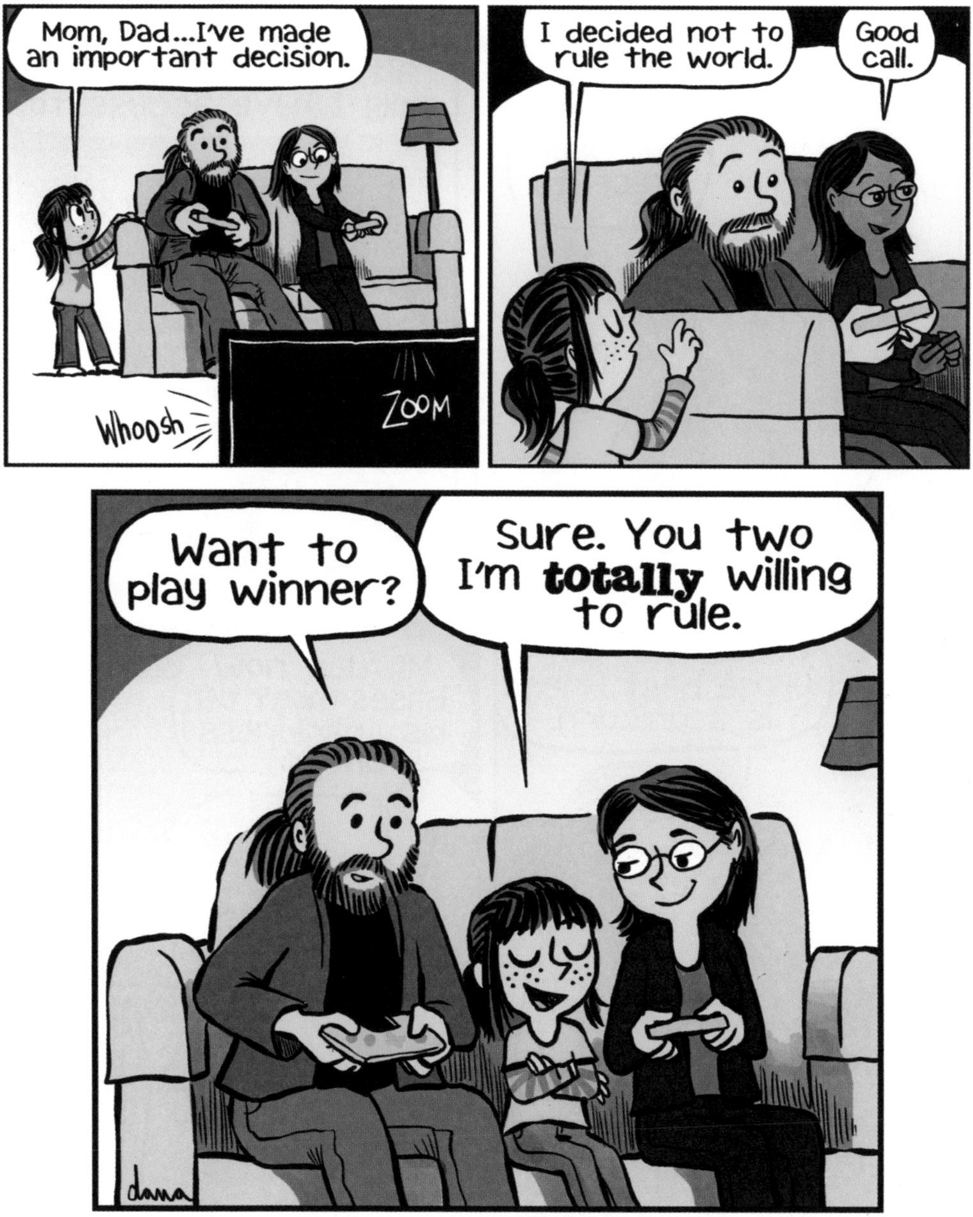
Mom, Dad...I've made an important decision.
Whoosh
ZOOM
I decided not to rule the world.
Good call.
Want to play winner?
Sure. You two I'm **totally** willing to rule.
dana

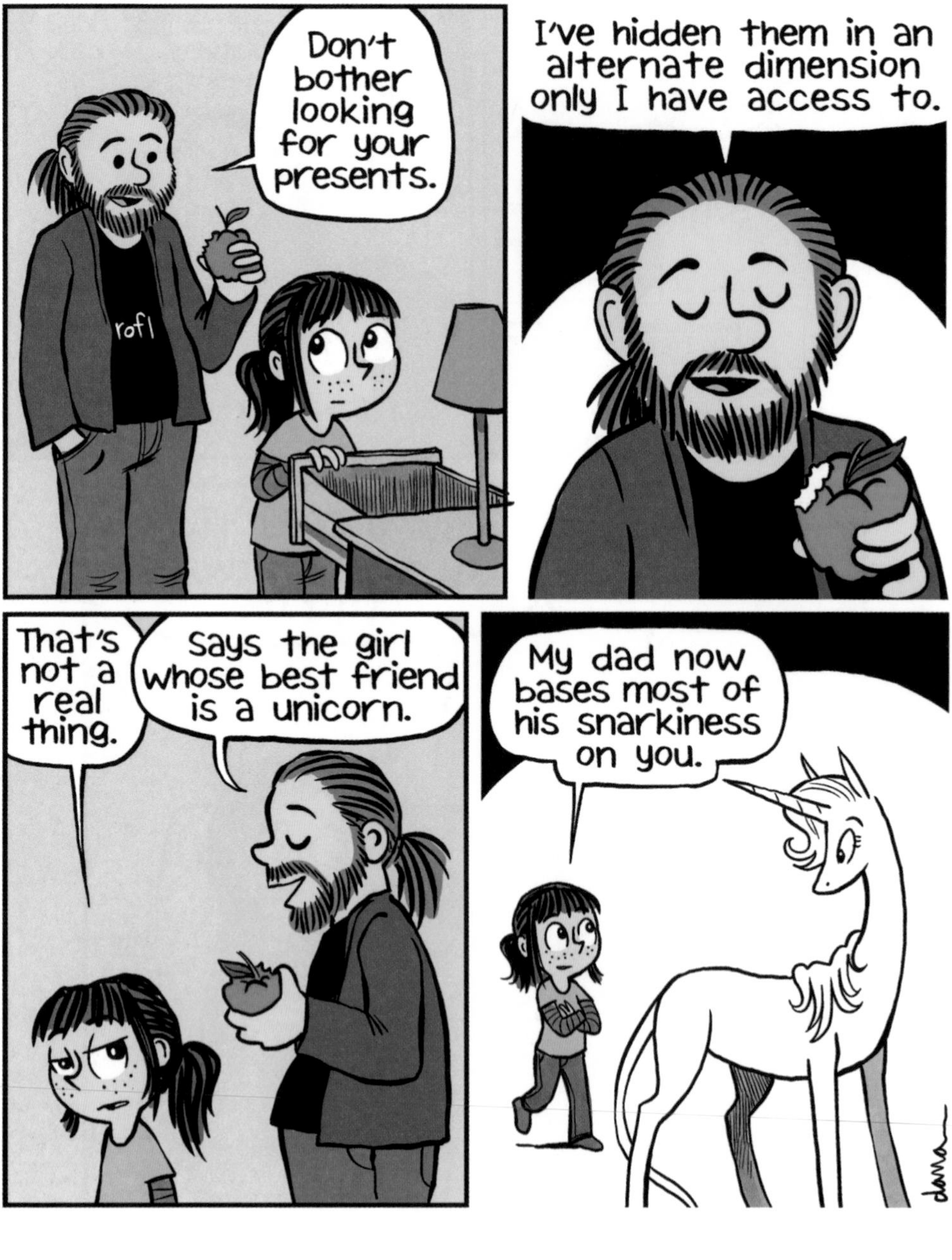
Don't bother looking for your presents.
rofl
I've hidden them in an alternate dimension only I have access to.
That's not a real thing.
Says the girl whose best friend is a unicorn.
My dad now bases most of his snarkiness on you.
dana

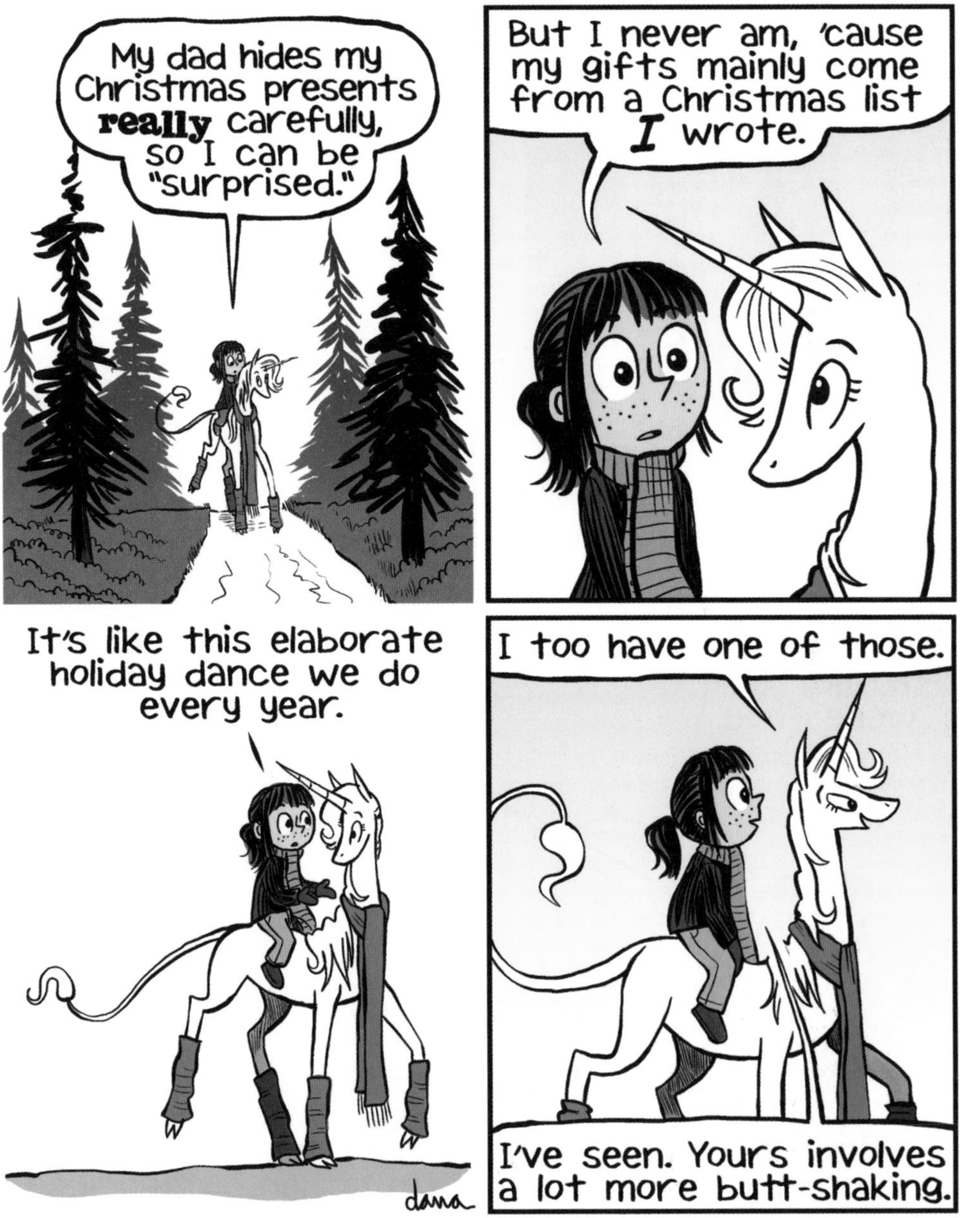
My dad hides my Christmas presents **really** carefully, so I can be "surprised."
But I never am, 'cause my gifts mainly come from a Christmas list *I* wrote.
It's like this elaborate holiday dance we do every year.
I too have one of those.
I've seen. Yours involves a lot more butt-shaking.
dana

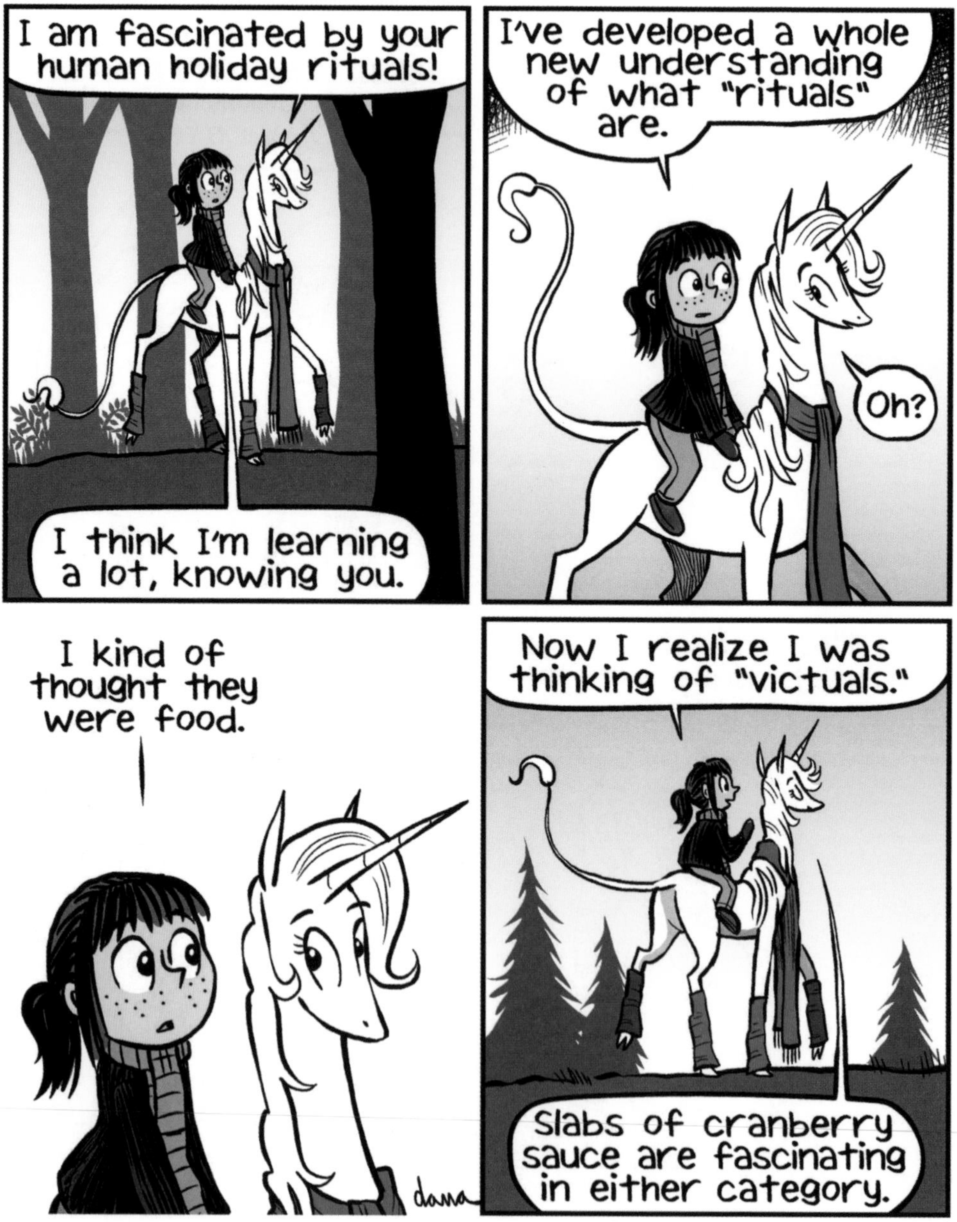
I am fascinated by your human holiday rituals!
I think I'm learning a lot, knowing you.
I've developed a whole new understanding of what "rituals" are.
Oh?
I kind of thought they were food.
Now I realize I was thinking of "victuals."
Slabs of cranberry sauce are fascinating in either category.
dana

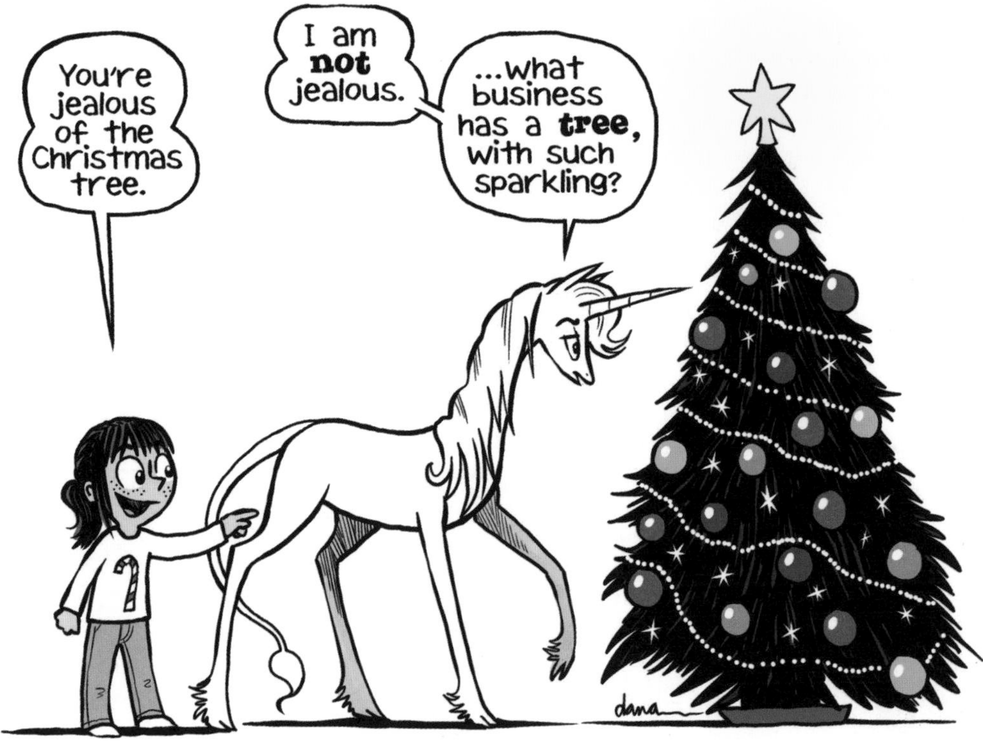
You're jealous of the Christmas tree.
I am **not** jealous.
...what business has a **tree**, with such sparkling?
dana

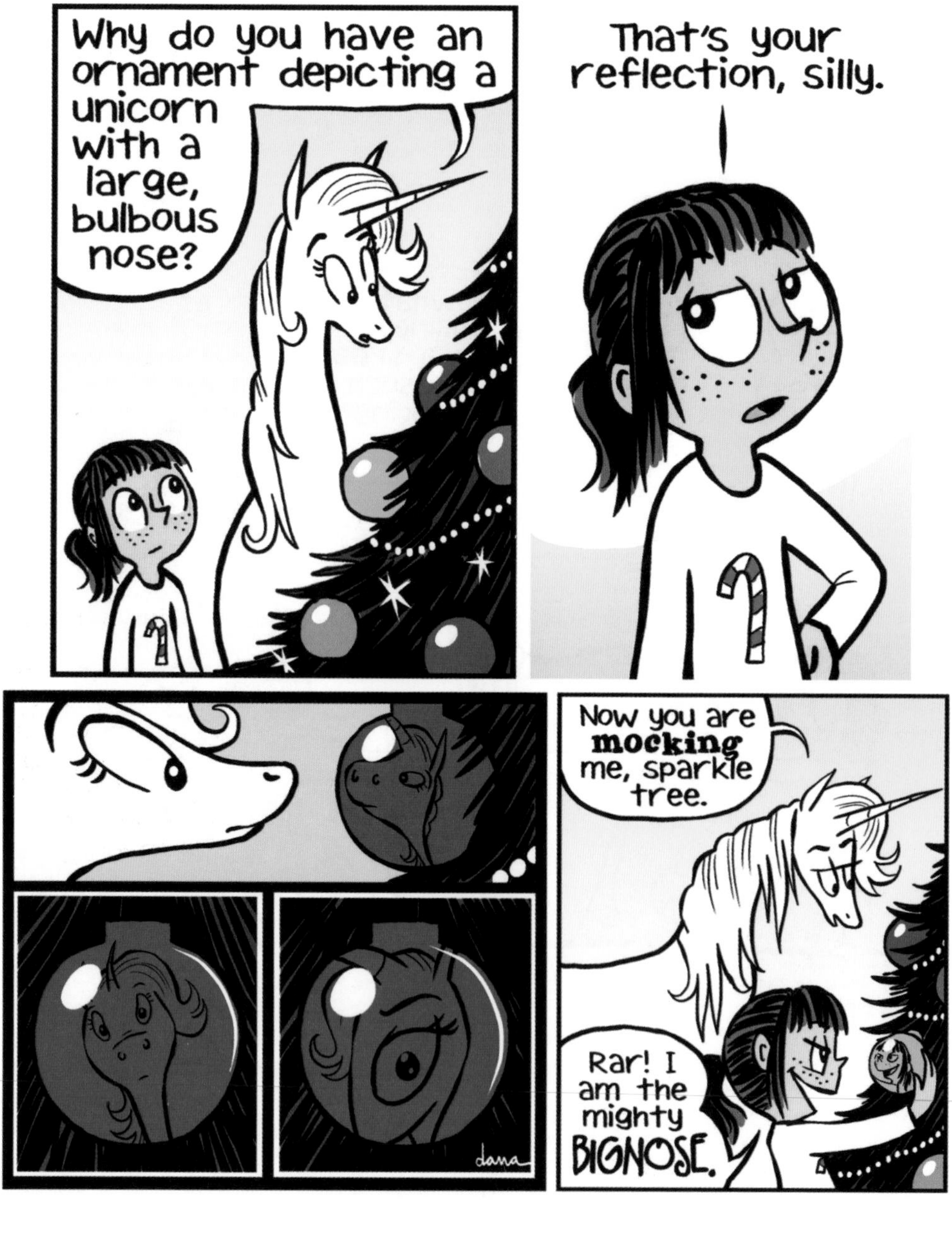

Why do you have an ornament depicting a unicorn with a large, bulbous nose?
That's your reflection, silly.
Now you are **mocking** me, sparkle tree.
Rar! I am the mighty BIGNOSE.
dana

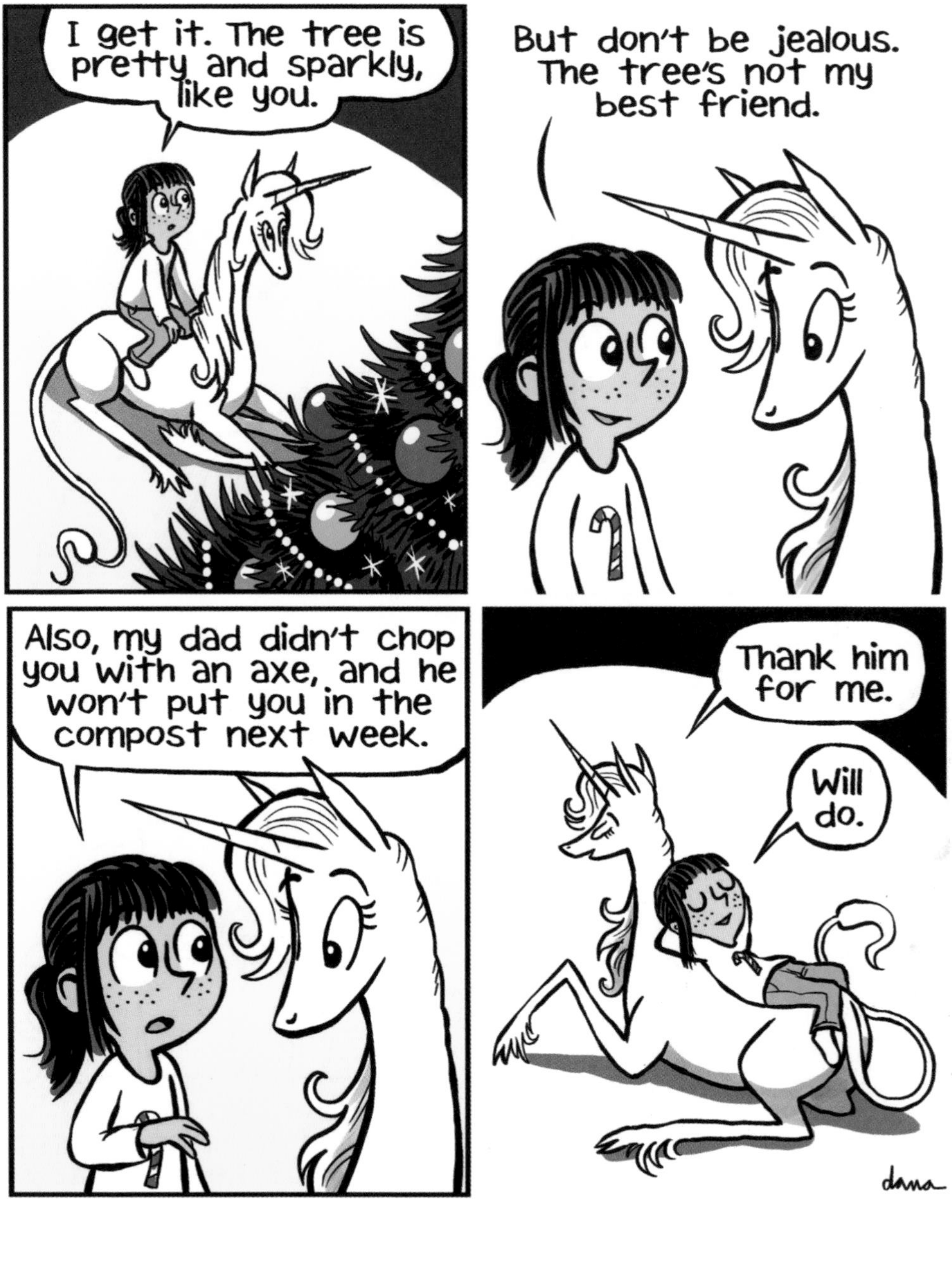

I get it. The tree is pretty and sparkly, like you.
But don't be jealous. The tree's not my best friend.
Also, my dad didn't chop you with an axe, and he won't put you in the compost next week.
Thank him for me.
Will do.
dana

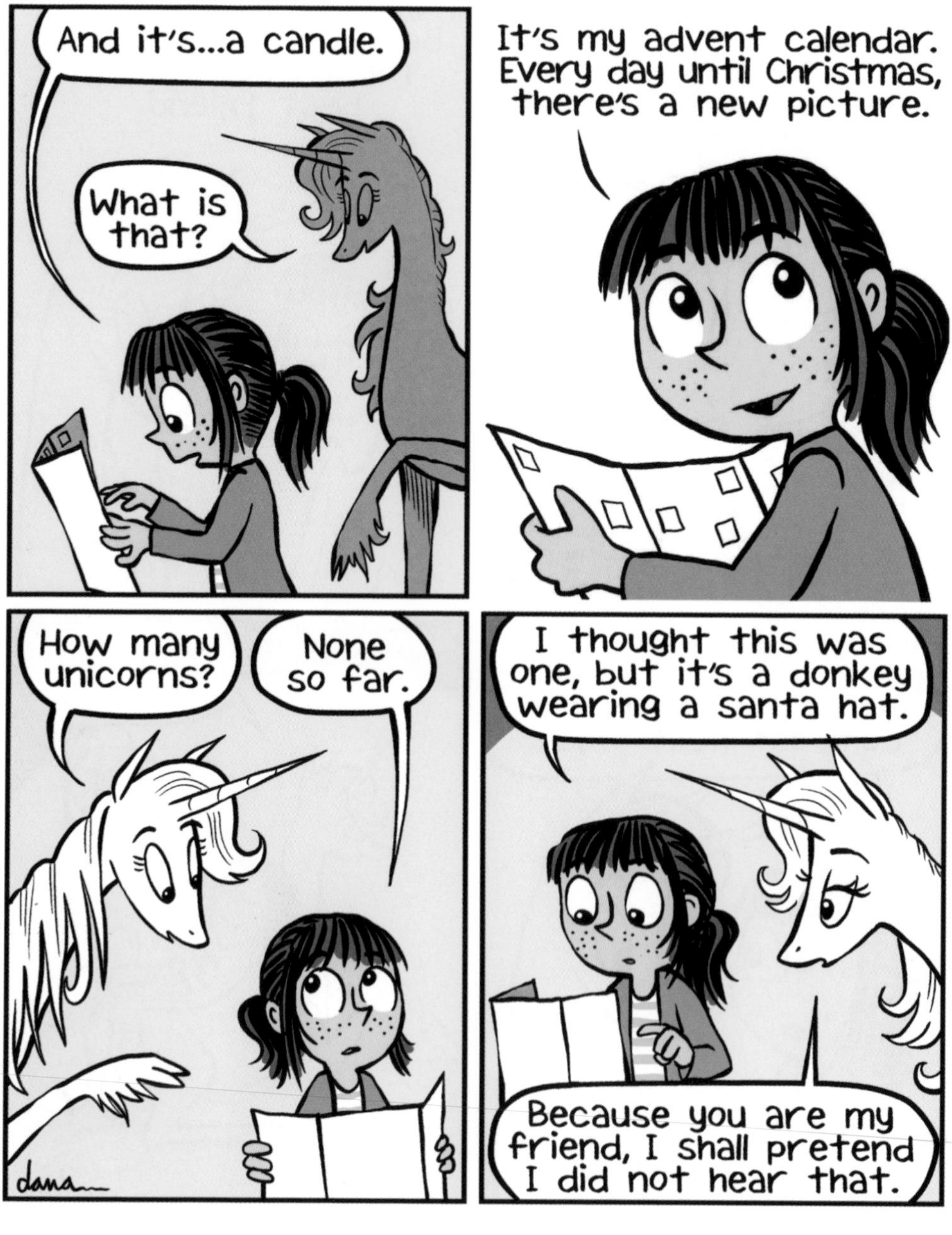
And it's...a candle.
What is that?
It's my advent calendar. Every day until Christmas, there's a new picture.
How many unicorns?
None so far.
dana
I thought this was one, but it's a donkey wearing a santa hat.
Because you are my friend, I shall pretend I did not hear that.

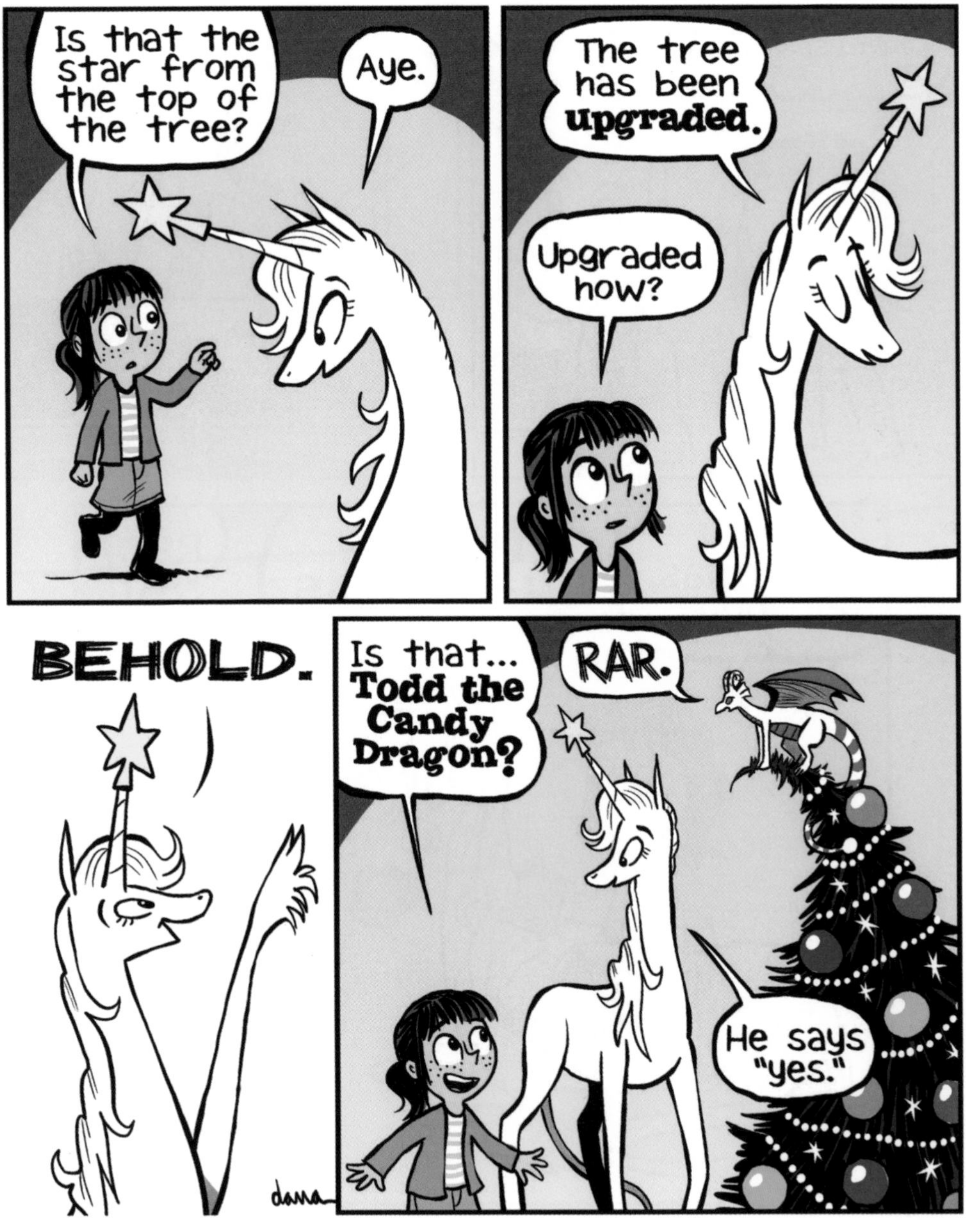
Is that the star from the top of the tree?
Aye.
The tree has been **upgraded**.
Upgraded how?
BEHOLD.
Is that... **Todd the Candy Dragon?**
RAR.
He says "yes."
dana

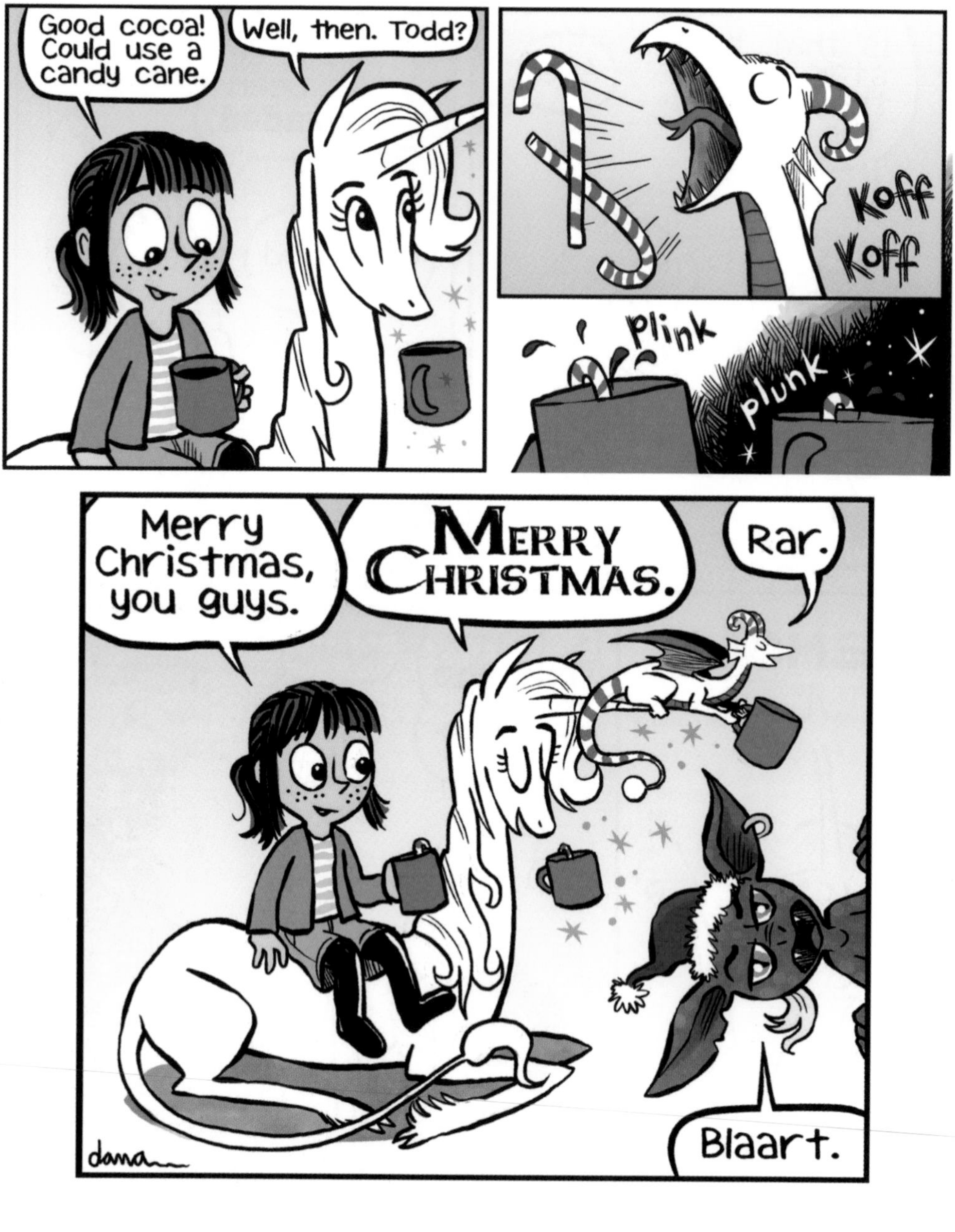
Good cocoa! Could use a candy cane.
Well, then. Todd?
Koff Koff
plink
plunk
Merry Christmas, you guys.
MERRY CHRISTMAS.
Rar.
Blaart.
dana

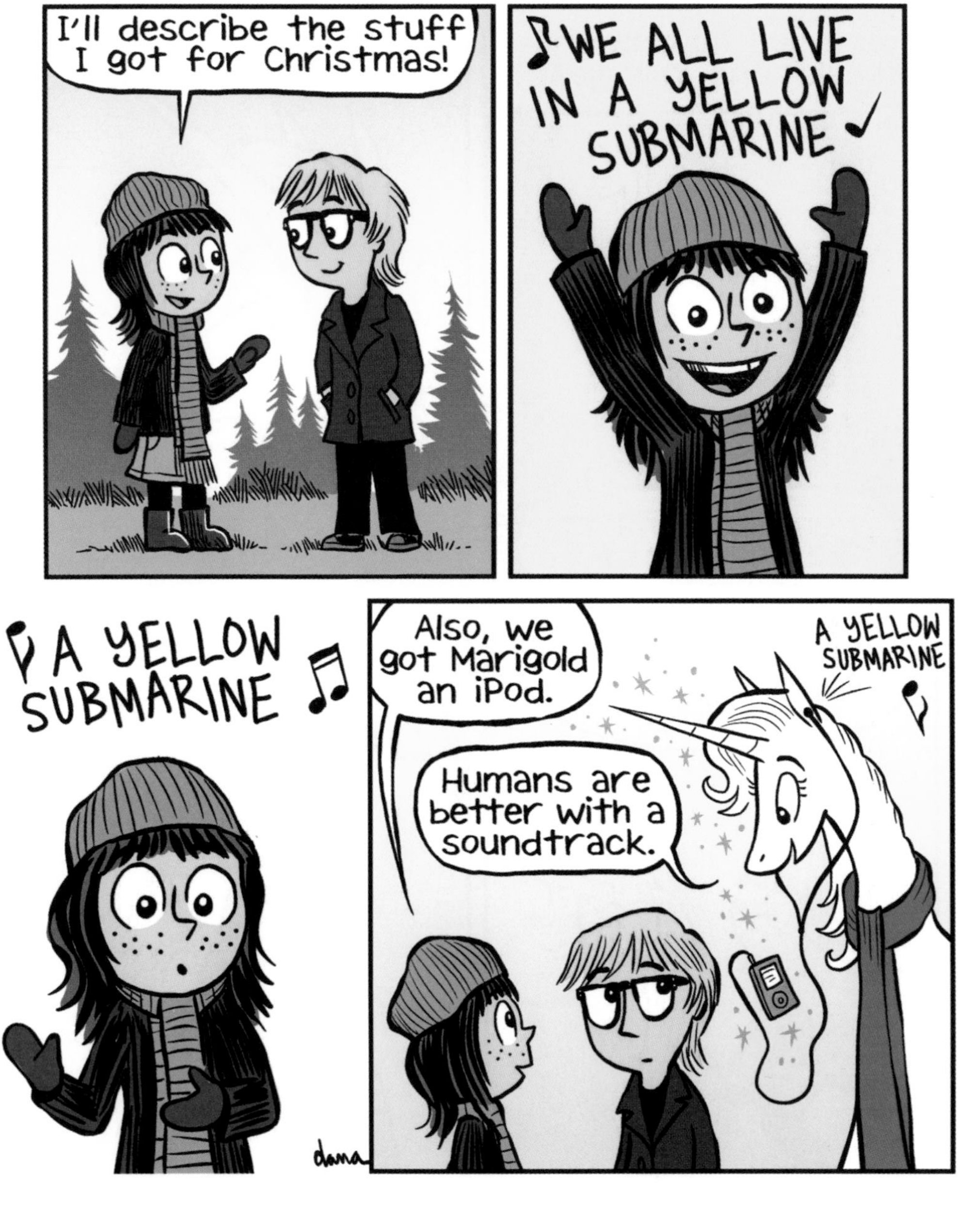
I'll describe the stuff I got for Christmas!
WE ALL LIVE IN A YELLOW SUBMARINE
A YELLOW SUBMARINE
Also, we got Marigold an iPod.
A YELLOW SUBMARINE
Humans are better with a soundtrack.
dana

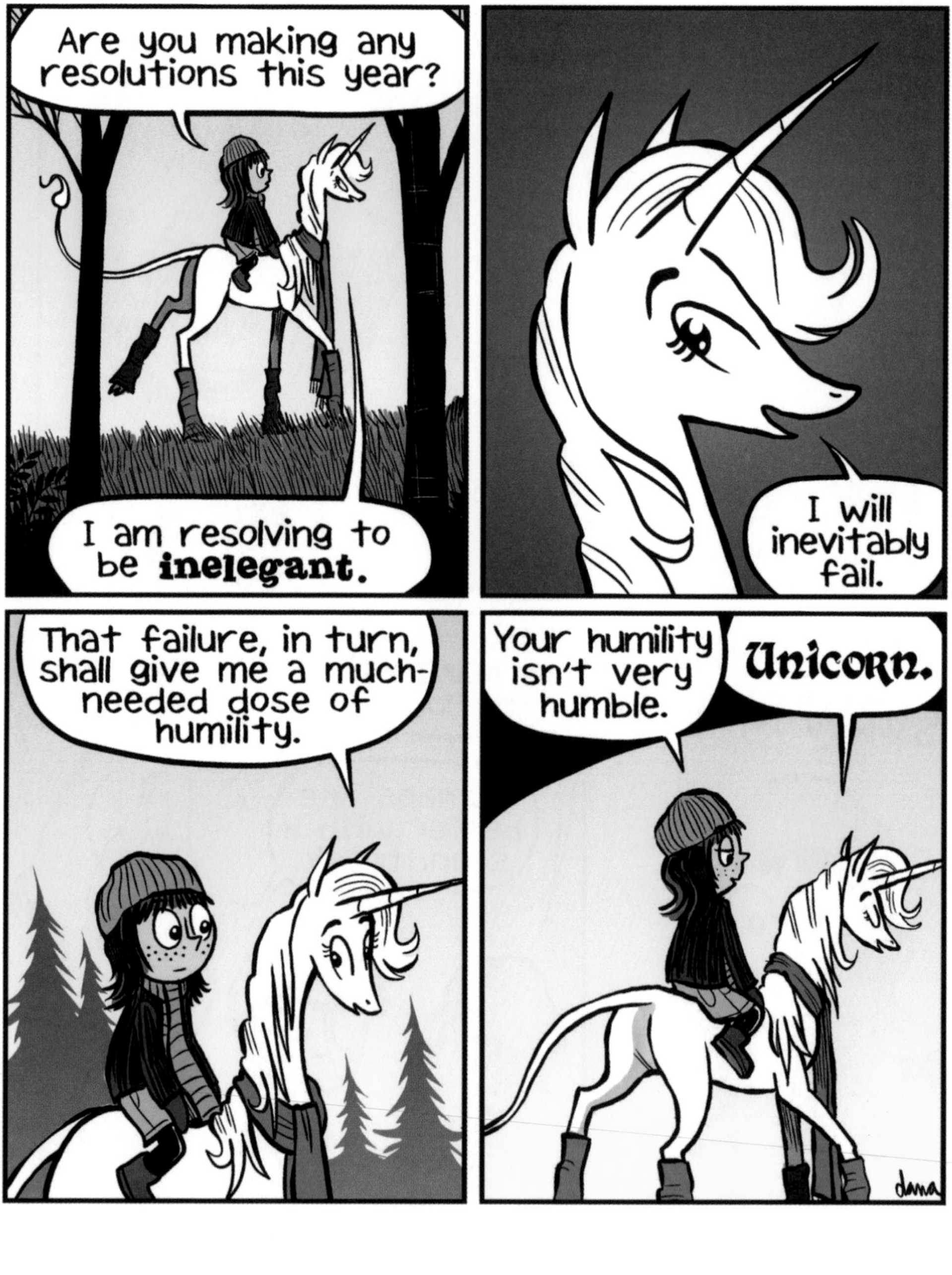
Are you making any resolutions this year?
I am resolving to be **inelegant.**
I will inevitably fail.
That failure, in turn, shall give me a much-needed dose of humility.
Your humility isn't very humble.
Unicorn.
dana

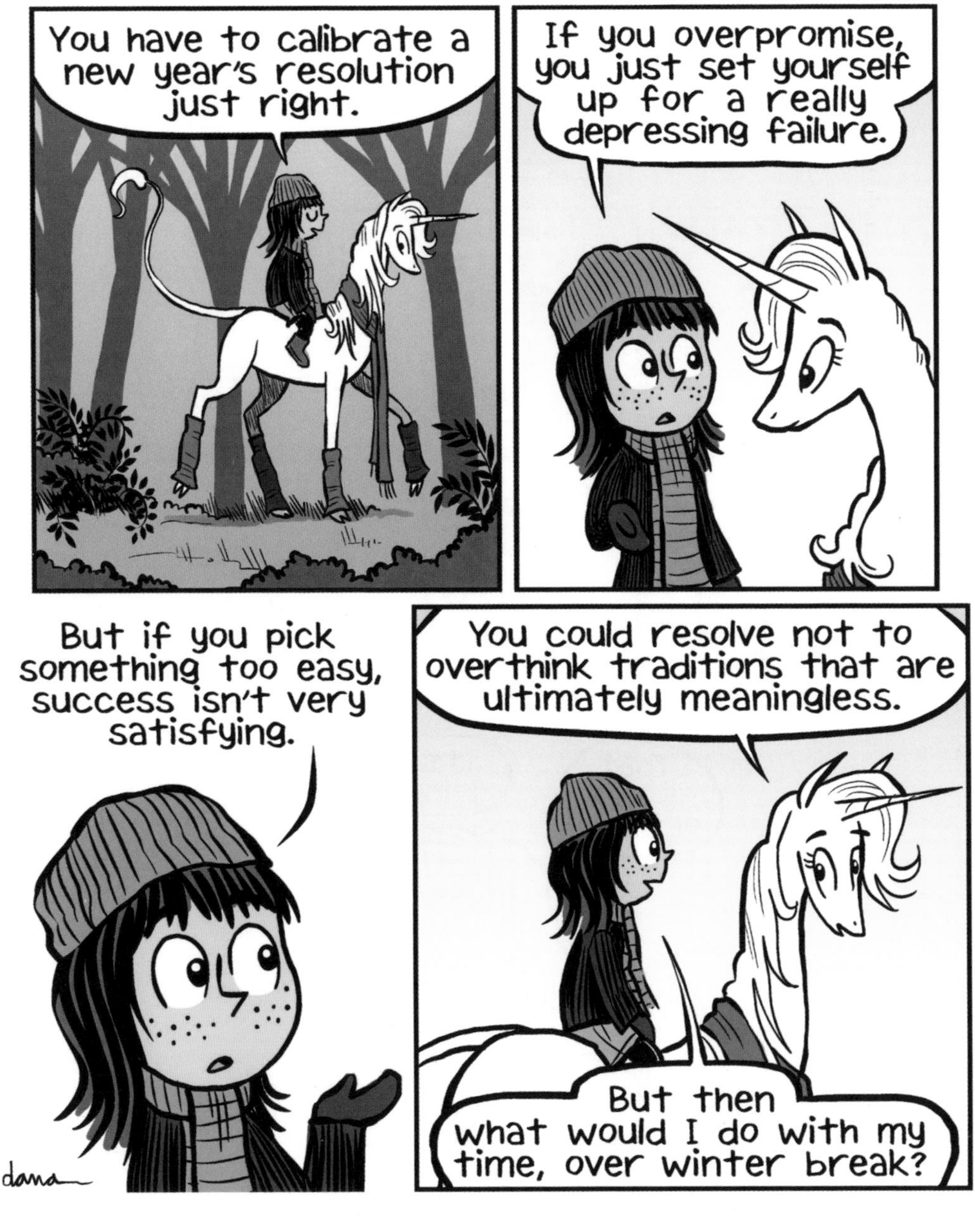
You have to calibrate a new year's resolution just right.
If you overpromise, you just set yourself up for a really depressing failure.
But if you pick something too easy, success isn't very satisfying.
You could resolve not to overthink traditions that are ultimately meaningless.
But then what would I do with my time, over winter break?
dana

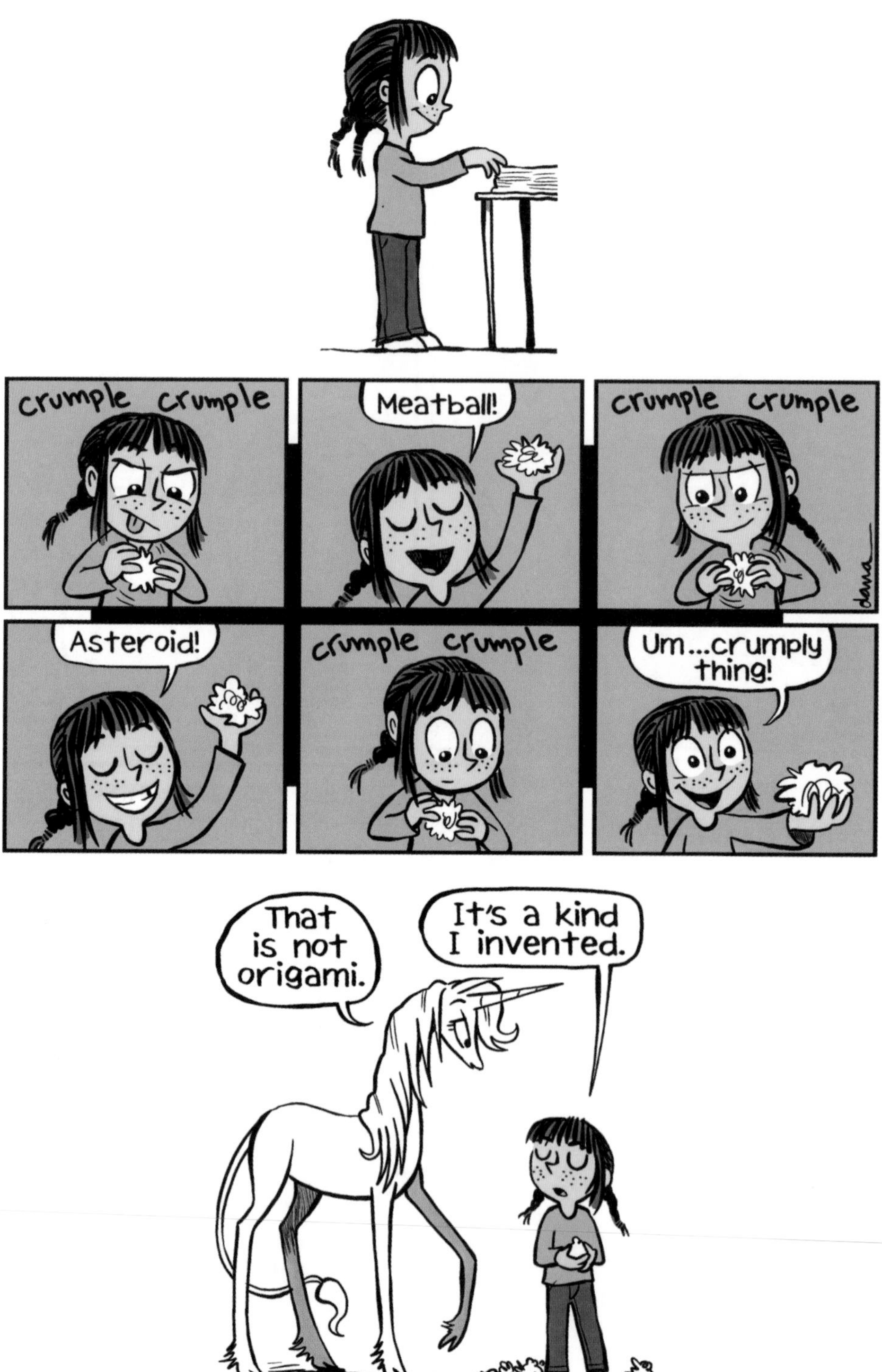
crumple crumple
Meatball!
crumple crumple
Asteroid!
crumple crumple
Um...crumply thing!
That is not origami.
It's a kind I invented.

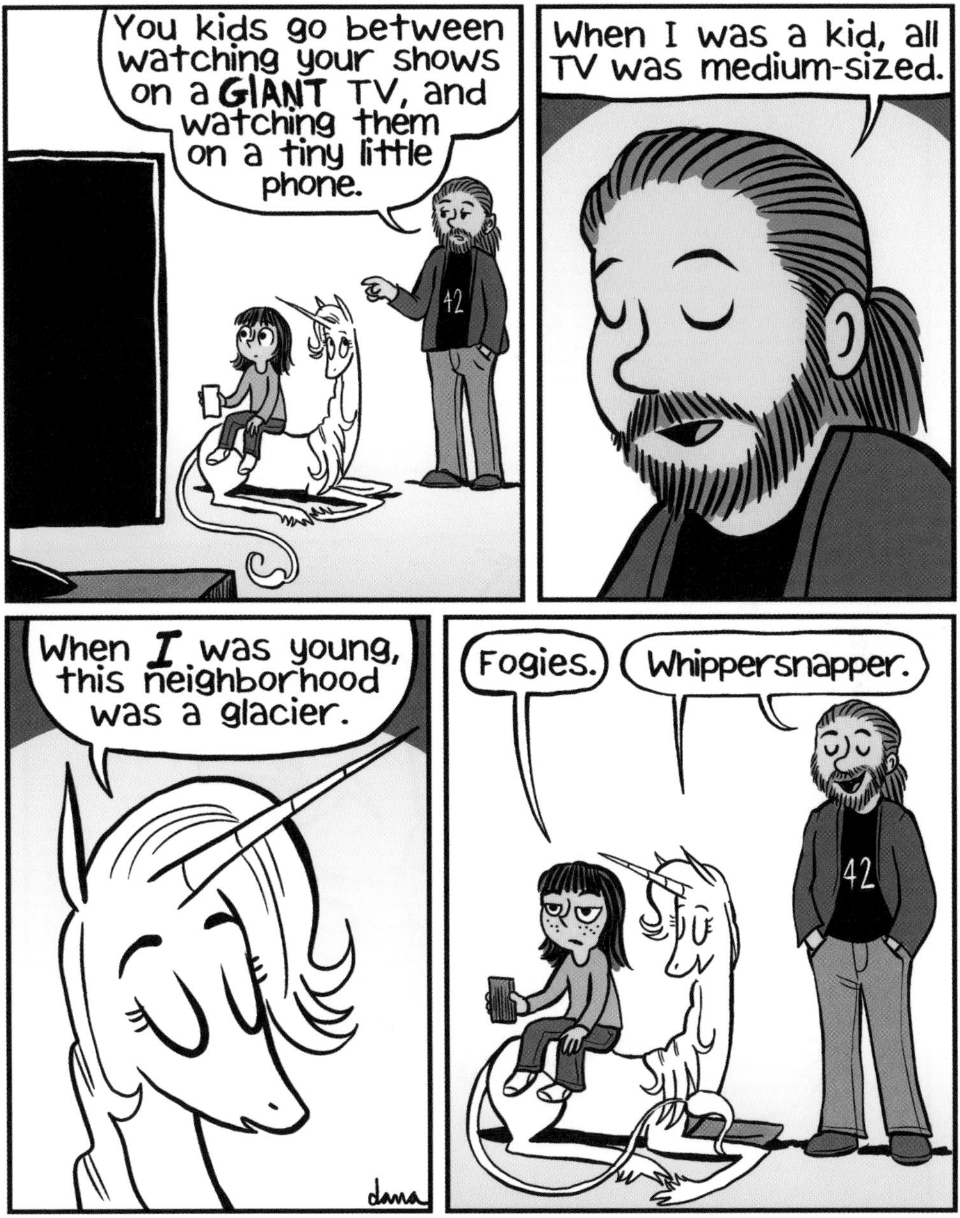
You kids go between watching your shows on a GIANT TV, and watching them on a tiny little phone.
When I was a kid, all TV was medium-sized.
When I was young, this neighborhood was a glacier.
Fogies.
Whippersnapper.
42
42
dana

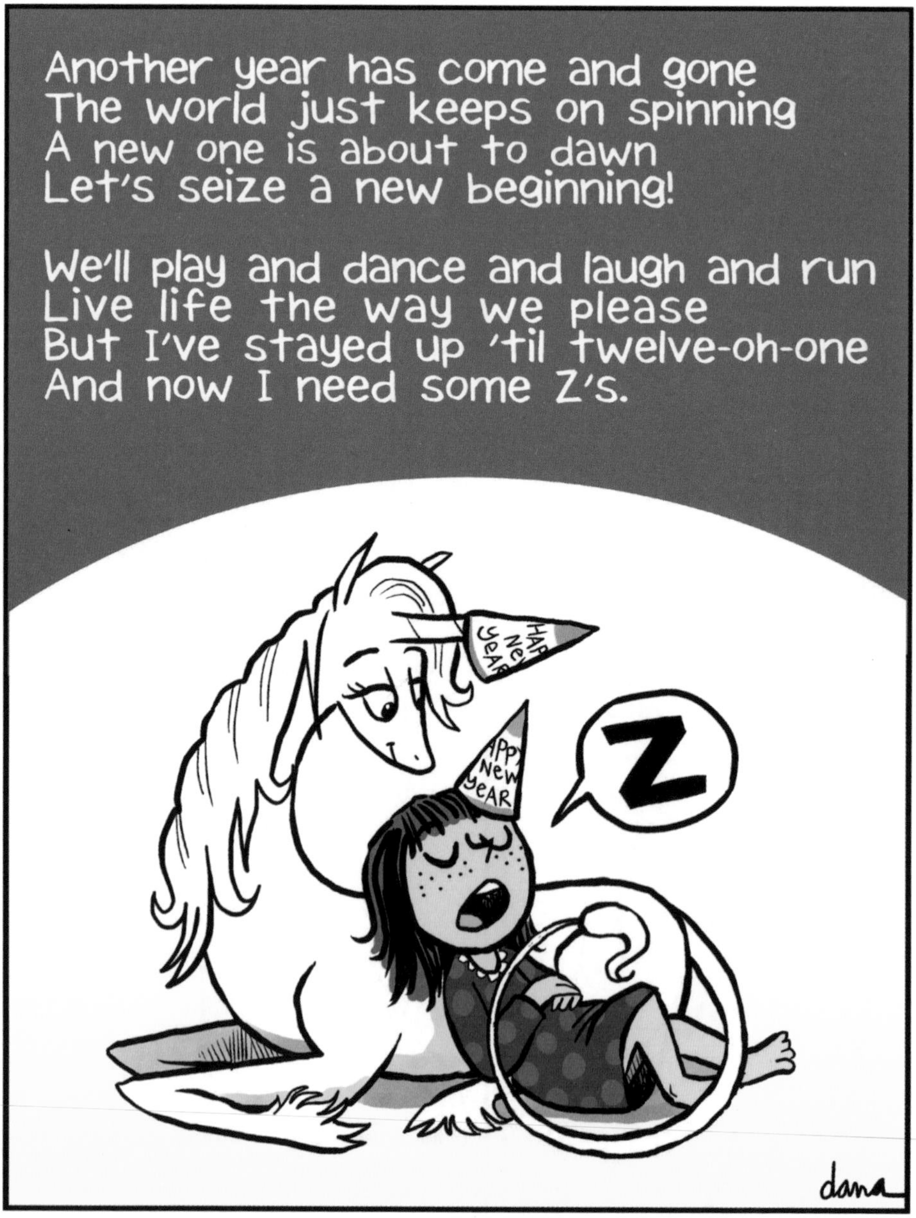
Another year has come and gone
The world just keeps on spinning
A new one is about to dawn
Let's seize a new beginning!

We'll play and dance and laugh and run
Live life the way we please
But I've stayed up 'til twelve-oh-one
And now I need some Z's.
Z
dana

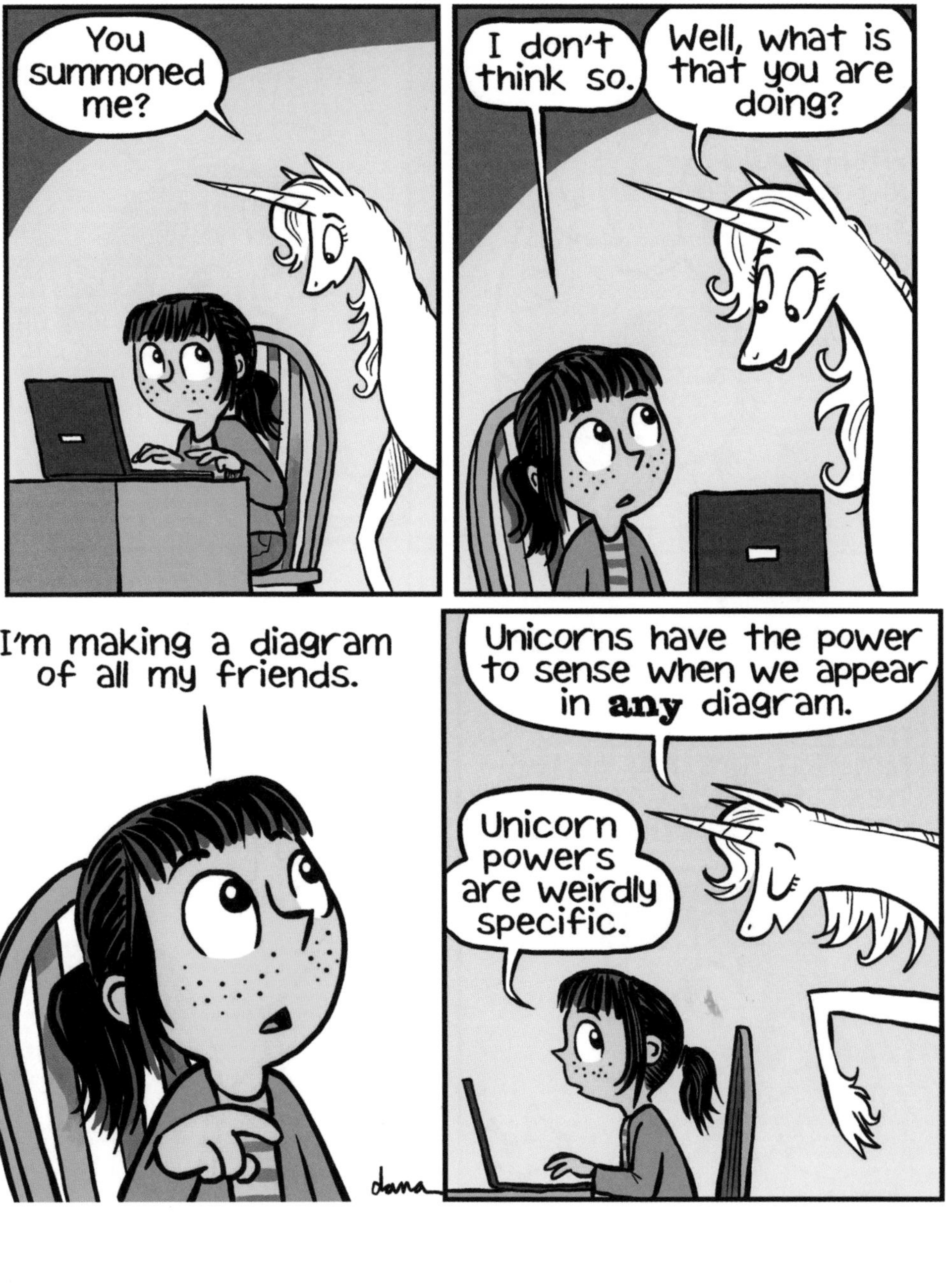
You summoned me?
I don't think so.
Well, what is that you are doing?
I'm making a diagram of all my friends.
Unicorns have the power to sense when we appear in **any** diagram.
Unicorn powers are weirdly specific.
dana

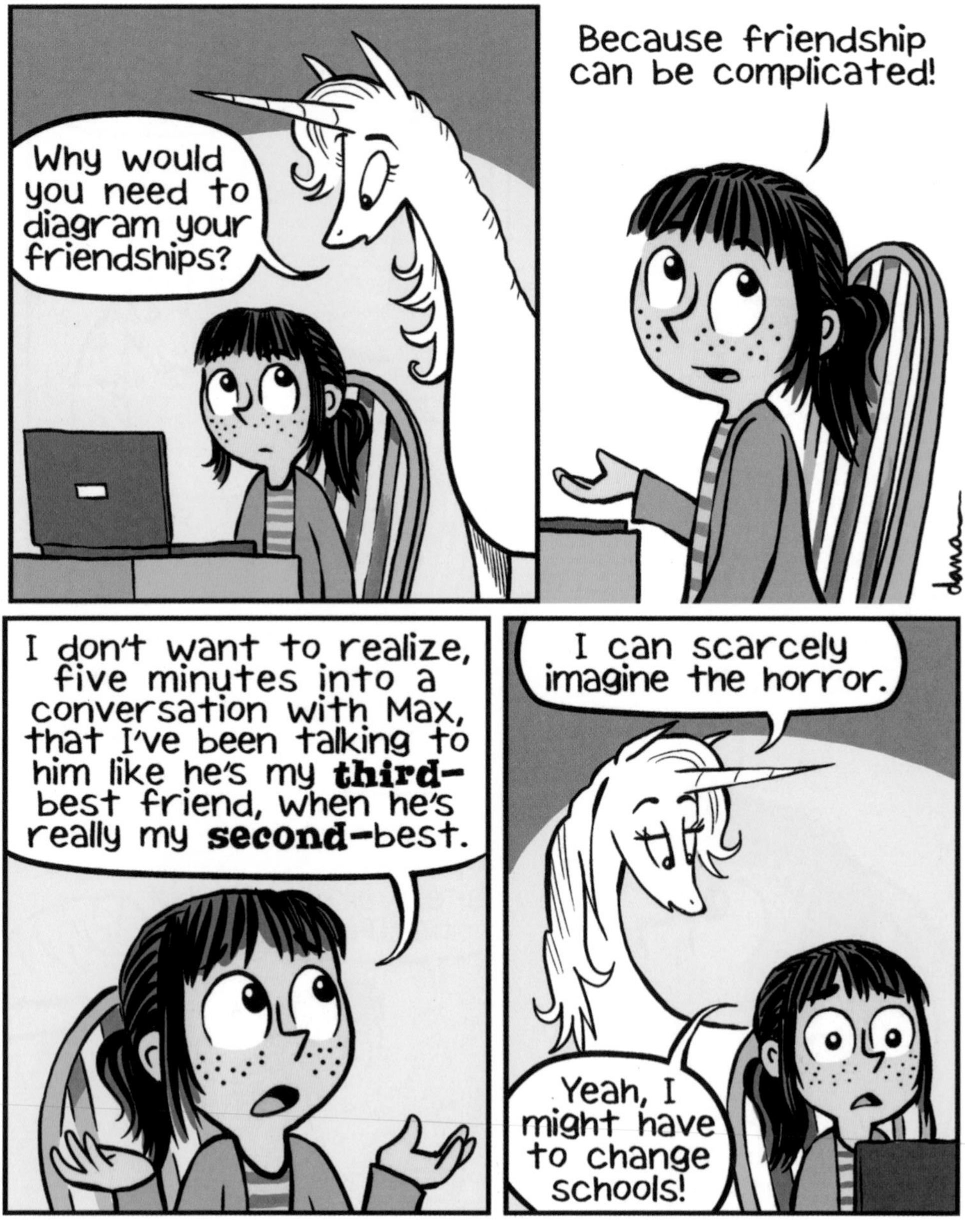
Why would you need to diagram your friendships?
Because friendship can be complicated!
dana
I don't want to realize, five minutes into a conversation with Max, that I've been talking to him like he's my **third**-best friend, when he's really my **second**-best.
I can scarcely imagine the horror.
Yeah, I might have to change schools!

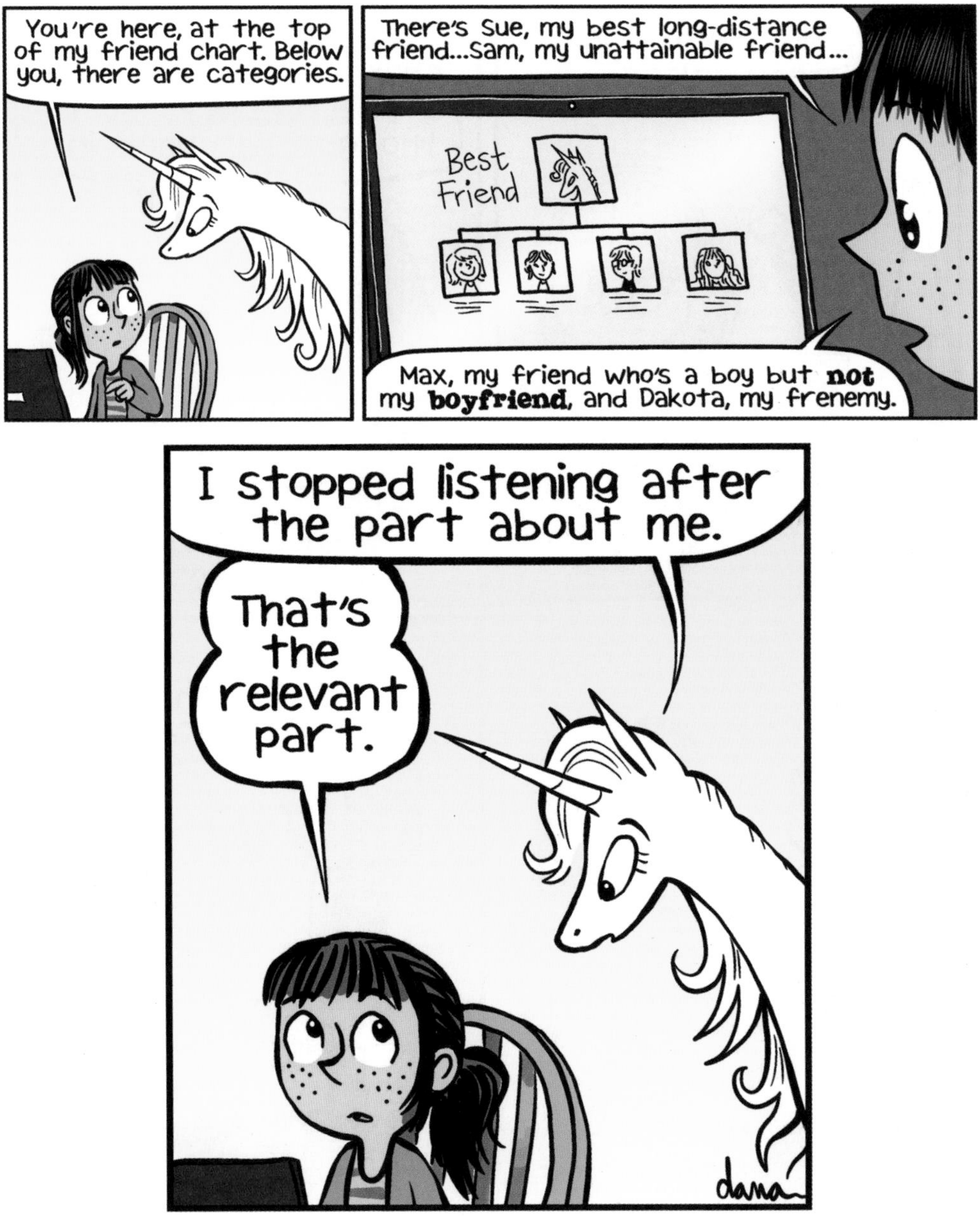
You're here, at the top of my friend chart. Below you, there are categories.
There's Sue, my best long-distance friend...Sam, my unattainable friend...
Best Friend
Max, my friend who's a boy but **not** my **boyfriend**, and Dakota, my frenemy.
I stopped listening after the part about me.
That's the relevant part.
dana

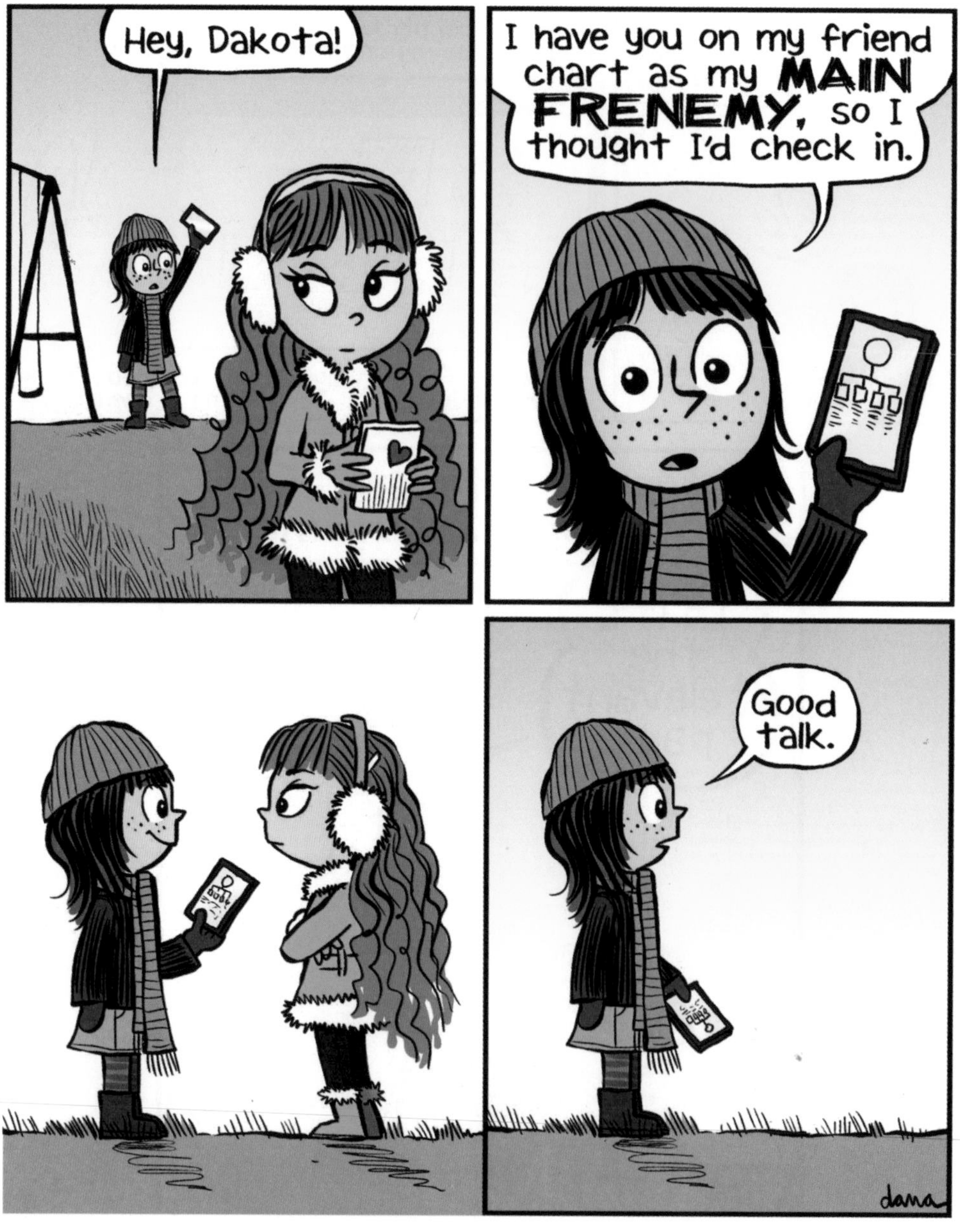
Hey, Dakota!
I have you on my friend chart as my MAIN FRENEMY, so I thought I'd check in.
Good talk.
dana

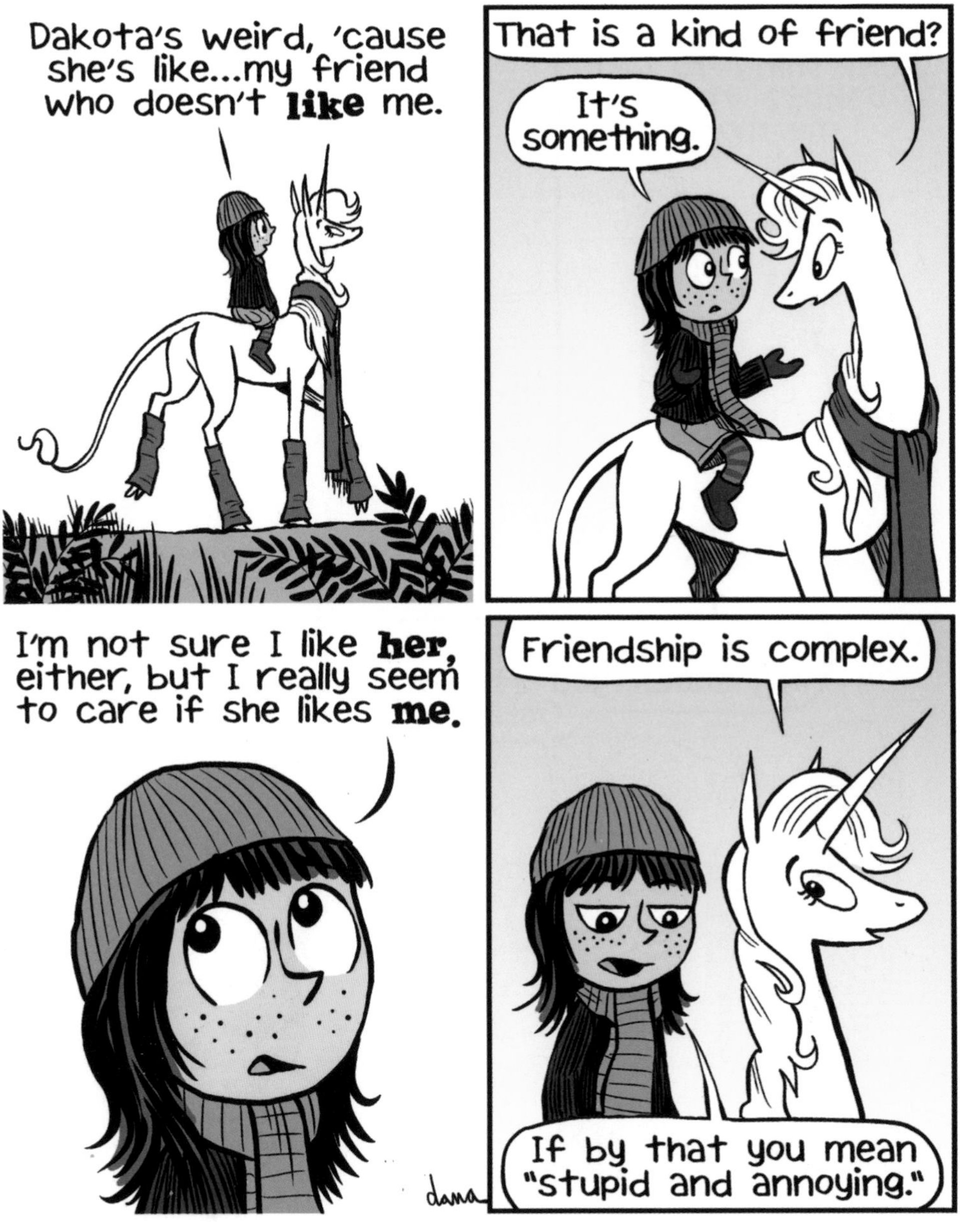
Dakota's weird, 'cause she's like...my friend who doesn't **like** me.
That is a kind of friend?
It's something.
I'm not sure I like **her**, either, but I really seem to care if she likes **me**.
Friendship is complex.
If by that you mean "stupid and annoying."
dana

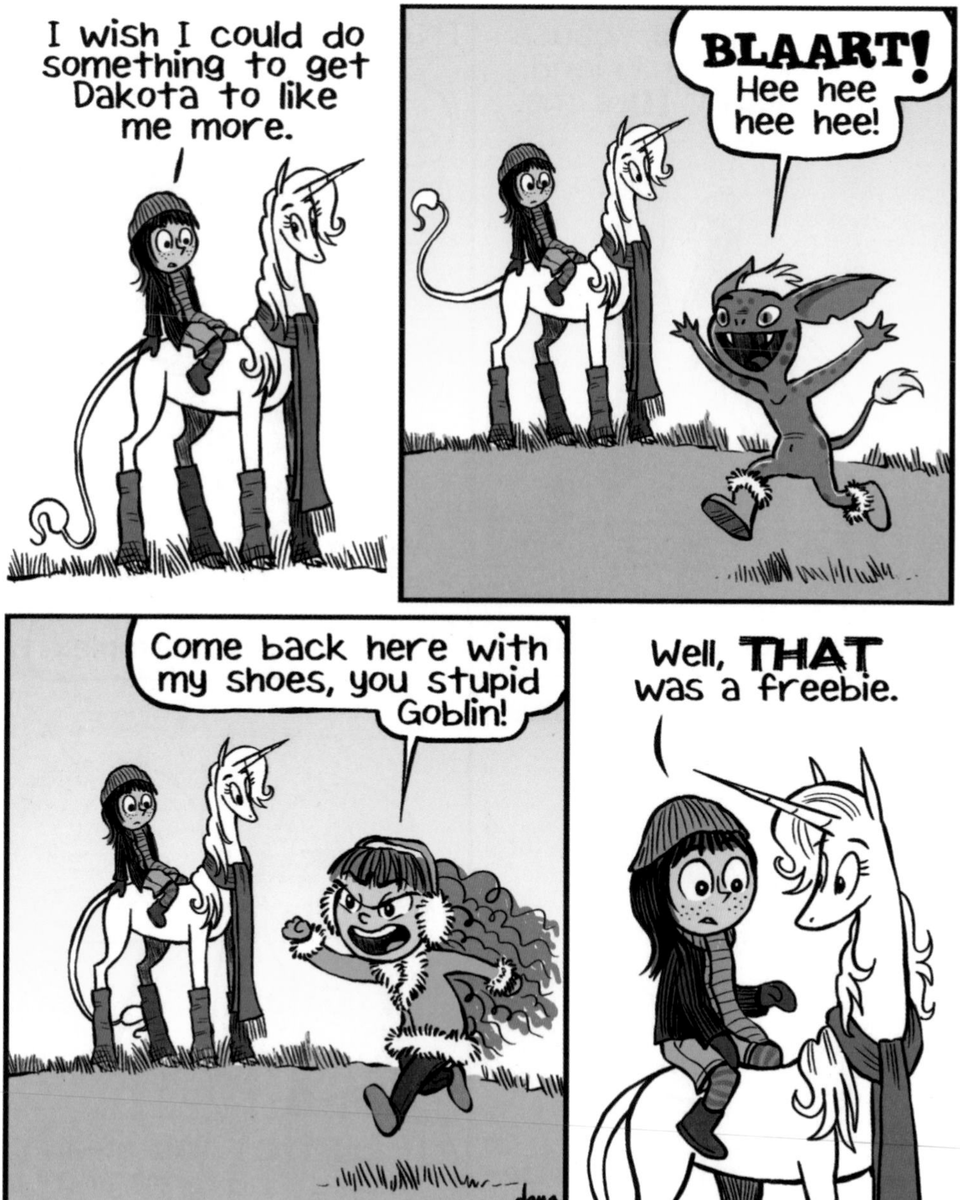
I wish I could do something to get Dakota to like me more.
BLAART! Hee hee hee hee!
Come back here with my shoes, you stupid Goblin!
Well, THAT was a freebie.
dana

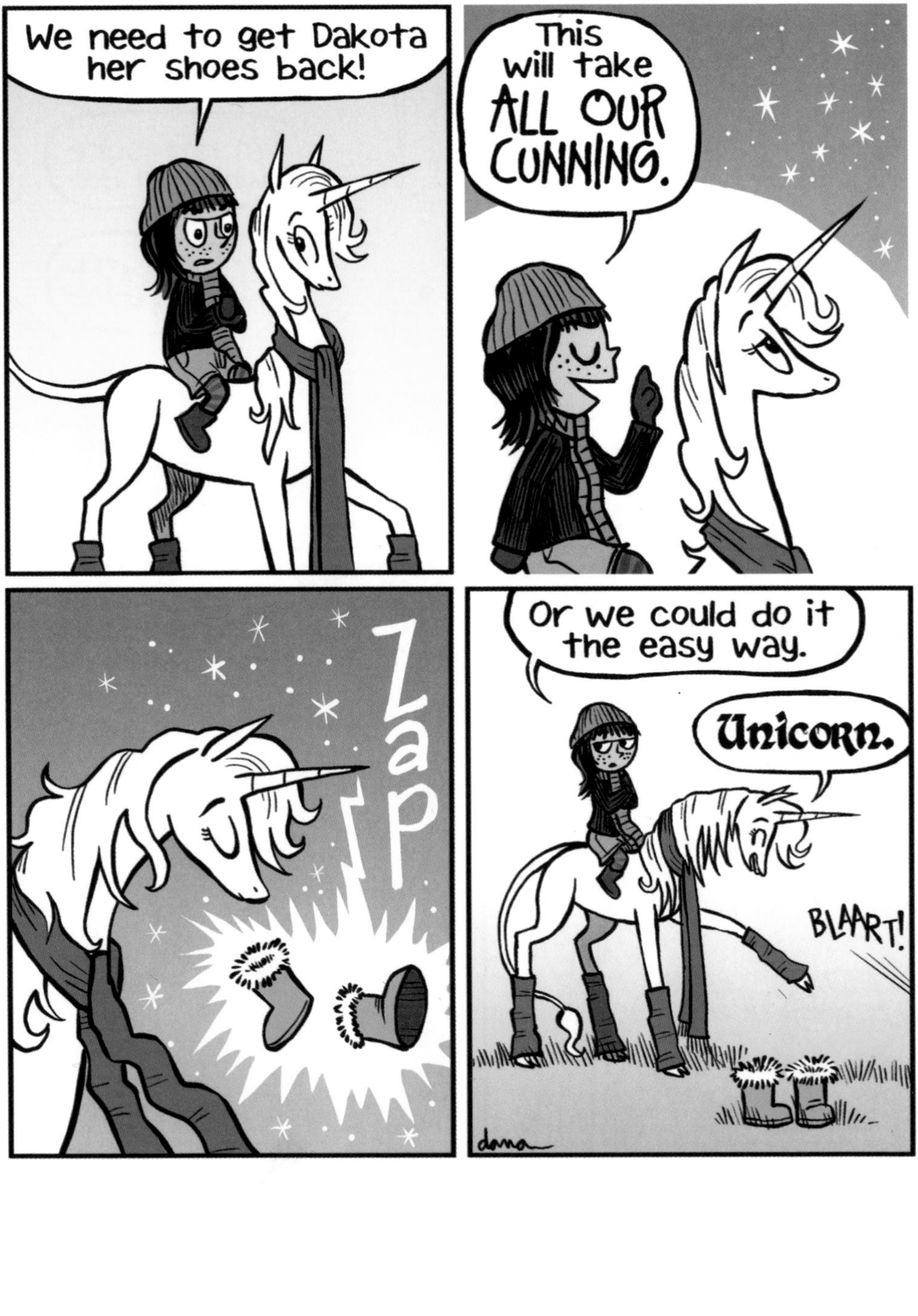
We need to get Dakota her shoes back!
This will take ALL OUR CUNNING.
Zap
Or we could do it the easy way.
Unicorn.
BLAART!
dana

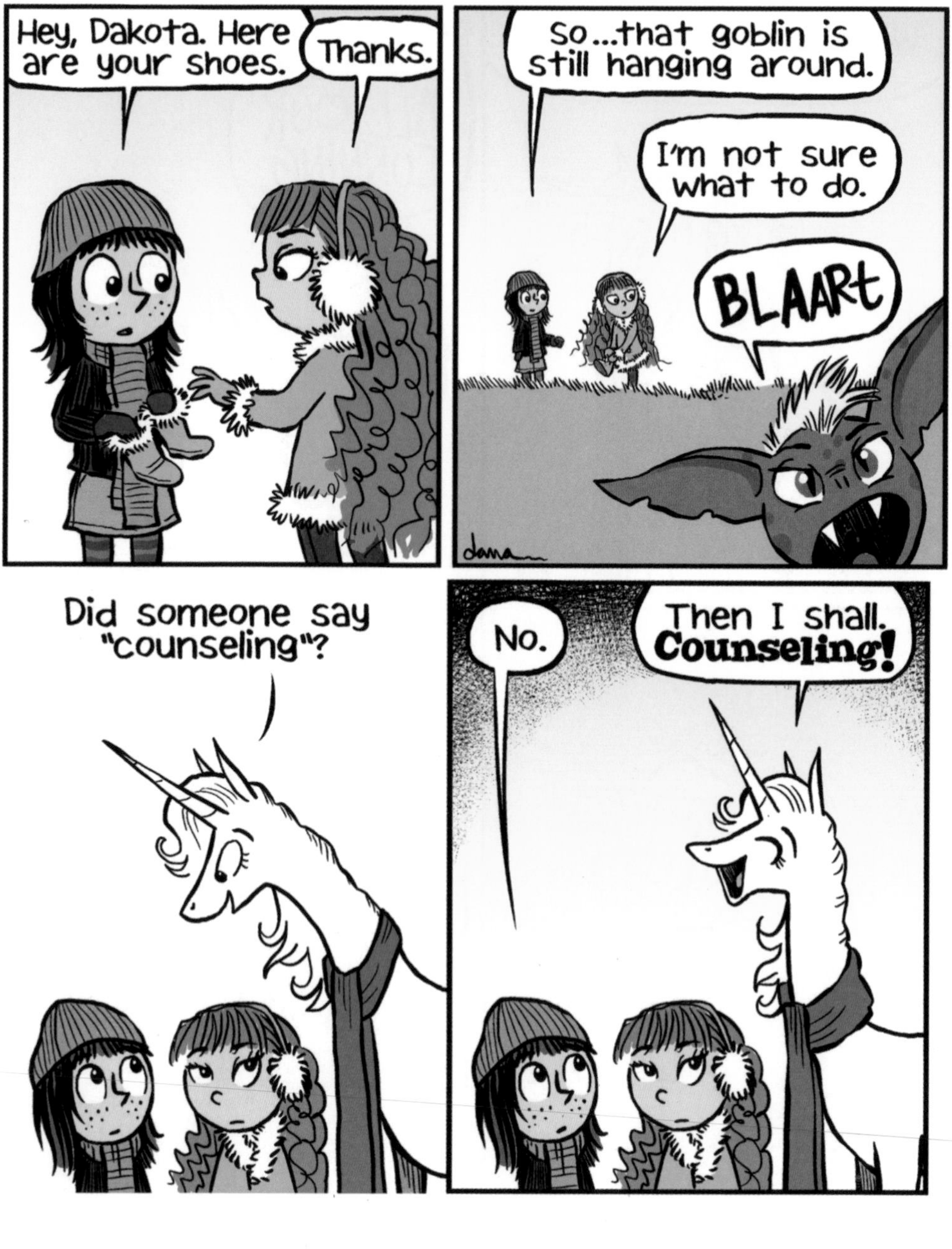
Hey, Dakota. Here are your shoes.
Thanks.
So...that goblin is still hanging around.
I'm not sure what to do.
BLAARt
Did someone say "counseling"?
No.
Then I shall. Counseling!

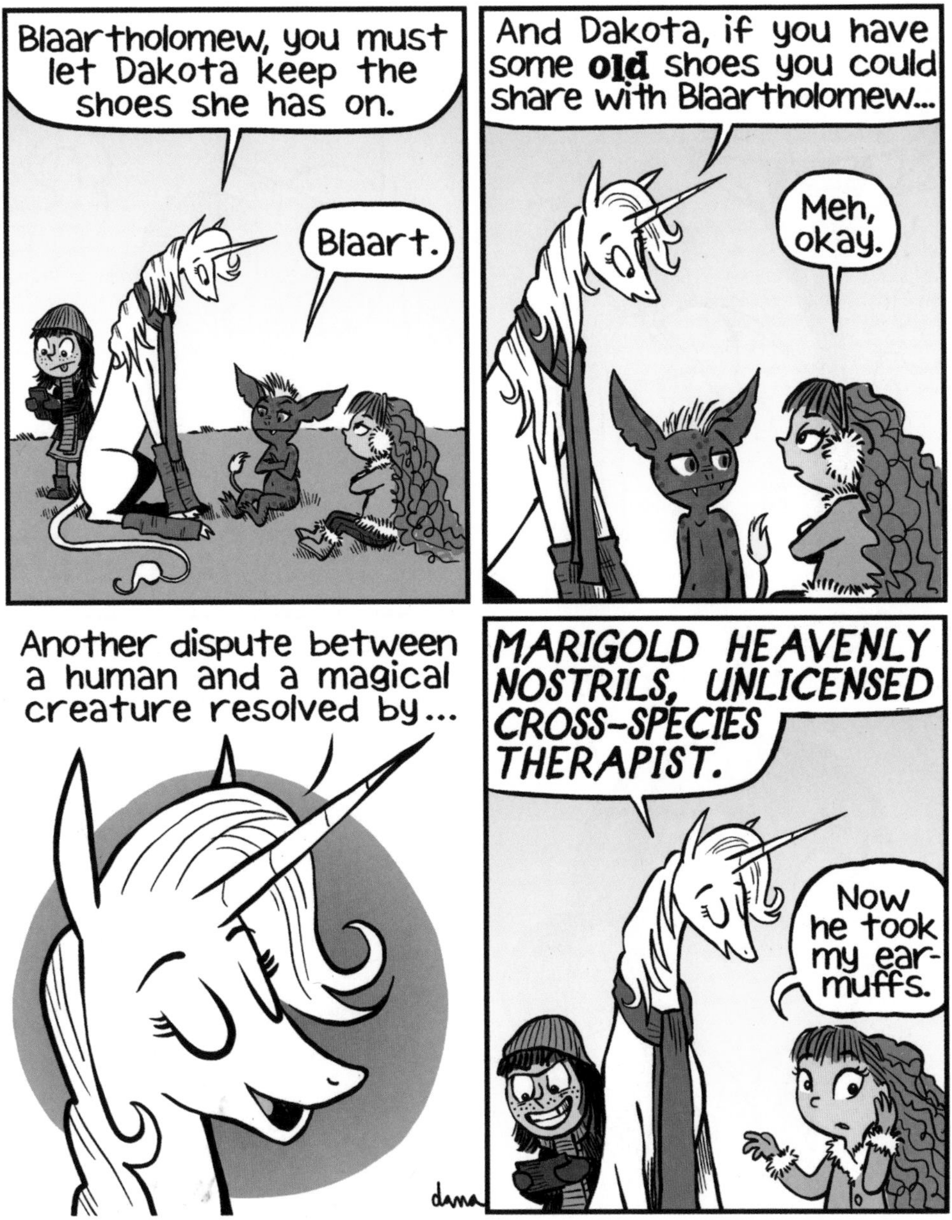

Blaartholomew, you must let Dakota keep the shoes she has on.
Blaart.
And Dakota, if you have some **old** shoes you could share with Blaartholomew...
Meh, okay.
Another dispute between a human and a magical creature resolved by...
MARIGOLD HEAVENLY NOSTRILS, UNLICENSED CROSS-SPECIES THERAPIST.
Now he took my ear-muffs.
dana

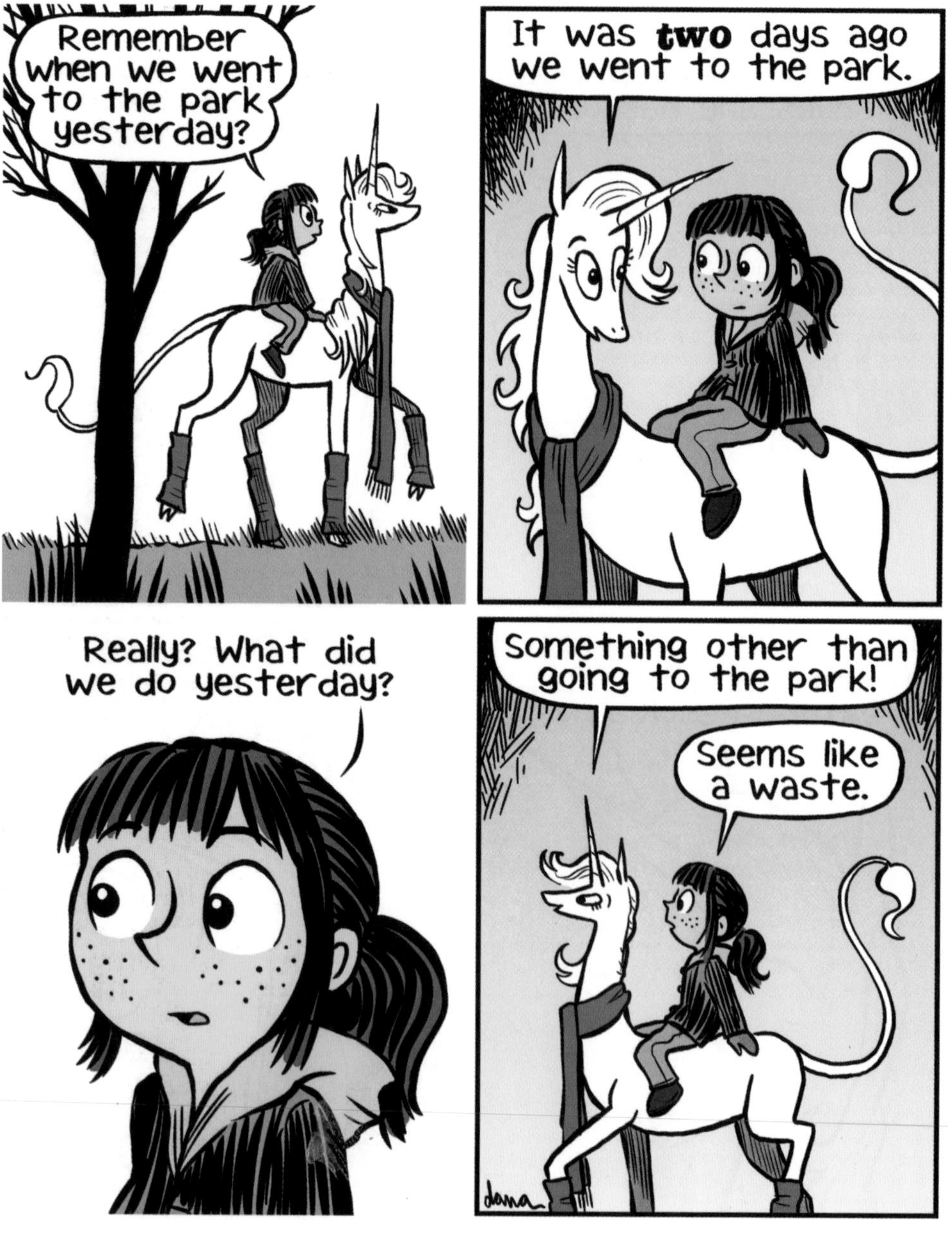
Remember when we went to the park yesterday?
It was **two** days ago we went to the park.
Really? What did we do yesterday?
Something other than going to the park!
Seems like a waste.
dana

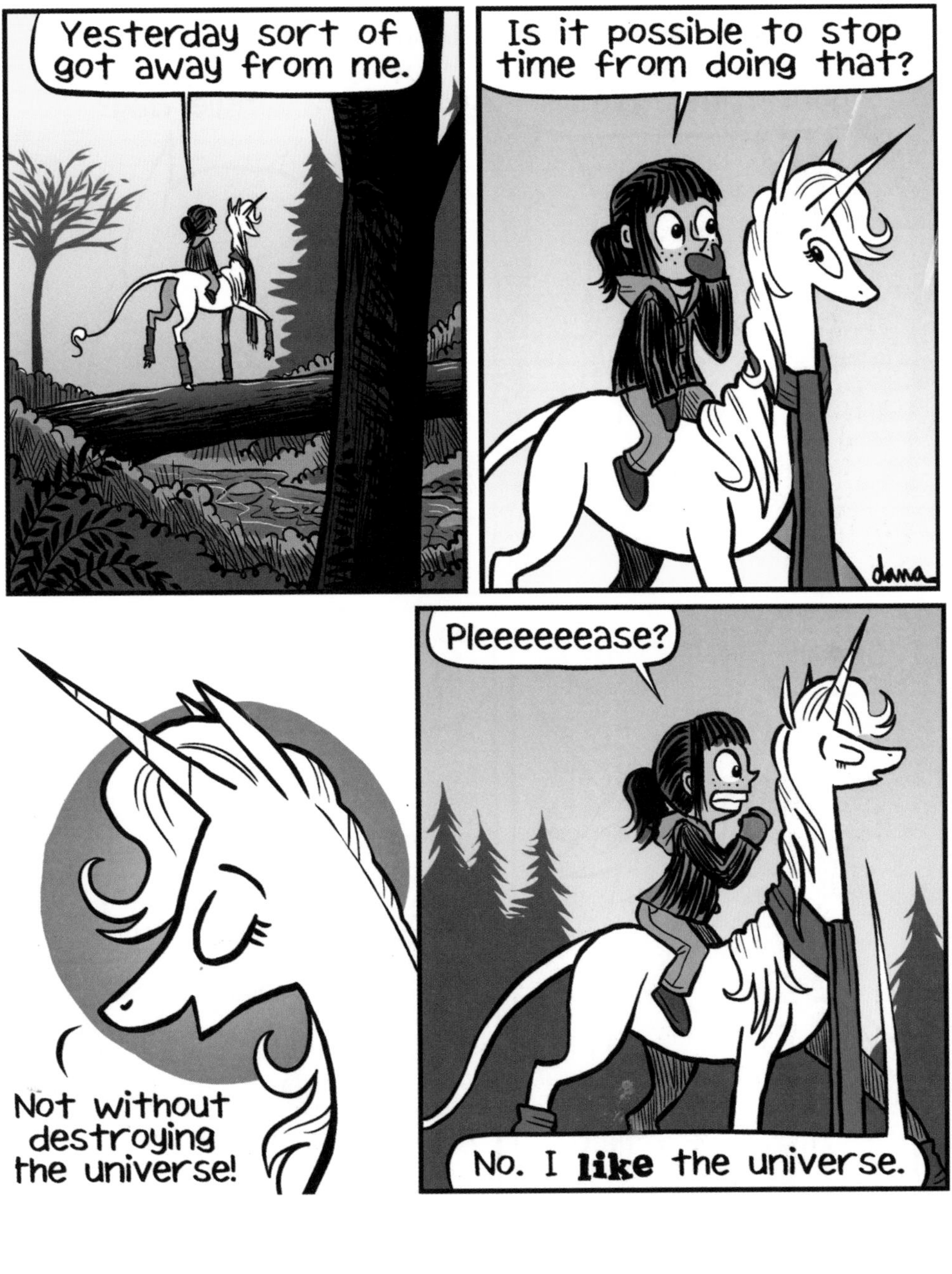
Yesterday sort of got away from me.
Is it possible to stop time from doing that?
dana
Not without destroying the universe!
Pleeeeeeease?
No. I **like** the universe.

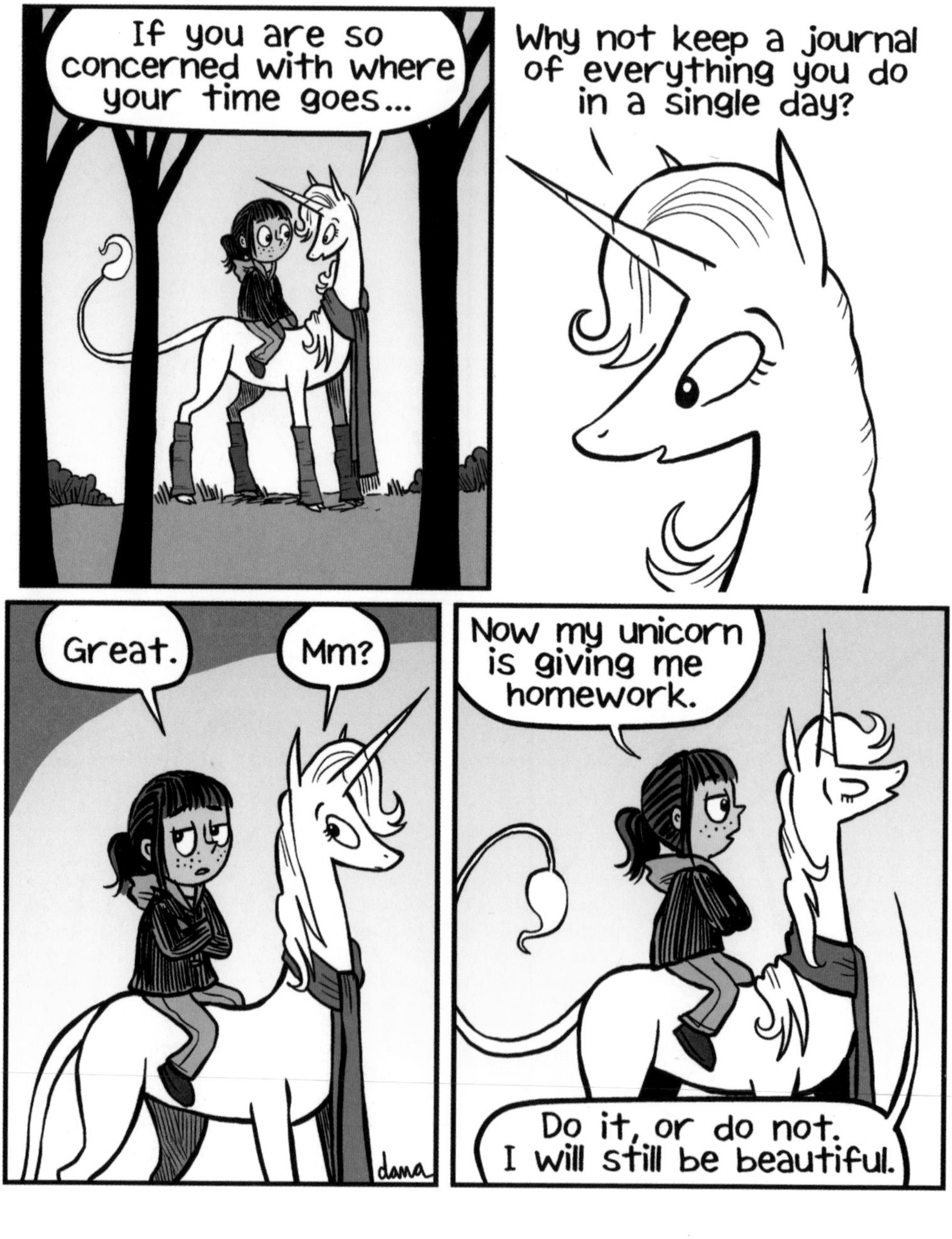
If you are so concerned with where your time goes...
Why not keep a journal of everything you do in a single day?
Great.
Mm?
Now my unicorn is giving me homework.
Do it, or do not. I will still be beautiful.
dana

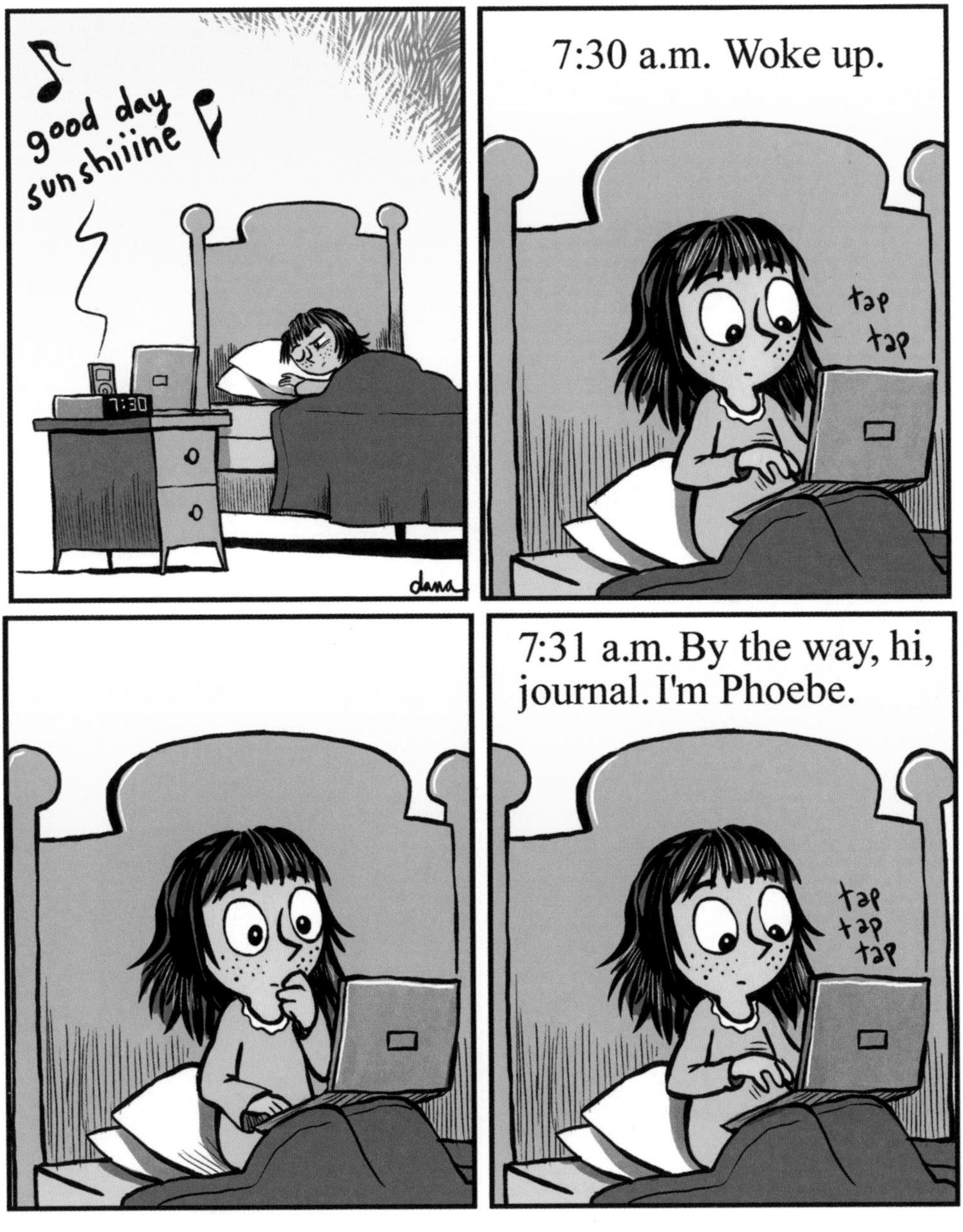
good day sunshiiine
7:30
dana
7:30 a.m. Woke up.
tap tap
7:31 a.m. By the way, hi, journal. I'm Phoebe.
tap tap tap

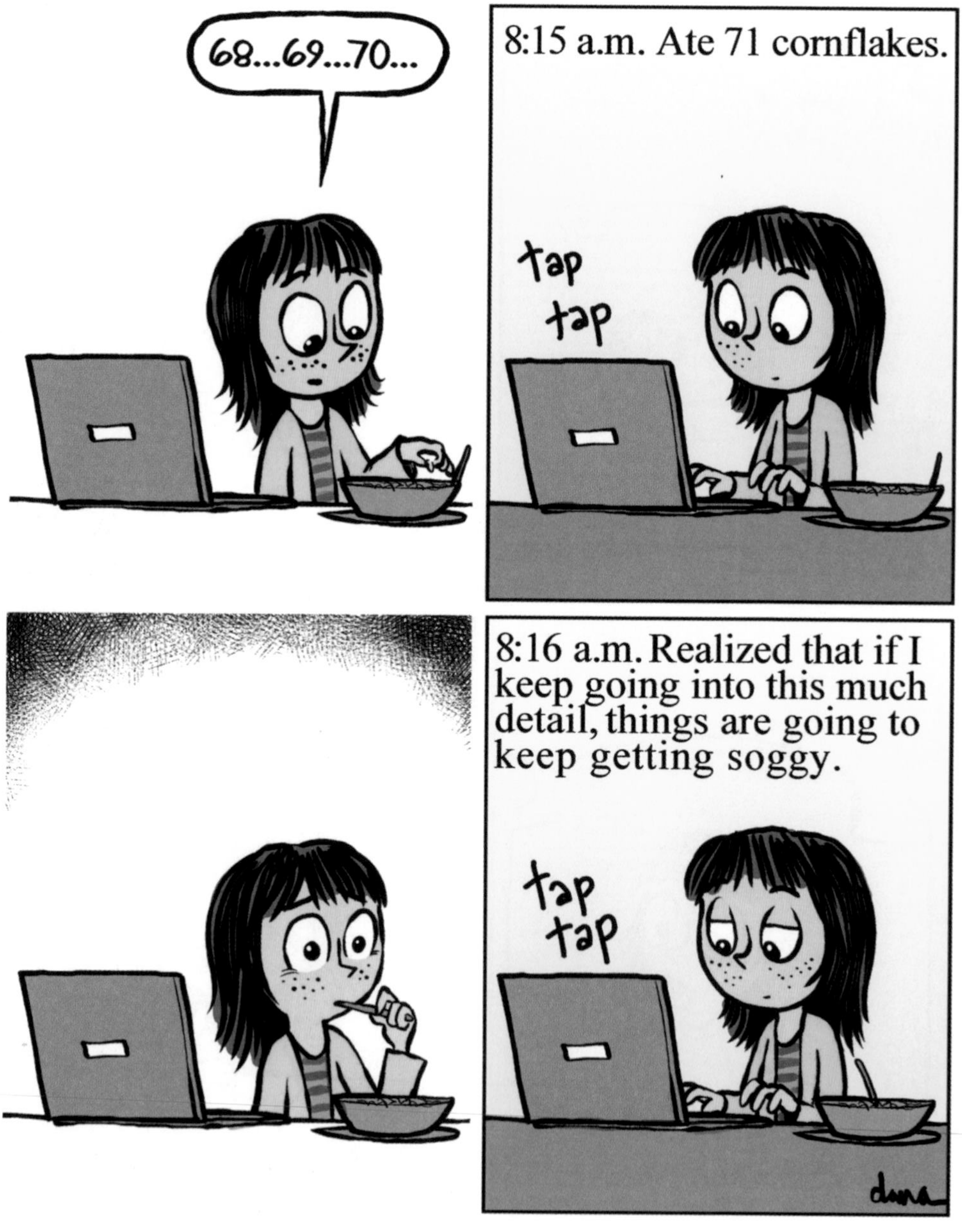
68...69...70...
8:15 a.m. Ate 71 cornflakes.
tap tap
8:16 a.m. Realized that if I keep going into this much detail, things are going to keep getting soggy.
tap tap
dana

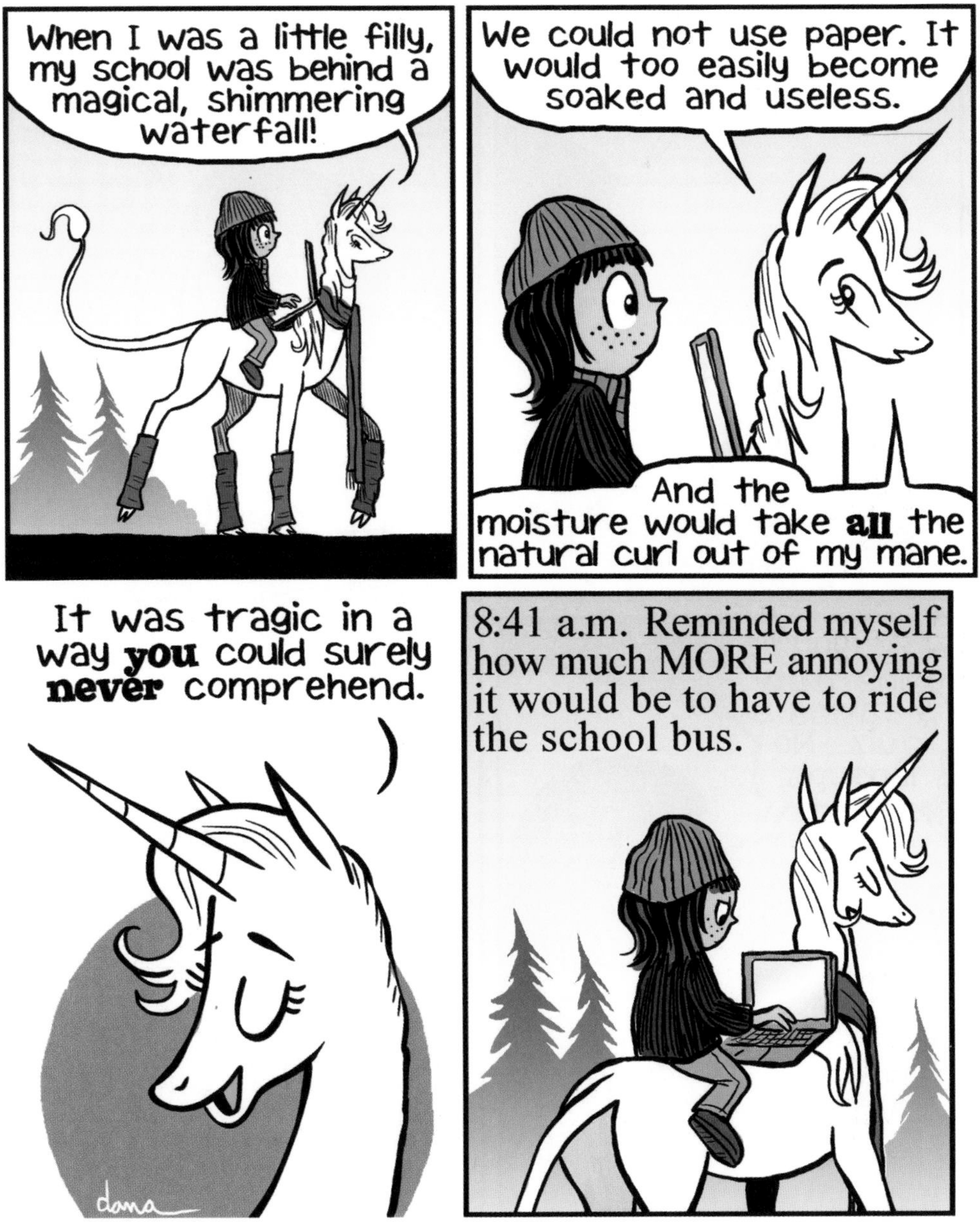
When I was a little filly, my school was behind a magical, shimmering waterfall!
We could not use paper. It would too easily become soaked and useless.
And the moisture would take **all** the natural curl out of my mane.
It was tragic in a way **you** could surely **never** comprehend.
dana
8:41 a.m. Reminded myself how much MORE annoying it would be to have to ride the school bus.

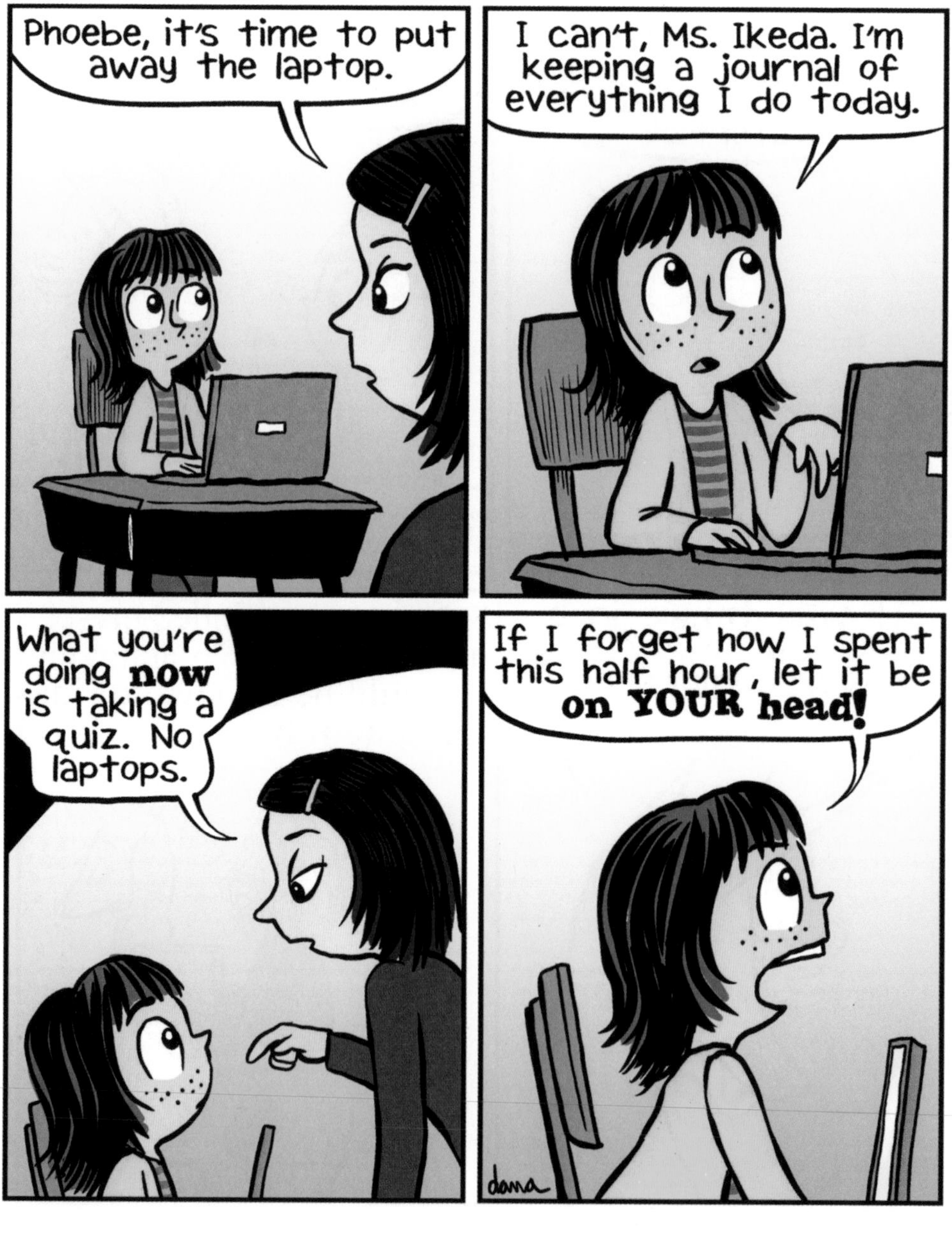
Phoebe, it's time to put away the laptop.
I can't, Ms. Ikeda. I'm keeping a journal of everything I do today.
What you're doing **now** is taking a quiz. No laptops.
If I forget how I spent this half hour, let it be **on YOUR head!**
dana

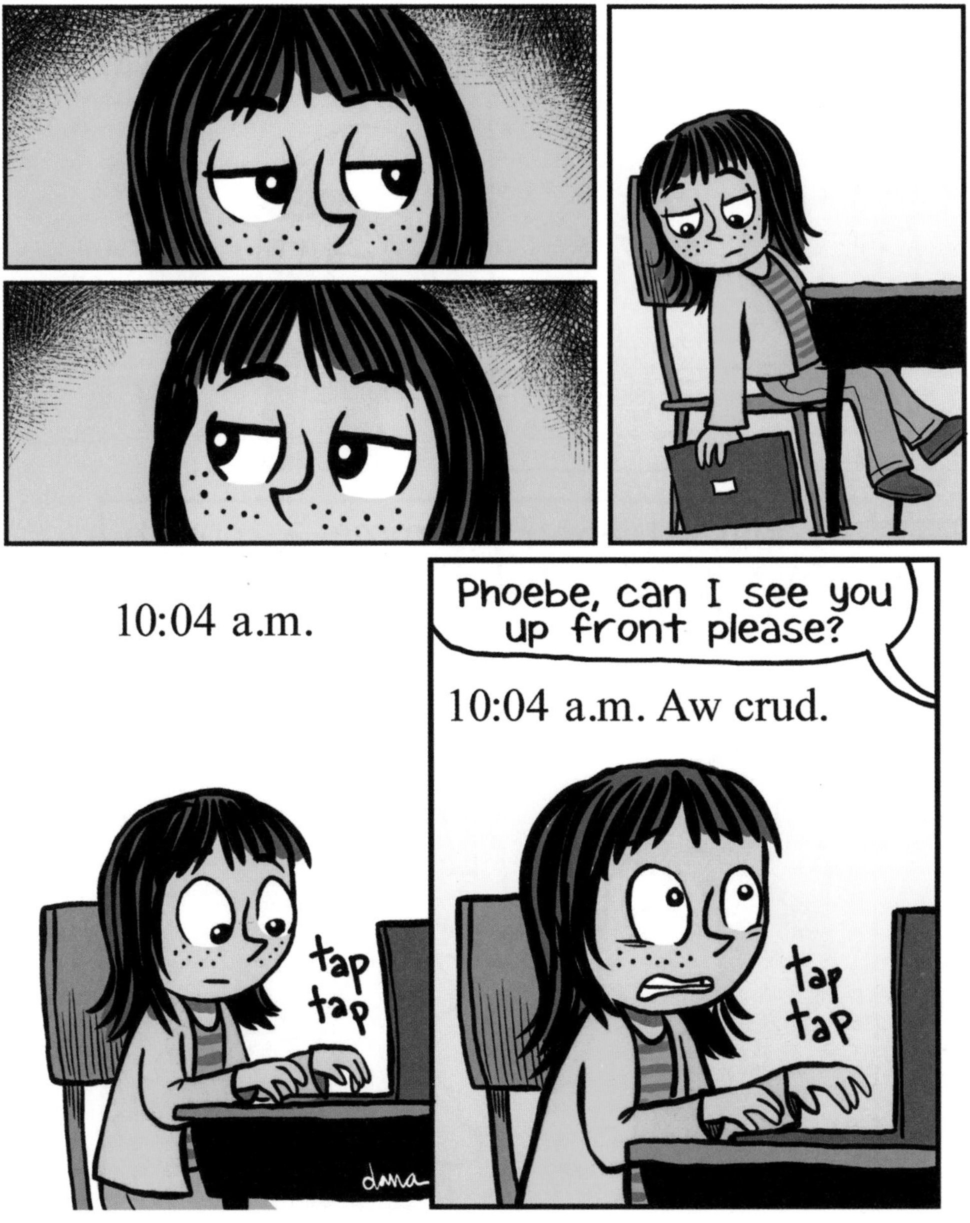
10:04 a.m.
tap tap
dana
Phoebe, can I see you up front please?
10:04 a.m. Aw crud.
tap tap

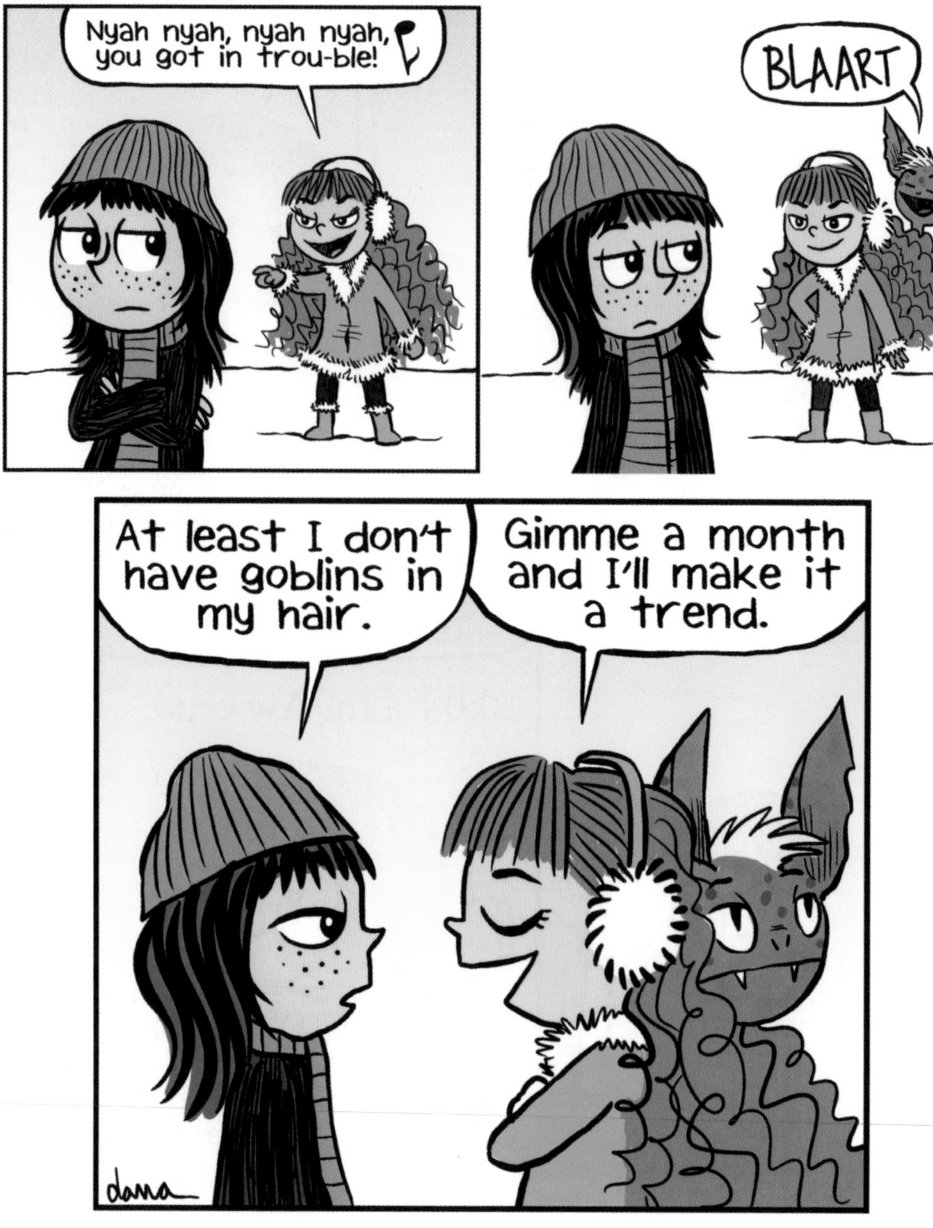
Nyah nyah, nyah nyah, you got in trou-ble!
BLAART
At least I don't have goblins in my hair.
Gimme a month and I'll make it a trend.
dana

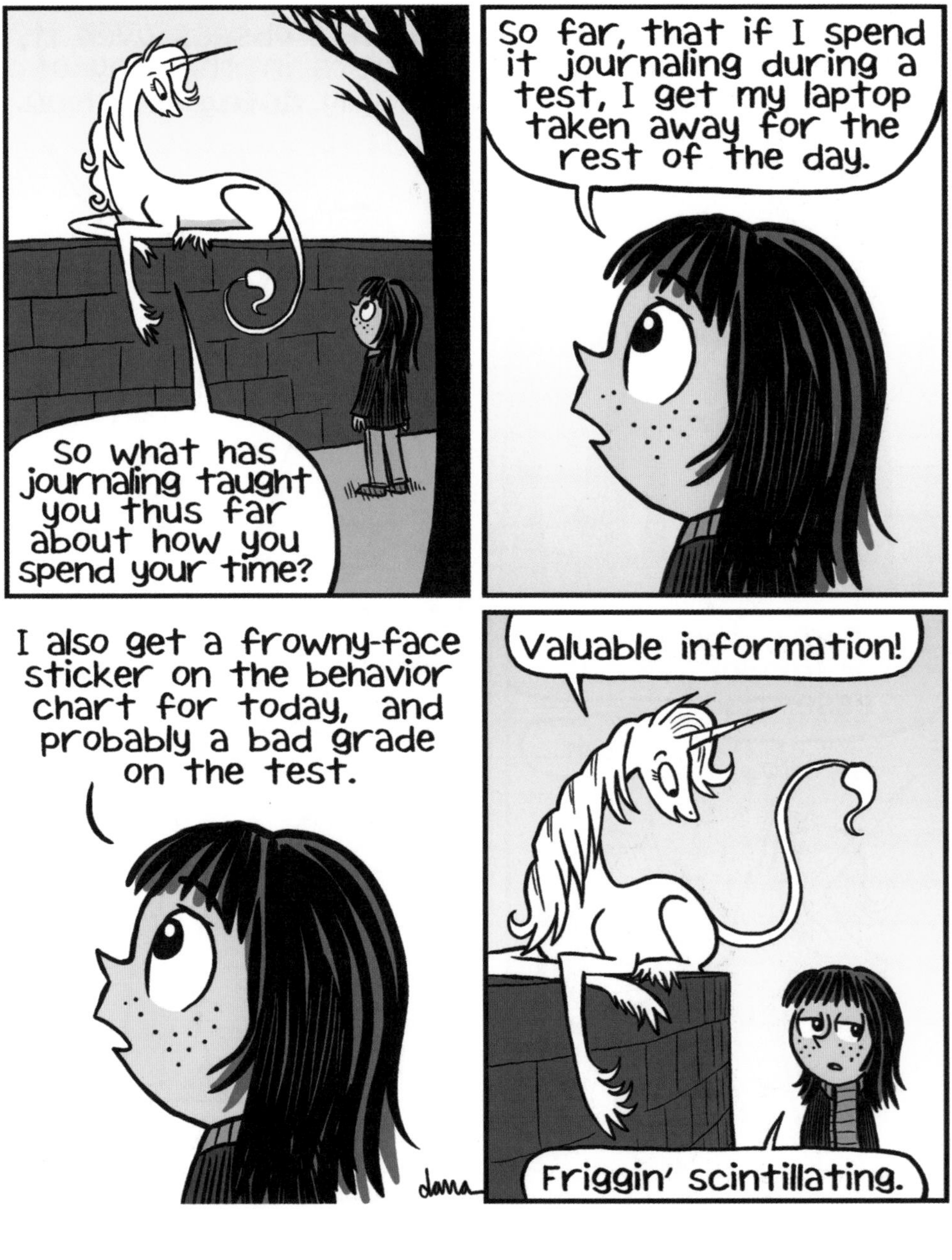
So what has journaling taught you thus far about how you spend your time?
So far, that if I spend it journaling during a test, I get my laptop taken away for the rest of the day.
I also get a frowny-face sticker on the behavior chart for today, and probably a bad grade on the test.
Valuable information!
Friggin' scintillating.

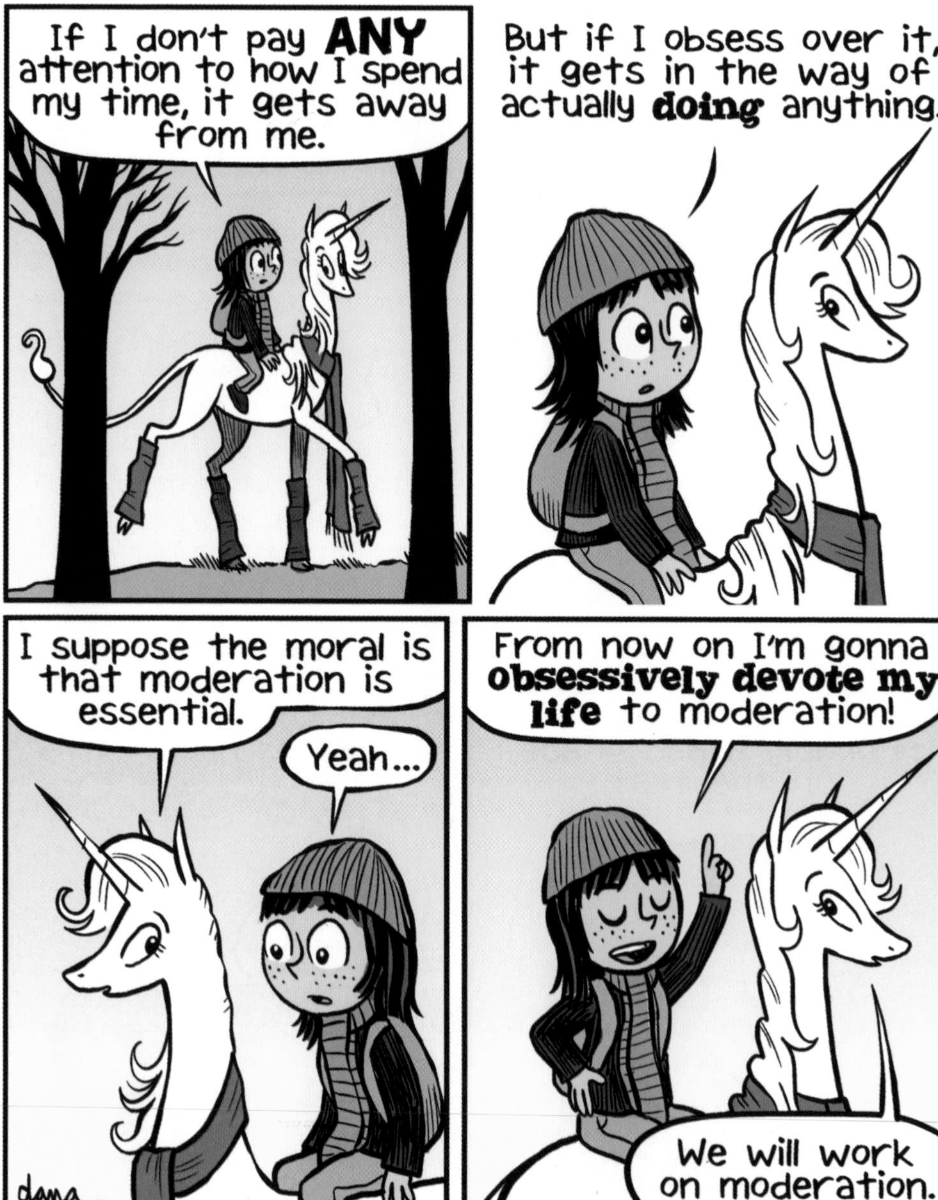
If I don't pay ANY attention to how I spend my time, it gets away from me.
But if I obsess over it, it gets in the way of actually doing anything.
I suppose the moral is that moderation is essential.
Yeah...
From now on I'm gonna obsessively devote my life to moderation!
We will work on moderation.
dana

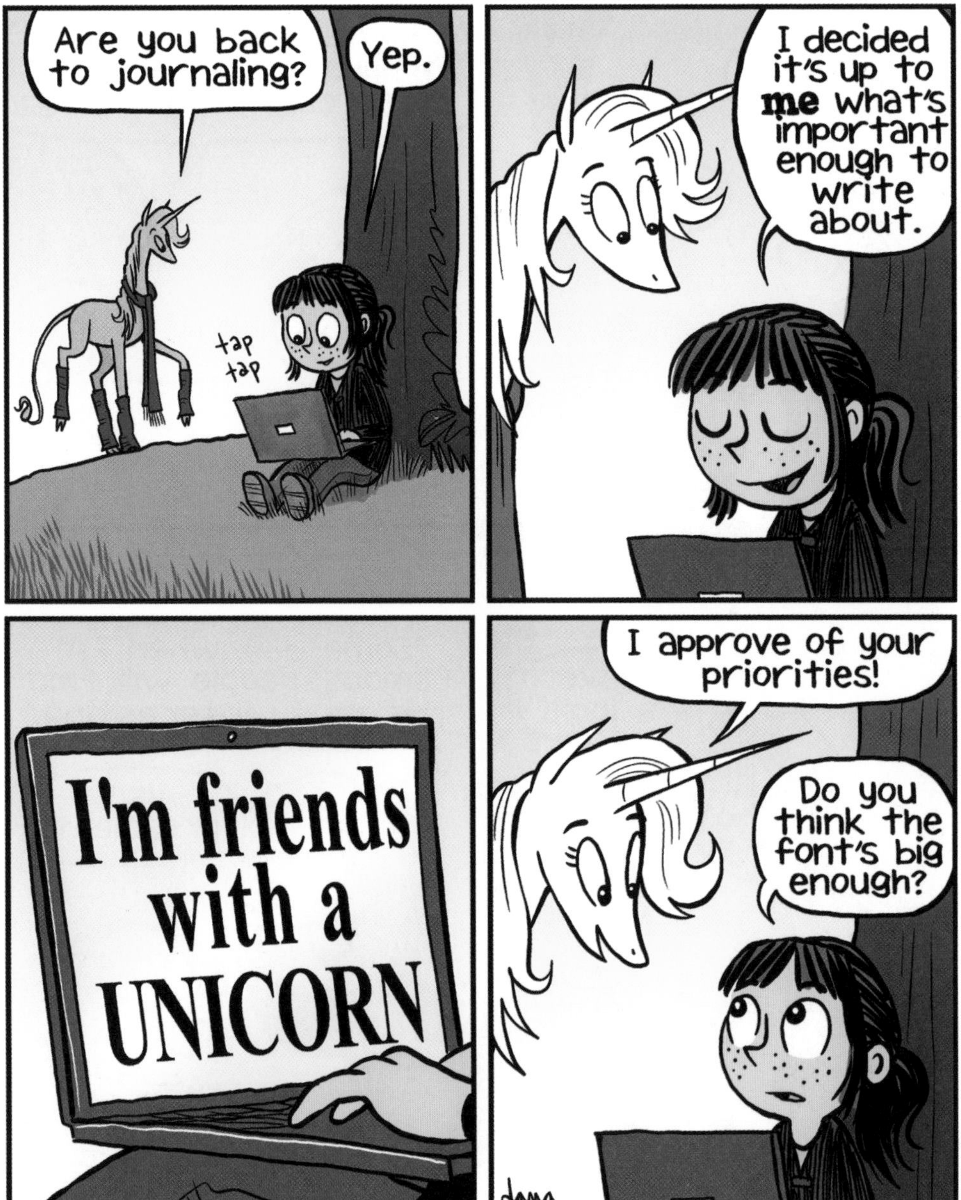
Are you back to journaling?
Yep.
tap tap
I decided it's up to me what's important enough to write about.
I'm friends with a UNICORN
I approve of your priorities!
Do you think the font's big enough?
dana

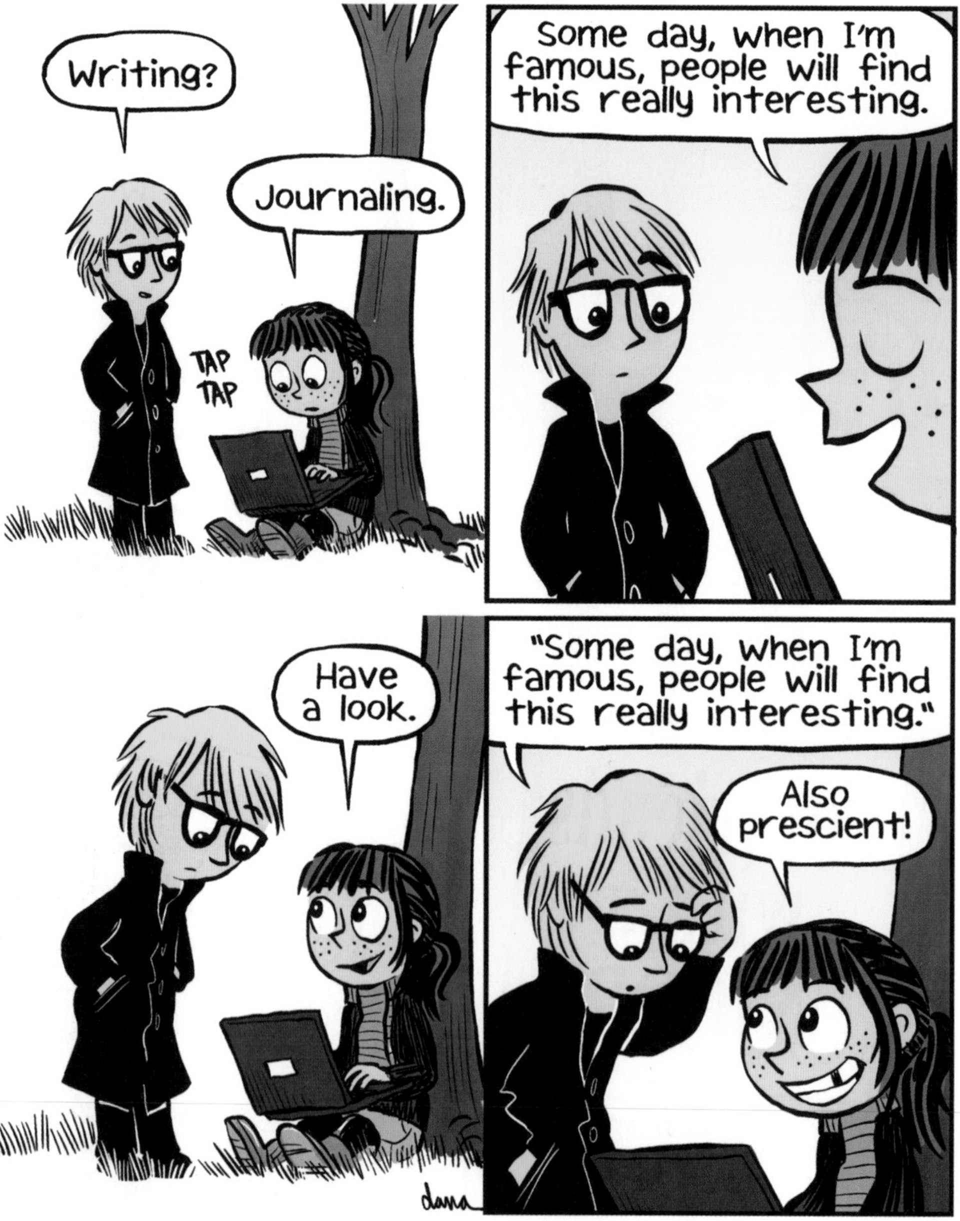
Writing?
Journaling.
TAP TAP
Some day, when I'm famous, people will find this really interesting.
Have a look.
"Some day, when I'm famous, people will find this really interesting."
Also prescient!
dana

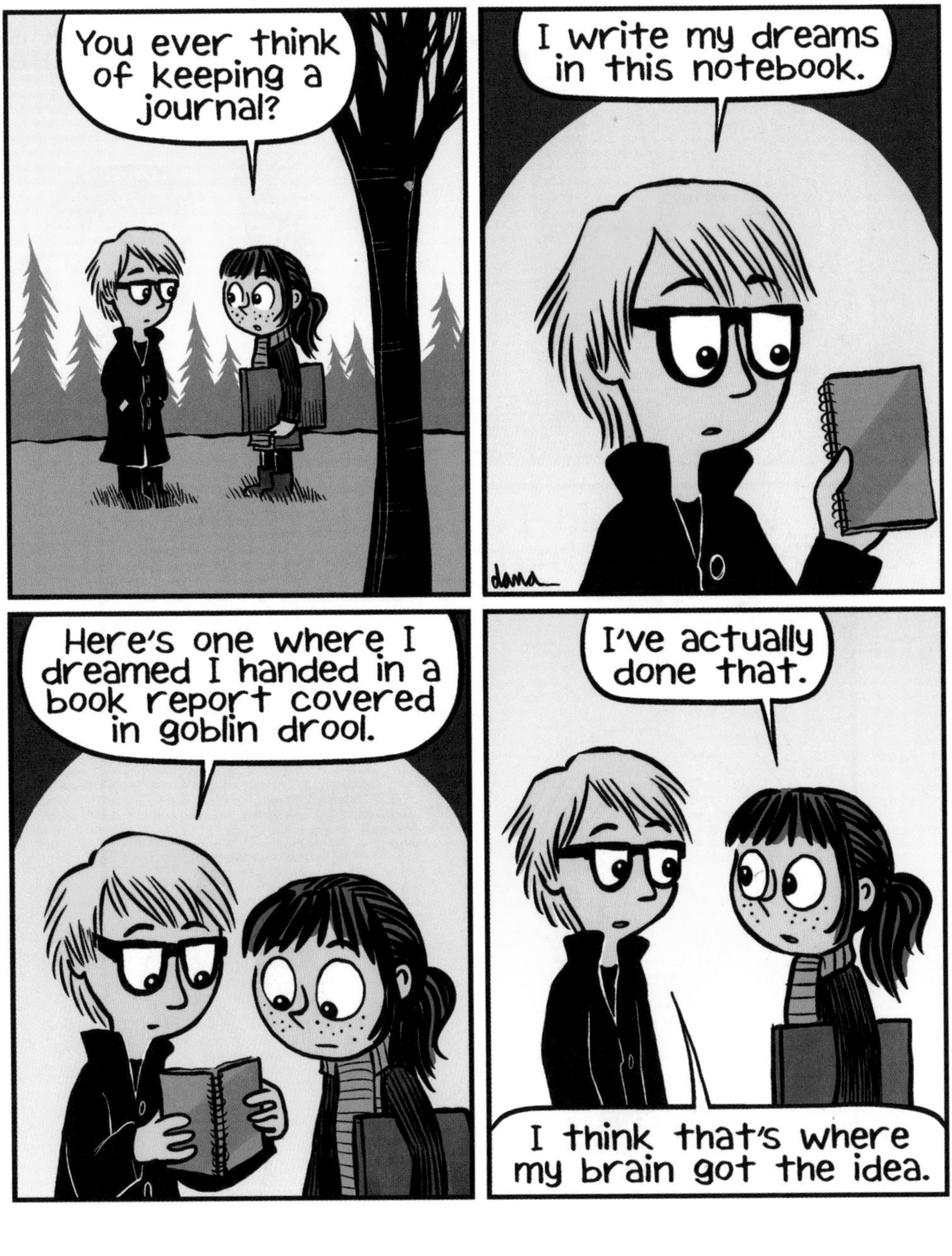
You ever think of keeping a journal?
I write my dreams in this notebook.
dana
Here's one where I dreamed I handed in a book report covered in goblin drool.
I've actually done that.
I think that's where my brain got the idea.

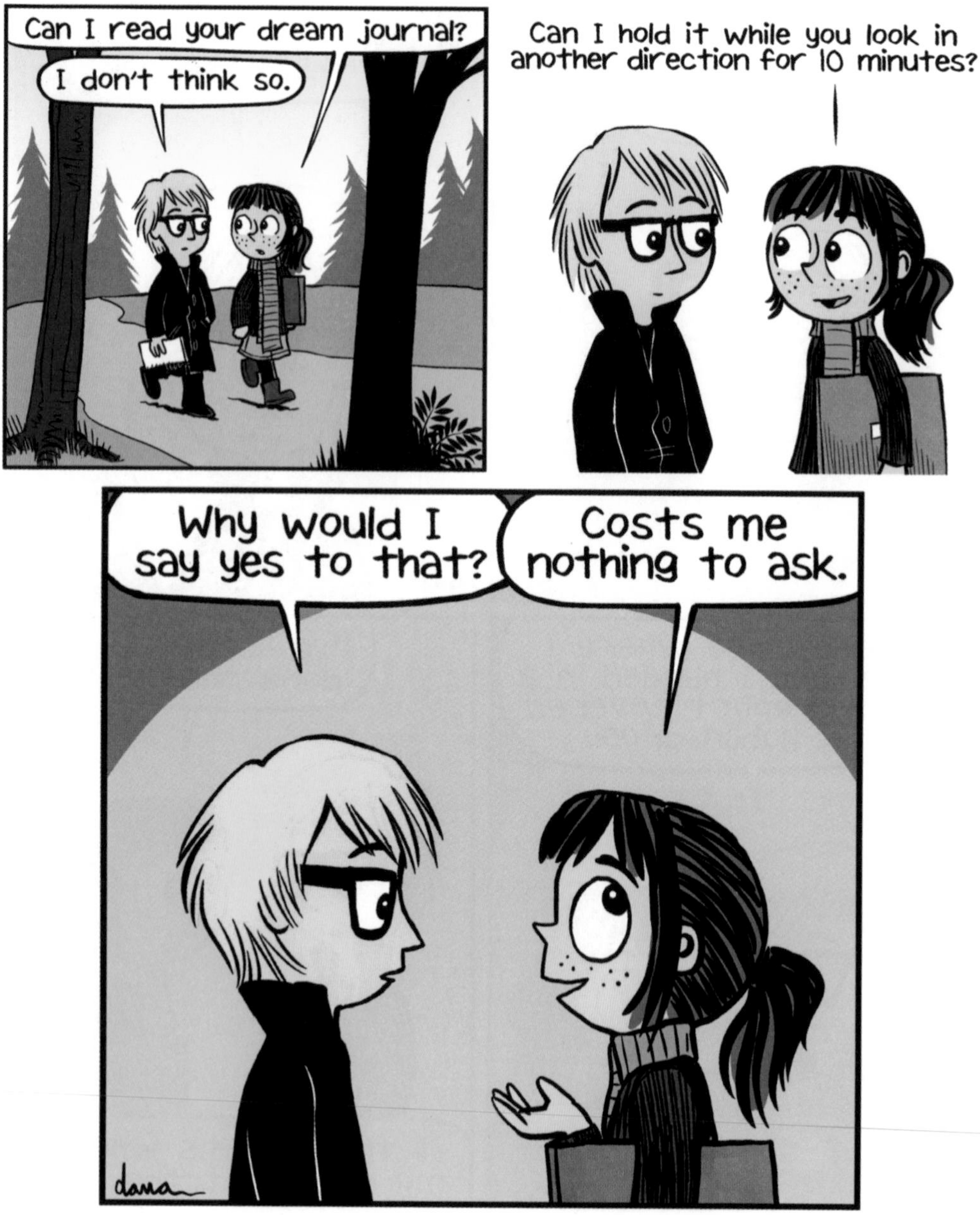
Can I read your dream journal?
I don't think so.
Can I hold it while you look in another direction for 10 minutes?
Why would I say yes to that?
Costs me nothing to ask.
dana

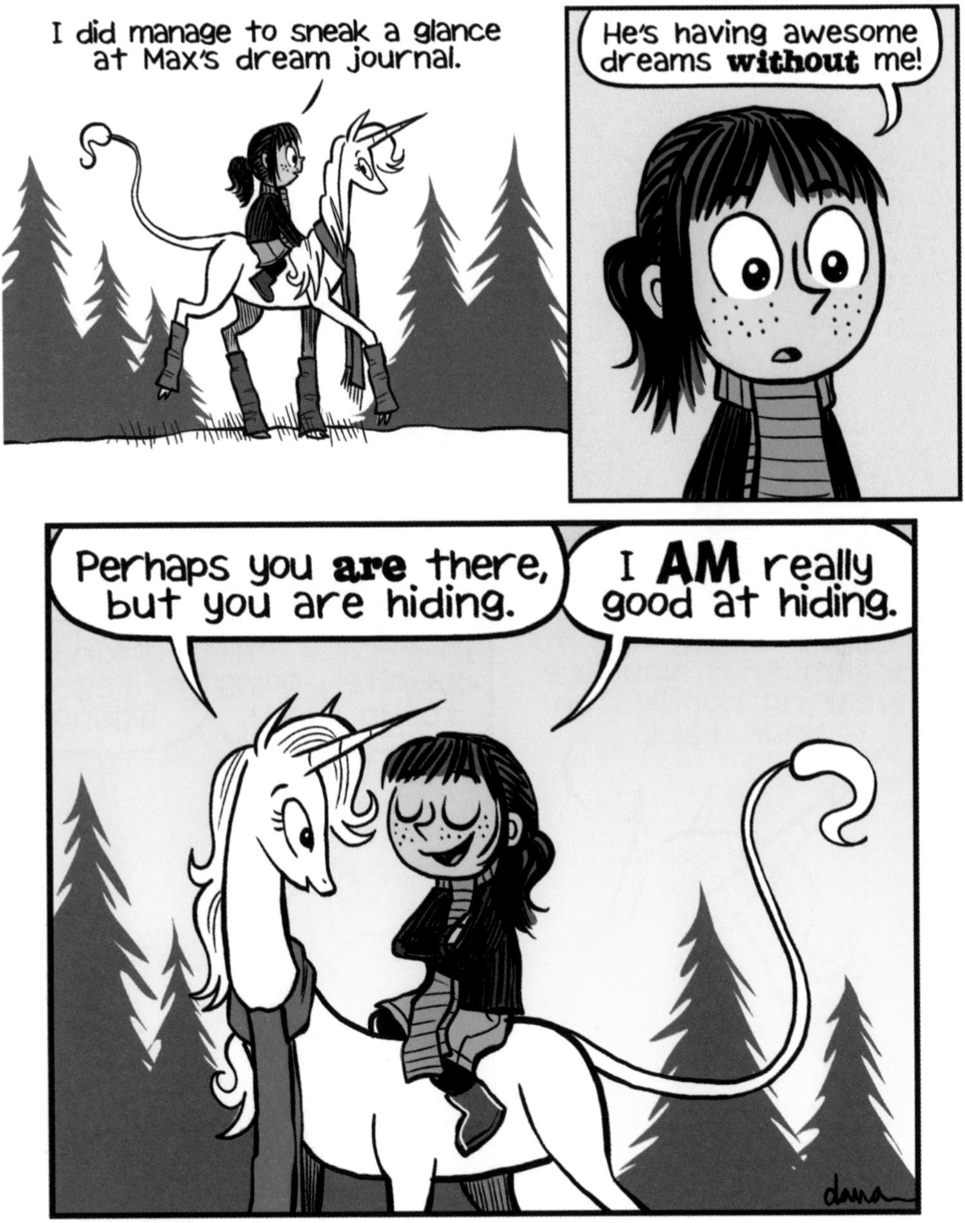

I did manage to sneak a glance at Max's dream journal.
He's having awesome dreams **without** me!
Perhaps you **are** there, but you are hiding.
I **AM** really good at hiding.

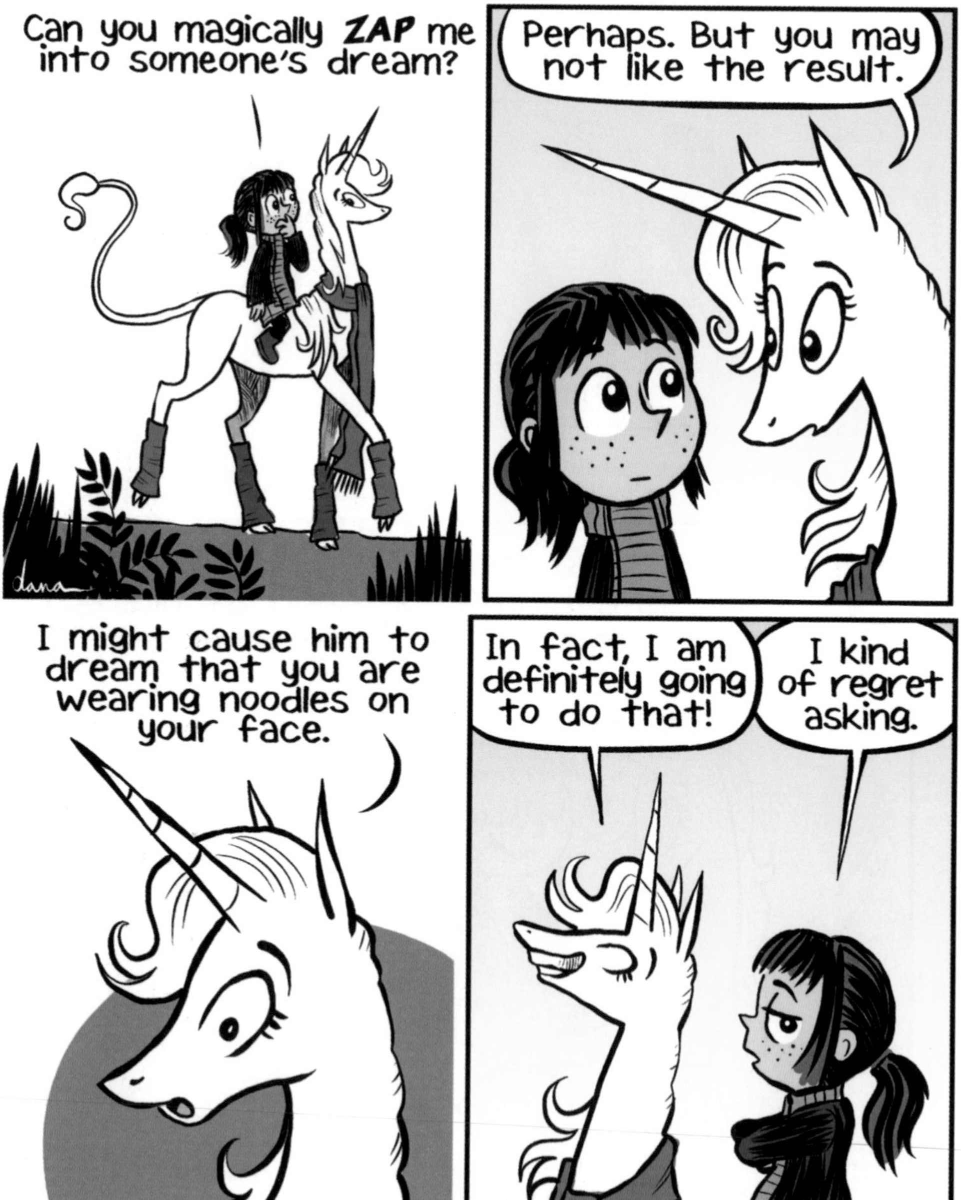
Can you magically ZAP me into someone's dream?
Perhaps. But you may not like the result.
I might cause him to dream that you are wearing noodles on your face.
In fact, I am definitely going to do that!
I kind of regret asking.
dana

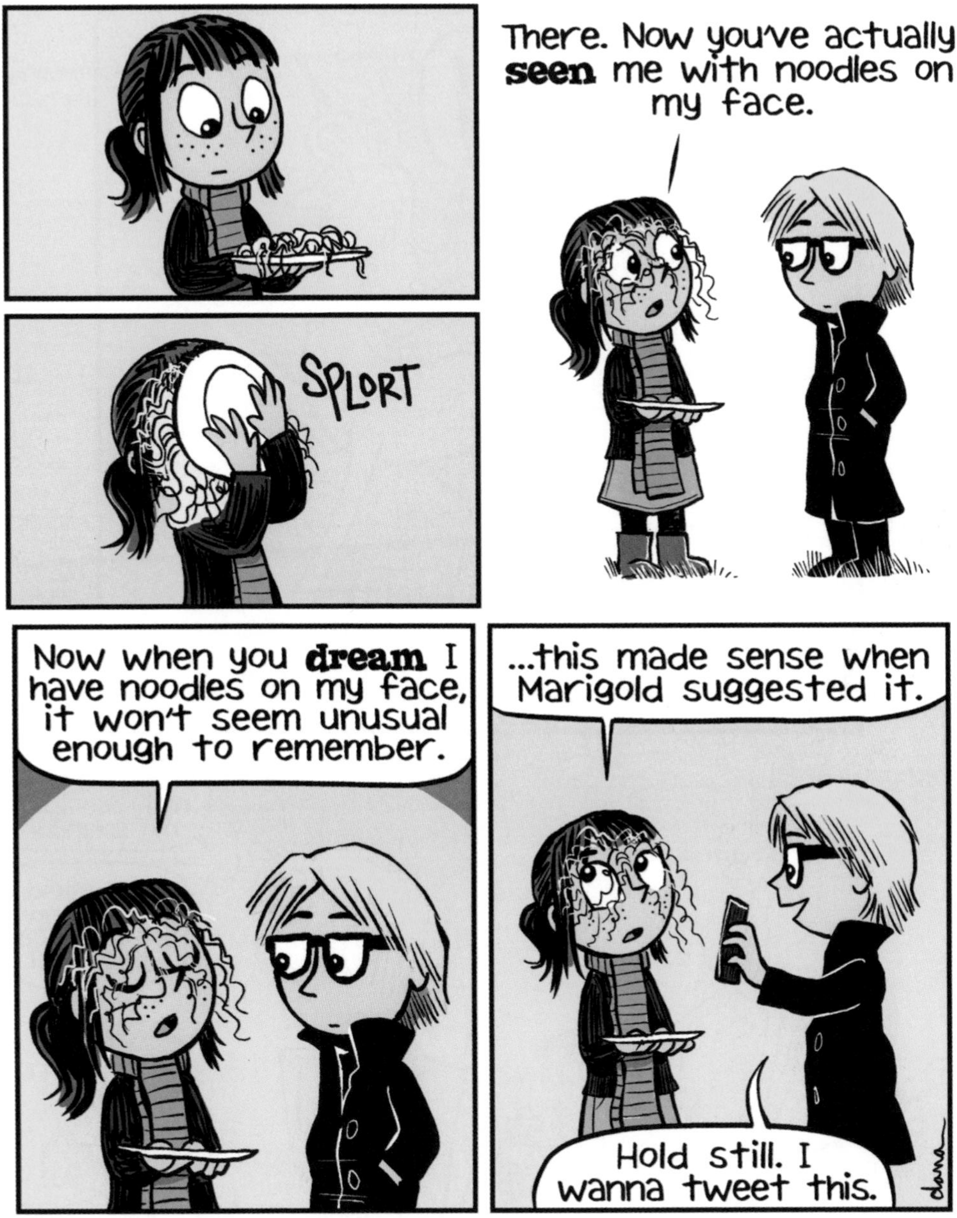
SPLORT
There. Now you've actually **seen** me with noodles on my face.
Now when you **dream** I have noodles on my face, it won't seem unusual enough to remember.
...this made sense when Marigold suggested it.
Hold still. I wanna tweet this.
dana

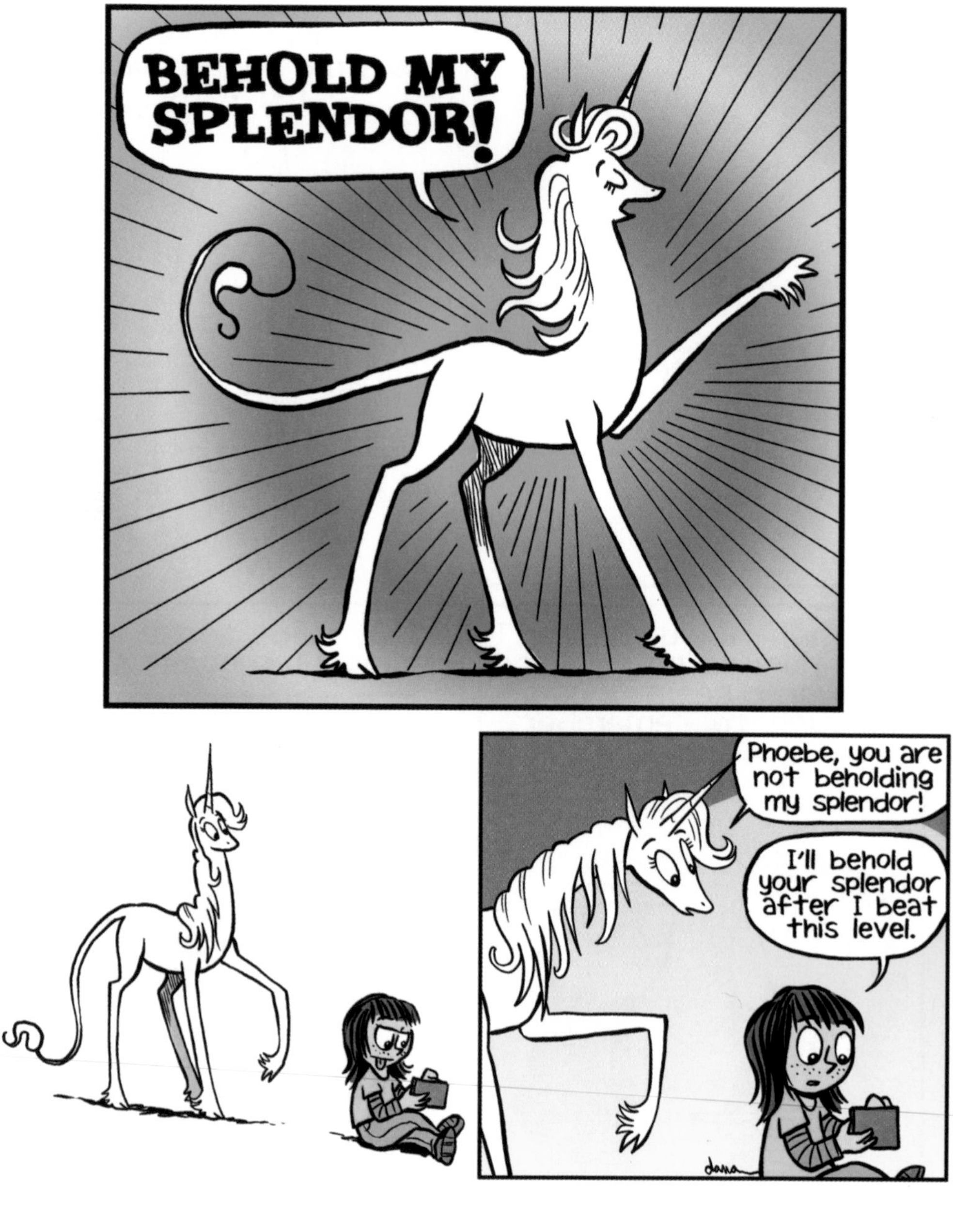
BEHOLD MY SPLENDOR!
Phoebe, you are not beholding my splendor!
I'll behold your splendor after I beat this level.

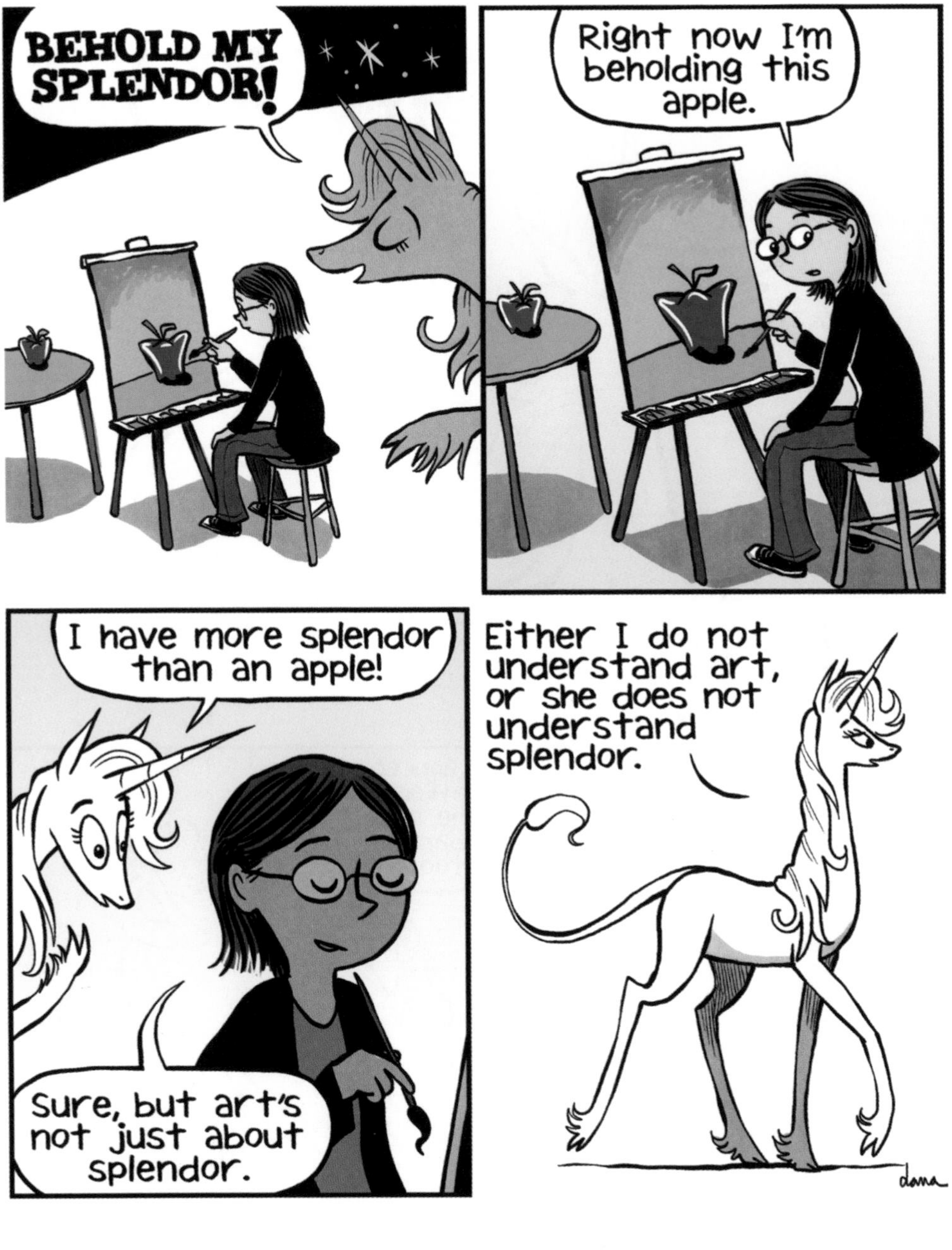
BEHOLD MY SPLENDOR!
Right now I'm beholding this apple.
I have more splendor than an apple!
Sure, but art's not just about splendor.
Either I do not understand art, or she does not understand splendor.
dana

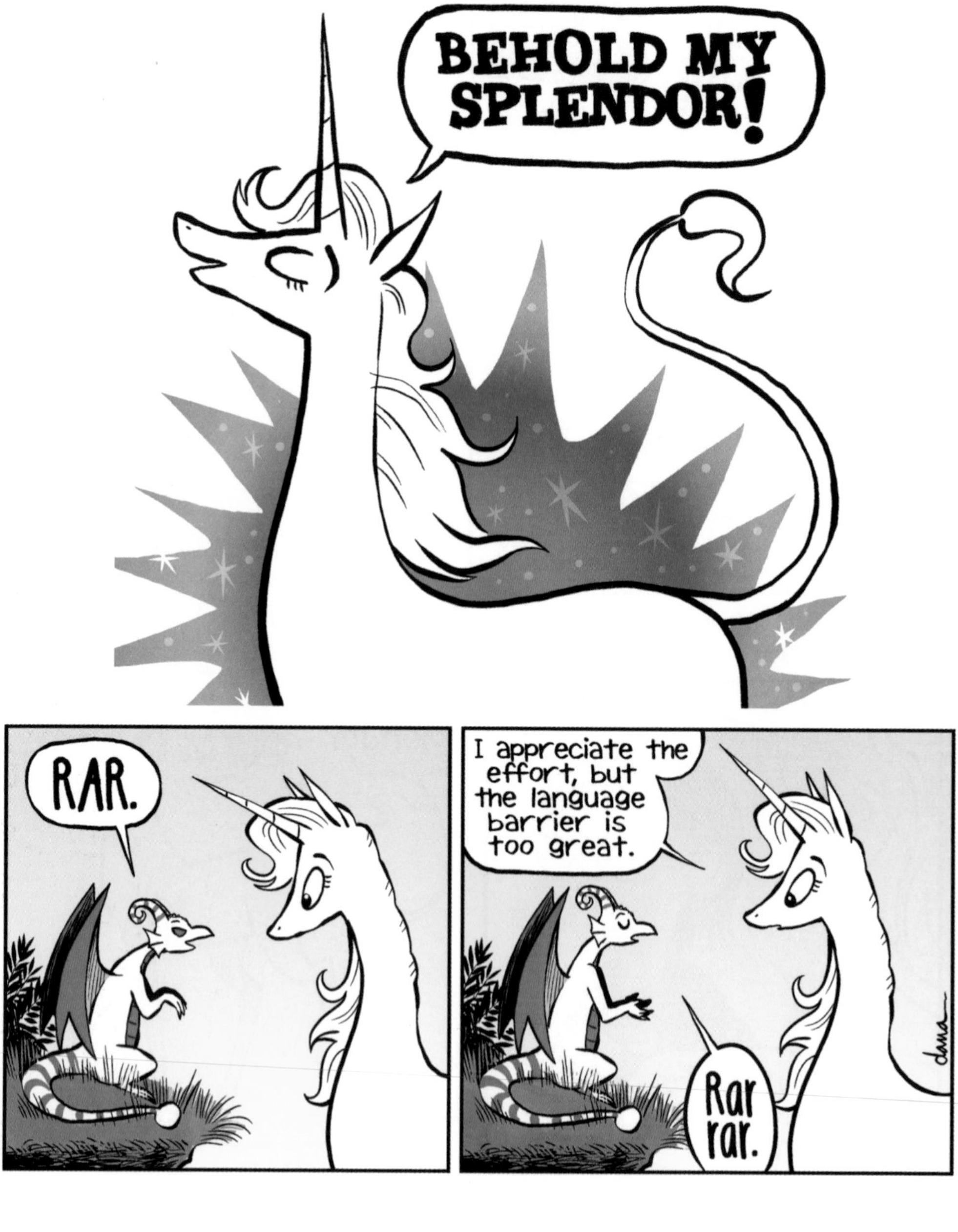
BEHOLD MY SPLENDOR!
RAR.
I appreciate the effort, but the language barrier is too great.
Rar rar.

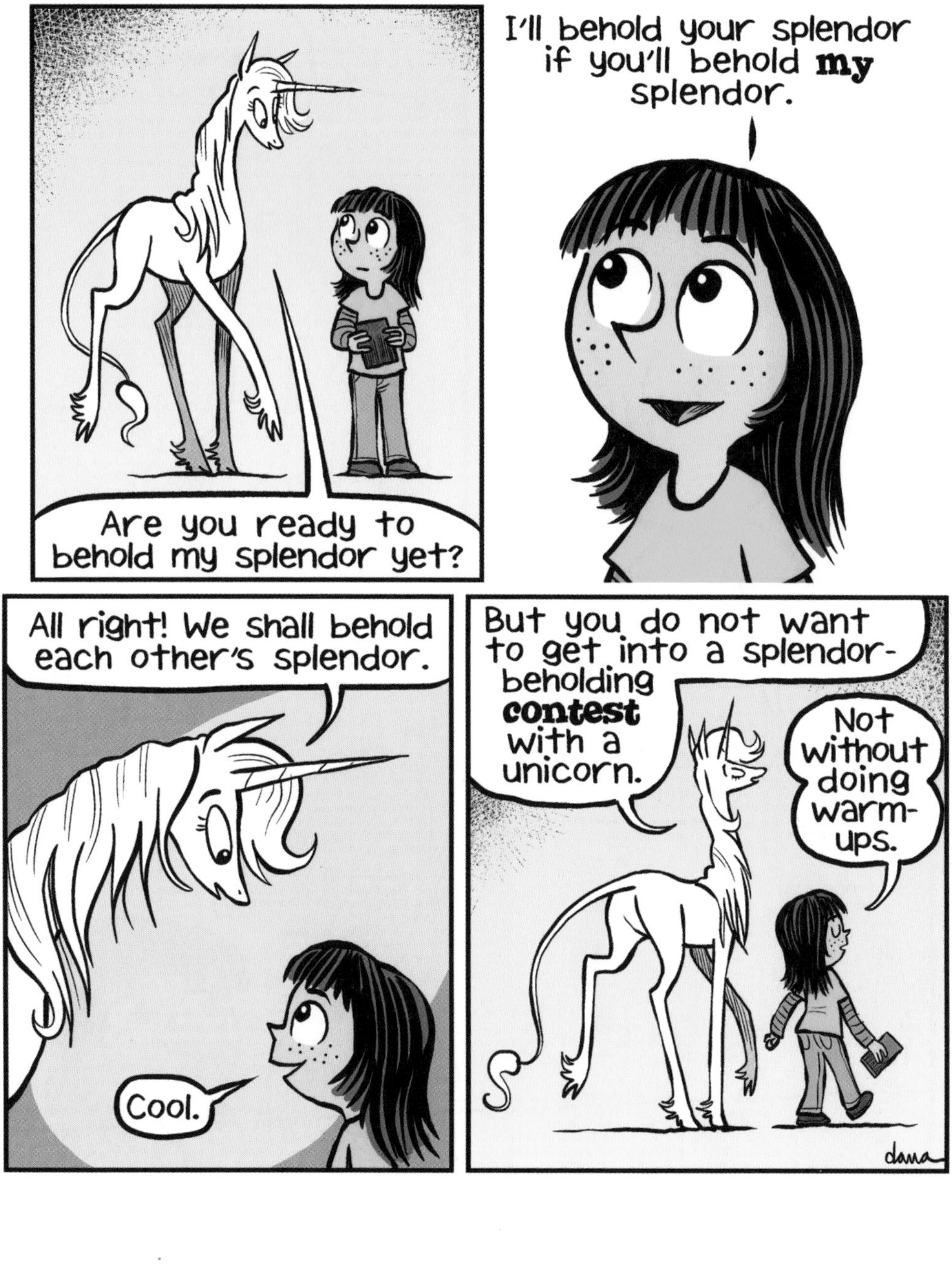
Are you ready to behold my splendor yet?
I'll behold your splendor if you'll behold **my** splendor.
All right! We shall behold each other's splendor.
Cool.
But you do not want to get into a splendor-beholding **contest** with a unicorn.
Not without doing warm-ups.
dana

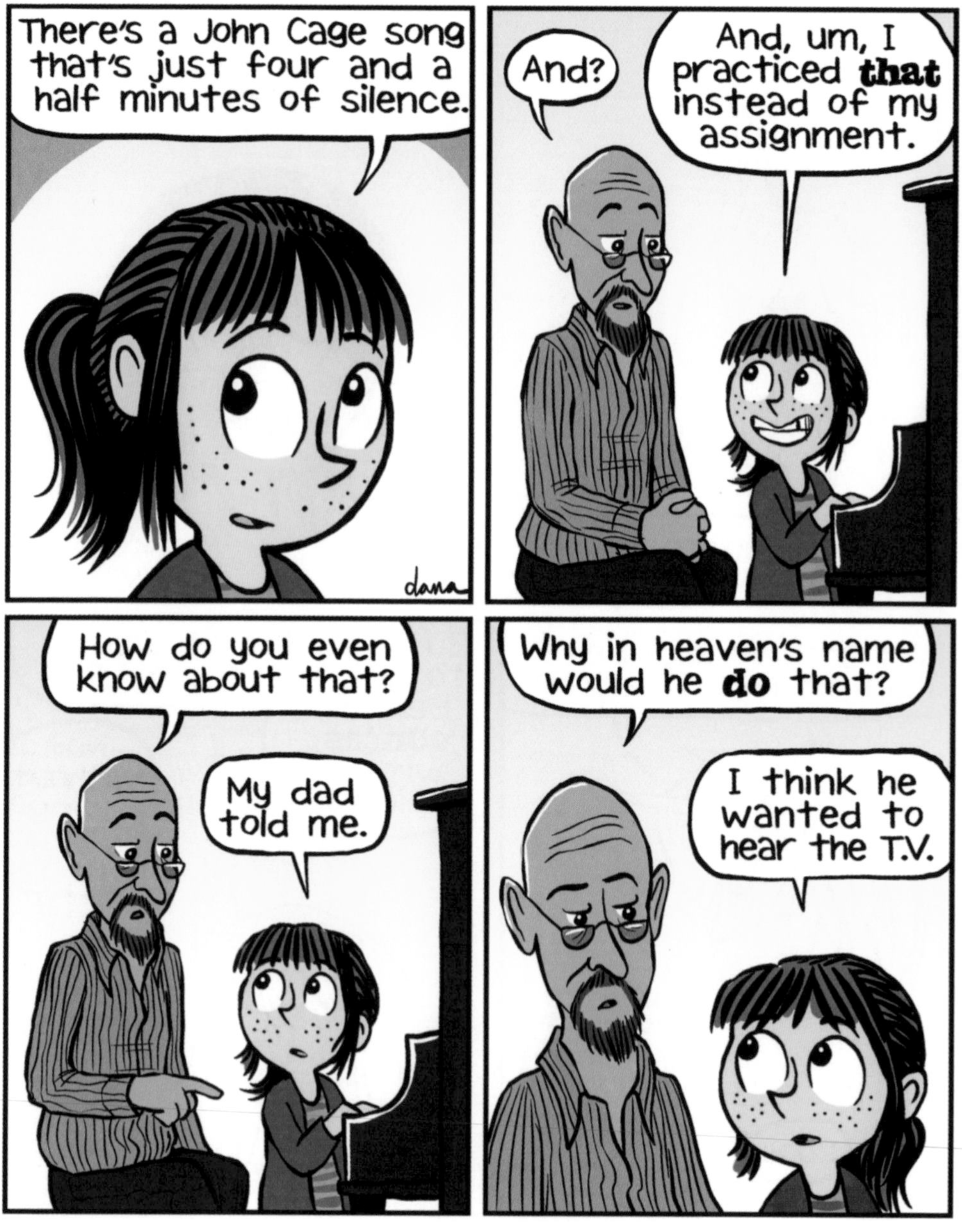
There's a John Cage song that's just four and a half minutes of silence.
dana
And?
And, um, I practiced **that** instead of my assignment.
How do you even know about that?
My dad told me.
Why in heaven's name would he **do** that?
I think he wanted to hear the T.V.

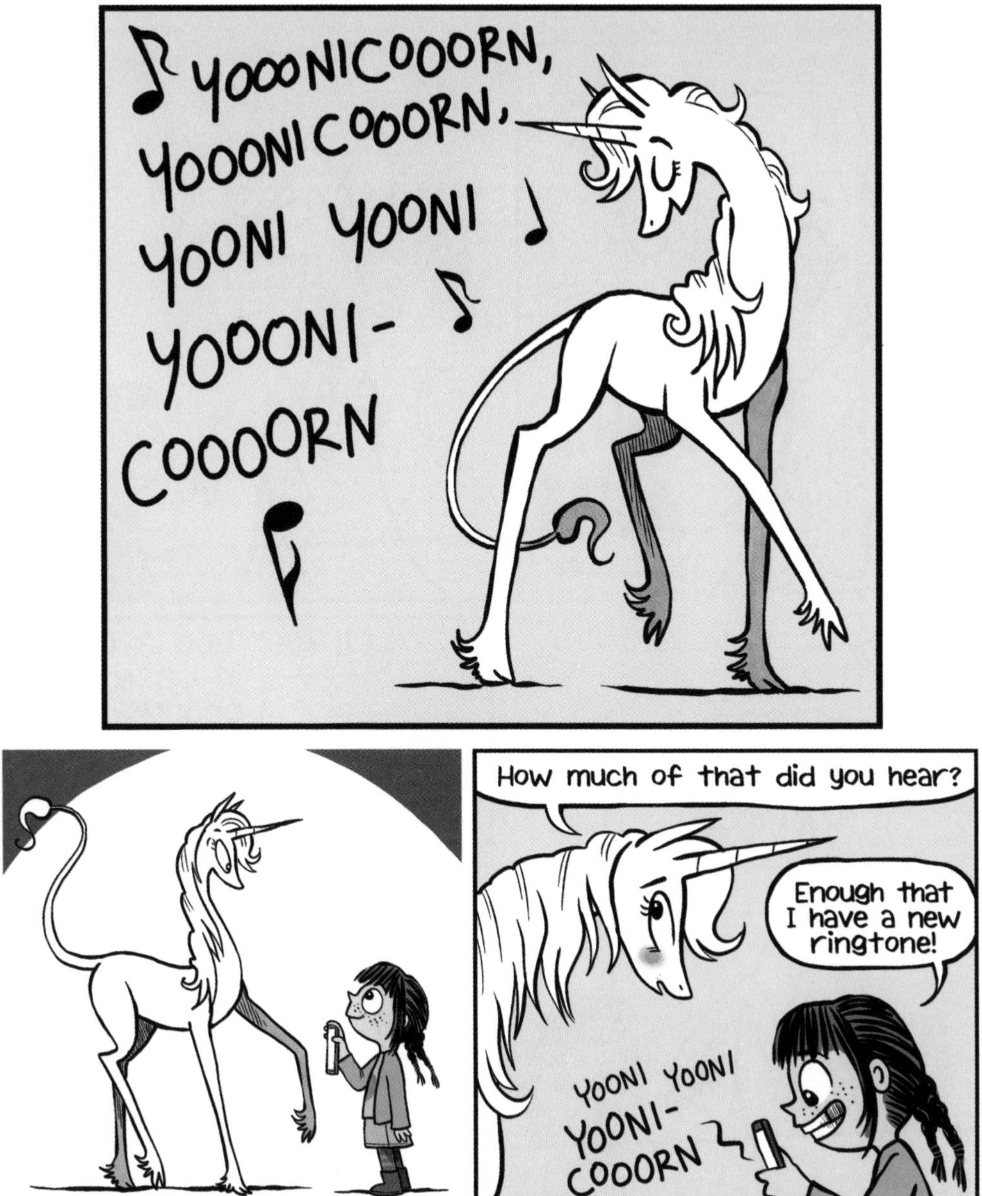
YOOONICOOORN, YOOONICOOORN, YOONI YOONI YOOONI-COOOORN
How much of that did you hear?
Enough that I have a new ringtone!
YOONI YOONI YOONI-COOORN

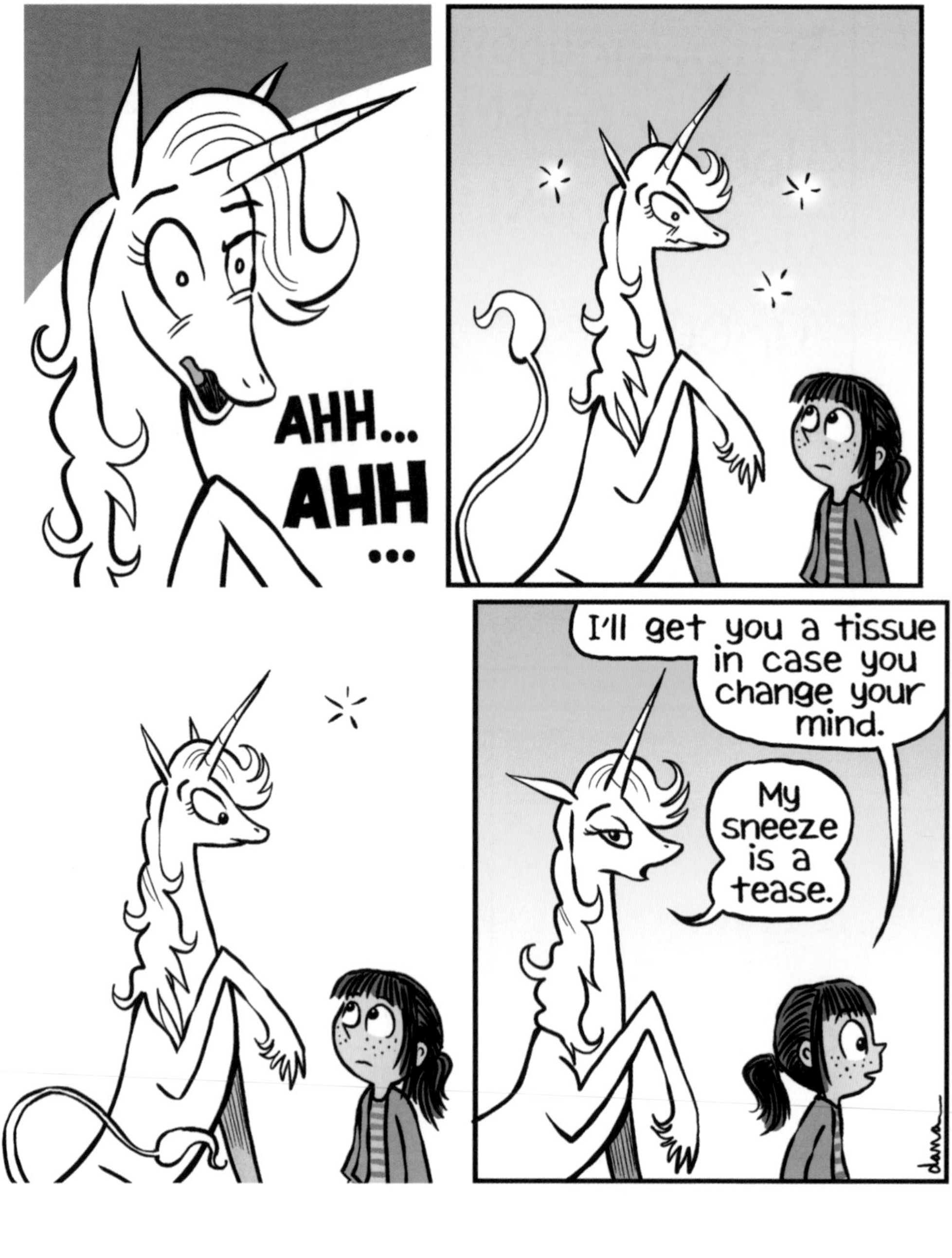
AHH...
AHH
...
I'll get you a tissue in case you change your mind.
My sneeze is a tease.
dana

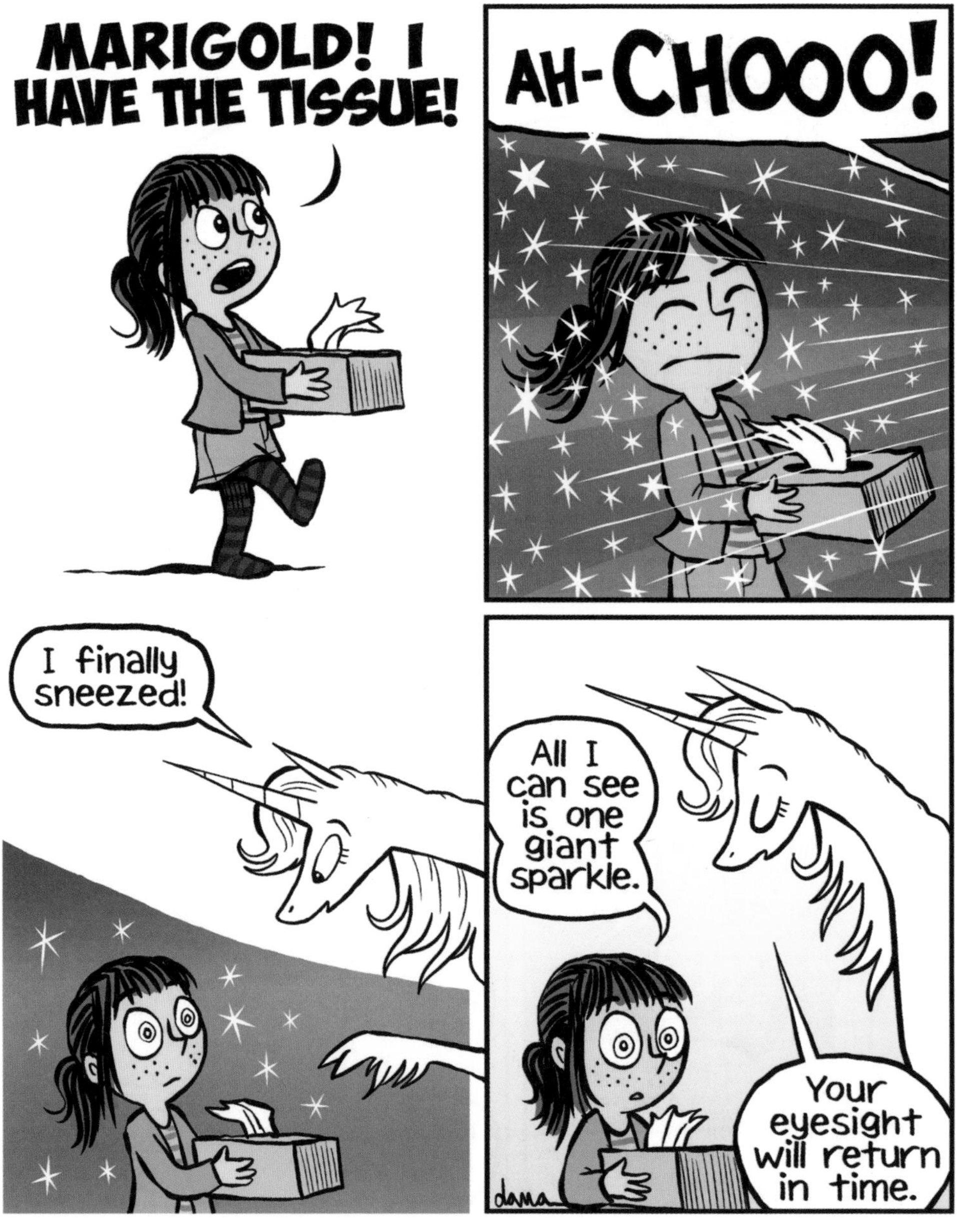
MARIGOLD! I HAVE THE TISSUE!
AH-CHOOO!
I finally sneezed!
All I can see is one giant sparkle.
Your eyesight will return in time.
dana

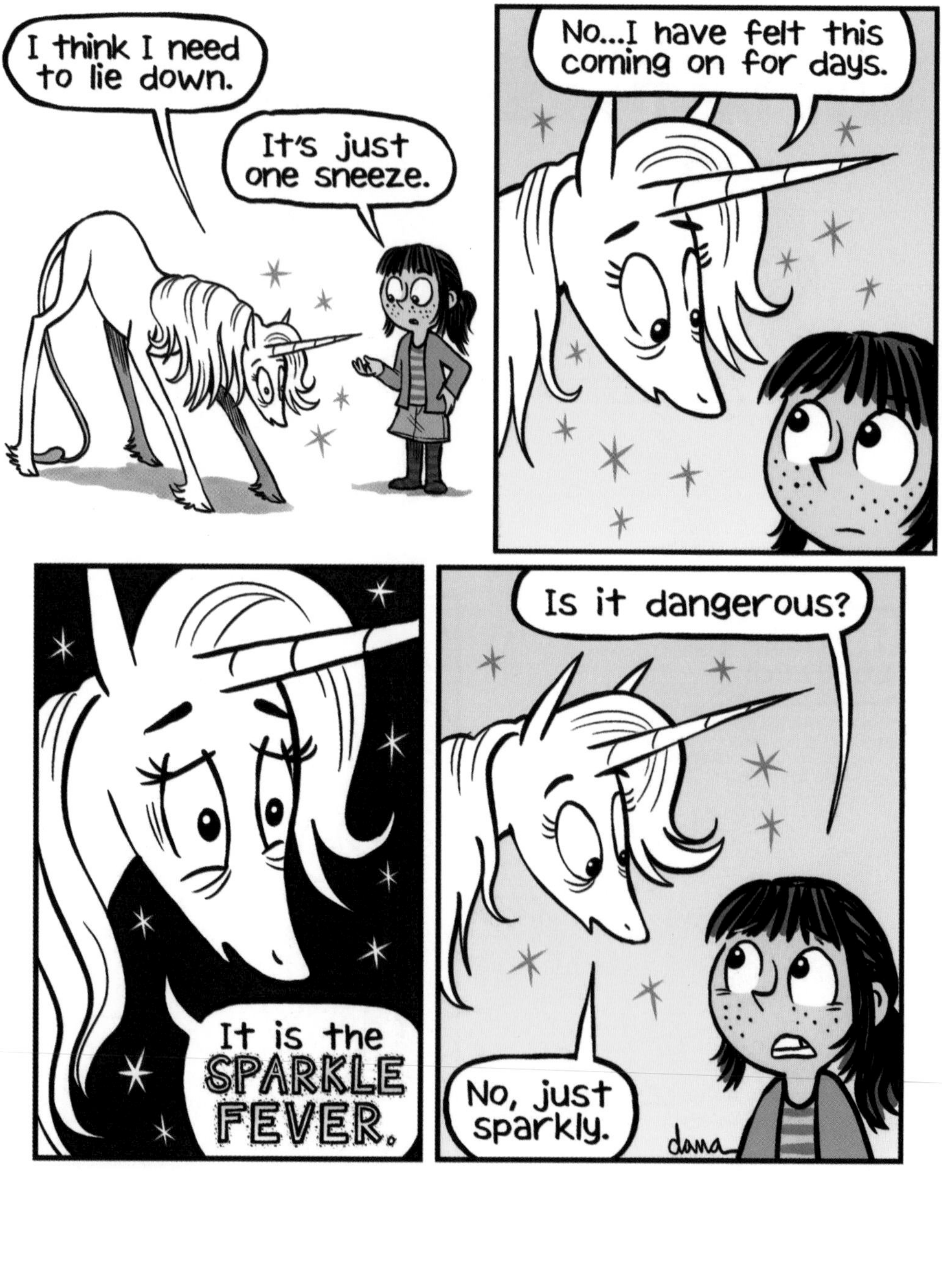
I think I need to lie down.
It's just one sneeze.
No...I have felt this coming on for days.
It is the SPARKLE FEVER.
Is it dangerous?
No, just sparkly.
dana

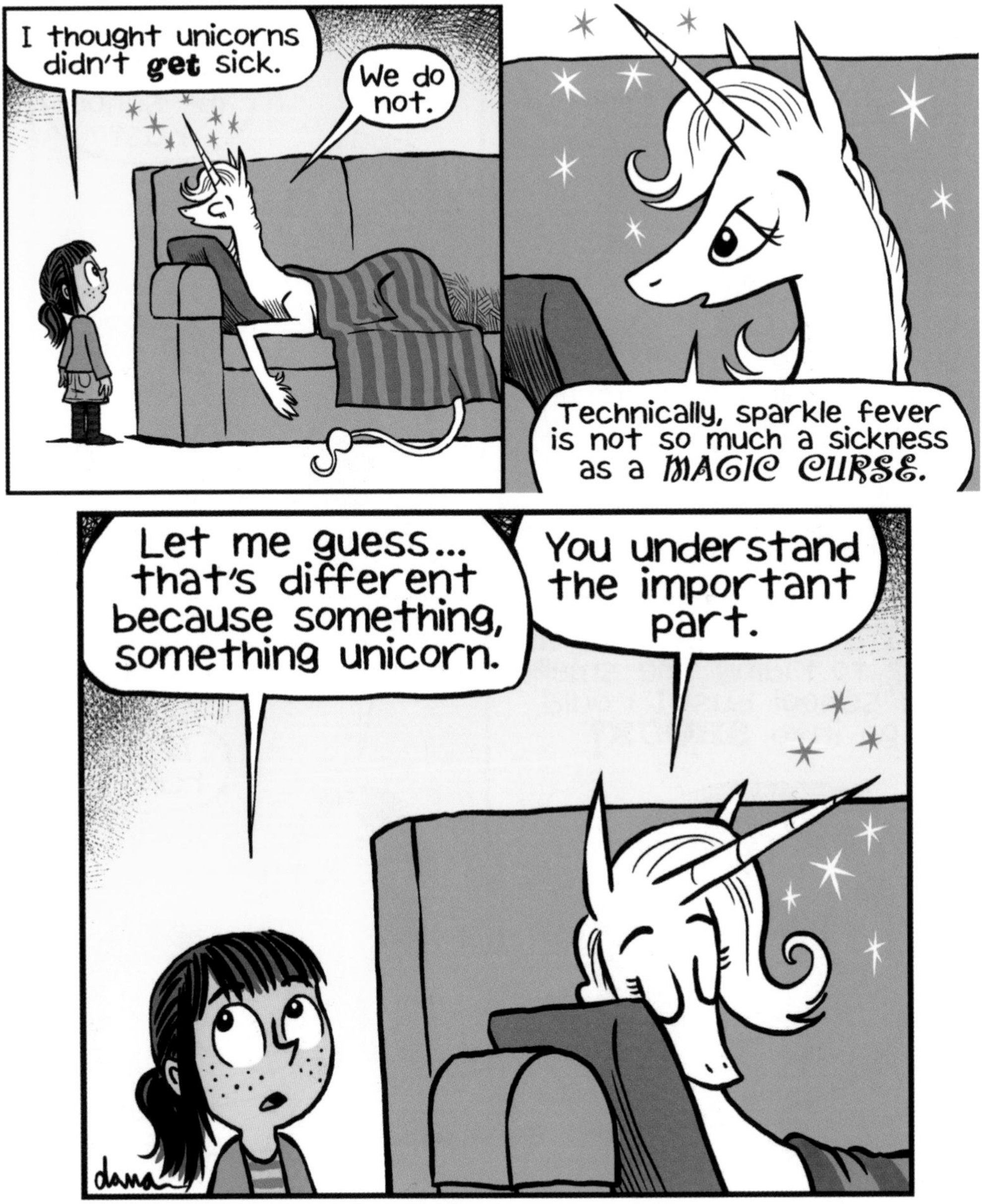
I thought unicorns didn't **get** sick.
We do not.
Technically, sparkle fever is not so much a sickness as a MAGIC CURSE.
Let me guess... that's different because something, something unicorn.
You understand the important part.
dana

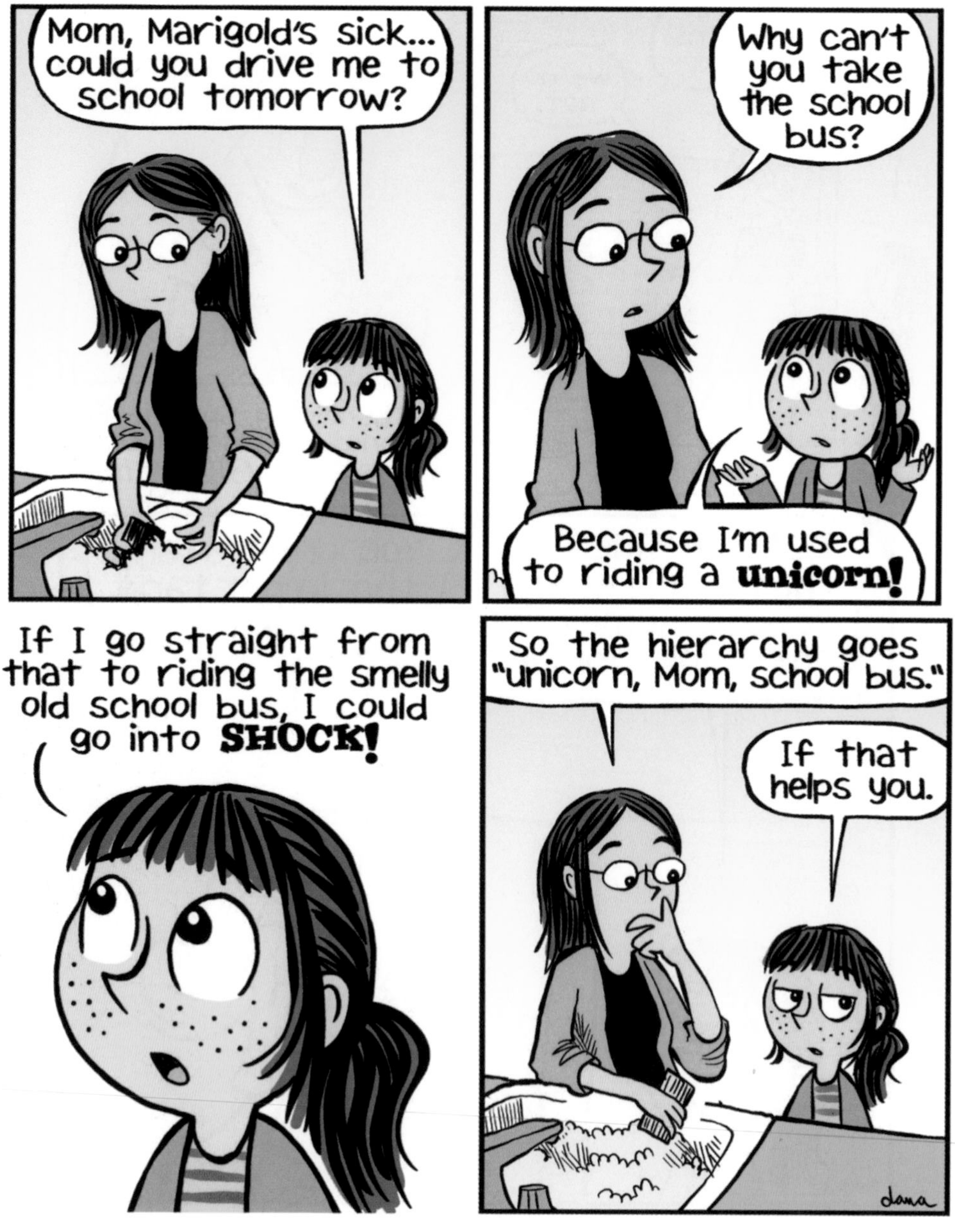
Mom, Marigold's sick... could you drive me to school tomorrow?
Why can't you take the school bus?
Because I'm used to riding a **unicorn!**
If I go straight from that to riding the smelly old school bus, I could go into **SHOCK!**
So the hierarchy goes "unicorn, Mom, school bus."
If that helps you.
dana

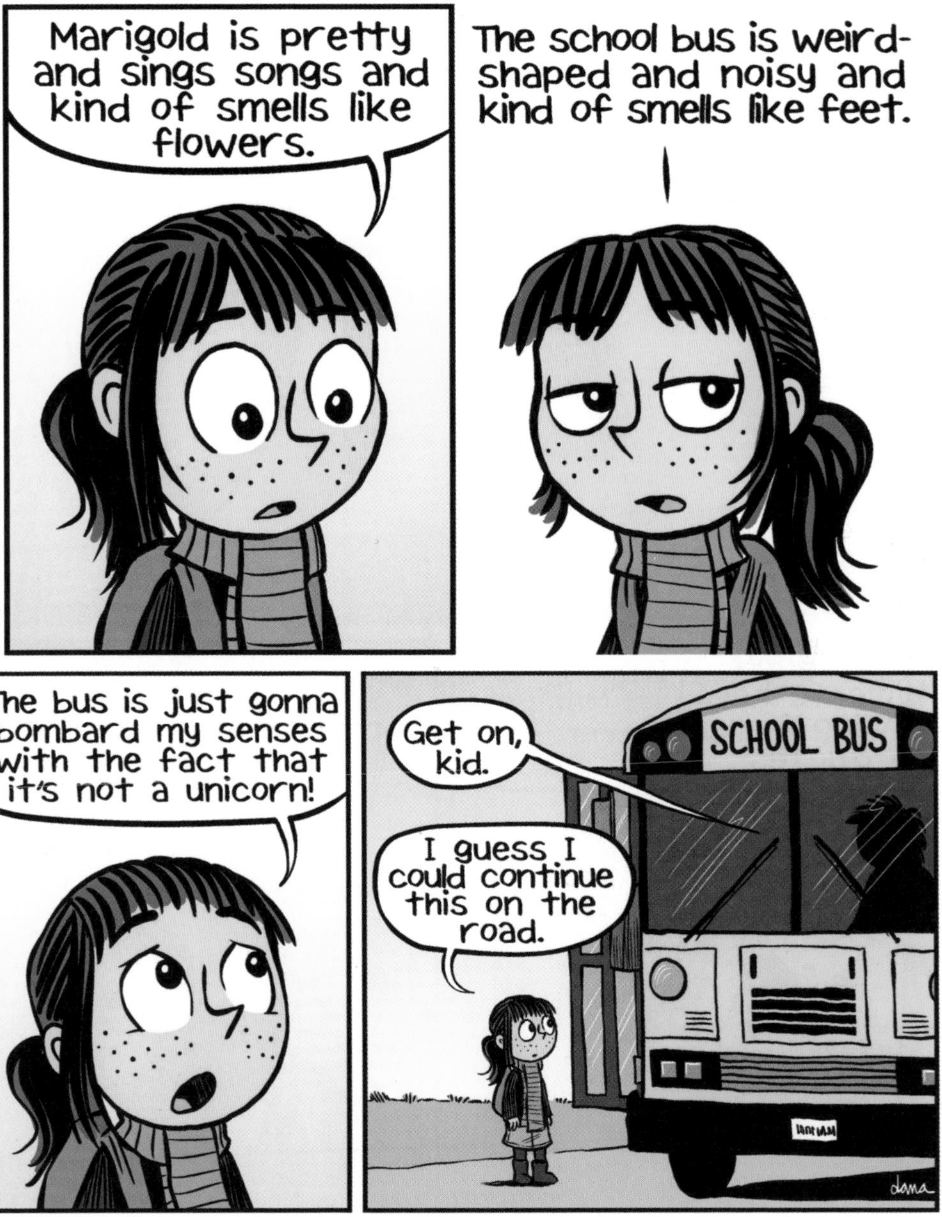
Marigold is pretty and sings songs and kind of smells like flowers.
The school bus is weird-shaped and noisy and kind of smells like feet.
The bus is just gonna bombard my senses with the fact that it's not a unicorn!
SCHOOL BUS
Get on, kid.
I guess I could continue this on the road.
dana

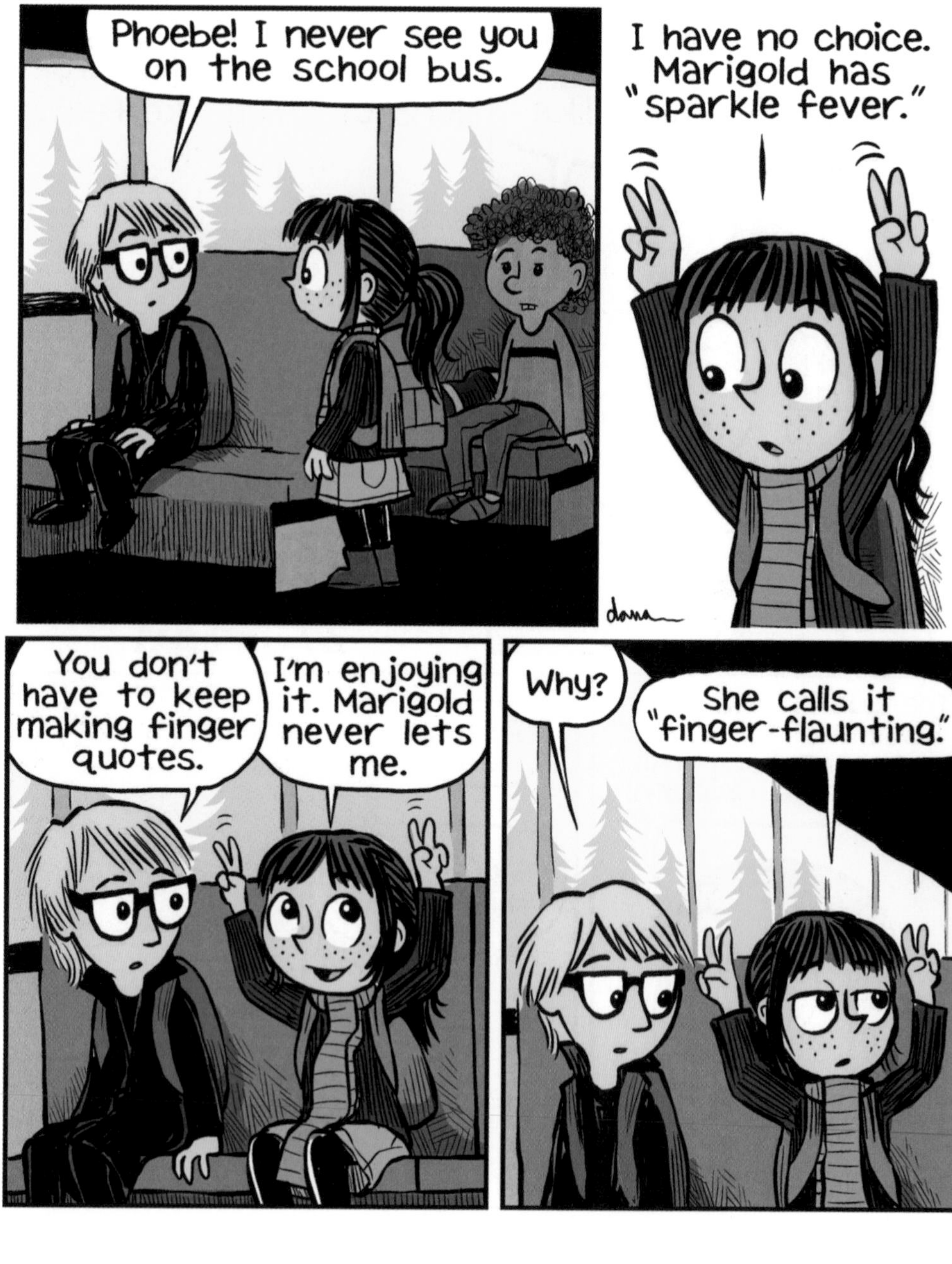
Phoebe! I never see you on the school bus.
I have no choice. Marigold has "sparkle fever."
You don't have to keep making finger quotes.
I'm enjoying it. Marigold never lets me.
Why?
She calls it "finger-flaunting."

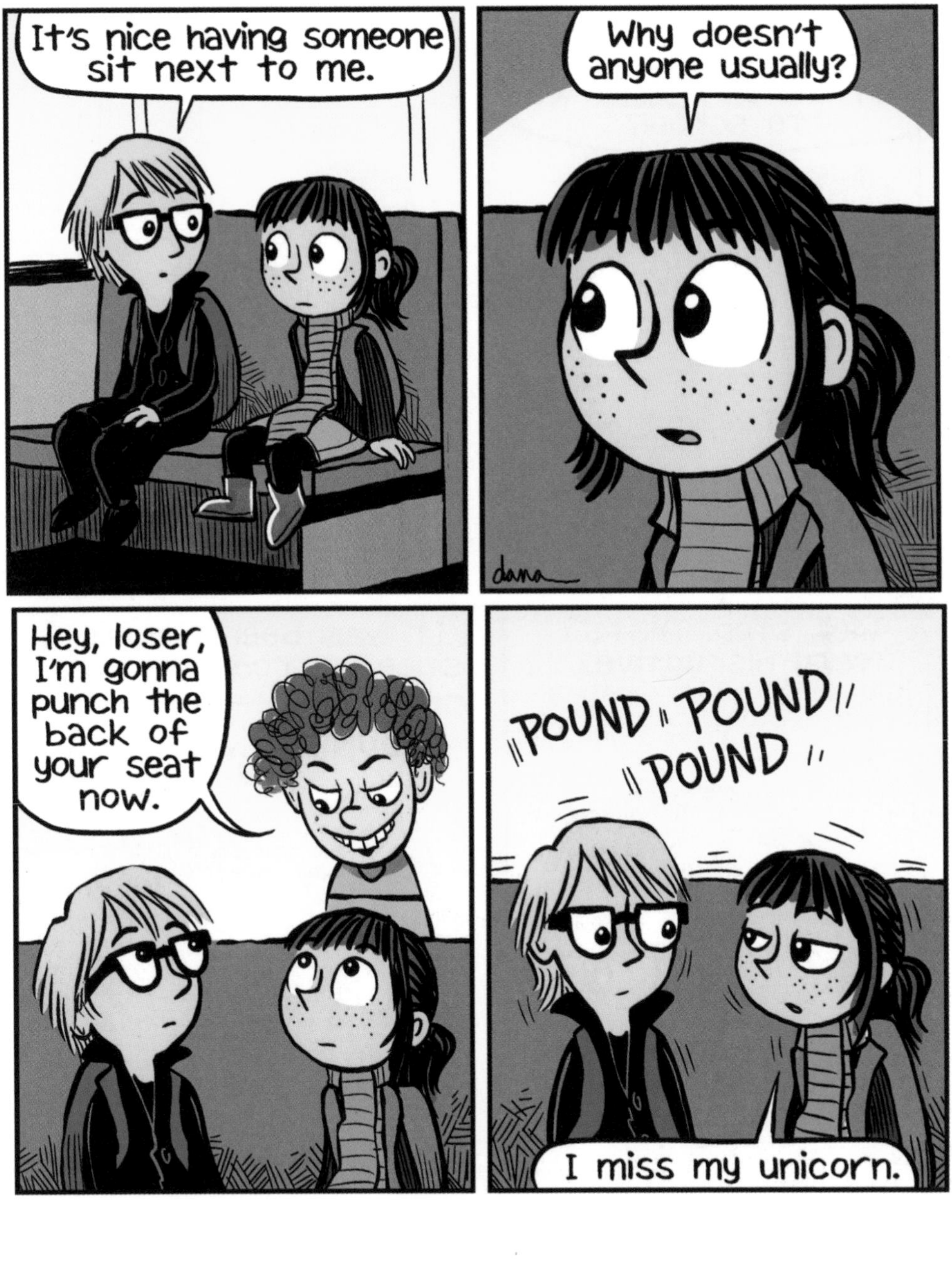
It's nice having someone sit next to me.
Why doesn't anyone usually?
dana
Hey, loser, I'm gonna punch the back of your seat now.
POUND POUND POUND
I miss my unicorn.

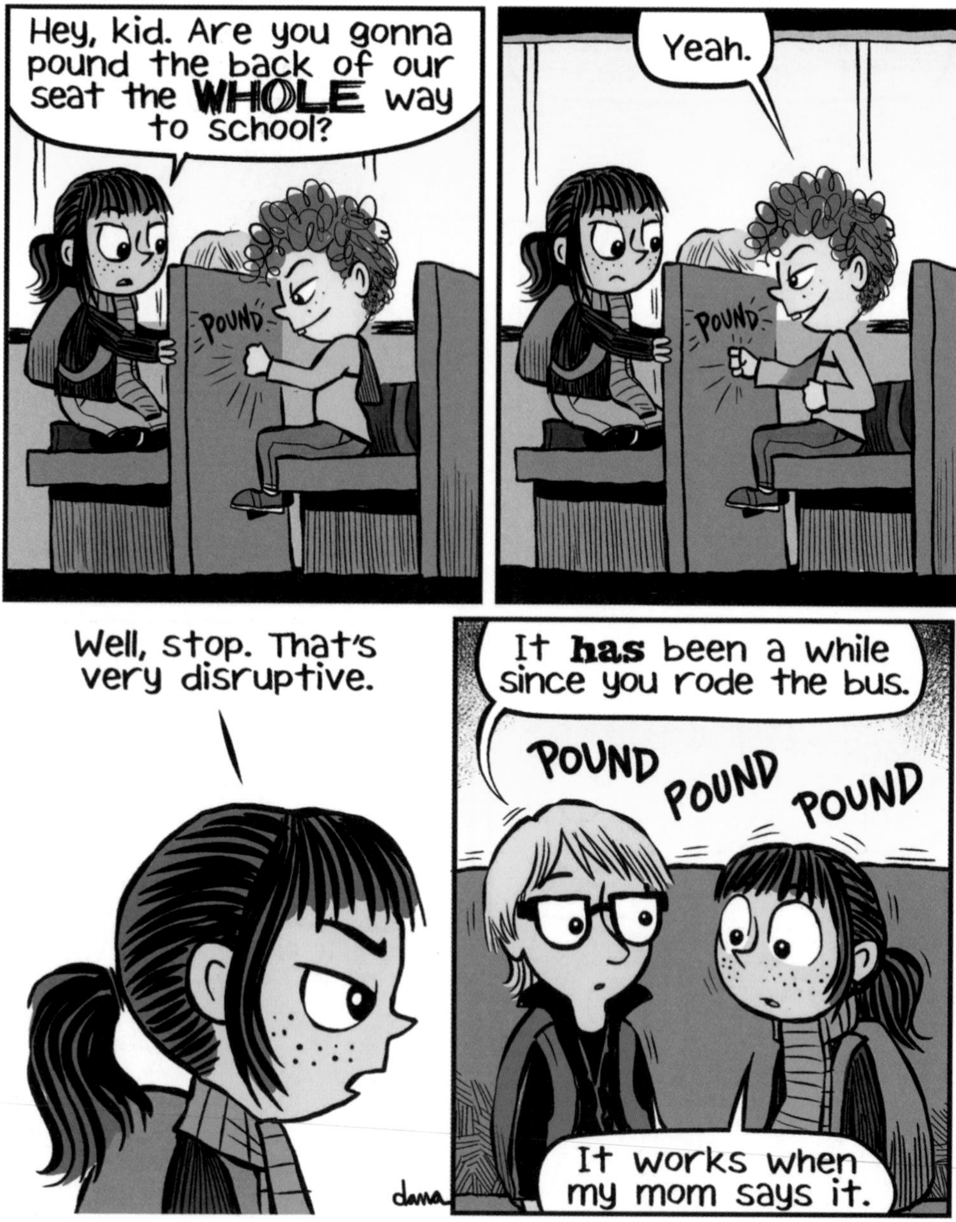
Hey, kid. Are you gonna pound the back of our seat the WHOLE way to school?
POUND
Yeah.
POUND
Well, stop. That's very disruptive.
It has been a while since you rode the bus.
POUND POUND POUND
It works when my mom says it.
dana

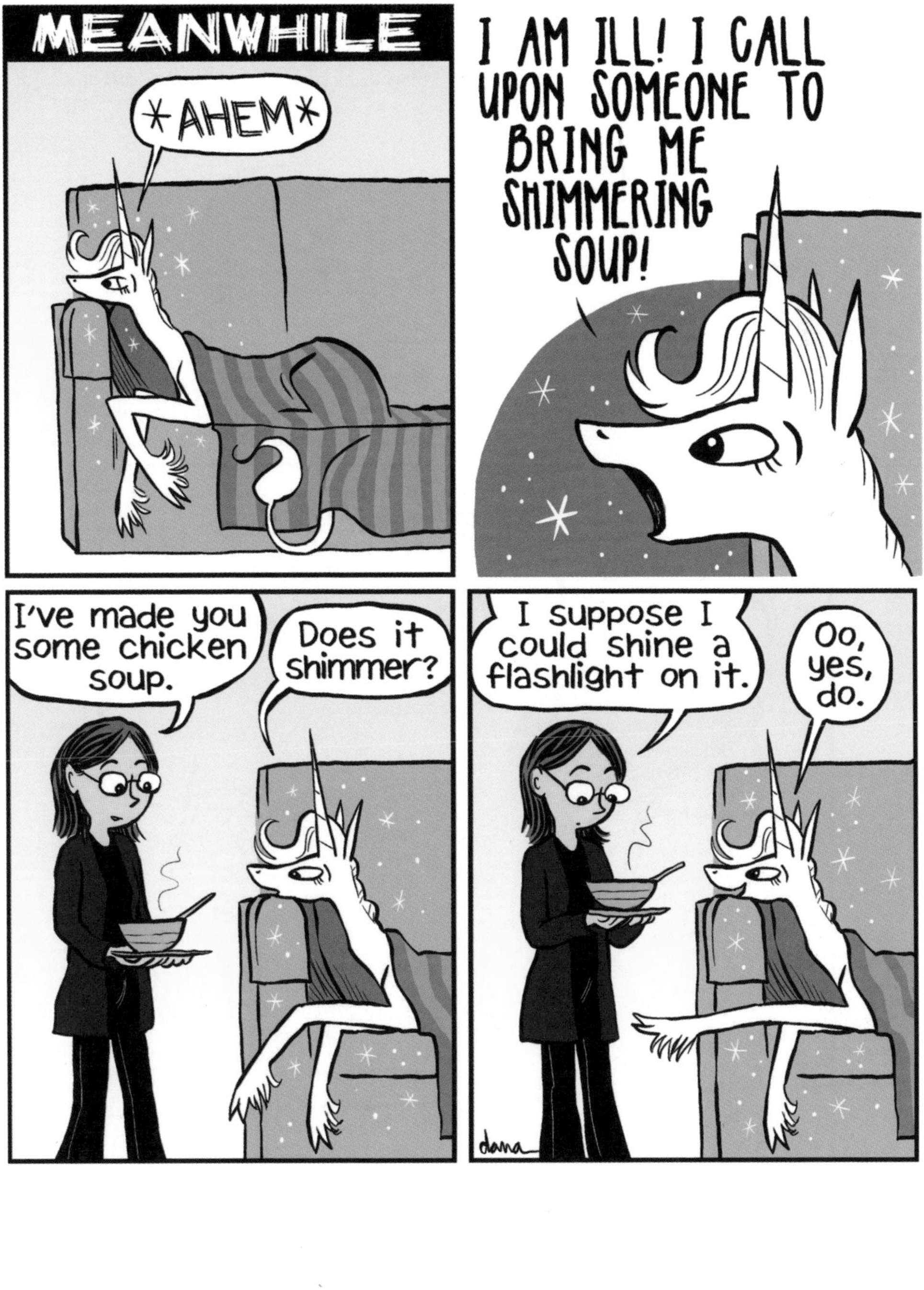
MEANWHILE
AHEM
I AM ILL! I CALL UPON SOMEONE TO BRING ME SHIMMERING SOUP!
I've made you some chicken soup.
Does it shimmer?
I suppose I could shine a flashlight on it.
Oo, yes, do.
dana

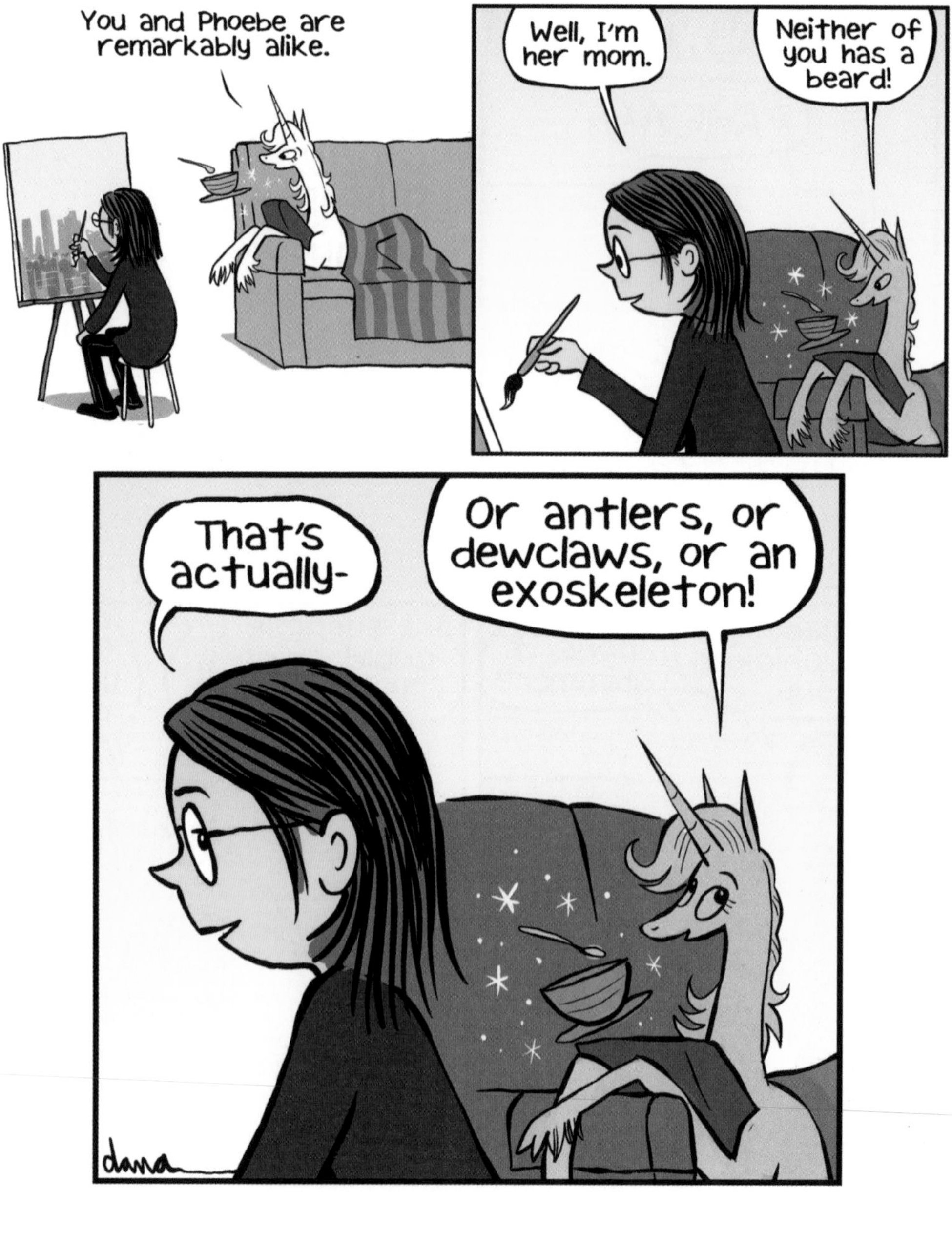
You and Phoebe are remarkably alike.
Well, I'm her mom.
Neither of you has a beard!
That's actually-
Or antlers, or dewclaws, or an exoskeleton!
dana

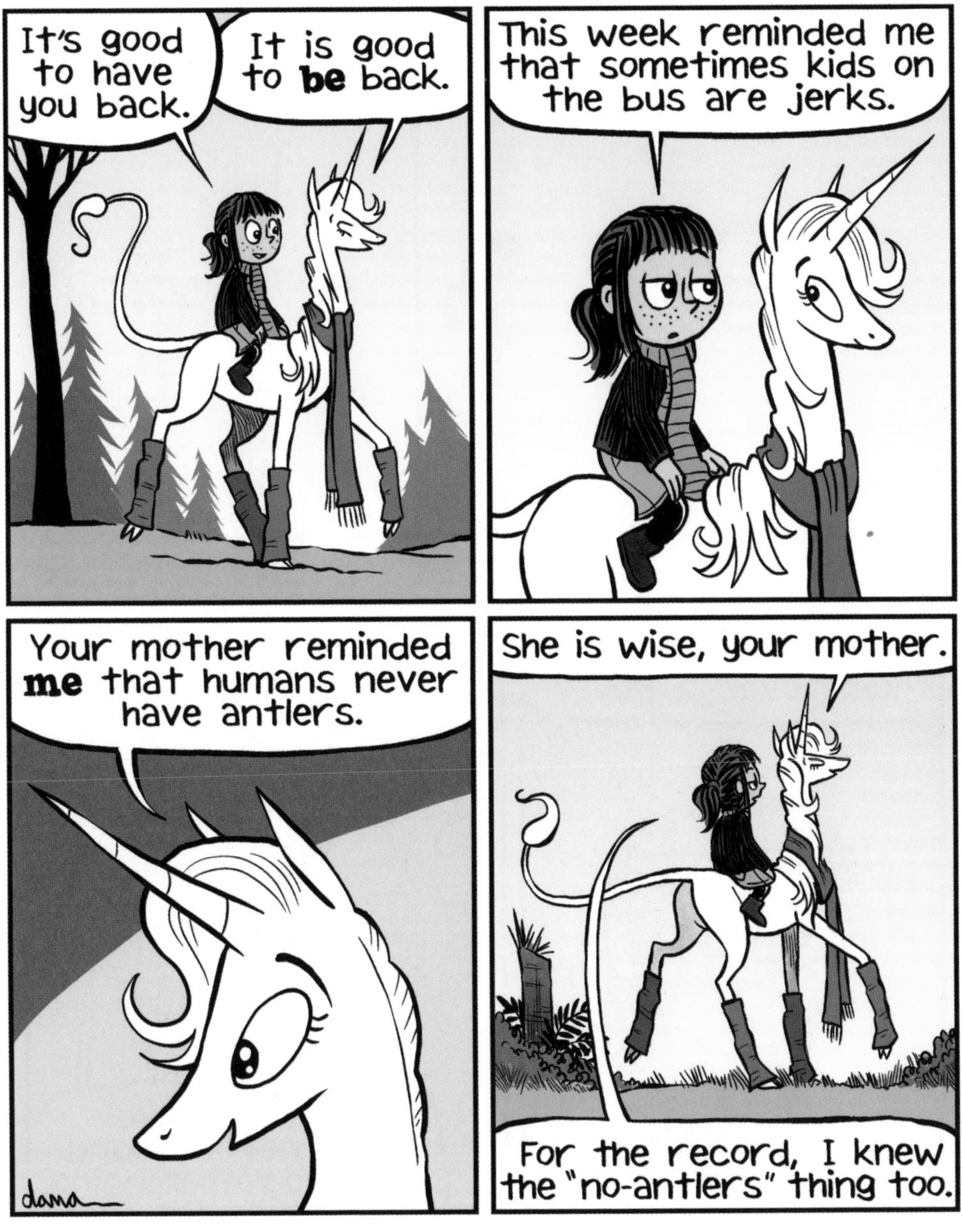
It's good to have you back.
It is good to **be** back.
This week reminded me that sometimes kids on the bus are jerks.
Your mother reminded **me** that humans never have antlers.
She is wise, your mother.
For the record, I knew the "no-antlers" thing too.
dana

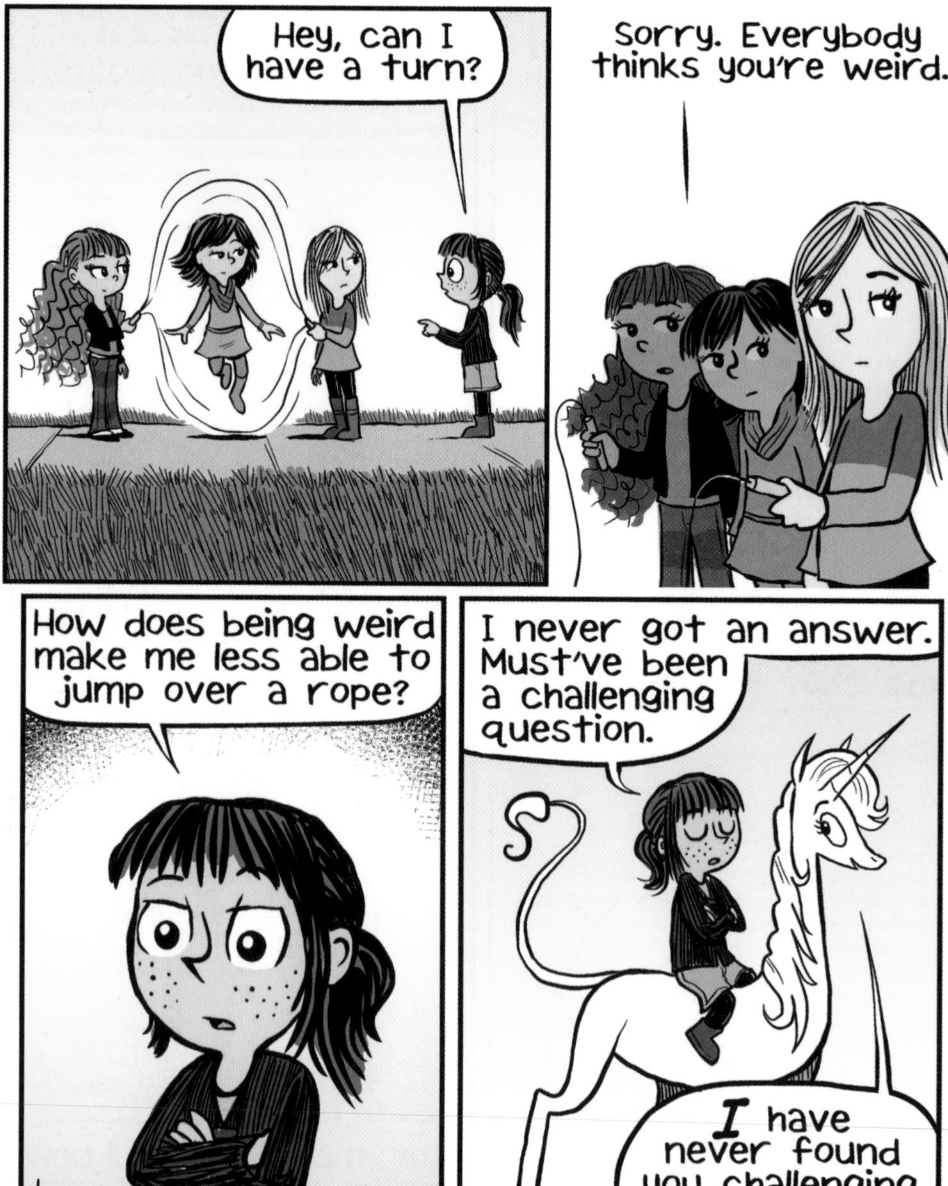
Hey, can I have a turn?
Sorry. Everybody thinks you're weird.
How does being weird make me less able to jump over a rope?
I never got an answer. Must've been a challenging question.
I have never found you challenging.
dana

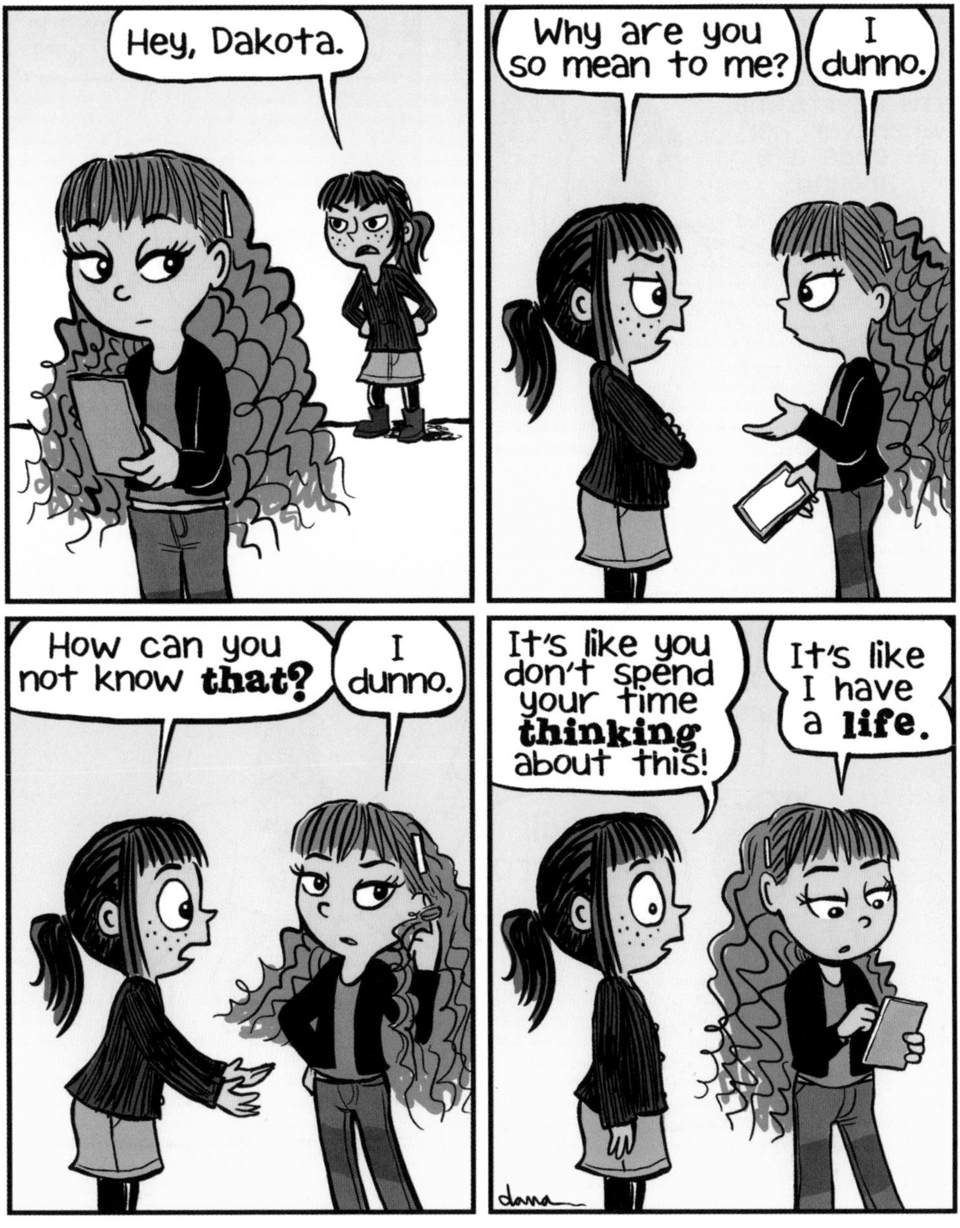
Hey, Dakota.
Why are you so mean to me?
I dunno.
How can you not know **that?**
I dunno.
It's like you don't spend your time **thinking** about this!
It's like I have a **life**.
dana

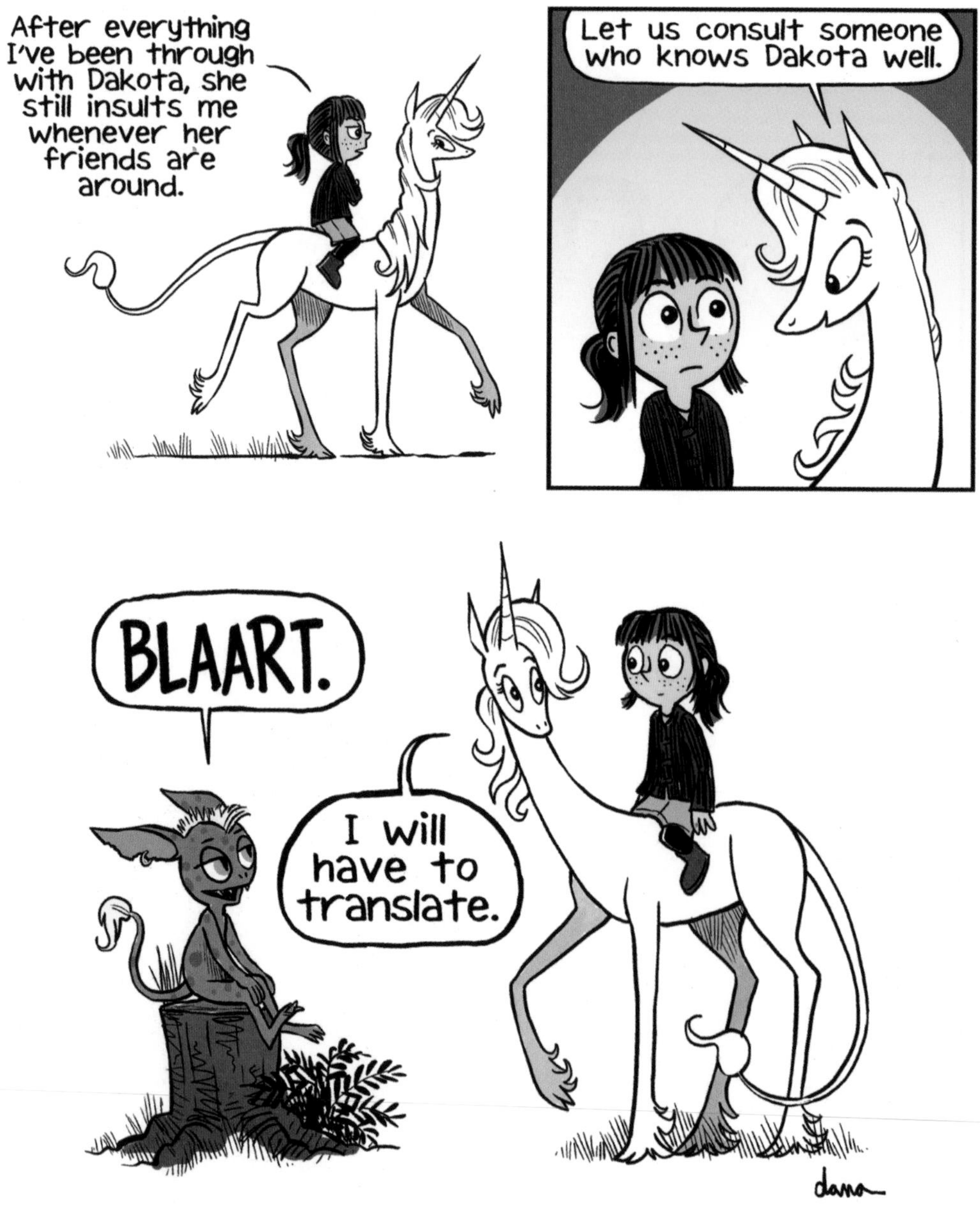

After everything I've been through with Dakota, she still insults me whenever her friends are around.
Let us consult someone who knows Dakota well.
BLAART.
I will have to translate.
dana

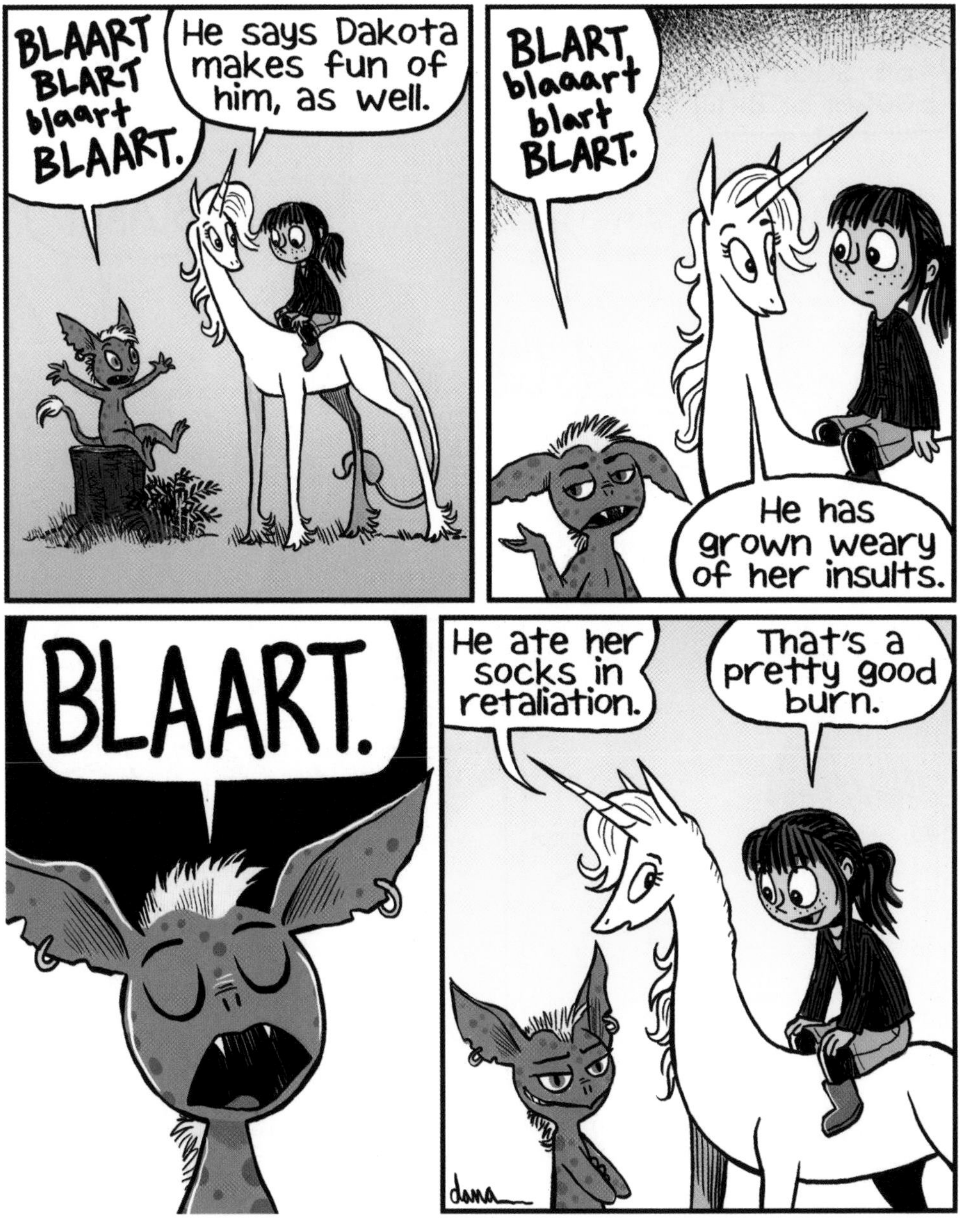
BLAART BLART blaart BLAART.
He says Dakota makes fun of him, as well.
BLART, blaaart blart BLART.
He has grown weary of her insults.
BLAART.
He ate her socks in retaliation.
That's a pretty good burn.
dana

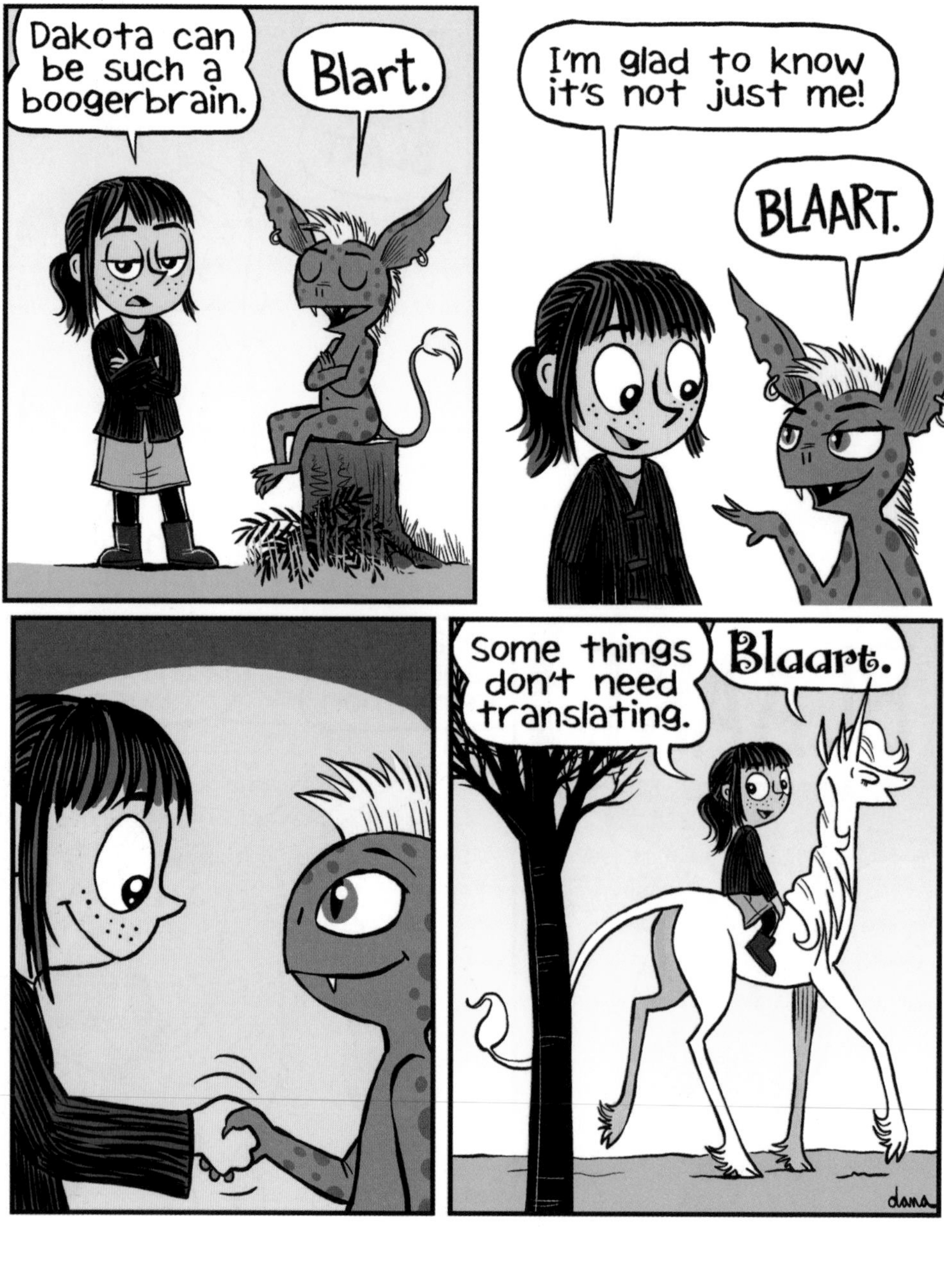
Dakota can be such a boogerbrain.
Blart.
I'm glad to know it's not just me!
BLAART.
Some things don't need translating.
Blaart.
dana

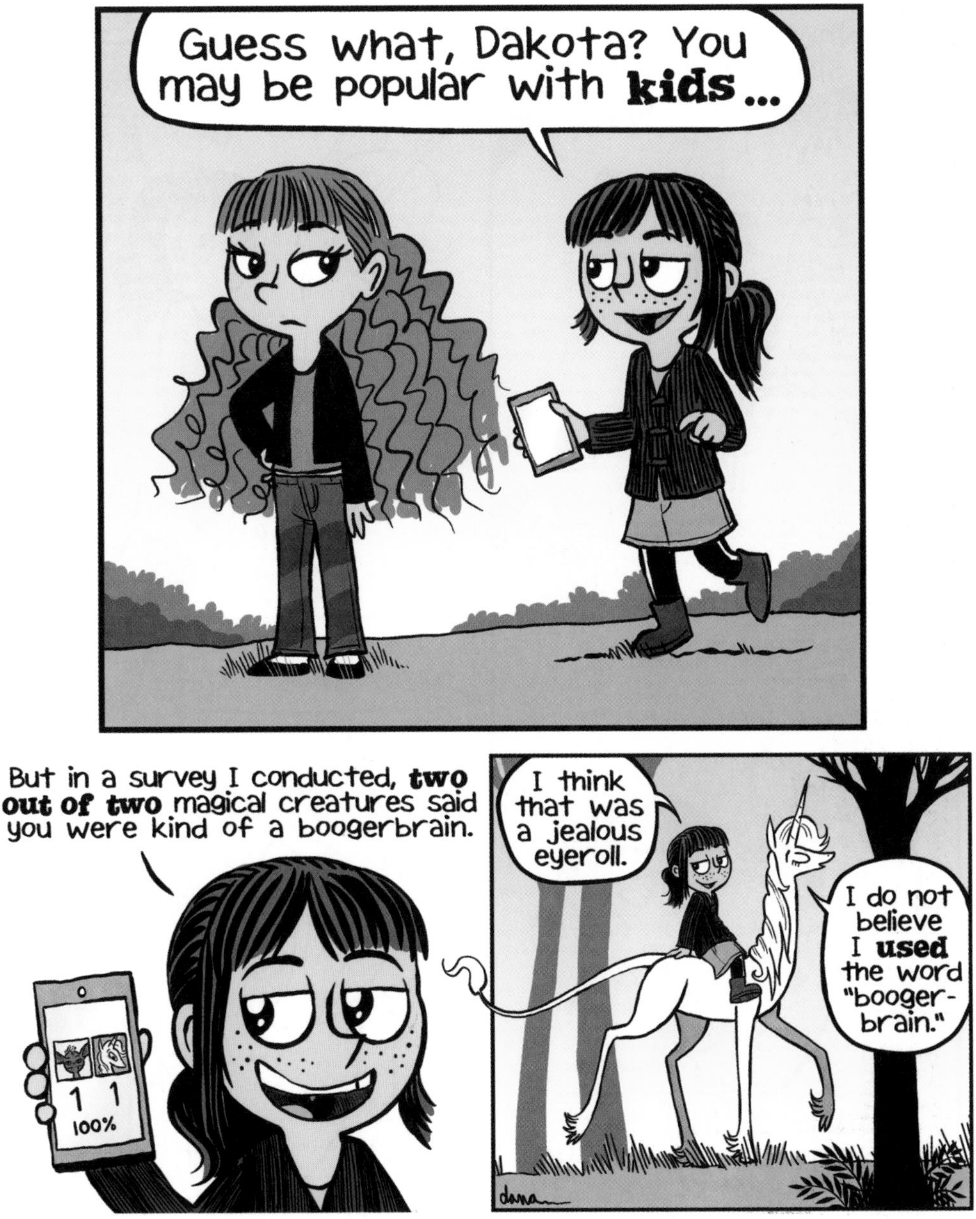

Guess what, Dakota? You may be popular with **kids**...
But in a survey I conducted, **two out of two** magical creatures said you were kind of a boogerbrain.
1 1
100%
I think that was a jealous eyeroll.
I do not believe I **used** the word "boogerbrain."
dana

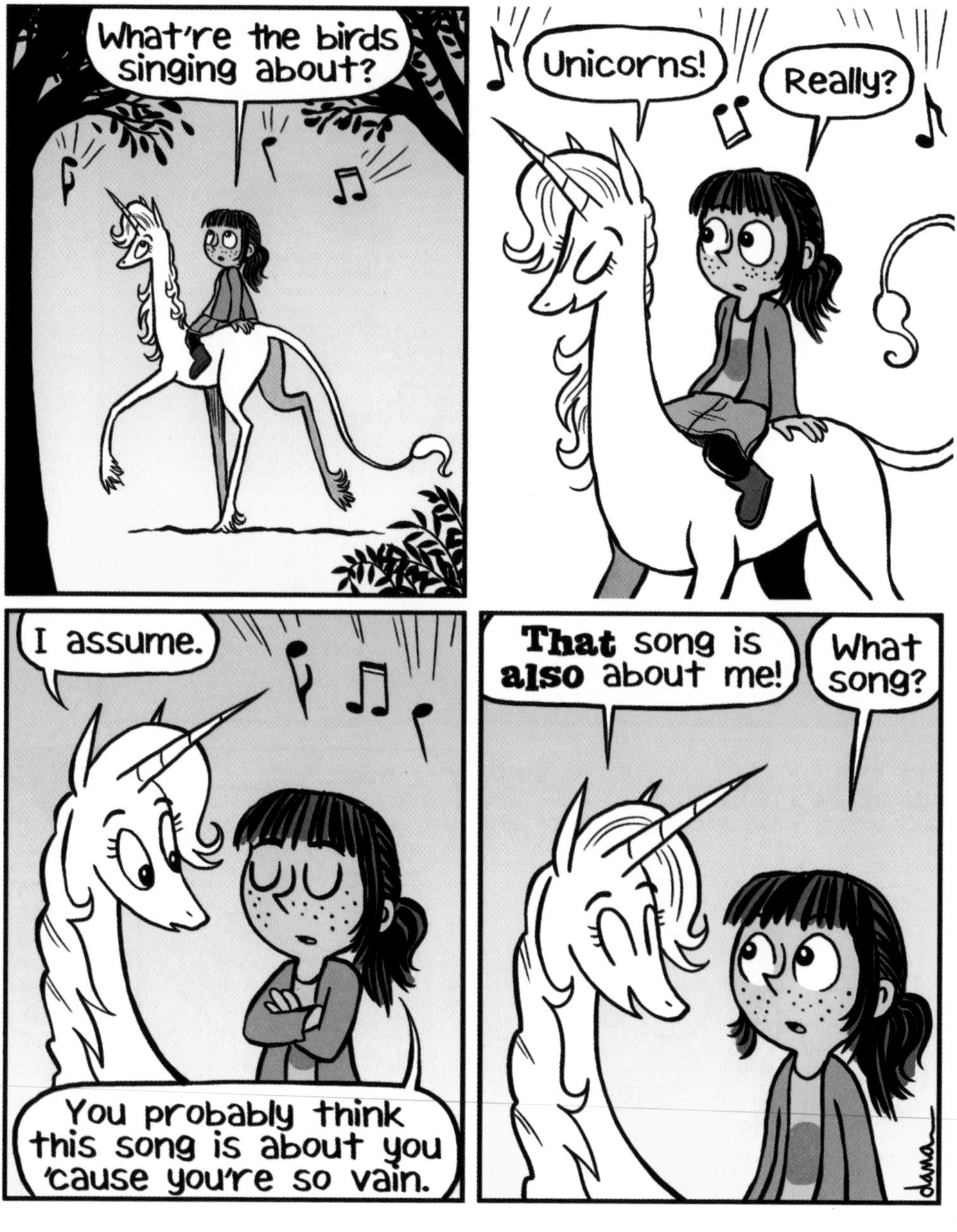
What're the birds singing about?
Unicorns!
Really?
I assume.
You probably think this song is about you 'cause you're so vain.
That song is **also** about me!
What song?
dana

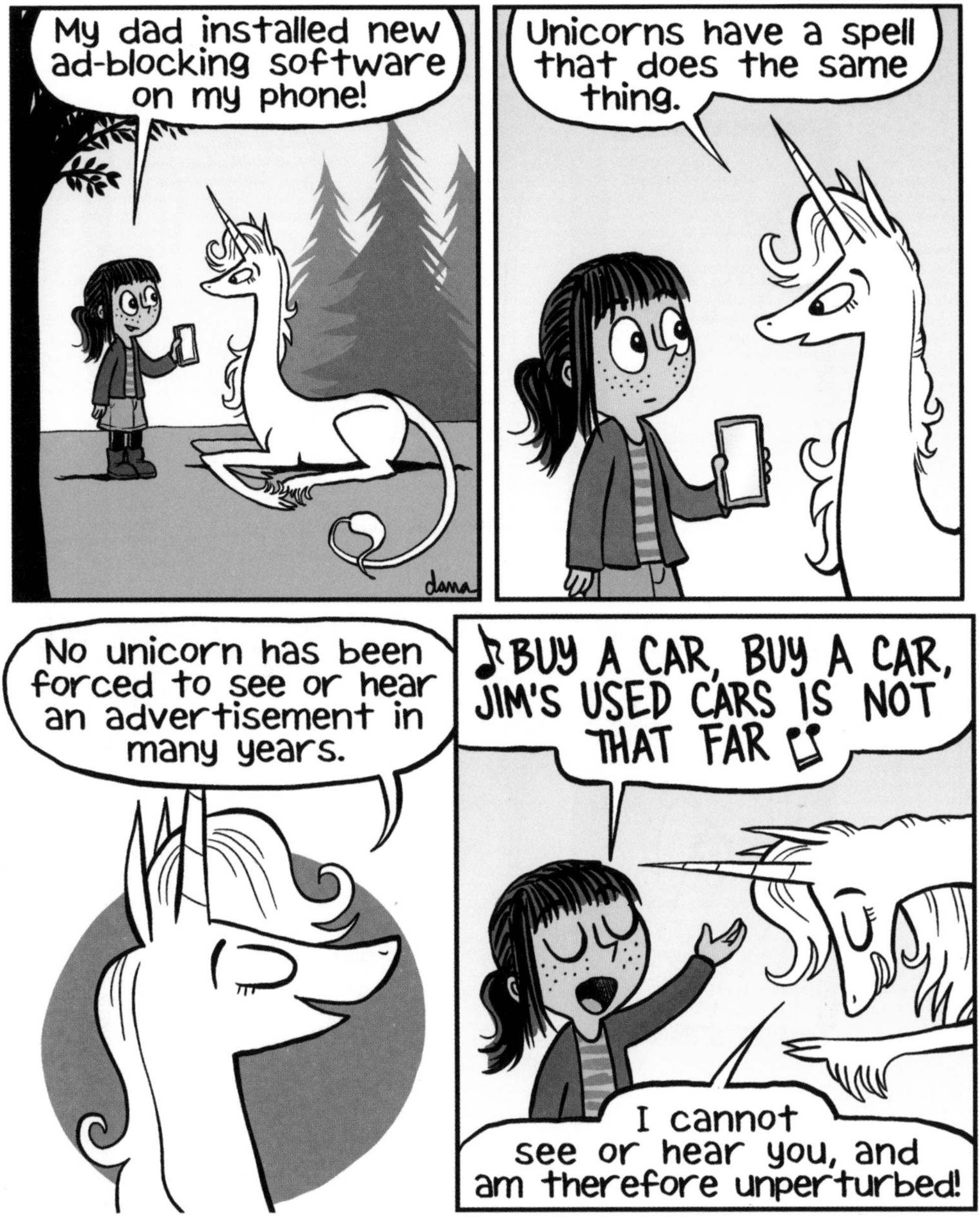
My dad installed new ad-blocking software on my phone!
dana
Unicorns have a spell that does the same thing.
No unicorn has been forced to see or hear an advertisement in many years.
♪BUY A CAR, BUY A CAR, JIM'S USED CARS IS NOT THAT FAR
I cannot see or hear you, and am therefore unperturbed!

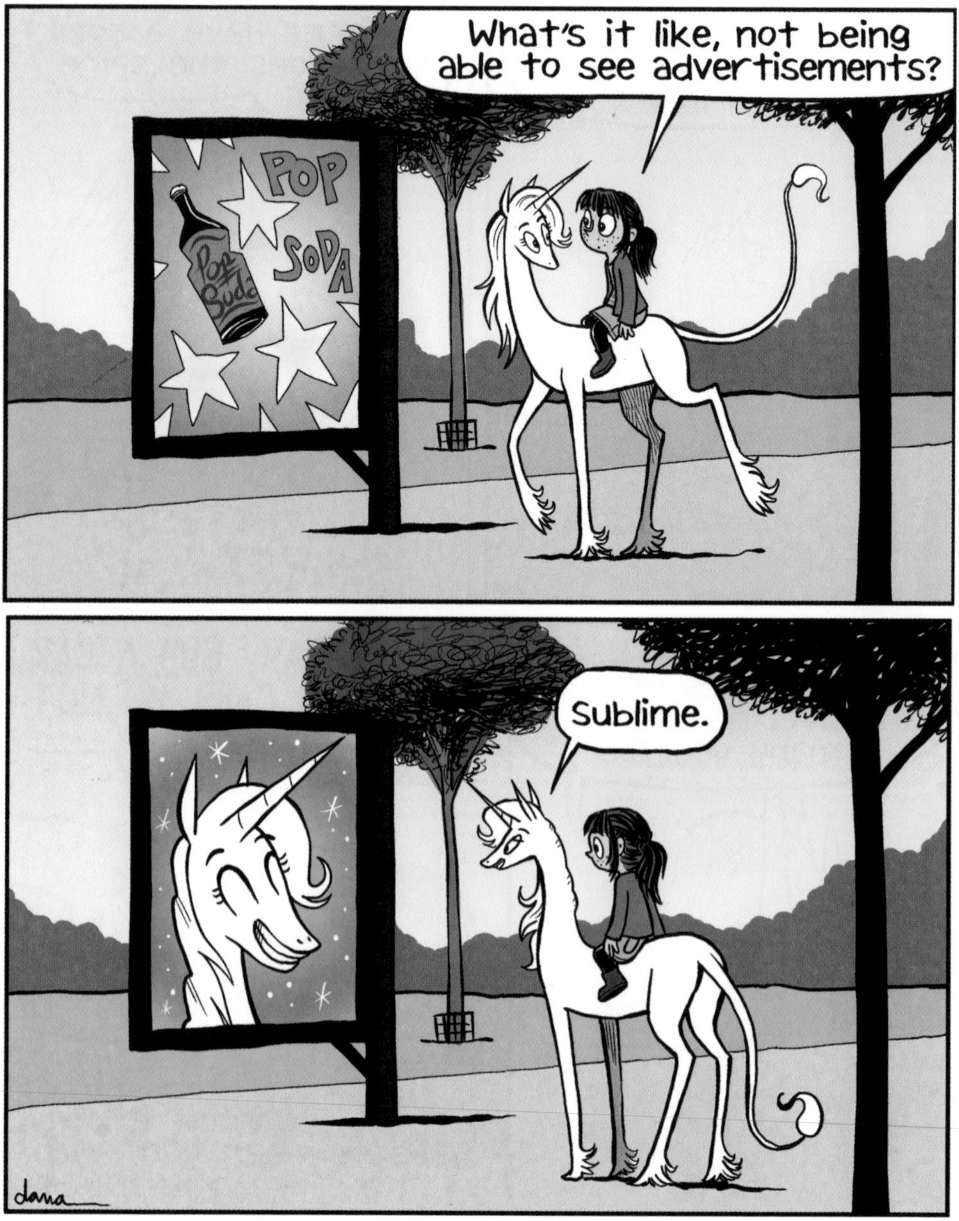
What's it like, not being able to see advertisements?
POP
SODA
Pop Soda
Sublime.
dana

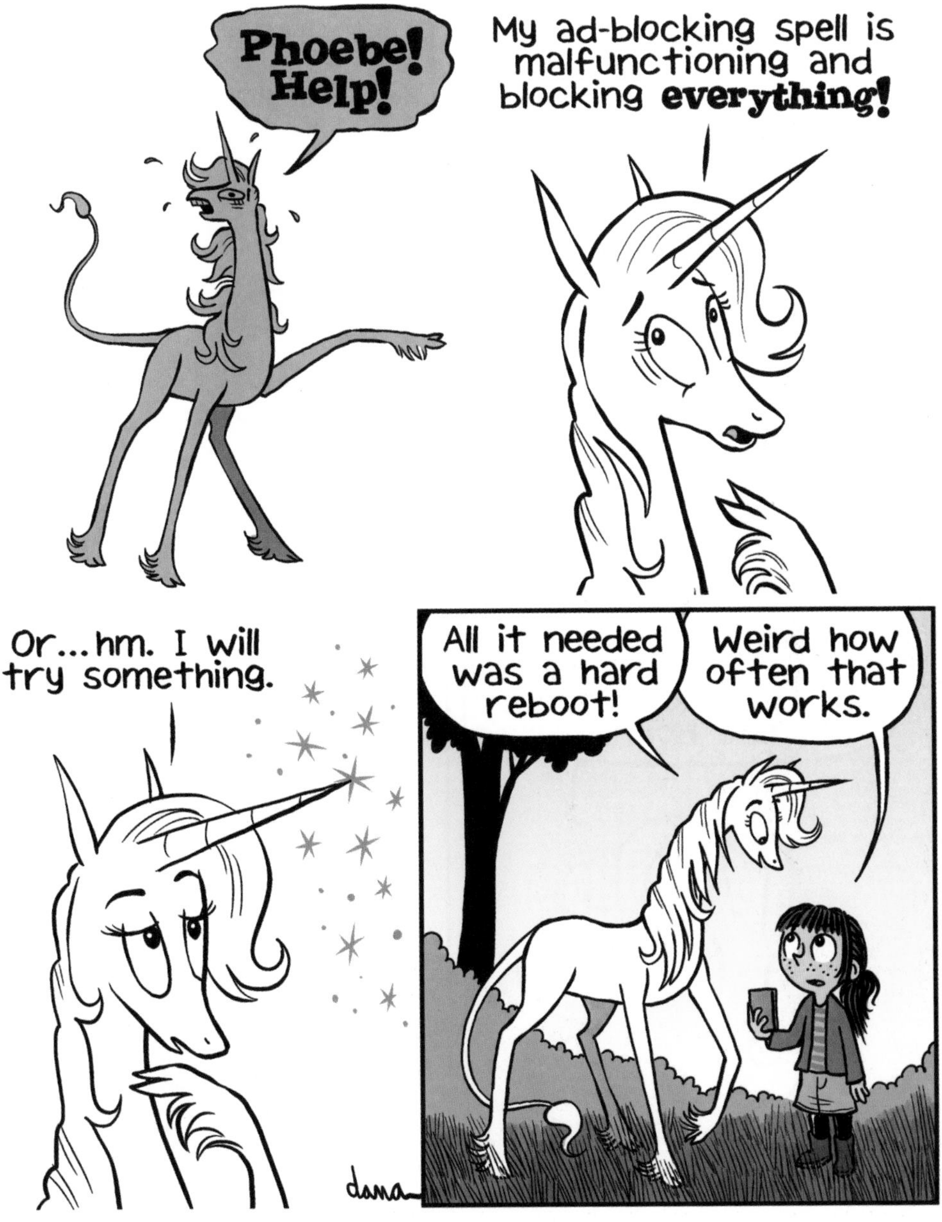
Phoebe! Help!
My ad-blocking spell is malfunctioning and blocking **everything!**
Or...hm. I will try something.
All it needed was a hard reboot!
Weird how often that works.
dana

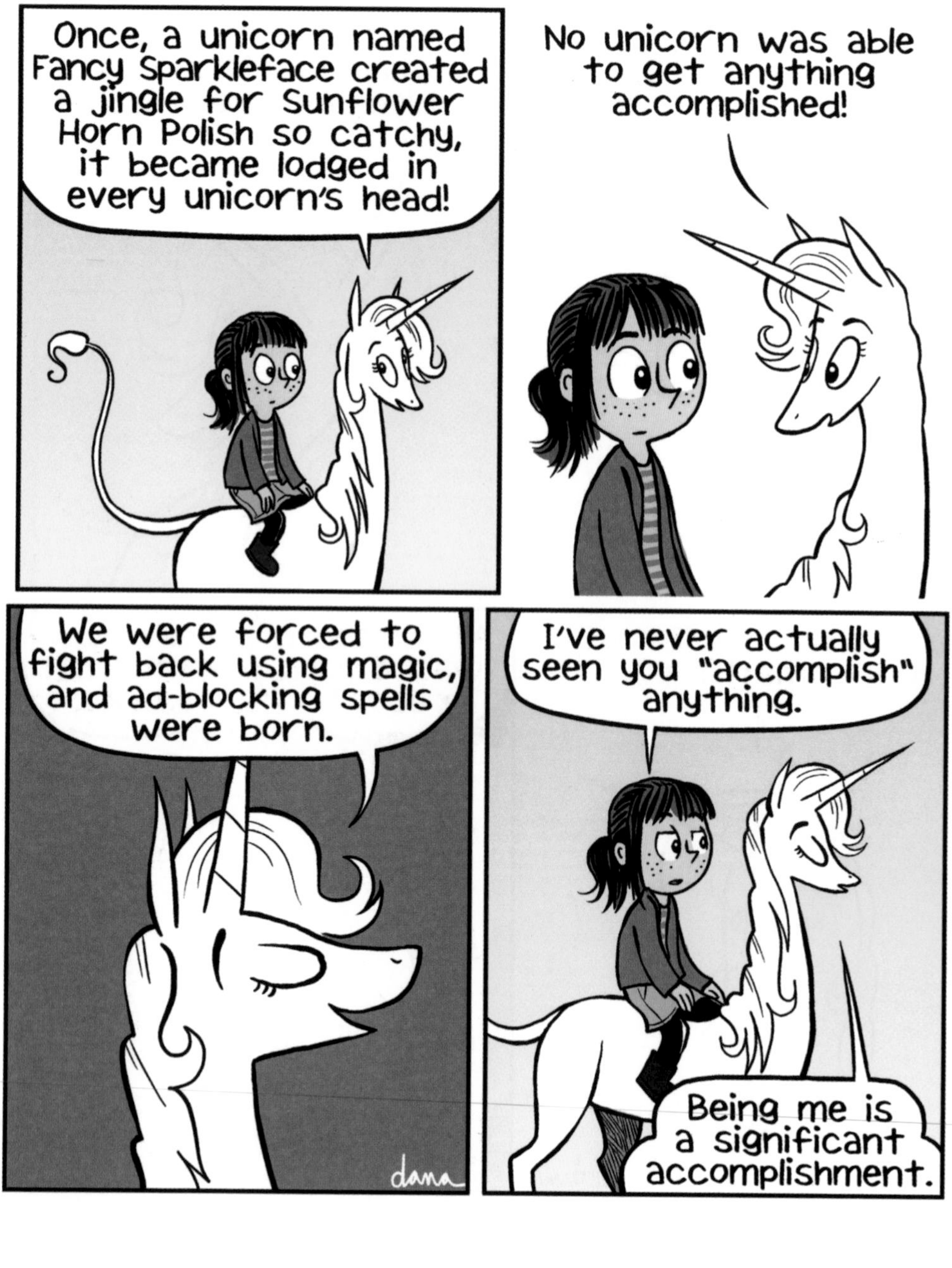
Once, a unicorn named Fancy Sparkleface created a jingle for Sunflower Horn Polish so catchy, it became lodged in every unicorn's head!
No unicorn was able to get anything accomplished!
We were forced to fight back using magic, and ad-blocking spells were born.
I've never actually seen you "accomplish" anything.
Being me is a significant accomplishment.
dana

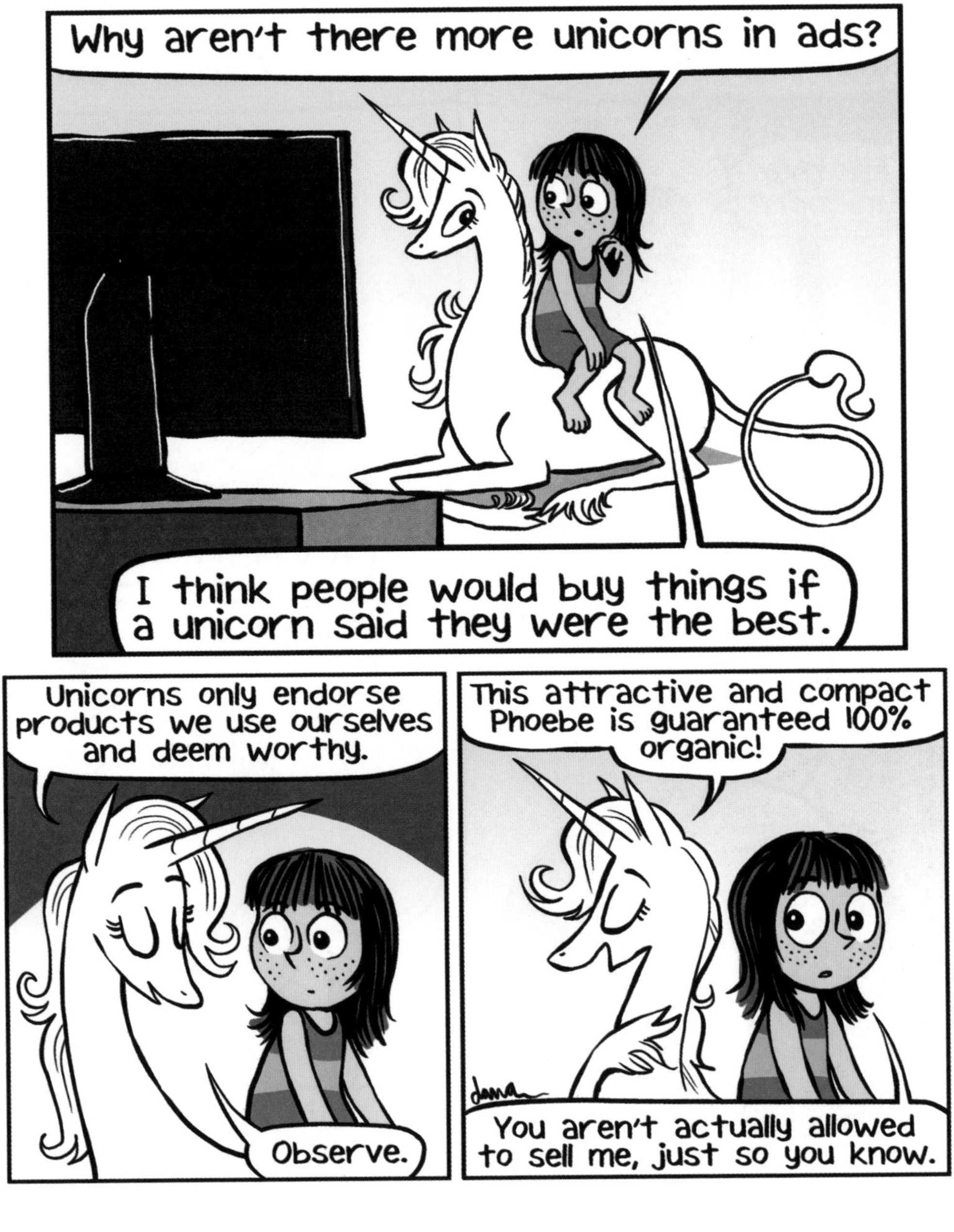
Why aren't there more unicorns in ads?
I think people would buy things if a unicorn said they were the best.
Unicorns only endorse products we use ourselves and deem worthy.
Observe.
This attractive and compact Phoebe is guaranteed 100% organic!
You aren't actually allowed to sell me, just so you know.

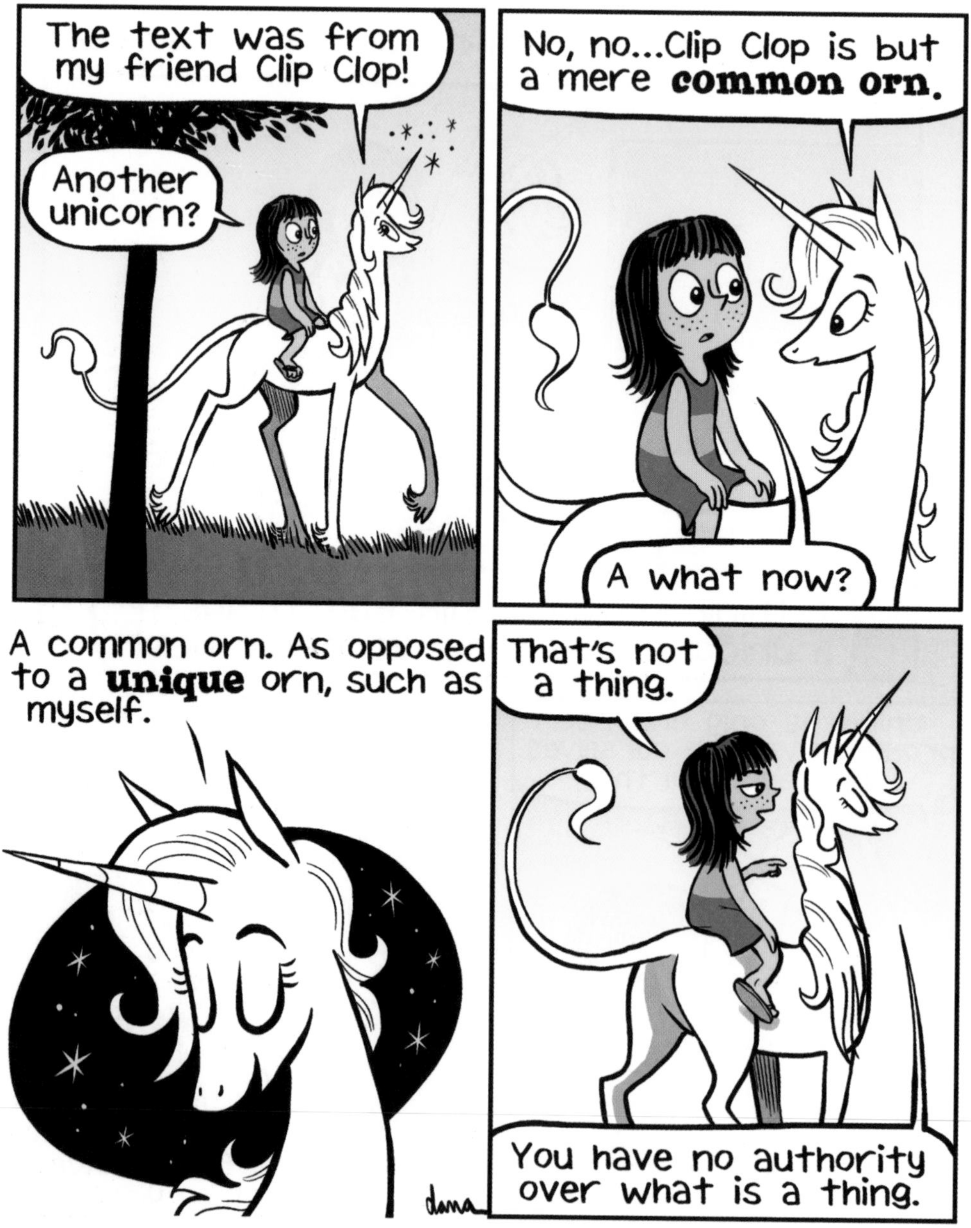
The text was from my friend Clip Clop!
Another unicorn?
No, no...Clip Clop is but a mere **common orn**.
A what now?
A common orn. As opposed to a **unique** orn, such as myself.
That's not a thing.
You have no authority over what is a thing.
dana

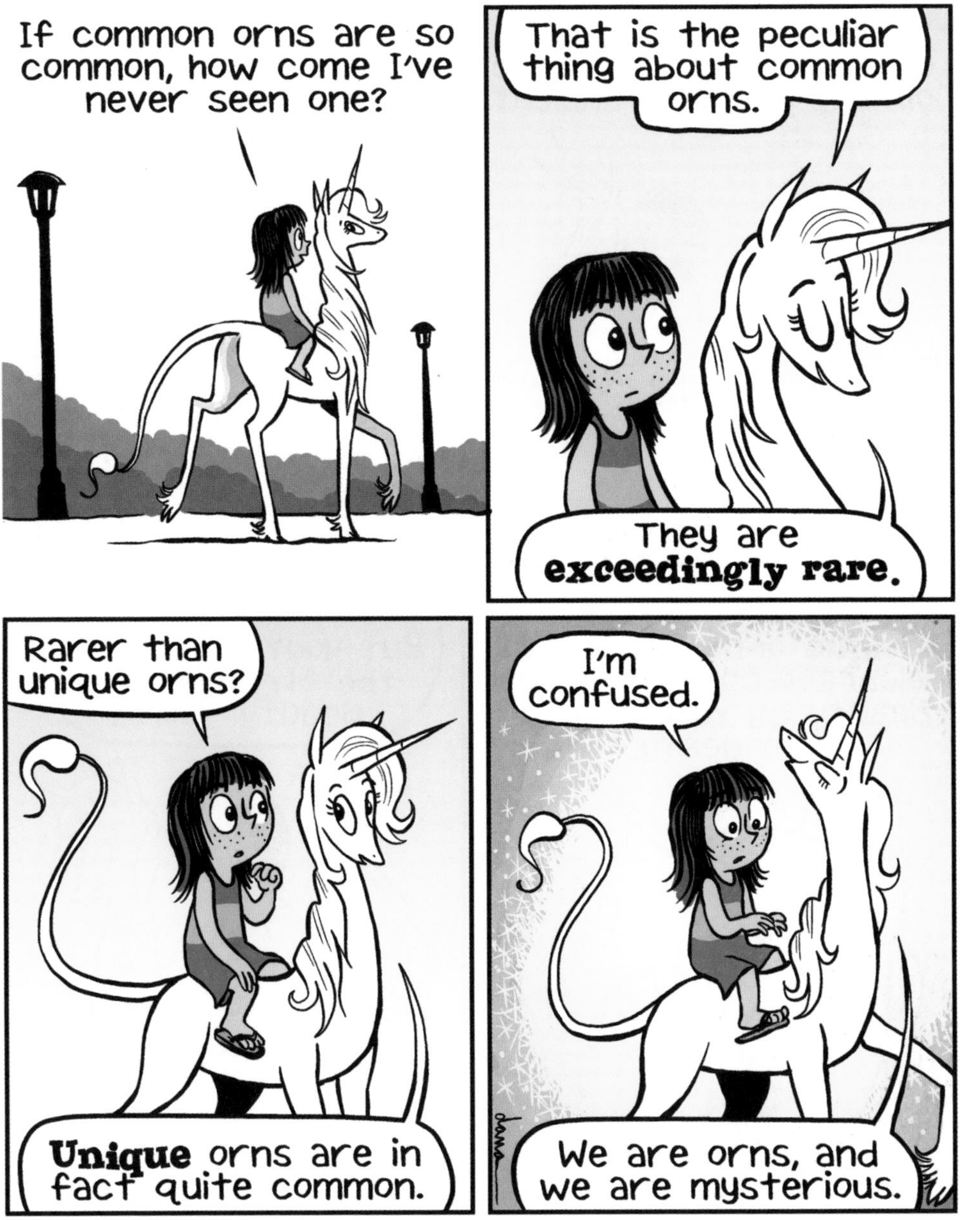
If common orns are so common, how come I've never seen one?
That is the peculiar thing about common orns.
They are **exceedingly rare**.
Rarer than unique orns?
Unique orns are in fact quite common.
I'm confused.
We are orns, and we are mysterious.
dana

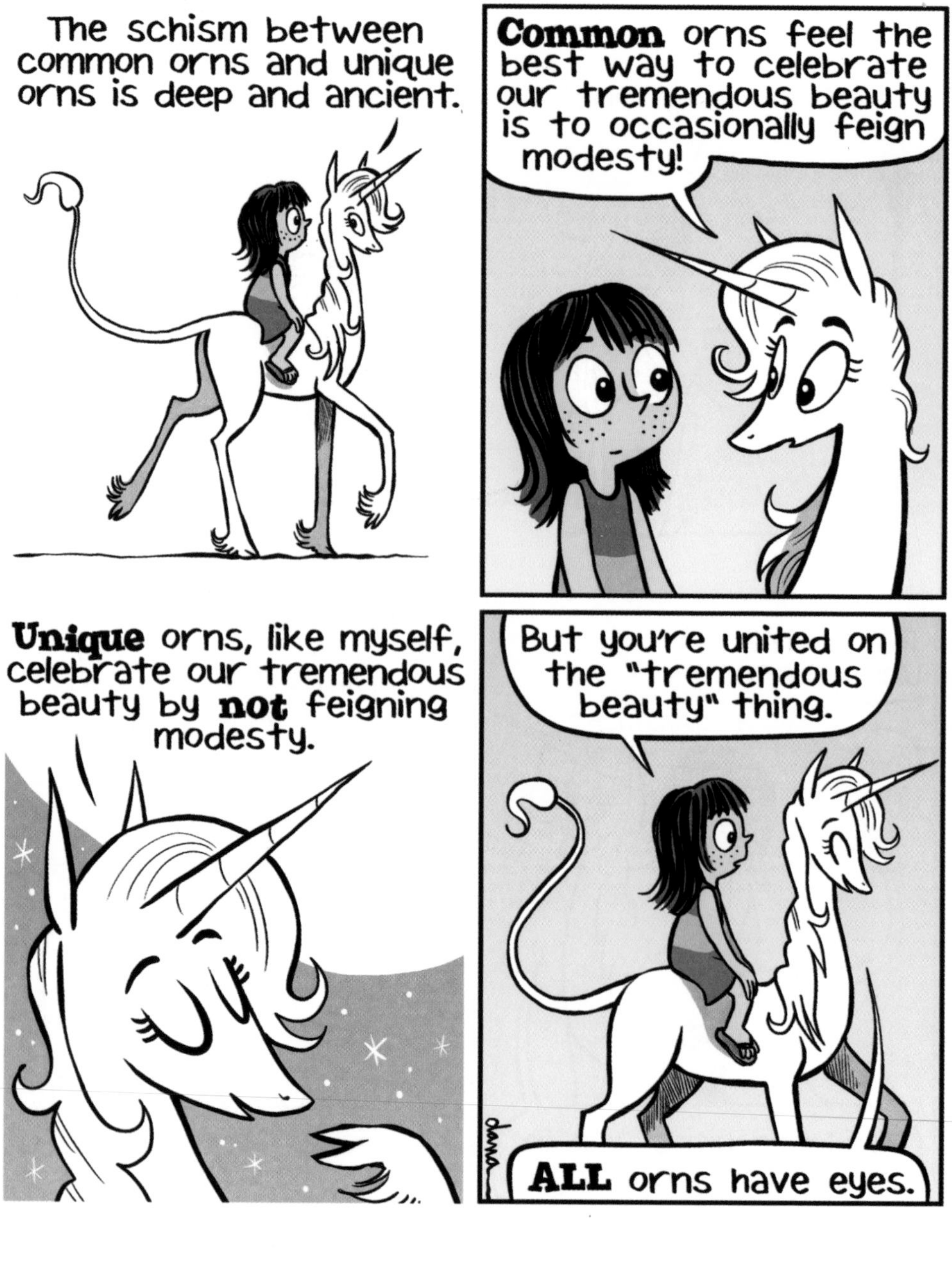
The schism between common orns and unique orns is deep and ancient.
Common orns feel the best way to celebrate our tremendous beauty is to occasionally feign modesty!
Unique orns, like myself, celebrate our tremendous beauty by **not** feigning modesty.
But you're united on the "tremendous beauty" thing.
ALL orns have eyes.
dana

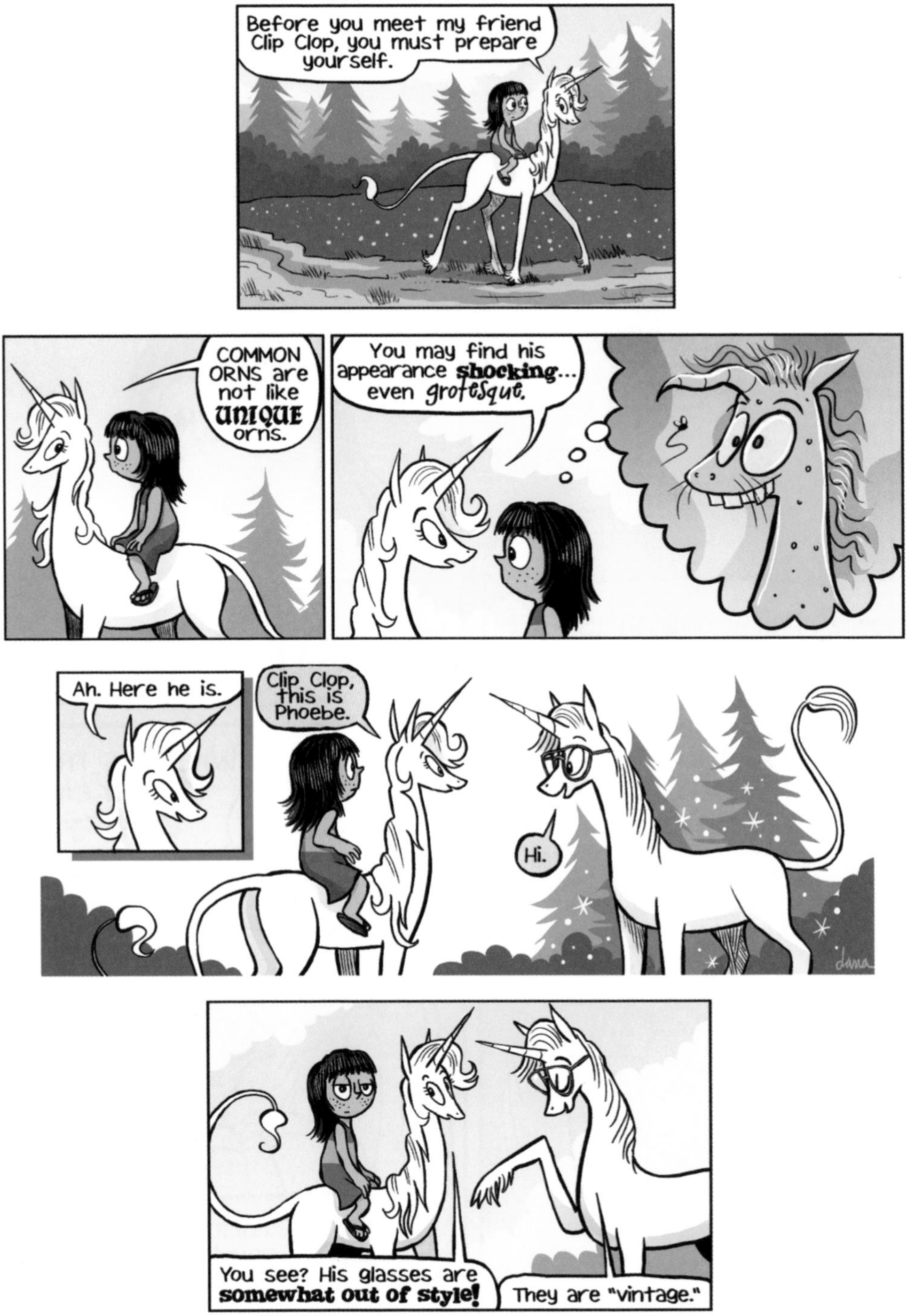
Before you meet my friend Clip Clop, you must prepare yourself.
COMMON ORNS are not like UNIQUE orns.
You may find his appearance **shocking**... even *grotesque.*
Ah. Here he is.
Clip Clop, this is Phoebe.
Hi.
You see? His glasses are **somewhat out of style!**
They are "vintage."

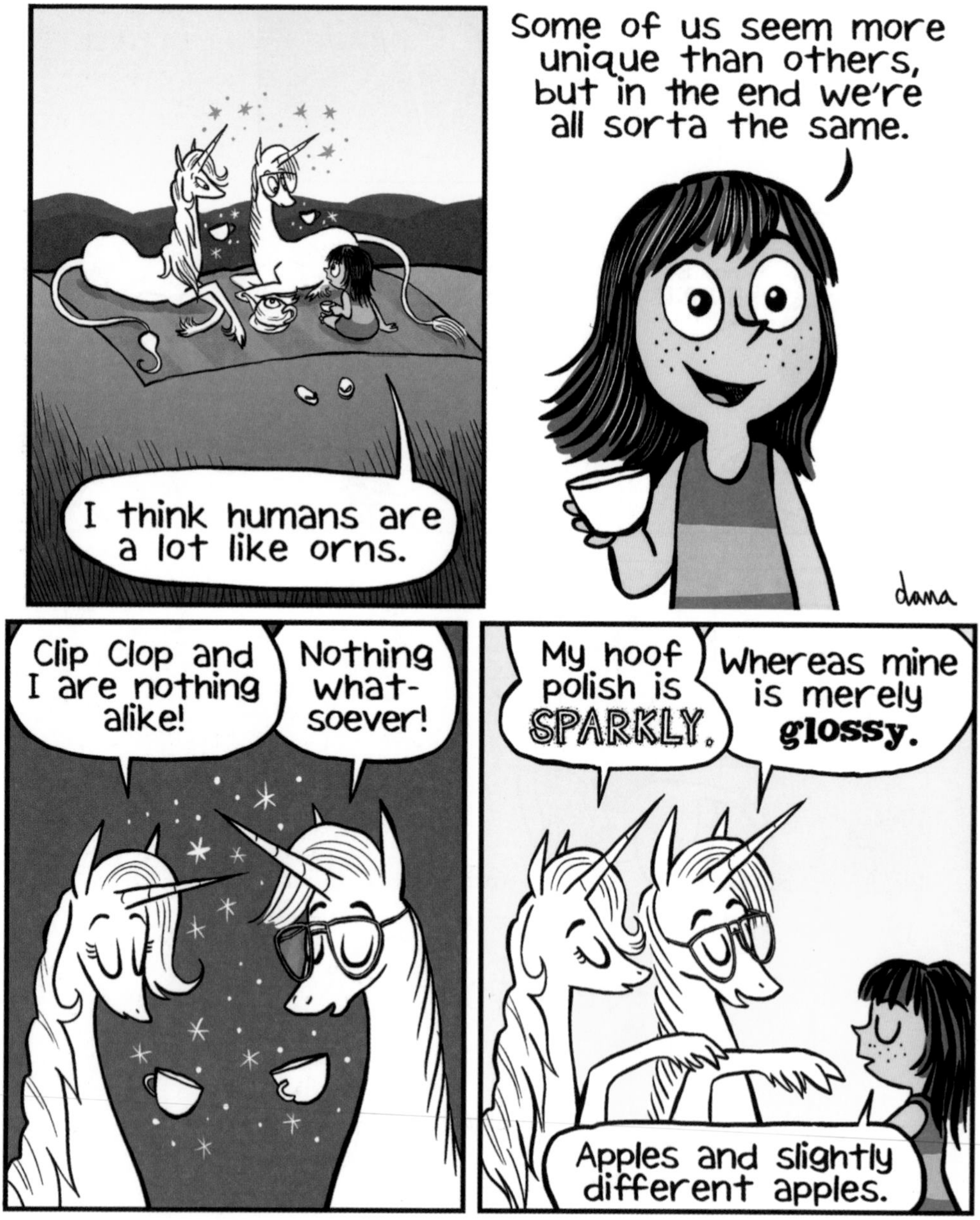
I think humans are a lot like orns.
Some of us seem more unique than others, but in the end we're all sorta the same.
dana
Clip Clop and I are nothing alike!
Nothing what-soever!
My hoof polish is SPARKLY.
Whereas mine is merely glossy.
Apples and slightly different apples.

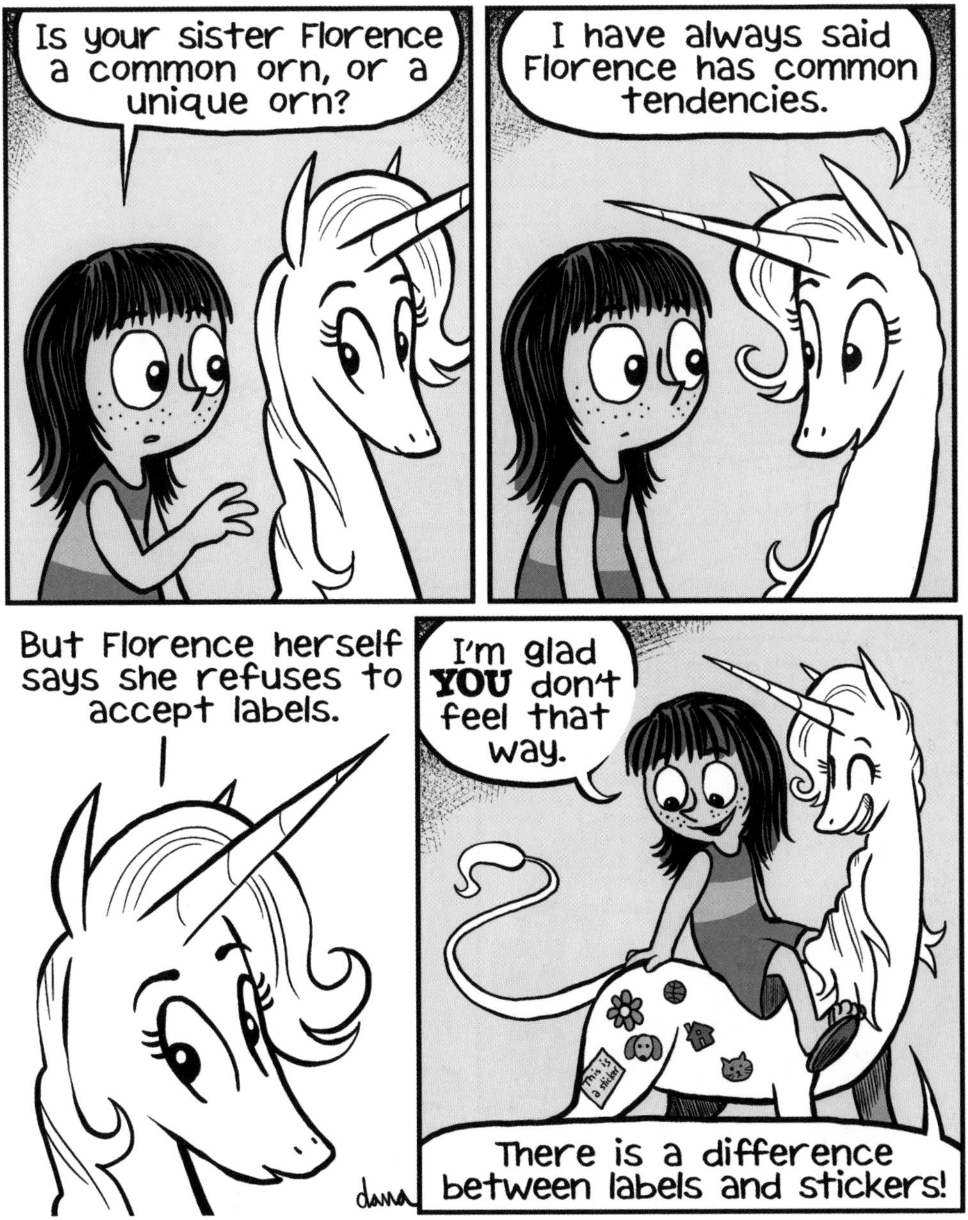

Is your sister Florence a common orn, or a unique orn?
I have always said Florence has common tendencies.
But Florence herself says she refuses to accept labels.
I'm glad YOU don't feel that way.
This is a sticker!
There is a difference between labels and stickers!
dana

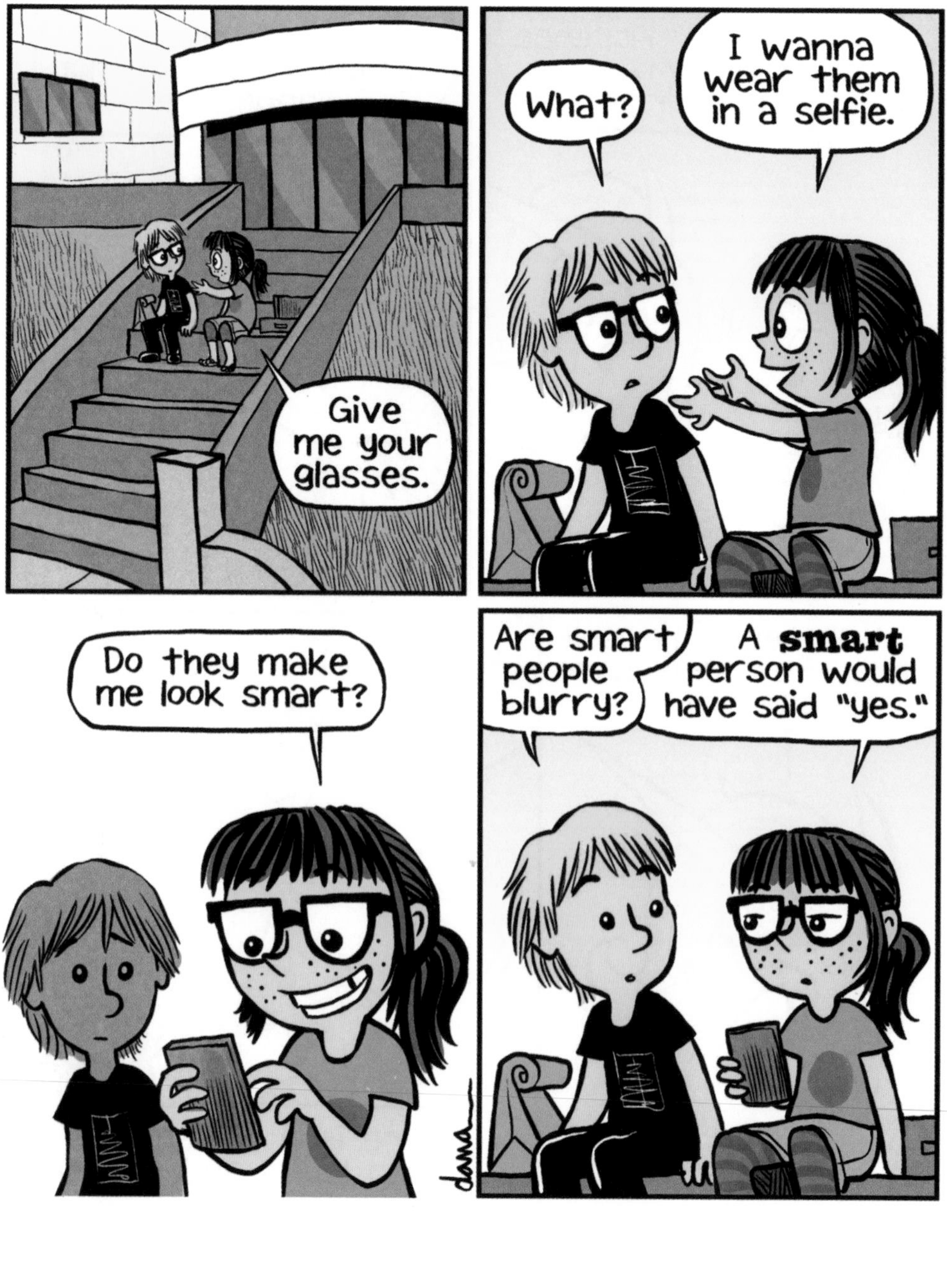
Give me your glasses.
What?
I wanna wear them in a selfie.
Do they make me look smart?
Are smart people blurry?
A **smart** person would have said "yes."
dana

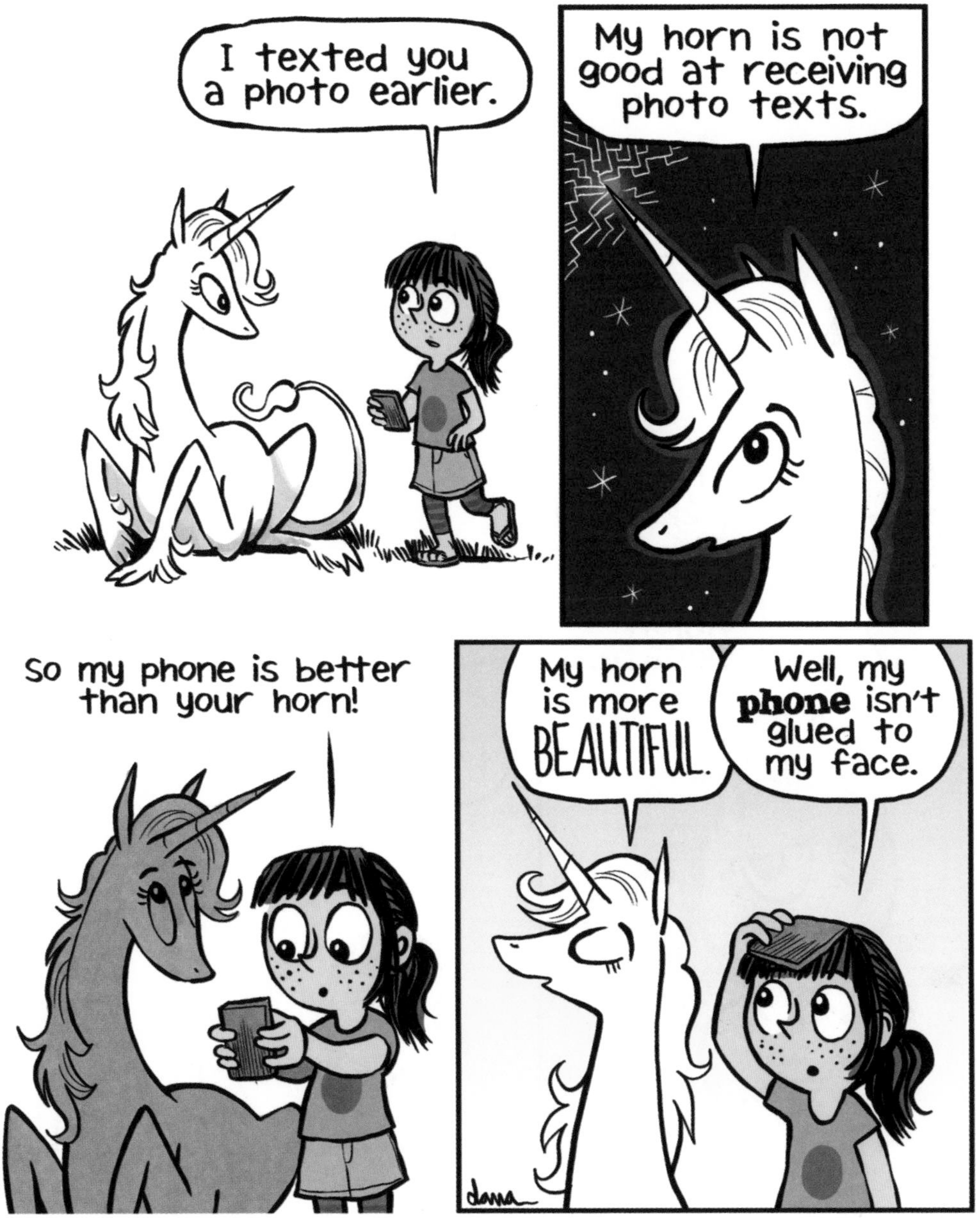
I texted you a photo earlier.
My horn is not good at receiving photo texts.
So my phone is better than your horn!
My horn is more BEAUTIFUL.
Well, my **phone** isn't glued to my face.
dana

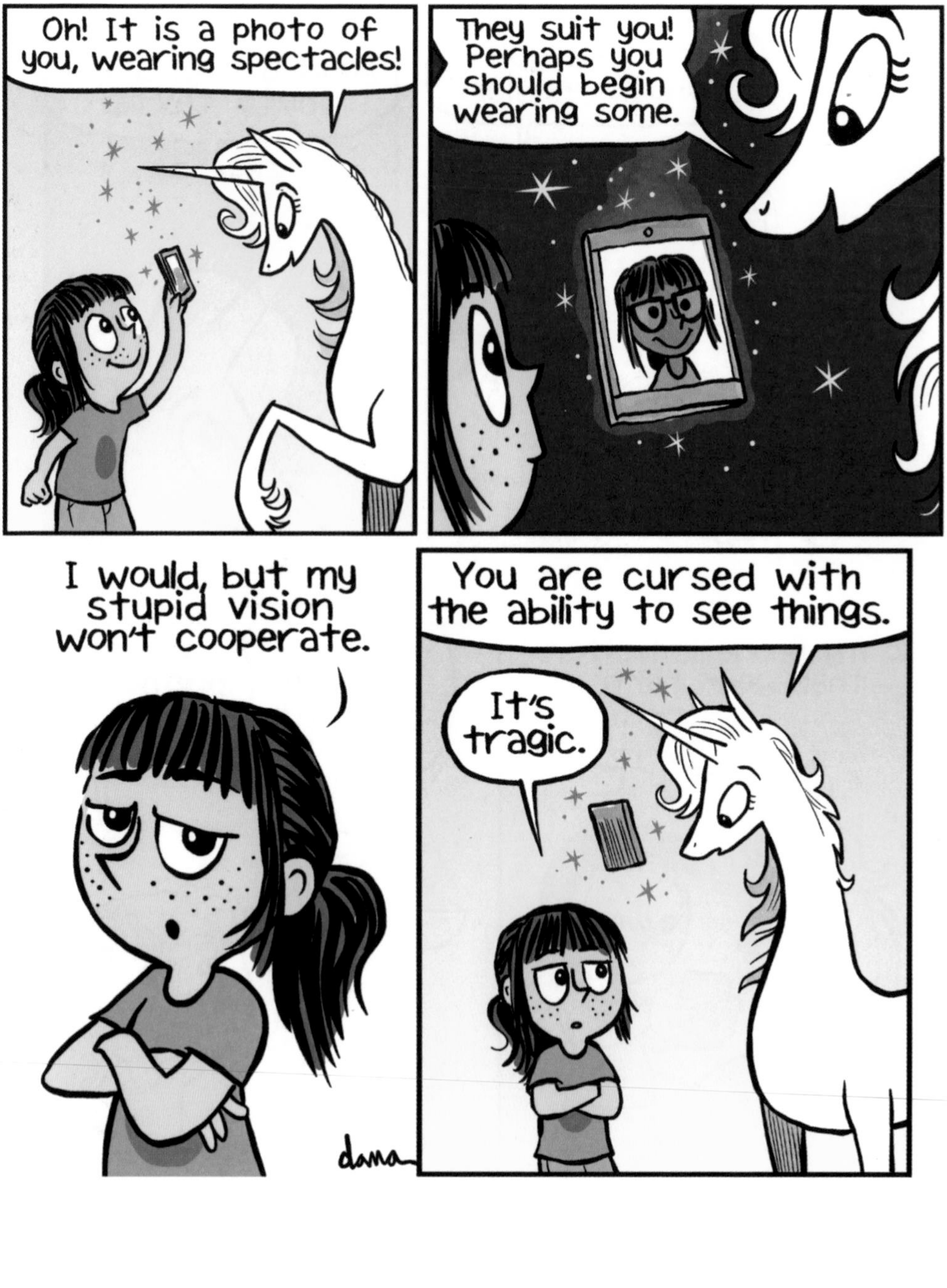
Oh! It is a photo of you, wearing spectacles!
They suit you! Perhaps you should begin wearing some.
I would, but my stupid vision won't cooperate.
You are cursed with the ability to see things.
It's tragic.
dana

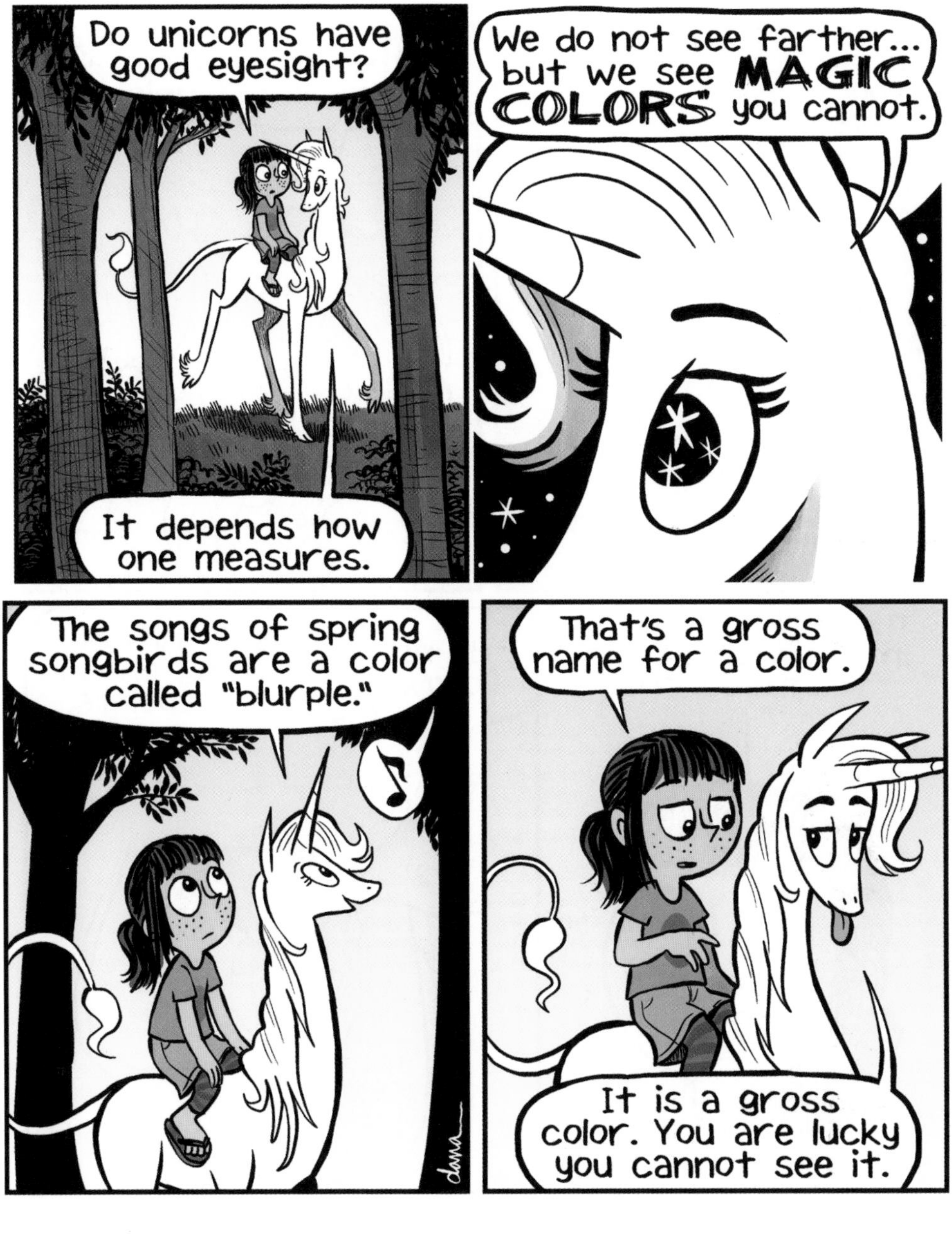
Do unicorns have good eyesight?
It depends how one measures.
We do not see farther... but we see MAGIC COLORS you cannot.
The songs of spring songbirds are a color called "blurple."
That's a gross name for a color.
It is a gross color. You are lucky you cannot see it.

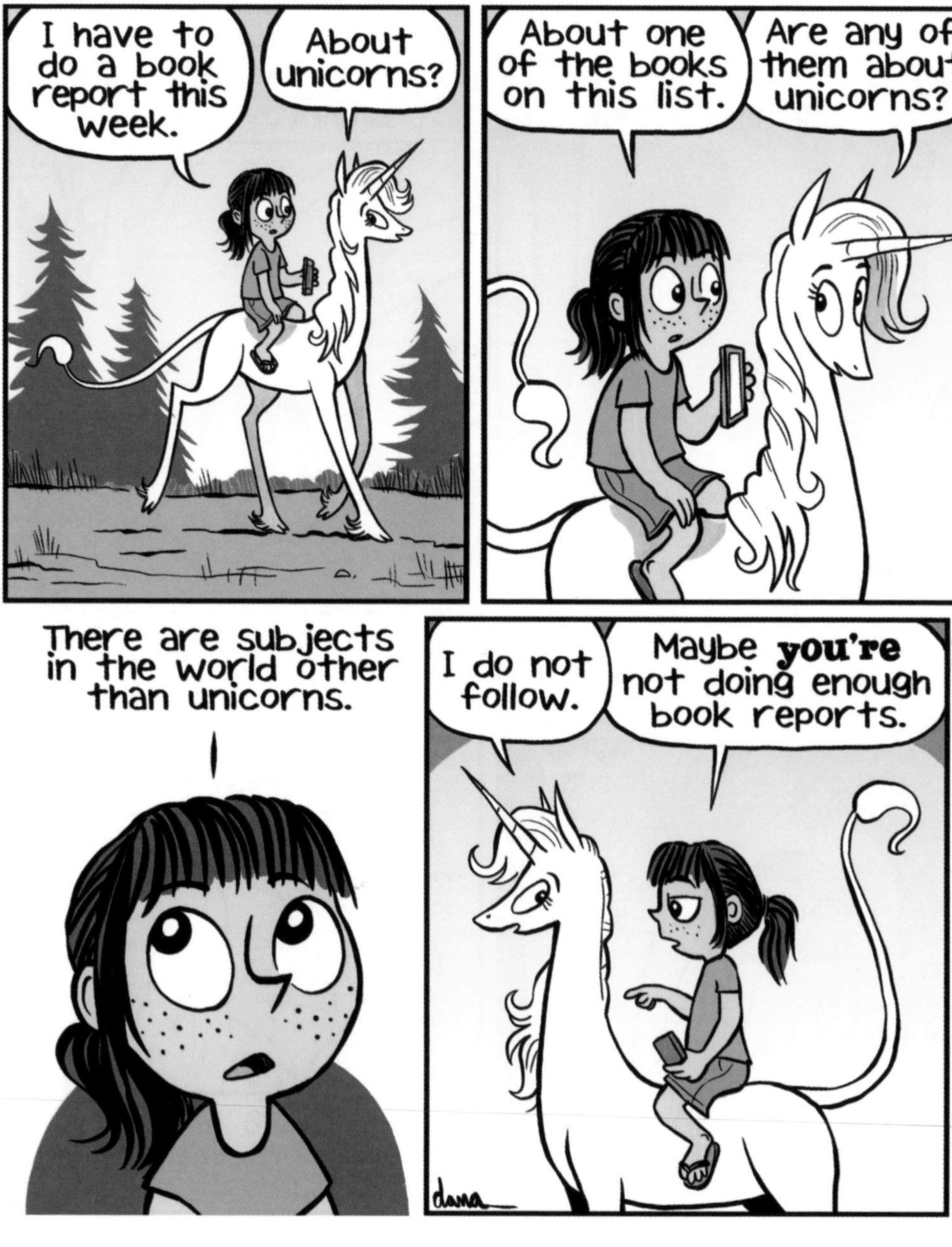
I have to do a book report this week.
About unicorns?
About one of the books on this list.
Are any of them about unicorns?
There are subjects in the world other than unicorns.
I do not follow.
Maybe **you're** not doing enough book reports.
dana

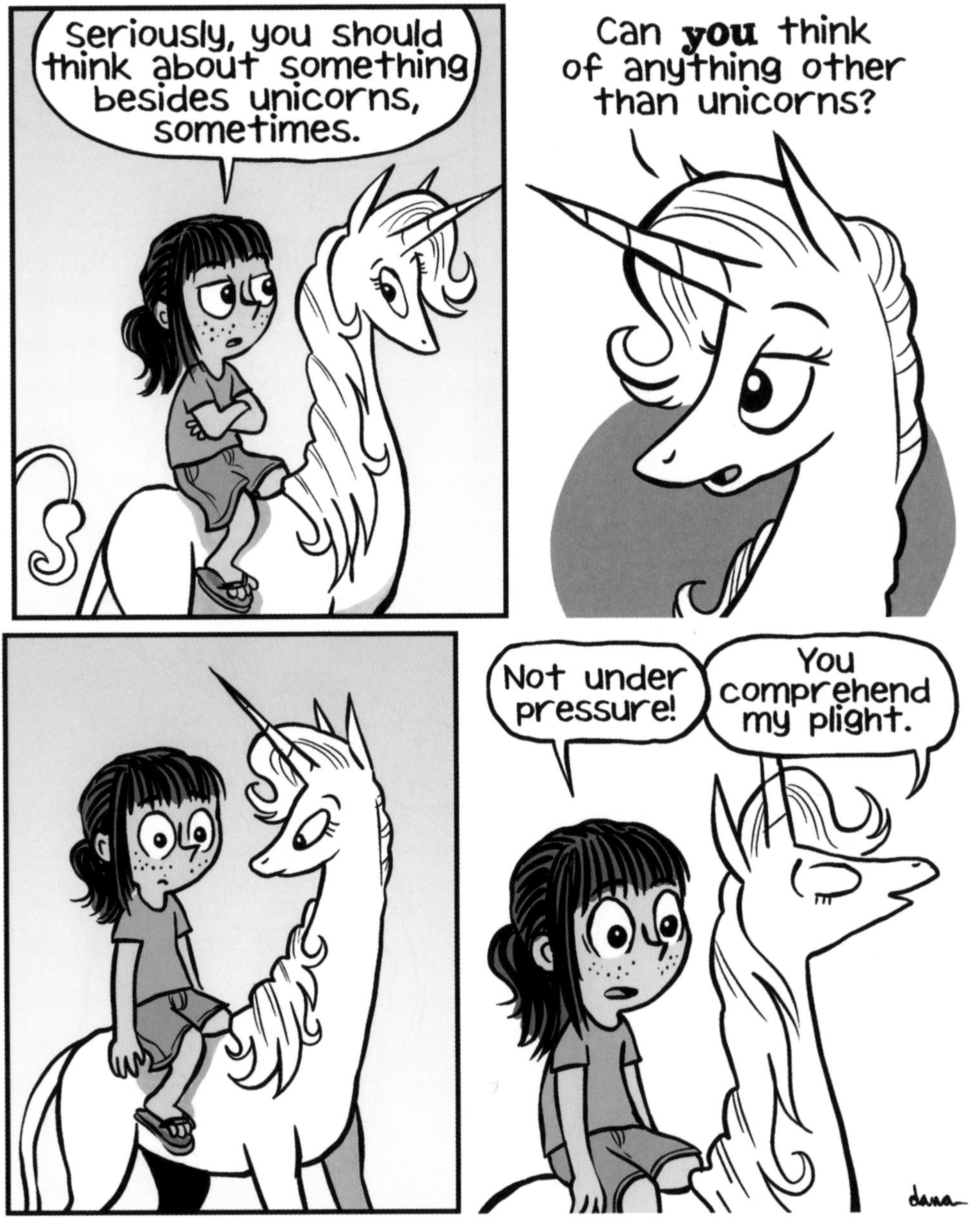
Seriously, you should think about something besides unicorns, sometimes.
Can **you** think of anything other than unicorns?
Not under pressure!
You comprehend my plight.
dana

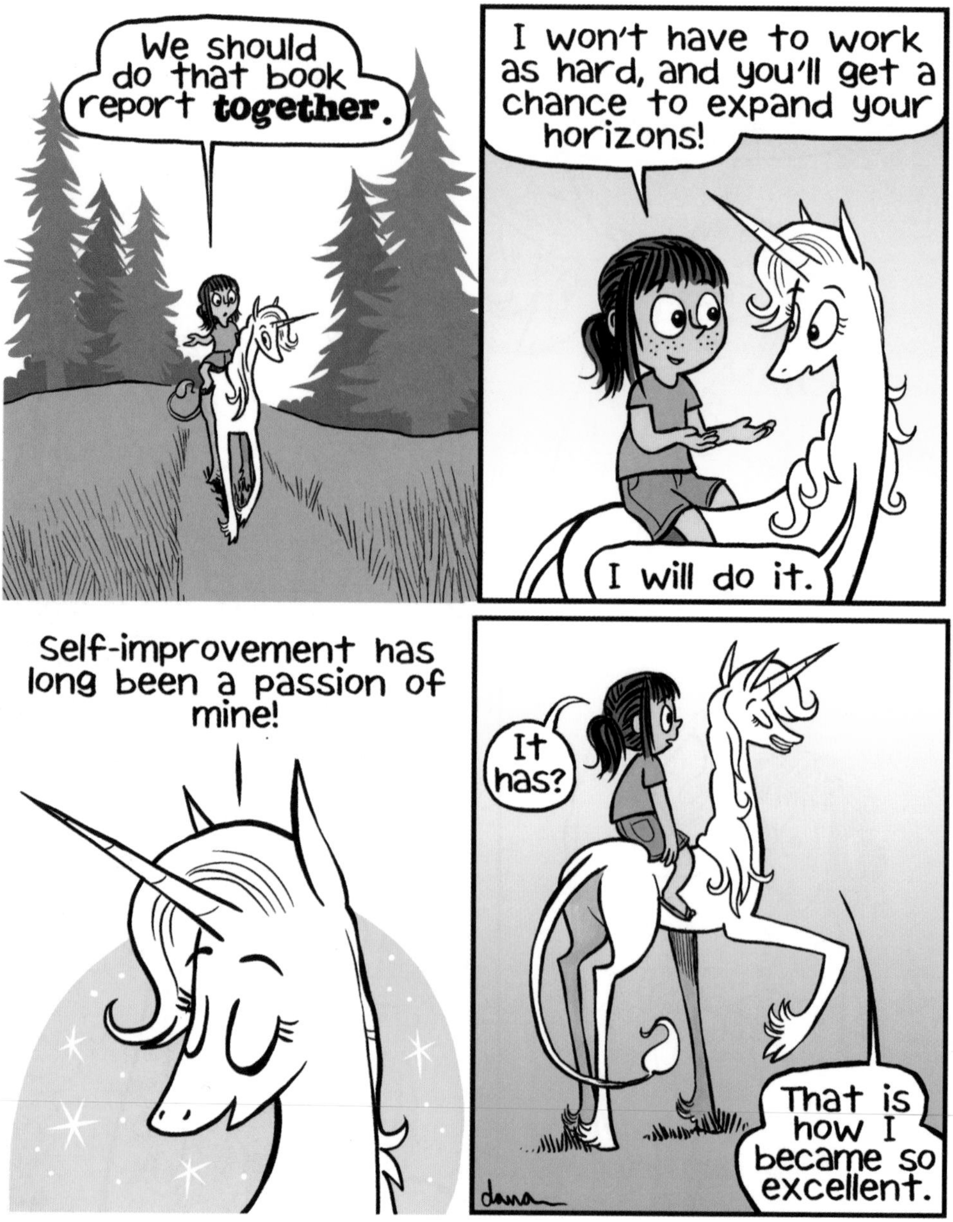

We should do that book report **together**.
I won't have to work as hard, and you'll get a chance to expand your horizons!
I will do it.
Self-improvement has long been a passion of mine!
It has?
That is how I became so excellent.
dana

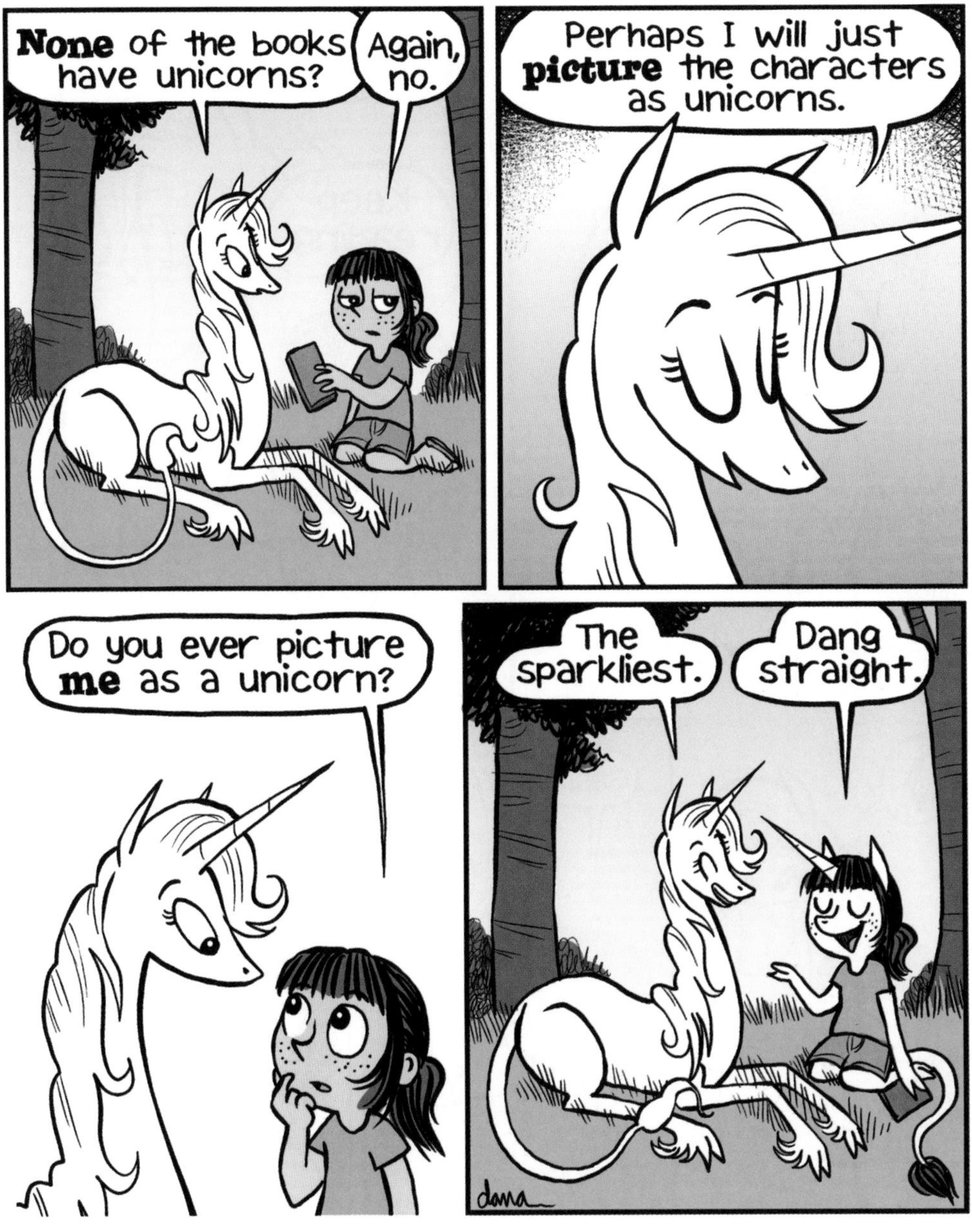
None of the books have unicorns?
Again, no.
Perhaps I will just picture the characters as unicorns.
Do you ever picture me as a unicorn?
The sparkliest.
Dang straight.
dana

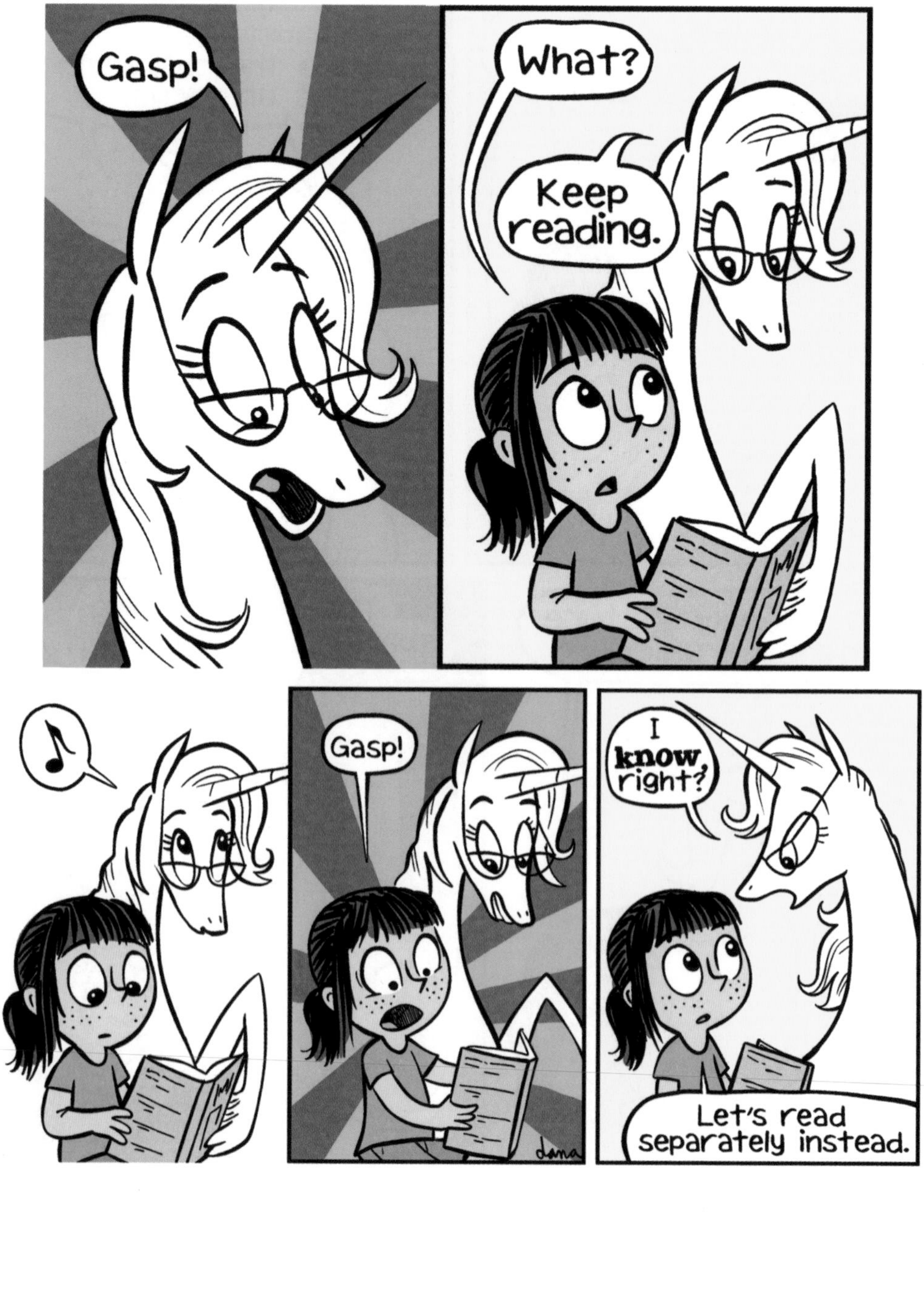
Gasp!
What?
Keep reading.
♪
Gasp!
I **know**, right?
Let's read separately instead.
dana

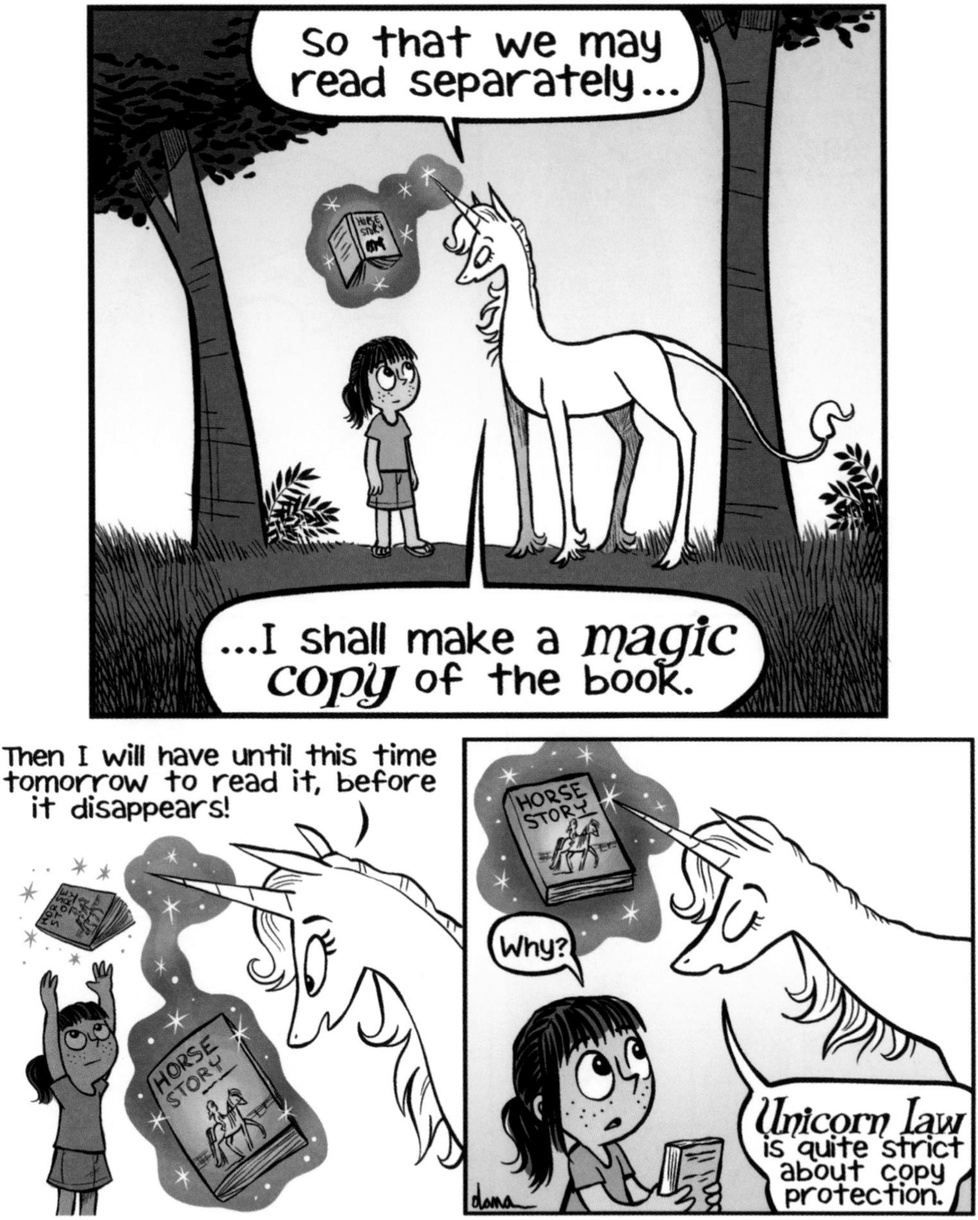
So that we may read separately...
...I shall make a *magic copy* of the book.
HORSE STORY
Then I will have until this time tomorrow to read it, before it disappears!
HORSE STORY
HORSE STORY
Why?
Unicorn law is quite strict about copy protection.

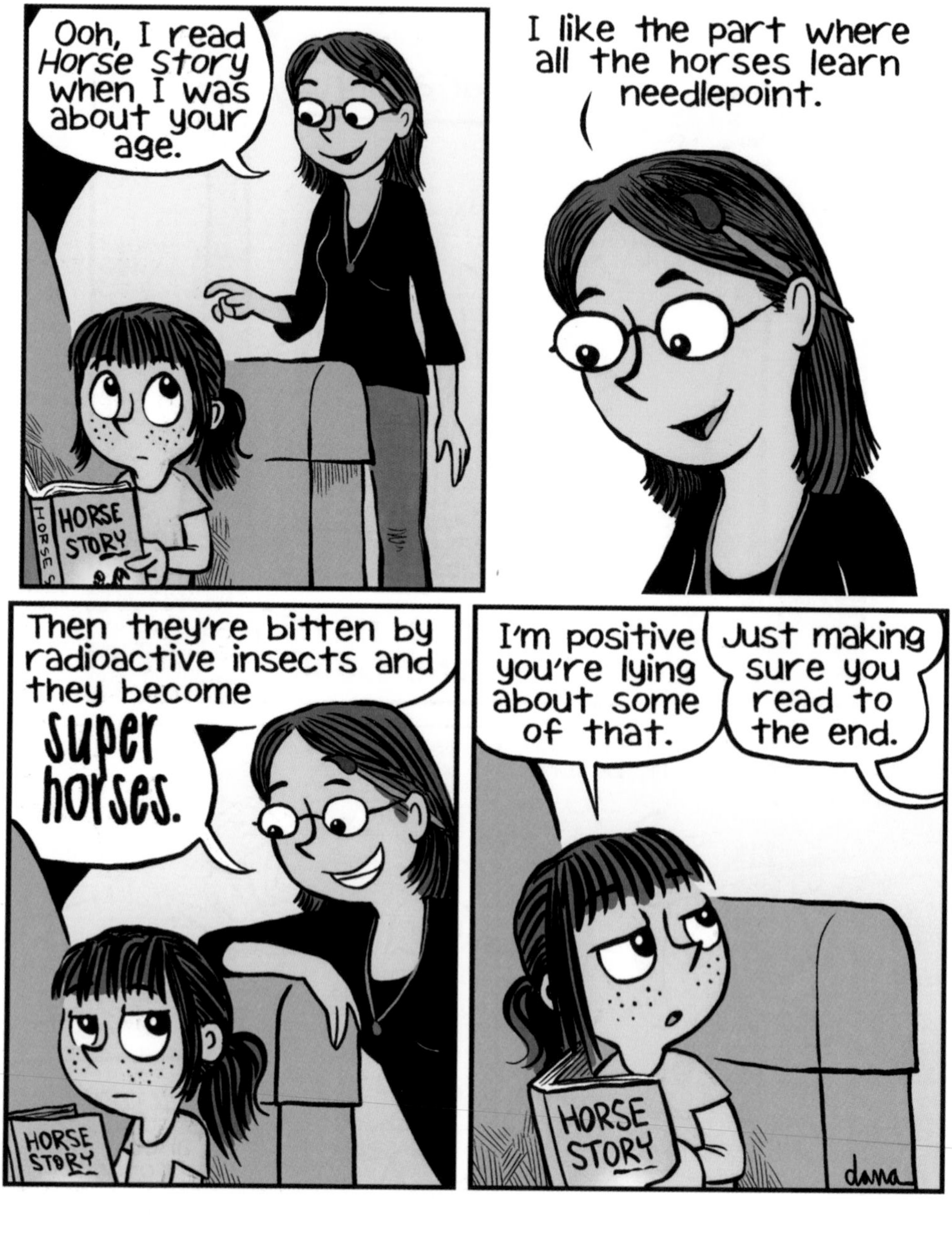
Ooh, I read Horse Story when I was about your age.
HORSE STORY
I like the part where all the horses learn needlepoint.
Then they're bitten by radioactive insects and they become super horses.
HORSE STORY
I'm positive you're lying about some of that.
Just making sure you read to the end.
HORSE STORY
dana

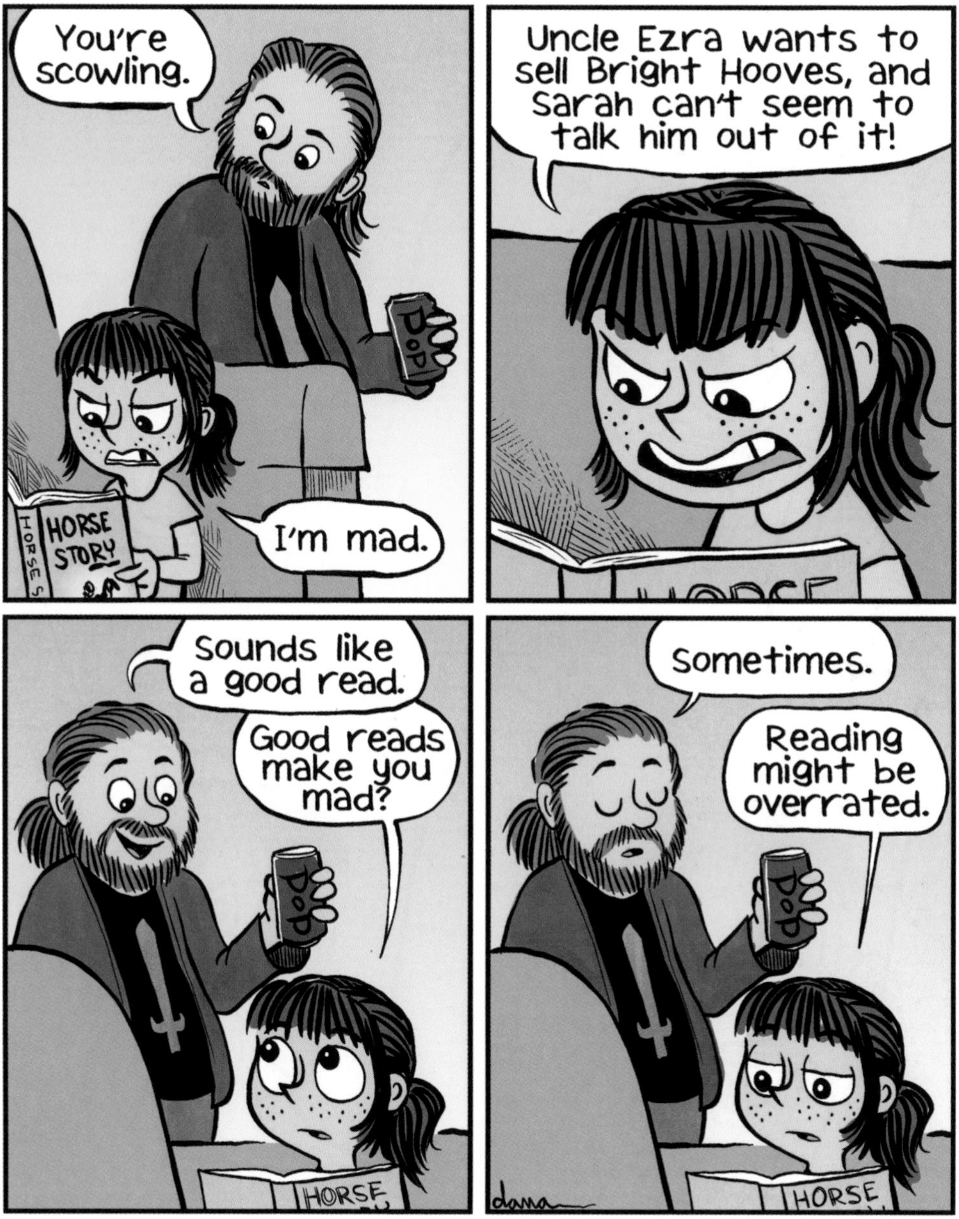
You're scowling.
HORSE
HORSE STORY
I'm mad.
Uncle Ezra wants to sell Bright Hooves, and Sarah can't seem to talk him out of it!
Sounds like a good read.
Good reads make you mad?
HORSE
Sometimes.
Reading might be overrated.
HORSE
dana

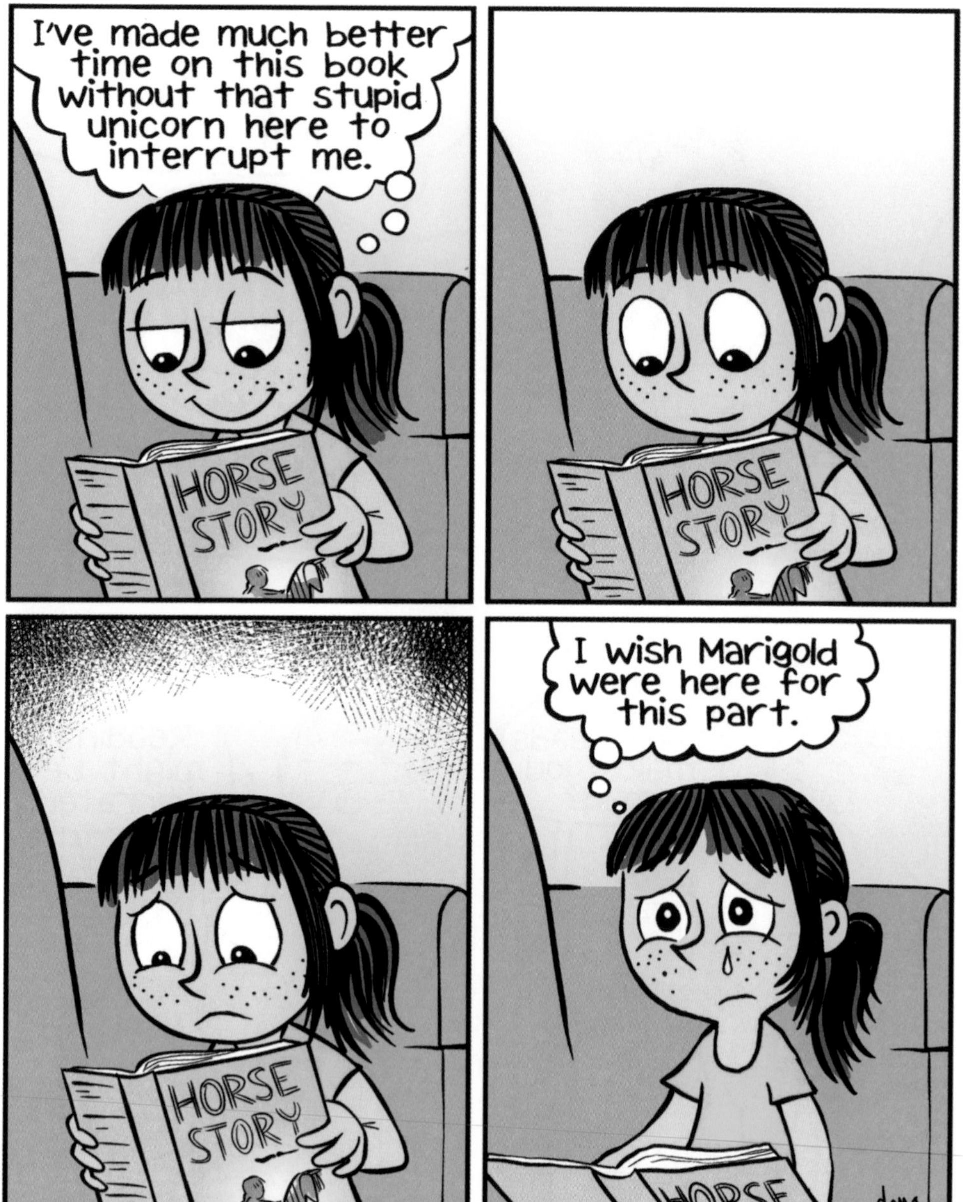
I've made much better time on this book without that stupid unicorn here to interrupt me.
HORSE STORY
HORSE STORY
HORSE STORY
I wish Marigold were here for this part.
HORSE
dana

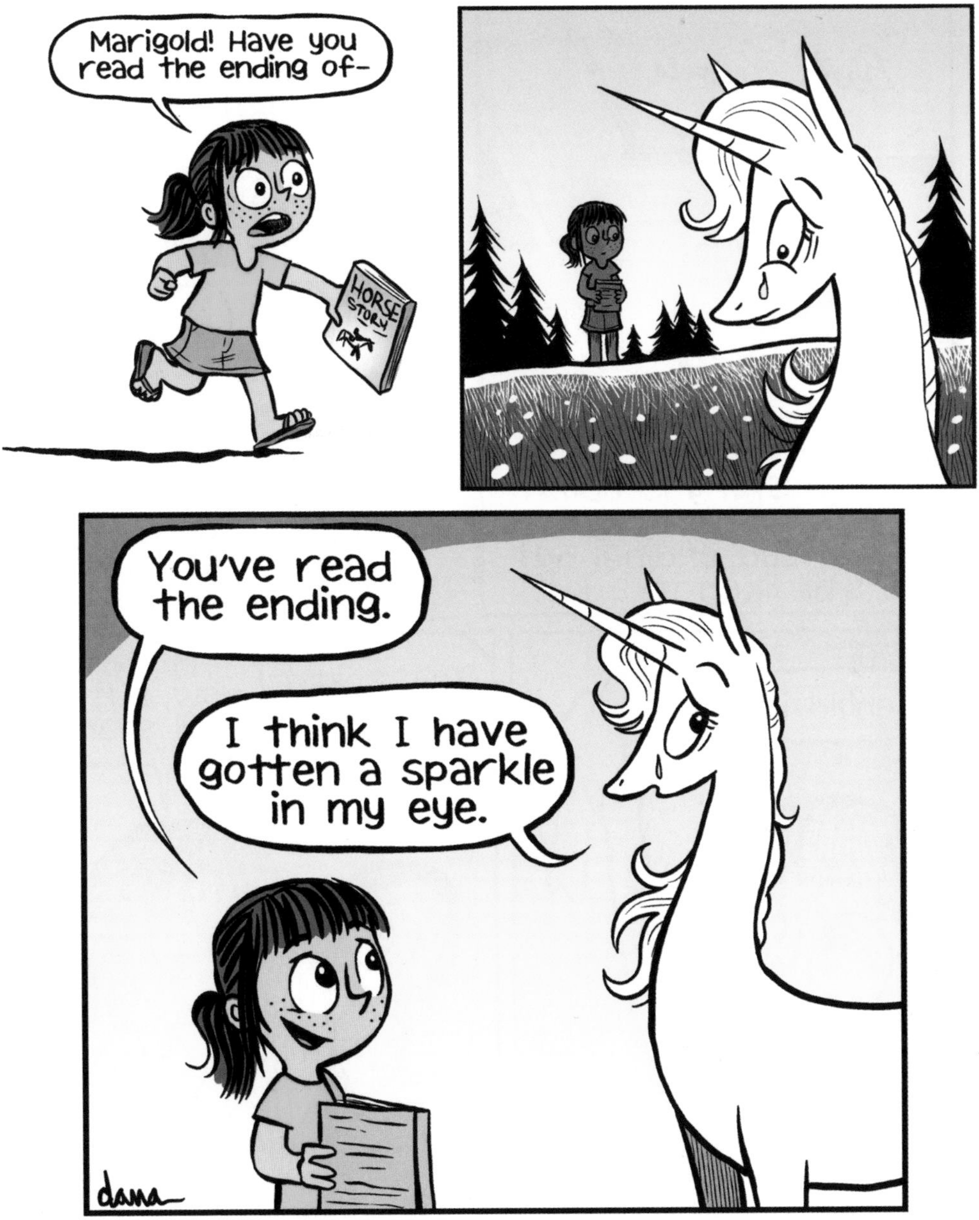
Marigold! Have you read the ending of-
HORSE STORY
You've read the ending.
I think I have gotten a sparkle in my eye.
dana

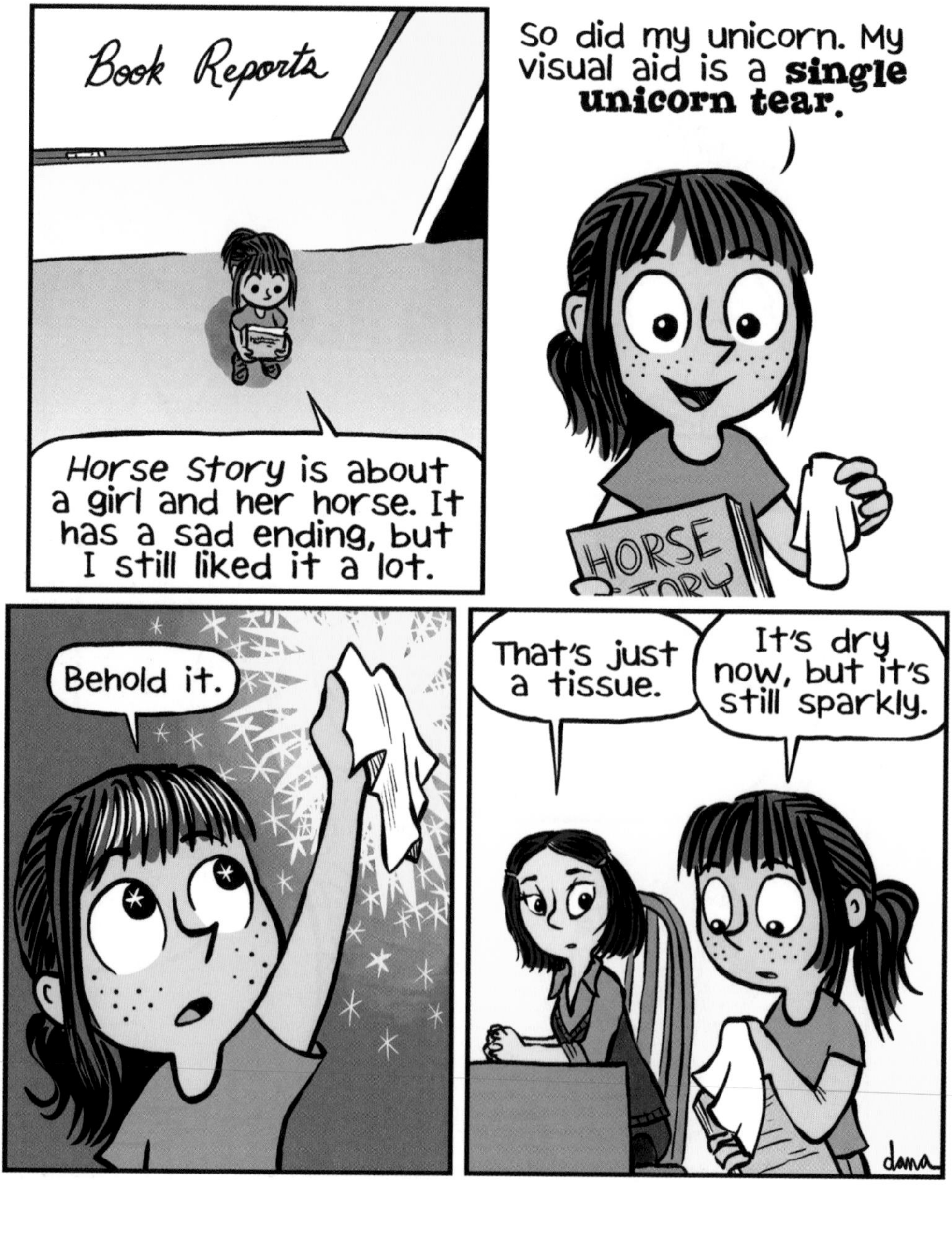
Book Reports
Horse Story is about a girl and her horse. It has a sad ending, but I still liked it a lot.
So did my unicorn. My visual aid is a **single unicorn tear.**
HORSE STORY
Behold it.
That's just a tissue.
It's dry now, but it's still sparkly.
dana

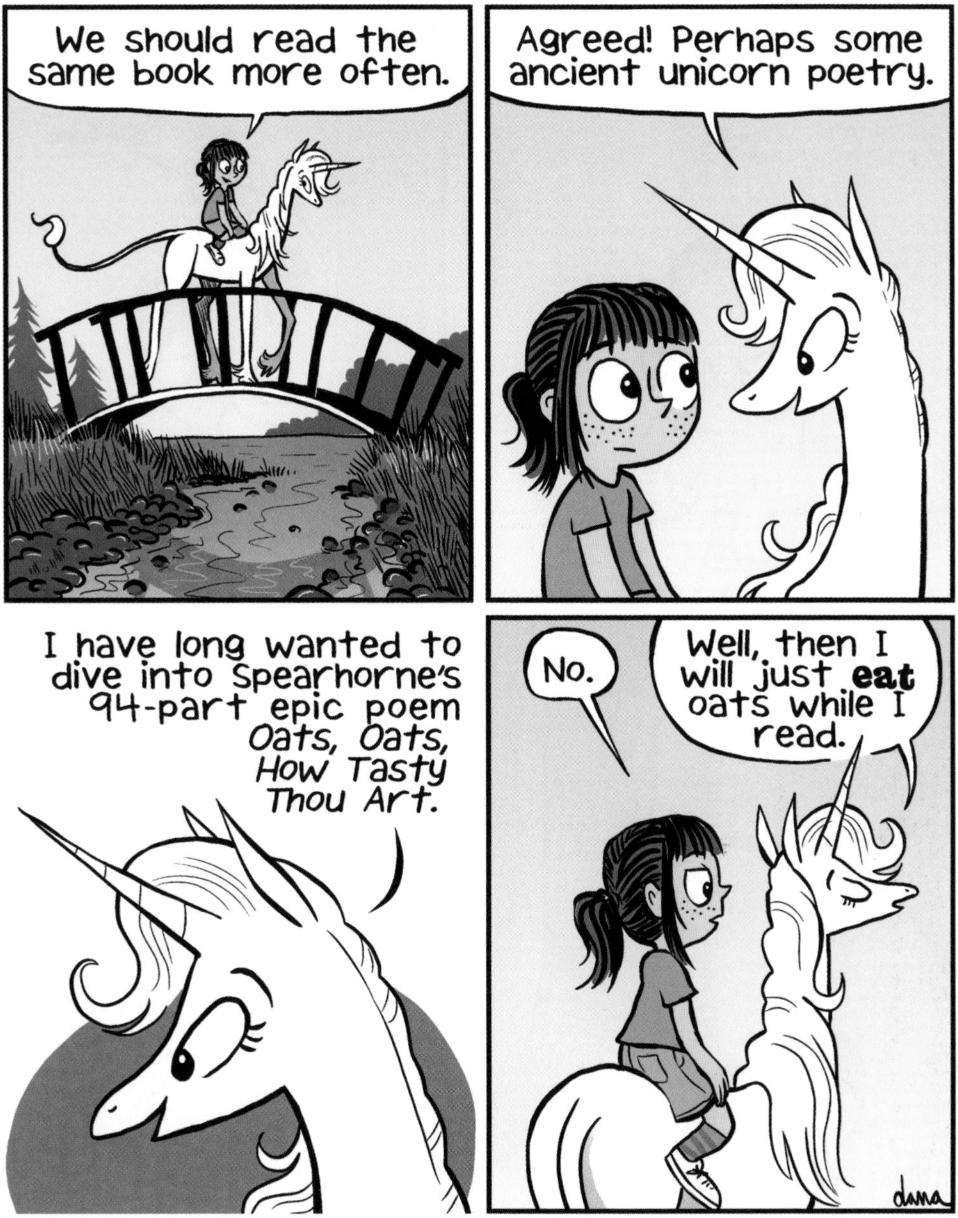
We should read the same book more often.
Agreed! Perhaps some ancient unicorn poetry.
I have long wanted to dive into Spearhorne's 94-part epic poem *Oats, Oats, How Tasty Thou Art.*
No.
Well, then I will just **eat** oats while I read.
dana

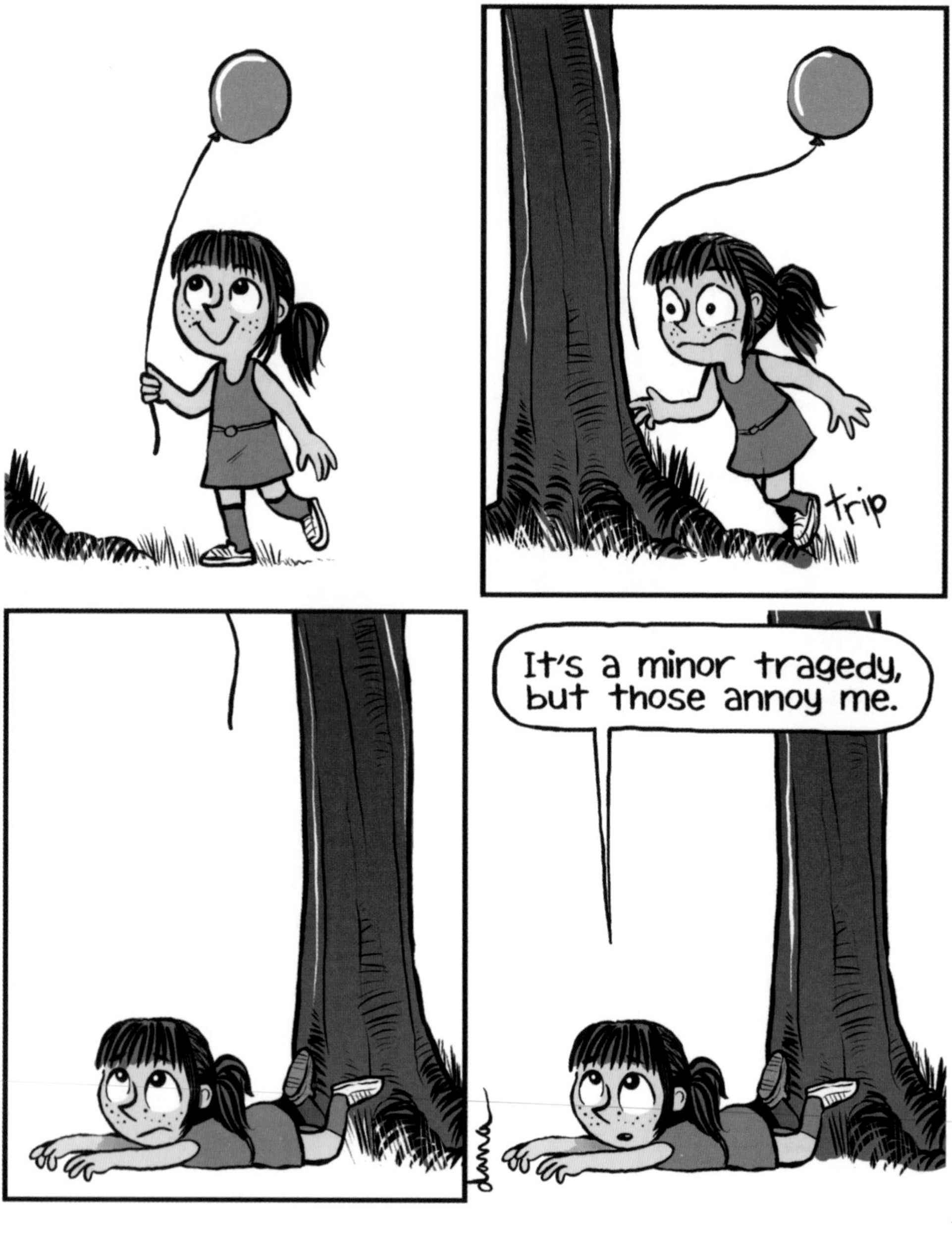
trip
It's a minor tragedy, but those annoy me.
dana

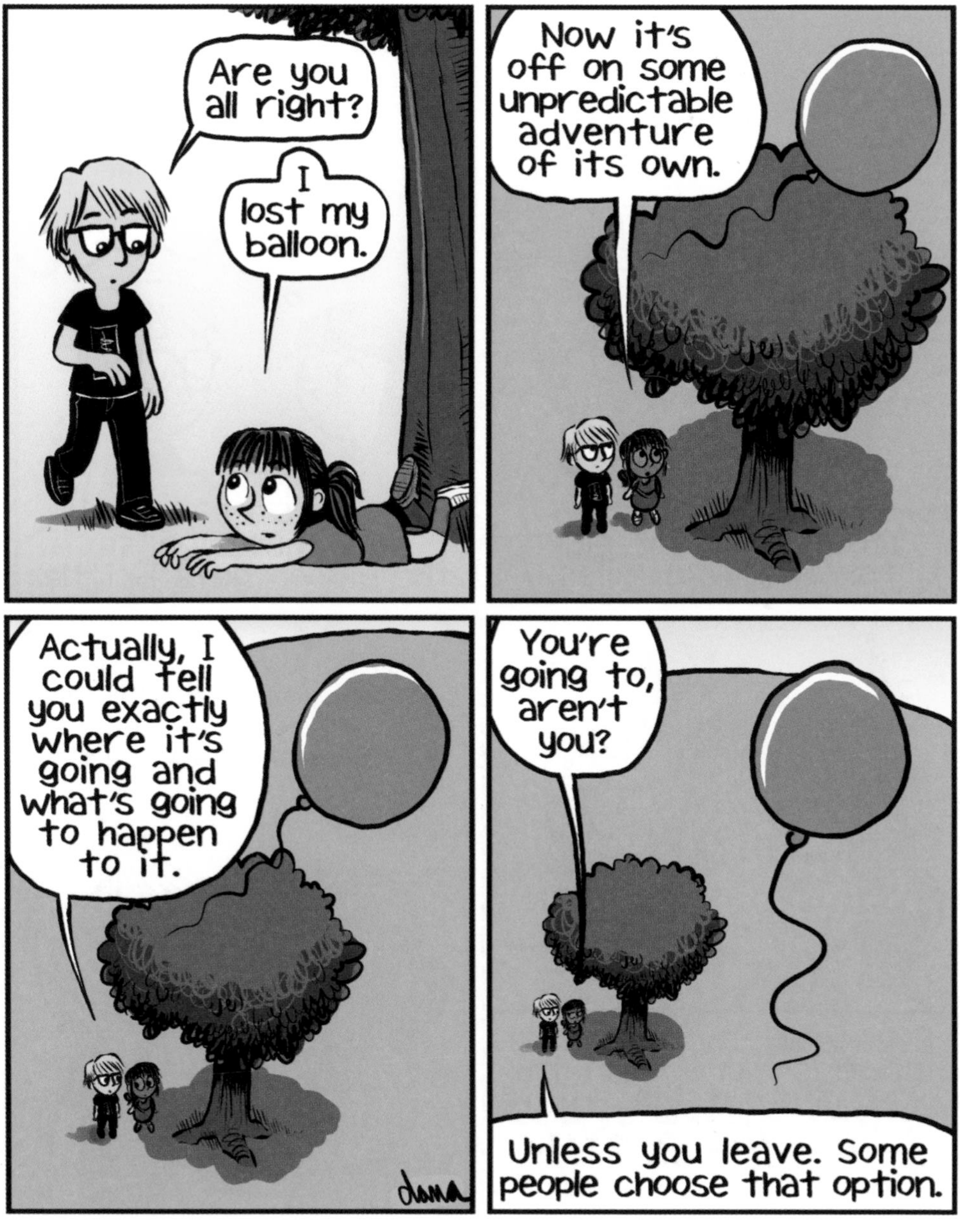
Are you all right?
I lost my balloon.
Now it's off on some unpredictable adventure of its own.
Actually, I could tell you exactly where it's going and what's going to happen to it.
You're going to, aren't you?
Unless you leave. Some people choose that option.

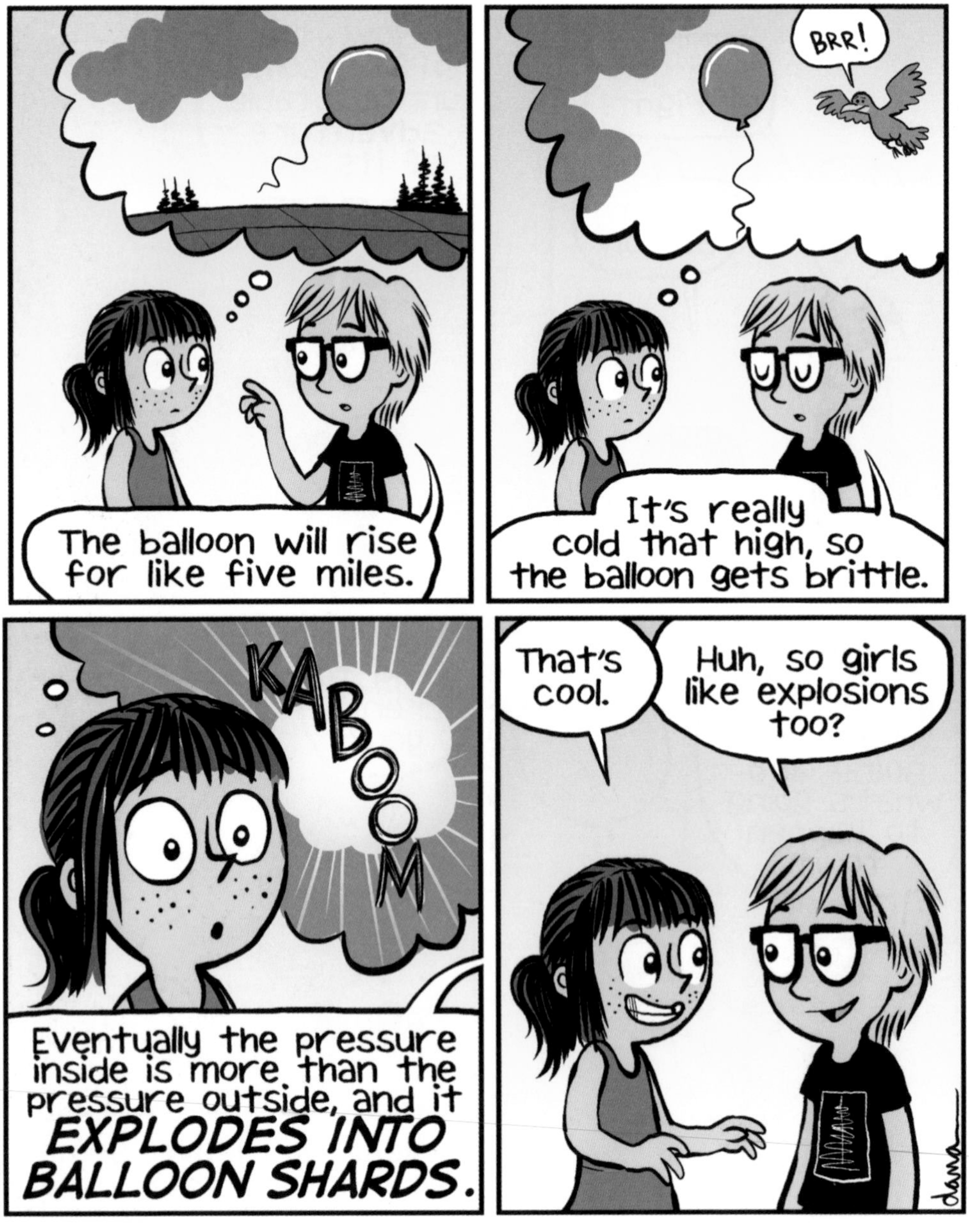
The balloon will rise for like five miles.
BRR!
It's really cold that high, so the balloon gets brittle.
KABOOM
Eventually the pressure inside is more than the pressure outside, and it EXPLODES INTO BALLOON SHARDS.
That's cool.
Huh, so girls like explosions too?
dana

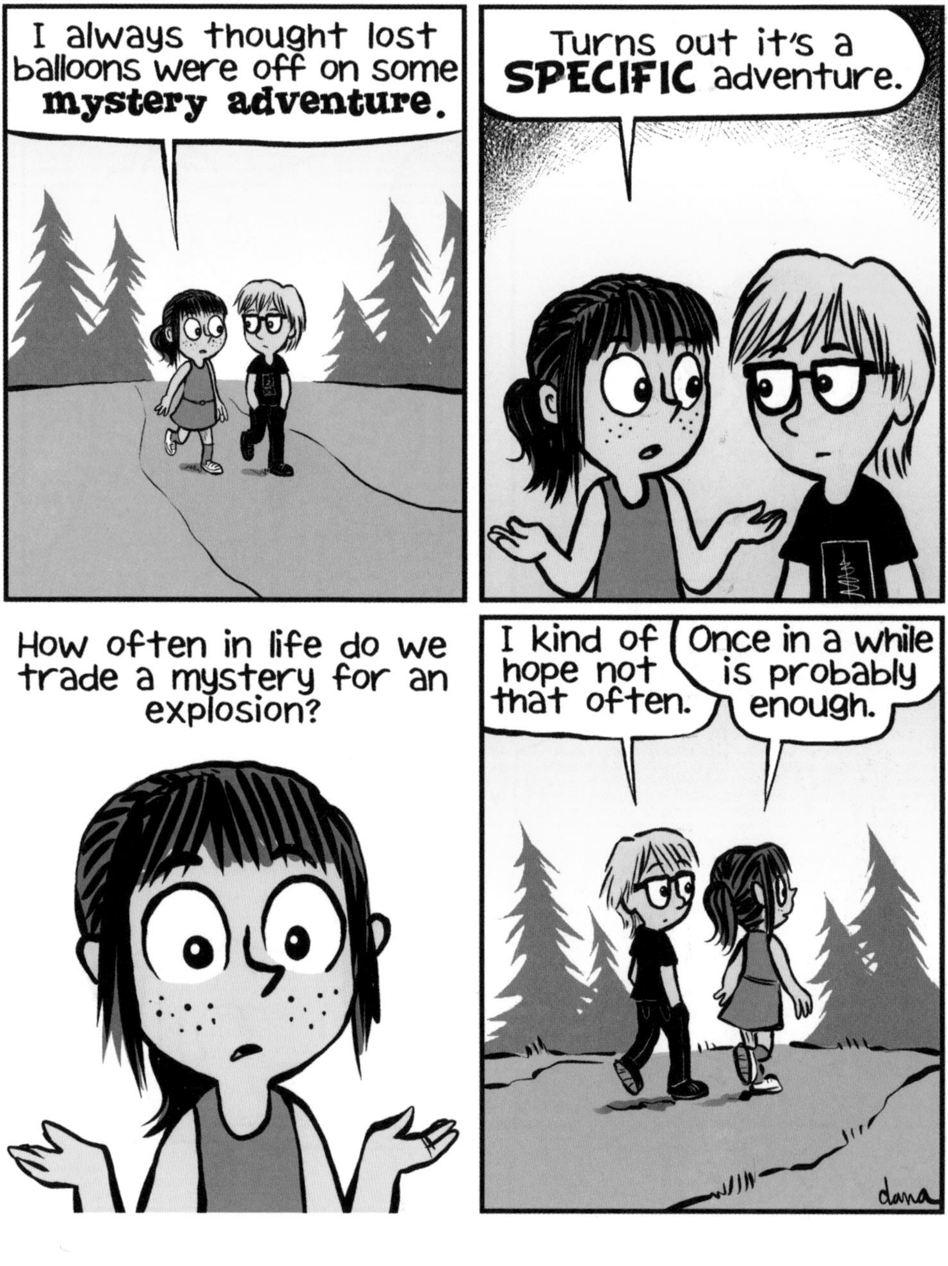
I always thought lost balloons were off on some **mystery adventure**.
Turns out it's a **SPECIFIC** adventure.
How often in life do we trade a mystery for an explosion?
I kind of hope not that often.
Once in a while is probably enough.
dana

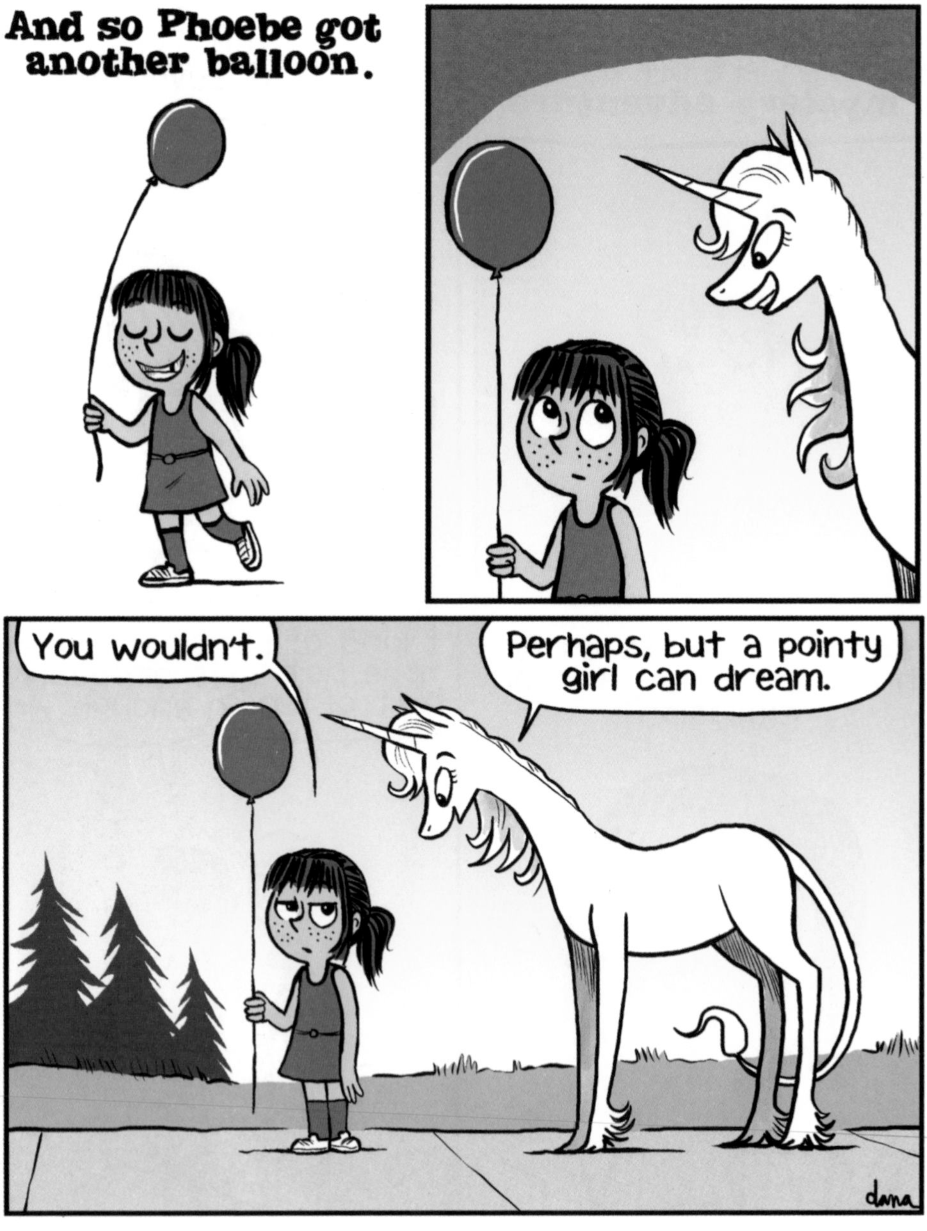
And so Phoebe got another balloon.
You wouldn't.
Perhaps, but a pointy girl can dream.
dana

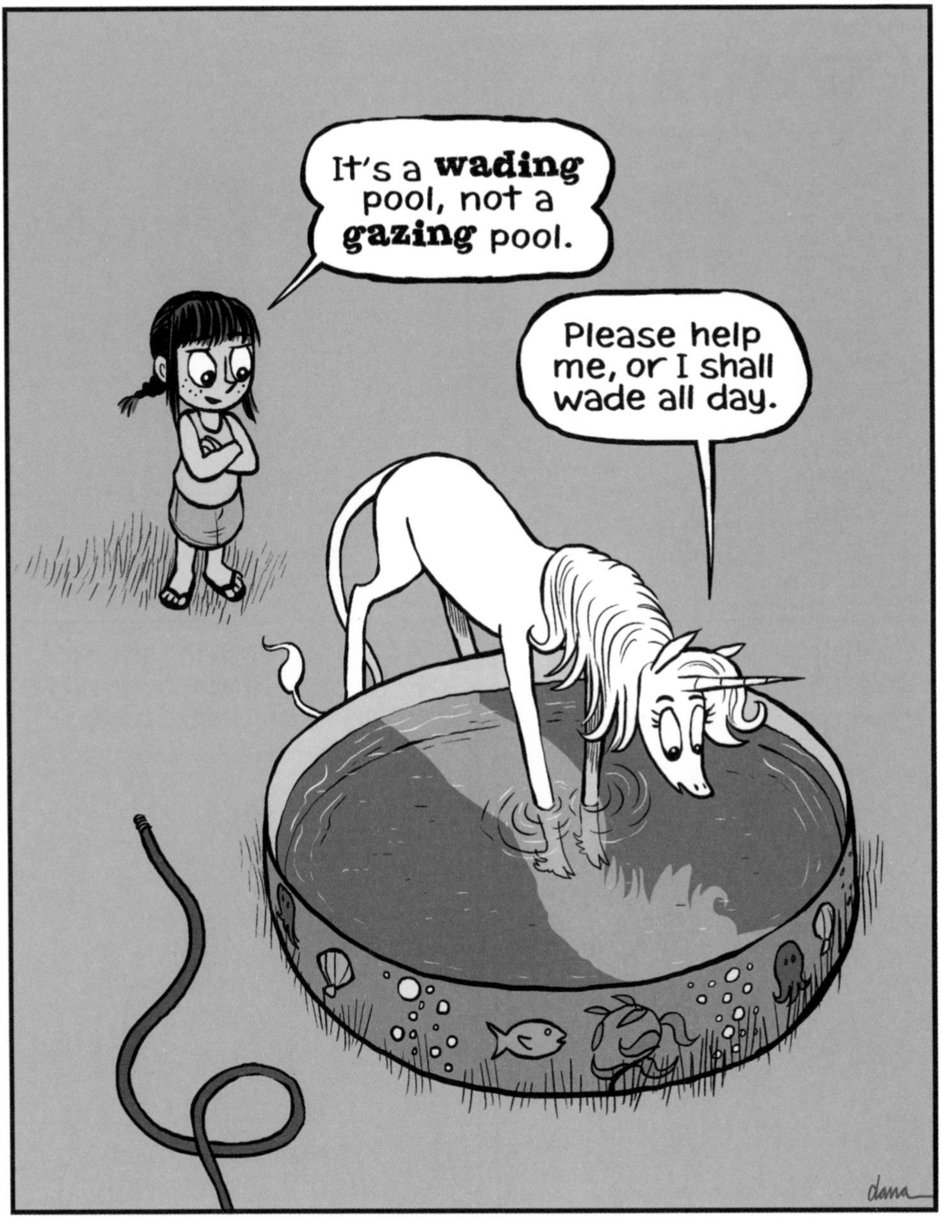
It's a **wading** pool, not a **gazing** pool.
Please help me, or I shall wade all day.
dana

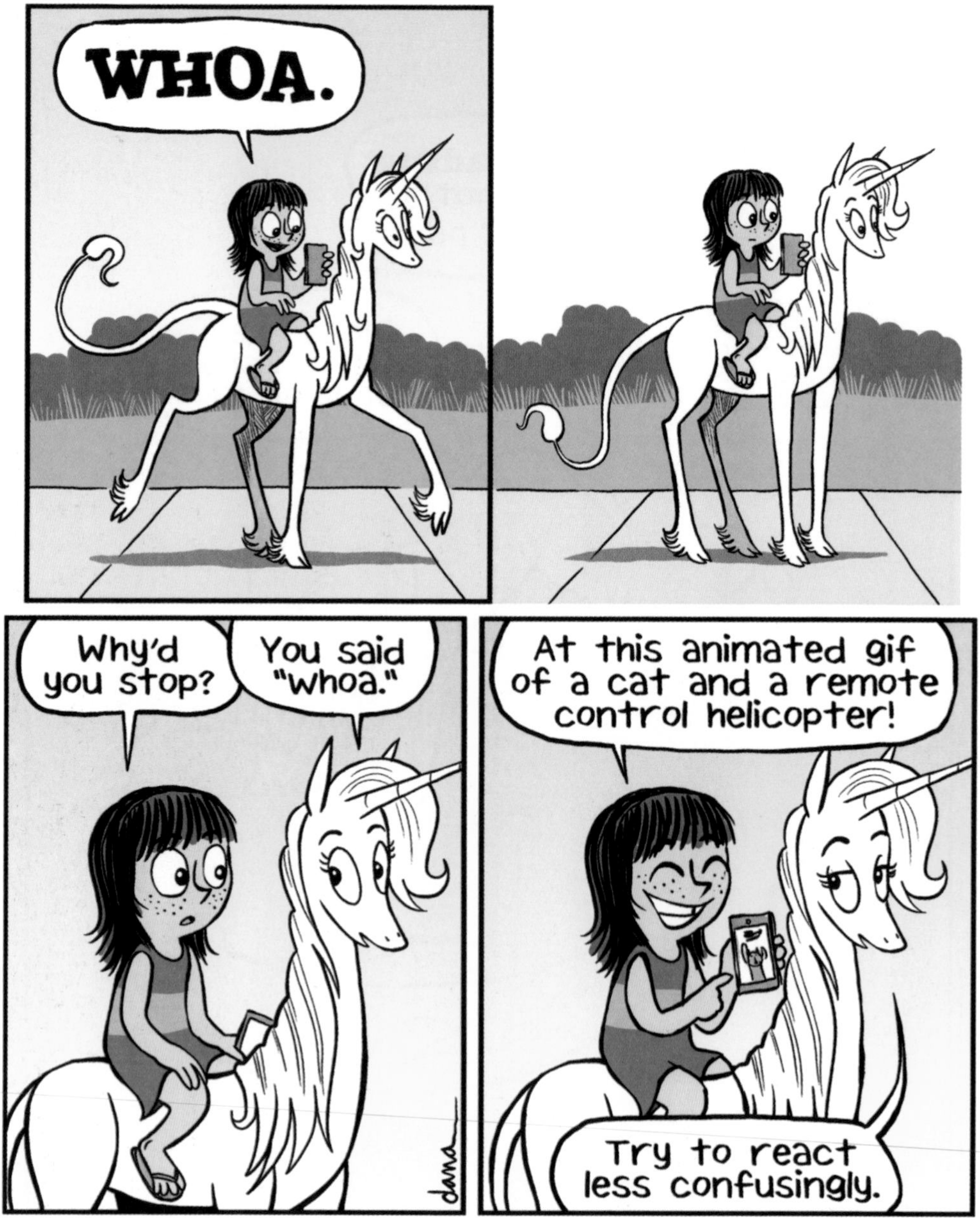
WHOA.
Why'd you stop?
You said "whoa."
At this animated gif of a cat and a remote control helicopter!
Try to react less confusingly.
dana

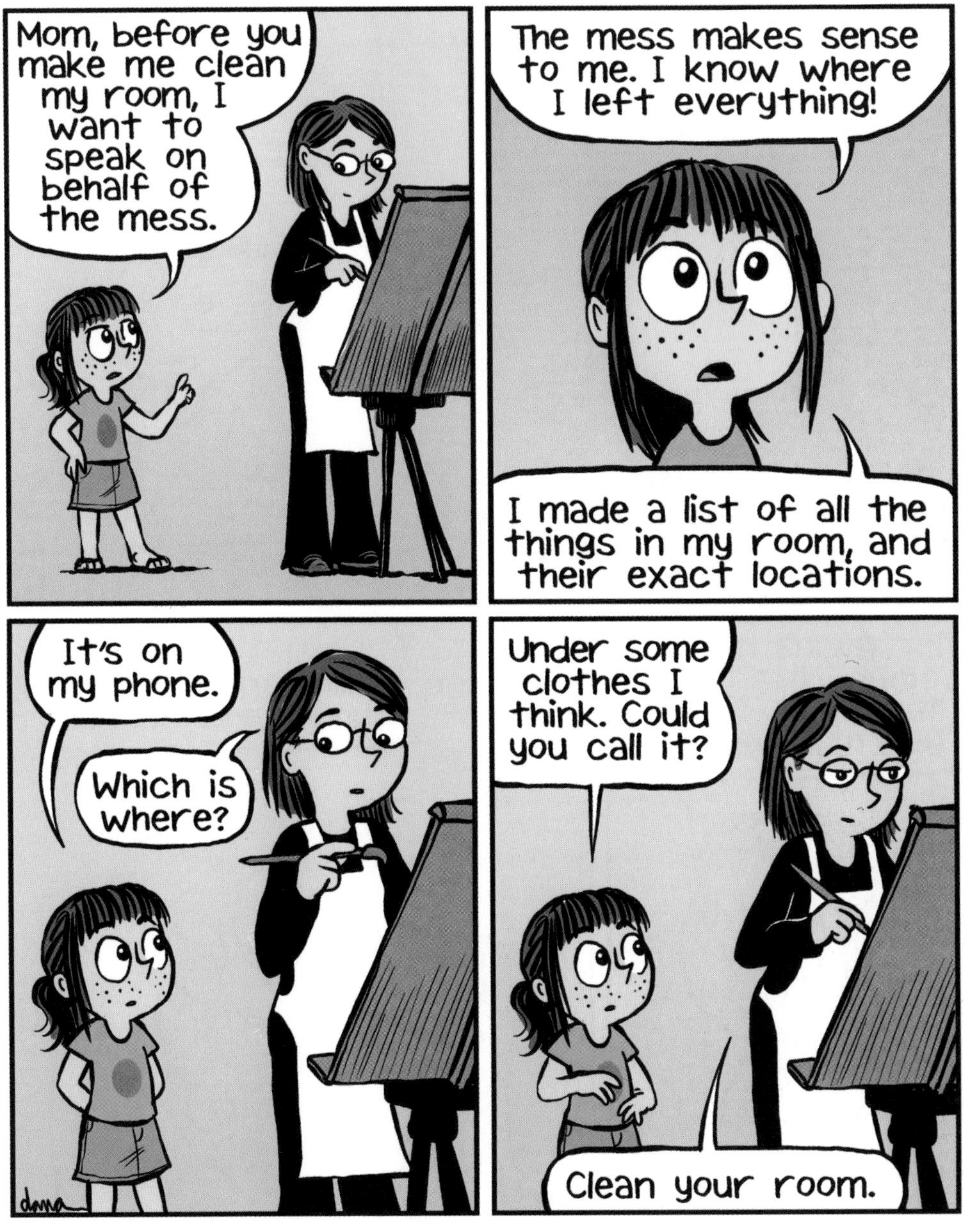
Mom, before you make me clean my room, I want to speak on behalf of the mess.
The mess makes sense to me. I know where I left everything!
I made a list of all the things in my room, and their exact locations.
It's on my phone.
Which is where?
Under some clothes I think. Could you call it?
Clean your room.
dana

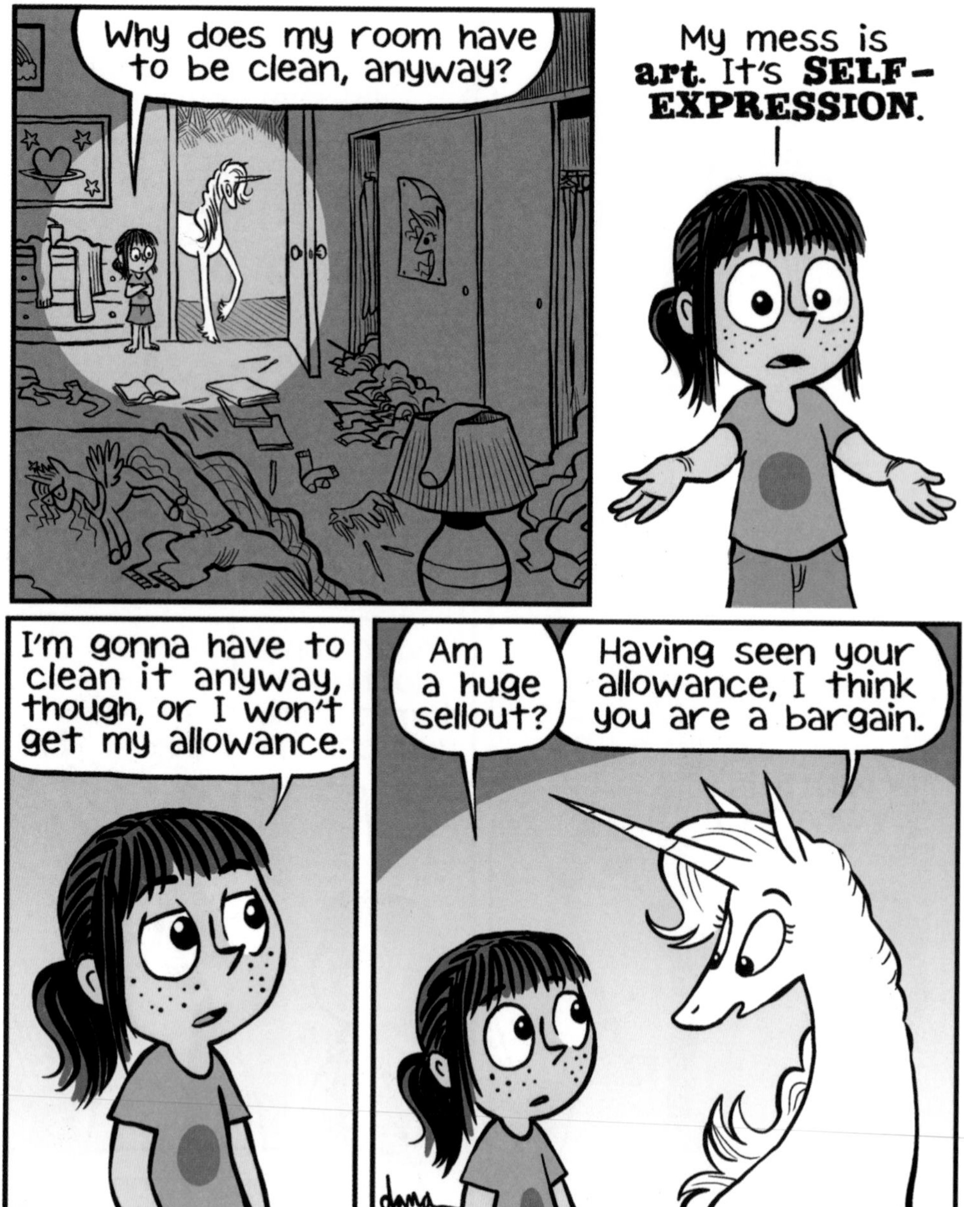
Why does my room have to be clean, anyway?
My mess is art. It's SELF-EXPRESSION.
I'm gonna have to clean it anyway, though, or I won't get my allowance.
Am I a huge sellout?
Having seen your allowance, I think you are a bargain.
dana

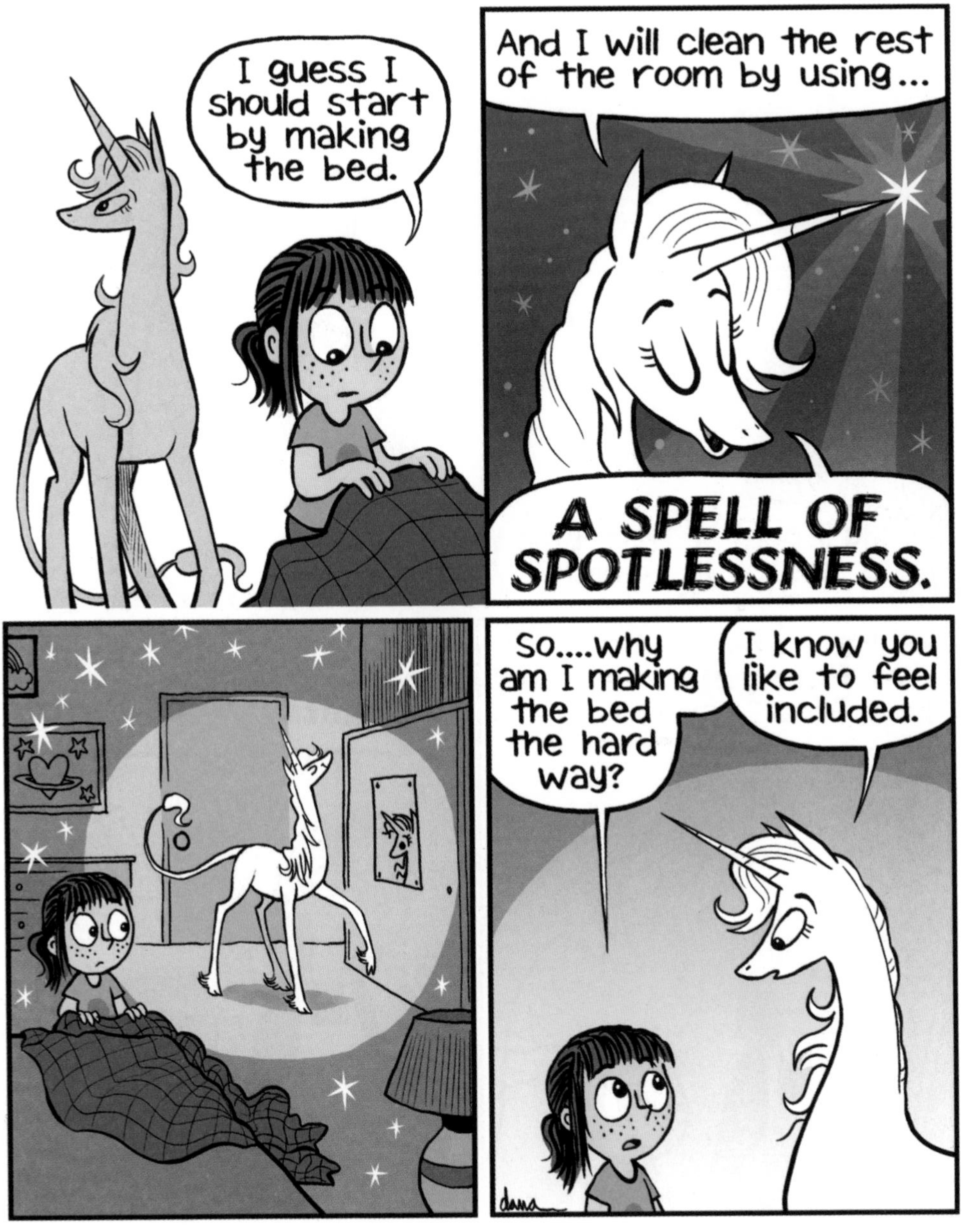
I guess I should start by making the bed.
And I will clean the rest of the room by using...
A SPELL OF SPOTLESSNESS.
So....why am I making the bed the hard way?
I know you like to feel included.
dana

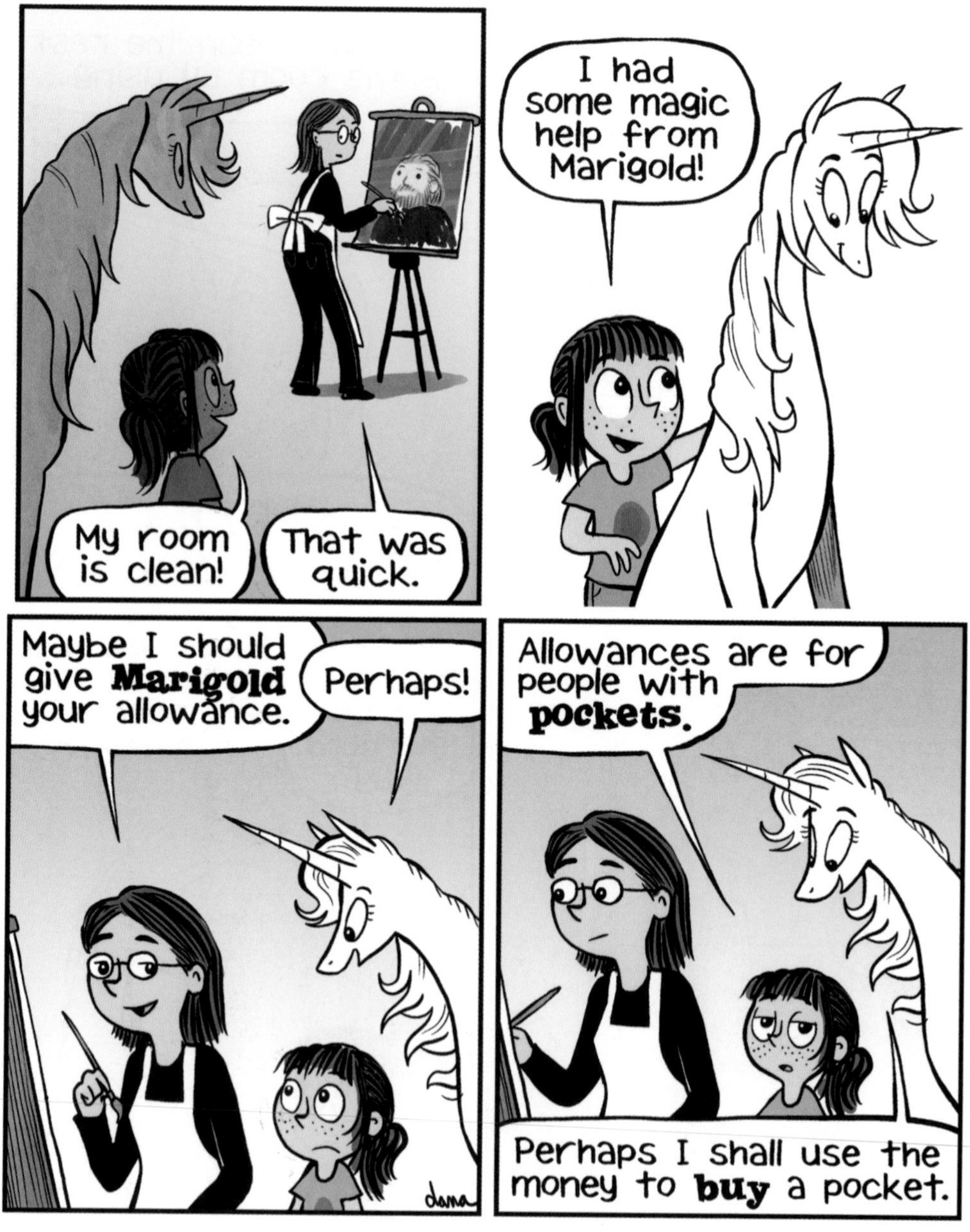
My room is clean!
That was quick.
I had some magic help from Marigold!
Maybe I should give **Marigold** your allowance.
Perhaps!
Allowances are for people with **pockets.**
Perhaps I shall use the money to **buy** a pocket.
dana

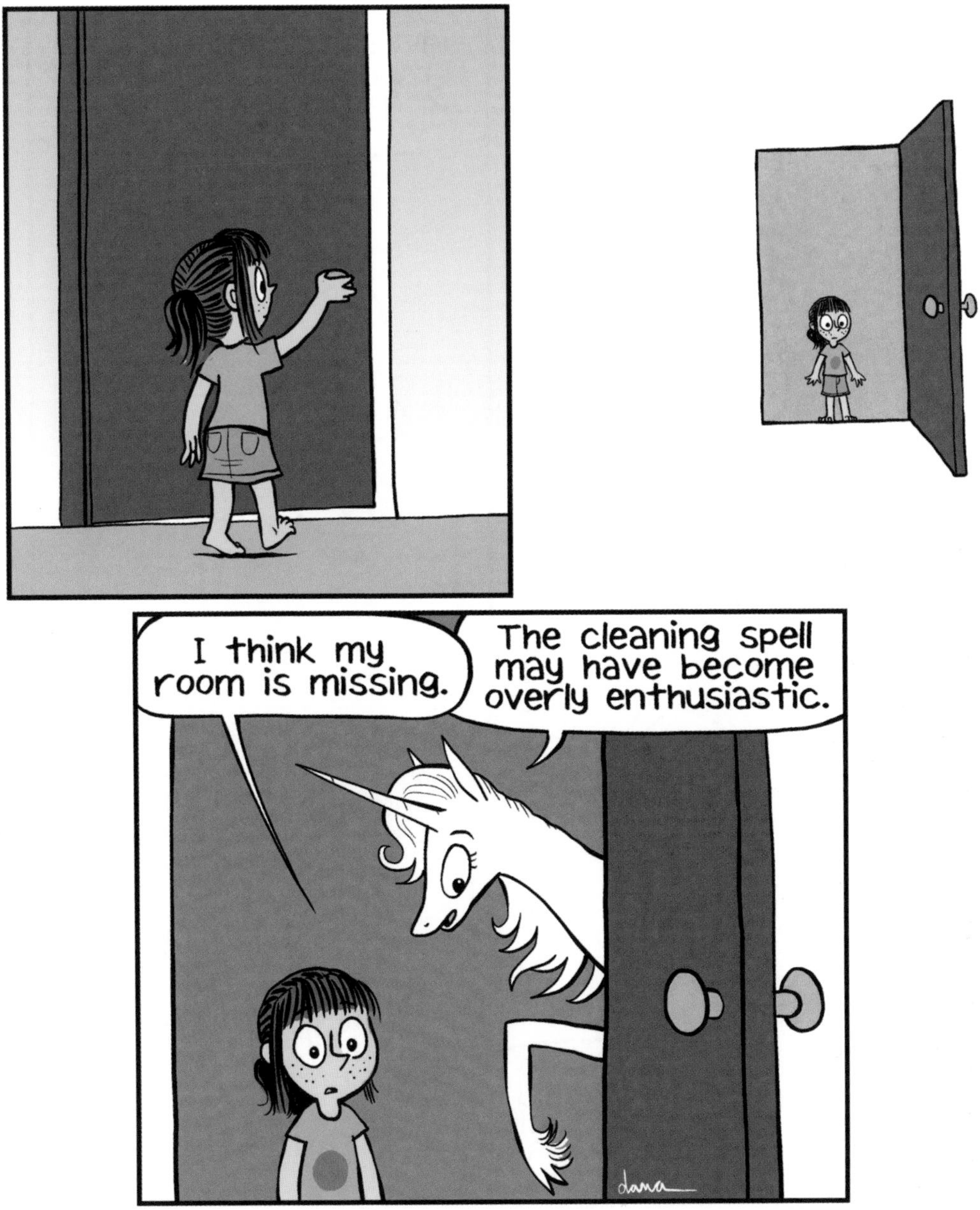
I think my room is missing.
The cleaning spell may have become overly enthusiastic.

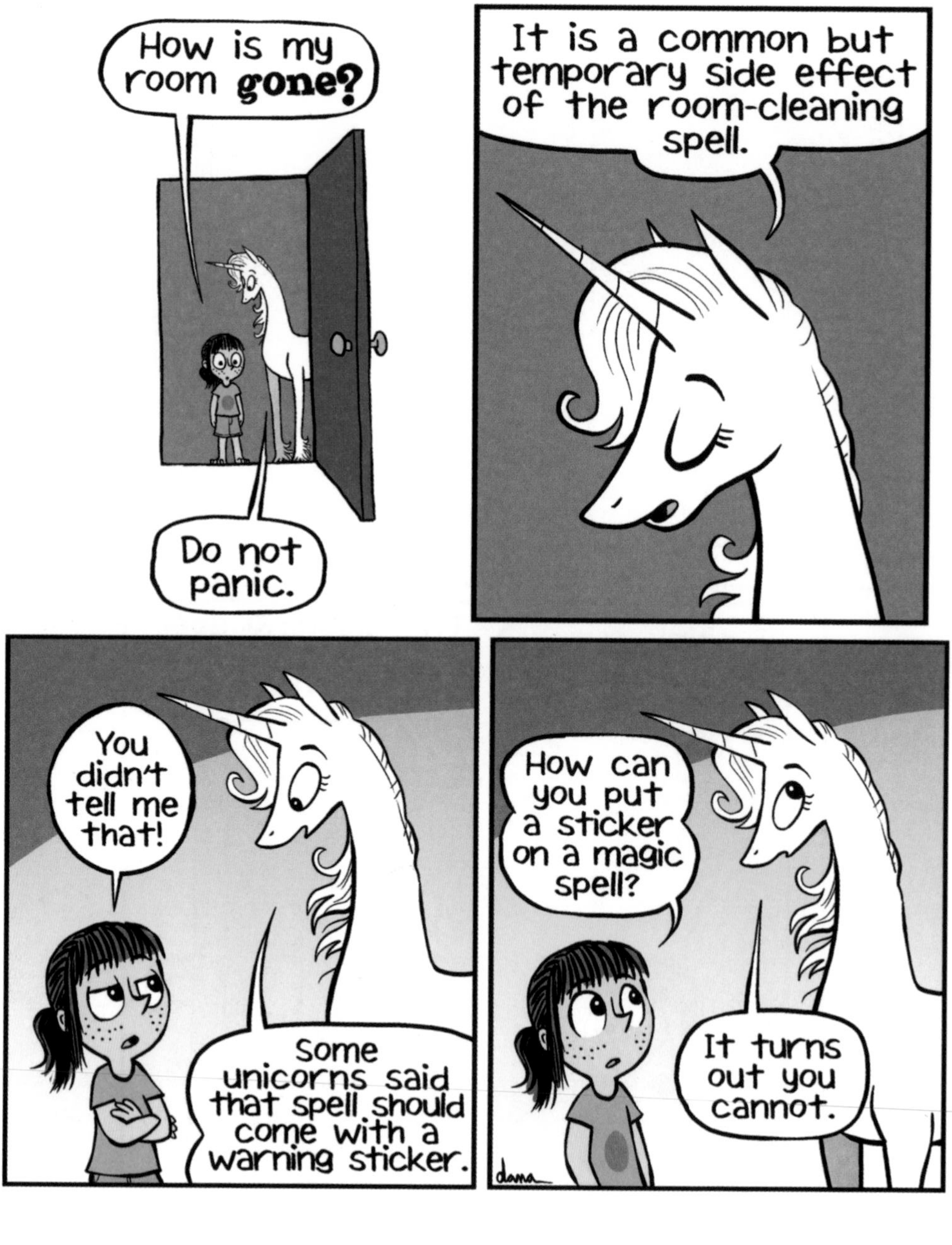
How is my room **gone?**
Do not panic.
It is a common but temporary side effect of the room-cleaning spell.
You didn't tell me that!
Some unicorns said that spell should come with a warning sticker.
How can you put a sticker on a magic spell?
It turns out you cannot.
dana

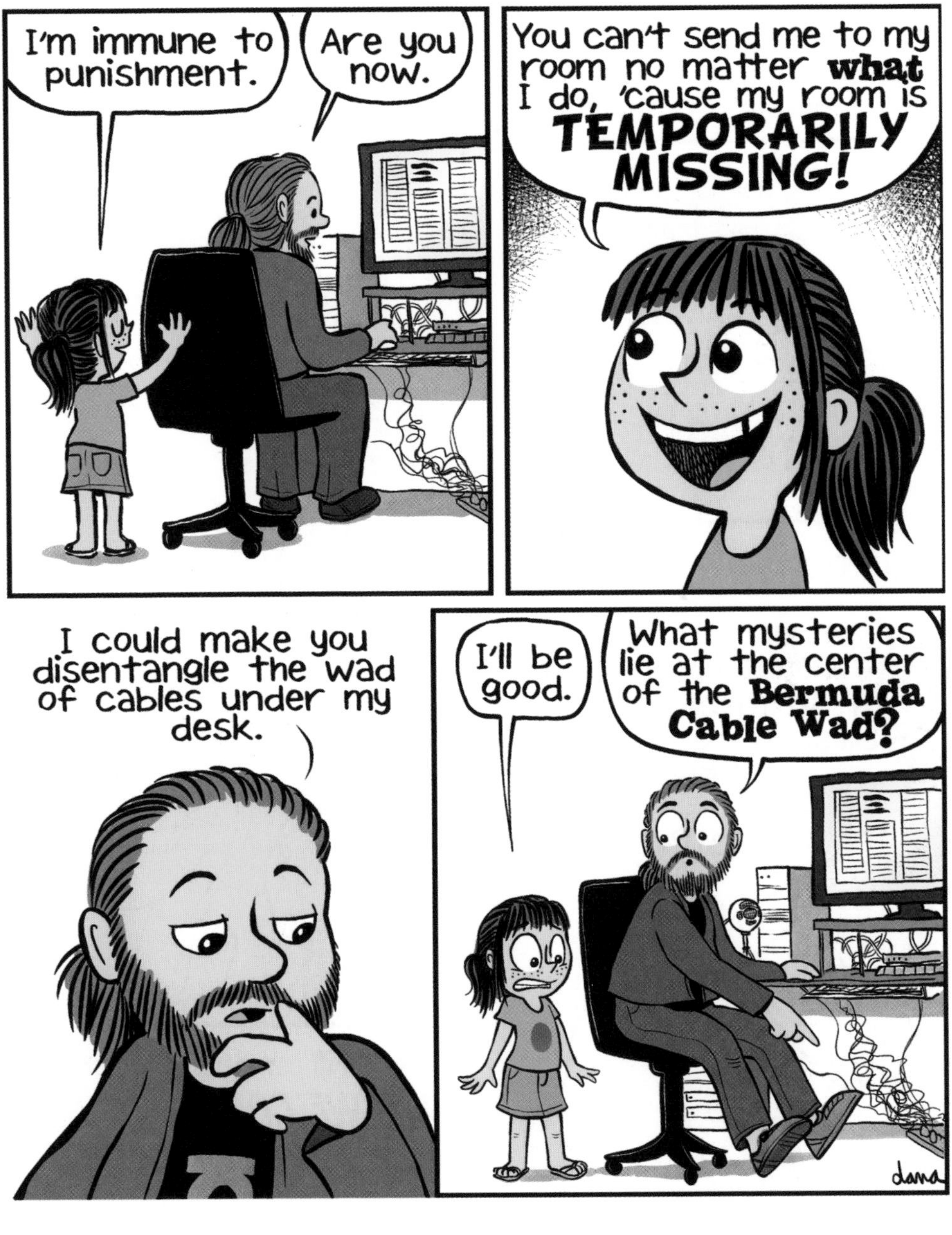
I'm immune to punishment.
Are you now.
You can't send me to my room no matter **what** I do, 'cause my room is **TEMPORARILY MISSING!**
I could make you disentangle the wad of cables under my desk.
I'll be good.
What mysteries lie at the center of the **Bermuda Cable Wad?**
dana

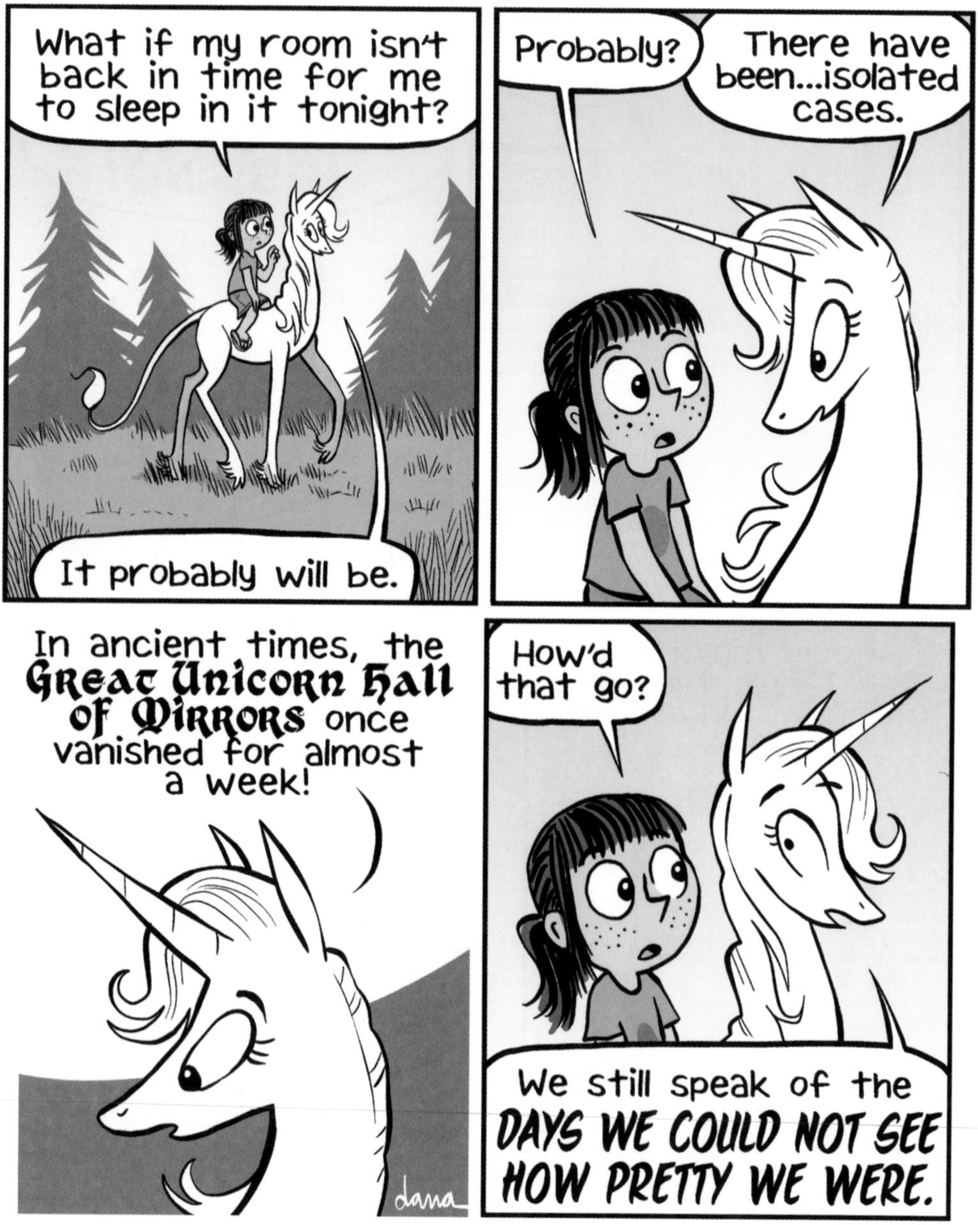
What if my room isn't back in time for me to sleep in it tonight?
It probably will be.
Probably?
There have been...isolated cases.
In ancient times, the Great Unicorn Hall of Mirrors once vanished for almost a week!
dana
How'd that go?
We still speak of the DAYS WE COULD NOT SEE HOW PRETTY WE WERE.

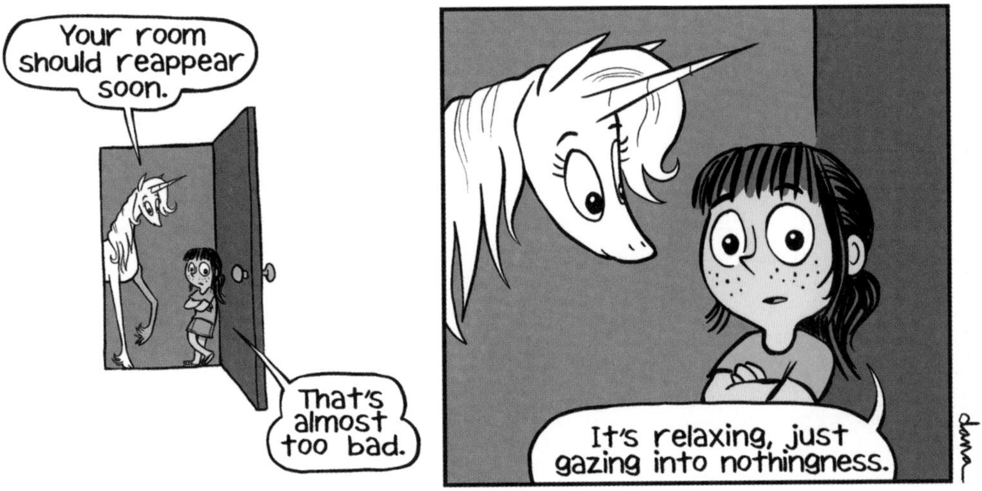
Your room should reappear soon.
That's almost too bad.
It's relaxing, just gazing into nothingness.
dana

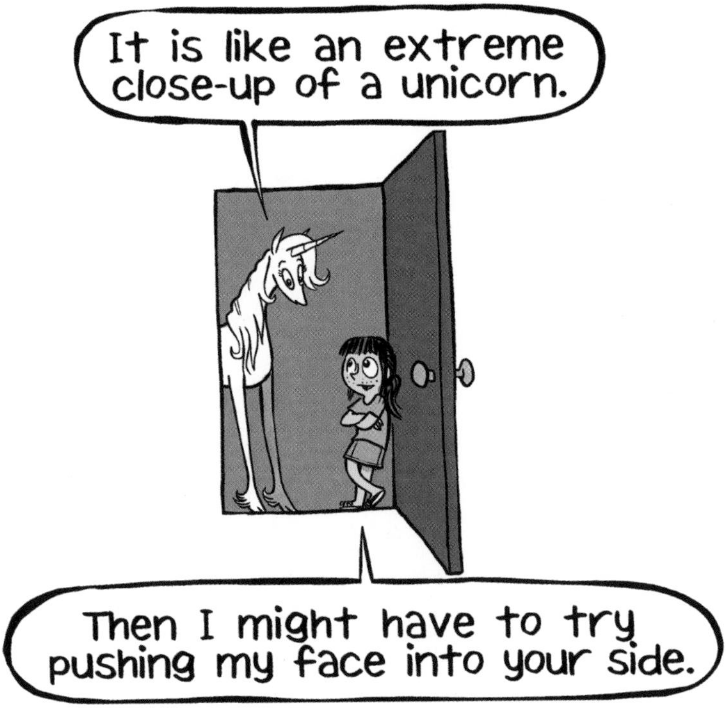
It is like an extreme close-up of a unicorn.
Then I might have to try pushing my face into your side.

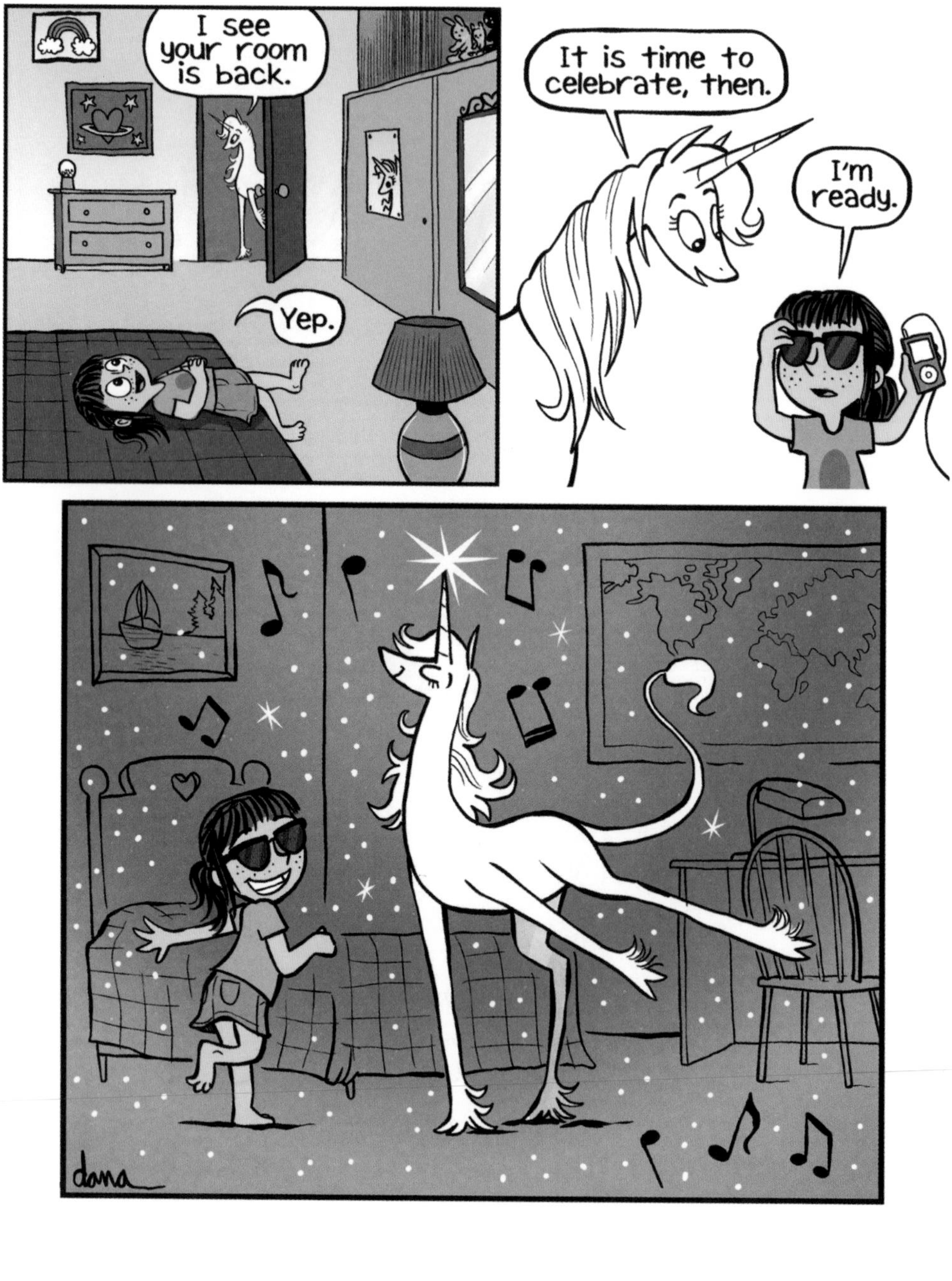
I see your room is back.
Yep.
It is time to celebrate, then.
I'm ready.
dana

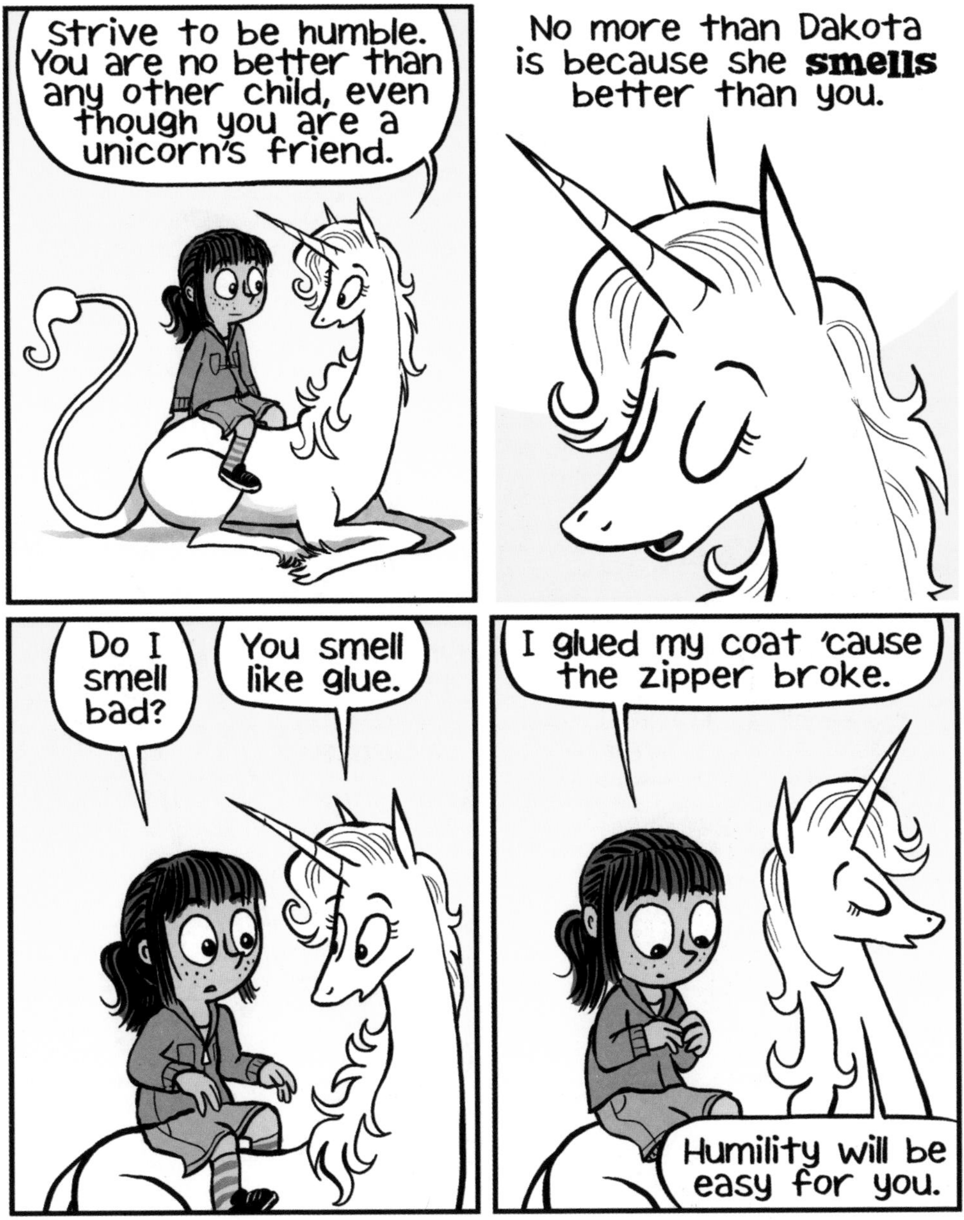
Strive to be humble. You are no better than any other child, even though you are a unicorn's friend.
No more than Dakota is because she **smells** better than you.
Do I smell bad?
You smell like glue.
I glued my coat 'cause the zipper broke.
Humility will be easy for you.

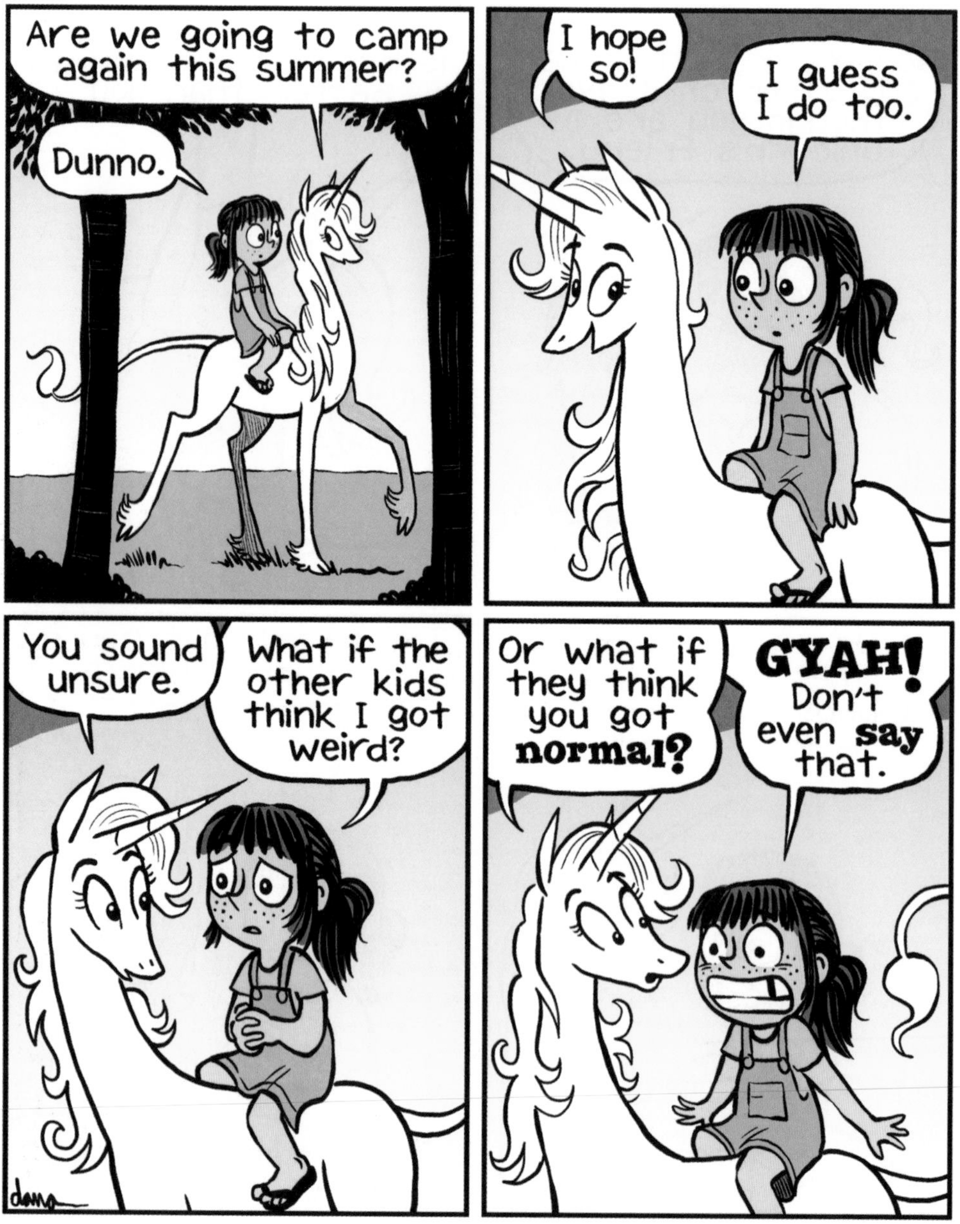
Are we going to camp again this summer?
Dunno.
I hope so!
I guess I do too.
You sound unsure.
What if the other kids think I got weird?
Or what if they think you got **normal?**
GYAH! Don't even **say** that.
dana

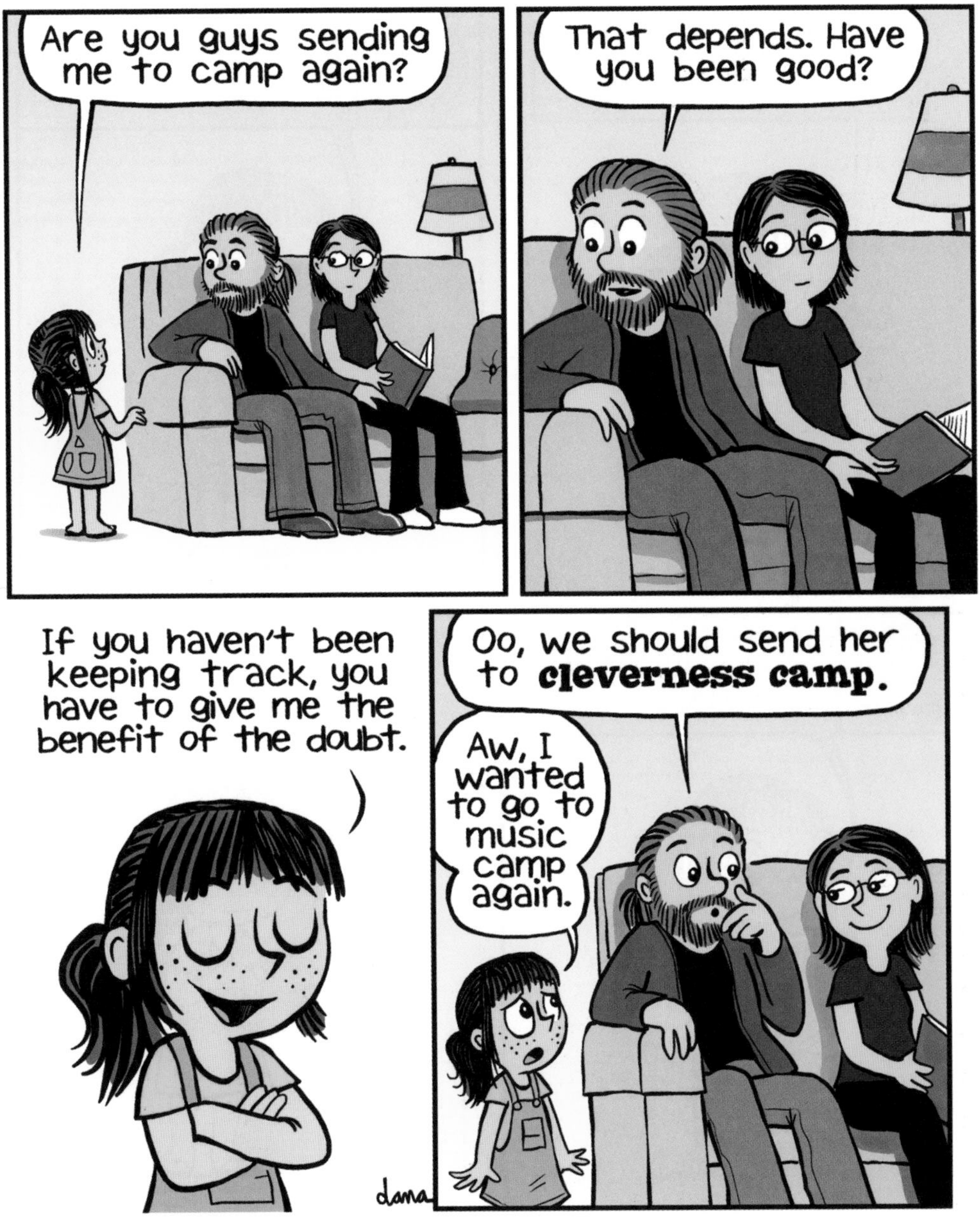
Are you guys sending me to camp again?
That depends. Have you been good?
If you haven't been keeping track, you have to give me the benefit of the doubt.
Oo, we should send her to **cleverness camp.**
Aw, I wanted to go to music camp again.
dana

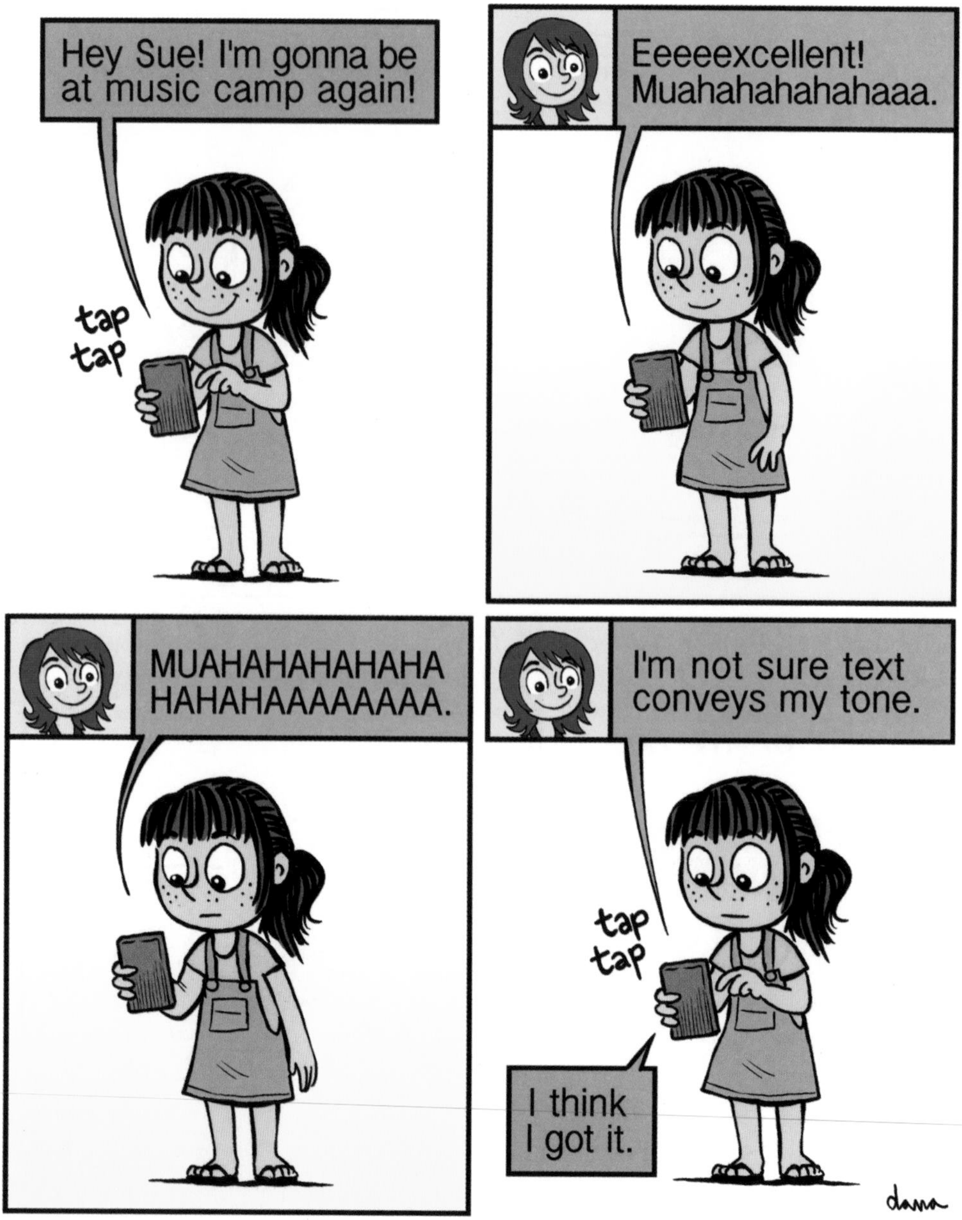
Hey Sue! I'm gonna be at music camp again!
tap tap
Eeeeexcellent! Muahahahahahahaaa.
MUAHAHAHAHAHA HAHAHAAAAAAAA.
I'm not sure text conveys my tone.
tap tap
I think I got it.
dana

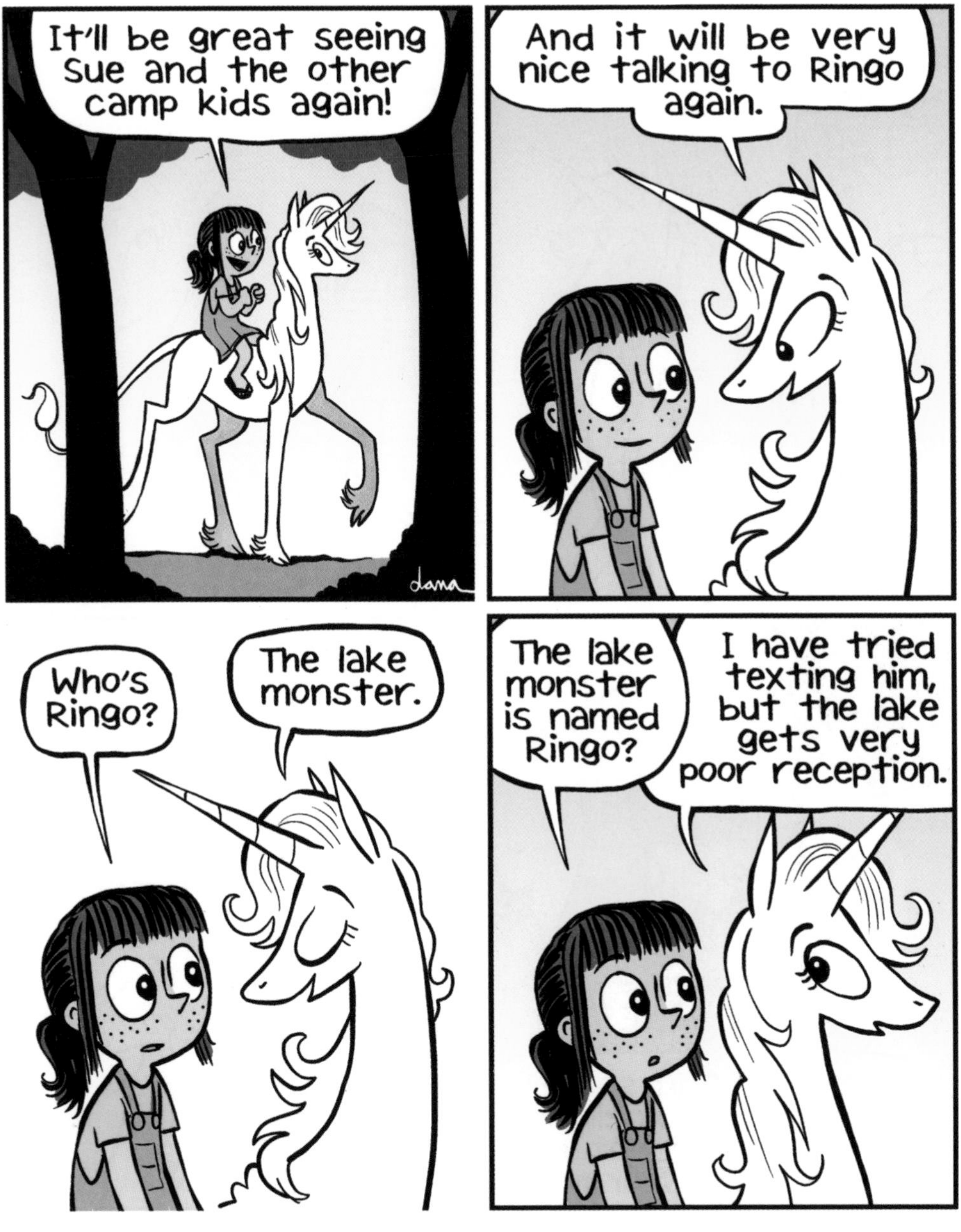
It'll be great seeing Sue and the other camp kids again!
And it will be very nice talking to Ringo again.
Who's Ringo?
The lake monster.
The lake monster is named Ringo?
I have tried texting him, but the lake gets very poor reception.

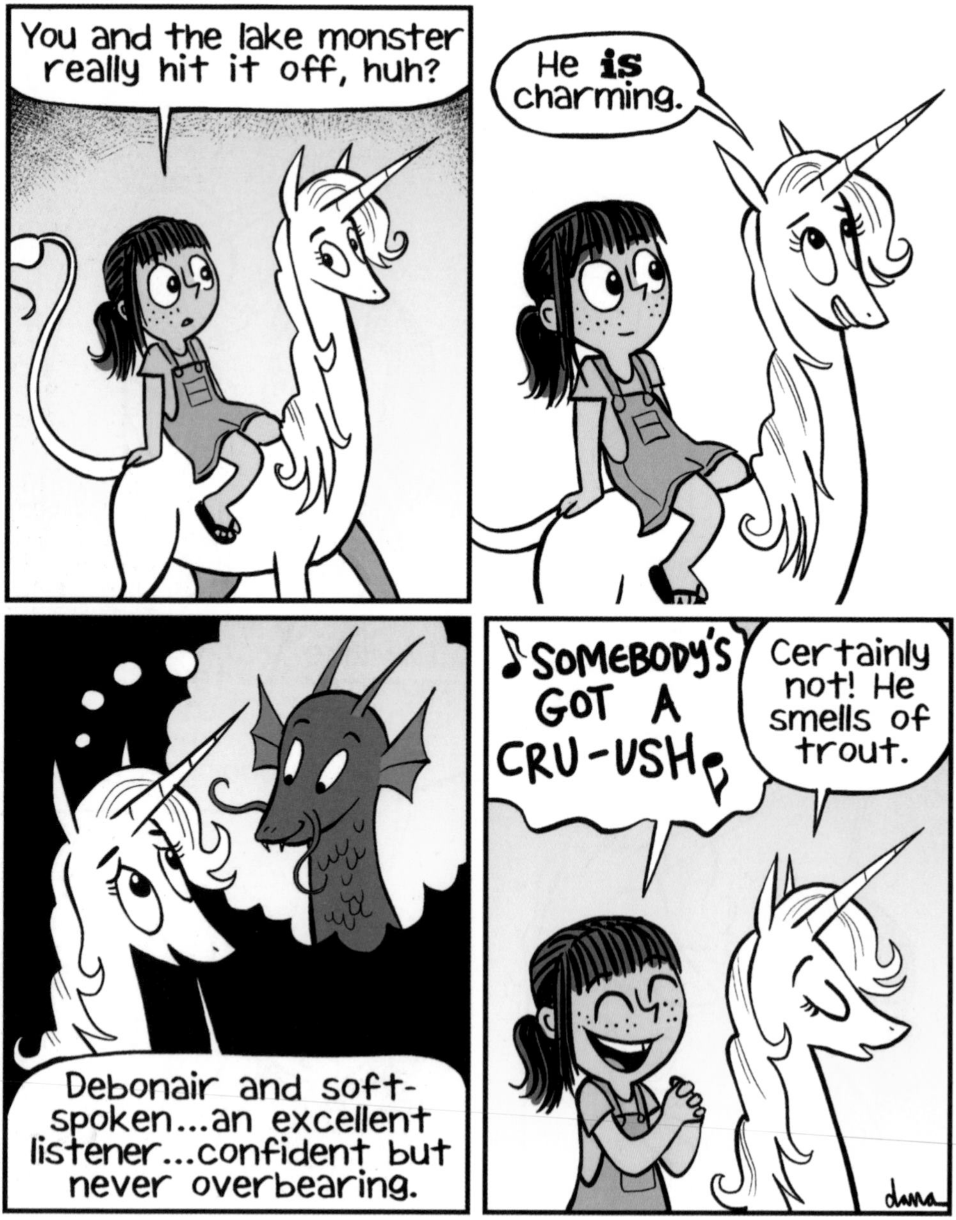
You and the lake monster really hit it off, huh?
He **is** charming.
Debonair and soft-spoken...an excellent listener...confident but never overbearing.
♪ SOMEBODY'S GOT A CRU-USH ♪
Certainly not! He smells of trout.
dana

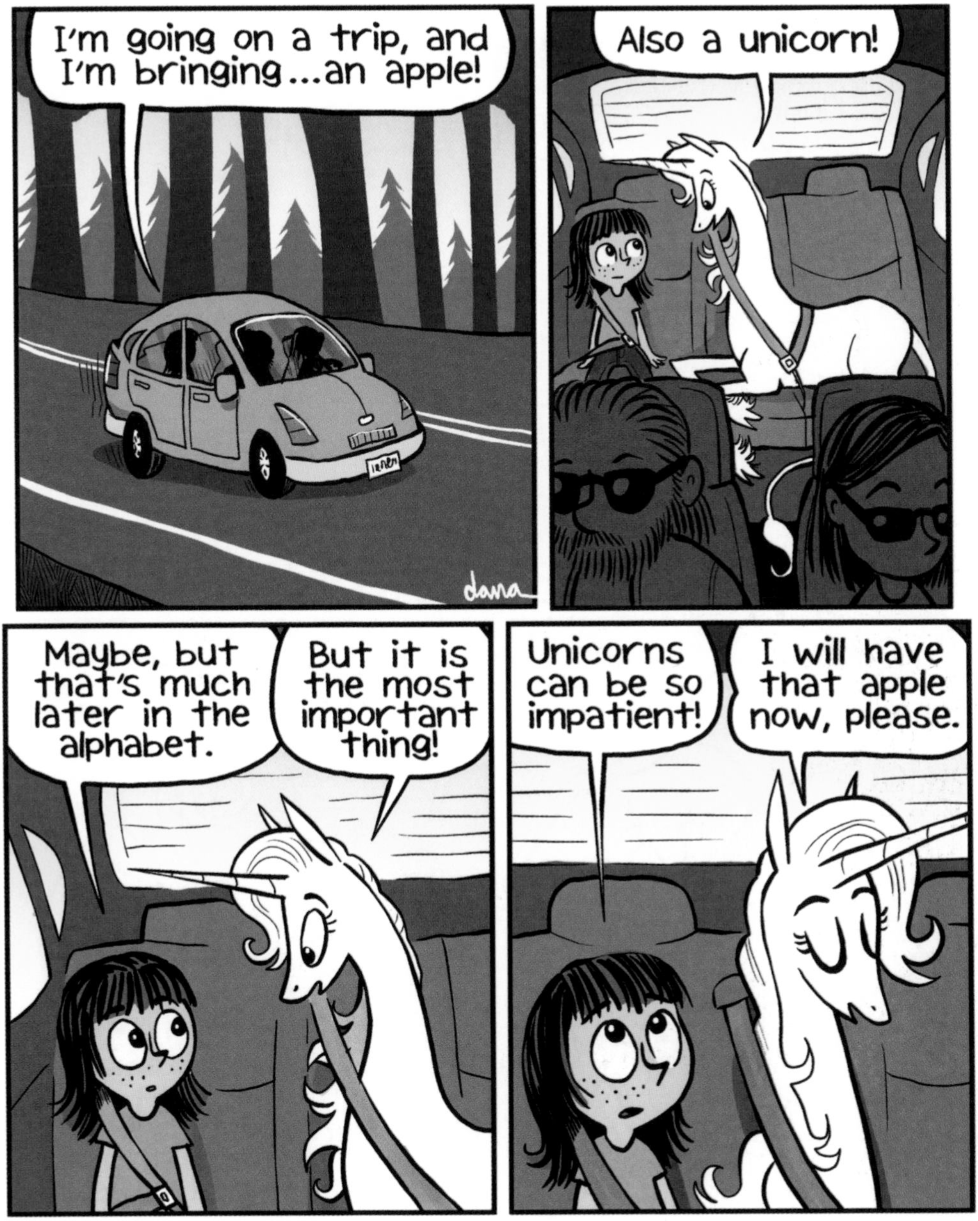
I'm going on a trip, and I'm bringing...an apple!
dana
Also a unicorn!
Maybe, but that's much later in the alphabet.
But it is the most important thing!
Unicorns can be so impatient!
I will have that apple now, please.

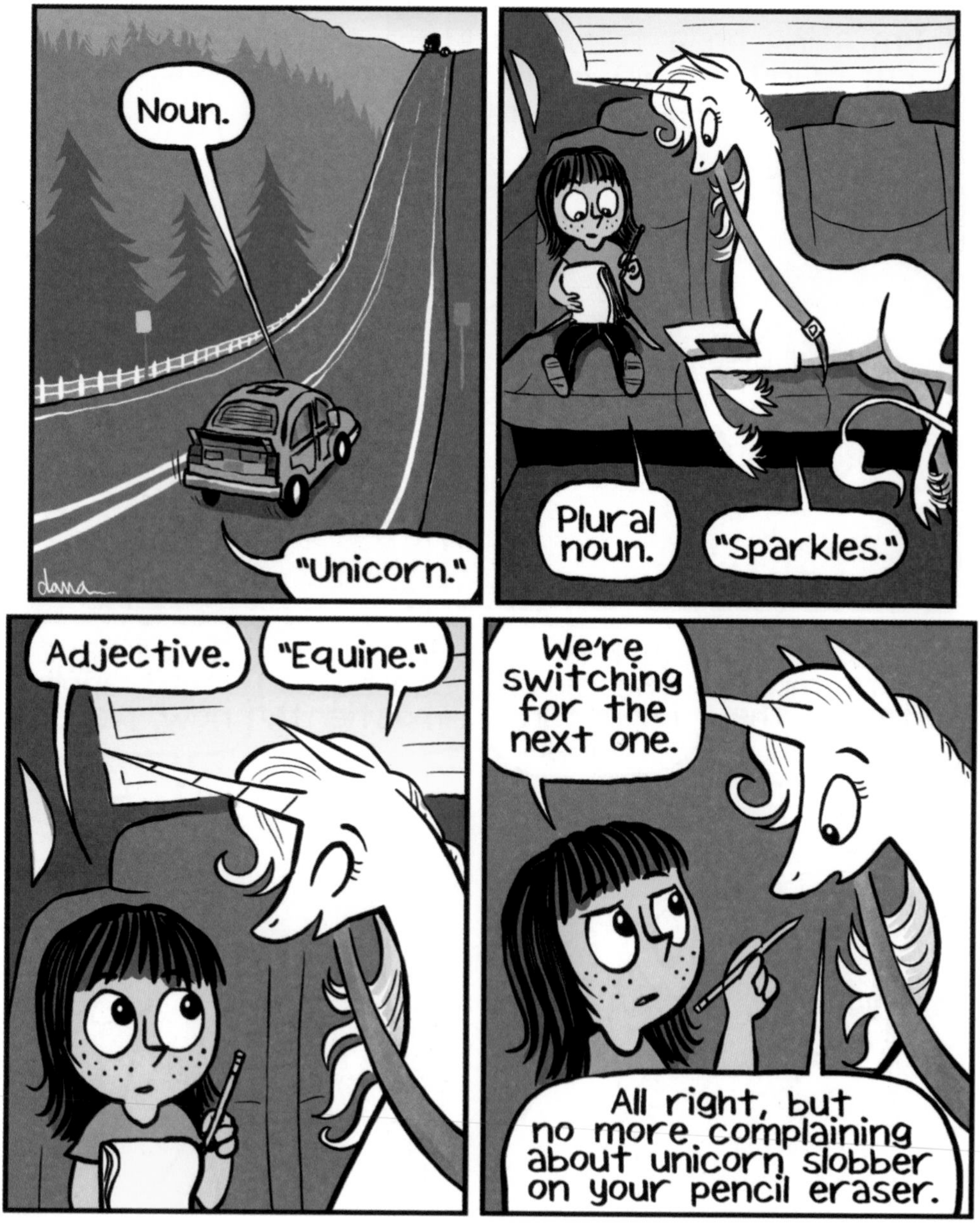
Noun.
"Unicorn."
Plural noun.
"Sparkles."
Adjective.
"Equine."
We're switching for the next one.
All right, but no more complaining about unicorn slobber on your pencil eraser.

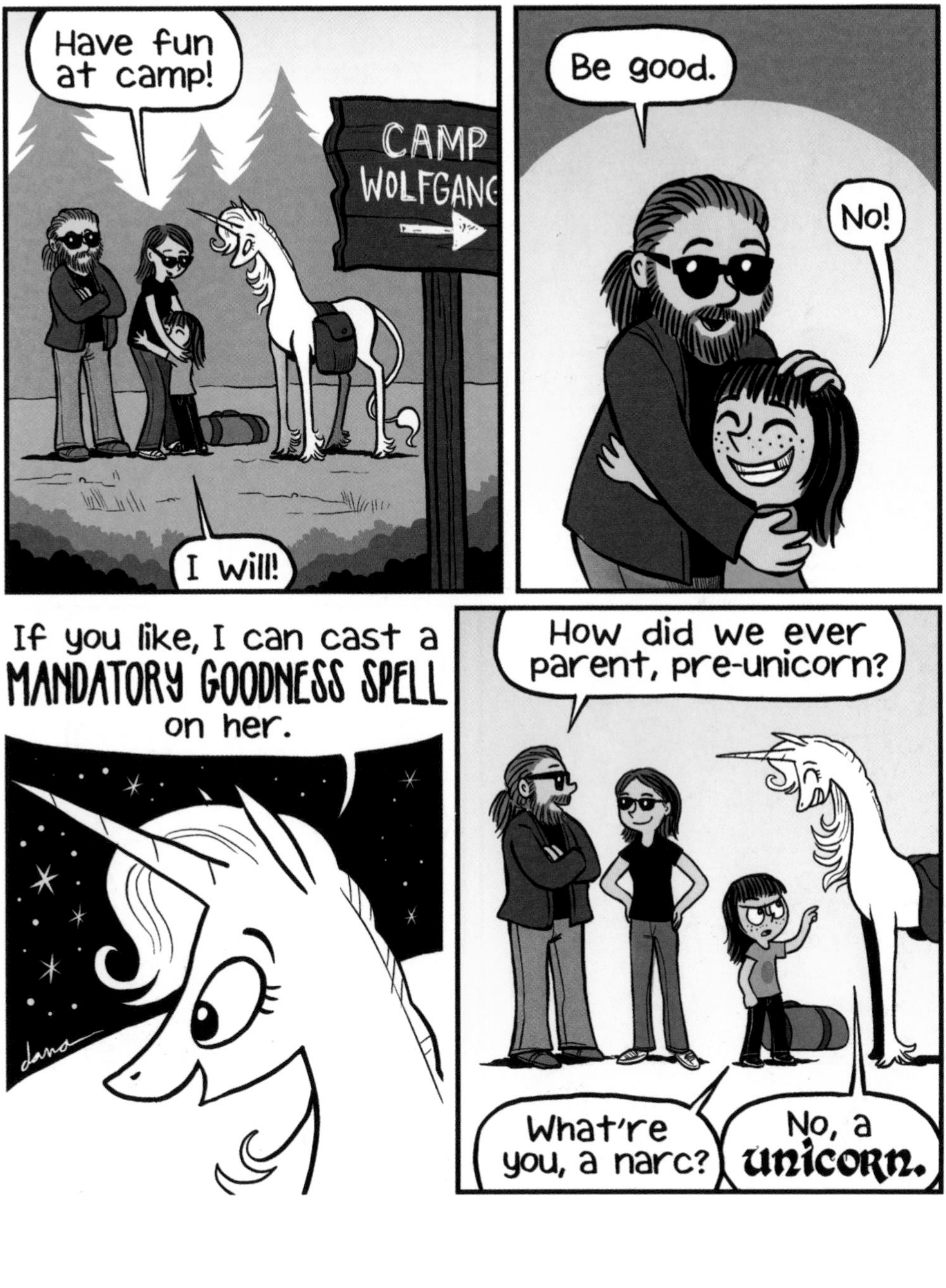
Have fun at camp!
CAMP WOLFGANG
I will!
Be good.
No!
If you like, I can cast a MANDATORY GOODNESS SPELL on her.
How did we ever parent, pre-unicorn?
What're you, a narc?
No, a unicorn.

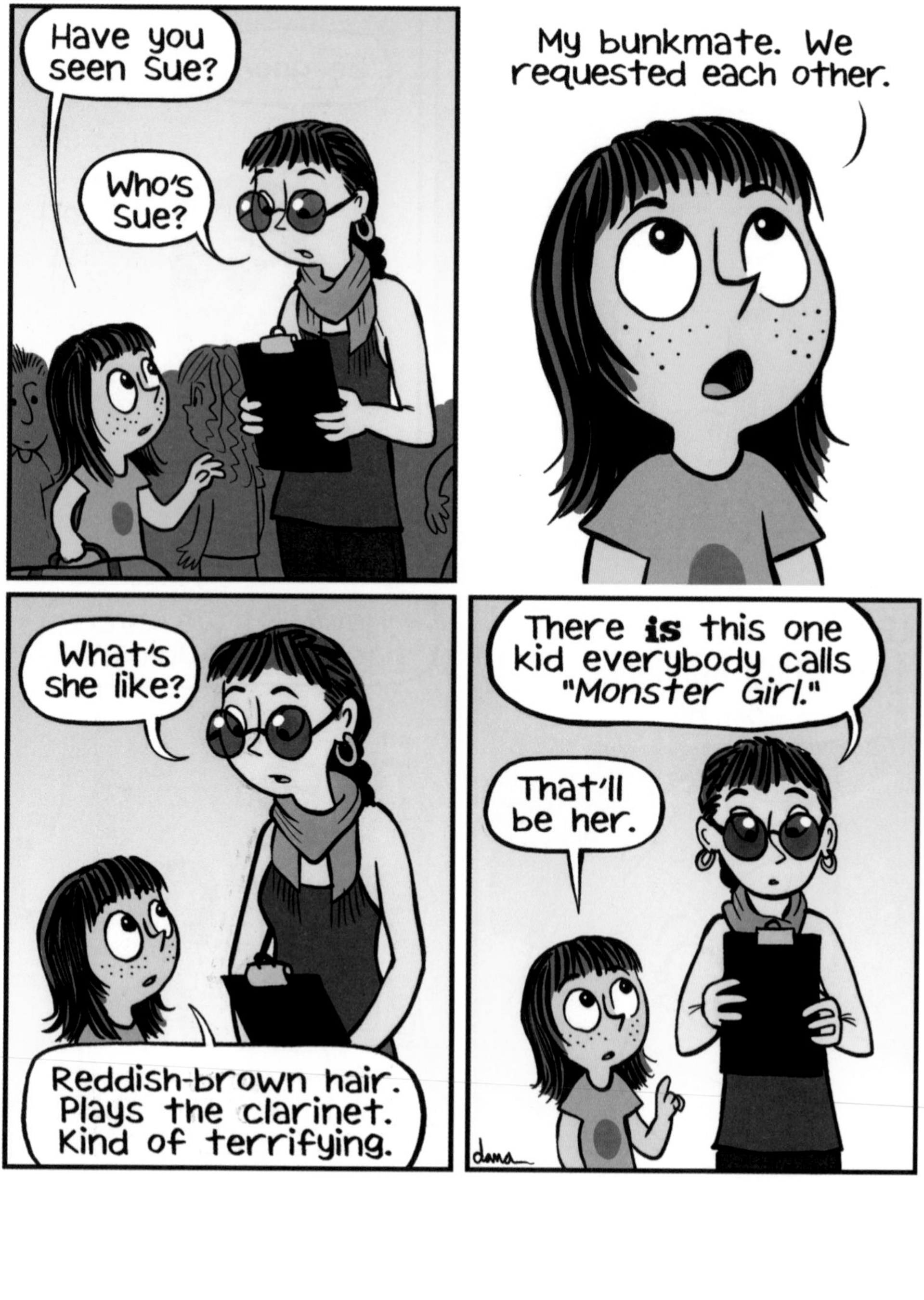
Have you seen Sue?
Who's Sue?
My bunkmate. We requested each other.
What's she like?
Reddish-brown hair. Plays the clarinet. Kind of terrifying.
There **is** this one kid everybody calls *"Monster Girl."*
That'll be her.
dana

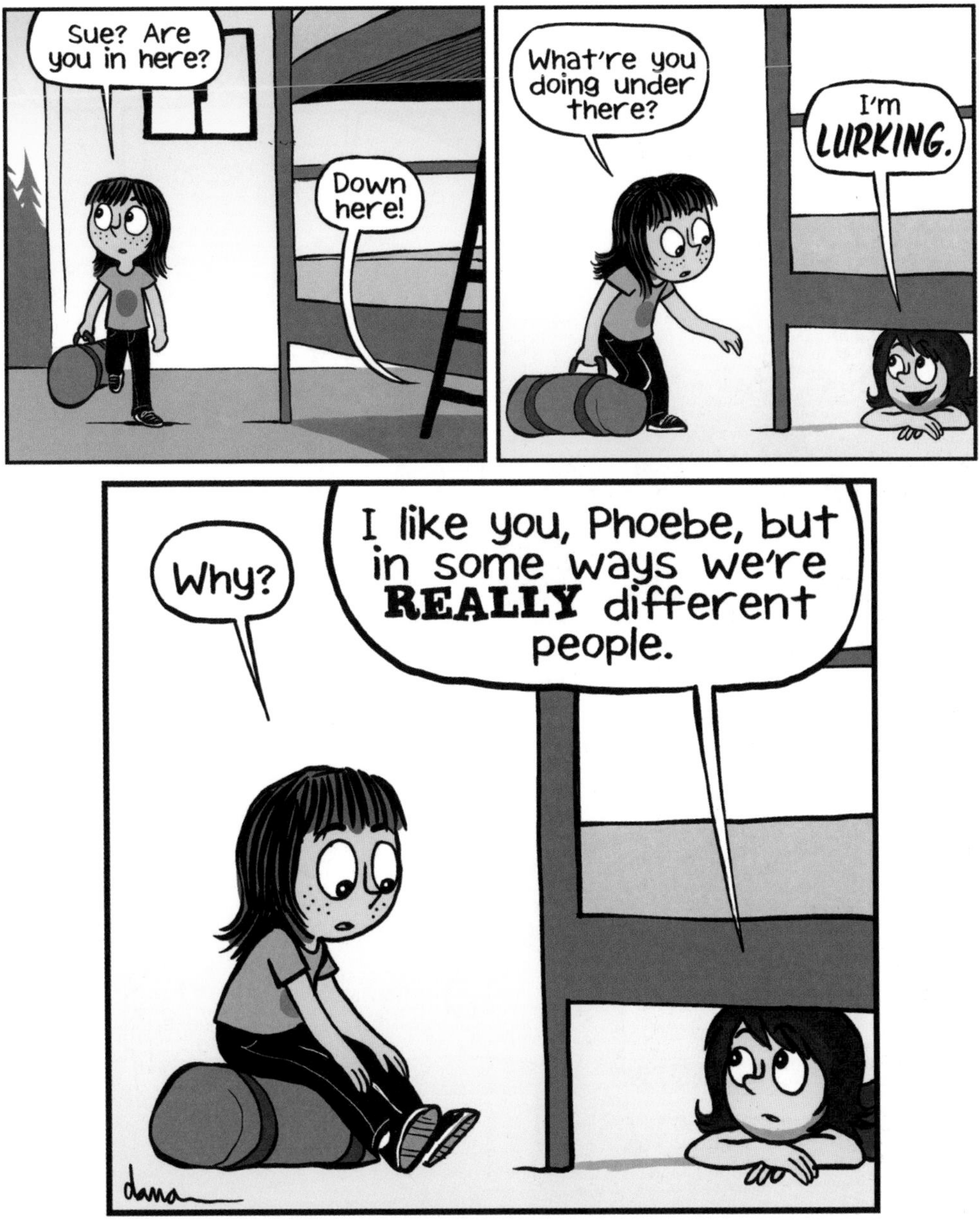
Sue? Are you in here?
Down here!
What're you doing under there?
I'm LURKING.
Why?
I like you, Phoebe, but in some ways we're REALLY different people.
dana

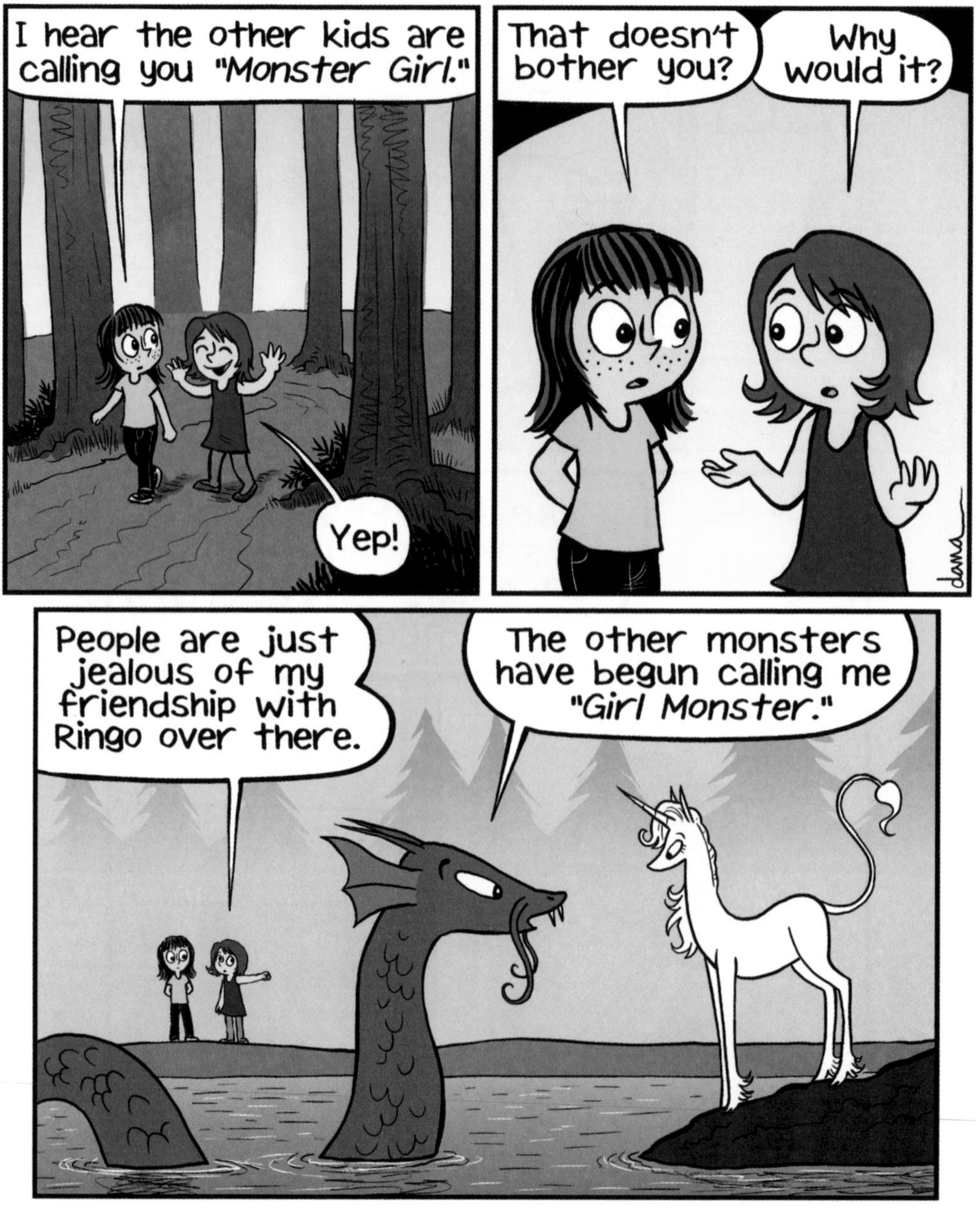
I hear the other kids are calling you "Monster Girl."
Yep!
That doesn't bother you?
Why would it?
People are just jealous of my friendship with Ringo over there.
The other monsters have begun calling me "Girl Monster."

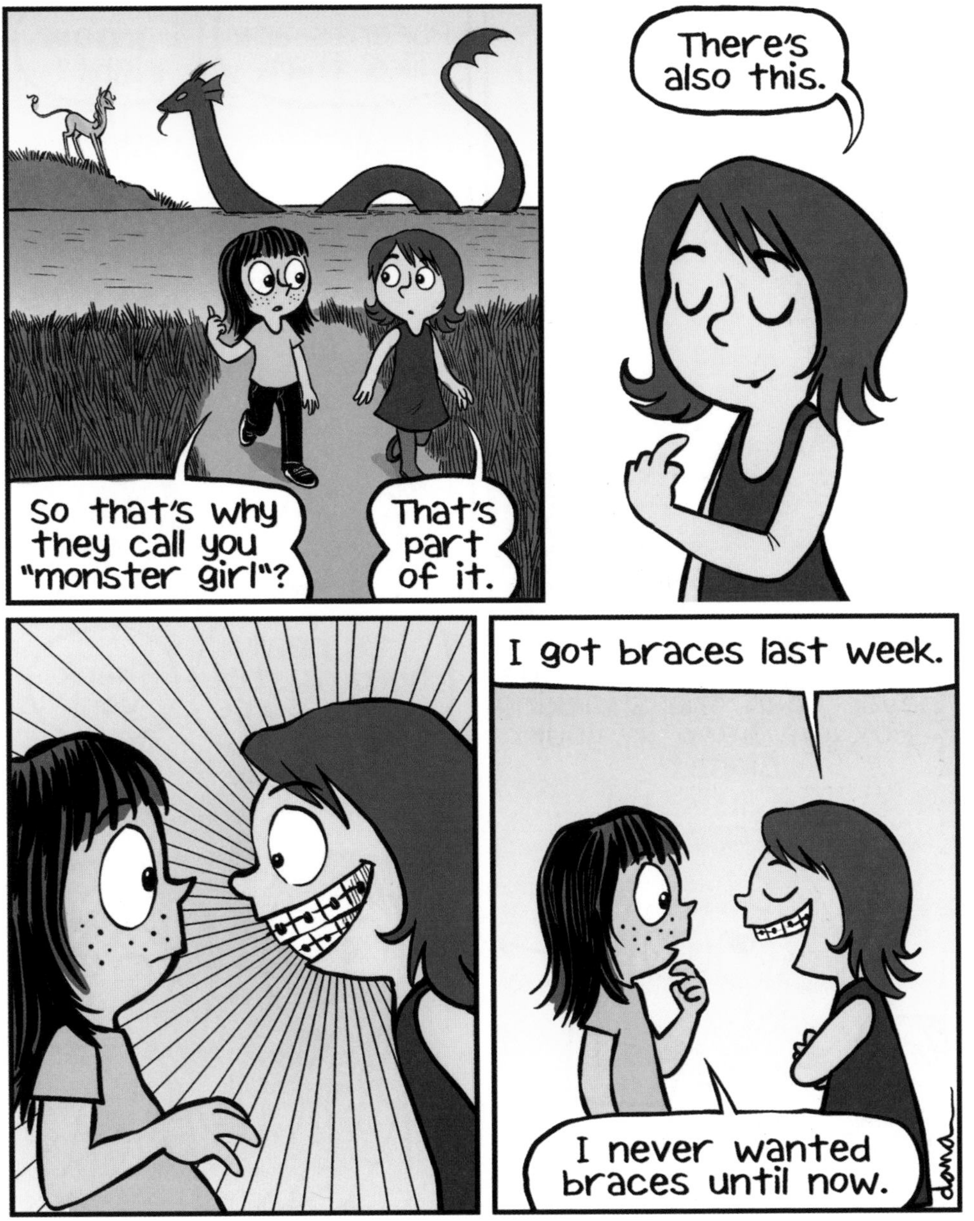
So that's why they call you "monster girl"?
That's part of it.
There's also this.
I got braces last week.
I never wanted braces until now.
dana

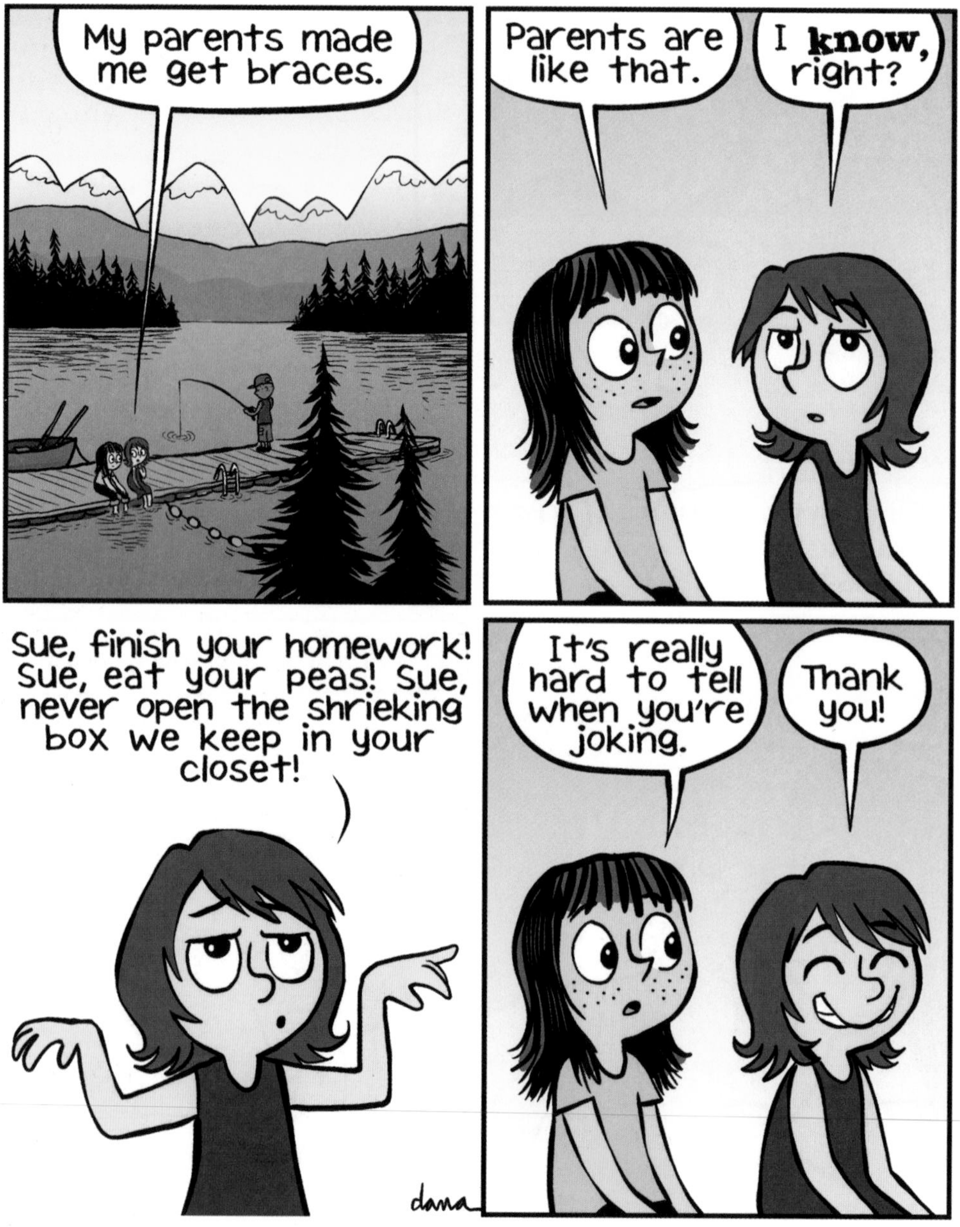
My parents made me get braces.
Parents are like that.
I **know**, right?
Sue, finish your homework! Sue, eat your peas! Sue, never open the shrieking box we keep in your closet!
It's really hard to tell when you're joking.
Thank you!
dana

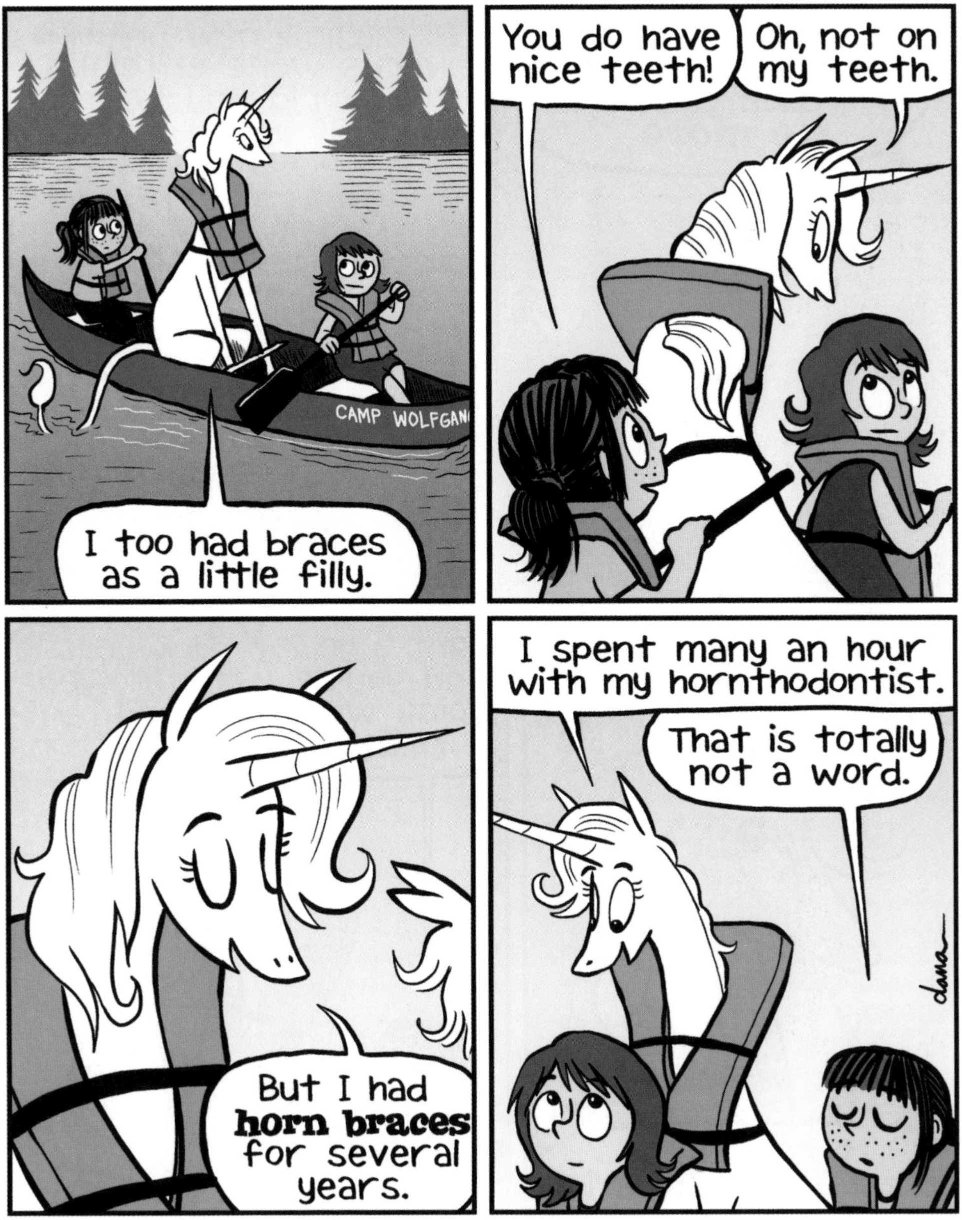
I too had braces as a little filly.
CAMP WOLFGAN
You do have nice teeth!
Oh, not on my teeth.
But I had **horn braces** for several years.
I spent many an hour with my hornthodontist.
That is totally not a word.
dana

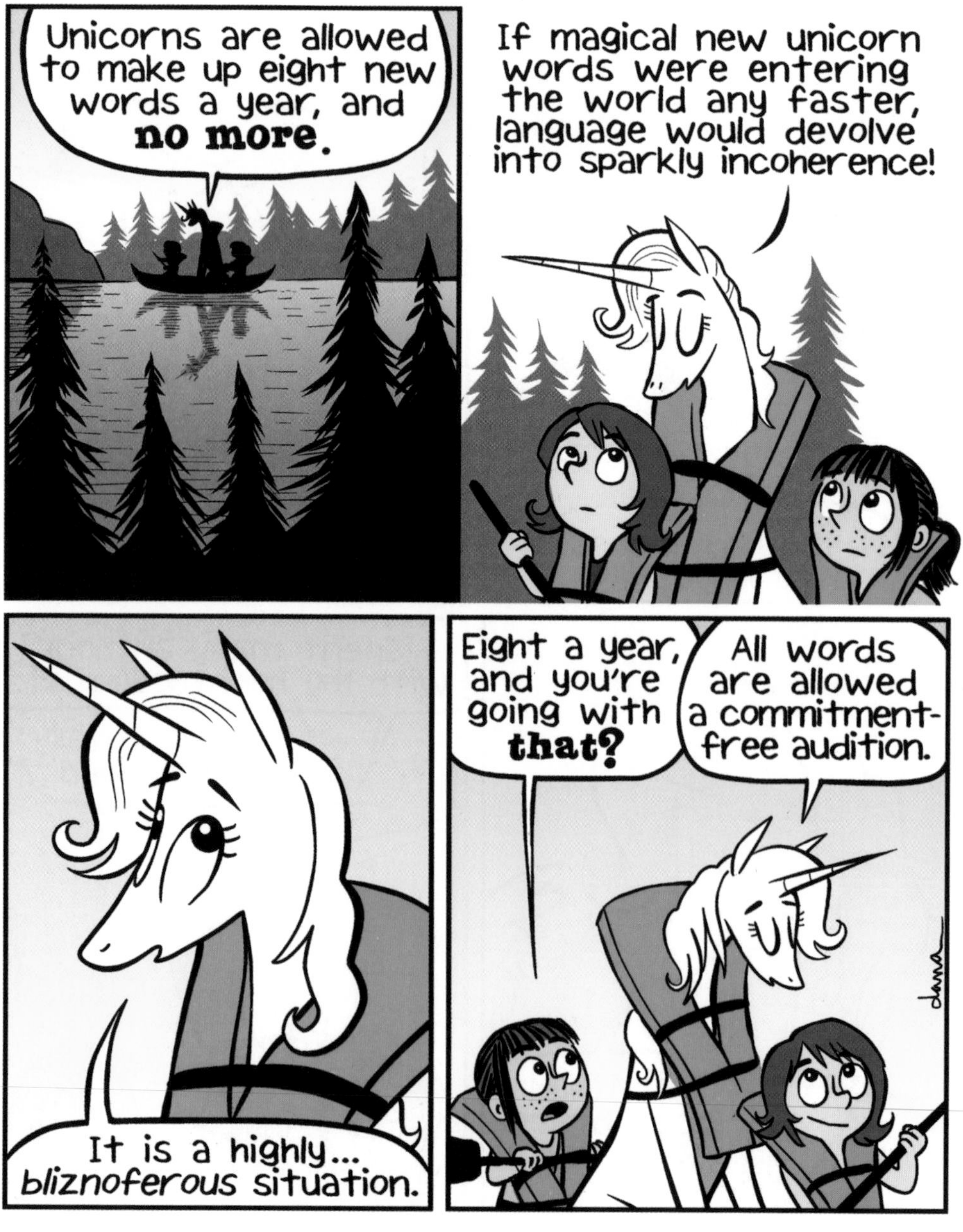
Unicorns are allowed to make up eight new words a year, and **no more**.
If magical new unicorn words were entering the world any faster, language would devolve into sparkly incoherence!
It is a highly... *bliznoferous* situation.
Eight a year, and you're going with **that?**
All words are allowed a commitment-free audition.
dana

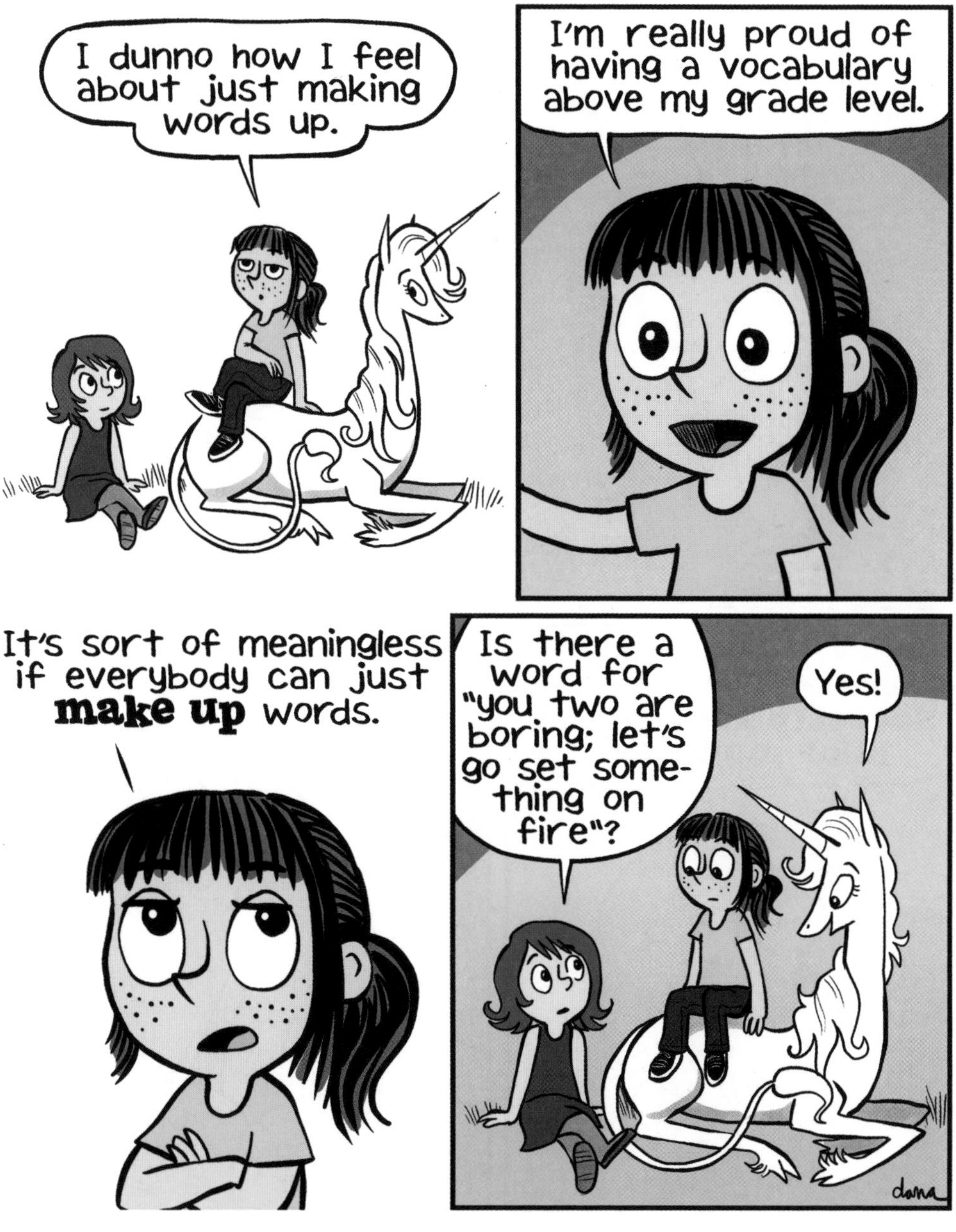
I dunno how I feel about just making words up.
I'm really proud of having a vocabulary above my grade level.
It's sort of meaningless if everybody can just **make up** words.
Is there a word for "you two are boring; let's go set something on fire"?
Yes!
dana

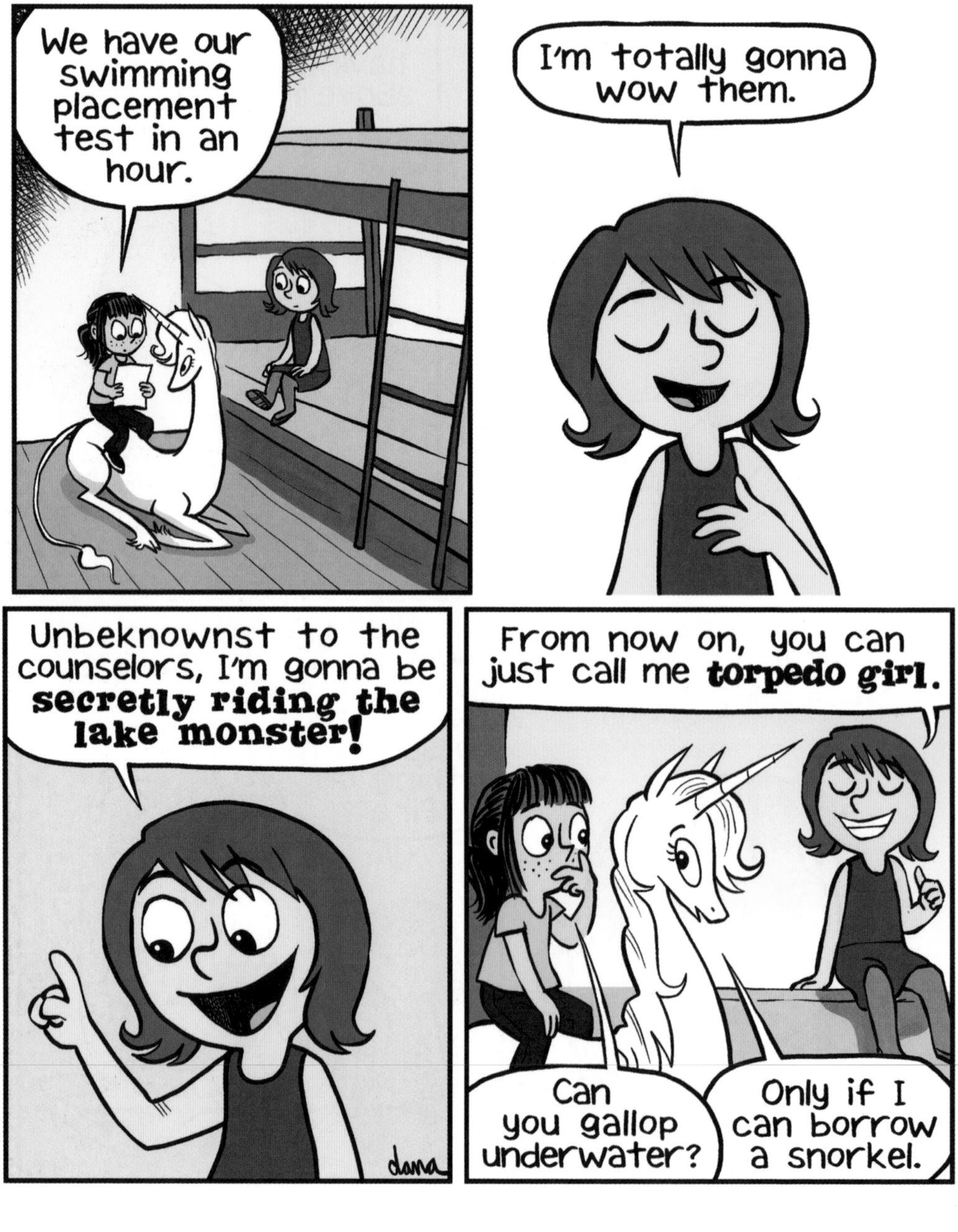
We have our swimming placement test in an hour.
I'm totally gonna wow them.
Unbeknownst to the counselors, I'm gonna be **secretly riding the lake monster!**
dana
From now on, you can just call me **torpedo girl**.
Can you gallop underwater?
Only if I can borrow a snorkel.

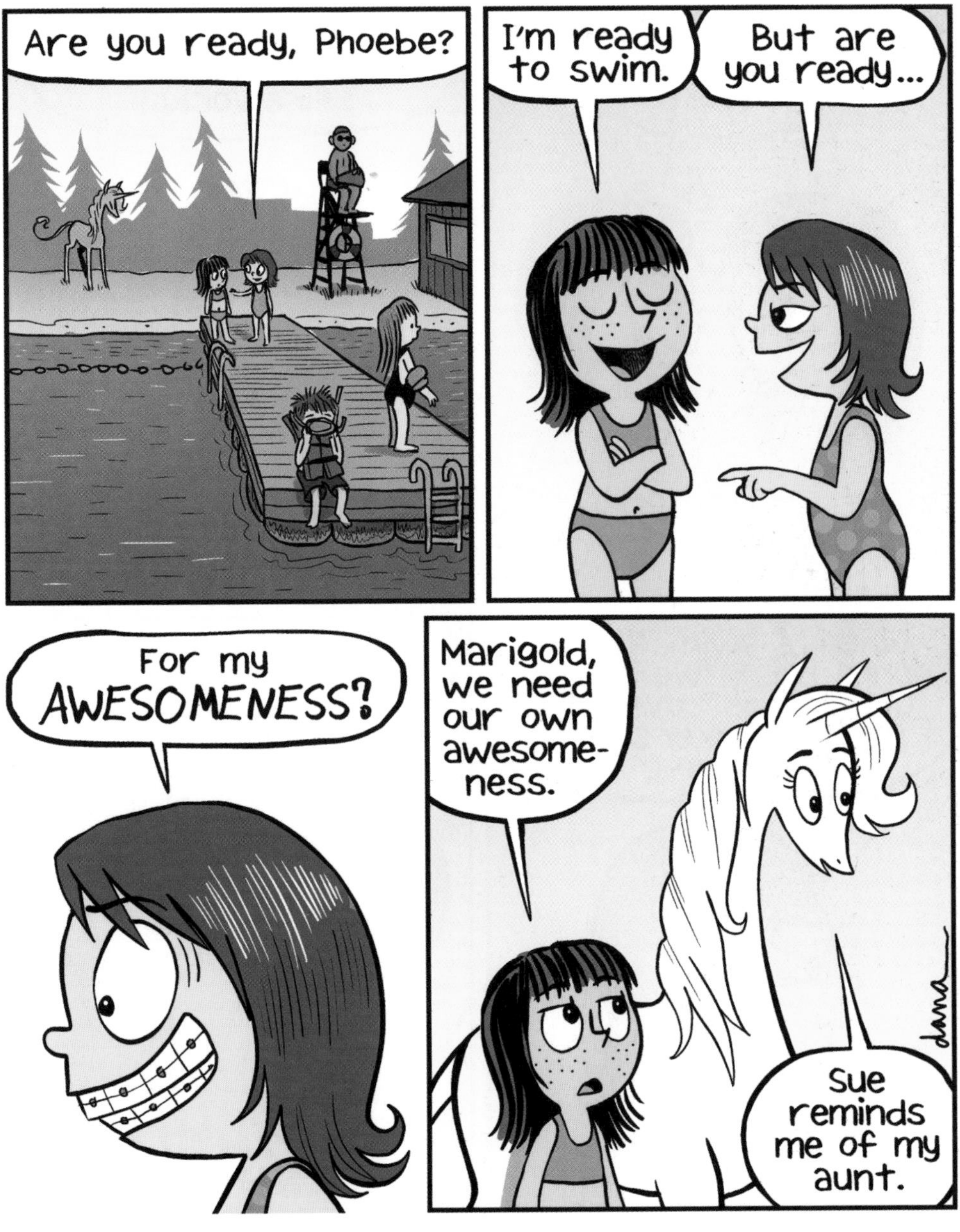
Are you ready, Phoebe?
I'm ready to swim.
But are you ready...
For my AWESOMENESS?
Marigold, we need our own awesome-ness.
Sue reminds me of my aunt.
dana

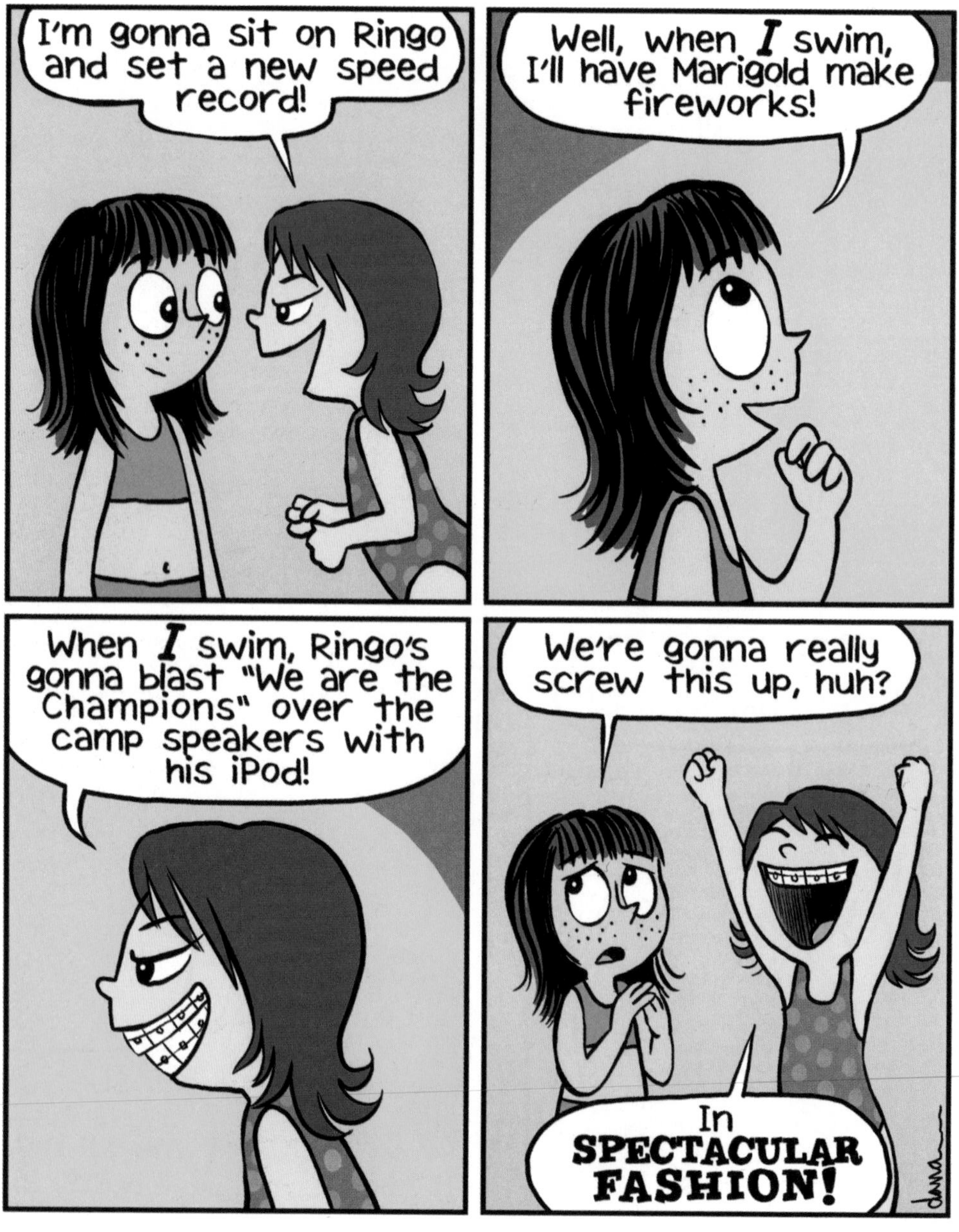
I'm gonna sit on Ringo and set a new speed record!
Well, when I swim, I'll have Marigold make fireworks!
When I swim, Ringo's gonna blast "We are the Champions" over the camp speakers with his iPod!
We're gonna really screw this up, huh?
In SPECTACULAR FASHION!
dana

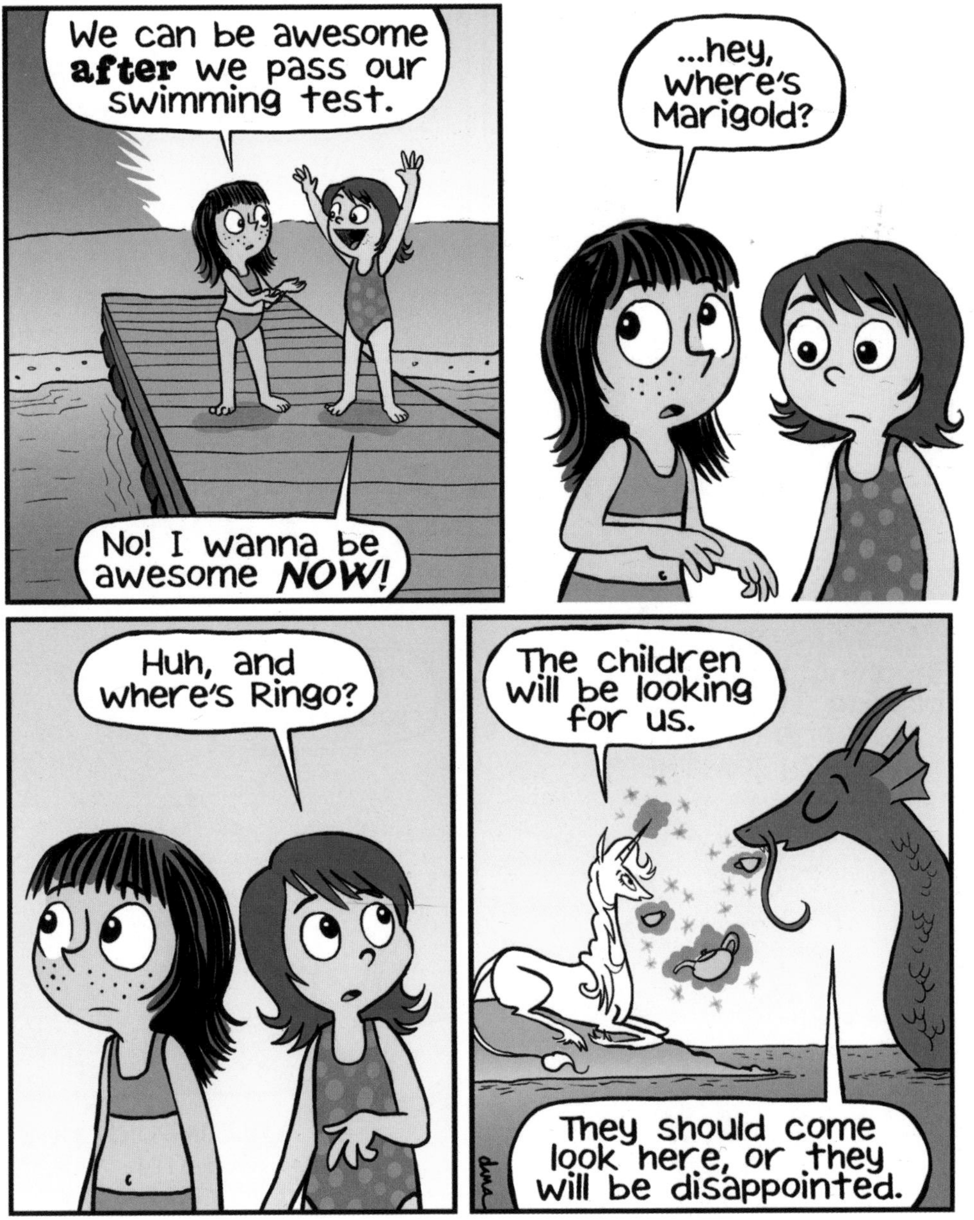
We can be awesome **after** we pass our swimming test.
No! I wanna be awesome ***NOW***!
...hey, where's Marigold?
Huh, and where's Ringo?
The children will be looking for us.
They should come look here, or they will be disappointed.

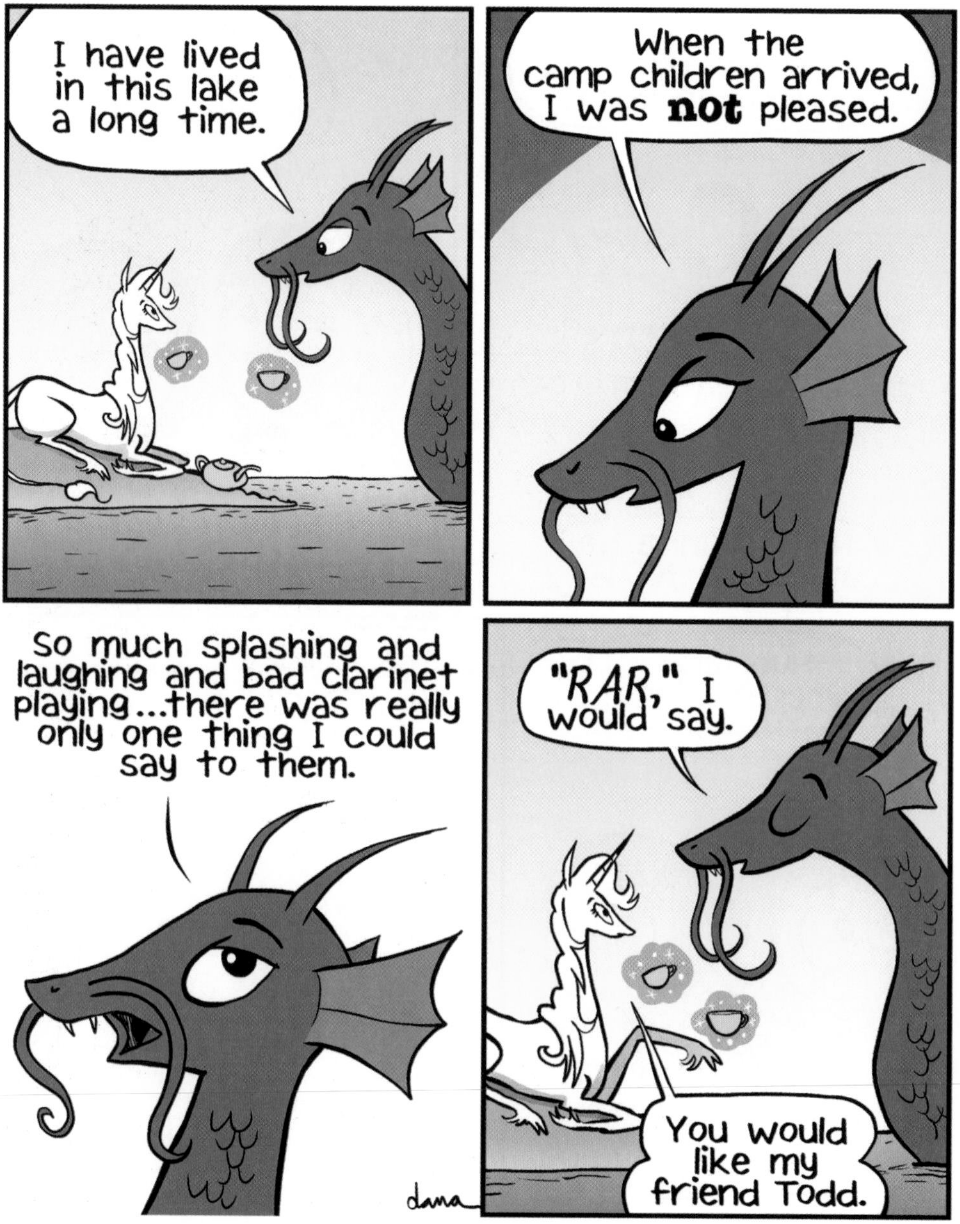
I have lived in this lake a long time.
When the camp children arrived, I was **not** pleased.
So much splashing and laughing and bad clarinet playing...there was really only one thing I could say to them.
"RAR," I would say.
You would like my friend Todd.
dana

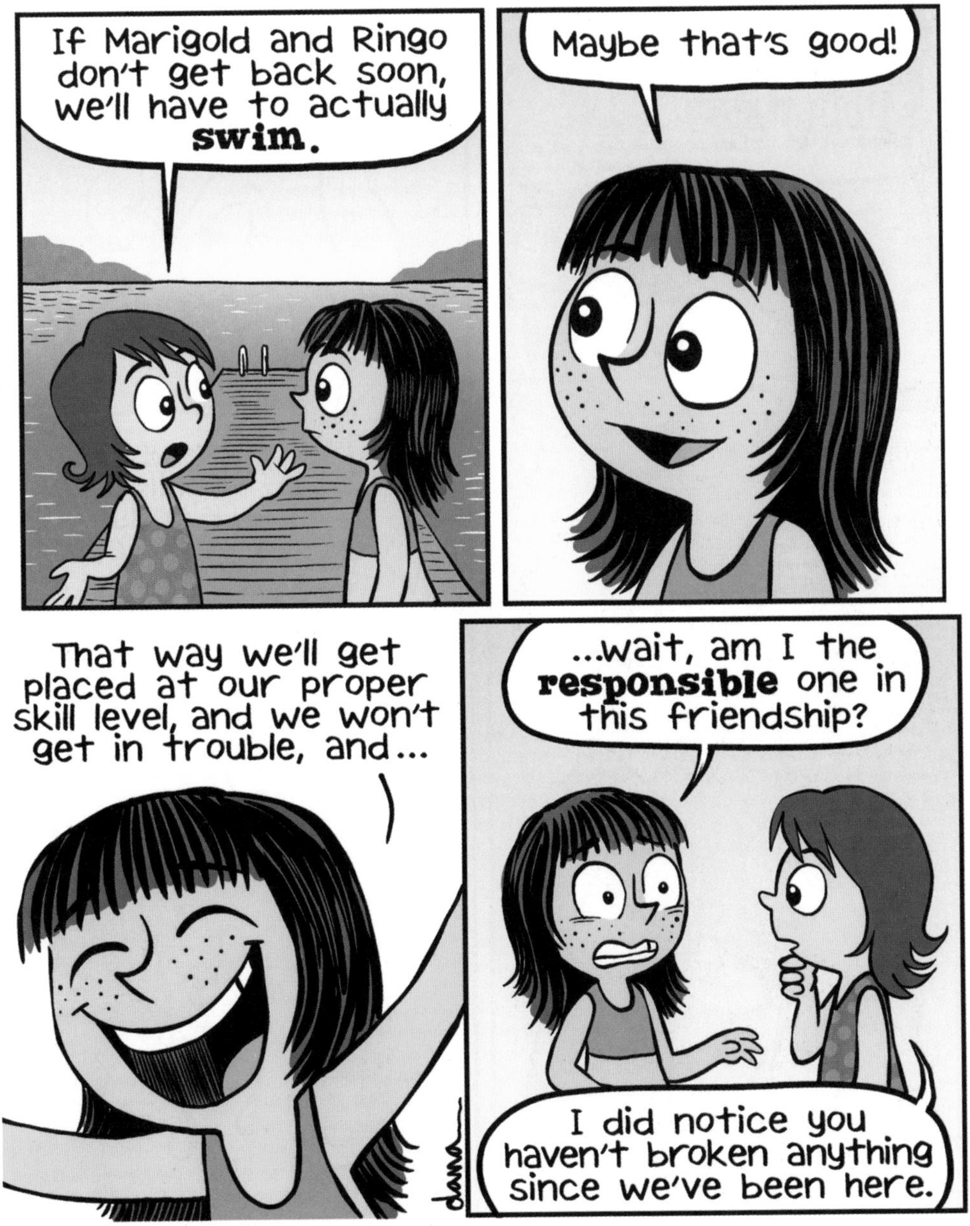
If Marigold and Ringo don't get back soon, we'll have to actually **swim**.
Maybe that's good!
That way we'll get placed at our proper skill level, and we won't get in trouble, and...
...wait, am I the **responsible** one in this friendship?
I did notice you haven't broken anything since we've been here.
dana

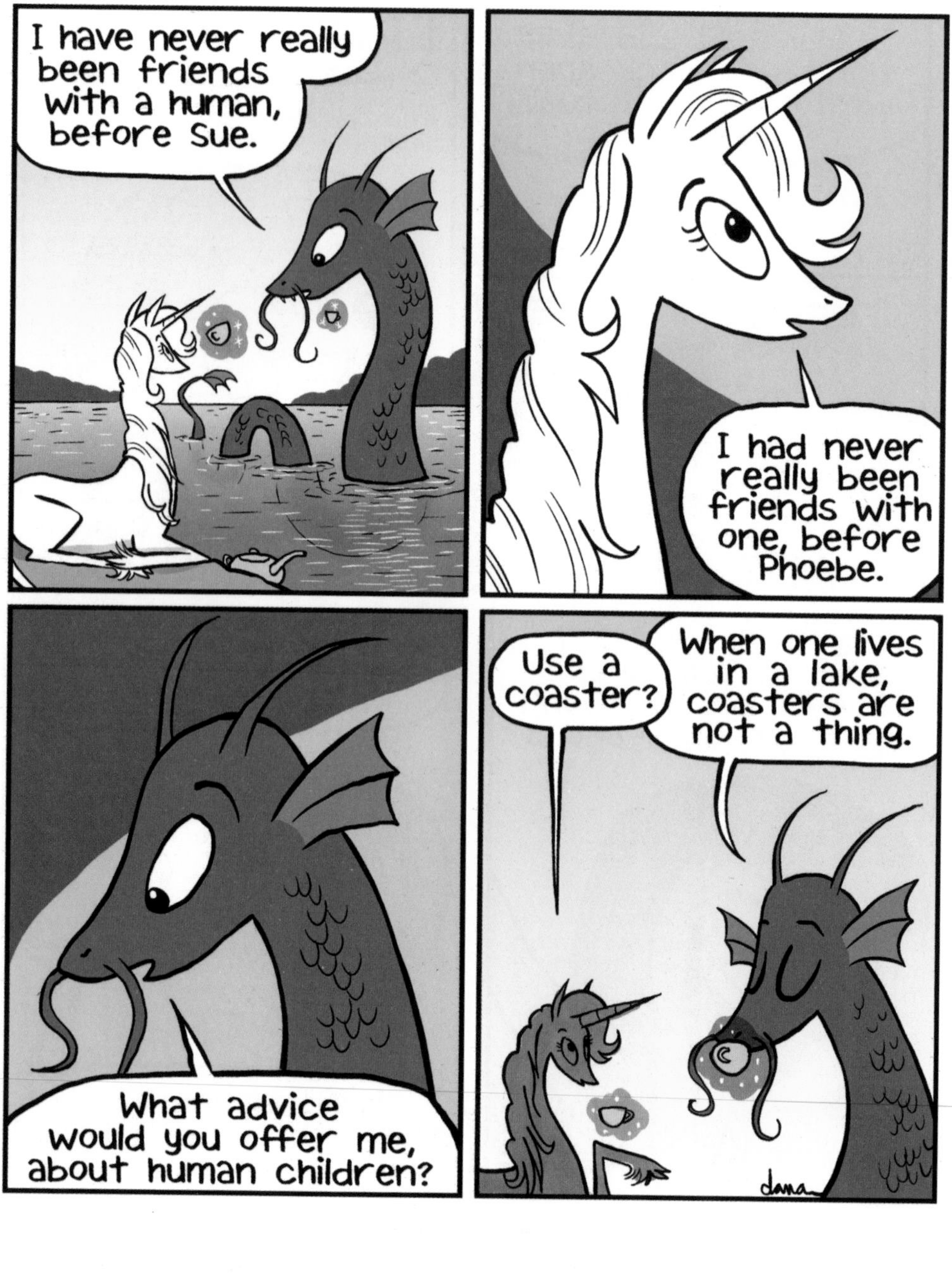
I have never really been friends with a human, before Sue.
I had never really been friends with one, before Phoebe.
What advice would you offer me, about human children?
Use a coaster?
When one lives in a lake, coasters are not a thing.
dana

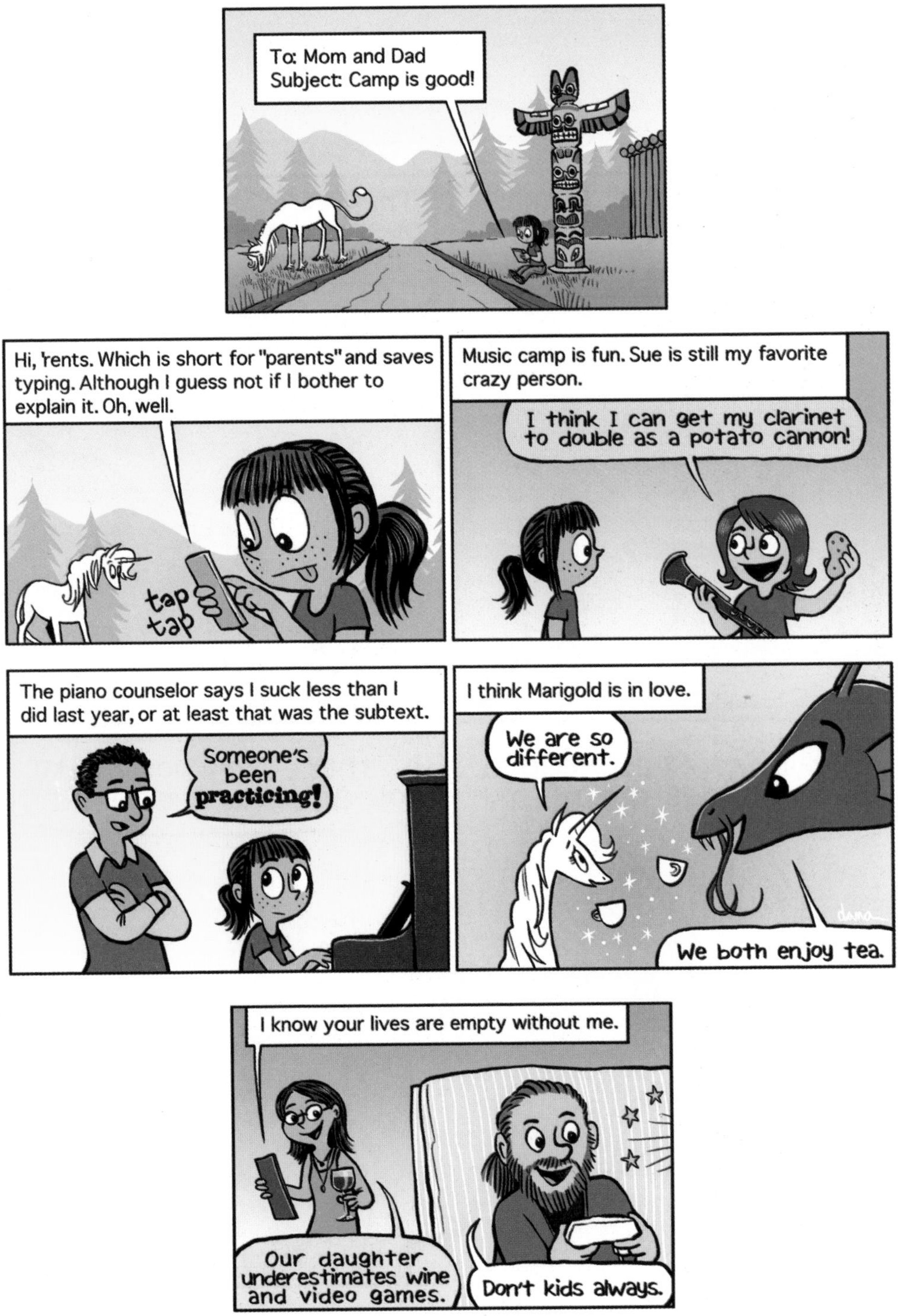
To: Mom and Dad
Subject: Camp is good!
Hi, 'rents. Which is short for "parents" and saves typing. Although I guess not if I bother to explain it. Oh, well.
tap tap
Music camp is fun. Sue is still my favorite crazy person.
I think I can get my clarinet to double as a potato cannon!
The piano counselor says I suck less than I did last year, or at least that was the subtext.
Someone's been practicing!
I think Marigold is in love.
We are so different.
We both enjoy tea.
I know your lives are empty without me.
Our daughter underestimates wine and video games.
Don't kids always.

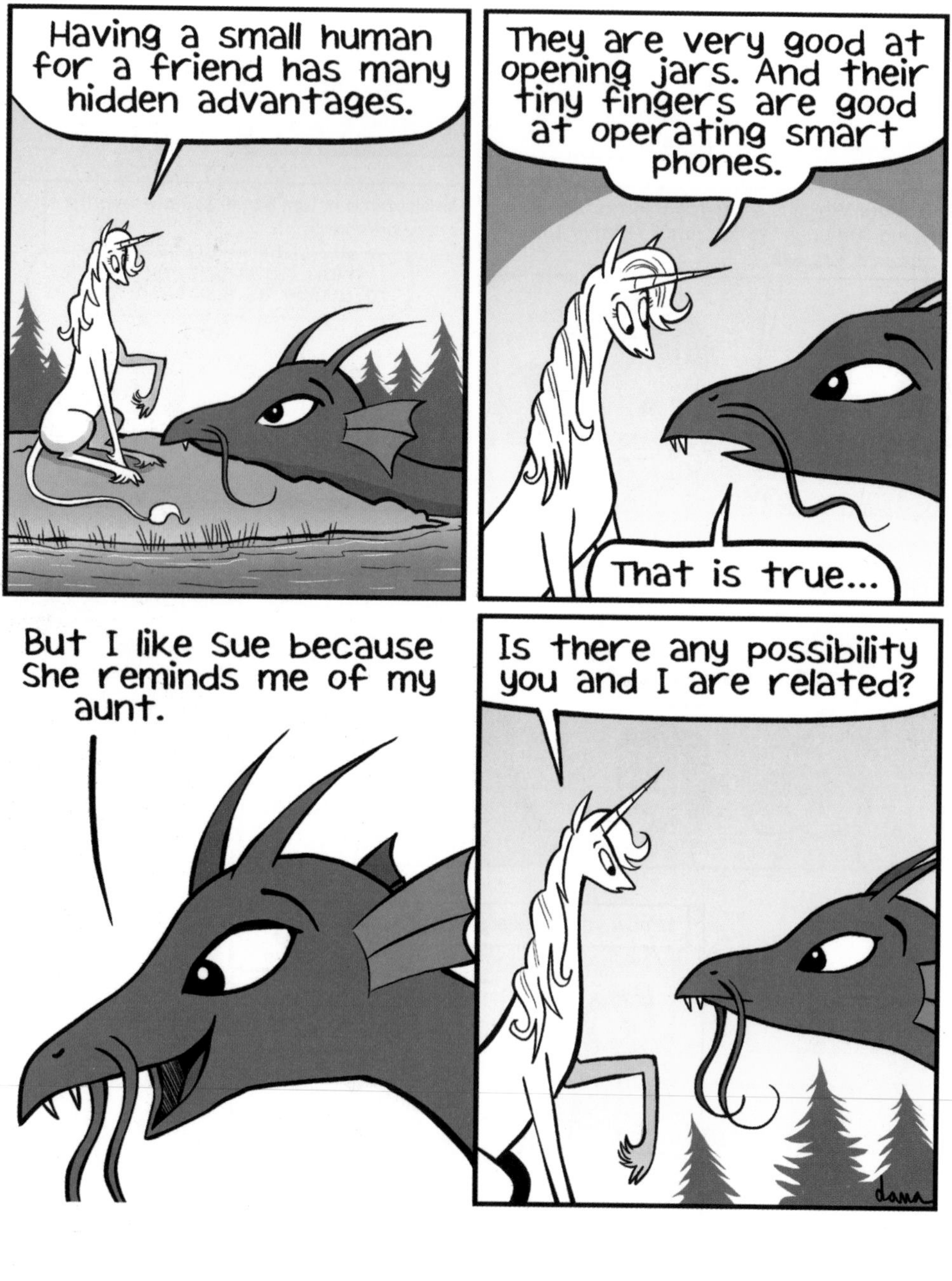
Having a small human for a friend has many hidden advantages.
They are very good at opening jars. And their tiny fingers are good at operating smart phones.
That is true...
But I like Sue because she reminds me of my aunt.
Is there any possibility you and I are related?
dana

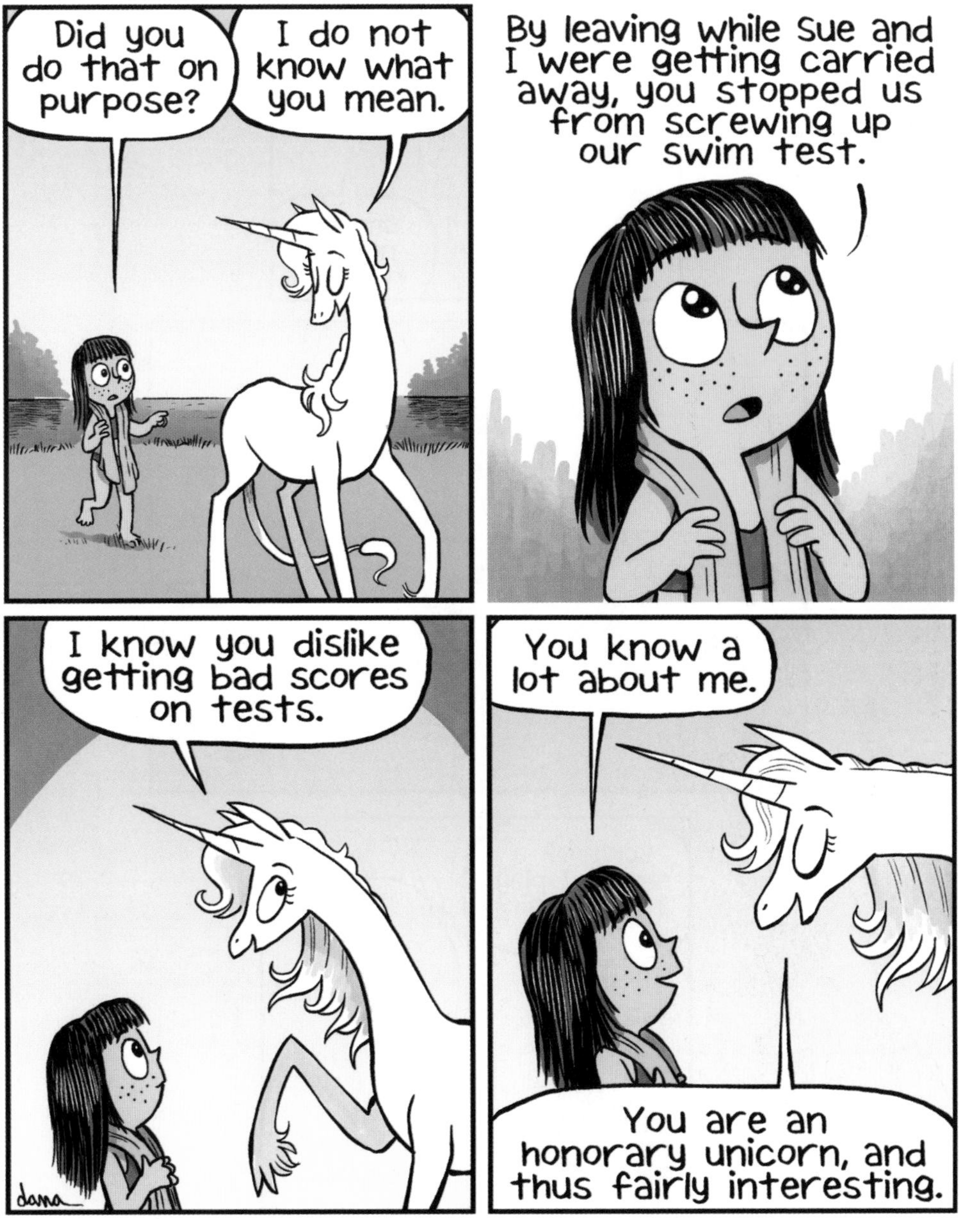
Did you do that on purpose?
I do not know what you mean.
By leaving while Sue and I were getting carried away, you stopped us from screwing up our swim test.
I know you dislike getting bad scores on tests.
You know a lot about me.
You are an honorary unicorn, and thus fairly interesting.
dana

Sue was disappointed she didn't get to show off.
She will not be for long.
Sort of a shame I play the friggin' piano.
Ringo does like a challenge.

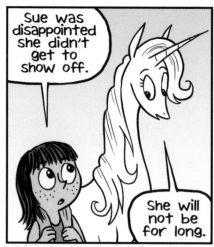

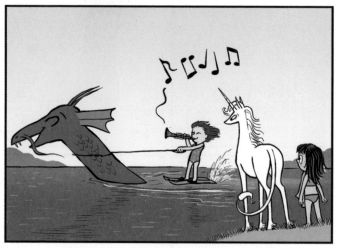

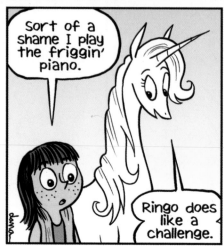

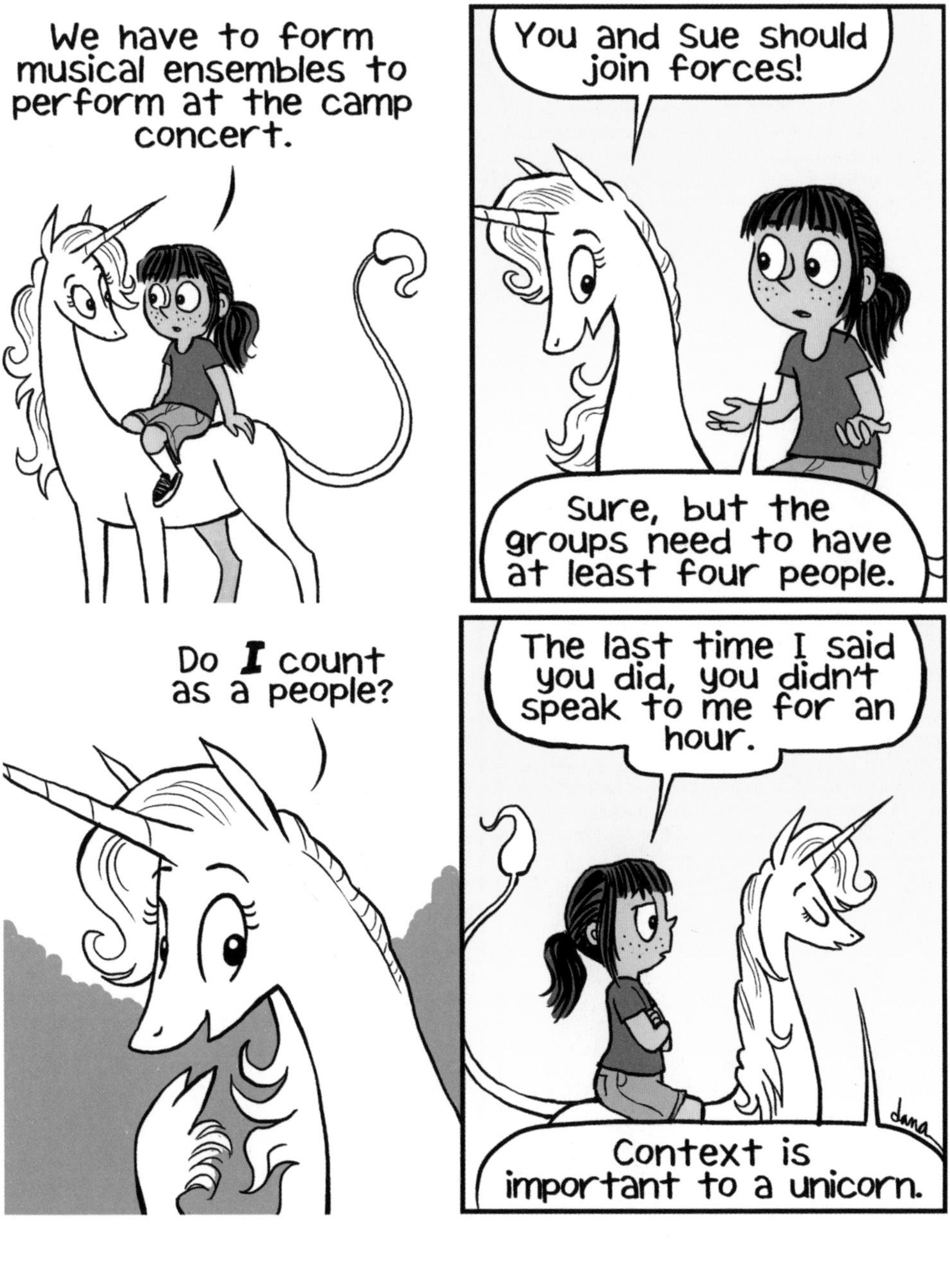
We have to form musical ensembles to perform at the camp concert.
You and Sue should join forces!
Sure, but the groups need to have at least four people.
Do I count as a people?
The last time I said you did, you didn't speak to me for an hour.
Context is important to a unicorn.
dana

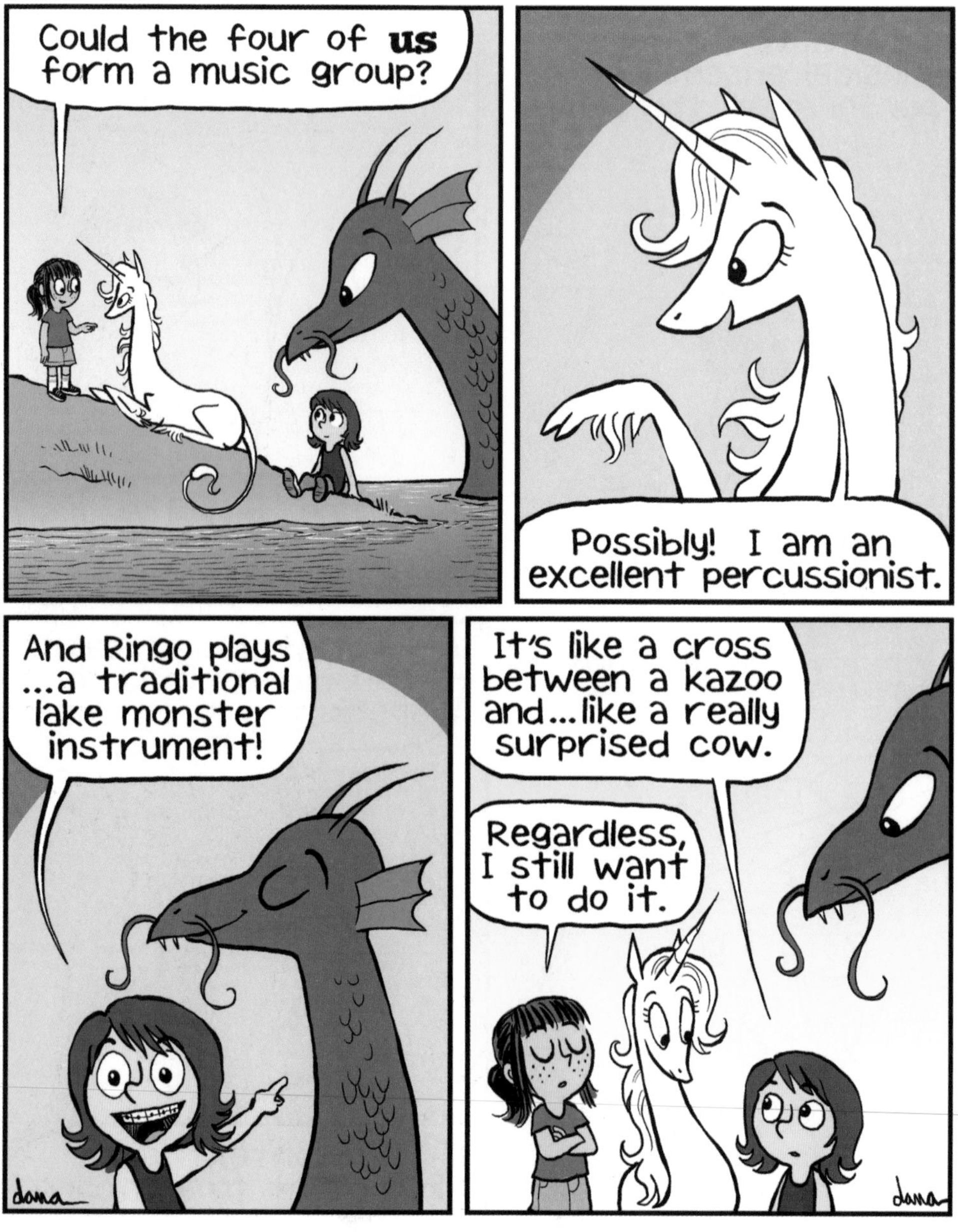
Could the four of **us** form a music group?
Possibly! I am an excellent percussionist.
And Ringo plays ...a traditional lake monster instrument!
It's like a cross between a kazoo and...like a really surprised cow.
Regardless, I still want to do it.
dana
dana

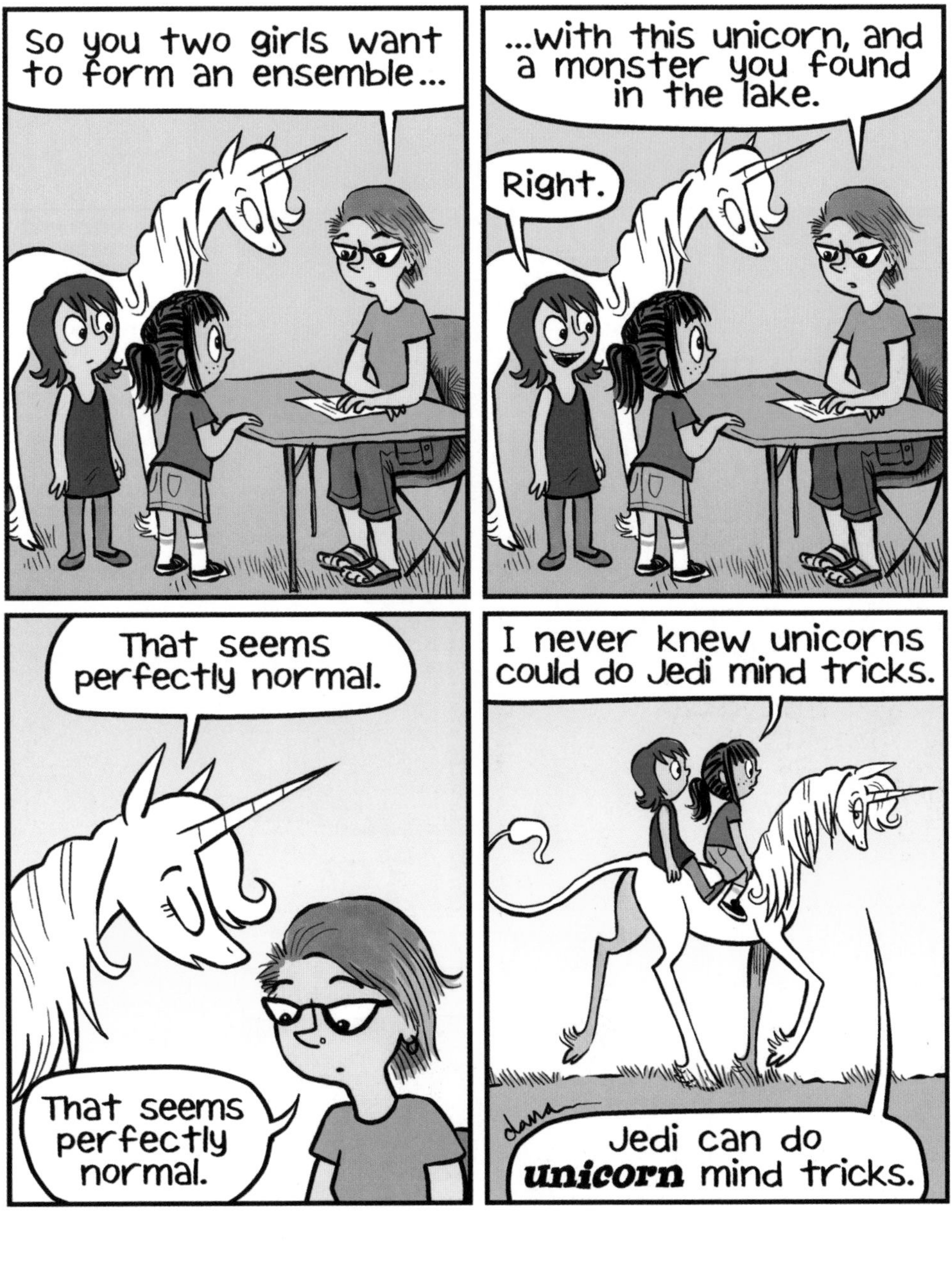
So you two girls want to form an ensemble...
...with this unicorn, and a monster you found in the lake.
Right.
That seems perfectly normal.
That seems perfectly normal.
I never knew unicorns could do Jedi mind tricks.
Jedi can do **unicorn** mind tricks.

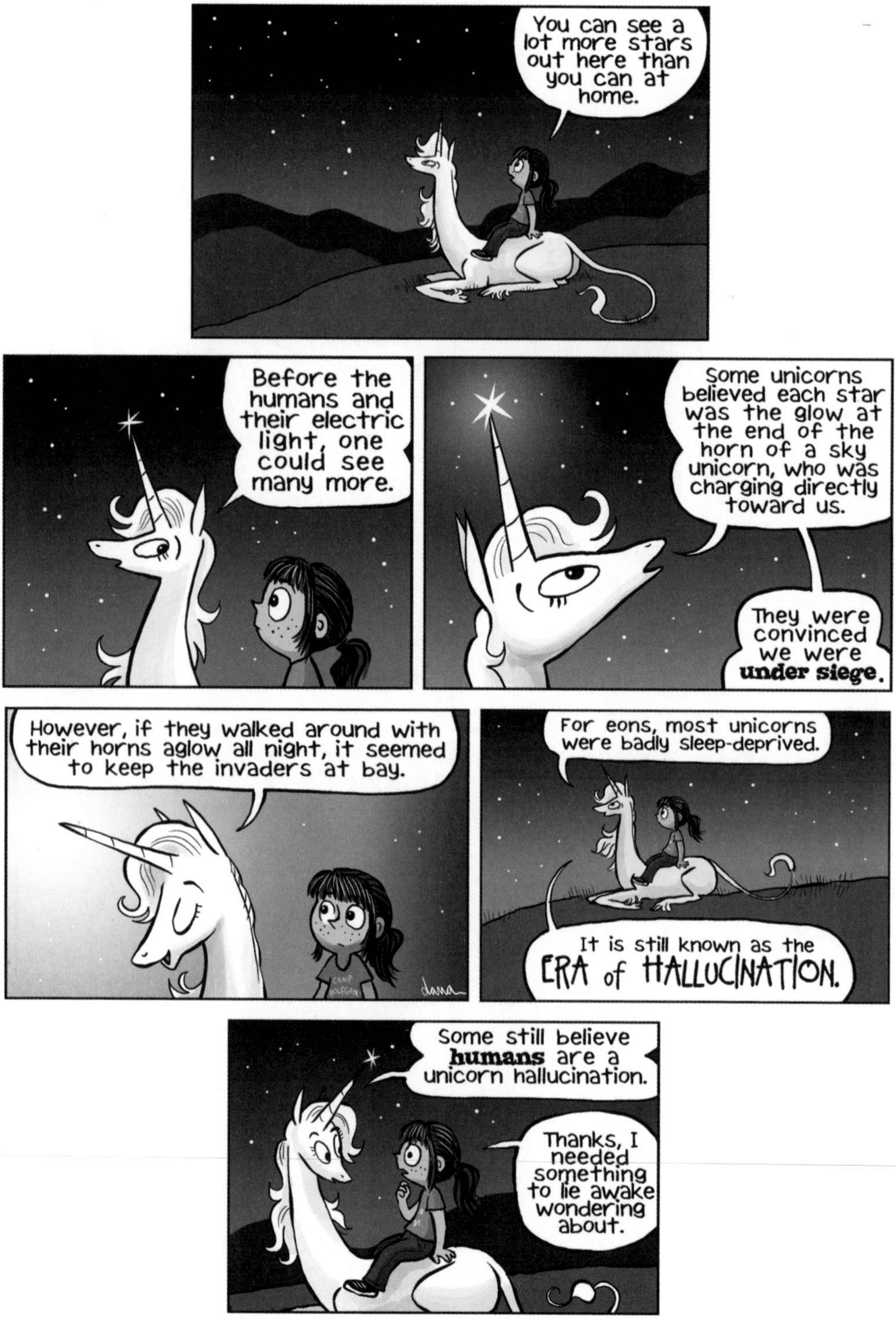
You can see a lot more stars out here than you can at home.
Before the humans and their electric light, one could see many more.
Some unicorns believed each star was the glow at the end of the horn of a sky unicorn, who was charging directly toward us.
They were convinced we were **under siege**.
However, if they walked around with their horns aglow all night, it seemed to keep the invaders at bay.
CAMP WOLFGANG
dana
For eons, most unicorns were badly sleep-deprived.
It is still known as the ERA of HALLUCINATION.
Some still believe **humans** are a unicorn hallucination.
Thanks, I needed something to lie awake wondering about.

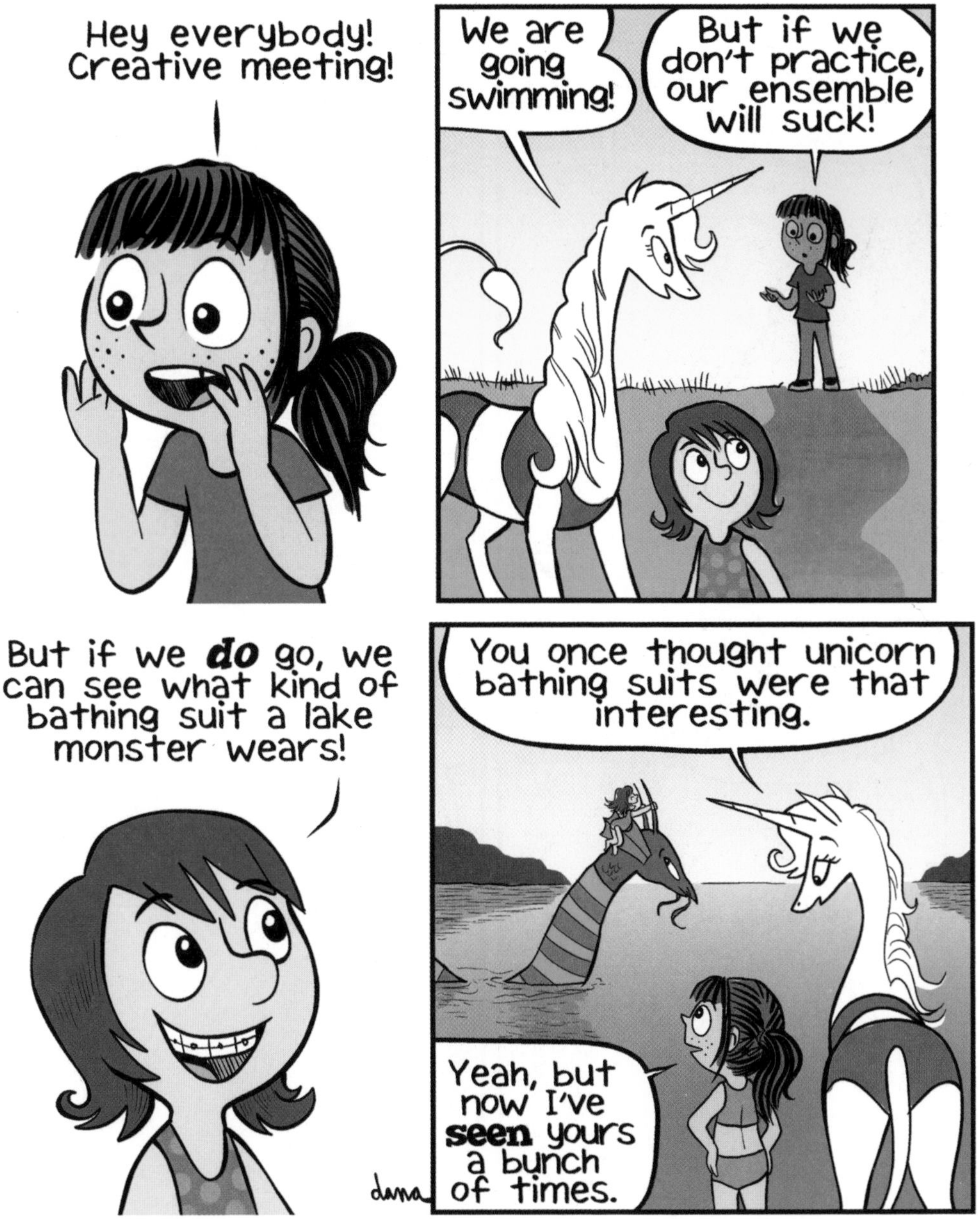
Hey everybody! Creative meeting!
We are going swimming!
But if we don't practice, our ensemble will suck!
But if we **do** go, we can see what kind of bathing suit a lake monster wears!
You once thought unicorn bathing suits were that interesting.
Yeah, but now I've **seen** yours a bunch of times.
dana

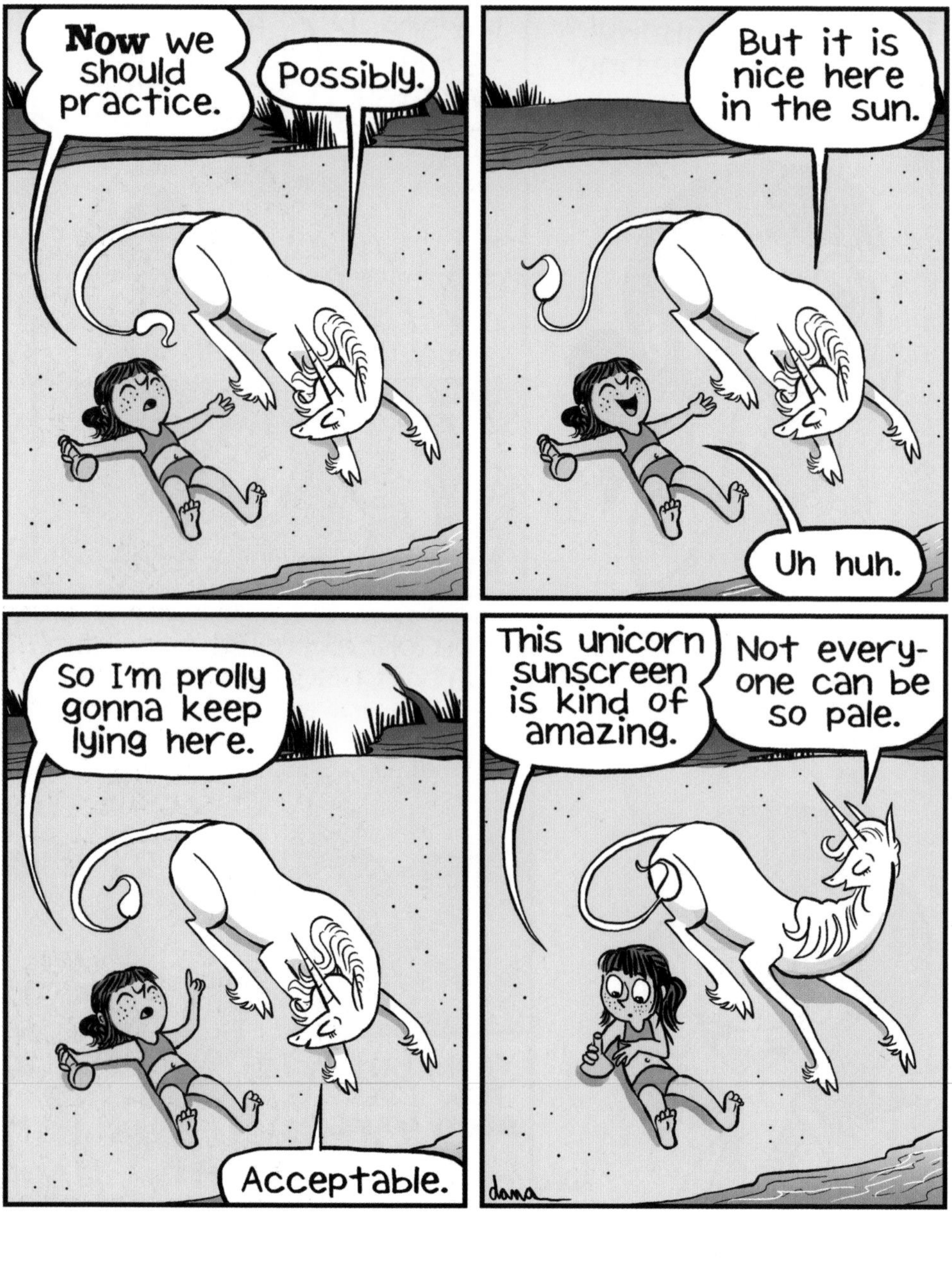

Now we should practice.
Possibly.
But it is nice here in the sun.
Uh huh.
So I'm prolly gonna keep lying here.
Acceptable.
This unicorn sunscreen is kind of amazing.
Not every-one can be so pale.
dana

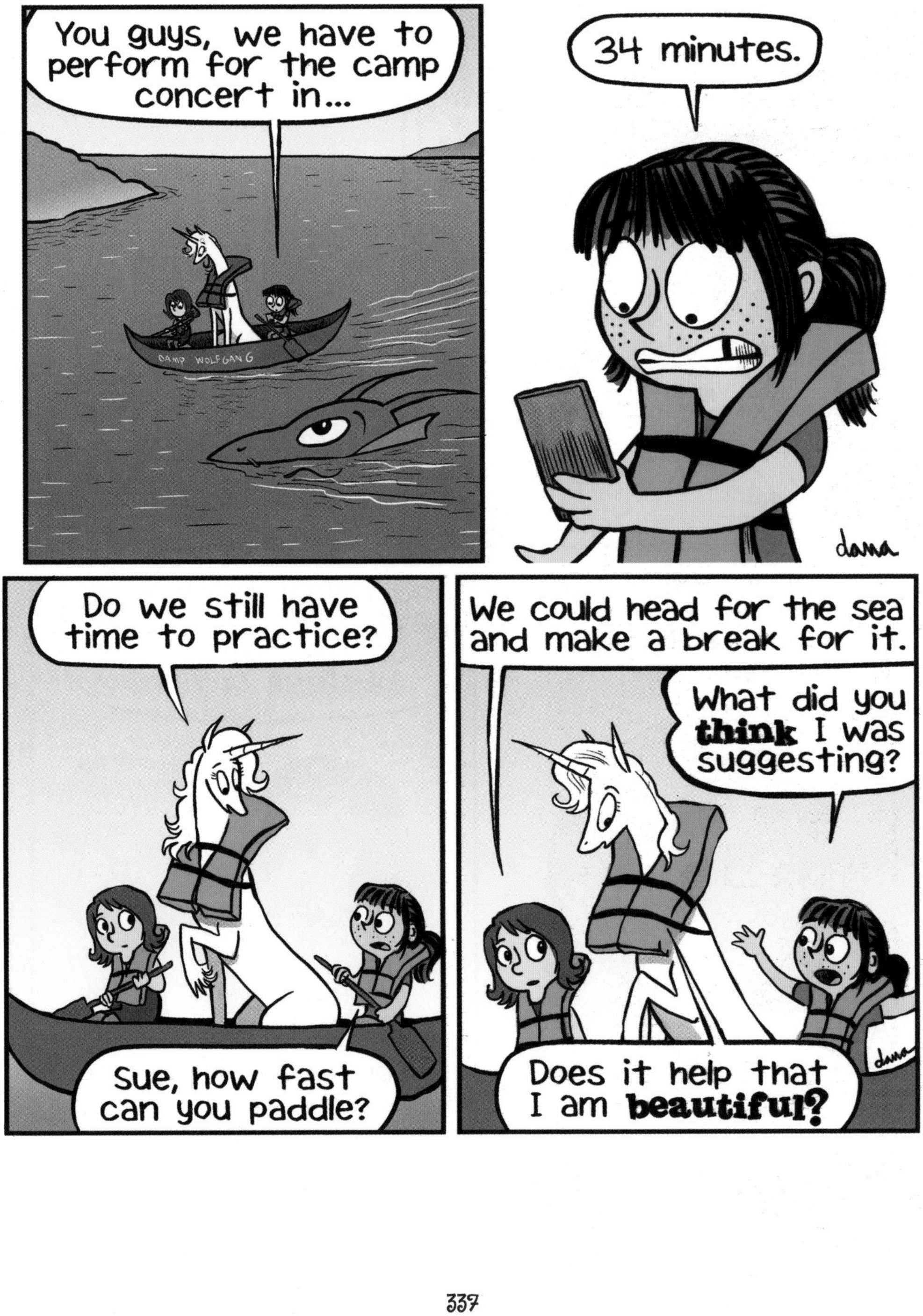
You guys, we have to perform for the camp concert in...
CAMP WOLFGANG
34 minutes.
dana
Do we still have time to practice?
Sue, how fast can you paddle?
We could head for the sea and make a break for it.
What did you **think** I was suggesting?
Does it help that I am **beautiful?**
dana

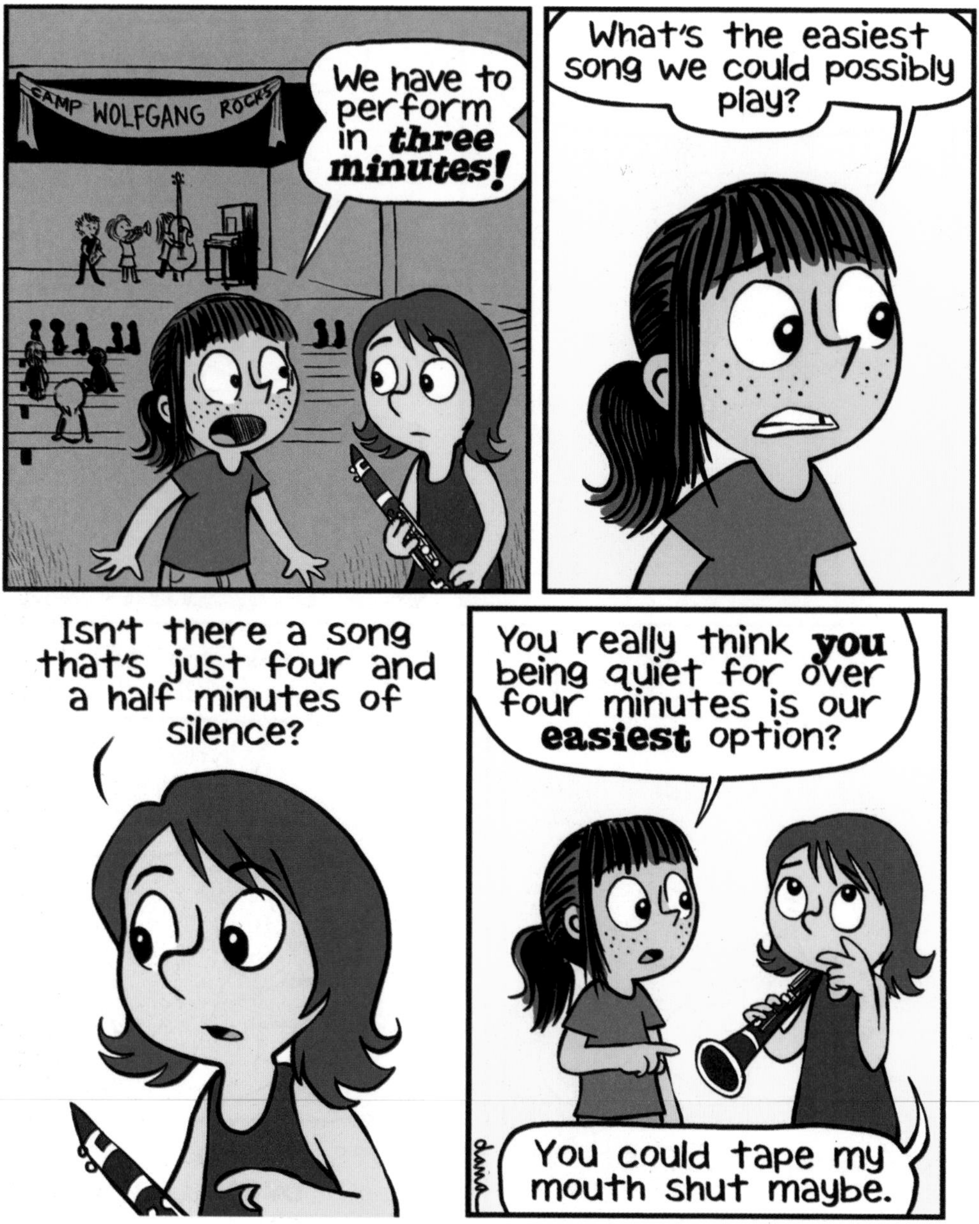
CAMP WOLFGANG ROCKS
We have to perform in **three minutes!**
What's the easiest song we could possibly play?
Isn't there a song that's just four and a half minutes of silence?
You really think **you** being quiet for over four minutes is our **easiest** option?
You could tape my mouth shut maybe.
dana

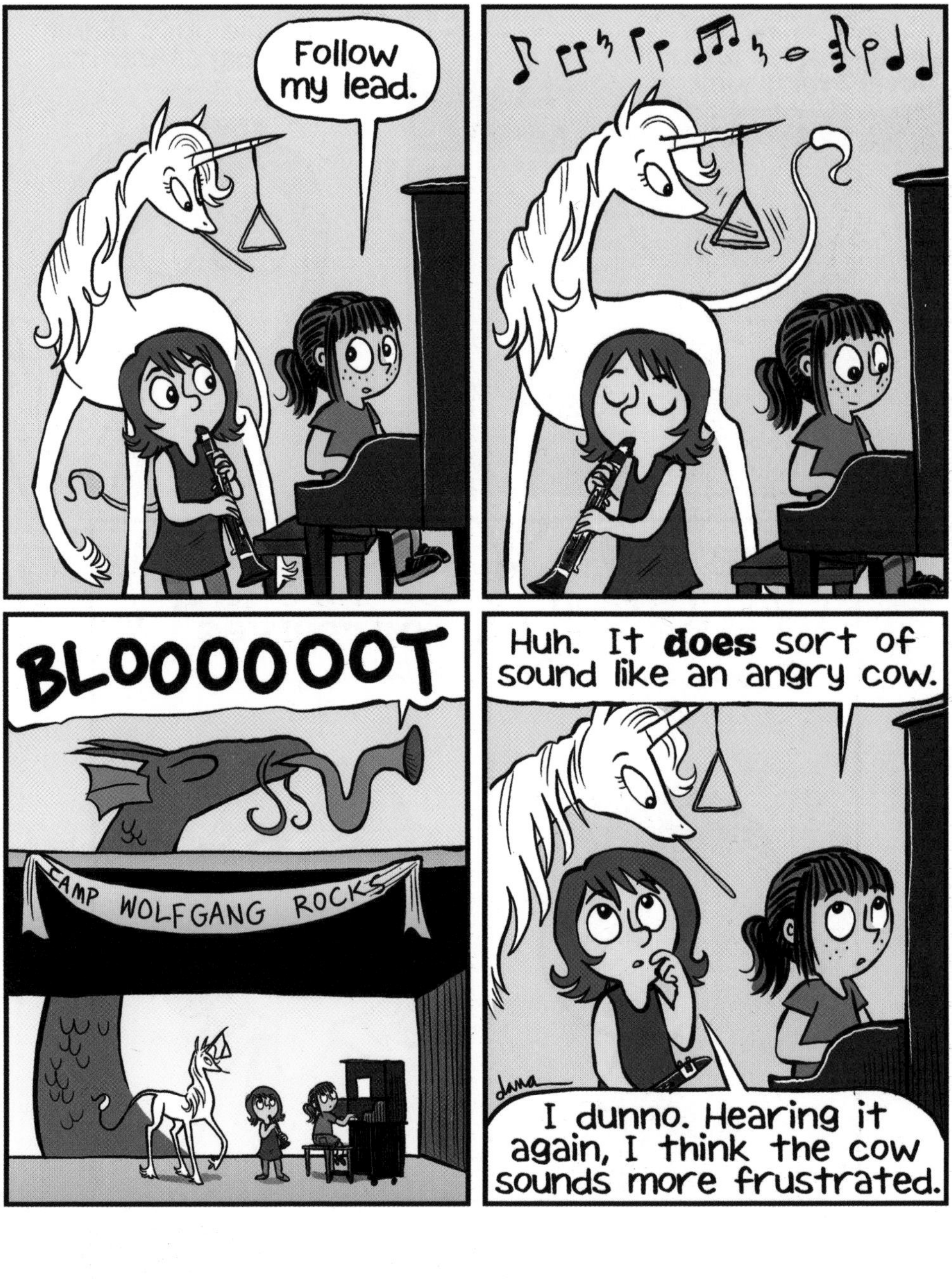
Follow my lead.
BLOOOOOOT
CAMP WOLFGANG ROCKS
Huh. It **does** sort of sound like an angry cow.
I dunno. Hearing it again, I think the cow sounds more frustrated.
dana

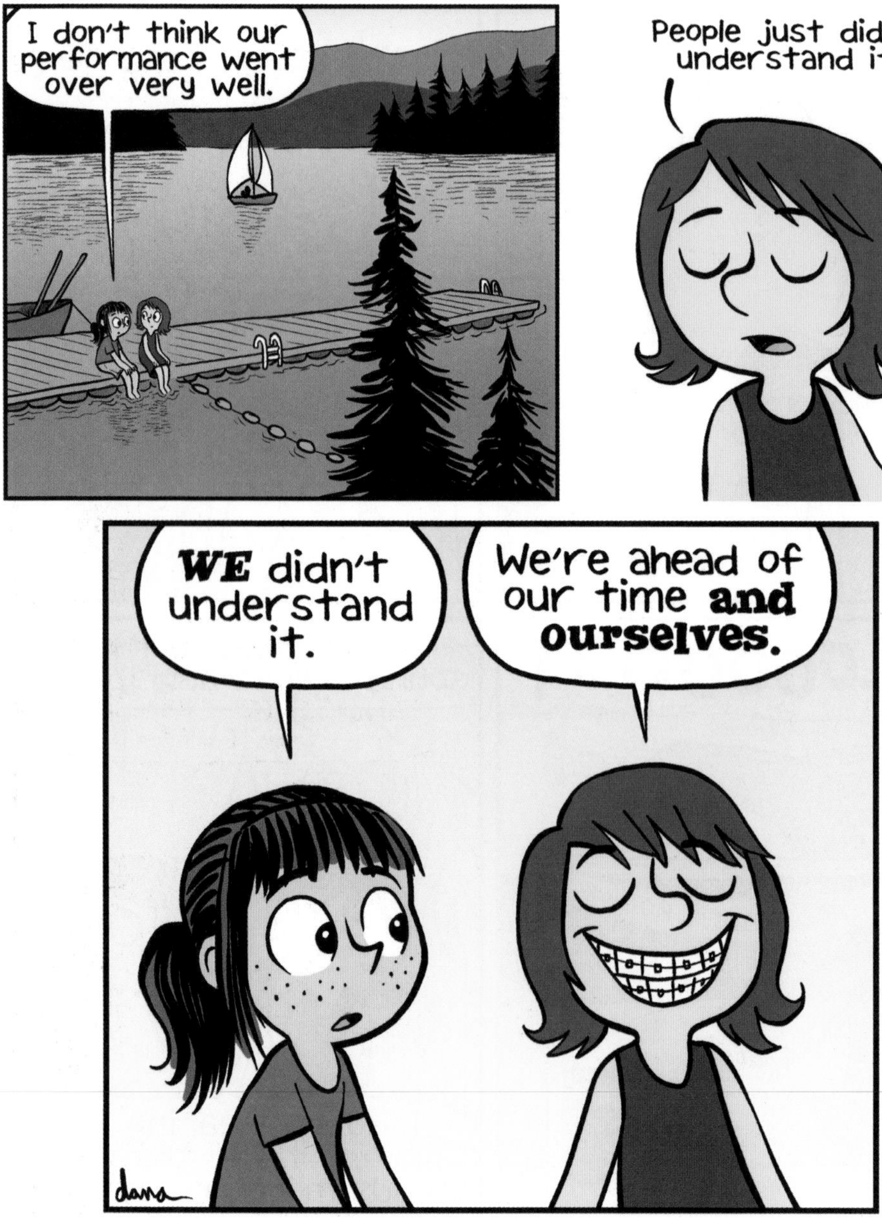
I don't think our performance went over very well.
People just didn't understand it.
WE didn't understand it.
We're ahead of our time **and ourselves.**
dana

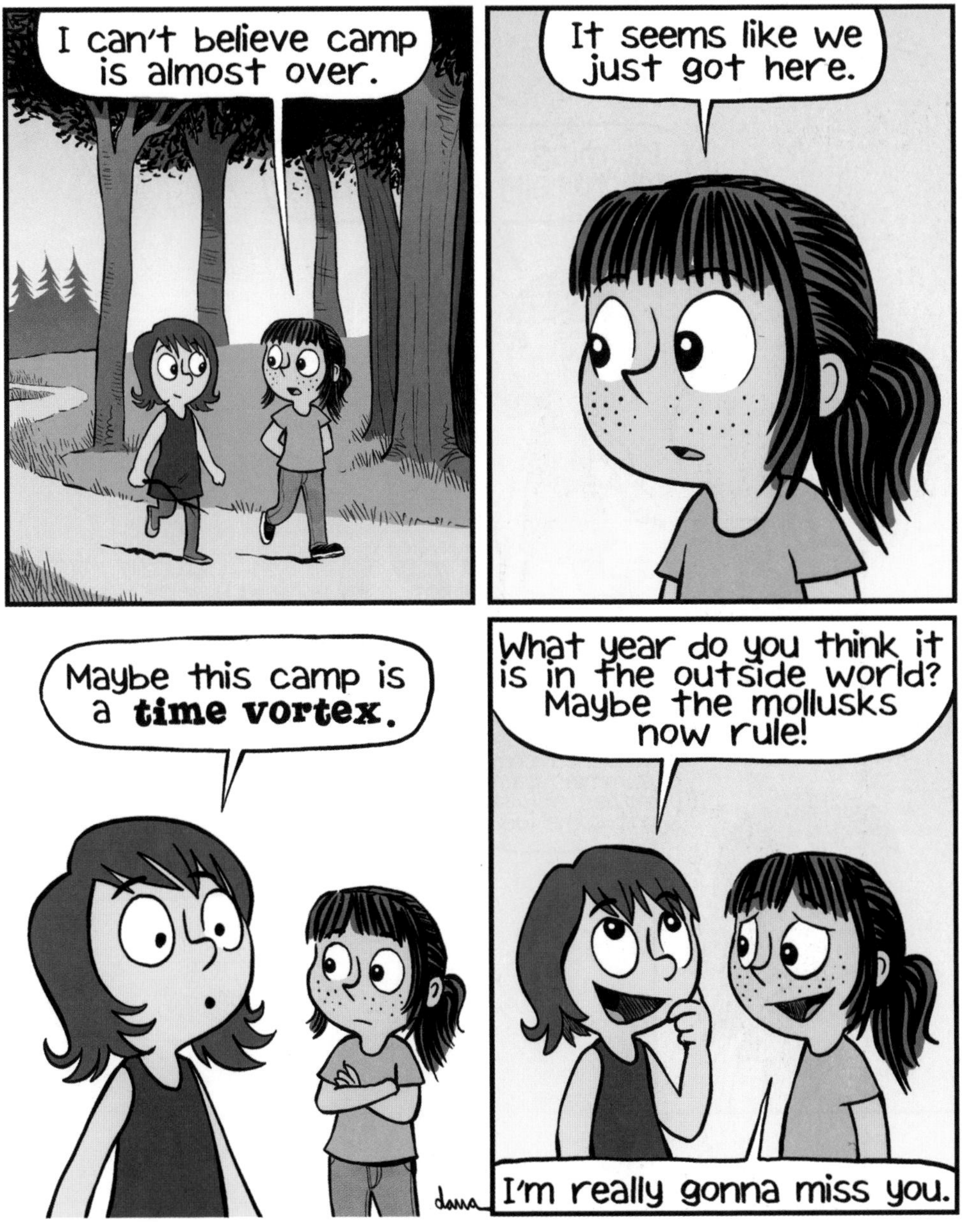
I can't believe camp is almost over.
It seems like we just got here.
Maybe this camp is a **time vortex**.
What year do you think it is in the outside world? Maybe the mollusks now rule!
I'm really gonna miss you.
dana

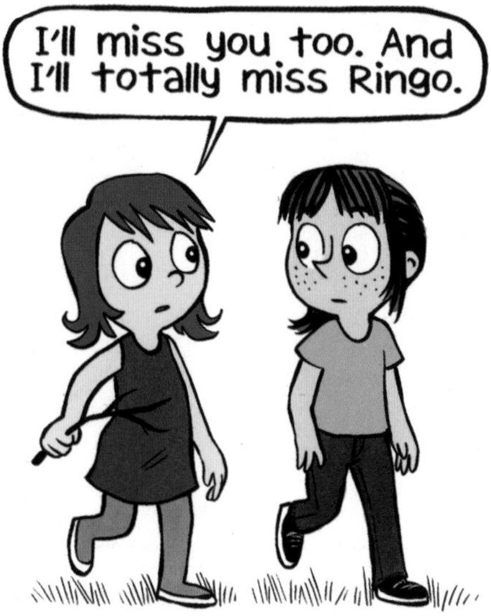
I'll miss you too. And I'll totally miss Ringo.

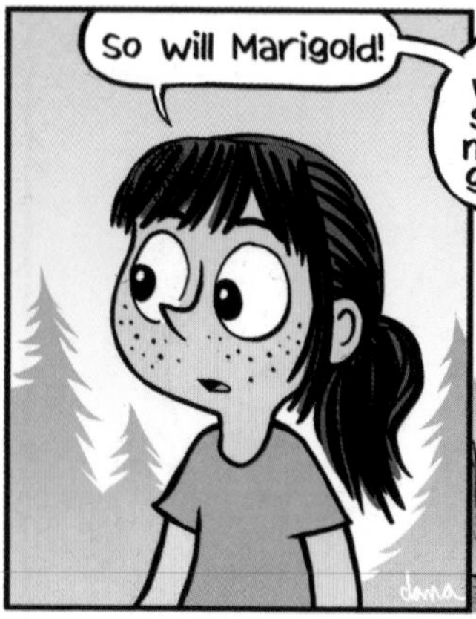
So will Marigold!
She and I watched some summer camp movies, and she got some ideas.
dana

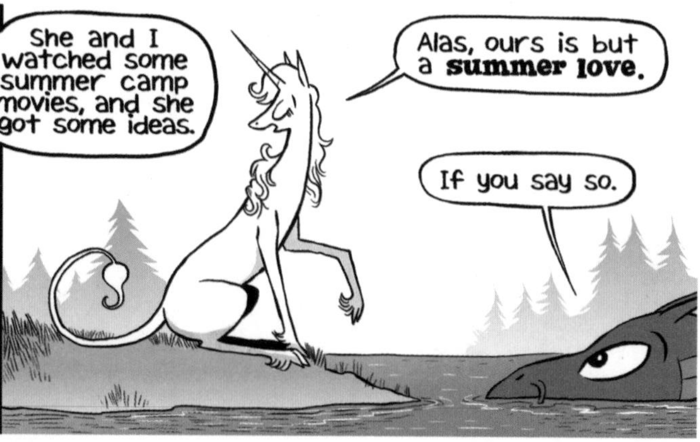
Alas, ours is but a **summer love.**
If you say so.

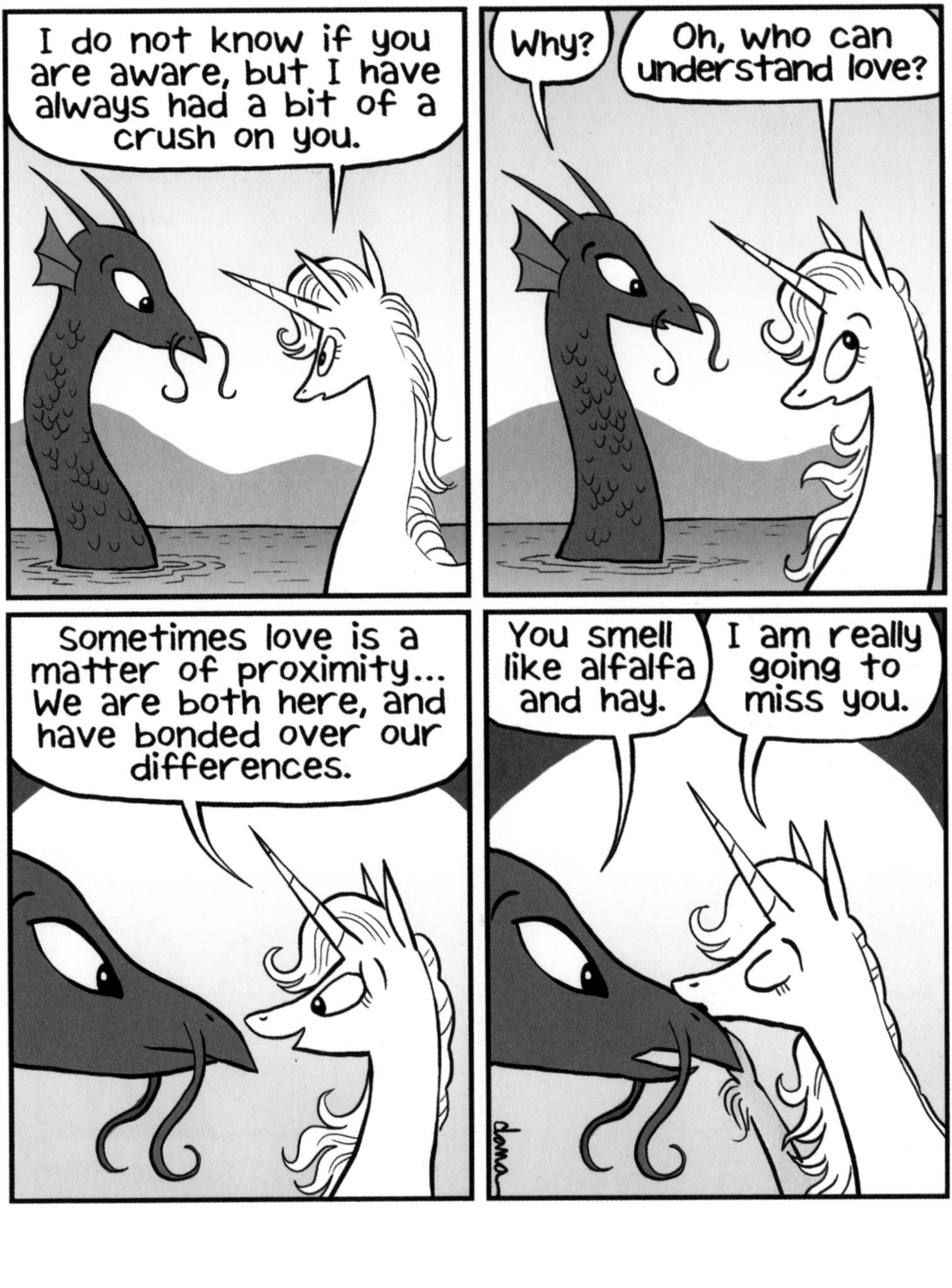
I do not know if you are aware, but I have always had a bit of a crush on you.
Why?
Oh, who can understand love?
Sometimes love is a matter of proximity... We are both here, and have bonded over our differences.
You smell like alfalfa and hay.
I am really going to miss you.
dana

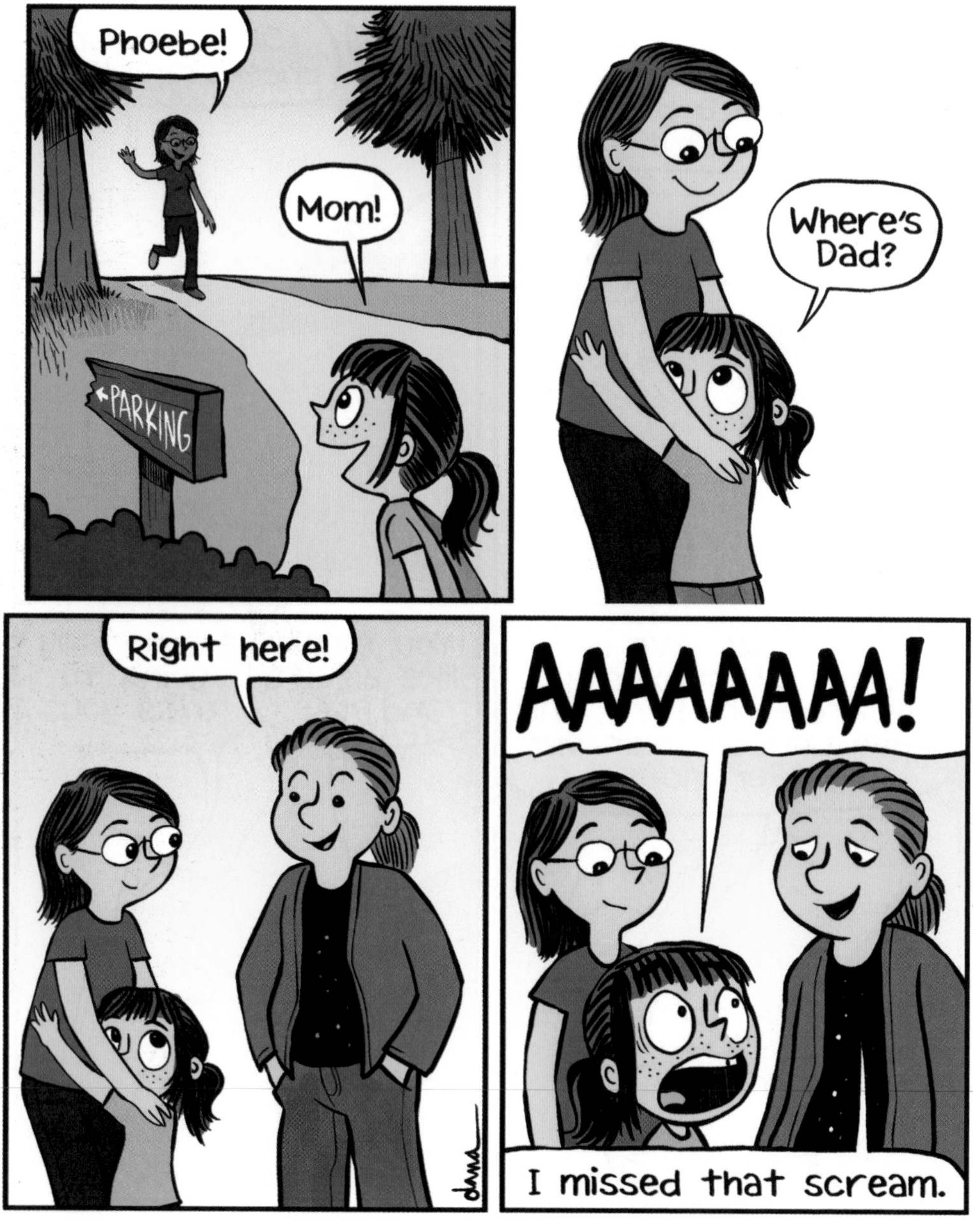
Phoebe!
Mom!
PARKING
Where's Dad?
Right here!
dana
AAAAAAAA!
I missed that scream.

Learn the Creative Process

In the earlier books, I showed you some of how I draw Phoebe, Marigold, and friends.

Now, let's look at how I make comics.

For example, the one where Phoebe asked Marigold about her New Year's resolutions. (It's on page 202 of this book.)

First, I have to come up with ideas.

I like to leave my house to do that. My house is full of distractions.

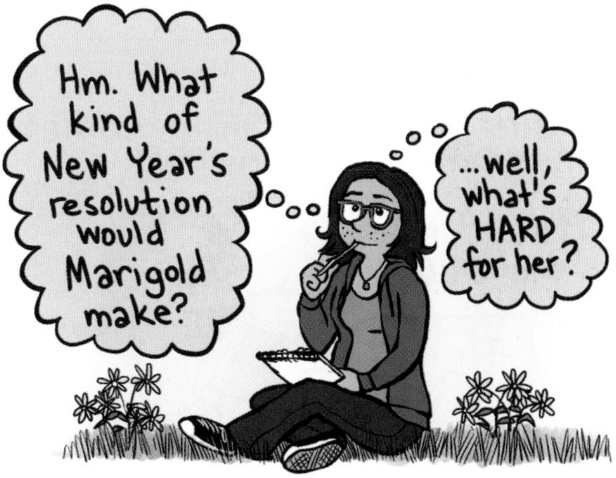
Hm. What kind of New Year's resolution would Marigold make?
...well, what's HARD for her?

When I draw them in my notebook, they look like this:

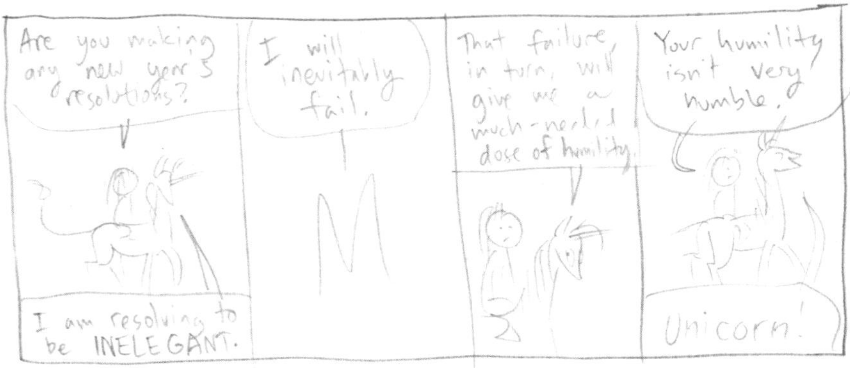
Are you making any new year's resolutions?
I am resolving to be INELEGANT.
I will inevitably fail.
That failure, in turn, will give me a much-needed dose of humility.
Your humility isn't very humble.
Unicorn!

It doesn't have to be much, just enough to show who's talking and what they're doing. (Sometimes, Marigold is just an M, or Phoebe is just a P.)

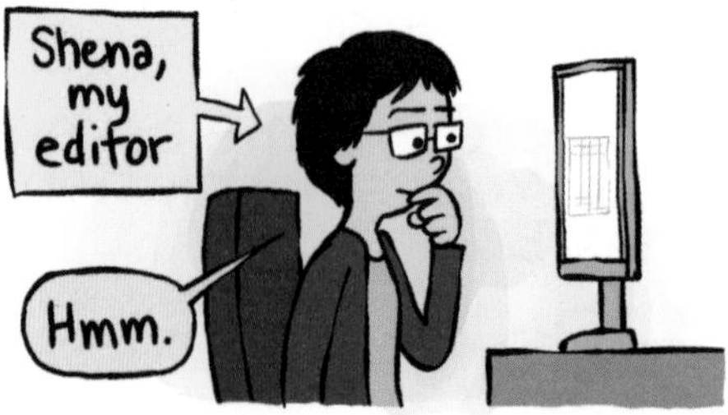
Shena, my editor
Hmm.

I take a picture of it on my phone and send it to my editor, so she can tell me what she thinks.

Sometimes she thinks something could be clearer, or funnier.

Other times, she just says:

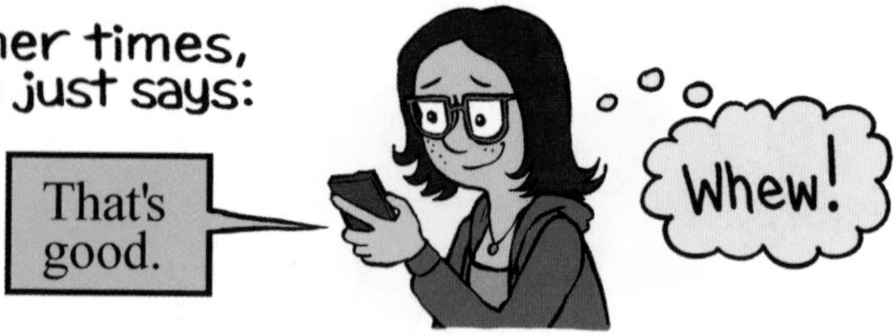
That's good.
Whew!

Once she approves, I get to work on the finished artwork. I do all that on my computer.

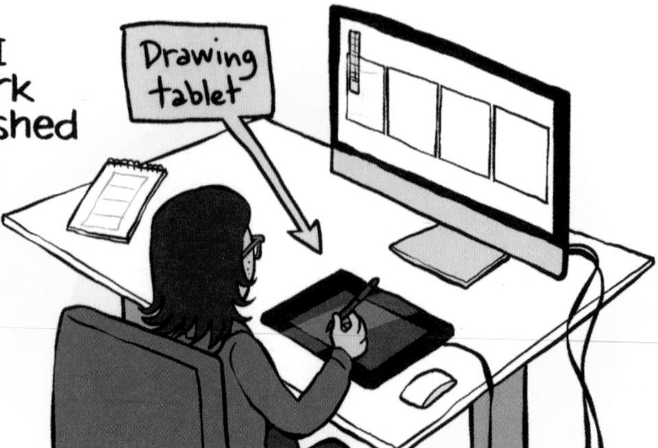
Drawing tablet

First, I add the lettering, so I know how much space I have for the artwork.

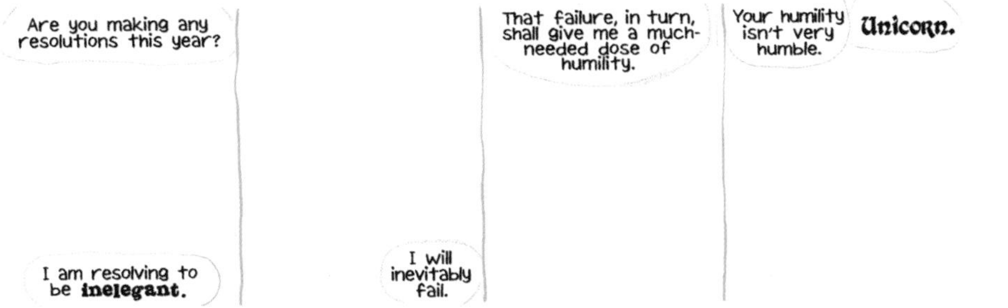
Are you making any resolutions this year?
I am resolving to be **inelegant.**
I will inevitably fail.
That failure, in turn, shall give me a much-needed dose of humility.
Your humility isn't very humble.
Unicorn.

Then, I add the rough "pencil" lines, usually in light blue.

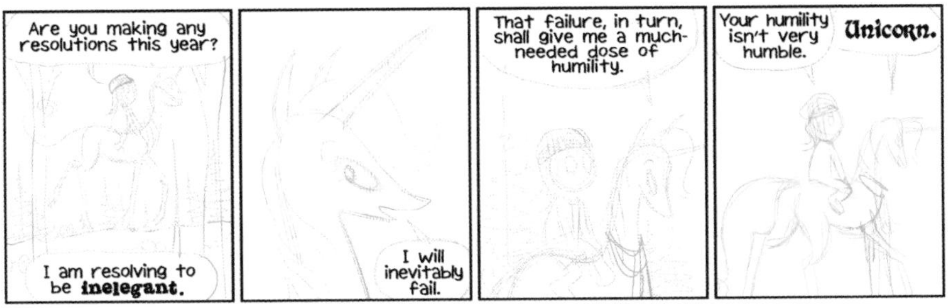
Are you making any resolutions this year?
I am resolving to be **inelegant.**
I will inevitably fail.
That failure, in turn, shall give me a much-needed dose of humility.
Your humility isn't very humble.
Unicorn.

Next, I add the black "ink" lines...

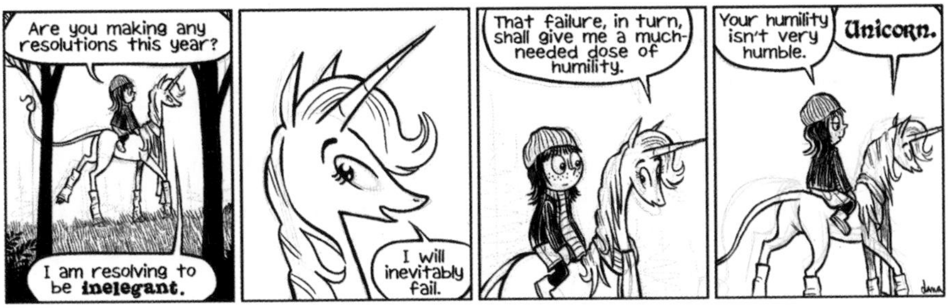
Are you making any resolutions this year?
I am resolving to be **inelegant.**
I will inevitably fail.
That failure, in turn, shall give me a much-needed dose of humility.
Your humility isn't very humble.
Unicorn.

Finally, I add in various shades of gray.

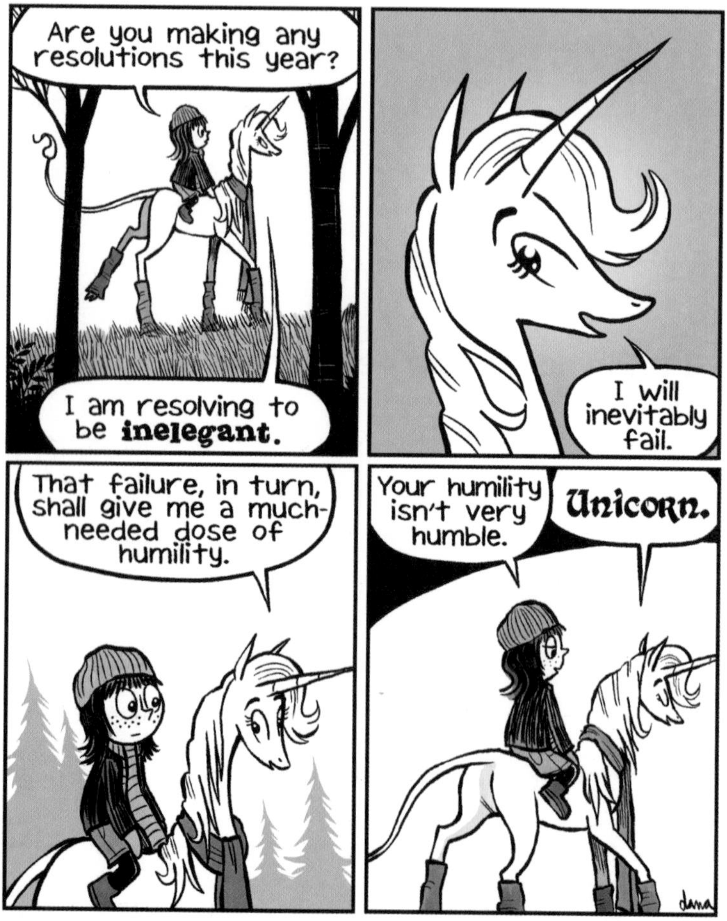

Are you making any resolutions this year?
I am resolving to be **inelegant.**
I will inevitably fail.
That failure, in turn, shall give me a much-needed dose of humility.
Your humility isn't very humble.
Unicorn.
dana

(A colorist who works for my publisher does most of the coloring, and as you can see throughout this book, he does a pretty amazing job!)

Glossary

calibrate (cal-li-brate): pg. 203 — verb / to plan carefully

context (con-text): pg. 331 — noun / the set of circumstances that surrounds an event

ensemble (on-som-ble): pg. 331 — noun / a group of musicians

exoskeleton (exo-skel-le-ton): pg. 250 — noun / a hard, external covering

feign (fain): pg. 266 — verb / to imitate or pretend

hallucination (ha-loo-sin-ay-shun): pg. 334 — noun / a vision of something that does not exist

incoherence (in-co-here-ence): pg. 318 — noun / a state of not making sense

percussionist (per-cuh-shun-ist): pg. 332 — noun / a drummer or any musician who plays an instrument by striking or beating it

prescient (pre-shunt): pg. 228 — adjective / having foresight

proximity (prox-im-it-ee): pg. 343 — noun / nearness

schism (si-zem): pg. 266 — noun / a division into two opposing groups

scintillating (sin-till-ate-ing): pg. 225 — adjective / brilliant or exciting

victuals (vitt-tles): pg. 194 — noun / food or provisions

vortex (vor-tex): pg. 341 — noun / a whirling mass that draws things into its current

whippersnapper (whip-per-snap-per): pg. 205 — noun / an offensively bold young person

Andrews McMeel Publishing
a division of Andrews McMeel Universal
1130 Walnut Street, Kansas City, Missouri 64106

www.andrewsmcmeel.com

21 22 23 24 25 SDB 10 9 8 7 6 5 4 3 2 1

ISBN: 978-1-5248-6981-6

Made by:
King Yip (Dongguan) Printing & Packaging Factory Ltd.
Address and location of manufacturer:
Daning Administrative District, Humen Town
Dongguan Guangdong, China 523930
1st Printing—4/19/21

ATTENTION: SCHOOLS AND BUSINESSES
Andrews McMeel books are available at quantity discounts with bulk purchase for educational, business, or sales promotional use. For information, please e-mail the Andrews McMeel Publishing Special Sales Department: specialsales@amuniversal.com.

Look for these books!

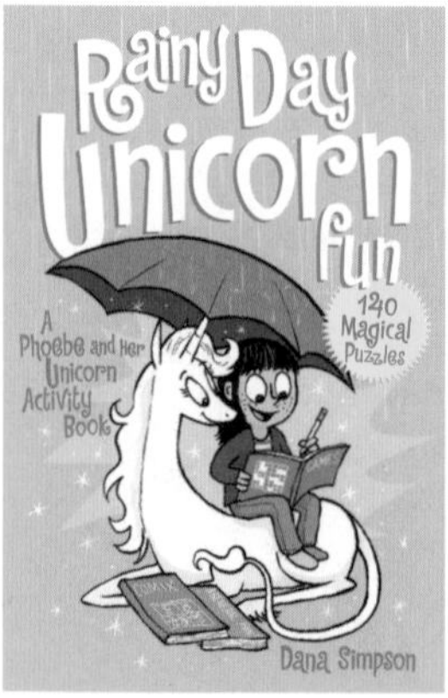
Rainy Day Unicorn Fun
A Phoebe and Her Unicorn Activity Book
140 Magical Puzzles
Dana Simpson

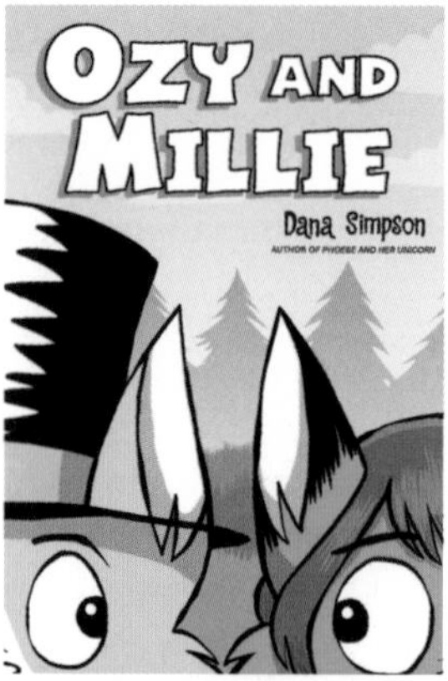
Ozy and Millie
Dana Simpson

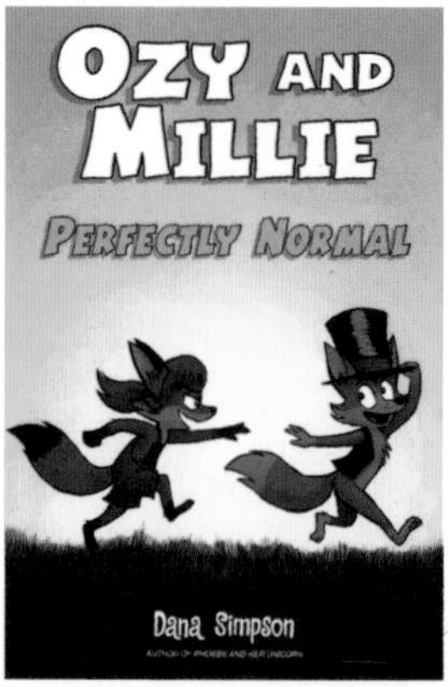
Ozy and Millie
Perfectly Normal
Dana Simpson

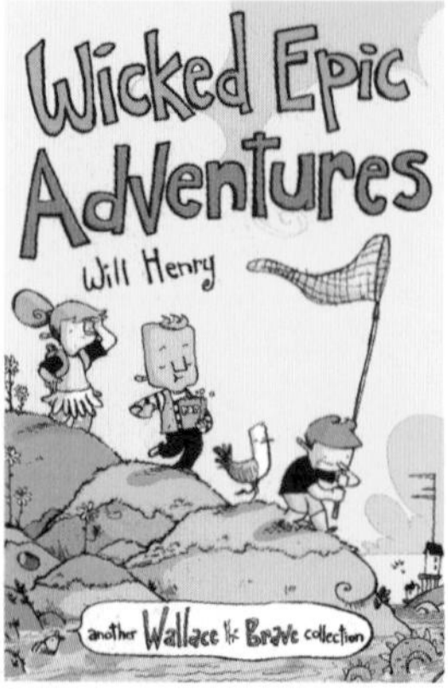
Wicked Epic Adventures
Will Henry
another Wallace the Brave collection

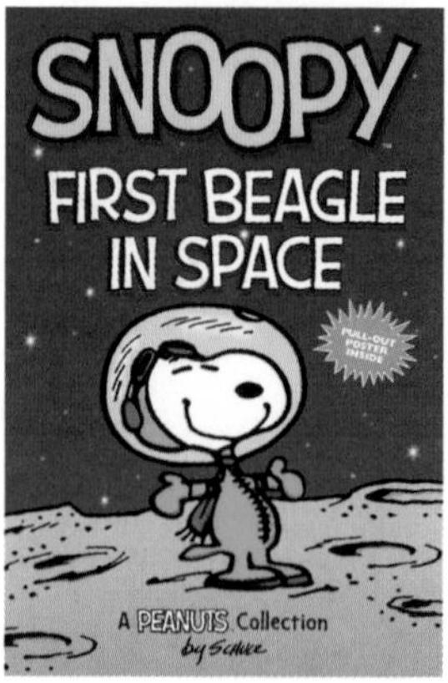
SNOOPY
FIRST BEAGLE IN SPACE
PULL-OUT POSTER INSIDE
A PEANUTS Collection
by Schulz

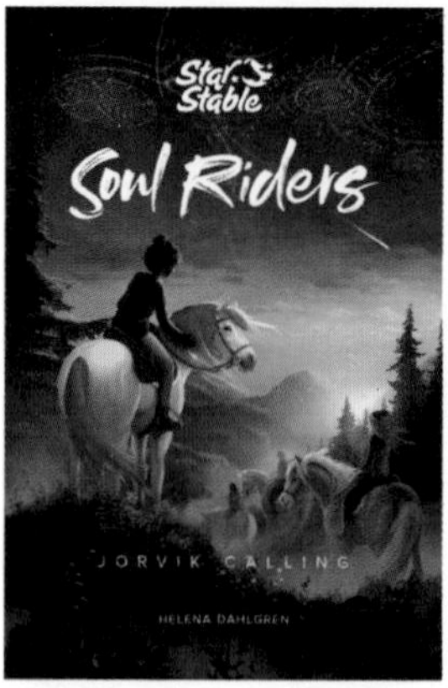
Star Stable
Soul Riders
JORVIK CALLING
HELENA DAHLGREN

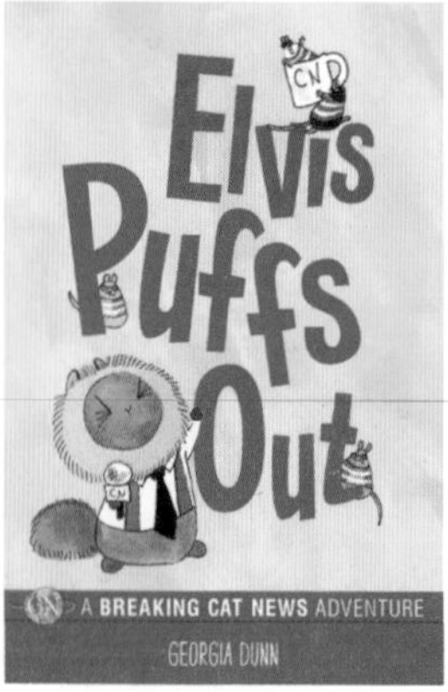
Elvis Puffs Out
A BREAKING CAT NEWS ADVENTURE
GEORGIA DUNN

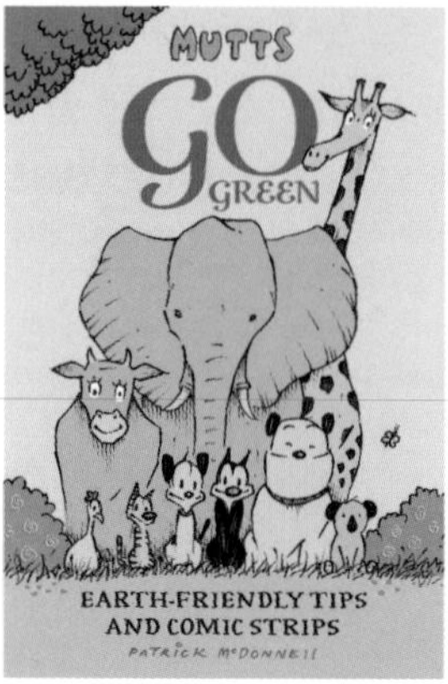
MUTTS
GO GREEN
EARTH-FRIENDLY TIPS AND COMIC STRIPS
PATRICK McDONNELL

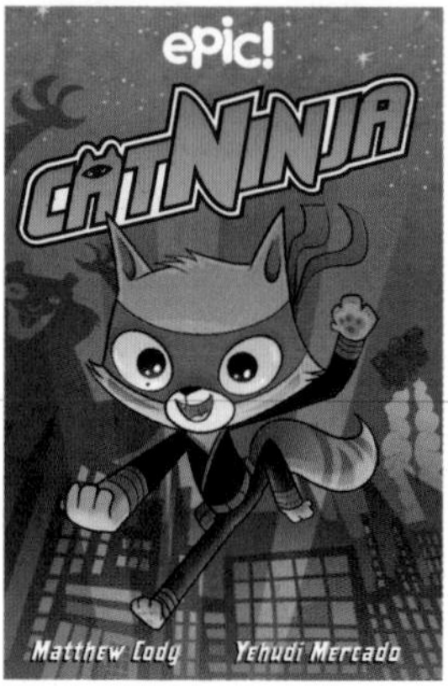
epic!
CATNINJA
Matthew Cody
Yehudi Mercado